JINX BALLOU BOUNTY HUNTER

JINX BALLOU BOUNTY HUNTER

BOOKS 1-3

DHARMA KELLEHER

Dark Pariah Press, Phoenix, Arizona

eBook ISBN: 978-1-952128-00-4

Print ISBN: 978-1-952128-05-9

CHASER

JINX BALLOU SERIES - BOOK 1

1

A blond woman opened the door, her swollen left eye shining with the rich color and texture of an overripe eggplant. Dried blood trailed from her twisted nose, over her split lip, and onto her faded Disney Cinderella T-shirt. Purple, green, and yellow bruises on her arms and legs documented a history of abuse.

"Jesus Christ! That looks like it hurts." I stood on her doorstep in Phoenix's Sunnyslope neighborhood, sweat beading on my skin in the late-afternoon heat. "Freddie do that to you?"

"What do you want?" Her fat lip and broken nose made it sound more like "Wuh you wuhn?" She glared at me from her open doorway, resting a hand on her hip.

"You're Vanessa Nealey, right?"

"Who wants to know?"

"Gee, I figured the words 'Bail Enforcement Agent' printed in big yellow letters on my Kevlar vest would've given it away." I handed her my business card with a sardonic grin. "Jinx Ballou, friendly neighborhood bounty hunter. Your boyfriend, Freddie Colton, missed his court date. Big Bobby Mills at Liberty Bail Bonds hired me to pick him up. Is he here?"

Vanessa crumpled the business card and tossed it at my feet. "Go to hell, lady." She started to shut the door, but I caught it with the toe of my boot.

"Listen up, princess! You put your home up as collateral. If Prince Charming doesn't come along with me, your bond is forfeit. Know what that means? It means no happily ever after. Liberty Bail Bonds will take your house, and you'll be on the street. Is Freddie really worth all that?"

She held my gaze for several seconds before her expression softened. "He ain't here."

"You sure about that?"

Vanessa stepped aside. "You wanna look around? Be my guest."

I was tempted to take her up on her offer, just in case she was bluffing. Technically, I didn't need her permission or even a warrant. By law, people on bail were still considered to be in custody, which was one of several reasons I quit the Phoenix PD years ago to be a bounty hunter. Too many regs. Too much paperwork.

My gut told me Vanessa was telling the truth. Freddie's Trans Am wasn't in the carport, and I didn't get the impression she was ready to lose her home just yet. "Where is he?"

"Out drinking, prob'ly."

I rolled my eyes. Sometimes my job was like pulling teeth. "Out drinking *where*?"

"Don't know. Don't care. We done here?"

I considered pressing her, but the sun was turning the back of my neck into bacon. I retrieved my crumpled business card and planted it in her hand. "Might want to hold onto this. If Freddie shows up, you'll want to call me. Unless you'd prefer living on the street when it's a hundred and ten out."

I turned to go, then pivoted to face her again. "Tell me something. Why do you put up with his bullshit? How many times has he been arrested for beating you up? Six, seven times at least, according to his sheet. And yet you keep posting his bail, dropping the charges, and letting him back in to do it all over again. I don't get it."

"Freddie loves me." She raised her chin with royal indignation.

"Geez, you really believe that, don't you?"

"We done here?"

"Do yourself a favor, Vanessa. Toss his crap onto the sidewalk, change the locks, and don't bail him out again. He isn't worth it."

"Mind your own damn business, lady." She shoved me away and slammed the door.

I wiped the sweat from my face and pulled my walkie-talkie from my tactical belt. "Okay, guys! Let's pack it up. Girlfriend says he ain't here."

"Bullshit!" came a gravelly reply from my associate, Fiddler. "When've you ever taken the word of a skip's girlfriend, Jinx?"

"Not usually, but this time I think she's telling the truth. Car's gone. Looks like he beat the ever-lovin' shit out of her—again—and went out drinking."

Fiddler, whose real name was Robert Dixon, was a bounty hunter from way back and was considered a legend in the business. Medical issues had forced him to give up leading his own team. But he could still guard a back door, and his prowess as a fugitive hunter was an invaluable resource. At least when I listened to him.

"I bet money he's in there hiding like the little pissant he is." Fiddler shuffled around from the backyard, his beer gut bouncing with each stride. Gray hair hung like ragged curtains from his jawline and down the back of his denim shirt.

Nathaniel "Rodeo" Kwan, an army veteran I'd been training for the past few months, approached from the east side of the house. He was a slim guy, a few years younger than me, sporting a straw Stetson on his head and a shotgun loaded with beanbag rounds slung over his shoulder. "If he ain't in there, where's he at?"

"Not sure." I led them back to my seven-year-old silver Nissan

Pathfinder. Nicknamed the Gray Ghost, it featured an extensive collection of dents, scrapes, missing trim, and peeling paint that rendered it invisible when I was looking for defendants on bail who'd missed their court dates.

I hopped into the front seat and started the engine. The blast of hot air from the vents made me wince. Rodeo claimed the seat next to me. Fiddler slid into the back.

Flipping through Freddie's paperwork didn't yield any clues about his usual hangouts. I pulled out my phone and checked his social media accounts.

"Ha! You can run, but you're too stupid to hide." I held out the phone to Rodeo, showing a status update posted twenty minutes earlier. "He's at some place called One-Eyed Jack's. Dunlap and Nineteenth. I love dumb criminals, don't you?"

"One-Eyed Jack's?" Fiddler harrumphed. "Jesus! That place is a bucket of blood."

"It's that bad, huh?" I asked.

"Bad?" Fiddler laughed darkly. "Used to be called Jack's Saloon till the owner lost an eye in a bar fight. Friend of mine took a knife in the belly there for ogling some dude's girl."

"Friend of yours, huh?" I shook my head as I navigated out of the neighborhood and turned north on Seventh Avenue toward Dunlap. "You hang out with some choice people, Fiddler."

"All turned out for the best, though," he continued. "After my friend got outta the hospital, he never cheated on his old lady again."

Rough bars didn't scare me. Okay, maybe they did a little. But after my high school boyfriend's father beat me half to death on our graduation night, I'd made it my mission to learn how to handle myself. I'd trained for years in krav maga and aikido. I also practiced parkour to help me escape situations that got out of control.

In my eight years as a bounty hunter, I'd been in countless fights, often with guys much bigger than I am. I'd been stabbed a few times. Caught bird shot in the shoulder once. A moon-shaped scar on my lower back marked where a .44 Magnum slug had clipped the edge of my Kevlar vest. Typical hazards of the trade.

Nevertheless, I was the team leader. It was on me to determine how to take Freddie the abusive asshole into custody, ideally without starting a brawl with a bar full of his drinking buddies.

A plan formed as I waited for the light on Dunlap and Fifteenth Avenue to turn green. I'd tried it a few times before with mixed success, but it beat any alternatives I could come up with. "Okay, kiddos, we're going with a honey trap," I announced.

"Aw, shit!" Rodeo and Fiddler said in unison.

2

"You lost your damn mind, girl?" Fiddler growled. "Those animals'll eat you alive and ask for seconds. Besides, Conor would have my ass if I let you go into that bar alone."

Conor Doyle was my boyfriend and a fellow bounty hunter who had worked with Fiddler back in the day. Until we started dating a year ago, Conor was also my boss. When our relationship caused friction among the other team members, I started my own fugitive apprehension crew with Conor's help.

"In case you hadn't noticed, Fiddler, this is *my* crew, not Conor's." I balked. "*I* sign your paychecks. I call the shots."

"With all due respect, Jinx," Rodeo said, "a honey pot doesn't sound like a smart strategy for this situation. Too many ways it can go sideways. I'd hate to see you get hurt."

I wiped the sweat from my face. "I'm open to suggestions."

"I say we go in with guns drawn and drag his sorry ass out of that shit hole they call a bar." Fiddler chucked Rodeo on the shoulder. "Give 'em a little shock and awe, right, soldier boy?"

"Yeah, right," I scoffed. "One of us might even get out alive to collect the bounty."

"GPS says One-Eyed Jack's is over there." Rodeo pointed at a shopping center to our left, and I slipped into the turn lane. "A more prudent approach would be to wait and grab him as he's leaving. Maybe he'll be too soused to put up much resistance by then."

I shook my head. "That could take hours. Phoenix Comicon starts tomorrow. I'm not cosplaying as Wonder Woman with bags under my eyes. Nobody wants to see that."

I turned in to the shopping center lot and parked on the other side of Colton's Trans Am, out of sight of the bar's front door. The AC was only now blowing cold. I leaned in and savored the cool air on my face.

"We're going with the honey trap. So you got a choice. Either be my backup and get paid, or you can catch an Uber home and I'll keep the whole bounty for myself."

"I got your six, Jinx," Rodeo said after a tense moment of silence. "Honey trap it is."

Fiddler's phone rang. He answered it in hushed, angry tones. I couldn't make out the words but figured it was one of his ex-wives calling to bitch about something.

When he hung up, I asked, "Which one of the former Mrs. Fiddlers was that? Molly, Daisy, or Daphne?"

"Huh? Oh, uh, Daisy."

"Child support again?" Rodeo asked with a smirk.

"Something like that."

"So you in or out, Fiddler?" I turned in my seat to look at him directly. I'd been getting tired of his nonsense lately. Half the time he didn't answer his phone when I called. And when he did show up, he smelled like the crowd at a Phish concert.

"Aw, what the hell! I'm in," he grumbled. "But don't say I didn't warn ya."

"Duly noted." I pulled off my ballistic vest and handed it to Rodeo.

"I got a bad feeling about this, Jinx," Rodeo said.

"Zip it, Han Solo. We each do our jobs, no one gets hurt." I handed him my Ruger .40 caliber, my Taser, and my tactical belt. "Toss me my purse."

He pulled my black cloth purse from the glove box and offered it to me. "But if what Fiddler says about this place is true—"

"Relax, I still have the .357 revolver in my ankle holster if things go sideways. Hand me the cuffs from my tactical belt." He did, and I slipped them into my back pocket.

"Now for a little macho-man kryptonite." With the makeup kit from my purse, I added some smoky eye shadow and thickened my lashes and eyeliner to make my eyes pop. I finished off the look with some slutty red lipstick. Normally, I was more sporty gal than girly girl, keeping the makeup to a minimum. But I could still crank up the femme when the job called for it. "How do I look?" I asked.

Rodeo studied my outfit and makeup, turning my face one way then another. He removed the band from my ponytail and let my black hair fall loose on my shoulders.

"Makeup's good—hot but not too over-the-top trailer trash. The oversized Diamondbacks jersey is okay, barely. But the dad jeans and biker boots don't exactly scream 'sexy,' especially for pulling a honey trap. A lacy blouse, Daisy Dukes, and strappy sandals would be better."

"Yeah, well, I don't have any of those with me, do I, Mr. Project Runway?"

He tilted his head, squinted, then tied a knot in the bottom of my jersey, exposing my midriff. "Gonna have to show some skin, girl." He flicked open a jackknife and pointed it at my chest.

My eyes widened. "What the hell?"

"Chill, girl." He pulled at the front of my collar with his free hand, cut a six-inch vertical slit in the top of the jersey, then folded under the newly made corners. "Just exposing a little cleavage. If you're gonna go fishing, you gotta use the right bait."

"Dude, I borrowed this jersey from my brother. Cost him a hundred bucks. He's going to kill me."

"Yeah, but now you look less like a construction worker." He popped his Stetson onto my head. "And more like a hot piece of ass."

I smirked, unsure how to take his comment. "Thanks, I guess."

"Enough with the fashion show," Fiddler grumbled. "We gonna do this or not? I got shit to do."

"Fine. I'll go in and draw Freddie out. Rodeo, I want you in front to help me muscle him into the Gray Ghost. Fiddler, guard the rear door in case Freddie makes me and bolts out the back."

I turned off the ignition, and we climbed out. The heat hit me like a blast from a hot oven. I hoped my face didn't melt before I got inside.

"All right, everybody in position. Let's take this guy down and call it a day."

Fiddler moseyed past the Subway shop at the end of the strip mall on his way around to the back of the bar. Rodeo took a position near a support column, shotgun at his side, where he watched me hustle toward the entrance.

A mountain of a bouncer sat on a stool beside the door, staring at his cellphone. As I approached, he stood and looked up. "ID?"

I handed him my driver's license. The bouncer glanced at it, then looked me up and down.

A tremor of nervousness rippled through me, accompanied by a memory of me with my best friend, Becca Alvarez, on our way to see the movie *Anywhere but Here* at the dollar theater. I was eleven and still new to going out dressed as a girl. Despite Becca's reassurances that I looked very feminine, I was terrified someone would figure out I was transgender.

I had handed our tickets to the woman in the theater lobby. She looked down at me and stopped in the middle of tearing the tickets, no doubt deciding whether I was a boy or a girl.

I stood there feeling like a deer in the headlights until Becca nudged me and whispered, "Smile."

I did. The ticket taker reciprocated. "Enjoy the movie, girls."

I brought my mind back to the present and forced a smile. The bouncer handed me my driver's license without a word and returned to his phone.

I breathed a sigh of relief and opened the heavy front door. As my eyes adjusted to the dim interior, I realized Fiddler wasn't kidding about the clientele.

A dozen or so men looking like escapees from a supermax prison sat at mismatched tables, their eyes following me to the bar. Some chatted up young women with a definite pay-for-play vibe. A couple of bikers in leather vests and bandanas crowded around a pool table along the far wall. The place reeked of stale beer and dollar store perfume, with a metallic undertone I suspected was blood.

On a flat screen mounted above the bar, the Arizona Diamondbacks were losing to the Phillies, while Keith Urban belted out a tune on the sound system.

It wasn't the first time I'd been in a place like this. Certainly not the last considering my line of work. I should've been terrified. Not the kind of joint a trans woman should linger in if she valued her life. But I was on the job, and my pulse raced with the thrill of the hunt.

3

My quarry, Freddie Colton, sat at the bar, nibbling pretzels and nursing a bottle of Bud Light. He looked to be in his midthirties, tall with muscular arms and wearing a royal-blue work shirt with his name stitched above the left pocket. His mug shot didn't do him justice. Few did, I supposed. But he was definitely easy on the eyes in a rugged, Brad-Pitt-gone-bad sort of way. A girl could get herself in trouble if she didn't know better.

His eyes were glued to the ball game on the flat screen. I hopped onto the barstool between Freddie and the TV and flashed him a polite smile before waving down the bartender.

The bartender had the face of a horse, a patch over one eye, and the scowl of a drill instructor. His cutoff denim shirt revealed a tattoo of a buxom woman waving a Confederate flag. I asked him for a Michelob.

Freddie angled his body toward me. "Jack, her drink's on me," he said in a baritone as smooth as silk. He met my gaze after a longing glance at my chest. "Don't think we've met. The name's Freddie. What's yours, sweet cheeks?"

"Hi, I'm Melody!" I cranked the pitch of my voice and my Southern accent up to bubbly bimbo levels.

"Melody? What a sexy name for a sexy babe. Damn glad to meet ya."

"Yo, honey!" a young guy shouted from one of the tables, patting his own lap. His tongue flicked across his upper lip. "Don't waste your time with Freddie. He's old. Come party with me. I'll show you a real good time."

"Quit trying to cut in on my action, Mancini!" Freddie's face colored with indignation. "Don't mind him, Melody. He's a dumb ass."

His action, I thought. *Keep dreaming, buddy.*

"How come I ain't never seen you here before, girl?" He shifted closer to me and slipped a hand onto my thigh.

My internal warning system went off with a surge of adrenaline. I resisted the urge to twist his wrist in a pinch hold and drive the heel of my palm into his nose. Instead, I plastered a coy smile on my face. "Just moved to town."

He leaned in, inches from my face. "Oh yeah? Where from?"

"A little place in Texas no one ever heard of." His cologne smelled like an earthy blend of fine leather, moss, and musk, causing my body to respond in ways it shouldn't with a guy like him.

"What brings you to Phoenix this time o' year?"

"I'm a nurse. I start work at John C. Lincoln on Monday." It was a story I'd used before. My mother was an RN, so I knew enough medical lingo to bluff my way with a guy like Freddie.

"Is that so? Well, welcome to Valley of the Sun, Nurse Melody." His hand slipped farther up my thigh, causing the grip on my beer bottle to tighten. "You're just in time for summer."

"Yeah, can't believe it's hit a hundred and ten already and it's only June."

"I think things are 'bout to get a whole lot hotter." He squeezed my thigh, sending an unexpected wave of heat into my pelvis.

"Hotter. Yeah, uh, sure is." It came out breathier than I intended. *What the hell's wrong with you, girl? Keep your mind on the job.*

"Wanna continue this conversation in private?"

"Um, definitely."

"I'd invite you to my house, but my roommate ... Not a lot of privacy, you understand."

You are such a liar, Freddie Colton. "I have a motel room just off I-17. Will that do?"

His gaze narrowed. "You ain't hustling me, are you? Cause I ain't the kind of man to have to pay for it."

"What? You think I'm a hooker? As if. I'm a medical professional." I turned to leave.

He grabbed my arm with a grip strong enough to leave a bruise then released it. "Shit, I'm sorry. Don't know what I was thinking. Forget I said it."

I gave him a side-eye and a reluctant, forgiving smile to replant the hook firmly into my prey. "Well, okay."

"That mean your offer still stands, Nurse Melody? I'd love to see your bedside manner." He set some bills on the bar to pay for our drinks.

"Sure, why not."

He held the door for me as we stepped outside into the glaring sunlight.

"My Trans Am's over here." Freddie pointed across the parking lot.

I let him take the lead as I reached for the handcuffs in my pocket. Rodeo stepped into our path, shotgun raised. "Freddie Colton, you're under arrest."

"Aw, hell no!" Freddie nearly knocked me over as he pivoted and raced back into the bar. I chased after him with Rodeo on my heels.

Freddie overturned tables and chairs in his wake. I used my parkour skills to maneuver past them, dodging pissed-off patrons along the way. I followed him down a narrow hallway, past the restrooms. He was thirty feet ahead of me when he blasted out the back door. I hoped Fiddler was ready to grab him on the other side.

When I rushed out the exit, Freddie was hightailing it down the alley with Fiddler nowhere in sight. I took off after Freddie, cursing Fiddler under my breath.

I quickly gained on him, but bringing him down wasn't going to be easy. He was a big guy, and his rap sheet told me he was a scrapper. I scrambled up a stack of wooden pallets onto a dumpster and vaulted into the air. I landed on his back like a cougar taking down an elk. He fell face-first onto the pavement and struggled to throw me off. I slapped the cuffs on him.

"Jesus Christ! What the fuck, Melody?" He tried to get up, and I put a knee in his back.

"Bail enforcement, asshole! You missed your court date. You're going back to jail."

"Like hell I am." Freddie tried to buck me off. "I'm gonna beat you bloody."

I drew my revolver and pressed it against his cheek. "Settle down, Freddie. I'd hate to have to shoot you."

"Can't collect your bounty if you kill me, bitch."

"Who said anything about killing you?" I flipped him over to face me. "I could put a .357 slug in your elbow or in your knee. Won't kill you, but it'll hurt like hell for a very long time." I pressed the nose of the revolver against his crotch. "Or maybe here. After all the times you beat up Vanessa, it's the least you deserve."

"You cunts are all alike. It's a goddamned conspiracy."

"Conspiracy! You're so full of shit." A laugh escaped my throat. "What'll it be, Freddie? You going to come along peacefully, or do I blast your junk into steak tartare?"

His eyes blazed at me until I pressed the gun harder into his crotch. "Five seconds. Four. Three. Two."

"All right, all right! I'll come along peaceful. Just don't shoot."

"Good dog." I patted him on the head and pulled him to his feet, keeping a firm grip on his arm. "I knew you'd see reason."

The pounding of boots on pavement approached from behind. I pivoted and raised the revolver only to see Rodeo rushing toward us, shotgun in hand.

"Ya got him?" he asked.

"I got him. What took you so long?"

"Got kinda crazy in there. Where the hell's Fiddler?"

Before I could answer, a mob burst out the bar's back door and headed in our direction. Jack the bartender marched in the lead with a sawed-off twelve-gauge leveled at us. Freddie's buddy, Mancini, swung a baseball bat menacingly. Others brandished an assortment of knives, broken bottles, and pool cues.

Rodeo and I pointed our weapons at the approaching throng. I held Colton by the back of his collar, using his body as a shield.

"Stop right there! Bail enforcement!" I shouted in my most commanding voice. "Drop your weapons and go back inside."

They stopped but didn't drop their weapons.

"Let him go, sweetheart," Jack said, "and we may just let you live."

"Yeah, after we fuck y'all up good," Mancini added.

"The lady told you to put down your weapons," Rodeo said. "I suggest you do it."

"Fuck you!" Mancini replied, whacking his bat on the ground.

"Which one of you wants to die first?" I aimed the .357 at Mancini. "How about you, Babe Ruth? Wanna try my fastball?"

Mancini glared at me for a few seconds, then dropped the bat with a hollow clunk that echoed in the alley. He held up his hands in surrender.

"Didn't think so. How about you, Jackie Boy? Wanna take one for the team? Show 'em what a tough guy you are?"

Jack tossed his shotgun on the ground. The other men dropped their weapons and held up their hands.

I smiled. "Good boys. Now go back inside."

With a lot of cursing, grumbling, and single-finger salutes, they complied.

Once the back door had shut, I breathed a sigh of relief and turned to Rodeo. "Well, that was exciting."

"Ya think?" He smirked, reclaimed his Stetson, and gathered up Jack's sawed-off and Mancini's bat. "Where's Fiddler?"

"Son of a bitch was gone when I got out here." I kicked a discarded whiskey bottle, sending it smashing into the back wall of the building. "I'm going to wring his fat neck next time I see him. So sick of his bullshit."

"The other day, he told me he was working the Holly Schwartz job. Maybe that call he got was a tip. Not that it justifies him going AWOL."

The Schwartz case had been a recent news sensation. Holly Schwartz was a seventeen-year-old with a rare neuromuscular condition that left her wheelchair-bound and mentally impaired. She and her mother, Bonnie, were darlings of the charity fundraising scene, appearing on countless telethons and national talk shows to entertain, inspire hope, and attract donations.

Six months ago, Bonnie was murdered. According to the news, a black man had broken in to abducted her. Her mother was stabbed and killed fending him off. Holly escaped somehow and called 911.

The situation went from tragic to bizarre when Phoenix police arrested Holly for her mother's murder. Fans of the mother-daughter duo protested, claiming police were further victimizing a traumatized orphaned girl. The latest development was that Holly had vanished shortly before a competency hearing.

"Did Liberty post Schwartz's bond?" I asked.

"No, some other agency did. Not sure who," Rodeo said as we perp-walked Freddie around the back of the building.

"But Fiddler's working the job? On his own?"

"For the past few weeks." Rodeo shrugged. "He's been having

money problems, Jinx. Combination of medical expenses and gambling debts."

"Why am I just now hearing about this?"

Freddie guffawed.

I smacked him on the back of the head. "Shut the hell up."

"Fiddler and I met for beers last Saturday," Rodeo explained. "He gets chatty after he's had a few. That's when he told me."

"Well, he can take his gambling problems and shove them up his ass. I'm done with him. I need people I can depend on."

We rounded the corner and approached the Gray Ghost. Rodeo opened the back hatch and tossed in the shotguns and the bat. "By the way, when's *Phoenix Living* publishing that article about you?"

Phoenix Living was an alternative weekly covering local culture, news, and politics. A month earlier, Thom Hensley, one of their reporters, had interviewed me for a cover story on female bounty hunters.

I grinned. "Comes out tomorrow. I gotta admit, I'm a little excited to see what Hensley wrote."

"Our very own celebrity." Rodeo patted me on the back. "Try not to get too big a head."

"Yeah, right. I'm just hoping some other bail bond agencies read it and send some jobs our way. Liberty's been a bit lean lately."

4

———

Shortly after sundown, we delivered Freddie Colton without incident to the Madison Street Jail in downtown Phoenix. The duty officer gave me a body receipt, which I would turn over to Liberty Bail Bonds the next morning in exchange for a six-thousand-dollar check. Not bad for a few days' work.

On the way home, I dropped Rodeo off to pick up his turquoise Mazda Miata at the Hub, a coworking space a couple of miles north of the jail, where I rented a desk.

"Dude, when are you going to buy a real car?" I teased when I pulled into the lot next to his car.

"Are you kidding? My Miata gets me plenty o' action."

"Oh really? From where? The Lollipop Guild? That car's so tiny it should have the Hot Wheels logo plastered on the side."

"Trust me, it ain't the size that matters. It's all in the ride." Rodeo grinned like the Cheshire cat. "Speaking of which, wanna go grab a drink somewhere? Stallions, maybe?"

Stallions was a country-style gay bar with a mostly male clientele, though it wasn't unusual to see women there too. I'd been several times to dance and drink. Even brought Conor once or twice. Fun place with good music and nice people, but I wasn't in the mood tonight.

"Thanks, but my skin feels like the salted rim of a margarita glass. I just want to go home and take a shower." Especially after Freddie had been pawing all over me. "Besides, Conor's coming over later. Rain check?"

"Date night. Got it." Rodeo smiled knowingly. He stepped out of the truck and grabbed his shotgun from the back.

I rolled down the window. "I'll deliver the body receipt to Big Bobby first thing tomorrow. Should have a check for you no later than ten."

"Copy that. Have a good night, Jinx." He gave me a fist bump.

"You too."

He locked his shotgun in his trunk and got settled in the driver seat. As I waited for him to start his car before taking off, I checked my phone and noticed Conor had left me a voicemail an hour or so earlier. I played it.

"Sorry, love, but I won't make it tonight. I'm on a stakeout, looking for one of my skips. Could be an all-nighter. Cheeky bastard's been giving me the slip at every turn. I'll catch up with ya in the morning before ya go off with your geeky mates at Comicon. See ya!"

So much for date night, I thought grimly. Since Conor and I had started dating, we saw each other less than when I worked for him. Didn't seem right, but there wasn't much either of us could do about it.

With Conor a no-show, I opted for plan B, which involved devouring an entire pint of raspberry sorbet while marathoning the latest season of *Orange is the New Black*. After a much-needed shower, of course. Yeah, this girl knows how to live.

I walked through the front door of my house on Cypress Street in Phoenix's quaint—and grossly overpriced—Willo District. My brother, Jake, who renovated and flipped houses for a living, got it for well below market value. It was in the Central Corridor, a stone's throw north of downtown, and was the closest thing to an LGBT-friendly neighborhood I'd found in Phoenix. Conor lived only a half mile away, so who was I to complain?

I shuffled through the living room and down a short hallway to my bedroom. The artichoke-style ceiling light above my futon filled the room with a golden glow. I wriggled out of my clothes, stepped into the bathroom, and turned on the shower.

As the hot water washed off a day's worth of sweat—and the lingering memory of Freddie's hand on my thigh drained away—a loud noise elsewhere in the house caught my attention. A thunk followed by a man cursing. A chill ran through me. Conor was on his stakeout. No one else was expected. So who the hell was in my house?

I left the water running so as not to tip off my uninvited guest that I was on to him. I slipped out of the shower and pulled out a Glock I kept stashed under a stack of hand towels in a drawer by the sink. The pistol's slide sounded deafening as I chambered a round.

I froze and listened to get a fix on my intruder's location. A kitchen drawer banged open—the junk drawer, from the sound of it—then slammed shut. Then another drawer rattled open.

Go time! I charged down the short hallway and leveled the gun at a large man standing with his back to me in the dark kitchen. "Down on the ground, now! Hands behind your head!"

It wasn't until the man held up his hands in surrender that I noticed the coppery curls atop his head. In one hand was a bottle of wine. In the other, a corkscrew.

"Don't shoot me, mum," he said in a thick Irish brogue. "I'll go quietly." He turned to face me with a cheesy smile on his face.

I lowered the Glock, catching my breath as my heart thundered in my chest. "Jesus, Conor. What the hell? I thought you were on a stakeout."

"The bloke showed up. We grabbed him and took him to Glendale lockup." His grin deepened. "Shite! Look at ya! All naked and deadly."

I rolled my eyes, a little embarrassed, then marched back to the bathroom to put away the Glock and grab my robe.

Conor hugged me from behind, whispering, "Now that we're both excited, how about a ride, eh, love?" He kissed my ear. I could feel him getting hard against my hip.

"After you scared me half to death? Fat chance, buddy boy!" I said with a chuckle. I slipped out of his grip, pulled on my robe, and tied the sash in a loose bow.

He sat on the toilet, looking up at me. "Scared *you*? I was the one staring down the business end of a Glock. Almost shat myself."

"Serves you right for sneaking in." I sat in his lap. Damn, he smelled good. My body literally ached to feel him inside me.

"Can ya blame me, love? You're gonna be spending all weekend half naked with your geeky mates wantin' to cop a feel of Superwoman."

I playfully swatted him. "First off, it's Wonder Woman, not Superwoman. And second, I won't be half naked. Just showing a little cleavage. I can try on the costume for you if you don't believe me."

"That's all right. I saw it when you first made it. And it's brilliant. But right now, I'm in the mood for more than a little cleavage." His deft fingers untied the bow on my robe's sash.

We made our way to the bedroom and spent the next hour loosening all the knots that a day pursuing fugitives can put into a body. It always amazed me that a man as strong as Conor could be so gentle. His fingers and lips played my body with the skill of a jazz musician, leaving me gasping with pleasure. When he slid into me, I grabbed his butt cheeks and pulled him in even deeper, rocking into a rhythm that sent my mind shooting into the stratosphere.

By the time we were done, I lay next to him, floating on the lingering buzz of two orgasms, my hand resting on the ginger curls of hair covering his belly.

"You hungry?" I asked, gazing absently at the scars on his chest caused years earlier by an IED explosion overseas.

He took a deep sigh. "What? Ya want to go again?"

"Not for me, silly. For food. I could make us some stir-fry or something."

He opened his eyes. "That sounds brilliant."

I threw on a worn gray tank top and matching yoga pants, made my way to the kitchen, and chopped up some vegetables and a chicken breast. As I fired up the gas stove and added some peanut oil to the wok, Conor wandered in wearing my robe.

"Don't you look cute." I tossed the chicken into the hot oil and stirred it as it sizzled. "Though the pink kinda clashes with your red hair."

"I suppose it does." He shrugged.

"You know that article comes out tomorrow. The one in *Phoenix Living* Thom Hensley interviewed me for. I'm excited to see what he wrote."

His smile faded ever so slightly. "Oh yeah? That's great, love."

"Something wrong?"

"Naw, nothing's wrong." Conor shrugged and snatched a piece of broccoli from the cutting board. "I'm glad you're excited."

A slight hesitation in his voice told me he was hiding something. I set down the spatula and faced him, hands on my hips. "What aren't you telling me?"

"Nothing, love. Swear to Christ."

"Don't lie to me, mister. You're so full of shit your emerald eyes are turning brown. Now spill!"

"It's just . . . in the bail enforcement biz, it's a good idea to maintain a low profile, especially with the press. Those dodgy blokes'll do a number on ya, sure as shoot ya. You in particular don't need guys like Thom Hensley digging up your past."

"Good grief, you think I told him I was trans? Not a chance. All we talked about was how I got into bounty hunting and what it's like being a woman in a male-dominated business. Period."

He kissed me on the forehead. "It's just I've read this guy's work. He doesn't write fluff stories, Jinxie. He writes hit pieces. Exposés about bad cops, corrupt politicians, and evil corporations. He did that series on Sheriff Joe last year. Wrote one last month about a strip club owner who's running a human trafficking ring."

"This isn't a hit piece, Conor. Thom's a nice guy. You'll see." I tossed in the veggies and my secret combination of sauces, though I was starting to lose my appetite.

"Don't be cross, love. I'm just worried about ya is all."

"I'd rather you be excited for me."

He hugged me from behind and gently kissed my ear. "Then excited I am."

I dished up two plates and handed him one. "Let's eat."

"How'd your night go?" he asked between bites. "D'ya get your guy?"

"Rodeo and I did." I picked at my food. "Fiddler was on the back door. But when the shit went down, he was MIA. Rodeo thinks he's working that Holly Schwartz case."

"That bloody prick! Don't know what's gotten into him lately. Ya want I should kick his arse?"

"Naw, I got it handled."

"That's my girl!" He grabbed my hand and squeezed gently, making it impossible to stay mad at him.

"After I turn in the body receipt to Liberty in the morning, I'm grabbing a bunch of copies of *Phoenix Living*. Want me to get you one?"

Conor paused mid-chew, shrugged, and shook his head a little too vigorously. "Naw, I'll just read yours."

"You really think he's going to out me, don't you? Why would you think that? Is there something you're not telling me?"

"Just me being paranoid is all."

"Paranoid and overprotective."

"What can I say? Ya mean the world to me, love." A smile bloomed across his face, but it had no effect on me.

"Well, cut it out. It's getting on my nerves. I'm not a child. I'm a grown woman." I pushed my plate aside. Conor's paranoia and a day of chasing down fugitives in the heat were taking their toll on my body as well as my mood.

He winked at me. "On that we can definitely agree."

"I'm tired. I think I'll turn in early. You coming?"

"I'd love to, but there's some paperwork I have to finish up at my place. Deez and the boys'll be pissed if I don't have their checks ready for them in the morning." He walked over and kissed me. "Don't worry. I'm sure the article will be brilliant."

"Thanks." I hugged him. "I love you."

"Love ya too. Get some rest. I'll clean up the kitchen before I go."

5

There were so many things I loved about being a bounty
hunter. I set my own hours, though sometimes that
involved spending long nights sitting in a car, bored out
of my skull and hoping I didn't have to pee. Also, I didn't have to
wear a uniform or worry about warrants or writing up arrest
reports. And there was nothing like the thrill of slapping the cuffs
on a fugitive and bringing him in. The only thing better was
getting paid to do it.

The next morning, I showed up at Liberty Bail Bonds on
Jackson Street in downtown Phoenix. Big Bobby Mills, the owner,
had run the agency there since Biblical times, or so he told
people. The office always reminded me of a cross between a man
cave and a barbershop, wrapped in wood paneling, circa 1975.

A half dozen wooden folding chairs formed a small lobby at
the front of the office. Autographed photos of Big Bobby posing
with various celebrities hung on one wall, his favorite showing
him arm in arm with members of Lynyrd Skynyrd after he'd
bailed them out for disorderly conduct and possession of a
controlled substance.

Big Bobby's wife, Sara Jean, sat at an antique walnut desk

separating the lobby from the rest of the office. She worked as the office manager, providing me with files for defendants who'd missed their court dates—and paychecks, after I'd delivered them back to jail.

Sara Jean was a sizable woman with a smile that could fill a room with warm fuzzies, and a Southern drawl as sweet as fresh-picked peaches. Whenever I stopped by, she'd fill me in on the latest about her grandkids, whose photos surrounded her workstation. As the only two women affiliated with the agency, we had formed a bond.

Above her desk hung a constellation of plaques and framed certificates recognizing the agency's contributions to local nonprofits including Valley Big Brothers Big Sisters, Phoenix Children's Hospital, and St. Mary's Food Bank.

When Sara Jean didn't smile at me as I walked in with Freddie Colton's body receipt, I knew something was bothering her.

"What's wrong?" I asked as I sat in the chair in front of her desk. "One of your grandkids sick again?"

"No." She kept her eyes on her computer monitor, typing away.

I set the body receipt on the desk. She glanced at it and kept typing.

"You and Big Bobby have a fight?"

"No."

I started to worry. Had I said or done something wrong? Last time we spoke a few days earlier, she'd been telling me about having lost three pounds. I'd joked that soon she'd be beating off the boys with a stick. Maybe she'd thought I was mocking her.

"You upset with me about something?"

Her fingers froze above the computer keys. Her eyes locked with mine, and I saw a self-righteous anger that made me scooch my chair back a few inches. Without a word, she pulled the new issue of *Phoenix Living* out of a desk drawer and slapped it down. My goofy mug was on the cover, though to be honest, I thought the photo made me look better than I did in real life.

"Okay. Was there something in the article that bothered you?" Had I said something negative about Liberty Bail Bonds? I didn't think so.

Sara Jean looked away. "All this time I thought you were a girl."

I glanced at the cover again and felt as if I'd been punched in the gut. The teaser headline read "Tranny Bounty Hunter Cleans Up the Town." *Aw, shit!*

"Sara Jean, I *am* a girl." I stood up, arms spread wide. "I mean, look at me. Do I look like a boy? Do I sound like a boy?"

"No, but according to this . . . " She pounded the magazine with her finger so hard, I thought she'd break one of her manicured nails. "You got one of them sex changes."

I sighed, even as my heart revved in my chest like a race car engine. "I've always been a girl, Sara Jean. It's just that through some crazy mix-up of biochemistry or genetics, I was born with a boy's body. It's hard to explain."

She fixed her gaze on me once again. "Ain't nothing to explain. Boys is boys, and girls is girls. God made you what you are. Ain't no changing it."

"I wish it were that simple, Sara Jean, but it's not. I'm—"

"Perverts like you's what's wrong with this world. Making it dangerous for God-fearing folks to use public restrooms."

"A pervert? Seriously, Sara Jean, is that what you think I am?" I rolled my eyes. "Wanna know what trans people do in public restrooms? We pee. We poop. And we wash our hands, which is more than I can say for *some* people."

Her hands disappeared under her desk. "Don't know what you're talking about."

"What we *don't* do, Miss Dirty Hands, is obsess about what's between someone else's legs because trans people are smart enough to know it's none of our goddamned business."

Her face colored with indignation. "Ha! That's what the fake liberal media wants people to think. Like y'all are just poor innocent victims. But I see y'all for what you are—wolves in sheep's clothing. Or women's clothing."

I pressed my palm against my forehead. I wasn't going to win this argument. As much as I liked Sara Jean, I'd known people like her my whole life—mindless drones who'd been fed a steady diet of hate-filled bullshit and self-righteous hypocrisy so long they refused to hear anything close to the truth.

"Fine. You want to think I'm some deviant out to destroy Western civilization, so be it. I just want to get paid, okay? Can we at least keep this professional?" I slid the body receipt closer to her.

She glanced at the paper, then at me, her mouth a thin line of bitterness. She snorted, pulled out the company checkbook, and wrote out a check with such ferocious pen strokes I thought she'd set the paper on fire. With a snap, she ripped the check loose and handed it to me. "Here's your check, *sir*. Don't come back."

My jaw tensed. If there was one thing that pissed me off, it was being intentionally misgendered, especially by friends. Or former friends. "I'd like to talk to Big Bobby."

"Bobby don't wanna talk to you. He gave me explicit instructions. He ain't hiring you no more. We are good Christians and don't take kindly to deceivers and perverts coming in here acting all unnatural. All these years I trusted you. I shared things with you. Intimate things with you, you . . . you thing."

Okay, that did it. Gloves were off.

I stood up and glared at her. "Look here, you ignorant transphobic bitch! Maybe if you pulled your holier-than-thou head out of your ass once in a while, you'd see not everyone is as privileged as you, that the rest of us are just doing our best to survive."

My rant was apparently loud enough to draw Big Bobby charging out of his office looking like a bull. He pointed a thick finger at me. "Get outta my office, you degenerate! Don't you never come back."

"I'm still working some of your cases, Bobby. So I will be—"

"We can handle them without you. Don't you worry your pretty, little, uh . . ."

I smirked. "Aw, Big Bobby. You called me pretty. Are you sweet on me?"

His face resembled a blood blister about to pop. "Get out!"

I'd said my piece, and I'd been paid. "Fine." I kicked open the door, stormed out into the heat, and sat in the Gray Ghost, wrestling with a combination of anger, humiliation, and hurt.

I had dirt on both of them. Maybe it would get me my job back, maybe it wouldn't. But even if it did, did I want to work with such bigoted assholes? I really didn't.

Bile rose in my throat as the salacious headline on the *Phoenix Living* cover flashed back into my mind. How had I not seen this coming? Was I not allowed to leave that part of my past behind? Would it haunt me for the rest of my life? I pounded the dash until the throbbing in my hand pulled me from that spiral of endless, unanswerable questions.

I took a deep breath. I focused on my mantra—WWWWD. What Would Wonder Woman Do? She'd let it go. She'd focus on the task at hand, which in my case meant finding a job. While I'd freelanced for several bail bond agencies over the years, the majority of my revenue had been coming from Liberty. With Big Bobby and Sara Jean giving me the heave-ho, I'd have to hustle up new business with my old contacts to make up the loss.

But first, I needed to get a copy of *Phoenix Living* and find out what in hell Thom Hensley had written about me.

6

I picked up a copy of *Phoenix Living* at a QT convenience store on McDowell. The clerk smiled, glanced at the cover, then back at me with a surprised look on his face. "Is that you?"

I nodded, impatient to read the article. "Yeah, it's me."

"So you're—"

"Really in a hurry. Thanks!" I hustled out the door for the sanctuary of the Gray Ghost.

I frantically flipped to the article. My heart thundered in my chest. My gaze danced erratically across the page. *Goddammit, girl, just chill out and focus.* I took a deep breath and started reading.

Most of what Thom Hensley had written came from our interviews. But then I came across the sentence: "Not only is Jinx Ballou among the few female bounty hunters in Arizona, she is also the only one openly transgender."

Openly transgender? What the hell? I pounded the dashboard so hard it sent a jolt of pain through my arm to my shoulder.

I'd met with Hensley three times, once at an upscale restaurant in Scottsdale, then twice more at his office for follow-up questions. He'd been charming and respectful, displaying a critical yet open mind and an attention to details.

"I find the idea of a female bounty hunter intriguing and encouraging," he told me over blue corn taquitos at our first meeting, setting a digital recorder between us. "We need more people like you breaking glass ceilings."

"Everybody's got to earn a paycheck somehow," I joked. "Besides, it's not like I'm the only woman in the business."

"You ever meet Domino Harvey?"

"No. She died a few years before I became a bounty hunter."

"What about that gal up in New Jersey? God, what's her name?"

"I know who you mean. Met her once when one of my fugitives fled to Trenton." I chuckled sardonically. "Not the most professional bounty hunter I've worked with, but she gets the job done."

"What inspired you to become a bounty hunter?"

My face warmed with embarrassment. "I was a nerdy kid reading comic books, dreaming of becoming a real-life Wonder Woman. When I realized at age six that wouldn't happen, I set my sights on becoming a homicide detective. I earned a bachelor's in criminology from Arizona State, then joined Phoenix PD."

"You were a cop?" He cocked an eyebrow. "Why'd you leave?"

"Funny thing about police departments. They don't let you go straight from the academy to being a plainclothes detective."

"You don't say," he replied with a chuckle.

"I knew this, obviously. But what I didn't realize was how miserable I'd be as a patrol officer. Me and uniforms? Not so much. Then there're all the rules and regs I had to follow. Wonder Woman never bothered with probable cause or arrest reports."

I stared blankly across the room, the memories replaying vividly in my mind. "The turning point came when my partner, Officer Luis Garza, and I responded to a violent confrontation between two rival gang members at Grumpy's Bar and Grill on the 300 block of West McDowell. By the time we arrived on scene, the suspects had been subdued by a couple of patrons—Conor Doyle and Robert 'Fiddler' Dixon.

"I took Conor's statement and learned he worked as a bounty hunter. I was intrigued. After two other uniforms transported the suspects to lockup, I questioned Conor further about his work. He explained he didn't have to wear a uniform, request warrants, or fill out arrest reports. I turned in my badge and joined his team a month later."

What I left out of my interviews with Hensley was that my aversion to uniforms and the regimental aspects of cop life stemmed from a near fatal semester at Phoenix Junior High Military Academy.

Before coming out as trans, I'd been acting out a lot. Drinking. Cigarettes. Weed. Anything to avoid dealing with my feelings of being a girl. When I got caught shoplifting a dress, my father, a psychologist, decided the discipline of a military academy would straighten me out and make a man out of me.

Instead, it sent me into a depression spiral that culminated in me breaking into the commandant's office, looking for a gun to kill myself with. All I found was a bottle of Vicodin. I washed down two dozen pills with a bottle of twelve-year-old scotch. Not that I really wanted to die. I just wanted to stop the soul-crushing pain I'd been struggling with my entire life.

I woke hours later in the infirmary, my throat sore from having my stomach pumped. My distraught father soon showed up, desperate to understand why I wanted to kill myself. With my defenses down from the Vicodin and the humiliation of the failed suicide attempt, I shared my dark secret with him—that despite outward appearances, I'd always known I was a girl.

To my surprise, he didn't freak. Apparently, he'd suspected something was going on and had been doing research. After I was sent home, he rallied my mother and brother around me and got me started on androgen blockers. The next semester, I enrolled at Discovery Charter Middle School as a girl.

I stared at the newspaper, entertaining visions of exacting my revenge on Hensley—running him over with my truck, riddling his body with bullets Bonnie-and-Clyde style, pushing him off Camelback Mountain and enjoying the sickening splat as he hit the valley floor a thousand feet below.

How he'd discovered my transgender history was beyond me. Only a few people knew. One of them had spilled the beans, and I was determined to find out who.

When I finally calmed down, I drove north to *Phoenix Living*'s editorial offices in the Sun Glow Building on the corner of Third Street and Earll Drive. I pulled into the underground garage and locked my guns in the glove box, in case I was tempted to turn my murder fantasies into reality. Being fired was bad enough. Didn't need to get arrested for first-degree murder.

After a short ride on the elevator, I stormed into the offices with my copy of the paper rolled in my fist. "I need to speak to Thom Hensley," I said to the receptionist as calmly as I could manage.

Moments later, Thom came out wearing a pale-gray suit and a lime-green dress shirt.

"Hey! How's my favorite bounty hunter?" He extended his hand, looking extremely chipper. I wanted to put *him* through a chipper.

"What the fuck, Thom?" I shook the paper at him.

"Excuse me? Something wrong with the article?"

"What gave you the right to out me?"

"Ah." He frowned and gestured toward a hallway. "Let's talk in my office."

My face burned. I felt like screaming but accepted his invitation. He led me to a glass-enclosed office and drew the blinds. The office was small but smartly decorated. Journalism awards lined a walnut bookshelf along one wall. He settled behind his modern black desk and invited me to sit in one of the upholstered guest chairs. I remained standing.

"How dare you do this to me, you slimy little hack! Bad

enough you out me, but you call me a tranny on the front page? You have any idea how offensive that word is?"

"I apologize for the use of that term. My copy editor writes the headlines, not me."

"I don't care if it was the pope. You had no right bringing up the subject in the first place."

He leaned forward, extending his hands in a conciliatory gesture. "Jinxie, sweetie, I did you and the transgender community a favor. Visibility is vital to greater acceptance. Look at Laverne Cox, Jamie Clayton, and Chaz Bono. They're not hiding who they are."

"Doesn't give you the right to out me. I got fired because of your story."

He pursed his lips in an apologetic pout. "Look, I'm sorry."

"Sorry doesn't help me. I want to know who told you."

"I'm afraid I can't reveal my sources. You understand."

I leaned over his desk, shaking the rolled-up paper at him as if he were a misbehaving puppy. "What I understand is that you're going to give me their name or you'll wish you had."

"Do I have to call security?" His hand hovered over a red button on his desk phone.

I gritted my teeth. A voice in the back of my head told me to chill. I sat in the chair. "Look, I just want to know who told. This is my life. Not some byline."

"Jinx, believe me when I say I never meant to hurt you or cost you your job. I know it's tough. But I have the utmost respect for your kind."

"My *kind*? What the hell do you know about my kind? Are you trans?"

"Well, no." He placed a hand on mine. "But look at the bigger picture. You're a trailblazer, paving the way for other transgender people to enter the profession. You should be proud."

I pulled my hand away while my grip on the paper tightened. "Don't try to charm me, Hensley. I want the person's name, and I want a public apology from you printed in next week's issue."

"Sorry. No can do."

"I'm going to sue your ass for defamation of character. You, your copy editor, the whole fucking newspaper."

"You can try, but you'd only win if what I wrote wasn't true. Problem is, everything in that article is factual. And eventually, you'll realize I did you a favor."

"How 'bout I do the world a favor and jam this paper up your ass?"

His hand pressed the red button. "You should leave now."

I stood, my hands trembling, while my murder fantasies played on a loop in my head. "You're going to regret this, dipshit."

I stormed out of the office as two sides of beef dressed in black polo shirts appeared by the receptionist's desk. "Relax, boys. I'm leaving."

The security guards escorted me down the elevator and out to my truck, going so far as to watch me drive to the booth to pay for parking. In the ruckus, I hadn't gotten my parking ticket validated, so I had to pay ten bucks for the privilege of giving Hensley a piece of my mind. *Insult, meet injury.*

I hit the streets, unsure where I was going. *I should call Conor,* I thought. But I couldn't bring myself to do it. I kept hearing his voice in my head, warning me not to get too excited about the article.

Was this what Conor was hinting at last night? Did he tip off Hensley about my trans history? Surely Conor wouldn't betray me like that. But if not him, who?

The questions raced round and round my head like coked-up hamsters on an exercise wheel, until I decided to talk with the one person who could understand my predicament—my fairy drag mother, Tía Juana.

7

Juanita Valdez came up through the Phoenix drag scene in the 1970s and '80s, performing under the name Tía Juana. In the early '90s, she transitioned to living full-time as a woman. Eventually she became the owner of the Main Drag, one of the valley's biggest queer bars, where she also served as mistress of ceremonies a few nights a week.

I met Juanita when I joined the local transgender support group as a teenager. She took an immediate liking to me, declaring herself my fairy drag mother. She taught me how to walk and talk and blend in with the rest of the female population.

"You gotta work it, Miss Thang. Don't let them boys clock you as anything but total fish. Your survival depends on it," she'd warn me, usually after chastising me for not looking or acting femme enough.

Shortly after my reassignment surgery, she bestowed upon me my nickname, Jinx—a mash-up of my first and middle names, Jenna Christina.

Juanita lived in an elegant four-bedroom house off Seventh Street near North Mountain, where she offered housing to an ever-changing roster of trans people left homeless by their families.

I passed under an arch of climbing vines sheltering Juanita's front door from the morning sun. My watch read just past eleven, a decent hour for most respectable folks. Juanita, however, tended to sleep till the crack of noon due to the late hours she kept at the bar. I rang her doorbell, anyway.

Moments later, the door opened. Juanita stood tall and thin, combining the elegance of Lena Horne with the flamboyance and sultry voice of Tina Turner. Her brightly colored silk robe revealed long, dark legs, still shapely for someone in her midsixties.

She was not wearing makeup, a rarity for her and not a good sign. She could be moody before she'd had coffee and put on her face. Like, rabid-dog-psycho-killer moody. So I opted to tread lightly.

"Morning, *tía*. Did I wake you?"

"Please, *chica*, tell me that wasn't you leaning on my doorbell at this god-awful hour." She gazed at me, bleary eyed. "Haven't even put on my war paint yet."

"You look beautiful, anyway. Truly."

"Ain't you sweet. Full o' bullshit but sweet." She sighed and stepped out of the doorway. "Come on in, sweetie. Don't need you melting on my front stoop."

I followed her down a short hallway to a spacious, brightly lit kitchen that looked out onto a courtyard bursting with oleander, hibiscus, and Mexican bird of paradise. I took a seat at the breakfast bar while she filled two earthenware mugs with coffee. A copy of *Phoenix Living* lay facedown on the bar nearby.

"Cream or sugar, sugar?" she asked.

"A little cream, if you don't mind."

"You know I never do." She poured a smidge of half-and-half into the mug, then slid it over to me. "I always have mine black. This tired old queen needs all the kick she can get."

"Where are your housemates?"

"Rosalyn's at a job interview. Caden had a doctor's appointment. I think he's starting T soon." T was slang for testosterone injections.

"How's Ciara's new bookkeeping job working out?"

Juanita's mouth twisted into a cruel scar. "You didn't hear?"

"No."

"Some motherfucker beat her near to death last week in the parking lot where she worked."

"Shit. That was her?" My chest ached. "I can't believe it. How's she doing?"

"She came outta the coma after two days. Face is beat all to shit. Broken arm. Docs saying she may come home tomorrow."

"Damn. The police know who did it?"

"Cops don't know shit. No one saw nothing."

"You want me to ask around? Talk to some of my old contacts on the force?"

"Anything you can do would be appreciated, sweetie." Juanita settled onto a stool on the other side of the bar, cradling her coffee. "So what brings Miss Jinx Ballou to Casa Valdez this depressingly sunny morning?"

A dust devil of rage and humiliation twisted up through my mind. I flipped over the *Phoenix Living*. "I got outed."

"Oh my heavens!" she exclaimed in mock horror. "Someone call the queer police. There's been an outing! Should I administer mouth-to-mouth?"

"Gee, thanks. Just what I need is to be mocked." I slipped the issue closer to her. "Look at this shit. It's humiliating."

She tilted her head and met my gaze. "Humiliating? Why? Because now everyone knows the valley's badass female bounty hunter is a hot little tranny?"

"*Tía*, stop! You know I hate that word." Angry tears prickled behind my eyes. I was not going to cry in front of her, no matter how she pressed my buttons.

Her gentle hand touched my cheek. "My dear little princess warrior, I'm sorry, but there's nothing humiliating about people knowing you're transgender."

"It puts a target on my back. You were the one who pounded it into my head that my survival depended on people not knowing I was trans. Look what happened to Ciara."

"True, I did tell you that, but that was a long time ago. Things have changed. Time for hiding in closets is over for seasoned warriors like you and me. We got to stand up and make a show of force. Let these motherfuckers know we're not going away." She tossed the copy of *Phoenix Living* across the breakfast bar. "Honestly, Jinx, I think you're just upset your little bubble of passing privilege got burst. A lot of us couldn't pass as cisgender if we tried."

"Maybe you're right, except the bail bond agent I work for fired me over the article."

"Well, fuck them! You'll find someone else to work for. You're good at what you do, right?"

I stared at my coffee. "Yeah, I suppose."

"And you're still dating that fine slab of Irish corned beefcake, are you not?"

I couldn't help but blush. "I am."

"You have a family that loves you and embraces you for who you are."

"Yeah."

"You have a roof over your head. Food to eat. A car to get you from point A to point B, yes?"

"Technically a truck, but yes."

"Then what the hell you bitchin' about, *chica*? You got a shit-load more than most of us. I mean, damn, you transitioned before you hit puberty. Your folks paid for your surgery. You won the fucking lottery."

"I know, I know, but—"

"Look at me, Jinx. I'm sixty-four years old and can't get

surgery because I'm HIV positive. Ciara, bless her tender heart, was nearly murdered. And you're whining about some crappy article and a narrow-minded bail bond agent? Bitch, please! Jinx Ballou, pity party for one!"

I felt sick and properly put in my place. I'd shown up here like a spoiled child with a broken toy when so many in the trans community faced homelessness, brutality, and worse on a daily basis. The room was silent for several minutes except for the chirping of a family of quail in the courtyard outside, the hen herding a half dozen bug-sized chicks to the shelter of the bushes.

Juanita broke the silence. "So why's *Phoenix Living* writing about you in the first place?"

I shrugged. "Thom Hensley called wanting to do a cover story about female bounty hunters. I said yes, figuring it'd boost business. But I never mentioned anything about being trans."

"Miss Thang, Hensley's an investigative reporter. He writes about corrupt politicians and Russian gangsters. You sat down with him and are surprised he dug up your little secret? *Chica*, please!"

"Okay, maybe I was a little naïve."

"A little?"

"Okay, a lot naïve. But still, I'd like to know who outed me to Hensley."

"Sure wasn't me. I never spoke to the man. Maybe that sweet boyfriend of yours."

I thought more about the night before, and my stomach soured. "He was acting squirrelly last night when I brought up the article."

"Then I suggest you ask him."

"I can't."

"Why the hell not? He's your boyfriend, ain't he?"

"I don't want him thinking I don't trust him."

"*Do* you trust him?"

"Yes. Maybe."

"Just ask the man. Don't play these mind games. Life's too short for that nonsense."

I finished my coffee. "You're right."

"Of course I'm right. Tía Juana is *always* right. Now"—Juanita gestured at my faded Pearl Jam concert T-shirt—"what is up with this outfit? Please tell me '90s grunge is not making a comeback. And where the hell is your war paint?"

"This is what bounty hunters wear. And it's too freakin' hot for makeup."

"Miss Thang, listen to your fairy drag mother and listen good. It is *never* too hot for makeup. A little waterproof eyeliner and some lipstick, at least." She tugged on my naked earlobes. "And did you learn nothing about accessorizing, or was I talking to myself all those years? I can loan you a pair of hoop earrings that would at least add some class to this sad little tomboy look you got going."

"Hoop earrings are too easy to get caught on something. Besides, I have some accessories in the Gray Ghost."

"Oh really? Such as?"

I smirked. "Black leather tactical belt from Bianchi with a molded plastic holster for my Ruger and two magazine pouches."

"Lord almighty, just kill me now."

"And I have bracelets."

She folded her arms and gave me a suspicious stare. "Really? Show me."

I pulled a pair of handcuffs from my back pocket. "See?"

"Out!" She pointed toward the front door. "I can stand this heresy no longer."

She was teasing, at least I thought she was. Sometimes it was hard to tell with her. But I needed to get going, anyway. I had to find a bail bond agency willing to hire me now that my big secret was out there.

At the door, I hugged her. "Thanks, *tía*. I can always count on you for a reality check."

"Darlin', my reality check bounced years ago." She cradled my face in her long, delicate fingers. "Go out there and get you a new client. Show those *pendejos* you won't be bullied."

"I will."

"And be safe out there in that crazy-ass world, you hear?"

"Always."

8

After Juanita's, I dropped by my house for a change of clothes. Since I was trying to drum up business, something a little dressier than my Pearl Jam shirt and jeans was called for. I was no fashionista, so my selection of business attire was limited. I debated between the federal agent style of a dark suit and blouse or something more casual like a polo shirt and jeans. I compromised with a white button-down shirt and khakis.

Juanita's comments inspired me to put on some makeup, but I kept it minimal. A little eyeliner. Mascara. Neutral lipstick. I was proud to be a woman, but I tended to follow my mother's philosophy of "less is more." As for my hair, I went with a simple ponytail. I was applying to be a bounty hunter, not a receptionist.

When I was satisfied with my look, I headed out into the blistering summer heat with a leather notebook filled with a thrown-together résumé and copies of body receipts I'd earned over the years.

One by one, I worked my way down a list of bail bond agencies I'd contracted with in the past, starting in downtown

Phoenix, then heading east to Scottsdale, Gilbert, Tempe, and Mesa. When that yielded nothing, I doubled back and tried bail bond shops in Avondale, Goodyear, Glendale, Peoria, and Surprise.

None of my conversations were as confrontational as the one I'd had with Sara Jean and Big Bobby, but the bail bond agents' averted eyes and clipped tones told me everything their words didn't—I'd been blackballed.

By midafternoon, I'd had enough. My voicemail showed three messages from Conor. I ignored them. I should have been slipping into my Wonder Woman outfit and celebrating sci-fi/fantasy culture with the costumed hordes at Phoenix Comicon. But even that held no appeal when I had no idea when I'd get my next paycheck.

While I calculated my next move, my phone rang. Caller ID showed it was my father.

"Hi, Dad, what's up?"

"Hey, cupcake. I'm calling to say how impressed your mom and I are with the article in *Phoenix Living*. When you told us you were interviewed, I didn't realize you talked about being transgender. Kudos to you for being so bold."

"Yeah," I grumbled. "Wasn't exactly how I planned it."

"Why? What's wrong?"

"I never told that reporter I was trans. He dug it up some other way."

"How do you feel about that?" My father, ever the psychologist.

"Angry, hurt, maybe a little scared. The bail bond agency I worked for fired me when they found out. I've been banging on doors all day trying to find work."

"Maybe it's for the best."

"The best? How is this for the best? How'm I supposed to pay my bills if I can't find work?"

"Being in the closet is no way to live, always afraid someone's going to find out your deep, dark secret. Before you came out to us, you were so miserable. Living with a secret is like a cancer. It eats away at your self-esteem and peace of mind. You're a beautiful, smart woman who happens to be transgender. I want my daughter to be proud of who she is."

I sighed. "I am proud, Dad. It's just I work in a very macho, testosterone-driven business. Not everyone gets it, you know?"

"Maybe you could go back to being a cop."

"I don't want to be a cop. I like what I do."

"And that's important, I know." I heard him sigh. "Trust the process, sweetheart. One thing this transition taught you was that you can get through anything. It made you tough. Sometimes I wonder if it made you too tough."

"I'm okay, Dad. I'll figure this out."

"I know you will. Oh, by the way, your mother wanted me to tell you she's been shopping again for you."

"Dad, no! I told her to stop. She keeps buying me those god-awful polyester dresses that look like they're from the 1950s."

"She's trying to be supportive. Just humor her next time you see her."

"I'd hate to reinforce bad behavior. Isn't that what you always say?"

"You got me there, cupcake." He laughed. "I'll try to talk to her. You'll be by for Sunday brunch?"

"I will."

"See you then, sweetie. Love you."

"Love you too, Dad."

When I hung up, I decided a little bang-bang therapy might improve my mood. I drove north to Glendale and spent two hours punching holes in paper targets at the Westgate Shooting Range. There was something deeply satisfying about the explosive power of firing off a few boxes of ammo. Especially when the figures on the targets looked a lot like Big Bobby Mills.

By the time I was done, my wrist was throbbing and my bank

account was a hundred bucks leaner. But I no longer felt the need to go all Bruce Willis on anyone, so the world was that much safer for everybody.

I hopped into the Gray Ghost and sent texts to Becca and Conor, saying I'd had a crappy day and asking them to meet me at Grumpy's Bar and Grill. Both responded with confirmations they'd be there. Becca rapid-fire texted me, desperate to know what was wrong. I replied that I'd fill her in at Grumpy's.

With my dinner plans in place, I called Rodeo. He answered after a couple of rings.

"Jinx. Uh, hey."

"I got paid for the Colton job. You can pick up your check tomorrow at the Hub."

"Just mail it. You got my address."

I sighed. "You know, don't you?"

"Know what?"

"Don't be coy with me, Rodeo. You heard Big Bobby fired me."

"He called me down to the office and told me. I'm sorry, Jinx. But you had to know there'd be consequences for coming out so publicly as . . . well, you know."

"Come on, Rodeo. You're a big boy. You can say the word. I'm transgender. Big friggin' deal. Is this going to be a problem between us?"

"Of course not. Happy to have you as part of the LGBTQ family. Truth be told, I'm a little disappointed you told that reporter before you told me."

"I never told that reporter I was trans." My grip tightened on the phone. I took a deep breath, not wanting to go down that rabbit hole again. "Anyway, I've been beating the bushes all day to drum up some new business for us. Should have something lined up soon." I hoped.

He didn't respond right away. I wondered if the call had dropped. "Rodeo? You still there?"

"Actually, I'm still working for Liberty." His voice was pinched.

"You what? How?"

"Big Bobby hired Fiddler and me as full-time employees. He's bringing everything in-house. I'll get a regular salary, health insurance, paid time off, the works."

"But you work for *me*, Rodeo," I said between clenched teeth. "I've been training you for six months."

"And I'm grateful. It's just that. . ."

"What?"

"Big Bobby said if I continued to work for you, he'd blackball me as well. I'm sorry, I can't risk it."

"How can you, as a gay man, turn a blind eye to what he's doing to me? What happened to loyalty and community solidarity?" My eyes felt as if they were throbbing.

"First off, I'm not gay, Jinx. I'm bi."

My face warmed at my misguided assumption. "Sorry. My bad."

"Second, loyalty doesn't pay the bills. I need the money and the bennies. My daughter's got severe nut allergies. Have you seen the price of EpiPens lately? So unless you've got big-paying jobs already lined up—"

"I got some leads," I lied. "And I've still got a few smaller outstanding jobs from Liberty."

"Jinx, they've been reassigned to Fiddler. He's the one leading the Liberty in-house team."

"Fiddler's *leading* the team? After he left us in the lurch on the Colton job?"

"He had an emergency come up."

"Yeah, an emergency. He's been having a lot of those lately. Working on his crew is the worst idea in the history of shitty ideas. You're an idiot if you can't see that."

"You think insulting me will get me to change my mind?"

"Rodeo, you're gonna get yourself killed working with him. What'll your daughter do then?"

"I survived Afghanistan. I can handle Fiddler. And FYI, he wants you to mail him his check too."

"Fiddler can kiss my ass. I'm not paying him squat after he disappeared yesterday."

"He's not going to be happy, but I'll let him know."

"You do that, Mr. Benedict Arnold." I hung up. I hadn't eaten since breakfast and was feeling seriously hangry. I needed food and friendly company.

9

―――

I threaded my way south through rush hour traffic to Grumpy's. The place was packed. I nabbed the last empty booth and ordered my usual—a Grumpy Burger all the way, Cajun fries, and a Four Peaks White Ale to wash it down.

Grumpy, a pudgy Vietnam Vet with silver mutton chop side-burns, had opened the bar and grill after being discharged from the army in 1973. The place had become a local landmark, having won *Phoenix Living*'s "Best of Phoenix" award in the Bar and Grill category more than twenty times.

As I waited for Becca and Conor, my mind drifted back to the article and my argument with Hensley. I tried to compile a list of people who might have outed me. The thought that any of my close friends or family might have blabbed to Hensley about my trans past decimated my appetite.

I looked up and caught Grumpy looming over me as I nibbled unenthusiastically on a french fry.

"Something wrong with my cookin', kitten?" He chewed absently on an unlit cigar.

"Don't start with me, Grumpy. I've had a crap day."

"That so? Something 'bout that article in *Phoenix Living*, I reckon."

I buried my head in my hands. "Geez Louise, not you too."

"Ah, don't go fretting, girl. I don't care what you are or what you been. Long as your money's green, you're all right in my book."

I sighed and offered him a weak smile. "Thanks, Grumpy. At least somebody doesn't think I'm trying to corrupt Western civilization. Big Bobby at Liberty Bail Bonds fired me over this. Can you believe it?"

Grumpy huffed. "World's full of assholes, kitten. Just gotta move on." He raised an eyebrow. "You can still pay for that dinner, right?"

"Yes!" I laughed sardonically. "I'm fired but not broke. Not yet, anyway."

"Good." He wandered toward the kitchen. "You're a smart girl. I'm shore you'll figure it out."

"Sorry I'm late." Becca slid into the other side of the booth. She fanned her flushed, sweaty face with a menu. "Traffic's a bitch, it's a hundred and eight outside, and my car's AC chooses today to crap out."

"Guess I'm not the only one having a lousy day."

"Yeah, you mentioned that in your text. What's going on? You and Conor having trouble?"

After she placed her order for a black-bean-and-corn salad, I filled her in on the day's events, including my suspicions about Conor.

"Oh, sweetie, I'm so sorry. You'd think *Phoenix Living* would know better than to out someone," she said between bites of salad. "And why would Liberty care about you being trans? It's ancient history."

"Beats me. And people wonder why I keep it private." I buried my head in my hands.

"You don't really think Conor told, do you?"

"I don't know. Someone did."

"It wasn't me. When that reporter guy called—"

"Wait!" My heart skipped a beat, and I looked up at her. "Hensley called you?"

"Yeah, said he was doing background research."

"How'd he get your number?"

"I figured you gave it to him."

"Geez, who is this guy? Anderson Cooper? What'd you tell him?"

"That we both work at the Hub, you doing your bounty hunter thing and me working as an IT security consultant. What else? I mentioned I sometimes do skip tracing for you. He asked how we met. I said we'd been best friends since junior high. But not a word about you being trans. I'd never betray your trust, I swear." She held up her hand as if taking an oath.

"I know you wouldn't. But someone did, and it's bugging the hell out of me. And the way Conor was acting last night . . ." Bile burned in my throat.

Conor slid into the booth next to me, which suddenly felt very cramped.

"Jesus, love, ya look wrecked."

He started to put his arm around me, but I pushed it away, unable to meet his gaze.

"What's going on, Jinxie? Is this about the bit in *Phoenix Living*?"

"So you read it?" It came out harsher than I intended. I locked eyes with him.

"I did. On balance, I thought it was a great story. Painted ya as the brilliant, badass bounty hunter you are."

"Yeah," I said sardonically. "Except for the part where Hensley outed me and called me a tranny."

"Aye, except for that." He grimaced and let his gaze slide away.

"Did you tell him?"

"Tell him what? That you're trans? Ya know I'd never."

"But you knew he'd out me, right? That's why you were acting so weird last night."

Conor sighed. "Hensley called and asked what it's like dating a trans girl. Don't know how he knew, but I told him it was none of his bloody business."

I punched him in the chest. "Why didn't you warn me?"

"I was hoping he wouldn't print it. Ya want me to have a go at him?"

"No, I already did. Tried to get him to tell who outed me, but he refused and had security escort me out of the building."

"I could try to hack into his computer remotely," Becca suggested with a devilish grin. "Maybe I can find out some answers for you."

I shook my head. "Don't bother. At this point, it doesn't really matter. It's out there. I just need to focus on getting some new clients now that Liberty fired me."

"They didn't!" Conor gasped. "Bloody bastards."

"Not only that, they hired my team out from under me. Rodeo and Fiddler are now Liberty Bail Bonds employees."

"I'm so sorry, love." He put his arms around me, and I let him this time. It felt good. "Ya still going to Comicon?"

I shrugged. "Maybe. Tomorrow's priority is to find someone willing to hire me, then assemble a new team. Right now the prospects aren't looking promising. Everyone I talked to today gave me the cold shoulder."

Conor kissed my ear. Becca clasped my hand. If nothing else, it was always good to know who had my back.

"Ya try Bennett Bail Bonds in Mesa?" Conor asked.

"Yes."

"West Valley Bail Bonds by the sheriff's substation in Surprise?"

"Told me they didn't have anything for me, but they'd 'keep me in mind,'" I replied with air quotes.

Conor nodded knowingly. "How about Second Chance down on Washington by the ball park?"

I nodded. "Same results."

"Why don't you go back to working on Conor's team?" Becca

asked. "You're always complaining how y'all never see each other."

Conor grimaced but didn't say anything.

"Definitely not," I answered after an uncomfortable pause. "Things got awkward after we started dating. Then when Deez got shot, everybody blamed me."

"Who's Deez again?" Becca asked.

"One of my guys." Conor shook his head. "And it wasn't your fault, Jinx."

"And yet suddenly I was Yoko Ono."

"Why? What happened?"

"We were making entry into a fugitive's house. He was a meth cook." Flashes of that day assaulted my mind. The reek of acetone and ammonia from a meth lab set up in a shed in the backyard. An explosion of glass as we made entry through an Arcadia door. A frightened child in the clutter-filled living room. Our team shouting commands to get on the ground, followed by people screaming.

"A guy in an upstairs bedroom got the jump on me and threw me to the ground. I should have been able to handle the situation, but I . . . I'd spent the night before at Conor's and was . . . I hadn't gotten enough sleep." I could hear my voice shake. My face felt hot. "Deez tried to pull the guy off me and got a bullet in the neck for his troubles. He spent two weeks in ICU."

"But he's right as rain now, love. All water under the bridge," Conor said. "Maybe Becca's right. Give it another go."

"I don't think so," I said with a weak smile. "Tommy Boy, Deez, and Byrd are all great guys. I just don't think it would work, especially now that I've been outed. Best I stick to running my own show."

"Well, shite." He doodled aimlessly with a french fry in the ketchup on his plate. "There's one place I don't think ya tried."

"Where?" I asked.

"Assurity Bail Bonds."

I scrunched my nose. "Didn't they go out of business a while ago?"

"The owner, Aaron Levinson, became ill a couple years ago and closed shop. After he died a few months back, his daughter, Sadie, opened a new office at the Arizona Center. Word on the street is she's got a defaulted bond worth a few hundred grand about to come due."

"Sweet." I grinned. "Best news I've heard all day."

"Just one thing." His mouth became a thin slit across his face. His gaze clouded with concern.

"What's that?"

He fidgeted in his seat. "Don't mention my name when ya talk to Sadie."

"Why not?"

"Just a misunderstanding from way back. Nothing important."

"Nothing important? Really?" I cocked my head. "So not important that I shouldn't even bring up your name? What kind of bullshit answer is that? Come on, dude, spill!"

"I can't, love. Honestly. Just trust me. She's a good person to work for. I doubt she'll care if you're trans. But keep my name out of it. It's all I'm asking."

"D'you sleep with her, big guy?" Becca asked, pointing her fork at him.

His face colored. "I'm not saying anything. If ya don't want to work for her, don't. Just trying to be helpful is all."

"Fine, I'll pay her a visit tomorrow." I eyed him suspiciously, unsettled by his need for secrecy. I needed the work.

10

———

fter dinner, I hugged Becca goodbye and followed Conor back to his place, just a half mile from my house.

Part of me needed some TLC after the lousy day I'd had. But I also hoped to uncover this mysterious history between him and Levinson. I didn't want to ask her for work only to get blindsided later by some bullshit in their collective past. Better to know what I was getting into beforehand.

The sun had dipped below the horizon as we pulled up to Conor's house, leaving the neighborhood in the soft, hazy glow of dusk. On the outside, his house looked like any other on the block. Brick facade with sage-green trim and a line of manicured shrubs, surrounded by a lawn of sun-scorched Bermuda grass. A few mesquite trees dotted the yard.

Inside the house, the walls were bare. No photos or artwork. No plants. Saltillo tile covered the floor throughout. His furniture was sparse but functional, consisting of a bed and nightstand in the bedroom, and two recliners and an entertainment center in the living room. His office had a bare IKEA desk, a metal folding chair, and a filing cabinet. The whole place was dull, empty, and lifeless—not so much a bachelor pad as a bunker.

"Ya want a drink?" he asked coolly as we stood in his kitchen, avoiding eye contact. It felt like our first date but more tense. He pulled a bottle of Jameson's from a cabinet.

"What I want is for you to tell me what happened between you and this Levinson woman. You have a bad breakup or something?"

His face colored. "I don't want to talk about it, Jinxie." He poured whiskey into a couple of glasses and offered me one.

I slammed my glass onto the counter hard enough to slosh whiskey onto the worn laminate surface. "You're always full of secrets, Conor, and I'm sick of it! You didn't tell me Hensley knew I was trans. I had to learn about it from Sara Jean Mills. And now this crap? Quit stalling and tell me. I'm your girlfriend, for Christ's sake."

"There are things I don't discuss. This is one of them." He drained his glass and poured another before taking it into the living room. He plopped down on a recliner and stared at the floor. I followed him.

"I get why you don't talk about growing up during the Troubles in Ireland or your experiences with Dark Horse Security in Iraq. But this? Give me a freakin' break, dude. Whatever happened between you and Levinson, I'm a big girl. I can take it."

"Leave it alone, Jinx! I'm not bloody telling ya!" He glared at me so hard it felt like a blow to my chest.

I took a step back. "Why you got to be so secretive?"

"We all got secrets, love. I kept yours all these years. I'm asking you to respect mine."

"Bullshit! I trusted you with my secret. But you won't trust me with yours."

"This ain't about trust, love," he growled. "What happened between Sadie and me's got nothing to do with you."

"If I'm going to be working with her and dating you, it sure as hell does. I need to know what I'm in the middle of because, sooner or later, it's going to come out. I'd rather find out now than get blindsided later."

"Then don't work with her."

"No one else will hire me!" My shouts echoed off the bare walls, followed by a silence broken only by the bass beat of my pulse in my ears.

"I don't know what to tell ya, love," he said, barely above a whisper. His expression softened as tears rimmed his eyes. "Just leave my bloody name out of it, if ya go see her. That's all I'm asking ya. Please, just let it go."

God damn him and his puppy dog eyes. My anger softened. I took his free hand in mine. "Fine, I'll let it go. For now."

I woke at three the next morning after dreaming I'd discovered who'd outed me to Hensley. Unfortunately, my betrayer's identity evaded my conscious mind. I lay there trying to pull it from the jumbled fragments of the dream, but whatever eureka moment I'd had was gone. Probably nonsense, anyway.

At three thirty, I climbed out of bed and fixed a pot of coffee. I felt untethered. My private medical history had been exposed for everyone to gawk at. My career was in free fall. And now my trust in Conor was crumbling. Juanita's reminder that some had it worse than me didn't make the raw ache in my soul any less.

By the second cup of coffee, I wasn't feeling any better. So I grabbed some shorts, a tank top, and spare running shoes I kept in Conor's closet and went for a parkour workout.

The Willo District where Conor and I lived offered mostly level ground with few obstacles to bounce off of. Not an ideal parkour playground. Residents weren't overly fond of *traceurs*, as we parkour practitioners called ourselves, vaulting over their cars or dashing through their backyards. Block walls, palm trees, and a neighborhood park had to suffice for practicing flips, climbs, and other maneuvers. Anything to get my heart pumping and my mind focused in the moment rather than on my troubles.

After an hour's workout, I returned to Conor's. By the time his alarm went off at six, I had showered, inhaled a liter of water, and scarfed down a bowl of cereal. I was sneaking out the front door when I heard, "Leaving without saying goodbye, love?"

He stood shirtless, leaning against a wall. Despite the old scars on his chest and legs, he looked sexy as hell. Part of me wanted to jump his bones. Another part wanted to strangle him until he confessed what had happened between him and Levinson.

"Morning, sweetie. Didn't want to wake you. Lots to do today."

"Gonna talk to Sadie about hiring ya?"

I sighed. "Right now, it's my best option. So, yeah." When he raised an eyebrow, I added, "And I won't mention you. Promise."

"That's my girl. Now c'mere and let me give ya a kiss for luck."

I stepped back inside and kissed him deeply, even as a laundry list of emotions twisted my insides.

When I pulled away a moment later, he asked, "Ya going to the convention afterwards?"

"Definitely, assuming Sadie hires me. I need to seriously geek out with the three *C*'s—cosplay, comic books, and my favorite celebs."

"Well, you're *my* favorite celeb."

My face flushed. "I'm just a girl who likes to catch fugitives and play dress up." I gave him a final peck on the lips and promised to let him know how it went with Sadie.

I stopped by my place for a change of dressy-ish clothes and stashed my Wonder Woman costume in a duffel bag before heading downtown to Assurity Bail Bonds's office at Arizona Center. If my meeting with Sadie Levinson went well, I could walk the half block south to the Phoenix Convention Center and enjoy the rest of Comicon. Tracking down Assurity's wayward defendants could wait until Monday.

The parking garage was near capacity when I arrived, no doubt packed with vehicles belonging to convention attendees. I found a space on the top floor, left the duffel on the passenger seat, and grabbed my notebook.

Assurity Bail Bonds was tucked in a corner on Arizona Center's second floor. A string of bells tied above the door jingled as I entered. The office consisted of a twenty-by-thirty-foot room with a single desk, three chairs, a coffee station, and a few vertical filing cabinets. Framed prints of paintings by Monet, Picasso, and Gaugin decorated the glossy white walls.

A slender woman in her forties with a no-nonsense expression on her face sat behind the desk with a stack of files beside her computer. Short wedge haircut. Red metallic framed glasses.

Tailored maroon jacket over a white button-down blouse. A model of the modern professional woman. I hated to admit she left me feeling a little intimidated.

"Sadie Levinson?" I asked.

She glanced up at me and put a hand to her chin. "Hmmm … too casual for an attorney. Too dressy to be posting someone's bail. Whatever you're selling, I'm not buying."

"Not selling anything, actually. I'm Jinx Ballou, bail enforcement agent. I understand you have a sizable bond that's defaulted."

She leaned back in her chair. "Who told you that?"

"Well, you know, people talk." I forced a laugh, trying to act casual as I sat in front of her desk.

"Indeed. Been talking quite a lot about you lately, Ms. Ballou." She pulled a copy of *Phoenix Living* out of the wastebasket by her desk. "Took me a moment, but I recognize you now."

Oh boy. Here we go again. "Look, Ms. Levinson, I'm a damn good bounty hunter with eight years' experience. I've tracked fugitives from one end of this country to the other. The fact that I transitioned nearly twenty years ago doesn't change that."

"You're right, it doesn't." She slid the newspaper to the corner of her desk. "Personally, I don't care what you are or what you have between your legs. I do care about not going out of business. Right now that's a real possibility if I have to pay this defaulted bond. The bounty hunter I originally hired for this case wasn't as reliable as I'd been led to believe."

"You're talking about Fiddler, right?"

"You know him?"

I scoffed. "Let's just say you're not alone in your assessment of him."

"I have a lot on the line with this bond. I need someone I can trust, someone who gets results."

"I get results." I pulled out copies of body receipts I'd accumulated over the years and set them in front of her. She looked them over. Our eyes locked, and I felt a connection as she pulled a file from the stack on her desk.

"Very well. I gather you're familiar with the Holly Schwartz case."

"The disabled teenager charged with stabbing her mother to death."

"That's her. She missed her competency hearing a month ago. I'm on the line for half a mill."

A half-million-dollar bond meant a bounty worth fifty grand. Cartoon dollar signs ka-chinged in my brain. "I'm listening."

"I need her back in custody no later than end of day Tuesday."

The dollar signs went thunk and vanished. "Tuesday? Are you freakin' kidding me? That's only five days from now, including today."

"I'm very aware of that fact."

Finding someone who'd been in the wind for a month was tough. Doing it in five days? The Catholic Church sainted people for lesser miracles. But considering my limited employment opportunities, I had little to lose and a whole lot to gain. "I'll take it."

She handed me the file. I scanned a copy of the arrest report, the bail application with Holly's photo, and printouts of emails from Fiddler updating Sadie on the case. Between his lack of punctuation, convoluted syntax, and rampant typos, much of what Fiddler wrote was incomprehensible. Honestly, didn't nobody learn this guy some English?

"What's your take on the aunt? What's her name?" I flipped back to the bail application. "Kimberly Morton."

"Until Bonnie Schwartz's death, Ms. Morton had very little contact with Holly, despite being Bonnie's sister. Even with all of the media appearances, Bonnie was very protective of her daughter, never letting her out of her sight for a minute."

"And yet Morton puts up her home as collateral for bail? That's awfully generous. You think she knows where Holly is?"

"Based on what Fiddler told me, Ms. Morton cares a lot for Holly and what she's been through, despite their estrangement. Would she risk losing her home to protect the girl? I don't know for sure, but I doubt it."

"You think Holly was kidnapped?"

"Morton never received a ransom request as far as I know. Still, Fiddler uncovered reports of two other young women in the Schwartzes' Maryvale neighborhood who've gone missing in the past year. According to the arrest report, Holly claimed a black man was trying to kidnap her when her mother was killed."

"Any idea who this mysterious black man might be?"

"Fiddler didn't turn up anything. The detective on the case believes Holly made up the story."

I flipped to the arrest report and found the name of the detective assigned to the case—Pierce Hardin. I stiffened. I did not want to talk to him if I could avoid it.

"All right, I'll try to bring Holly in by Tuesday."

"I don't need you to try." Sadie looked as if the weight of the world sat on her brow. "You need to bring her in by Tuesday, or we're both out of a job."

I stood and offered her my hand, which she shook. "Understood."

As I turned to leave, she said, "One more thing. I don't want Conor Doyle working on this."

I tried to look innocent. "Conor who?"

"Don't play coy with me, Ms. Ballou. I read the article." She held up the newspaper and waved it in the air. "I know Conor's your boyfriend."

"Okay, fine, he's my boyfriend. What the hell's the deal between you two, anyway? Y'all have a bad breakup? He boil your pet rabbit or something?"

Her face was a stone wall. "Suffice it to say, I don't trust him and neither should you. He's not who he says he is."

"What the hell's that supposed to mean?"

"I can't say any more. Just take my word for it."

"Now who's being coy? He's my boyfriend. If there's something I should know about Conor, I'd like to hear it."

She pulled off her glasses and pinched the bridge of her nose. "You want to date him, that's your choice. But I don't want him involved on this job. That's final."

"Look, lady, you want me to find Holly Schwartz—in five days, no less—I'm going to need help. Right now Conor's all I got."

Sadie held out her hand, reaching for the file. "Fine. I'll give the job to someone else. I'm not having Conor anywhere near my cases."

I grimaced. She was probably bluffing. She seemed as hard up as I was. Then again, I could really use the fifty grand, even if it was a long shot. "All right. I'll locate Holly without him."

"See that you do. I find out he's working with you on this, I'll pull it. You hear me?"

I held up a three-finger salute. "Scout's honor."

12

———————

I climbed the stairs of the parking garage, feeling conflicted about my new situation. On the one hand, I was happy to be working again, and with a bail agent who didn't care that I was transgender. The fifty-grand bounty wasn't anything to sneeze at, either.

On the other hand, what Sadie said about Conor bothered me. More than bothered me. It pissed me the fuck off. What the hell was she talking about? I didn't want to believe her. But there were parts of Conor's past that he didn't talk about. Like growing up during the Troubles in Ireland and some of the shit he saw in Afghanistan and Iraq. But what the hell did that have to do with who he was now?

When I reached the Gray Ghost, I flung the duffel bag with my Wonder Woman costume into the back so hard it bounced off the back window. No time to play superhero for the geeky masses. Comicon was on hold until I could track down a poor, orphaned, disabled girl and throw her back in jail. Sometimes this job fucking sucked.

Sitting in the driver's seat, I cranked the AC and opened Holly's file. Until the murder, she'd been living with her mom in a small house in the Maryvale neighborhood in west Phoenix. But after getting bailed out of jail, she'd been staying with her aunt, Kimberly Morton. That put Morton at the top of my list of people to talk to. I'd check out Holly's old house in Maryvale later, though it was unlikely she was there.

I dropped by my house to change into a Gin Wigmore T-shirt and some cargo pants, then punched Morton's address into my GPS. She lived in a fancy-schmancy neighborhood off Tatum Boulevard in Paradise Valley, just east of Phoenix. I put my phone on speaker and called Conor.

"Good news! I got the job," I said when he answered.

"That's brilliant, love. Ya want to meet for lunch to celebrate, or are ya headed to Comicon?"

"Neither, unfortunately. I'm working the Holly Schwartz case. Only got five days to track her down."

"Shite! Five days. So, what's the bounty on her?"

"Fifty grand."

"Oy! That's a pretty penny. All to find some girl in a wheelchair?"

"You want in on it?"

So what if I swore on my scout's honor not to bring in Conor. The truth was, I never was one of those cookie-peddling Girl Scouts, anyway. Sure as hell was never a Boy Scout. Besides, something about this case didn't feel right.

If she was hiding out at Auntie Kimberly's house, Fiddler would have dragged her ass back to jail a long time ago. So either Kim Morton had connections with people who knew how to hide someone, or something seriously fucked up was going on. Going it alone could get dangerous either way.

"Ya didn't mention my name, did ya, love?"

"Not technically," I hedged.

"Jinxie, ya promised me ya wouldn't."

"Don't get your boxers in a bunch, dude. *She* brought up your name, not me. She knew we were dating from the *Phoenix Living* article. Maybe you shouldn't have gotten all blabby with Hensley, huh?"

I heard him sigh. "So she's cool with me being on the job?"

"Not so much. In fact, she expressly forbade it." My fists tightened on the steering wheel, and I cut off some guy in a shiny new Beemer to get around a slow-moving landscaping truck. "Point of fact, she said you weren't who you said you are. What's she talking about, Conor?"

"Bollocks!"

"That's all you have to say? Bollocks?"

"She's daft, Jinxie. You've known me for years. Do ya honestly think I'm not who I say I am?"

"I didn't until all this bullshit. What happened between you two? I want an answer."

"Perhaps I should stay out of it. Don't want to jeopardize your business with Sadie."

I sighed. This wasn't going where I wanted it to. "Forget Sadie, Conor. I need backup on this, all right?"

"What's wrong, Jinxie?" he asked with a forced chuckle. "Ya worried a little girl in a wheelchair can take ya?"

"Yeah, right. Not her I'm worried about. There's something seriously hinky about this case. A disabled girl vanishes days before a hearing on her mother's murder? And after a month of hunting, Fiddler still can't find her? I got a bad feeling about this one. So are you in or what?"

"I've always got your back, love. Especially when things get dodgy. What's the plan?"

I told him to meet me at the aunt's house in Paradise Valley and gave him the address.

"I'll be there. But don't blame me if Sadie goes batshite crazy when she finds out I'm helping you."

"I won't tell if you won't."

Paradise Valley was an upscale suburb wedged between Phoenix and Scottsdale. Kimberly Morton's neighborhood, at the base of Mummy Mountain, consisted of sprawling stucco-covered ranch houses in various shades of tan, topped with red Spanish tile roofs and surrounded by manicured desert landscaping. Among the shiny Porsches, Teslas, and Bentleys, my scruffy-looking SUV stuck out like a turd in a champagne fountain.

I parked on the street next to Morton's semicircular driveway and tried again to decipher Fiddler's email updates to Sadie while I waited for Conor. I didn't learn much. Much of what he wrote was incomprehensible word salad. There were mentions of the house where Holly and Bonnie lived and a black van but nothing that made any sense. He'd smelled like weed when we'd gone after Freddie Colton. Maybe he was stoned when he wrote the emails. Maybe that was why he hadn't found Holly.

Ten minutes later, Conor pulled up behind me in his restored '68 black Dodge Charger. I grabbed my paperwork and put on my body armor and tactical belt, with my Taser on the right and my Ruger on the left in a cross-draw holster. A pair of wraparound shades and fingerless black leather gloves completed the ensemble.

The moment I opened the truck's door, the morning heat slapped me in the face like a wave. "God help me when monsoon season gets here."

"Hey, love," Conor said as we met by his car. He wore a tan polo shirt with the logo of his company, Viper Fugitive Recovery, embroidered in the left corner. "Ya look like you're ready to storm the castle. Ya expecting trouble from the aunt?"

"Not taking any chances." I adjusted the Velcro straps on the side of my vest. "Besides, I want her to know we mean business."

"Fair enough. I think I'll chance it without a vest in this swanky neighborhood."

"Suit yourself."

"So how do ya want to handle it? Ya want me around back?"

I shook my head. "I doubt Holly's here. But even if she is, she's not likely to outrun us in a wheelchair. Let's stick together for now, see what Auntie Kim has to say."

"Works for me."

We followed a flagstone walk to the front porch. I jabbed at the doorbell a couple of times, then banged on the security screen door. "Open up! Bail enforcement!"

Moments later, a woman resembling a slender, uptown version of Bonnie Schwartz appeared on the other side of the security door. She was dressed in a brightly colored flowing silk sundress. The fancy threads contrasted with the haunted expression in her eyes. Her skin was sallow, and she looked as if she hadn't slept or eaten in weeks.

"Can I help you?" Her voice was a hoarse, lifeless whisper.

"Kimberly Morton?"

"Yes." Her gaze switched from me to Conor and back again. "If this is about my niece, I told the last guy, she isn't here."

"Look, lady, enough of this bullshit. You posted her bond with Assurity Bail Bonds, and Holly missed her court date last month. If I don't return her to custody immediately, you're going to lose your pretty little mansion." I waved the paperwork authorizing me to arrest Holly and slapped it against the screen.

Morton blinked back tears. "If I knew where she was, I'd tell you. Someone took her. That's all I know. I called the police, but they won't help. No one cares."

If she was lying, she was damn good at it. I offered her a sympathetic smile as my nagging conscience got the best of me. "Fine. I'm sorry. Tell us what you know. Then maybe we can find her and return her safely to custody. All right?"

I could see the wheels turning in her head, trying to decide if she could trust us.

"We just wanna help you and your niece get things sorted out, mum," Conor said in his sexiest brogue. "She's already been through so much, don'cha think? Please let us help."

The woman's distraught demeanor softened. I was jealous of the way his accent mesmerized other women. Then again, I fell for him the same way, so who was I to complain? And if it got us in the door, all the better.

Morton sighed and opened the security door. "Come in."

13

———

She led us from the spacious entryway to a living room as big as my entire house. Unlike my place, all the furniture and decor was coordinated in a kaleidoscope of off-white, beige, tan, and taupe. Native American pottery and other artwork lined bookshelves. The only vibrant colors appeared in a collection of abstract paintings mounted on one wall—explosions of red, orange, and blue on canvas.

She led me to a tan Ultrasuede couch. "Can I offer the two of you something to drink?"

"Some water would be great." Anything to get the taste of the desert out of my mouth.

She strolled to a wet bar on the far end of the room and pulled two cobalt glass bottles from a mini fridge and offered one to each of us. The water was some fancy brand I'd never heard of. I unscrewed the cap and took a long pull. Didn't taste any better than Dasani, but it was cold and wet, and that was all I cared about.

"When was the last time you saw Holly?" I asked.

A cloud passed over her face. "Two days before her competency hearing was scheduled. Holly and I had an argument about our attorney's decision to have her declared not guilty by reason of mental defect. Holly hated that. Kept screaming how she wasn't crazy or stupid, and insisted she didn't kill her mother."

"But Holly is mentally disabled, right?" I watched her body language. So far, she seemed to be telling the truth.

"Last time I spoke with my sister, Bonnie—which was a few years ago—she said Holly had the mental capacity of a five-year-old. Holly was fourteen at the time. Personally, I think she's smarter than her mother gave her credit for."

"It's been three years since you've seen your sister?" Conor asked.

"As kids, we were thick as thieves, she being just a year older than me. But in junior high, she shut me out and started hanging with a rough crowd—skaters and junkies, mostly. She ran away at sixteen, and I didn't see her for several years.

"Then out of the blue, I got a call from her not long after my late husband passed. Bonnie was pregnant. I figured she'd have an abortion, but she believed the pregnancy was a sign from the universe to get her shit together. Despite my busy schedule as a Realtor, I tried to be there for her during the pregnancy best I could."

"That's very generous of you," I said. "So what happened? How did you two become estranged again?"

"When Holly was six months old, she got really sick. Bonnie said she spit everything up and was having horrible seizures. Medical tests didn't show anything specific, so her doctors dismissed Holly's symptoms. They treated my sister like she was imagining things."

"How horrible," Conor replied.

"Bonnie didn't give up. She spent every spare moment looking up rare medical conditions on the web and poring over medical journals. It got to the point where her own health was declining. I made the mistake of telling her she was becoming obsessed. She didn't take it well. From then on, my contact with Bonnie and Holly was sporadic at best."

"Who killed Bonnie?" Conor asked. His question surprised me. It wasn't our job to determine Holly's guilt or innocence. We just had to bring her in and let the courts figure out the rest.

"I only know what Holly told me. Bonnie was in their backyard, feeding the neighborhood cats. Holly was coloring at the dining room table when a large black man broke into the house. She screamed when he tried to drag her away. Bonnie came running and . . ." Tears streamed down her face. My throat grew tight as I watched the raw emotion tear away her composure.

"Bonnie grabbed a kitchen knife to stop him. But he took it from her. Stabbed her several times in the stomach. Holly managed to lock herself in the bathroom and call 911."

"Why'd the police arrest Holly?" I asked.

"The police interrogated her for hours, treating her like she was a hardened criminal instead of a mentally impaired teenager. When I got a call from her and learned what was going on, I phoned my friend Zach Swearingen to represent her. He normally handles corporate cases, but he's the only lawyer I know, and he did some pro bono criminal work when he was younger.

"Once he was there, I figured they'd let her go. Instead, they arrested her. She was the victim, and they had the nerve to arrest her. What's this world coming to?"

"What about the girl's da?" Conor asked. "Is he in the picture?"

"Her da?"

"Her father," I explained, giving Conor a look.

"Bonnie never told me his name. Just said he was some guy she used to sleep with in order to buy dope. Bonnie used to have a drug problem. I think that's what caused Holly's health problems. I never pressed her for the father's identity. Not my business, you understand."

Something about the story didn't sit right with me, but I couldn't put my finger on it. "You love your niece, I gather."

"Of course, she's a good kid. And she's family."

"You'd do anything for her. Pay for her lawyer. Post her bail."

"Naturally!" Morton started to come alive. "Someone needs to be there for her. Sure as hell hasn't been the police."

"Would you risk losing your house to keep her from going to trial?" I pressed.

Conor shot me a glare that said back off. I ignored it.

Morton's face flushed. "You think I'm hiding her? I told you, someone kidnapped her. I called the police, this Detective Hardin, but he hasn't done a damned thing. Won't even issue an AMBER Alert."

"Did he say why?" Conor asked.

"He refuses to believe she was taken against her will."

"No ransom demand, though?" I pressed.

"No." The fire in her eyes dwindled. "That's what scares me more than anything. If they don't want money, then why take her?"

Morton pulled a pill bottle out of her purse and swallowed a couple of capsules. "I keep hearing about these sex traffickers— these men who sell girls into slavery. It terrifies me to think what she must be going through."

"How'd the kidnappers get in?" Conor asked.

"They broke the backdoor window. Snatched her right out of her bed. Didn't even take her wheelchair, for God's sake. I was asleep in the next room, but somehow I didn't hear a thing."

Yeah, I wonder why, I thought, eyeing the pill bottle still in her hand.

Morton's gaze drifted out to the backyard, where sunlight danced off the water of their pool. "I'm honestly at my wit's end."

I glanced around the room, looking for a security system. "You have any surveillance cameras?"

"I do. But the system wasn't armed that night for some reason. I don't know if it crashed or maybe Holly accidentally turned it off." She wiped a tear from her eye. "I can't tell you how many times I've wished I'd checked it before I went to bed that night."

"Can we see the room where she was staying?" Conor gave her that smile of his.

The damned woman blushed and smiled as she wiped her cheek. "I suppose it couldn't hurt anything."

14

I followed Kimberly Morton down a hallway to a bedroom ablaze with sunlight filtered through ivory curtains. A painting of galloping horses hung on the wall above the queen-size sleigh bed. The floral comforter was pulled back, revealing pale-yellow sheets. A nearby bookshelf held a collection of DVDs, middle-grade chapter books, and animal-themed knickknacks.

"After her mother died, I did what I could to make this guest room feel like home. She loves animals, especially horses. We were talking about getting a puppy before she disappeared."

Along the opposite wall stood a wooden desk with a stack of coloring books and a cup full of colored pencils. I picked up a coloring book that featured forest animals on the cover and thumbed through it. The use of color and shading was impressive, not what I expected from a mentally impaired teenager. "Did Holly color these?"

"Yes. She's quite talented. Something that her diseases couldn't take away, thank goodness."

I flipped to a picture of a mother bear and a cub and paused. On top of the brown coloring of the fur, streaks of red cut across the cub's stomach and front legs. Holly had also drawn something the color of rotten avocado streaming out of the cub's mouth.

On the next page, a family of deer crept through the forest. Thick red slashes marked the body of one of the fawns, while green and black lines spewed from its mouth. Holly had added the same bizarre touches on the following page. "Geez! What's up with this?" I held the book up to show Morton. "Bleeding, puking animals?" *Maybe she* is *nuts,* I thought.

"Oh, that poor child." Kimberly took the book and placed a hand on one of the drawings. "Must be a response to the trauma she's experienced."

"Uh-huh." I explored the dresser next to the bed. The top drawer was empty. The bottom drawer contained only a couple of shirts, one pair of shorts, and three mismatched socks.

I glanced at Conor, who stood next to the open wall closet. A couple of dresses hung from the rack.

"These all the clothes she owns?" Conor asked. "Seems a bit empty, if ya ask me."

"What?" Kimberly looked in the closet, then in the dresser drawer I was holding open. "No, she has plenty of clothes. I don't understand where they could be."

"You didn't notice her clothes were gone until just now? Seriously?"

"I . . . I never thought to look in her closet. I just assumed they'd be here."

I shook my head. "Anything else missing that should be here?"

"No, not that I see." Kimberly's lower lip trembled as she looked around the room. *Is she for real, or is this all an act to throw us off the scent? How could she not have noticed this before?*

I stepped into the bathroom. Prescription pill bottles were lined up on the counter like a squad of orange plastic soldiers next to a weekly pill organizer. I looked at the labels but had no idea what they were for. "She take all these meds?"

Morton nodded. "That's what worries me most. She needs these. Without them she could . . . assuming . . . assuming she's still . . . oh God!" Emotion choked off the rest of her sentence. She covered her face with her hand and slumped onto the toilet seat. "She has so many health problems. She can't survive without her meds."

I faced her and put my arms on her shoulders. "Can you think of anyone who would have taken her?"

"No! Of course not!"

I tried to think of more questions but couldn't come up with anything. I looked at Conor, and he shrugged.

"I don't know where Holly is, Ms. Morton. Maybe you're hiding her."

"I'm not!"

"Maybe she was kidnapped like you say. Either way, I intend to find her." I placed my business card in her hand. She looked up, and I locked eyes with her. "Call me if you think of anything that might help."

"I just want her home safe," she said, staring blankly at the shower curtain.

"You know when I find her, I'm taking her to jail, right? What happens after that is out of my hands."

Morton nodded. "I know."

"Come on." I led Conor out of the bathroom and into the living room. "She knows more than she's saying. How could she not have noticed Holly's clothes were missing?"

"Aye. And why'd they take the girl's clothes but leave her meds and wheelchair behind? Seems a bit dodgy. How about we talk to the neighbors? You go west, I'll go east?"

I mulled it over. "Yeah, all right. Meet you back at the cars in ten."

"And Kimberly?"

I glanced back down the hallway. "What about her?"

"I hate to leave her like this."

"She's a grown woman. I'm sure she can take care of herself.

We got a fugitive to find and a bounty to collect. Come on. Let's canvass the neighbors."

"Whatever ya say, boss lady," he said with a grin.

I nudged him. "Don't you forget it."

When I stepped outside, my eyeballs felt as if they were boiling in my skull. Sweat trickled down my face as I hiked along the street for what felt like a mile but was probably closer to a couple of hundred feet. I pulled off my ballistic vest. My shirt looked as if I were competing in a wet T-shirt contest.

By the time I reached the neighbor's porch, my arms were bright red. I pressed the doorbell, and a moment later, a man in a green-striped shirt and chinos answered the door.

"If you're looking for landscaping work, I've already got somebody. Sorry."

"Seriously, dude? You think I'm here to trim your palm trees?" I held up my vest and pointed at the words Bail Enforcement Agent. "I'm a bounty hunter looking for your neighbor's niece. Her name's Holly Schwartz. Have you seen her?" I handed him Holly's photo.

He squinted at the picture and shook his head. "Nope. Doesn't look familiar."

"Really? She's been living next door for the past six months. Take another look."

He studied the photo for a minute. "Wait, I have seen her."

I felt a rush of hope. A break at last. "Really? Where?"

"On TV. 'Bout a year ago. One of them telethons, I think it was. That girl was on it, sitting in a wheelchair, singing 'God Bless America.' Skinny little thing."

I sighed. "Have you seen her recently? Say, in the past week or so?"

"Can't say as I have. Sorry." He handed me back the photo and shut the door before I could ask anything else.

I continued on to the next two houses, then doubled back to the neighbors on the other side of the street with similar results. Finally, I trudged back to our vehicles. My feet were so hot from the sidewalk, I thought my boots would melt. Conor was already waiting in his car, eating a bag of Flamin' Hot Cheetos.

I slipped into the passenger side and stuck my face in front of the vents blowing cool air. "Oh, thank goodness!"

"Any luck with the neighbors, love?"

"Asshole next door thought I was there to trim the bushes. Can you believe that shit?" I lifted the bottom of my shirt and shook it, trying to send some of the cool air across my chest. "I swear one of these days I'm moving to someplace cool, like Seattle or Portland. Maybe Canada."

"Anyone seen Holly?"

"Not in the past few weeks."

"Shite! No luck on my end either." I could hear the bag rustle in his hand. "Care for a Cheeto? I find it helps me think."

"No, thanks. Just want to cool off."

"Maybe we should talk to Detective Hardin," he said. "Find out why he arrested her."

The memory of Hardin's gruff voice chewing me out for doing something stupid on a domestic disturbance call rattled in my brain. "I'll pass, thanks."

"Why?"

"What's it matter to us why he arrested her? Our job isn't to find out whodunit. I just want to track her down and bring her in. End of story."

"Ya know him, don't you?"

"What? No!" I sighed. "Okay, yeah, I know him. He was my training officer when I joined Phoenix PD."

"Why don't ya want to talk to him?"

"Doesn't matter. Maybe Holly's lawyer knows where she is. This Swearingen guy."

"A lawyer ain't gonna tell ya shite about his client's whereabouts, Jinxie. Let's talk to Hardin. If we can persuade him to let us look at witness statements, it might give us a lead."

I turned away from the air vent to glare at him. "Who's running this case? Me or you?"

He gave me a pacifying look, as if I were a rabid bulldog. "You are, love."

"Damn straight!" I was being a bitch, but I was hot and frustrated about not being at Comicon. Not to mention being pissed at being outed. Poor Conor was in my line of fire.

"Holly's lawyer is bound by privilege. I doubt you'll get anything useful outta him."

"Then I'll just have to be very persuasive."

"Persuasive? What are ya gonna do? Threaten him? Charm it out of him?"

"I can be charming." I sneered at him. "When I want to be."

"Aye! Charming like a snake. And just as deadly."

"Hey, I charmed you, didn't I?"

"Aye, that ya did, love." He chuckled. "Care to place a wager?"

"I'll bet you fifty bucks I can get Swearingen to tell me where Holly is. Assuming he actually knows."

"I'll take that bloody bet."

15

Zach Swearingen's office was located in the Corporate Century Office Park on Shea Boulevard, just east of Scottsdale Road.

Conor was right. It was a long shot. Lawyers weren't chatty about their clients except in the courtroom. But I had a few ideas of how to loosen this one's lips. First, I had to get past his secretary. After canvassing Morton's neighbors, I looked like a wreck and smelled even worse. It was time to get creative. I parked the Gray Ghost in the office park parking lot, grabbed my purse from the glove box, and got to work.

Moments later, Conor knocked on my window. "Oy! Jinxie! We goin' in or what?"

I rolled down the tinted window, and he gasped.

"Jesus bloody Christ! What happened? Ya look like you've been battered."

I smiled. "That's the idea." I'd used a combination of purple eye shadow and smudged eyeliner to give the illusion of bruises. "You still got that bag of hot Cheetos?"

"Sorry, love, I ate them all."

"But you still have the bag, right?"

"Aye. How come?"

"I need it."

He went to his Charger and returned a moment later with the empty bag. I stuck my hand into it, coated my fingers with the spicy red powder, and rubbed my left eye with it. "Holy fuck, that hurts!" I gasped.

"Bloody hell, Jinxie!"

I clenched my fist and gritted my teeth as I waited for the fiery pain in my eye to subside. It didn't. At least not right away. I tried to distract myself by thinking of the things I could do with my half of the bounty. Didn't help. "Ugh, that really hurts."

I peeked at my reflection in the rearview mirror, at least with my right eye. My left eye was red, puffy, and tearing uncontrollably. I really did look as if I'd been punched.

"Have you gone completely mad? What'd ya do that for?"

"You'll see." I grabbed my purse, leaving all my bounty hunter gear on the passenger seat, then locked up the Gray Ghost. "Just follow my lead."

Conor and I joined a petite elderly woman in the elevator, and I punched the button for the fourth floor.

The woman glanced at me then gave Conor the evil eye. As the door opened onto the third floor, the woman wagged her finger at him. "You should learn to keep your damned hands to yourself." She marched out of the car, and the doors closed behind her.

I chuckled.

"Please tell me I'm not the villain in this daft scheme of yours."

"Of course not," I said. "Story is that you're my new lover, protecting me from my abusive, hopefully soon-to-be-ex husband."

"Bloody hell."

On the fourth floor, I led Conor through the glass doors of Miller, Crouch, and Swearingen.

A sharply dressed man with a soul patch, wire-framed

glasses, and a single diamond stud earring sat behind the receptionist desk. As soon as he saw me, a worried expression crossed his face. "Uh, can I help you?"

I drew on emotions from the darkest moments of my childhood. My jaw tensed. My throat tightened, and I blinked back tears.

"I . . . I do hope so," I said as I grasped Conor's hand. "I recently separated from my abusive husband. But he keeps coming after me and my new boyfriend."

"I'm so sorry." The receptionist offered me a box of tissues from his desk. I took one.

"Thanks. Unfortunately, the police won't do anything. I tried to get a restraining order, but it was quashed. My friend Kim Morton suggested I hire Mr. Swearingen to get it reinstated."

"I see. Well, do you have an appointment?"

"No, I . . . I'm just so afraid. He . . . he's threatened to kill me. Please, I must see Mr. Swearingen now."

"Of course." He picked up his phone and dialed an extension. "Mr. Swearingen, we have a woman in an emergency situation here. Says she was referred to you by Ms. Morton. Yes, certainly." He hung up. "You're in luck. One of Mr. Swearingen's court appearances got postponed. Go down the hall. Third door on your left." He pointed.

"Oh, bless you." I put my hand on his and gave him a teary smile.

As we walked toward Swearingen's office, Conor said, "Damn, love. That was Oscar-worthy. And more than a bit scary. Made me want to batter the imaginary wanker that done this to ya."

"Two years in the Aristotle Collegiate High Drama Club. You should have seen me as Rose in *Meet Me in St. Louis*." I used the tissue Chris had given me to wipe as much of the fake bruise makeup off my face as I could.

Zach Swearingen stood when we walked into his office. He wore a pin-striped black suit with a Rotary pin on his lapel. "Can I help you?"

I tossed the tissue in the trash can next to his mahogany desk. "Yes, we need help tracking down one of your clients."

"What? I thought you were a domestic violence victim."

"Sorry, didn't think your office manager would let us in if we told him we were bail enforcement agents."

"Bail enforcement agents? Get out of here before I call security."

"Why is everyone calling security on me these days? It's really rude."

"Maybe you should take a hint."

"Your client, Holly Schwartz, missed her court date last month," I said. "Assurity Bail Bonds hired us to bring her in. If we don't return her to custody by Tuesday, your friend Kim Morton loses her house."

"I have no idea where Holly Schwartz is. Most likely kidnapped by the man who murdered her mother. Maybe if the damned cops put out an AMBER Alert, we could find her."

Something about his gaze told me he was holding something back, but I had no idea what. Or maybe he was just a shifty-eyed lawyer. Or both.

"Mr. Swearingen," Conor said, "could ya tell us what ya know about her mother's attacker?"

He fiddled with a gold Cross pen on his desk. "According to Holly, he was about six-eight, medium-dark skin, wearing an orange shirt. Had a black wing tattoo on his right arm and a gold hoop earring in one ear."

"Anything else?" I asked.

"That's all she gave me."

"If ya think she's innocent, why are ya pleading that she's daft?"

Swearingen's face flushed. "Look, buddy, are you a lawyer?"

"Can't say as I am, no."

"Then don't tell me how to plead my case. You two clowns have wasted enough of my time." He stood and pointed toward his office door. "I want you gone."

"Fine," I said. "But if Kim Morton loses her house because of you—"

"Get out! And if you harm one hair on Holly Schwartz's head, I'll bring criminal charges against you both. You hear me?"

On the ride down the elevator, Conor held out his hand. "Pay up."

I rolled my eyes. "Yeah, right. He didn't know. That was a condition of the bet, remember?"

Conor harrumphed. "He knows where she is. I could see it in his eyes."

"There was certainly something he wasn't saying."

"So pay up. Fifty bucks."

"Good lord! I don't have it on me."

"Figures."

My eye was still irritated, and my head was starting to pound. "I'm calling Becca. See if she can do some skip tracing." I pulled out my phone and dialed her number.

"Not a bad idea," Conor said as we exited the elevator.

"This is Becca." She sounded glum.

"Yo, Becks, it's Jinx. I need you to do some skip tracing."

"Jinx." She groaned. "Today's not the best day. Can it wait?"

"Normally, I'd say yes, but I'm on a tight deadline. Got to catch my fugitive by Tuesday night. Chronic fatigue acting up?"

"Yeah. Not a good day. I'm all out of spoons."

She was telling me that her chronic fatigue syndrome was flaring up again and that her energy level was critically low. I felt bad about pushing her, but if I didn't locate Holly by the deadline, my career as a bounty hunter was over.

"I keep telling you, switch to knives. It's much more fun," I said, trying to cheer her up.

"Funny." She sighed. "I know I'll pay for it tomorrow, but for you, I'll risk it."

Years earlier, when she was first diagnosed with chronic fatigue—or myalgic encephalomyelitis, as it was formally known

—I was one of the few people who didn't think she was just being lazy. I also tried to be there for her whenever she had a flare-up to make sure she had food and other essentials that she didn't have the energy to get for herself. Just part of our pact as besties.

"You're a goddess."

"Yeah, Hypnos, Greek goddess of sleep. Who am I looking for?"

"Holly Schwartz."

"The girl in the wheelchair whose mother was killed?"

"That's her. I need whatever you can find on her, her mother, and her aunt, Kimberly Morton. Pull phone records. Bank records. Anything that shows some recent activity." I gave her the relevant information from the bail application.

"Okay, I'll let you know what I find out."

"Thanks, Becca. You need anything? Groceries? Fast food? Porno?"

She chuckled. "Naw, I'm set, but thanks for asking. I'll be in touch."

I hung up. "Okay, she's on it."

"Brilliant. Let's go to the Phoenix police and talk to Detective Hardin."

"Ugh," I groaned. "I'd rather eat glass."

"What's the deal between you two?"

I cocked my head. "Asks the man who doesn't want to spill about his torrid affair with Sadie Levinson."

"We never had an affair. I worked for her father. Things got complicated is all."

"Complicated? The more you dance around this, the more I want to know. You realize that, right?"

"Fine." He strolled out of the lobby into the parking lot. The hot air made my eye burn more. "Don't tell me about you and Hardin. I'll just go back to working with my own team."

"Wait! Wait."

He stopped and turned. "Yes?"

I stared at the pavement, kicking at loose bits of asphalt. "He was my training officer, okay? That's how I knew him."

"And what? He was a bad cop?"

"Just the opposite. He's top-notch. Very by the book. Thing was, he was always on my case, criticizing every little thing I did wrong. Some of the other officers called him Officer Hard Ass. Now I guess he's Detective Hard Ass."

"Really that bad, eh?"

I looked up at Conor. "When I quit the force, he chewed me out. Called me a disappointment and said I was throwing away a promising career. He raked me over the coals for turning my back on the opportunity to be the department's first transgender officer. We parted with a lot of bitter feelings between us."

"So he knew you were trans?"

"Not a lot of secrets that side of the blue line."

"Was that why he was such a tosser to ya?"

"No, he was a bastard to everybody. Good cop. Really knew how to control a bad situation. But he didn't put up with a lot of bullshit. Turned being rude and sarcastic into an art form."

"Ah, so that's where ya get it from!"

"Funny. Not."

"I think ya should face your fears and talk to the man about Holly Schwartz. Maybe something in the case file can point us in the right direction."

"Fine. Let's do this."

He glanced at his watch. "Actually, I've got something else I gotta take care of, love."

I raised an eyebrow. "What? You just talked me into seeing Hardin. Now you're bailing on me?"

He shook his head dismissively. "Just a minor errand. Shouldn't be long."

"Whatever. I don't want to know." I hopped into the Gray Ghost and started it up, letting the AC blow out all the hot air before closing the door.

Conor knocked on my window. I rolled it down. "Yes?"

"Where ya going after you talk to Hardin?"

"The Schwartzes' house in Maryvale."

"I've got the address. I'll try to meet ya there."

"Whatever." I rolled up the window before he could respond, and drove off.

16

___

I walked into the Phoenix Police Department building on Washington Street and found my buddy, Ortega, manning the front desk.

He glanced at me, and a smile opened up on his face. "How's it going, Ballou?"

I fist-bumped him. "Going well. I see you earned some stripes."

"Yeah," he said, patting the sergeant patches on his arm. "Passed the exam a few months ago. You looking good, mama."

"Shut the hell up, Ortega. God!" I blushed like a damned schoolgirl.

"You still chasing fugitives?"

"Matter of fact, that's why I'm here. I need to talk to Hardin about one of his cases. He in?"

"Should be at his desk." He handed me a visitor's badge. "Homicide unit. Third floor."

"Thanks." I attached the badge to my belt. "Good to see you, man."

My pulse quickened as I rode up the elevator and strolled through the homicide unit's maze of cubicles. Detective Pierce

Hardin looked as though he was not having the best of days, and that was saying something. His skin was ashen. His clothes looked slept in. And there was a bottle of Maalox on his desk.

"Rough day, dear?" I asked nervously, resting an arm on the cubicle partition.

He turned a weary eye to me. "Ballou. And here I thought we got rid of you years ago."

"I'm back."

"Like a bad case of herpes. What the hell you want? I'm busy."

"Need some information on the Holly Schwartz case."

"Why you want that?"

"She jumped bail, and I've been hired to apprehend her."

He rolled his eyes. "I've been up all night working a triple homicide, and you want me to help you do your job? Ha!"

"Hey, when the people you lock up don't show up for court, somebody's gotta track them down. We all have a job to do so that justice is served."

"Justice, huh?" He rubbed his face, leaned back in his chair, and folded his arms. "What information you looking for exactly?"

"For starters, why'd you charge her?" Since I was here, I figured it couldn't hurt to ask. I grabbed a swivel chair from a nearby desk. "She's a mentally disabled girl in a wheelchair, for God's sake."

He pulled out the murder book, a three-ring binder filled with reports, photos, and notes on the case, and flipped through it. "Several reasons. The ME report shows the stab wounds coming from someone who was short or in a seated position, like a wheelchair. If the mother'd been stabbed by a large man standing, the angle of the wounds would have been completely different."

"So you don't believe her story about a black man in an orange shirt? A black wing tattoo on his arm sounds like a rather detailed description, if you ask me."

"No evidence of forced entry. Also, when we found the girl, she was covered in blood."

"So? Holly could have tried to stop her mother's bleeding," I suggested.

"So she claimed. But the blood on her shirt and pants wasn't just from transfer. It showed directional spray, consistent with castoff from a knife."

"Why would she kill her own mother? Her aunt says the two were thick as thieves."

"From my interview with Holly, I learned her doctor was scheduled to put a feeding tube in her. Holly didn't want one despite suffering from malnourishment. Claimed she didn't need it, that her mother was poisoning her to make her too sick to keep food down. Thus, motive."

"That's one thing I don't get. You grilled a mentally disabled teenager for sixteen hours?"

"First of all, don't lecture me on procedure, Ballou. I can shit regulations better than you can recite them. Secondly, we had a child advocate present. And third, she's not as disabled as people think."

"Are you serious?"

"Don't get me wrong, she plays the part very well. But trust me, there's a sharp, wicked little mind in that head of hers. I am not letting her get away with murder."

I sat there stunned. I wouldn't have believed it from anyone but Hardin. "So she killed her mother because her mother was making her sick?"

"That's my theory. And the evidence backs me up."

"And there's no connection to these two other women who were abducted from Maryvale earlier this year?"

"Feds believe those cases are part of a human trafficking ring they're investigating. There's no connection with the Schwartz case other than location." He took a slurp of coffee and made a disgusted face. "Anything else? I have murders to solve."

"Where would Holly hide to avoid jail time?"

"Try the aunt. The one who hired the attorney."

"I did. Didn't get the impression she's hiding her. What about the Schwartzes' friends or neighbors? I assume you canvassed the neighborhood after the murder."

"We did. Everyone loved her. But would they risk jail time to hide her? I doubt it."

"Can I get a copy of the witness statements?"

"Hey, Hardin! The lieutenant wants to see you," a female detective called from across the room.

Hardin grumbled. "Wait here. And don't touch anything." He strolled into the lieutenant's glass-enclosed office and shut the door.

I figured he'd be in there a while. I grabbed the murder book and hustled to the photocopier in the corner of the bull pen. With a clack, I opened the binder and made copies of call logs from the victim's phone, fingerprint analysis, the medical examiner's report, and transcripts from interviews.

I heard the lieutenant's door open a crack.

"Shit." I stuffed the copies in my waistband under my shirt, put the originals back in the murder book, and hightailed it to Hardin's desk before he walked out of the office.

"Anything else you need to know?" Hardin asked when he returned. "I've got work to do."

"Yeah, how come you didn't issue an AMBER Alert?"

"Two reasons. One, she turns eighteen in a couple months. And two, I've seen no credible evidence that she'd been abducted. Either her aunt or someone else is hiding her. I did issue a BOLO, however. Notified the sheriff's department, state patrol, and border patrol. Anything else?"

"No, I'm good. Thanks for your help." I got up. "Good luck with the triple murder."

"Thanks. Nice article in *Phoenix Living*, by the way."

I rolled my eyes. "Don't remind me."

"What? I thought it was good. Nice to see people in your community getting decent representation. Especially in your line of work."

"Thanks, I guess." I started to walk away, then turned. "Hey, speaking of my community, you heard anything about the Ciara Vanderbilt case?"

He squinted. "Name's not familiar. Another one of your skips?"

"A friend of mine, actually. Trans woman beaten and left for dead in a corporate office parking lot."

"This is the homicide unit, Ballou. Unless she's actually dead, it's not my case."

"Oh well. Thought you might have heard something. Thanks, anyway."

"Good luck finding Holly Schwartz. You're gonna need it."

17

———————

When I reached the Gray Ghost, Becca called. She sounded so fragile.

"Ran the phone logs for the Schwartzes. Bank records too."

"Great! Anything interesting?"

"Bonnie's calls were mostly to doctors," she said as she took an audible breath. "A few to a company called Compassionate Care." Another breath. "A handful to charities. Rare Disease Foundation. Campaign for Neuromuscular Research."

"No surprises there."

"Not many calls on Holly's phone. Most to her mother. A couple to a George Peavey. Not sure who he is yet." She paused for a moment and moaned quietly. "Final calls were night of the murder. One to Richard Delgado. Visiting nurse, I think. Last call was 911."

"What about the bank records?"

"Expenses were typical household—Walmart, Safeway, utilities. Deposits were mostly disability payments and checks from charity orgs."

"Can you email me that information?"

"Yeah."

"Thanks, Becks. I know you need to take care of yourself. I'm just under such a time crunch."

"I know."

"When you're feeling better, see what you can dig up on Richard Delgado and George Peavey."

"Gotcha. Bye." She hung up.

I hated pushing her like that, but I didn't know anyone else who could get me the answers I needed. Unfortunately, none of the info I had so far gave me a clue where Holly might be or whether she was hiding from the law or had been kidnapped. Time to visit the scene of the crime.

The Schwartzes' Maryvale residence was ten miles northwest of downtown Phoenix. The cars parked along their street consisted of junkers with crumpled quarter panels, missing bumpers, and cracked windshields. In this environment, the Gray Ghost was invisible.

The house was tan with brick-red trim. Candy bar wrappers and empty beer bottles littered the yard. Weeds grew four feet tall in places, while sunbaked earth showed in other spots.

I suited up with my body armor, tactical belt, and weapons. I doubted Holly was hiding in the old family domicile, but it was a possibility. Didn't want to be caught unawares.

From the driveway, I followed a paved walkway into a narrow courtyard, which shielded me from anyone who wasn't standing directly in front of the house. An aluminum ramp rose six inches to the front doorstep. Faded, tattered fragments of the Phoenix PD crime scene seal clung to the door, warning people not to enter without permission. But the techs had finished their work months ago. My only barrier now was the dead bolt.

I could have used the ram I kept in the back of the Gray Ghost but preferred to make a more low-key entrance, considering I was alone. I fished a couple of picking tools out of a leather pouch I kept in my cargo pants and set to work on the lock. The security pins made it trickier than the typical door lock, but soon the cylinder turned and the door opened.

Sunlight filtered through gauzy blinds in the room to my left. Tiny black flies buzzed around my face and ears. Despite the passage of time, the stench of death lingered in the air, compounded by the suffocating heat from the lack of air conditioning. I made a conscious effort to breathe through my mouth. It didn't help much. It took all my willpower not to retch.

I flicked a light switch. No power. I pulled out an LED flashlight and swept the front room. A slate-blue couch stretched in front of the double window to my left. I crossed the room to a laminated wood bookshelf standing against the wall, filled with stacks of board games and stuffed animals. Nothing indicated where I would find Holly.

I stepped up to a dining area with a glass dinette table and four brass and cloth chairs. On the table, three colored pencils rested in the crack between pages of an open coloring book. No eviscerated animals in this one. Just beautifully colored abstract designs.

Next to the book lay a yellowing *Arizona Republic* newspaper featuring a photo of the Phoenix Suns' Cedric Wilson on the front page. The article reported that the basketball star had apparently undergone knee surgery following an ATV accident.

Something about Wilson's photo piqued my interest, but I wasn't sure why. I was a fair-weather sports fan at best. I scanned the article but didn't find anything relevant to my case and tossed it aside.

I entered the kitchen, where the puke-green countertops didn't help my growing sense of nausea. Neither did the dead maggots in a graveyard of dried refried beans occupying a saucepan atop the stove. *Why hasn't anyone cleaned up?* I wondered. Maybe the property was still in probate.

I moved on to the family room on the other side of the

kitchen's breakfast bar. The smell of death was intense here. A three-foot-wide brown-black stain on the floor marked where Bonnie Schwartz had met her end. I stared at the bloody carpet, playing out the multiple scenarios in my mind. Home invasion or domestic disturbance? Either way, it was a tragedy.

A stack of mail lay on a water-stained coffee table. I sorted through the envelopes and flyers, hoping for clues. Most of it was junk mail promising amazing deals on hearing aids, solar panels, and dental services. A few medical bills were marked past due. One was an envelope from Compassionate Care, LLC.

There were also letters and cards hand addressed to Holly. I opened one. It was from a fan thanking her for the inspiration after she appeared on a telethon. The others offered similar thanks and well wishes. A few included cash and checks.

The last one I read was printed from a computer. It started innocently enough but soon got creepy and sexually explicit. It was unsigned. According to the postmark, this creep was local. My skin crawled. The stale air felt suffocating. I could feel the stench of decomp in my lungs.

I stuffed the stalker letter, the fan mail, and the bills into a pocket in my cargo pants. I'd go through them later to see if they pointed to anything. Maybe Becca could help.

A hallway led to Holly's room, where an adjustable bed took up much of the space. Inspirational posters hung on the walls. *Hang in there! Believe in yourself. Life is a miracle.* Whatever. I checked the brightly painted chest of drawers and then the closet. Both were empty.

I continued my search in the guest bathroom, a spare bedroom, and the master bedroom without finding anything of note.

In the master bath, I discovered a sliding panel in the wall, concealed behind a wicker vanity shelf. I kneeled down with my flashlight to get a closer look.

"Find anything interesting?" someone asked behind me.

My flashlight clattered to the floor, and I nearly jumped out of my skin. Bile rose in my throat as I snapped to my feet, ready to fight.

"Holy fuck, Conor! You scared the shit out of me. Again. I should put a bell on you."

"Nothing to be scared of, love. Just the man of your dreams." He wrapped his arms around me and leaned in to kiss me.

I pushed him away. "More like my nightmares, the way you keep sneaking up on me."

"What's wrong, Jinxie? Can't a guy get some love?" he joked.

"Jesus, Conor, a woman died here, and her daughter is missing. Have some respect." I sat down on my heels and slid back the concealed panel. With the beam of the flashlight, I discovered a small money-counting machine. I pulled it out to show Conor.

"Now why do ya suppose they have a counting machine hidden away in the loo?" Conor asked.

"Someone was apparently making enough green they needed help counting it."

"Ya probably right. Unfortunately, it doesn't tell us where our girl is."

"No, it doesn't." My pulse slowed as disappointment settled in. "God, I wish I was at Comicon right now instead of this sweltering house of death."

"Naw, ya don't. I heard on the news some bloke inside the convention center got nicked with four loaded pistols and a shotgun. Security's been ramped up a hundredfold. All props are now banned."

"Geez! What the hell's wrong with people?"

"It's a mad, mad world, love." He offered me a hand and pulled me to my feet. "Any luck finding your fugitive?"

"Bits and pieces of information but no workable leads." I led him back down the hall and out the front door. I felt lightheaded. The oppressive heat and the god-awful stench were taking their toll. I managed one more glance around the front room and got the hell out of there.

It wasn't much cooler outside, but at least the air was fresh.

Well, as fresh as the air in Phoenix ever was, what with the brown cloud of smog and all. As my eyes adjusted to the glaring daylight, I noticed a skinny white woman with blond dreads standing by the Gray Ghost and eyeing me suspiciously.

18

The woman wore a lacy halter top, Daisy Dukes, and flip-flops. A muddy kaleidoscope of ink ran down each pale arm. I guessed she was in her forties, but she could have been younger.

"What're y'all doing in Bonnie and Holly's place? Y'all cops?" she asked through a mouth of rotten teeth as we approached. Her voice was like gravel in a blender.

"Not exactly," I replied. "Holly's gone missing. Her aunt's worried, so we're trying to find her. Did you know Bonnie and Holly well?"

"Yeah, I knowed 'em."

I perked up. "Any idea where Holly might be?"

She crossed her arms. "What's it worth to you?"

About fifty grand, I thought. I pulled my wallet out of my pocket. I didn't generally carry my purse when I worked. It was unwieldy and just something to lose. All I had in the wallet was a ten and three ones. I handed her the ten. She looked at me as if I'd kicked her dog.

"A ten? That's all Holly's worth to you? Damn, I get more than that for a hand job."

"Good lord." I nudged Conor. "Hey, ya got any cash on you?"

"Ya mean aside from the fifty ya owe me from our bet earlier?"

"Come on, man, cough up some green so Trixie here can buy herself a new set of teeth."

"For your info, my name ain't Trixie. It's Shartroose." She spelled it for me. "You know, like the color?"

I didn't know exactly how the color chartreuse was spelled, but I was pretty sure that wasn't it.

Conor pulled out a wad of twenties. I snatched it from him and counted out three, then handed back the rest. She reached for the cash, but I held it away.

"First tell us what you know. Then we'll see what it's worth."

"What I know is I saw a black creeper van parked in front of their house that night. I seen the same van there several times before."

"You see who was in it? Or get a license plate?"

"No."

"That's it? You saw a black van?"

"Who you think I am? Jessica Fletcher or some shit? I told you what I know. Now gimme my money."

"That little tidbit isn't worth sixty dollars. Not even worth the ten."

"It's worth something."

"It's worth crap." I strutted around to the driver's side of the Gray Ghost, fanning myself with the cash. Conor stood to the side with a bemused look on his face.

"All right, fine," Shartroose said, following me into the street. "Driver had brown skin, long black hair."

"Any distinguishing features? What was he wearing?"

"I don't know. I was busy getting ready for a date, and it was dark besides. I think I seen him wearing an orange shirt one time before, though."

So far he sounded like the guy Holly described. "How old was he?"

"How'm I supposed to know?"

"Guess."

"I dunno. Twenties, thirties, maybe."

"What was he doing when you saw him?"

"I just saw him pull up and walk to the front door. " Shartroose got quiet and mellow all of a sudden. "Makes me sad to think about it. Bonnie was real nice. Spent her life taking care of that poor girl. Then someone gone and kilt her."

"Have you seen Holly since then?"

"Not since that night. Heard she moved in with a relative in the East Valley."

I paused, hoping she'd offer something else. When she didn't say anything, I handed her a couple of the twenties. She looked at them as if they were trash.

"Forty lousy dollars? For all I told you?"

"Plus the ten I already gave you makes fifty. And trust me, that's being generous."

Conor grabbed the other twenty and handed it to her with his business card. "Thank ya, darlin', for all your help. Would ya give us a ring if ya see either Holly or the guy show up? We'll make it worth your trouble, I promise ya."

Shartroose's eyes got all sparkly as she nuzzled up to him. "Oooh, Mr. Lucky Charms, I like how you talk. I'll call even if I don't see them none. You and me can do a little partying."

I pulled her hand off Conor's thigh and shoved her away. "Thanks, but we got work to do." I turned to him. "Come on, Lucky Charms. Before I shoot you in your shillelagh."

"Bitch!" Shartroose shouted as she walked across the street.

Conor chuckled. "Not jealous are ya, love?"

I scoffed. "Of Shartroose and those nasty teeth of hers? Yeah, right. I'm sure you're just itching to kiss that mouth."

"Then why're ya getting your knickers in a twist?"

"Because it's four o'clock in the afternoon and I've spent the last hour in a house that smelled like hot death. If we don't come up with a lead soon, I'll miss out on fifty grand and any future jobs with Assurity Bail Bonds."

He put an arm around me, and I didn't resist. "Come on, Jinxie. I'll buy ya a beer at Grumpy's."

I was about to say yes when a man with long black braids and wearing a blue-plaid shirt came strolling down the sidewalk. He spotted me and took off running the other way.

I raced south after him. Conor's Charger roared to life behind me, but I was focused on the man I was chasing.

With the weight and bulk of my gear, I had trouble keeping up with him. Shortly before the road took a sharp right turn, he cut between the houses and hopped a block wall. I drew on my parkour skills and vaulted it with half the effort he used and spotted him running across the backyard, a Chihuahua yapping at his heels.

When he flipped over the opposite wall, the Chihuahua turned its attention to me. I breezed past the dog as I heard a loud splash. I cleared the wall and landed on a narrow strip of ground between the wall and a kidney-shaped pool. A tangle of green garden hose extended to the water's edge. My quarry splashed desperately in the pool, crying out for help.

I was tempted to let him drown, but if he knew where Holly was, I couldn't risk losing him. I extended a ten-foot leaf skimmer. He grabbed hold of it, and I pulled him to the edge of the pool.

"Jinx?" he sputtered as his braids floated in the water behind him. "Why you chasing me?"

"Why you running, Jessup?"

Before he could answer, a man came out of the house, pointing a double-barrel shotgun at the two of us. He was bald except for a wisp of white encircling his pale head. His plaid shorts were pulled up to his armpits. "What the hell you hooligans doing in my backyard?"

I raised my hands in surrender. "Hold your fire, mister. I'm a bail enforcement agent. Just fishing this guy out of your pool. Put down the gun, and we'll be on our way."

He looked from me to the man in the pool but didn't lower

the shotgun. "Y'all get on outta here b'fore I exercise my Second Amendment rights."

I pulled Jessup out of the pool and led him out the front gate, dripping water along the front driveway to the street. "How's the water?" I asked, keeping a grip on his arm.

"I ain't done nothing, and you know it."

"Then how come you ran? If I didn't know better, I'd say you have a guilty conscience."

"It's a nice day. Thought I'd get some exercise."

"Running in a hundred degree weather, followed by a dip in a pool? You training for a triathlon?"

"It's a free country. Besides, you ain't got no warrant on me."

"Actually, I'm looking for a missing girl. Rumor is she was taken by a light-skinned black man with long hair and a tattoo on his arm." Though I had to admit, the ink on Jessup's arm wasn't a wing but more a Samoan tribal design.

"You talking 'bout Holly, ain't ya?"

"Yep."

"And you think I took her? Shit, Jinx. I sling a little dope now and then, but I ain't never took nobody. You know I ain't like that. 'Specially that poor child."

I had to admit, for all the times I'd gone after Jessup for jumping bail, it was always for nonviolent drug-related offenses. Still, junkies and dealers weren't above learning new tricks. "Where were you a month ago?"

"Month ago? Oh, I remember." A smile spread across his face. "Vegas, baby! Wanna see pics?"

"Show me."

He pulled his phone from his back pocket. "Shore hope it didn't get fried from me skinny-dipping." He tapped the screen a few times. "Hey, hey! Looka here!"

I took the phone and flipped through a series of photos of him posing with a couple of showgirls. The time stamp matched the date that Holly went missing. "You win anything?"

"I was up about two grand, then I lost it all and them some. House always wins, you know what I'm saying?"

"Any idea who might've taken Holly?"

He stared at the ground as he wrung the water out of his Sean John plaid shirt. "Past few months, I heard word that someone's snatching girls off the street. Young ones, mostly. In a black van."

"I heard about the two. Feds are investigating it."

"Way I hear it, closer to ten I know about. Cops don't like to say. Don't wanna spook folks 'round here. But we know what's going down."

"You see that black van driving around? Or in front of Holly's house?"

"Possible. Not really sure." He looked up at me. "You gonna throw that girl in jail 'cause of her mama got kilt? Don't seem right."

I sighed. "Jessup, I got orders to pick her up. If she's in danger now, hopefully I can find her, return her to custody so her aunt can bail her back out. Maybe once they see she was kidnapped, they'll drop the charges."

"But you gotta do what you gotta do, huh?"

"'Fraid so, man."

He nodded. "I got your number from the last time. I hear anything, I call you, a'ight?"

"'Preciate, my friend."

He walked away and took off his shirt. The sunlight gleamed off his wet, dark skin.

I turned to stroll back toward the Schwartz house when he called out again. "Yo, Jinx! Just remembered something Holly say to me."

"What's that?"

"'Round Christmastime, we was all over at her mom's place. Holly say to me her daddy was gonna take her away to live in his mansion. Like he Daddy Warbucks or something."

"Her father? You sure?"

"What she said. 'Course she was a little loopy from the medication she was on. Maybe she made it up."

I stood there pondering. "She say his name or what he looked like?"

"Naw, nothing like that."

"Thanks. I'll catch ya later."

He flipped me a bird but was grinning while he did it. Then he passed between two houses into a vacant lot.

I met Conor driving his Charger coming from the other direction. "Ya lose him, love? I tried to intercept him with the car. Must've missed him."

"Wasn't our guy. Just Jessup."

"Shite! Get in. I'll drive ya back to the Ghost."

19

On the drive to Grumpy's, I called Detective Hardin again. Judging from his tone when he answered, his mood hadn't improved with the day. Then again, neither had mine.

"Hey, when you interviewed the Schwartzes' neighbors, d'you talk to a gal calling herself Shartroose?"

"The meth junkie? All I got from her was a lot of nonsense."

"She told me she saw a black van in front of the Schwartzes' house shortly before the murder. Driver matched Holly's description of the man who attacked her mother. African-American. Long hair. Orange shirt. Black creeper van. I think Holly's story may be legit." I chose not to mention the stalker letter or the money-counting machine. Reading other people's mail was a federal crime. And my breaking into the house when I had no reason to believe she was there was also frowned upon.

"You think suddenly after nineteen years I forgot how to do my job, Ballou? I got the ME telling me one thing. A junkie whore telling me something different. Who you think I'm gonna believe?"

"Just wondering if you overlooked something. How else is a

girl in a wheelchair going to suddenly disappear? Maybe human traffickers. I hear there've been a lot more missing girls than you let on."

"Ballou, I'm exhausted and don't have time to listen to you play armchair quarterback. You wanna solve homicide cases? Rejoin the force. Otherwise, do your speculating on your own time."

"This girl could be enduring God knows what."

"Goodbye, Ballou."

"Don't hang up on me, Hardin. Hello? Goddammit."

Grumpy's parking lot was already full by the time I got there. I parked the Gray Ghost on a nearby side street. Conor pulled in behind me. As we walked the half block to the restaurant, I filled Conor in on my conversations with Hardin and Jessup, as well as the creepy letter I found at Holly's house.

"I don't get it," I said as we walked across Grumpy's parking lot. "Hardin's absolutely convinced that this seventeen-year-old girl is guilty, even when most of the evidence points to someone else."

"Why da ya care what he thinks, love? We got to find the girl. Let the courts sort out her guilt or innocence."

"I know, but it pisses me off. I hate how people get railroaded when cops are too stubborn to look at evidence that contradicts their theory of the case." I pulled open the door. The air inside was cooler, but I still felt as if I were melting. Conor and I grabbed seats at the bar.

"Uh-oh! Here comes trouble!" Grumpy breezed past carrying a couple of plates of food, made less appetizing by that damned cigar dangling from his mouth.

"Don't start with me, Grumpy." I put my hair up into a ponytail to get it off my neck. "Could you crank up the AC, for Christ's sake?"

"I could, kitten, but then I'd have to double my prices. 'Lectricity ain't cheap." He handed the plates off to a server. "You want your usual?"

"Yeah, whatever."

He set down a couple of beers in front of Conor and me, then waltzed back into the kitchen. I pressed the bottle to my temple and gasped. The ice-cold glass against my sun-scorched skin was equally painful and orgasmic.

"Let's say ya find the girl," Conor said after a long pull on his beer. "Whatcha gonna do with your cut of the bounty?"

"Honestly, haven't thought much about it. You?"

"Pay off my second mortgage," he said. "I owe a lot on those renovations I did a while back."

"You're so damn practical. I think I'd like to buy a motorcycle."

"Ha! You'd look bloody deadly on a Harley."

"Fuck Harley. There's a shop north of the valley that sells custom motorcycles for women. I've seen the website. Amazing shit. And fast too."

"You'd look hot no matter what ya rode." He winked at me. "Now all we got to do is find where the little lass is hiding."

I pulled out the stalker letter I'd picked up at the Schwartzes'. "Look at this. He talks about adding her to his harem. Begs her to send him photos of her naked but warns her not to tell her mom. The girl's seventeen, for Christ's sake. Ugh!"

Conor took the letter and the envelope. His lips drew back in a snarl. "What a bloody gobshite! What kind of filth writes such a thing to a teenage girl?"

"I wonder if the author of this letter is the one who tried to grab Holly and killed her mother," I said.

"Could be. Maybe also connected to these kidnappings in Maryvale." He took a long pull on his beer. "But if it is the same bloke, why take the girl months later? From her aunt's house, no less?"

"To keep her from testifying? Who knows? But it's looking more and more like she was kidnapped. I have no idea where to look." I thought about it for a moment. "But I know someone who might."

I pulled out my phone. I still had Hensley's phone number from when we were arranging the interviews.

"Where would I find those sex traffickers you interviewed a while back?" I asked when he picked up the call.

"Who is this?"

"Jinx Ballou. Now answer the question," I growled.

"You trying to get me killed? Is that what this is?"

"No, I'm trying to save the life of a seventeen-year-old girl. Now where do I find these guys?"

"Like I told you before, I don't divulge my sources. Normally, it's for professional standards. But these human traffickers are sociopaths. They kill anyone considered a threat. They've murdered cops, judges, feds, you name it. I'm not putting my life at risk so you can collect a bounty."

"Hensley, either you can tell me, or I can find them myself, and when I do, I'll tell them you blabbed. Or you can tell me for real and I'll keep my mouth shut. I'm just trying to rescue someone they've taken."

"You're looking for Holly Schwartz, aren't you? I heard she missed a court hearing. You think she got kidnapped?"

"It's highly likely."

The line was silent for a moment, except for his breathing. I liked that he was sweating over this.

"Okay, here's what I know. There's a guy named Volkov. Used to run strip clubs down in Tucson, then a few years ago, he expanded up here. But the strip clubs are a cover. He's been running a human trafficking empire for the better part of two decades. His family runs a major crime syndicate in Chechnya.

"He drove out all his competition in Arizona and several surrounding states. Most of the coyotes running girls from Central America and Mexico work for him. But they also grab local girls too. They send them to drop houses all over the western US, where they're forced into domestic work if they're lucky. Sex work if they're not."

"Where do I find this Volkov?"

"He's got an office in downtown Phoenix. But it's just the corporate office for his strip clubs. He keeps the girls in an old warehouse elsewhere."

"Where?"

"I don't know. They blindfolded me."

"You've been there? And you didn't do anything to save those women?"

"What was I going to do? I'm a reporter, not a cop. I was unarmed. They had automatic weapons."

"And you have no idea where he keeps these women? East Valley? West Valley?"

"West, I think. Past Goodyear, if I had to guess. Could be the other side of the White Tanks for all I know."

"You're really useless, Hensley."

"Look, if you promise not to mention my name, I can put you in touch with someone who knows more than I do."

"Well, fuck, why didn't you say so before?"

"If word got out that I shared this, it could ruin me."

"After the crap you've put me through, you think I'm worried? You are at the top of my shit list, buddy. And so is whoever ratted me out to you."

"For your information, no one ratted you out. I *figured* it out. You were enrolled at one school as a boy. Then months later you show up at a new middle school as a girl. It wasn't rocket science. As for my Volkov source, I'm not telling you his name if you're going to betray my trust."

"Fine, I won't tell. Just give me the name."

"He's a concierge at the Harrington Arms Hotel."

"Seriously? The Harrington Arms?" It was a hotel built in downtown Phoenix the year Arizona became a state. A century later, its posh amenities and five-star service still attracted elite guests from around the world. I'd never even been in the lobby, much less stayed in a room.

"What's this concierge's name?"

"Ricky."

"Ricky who?"

Conor perked up at the name. "Ricky the concierge? I know that little wanker."

"Never mind," I told Hensley. "So they really allow sex slaves at the Harrington Arms?"

"It's very hush-hush. But apparently some of their guests are willing to pay handsomely to have certain less-than-savory urges satisfied," Hensley explained. "Ricky contacts someone in Volkov's organization to take care of them. A defenseless celebrity like Holly Schwartz would fetch a high price."

"How come you never mentioned the Harrington in your newspaper?"

"Because Volkov made me promise not to, and I'm rather attached to my head. "

"So you're getting paid while women are being exploited. Congratulations, you're a douchebag."

"Hey, I've shared what I know with the FBI, okay?"

"Oh, you're a real humanitarian."

"How long has Holly been missing?" Hensley asked.

"About a month. Why?"

"He likes to move around the girls every few weeks or so. Chances of her still being in Phoenix are slim, I'm afraid."

"Let's hope for your sake she's still in town."

"What's that mean? If this gets back to me—"

"Quit your whining, Hensley, you little bitch. If I can't get my career back on track with this job, Volkov'll be the least of your worries." I hung up before he could protest further and turned to Conor. "So you know this Ricky fellow?"

"Aye, I've squeezed him for info a few times. Skinny little weasel with a pompadour. Like some little rockabilly wannabe. Not surprised he's mixed up with the likes of Volkov."

"His last name isn't Delgado by chance, is it? There was a Richard Delgado on one of the Schwartzes' call logs."

"Naw, his last name's Harris." He picked at the label on his beer. "So ya think Volkov has your girl, eh?"

"About the only lead I got at this point."

"Bloody hell."

"Why? What do you know?"

"Guy's a fuckin' psychopath. I've heard stories of what he does to girls who try to escape. Carves them up slowly like a Thanksgiving turkey while forcing the other girls to watch. 'Course, no one can prove it. Every once in a while, the feds raid his clubs, hoping someone'll talk. No one does."

I finished off my beer and slapped him on the back. "Well, that's why they pay us the big money. To go after psychos and bring our fugitives to justice."

"You're bloody serious?"

"As a fucking heart attack. I got everything riding on this case. No punk-ass Chechen gangster's getting in my way."

He finished his beer and pounded the bar. "All right then, love. Let's go talk to Ricky the dodgy concierge and get our girl."

20

We dropped off Conor's car at his place and drove to the Harrington Arms in the Gray Ghost. It was going on six o'clock, and most of the traffic was heading away from downtown. We rode the elevator from the underground garage up to the cavernous lobby.

My jaw dropped. I felt as if I'd walked into a cross between Buckingham Palace and a neo-Gothic cathedral. The place shimmered with gold. Towering columns rose forty feet from the marble floors to support the elaborate vaulted ceiling, lit with crystal chandeliers the size of my truck.

A grand staircase flowed from the second floor, spreading out at the bottom like a river delta. Twenty-foot-tall Art Deco paintings depicting the Phoenix of yesteryear hung from the walls above arched doorways. In the center of it all was a lounge area decorated with luxurious rugs and couches. People from all corners of the globe milled about, speaking languages I could only guess at.

"Jesus fucking Christ, is this Arizona or Renaissance Italy?" I whispered as I followed Conor, trying not to gawk like a tourist. "Where's the concierge?"

"Follow me."

To the left of the sprawling mahogany registration desk, a guy in his midtwenties stood behind a podium with a Mac laptop. He was dressed in a burgundy suit and wore his hair in the pompadour Conor had mentioned.

He looked up with a smug smile, which soured as soon as he saw Conor. "How may I—oh no. Not you."

"Jinxie," Conor said, "meet my buddy Ricky, the concierge. Ricky, old boy, this here's my gal, Jinxie."

"No offense, Ms. Jinxie, but I am here to serve our guests." He glared at Conor. "Not scruffy ruffians. Do I need to call security?"

Conor put his arm around the concierge's shoulder. "Ricky here helps the Harrington's guests access all sorts of hard-to-acquire items. Tickets to sold-out Suns games, guest passes to TPC, reservations for a chef's table at the hottest restaurants. You want it, this bloke'll get it for ya. For a price, of course."

Ricky signaled to a wall of muscle dressed in black standing on the other side of the registration desk. He ambled toward us, his thick arms ready at his side.

Conor continued, paying no attention to the approaching man in black. "Our boy here also helps his clients satisfy their dodgier appetites. Drugs. Dog fights. Prostitution. S&M. Every sort of kink ya can imagine."

"Uh, Conor . . ." I pointed toward the security guard, who cracked his knuckles as he drew closer.

Conor beamed. "Ricky likes to indulge a bit too. I've got some lovely videos of him with the governor's granddaughter. What was her name, old boy?"

Ricky went rigid, his face coloring, his eyes locked on Conor. The concierge waved off the security guard, who returned to his post by the front desk. "What the hell you want?" he asked through gritted teeth.

"We're looking for a girl," I said.

"Hungry for a little threesome action, are we?"

"Not exactly." I held up a photo of Holly. "We're looking for this girl—Holly Schwartz."

Ricky cocked an eyebrow. "I know her. Why are you . . . oh, wait a minute, she's been in the news lately. Something about her mother getting murdered. *Très* sad." He gave a mocking pouty face, making his bottom lip look very punchable. I resisted. Barely.

"She's also missing," I said. "Most likely kidnapped by a human smuggler named Volkov."

Ricky shrugged with a disinterested look. "I know nothing of such things."

Conor slammed the laptop shut, almost catching the concierge's fingers in it. "Cara! That's Governor Denton's granddaughter's name, isn't it? She's a cutie, though a bit young even for you, Ricky boy. And unless ya help us out, I'm sending our madame governor a video file of the two of you."

"For your information, it was consensual."

"Bullshite. The girl's fifteen, ya little wanker. You're what? Thirty?"

"Twenty-seven. Ish." Ricky's left eye twitched. "I really hate you."

"Coming from a gobshite like yourself, I'll take that as a compliment. Where's Volkov keep the girls?"

"If I tell you, Volkov'll kill me."

I flicked open a black-bladed knife and leaned into the little maggot, pressing the tip of the blade into the belly of his heavily starched shirt. "How long you think you'll live when I eviscerate you? Intestines dumping onto the floor, blood and fecal matter all over your pretty white shirt? My guess is ten minutes, maybe twenty. The whole time, you'll be screaming in agony, knowing no one can save you. Conor, you want to time him?"

"All right, all right! Jesus!" He cowered, his eyes tightly shut, trembling like an overbred Yorkie in a thunderstorm. "I-I'll tell you."

"You got five seconds, or I start cutting."

"Th-There's a warehouse. West of Buckeye. Not far from Arlington."

"Address!"

"It's . . . it's in my laptop." He opened the Mac and brought up an address on Old US Highway 80.

Conor patted him on the back. "See? That wasn't so hard, was it, Ricky boy?"

"What about Holly Schwartz?" I pressed the tip of my knife harder. "Does he have her?"

Ricky winced. "The crippled girl?"

"Disabled," I corrected.

"There was a girl like that. Don't know if it was Holly." He swallowed hard. "But that was weeks ago. Volkov likes to move his girls around. Doesn't want 'em too comfortable."

"Let's hope for your sake he's still got her." I put away my knife and marched back toward the elevator.

"What's that supposed to mean?" Ricky cried. "Hey! Conor, what's she talking about?"

Conor caught up with me as I punched the down button between the two elevators. "Ya know, you're quite scary sometimes."

"People like him make me sick," I muttered, staring at the lit button. "I should have gutted him."

"If ya had, we couldn't go rescue Holly, now could we?" He put an arm on my shoulder. "By the way, if we're planning on stormin' the castle, we'll need some serious backup. Unfortunately, Deez and the boys are up in Salt Lake, chasing down a fugitive."

"Let me see what I can do." I pulled out my phone and hit a number on speed dial. On the third ring, I heard a familiar voice ask who was calling. "Rodeo, it's Jinx."

"Hey, Jinxie. How's it hanging? Oh, sorry. Was that inappropriate considering you're, uh, you know?"

"Oh good lord. Get over yourself." I sighed. "Listen, Conor and I need some support. You available?"

"I told you, Big Bobby won't allow me to work with you."

"Don't be such a pussy! Come on. We need you." The arrow on the antique floor indicator above the nearest elevator began dropping from fifteen. I doubted I'd get much signal once we stepped in the elevator. "We're hitting a Volkov warehouse to rescue Holly Schwartz."

"Wait, did you say Volkov? As in Milo Volkov?"

"You heard of him?"

"Only from reports of the mutilated bodies left in his wake. That's a whole lot of heat I don't need. I'll pass on this one."

"You chickening out, Rodeo?"

"Last time someone crossed Volkov, the guy's remains were scattered on top of Camelback Mountain."

"Volkov cremated him?"

"No, ran him through a wood chipper."

I cringed. But I was committed to saving this girl, especially since no one but her aunt seemed to give a shit. "Did I mention the bounty is fifty grand?"

"And how much of that can I spend when I'm dead? Not interested, Jinxie."

"Come on, Rodeo, think what this girl must be going through. What if it was your daughter?"

"But it's not. And I won't be much of a father if I've been ground into raw hamburger," he said firmly. "Good luck, Jinx. Try not to get yourself killed. I really like you." He hung up.

"Crap." I turned to Conor as the elevator door opened. "Rodeo's out."

"Smart man."

I gave him a sideways look while we rode down to our level in the parking garage. "You're not having second thoughts, are you?"

"Naw, but ya can't blame a bloke for not wanting to go up against a Chechen gangster."

"Suppose not. But I'm not giving up on this girl. I can't."

"I understand."

"Who else can we call?"

"Maybe it's better with just the two of us. Going in all guns blazing isn't the best strategy."

"So how we getting in?" The elevator door opened, and we stepped into the parking garage.

"I have an idea. You probably won't like it, though."

He explained his strategy. He was right. I didn't like it.

"That's your plan?" My voice echoed off the concrete walls and floor. "Are you fucking insane?"

"Ya got any better ideas, love?"

"Not at the moment, but I'm sure as hell not doing that." We climbed into the Gray Ghost. "Let's stop at your place, arm up, and see what we're up against."

21

The Gray Ghost's dashboard read eight o'clock when I pulled off the road a half mile from a fenced-in warehouse belonging to Eden Produce. Farmland stretched out in all directions, illuminated by silver moonlight. From the driver's seat, I stared at the front gate through a pair of binoculars.

The fifteen-foot chain-link fence was topped with razor wire. Inside the fence were parked two semis bearing the Eden Produce logo. It looked like one of dozens of produce warehouses in the area except for the armed guard manning the front gate.

"Guard at the gate's carrying an AK-47," I said. "No one along the fence as far as I can see." My phone rang. I checked the caller ID, saw it was my mom, and sent it to voicemail. I needed to focus on the task at hand.

Conor looked through his own binoculars. "Surveillance cameras along the fence and all visible points of entry into the warehouse."

"So I guess this is the place, huh?" I asked.

"Unless kale's gotten so pricey you need armed guards to keep out the crazed vegetarians, I'd say we're in the right spot."

"How many more inside, I wonder?"

"Crazed vegetarians?" he asked with a smirk.

"Armed guards, smart-ass."

"No way of knowing. Maybe this isn't such a good idea."

"I'm not giving up on this girl," I said.

"Darlin', it's not worth getting yourself killed. Not even for fifty grand."

"It's not about the money anymore. This kid's been either sick or abused her whole life, confined to a wheelchair. Her mother's been murdered. And now this? I don't care if I don't see a dime. I'm not abandoning her to a life as one of Volkov's sex slaves."

"And how ya propose we get past these blokes?"

"I guess we go with your plan," I said, although thinking about it made me nervous.

He shook his head. "I withdraw my suggested plan. Too risky."

"How else will we get in there?"

"It's not getting in I'm worried about. It's getting out."

"Since when have you backed down from a challenge?"

"This isn't a challenge, Jinxie. It's bloody suicide. I won't do it."

"Fine, I'll do this myself." I pulled off my ballistic vest and began mussing my hair. When I looked sufficiently feral, I hopped out of the truck and rubbed dirt on my face, clothes, and through my hair.

Conor sighed. "Jesus, Mary, and Joseph, woman. You can't do this by yourself. Won't work."

"Then work with me." I locked my gaze on him.

He walked up to me and cupped my face in his hand. "You're daft, ya know that? Completely mental."

"Aw, you say the nicest things." I forced a smile, even though my insides shook like Jell-O. I knew he was right. This whole thing was stupid. But I was sick of people telling me what I couldn't do, and pissed off at everyone turning a blind eye to the shit going on inside that warehouse.

"So your mind's made up, eh?"

"Damn straight."

"Then let's get on with this bloody nonsense." He lifted the back hatch of the Gray Ghost, pulled a Bushmaster M4A3 Carbine out of its case, and popped in a curved thirty-round magazine.

I tossed my tactical belt in the truck and stuffed the Ruger in the front of my waistband. My revolver was still in the ankle holster. I used my knife to cut a pair of zip tie cuffs in half, then slipped a cuff on each wrist. With the closed knife concealed in my right palm, I held my wrists together in front of me, giving the illusion I was restrained.

I looked up at Conor with my most defeated expression. Eyes lifeless. Shoulders slumped. "Convincing enough?"

He turned and cocked his head, studying me. "Hands should be behind your back."

I moved the Ruger to the small of my back and held my hands behind me, hoping the slower draw time on the Ruger wouldn't cost me my life. "Okay, how about now?"

I saw him shudder, though he tried to hide it. "I really don't like this."

"Why? You're the one with the assault rifle."

"Not me I'm worried about."

"I can take care of myself, big boy," I said. "Let's do this."

We climbed back into the Gray Ghost with Conor in the driver's seat.

22

———————

Conor pulled up to the gate. The guard shuffled over. "What the hell you want?"

"Caught this one trying to escape from one of the other drop houses," Conor said in his best American accent. "Boss man told me to bring her here."

"No one told me nothing."

Conor shrugged. "Don't believe me? Call Mr. Volkov, though I'm told he's wining and dining some bigwig Arab clients." He pronounced it "Ay-rab," and it was all I could do not to laugh. "I wouldn't disturb 'em if I was you."

"Please don't do this," I pleaded, playing the part. "Just let me go. I won't tell anyone."

"Shut the hell up!" Conor slammed me across the face hard enough to make me see stars. I tasted blood.

Conor's unexpected punch triggered long-forgotten memories. The trauma of getting pounded into a bloody pulp at my high school graduation party surfaced. Images flashed through my mind of a huge man driving his mallet-sized fists into my body, the antiseptic smell of a hospital, and the incessant beeping of a vitals monitor.

I'd been hit countless times in my work and always shook it off. *Why the hell is this any different?* I sobbed and hung my head in defeat. Part of the act, I told myself.

"Yeah, all right. I'll radio Perkins in the warehouse to have someone escort her inside." The guard reached for his radio.

"No can do, mate." Conor's American accent was slipping.

My gut twisted. *Don't blow it, dude,* I thought.

"I have orders to escort her all the way in personally," Conor said. "It's my arse if she gets away again."

The guard narrowed his gaze at Conor, then grunted his approval and waved us on. "Pull around back to the loading dock. Sanchez'll show you where to go."

"Thanks!" Conor drove through.

I took a deep breath, getting control of my emotions. One step closer to rescuing Holly.

"You okay, love?" There was concern in his voice. "Aw, shite! Your lip's bleedin'."

"I'm all right." My grip tightened on the folded jackknife behind my back. "We're committed now. Just stick to the plan."

He drove around the warehouse to a large concrete loading dock with a staircase on the side. A dark-skinned man guarded the back door. Sanchez, no doubt.

Conor climbed out. Sanchez raised his rifle and pointed it at Conor.

"Whoa! The guy at the gate told me to bring this one around back. Clever girl snuck out of one of the other drop houses." Conor walked around and opened my door and roughly dragged me out of the truck. I kept my eyes on the ground.

"Yeah, okay. Bring her up," Sanchez replied.

Conor poked me in the back with his Bushmaster. "Move, cunt!"

I trudged up the stairs to where Sanchez was standing. He slung his rifle over his shoulder and cupped my chin, turning my face this way and that. "What happened to this *puta's* face?"

"Put up a bit of a fight when we caught her."

"You think you smart, *puta*?" Sanchez licked his lips. "Not so smart now, eh?" He grabbed my right breast and twisted hard enough to make me gasp. My grip on my knife tightened as I resisted the urge to fight back.

"Easy, mate." Conor pushed himself between us. "Let's not damage the merchandise any more than necessary."

"Fuck you, *maricon!*" Sanchez shoved Conor aside and grabbed my shirt collar. His breath smelled of spiced meat and tequila.

When he reached for my crotch, I flicked open my blade and lunged at Sanchez. He grabbed my arm, and we grappled until he kicked me away, sending me teetering off the edge of the platform and landing on my butt five feet below. I vaulted back onto the platform, knife still in hand.

Conor had Sanchez in a choke hold, but the guard broke free with an elbow to Conor's midsection. Sanchez picked up Conor's rifle and was about to shoot when I drove my knife into his carotid. Warm blood sprayed all over me, the wall, and the ground. He collapsed on the platform. A moment later he was still.

My heart raced as I looked around to see if anyone else had heard the scuffle. We appeared to be alone for the moment. Score one for the good guys.

Conor eyed me suspiciously. "You okay, love?"

"More than okay." I wiped my face on my shirt and caught myself grinning. "Okay, folks, let's see what's behind door number two."

I stashed my knife in my pocket and pulled out the Ruger. Conor opened the door, and I followed him in. The interior was dark and chilly, with rows and rows of twenty-foot-high shelving stocked with boxes of produce on pallets. Two forklifts sat idle in a corner.

"Where to now?" I asked.

Conor pointed his rifle down the aisle along the left wall. "Let's try that way."

With my finger on the trigger, I led the way past the stacks of produce. At the other end of the row stood a large caged area filled with people. I caught a whiff of body odor and urine.

"Who the hell are you?" A broad-shouldered man with his AK-47 raised appeared at the end of the row, between us and the cage.

I raised my Ruger, put two in his chest, and raced past him to where women and children of various ages huddled inside the chain-link cage. A girl about twelve years old looked up at me. Her eyes went wide. "Look out!"

I ducked as a burst of automatic gunfire shook the air. Bullets rattled the fence and ricocheted off the back wall. I turned and saw two other guards shooting at us. I pulled off three shots at one guard, hitting him in the neck and chest. I aimed at the other and was about to pull the trigger when his head whipped back in a cloud of gore as Conor brought him down with his Bushmaster.

The door to the cage was secured with a padlock. "Where are the keys?" I called to the girl who had warned me about the other guard.

"He has them!" She pointed at the guy Conor had shot. I heard shouting and the pounding of boots on concrete coming from all around us.

"Cover me!" I told Conor.

I stashed my Ruger in my waistband and searched the dead guard, shuddering as bursts of gunfire ripped through the air. My hands found a cluster of keys attached to his belt. I cut the belt with my knife and located the one that looked like a padlock key.

I popped the lock as a spray of bullets hit the fence around me. The people in the cage screamed, and we all dropped to the floor. I turned with my Ruger out and dropped another guard raising his weapon at me.

"FBI! Drop your weapons! Get on the ground!" One of the guards held up a badge.

"What the—" I wasn't sure whether to believe him or not.

"Drop your weapons, now! Get on the ground!" A female

voice came from behind me in the cage. I turned. A woman with dirty-blond hair and fierce eyes had a Glock trained on me.

"Fuck." I set my gun on the floor and lay down with my hands behind my head. Conor did the same.

"We're bail enforcement agents," I said. "Looking for a fugitive." I felt myself being cuffed.

"Took us months to infiltrate this organization, and you two screw up the op because some jailbird jumped bail?" the female agent asked.

I looked over and saw the other agent cuff Conor. This was so not how I pictured it would go down.

The lady fed pulled me to my feet and escorted me to the warehouse office. Once inside, she closed the office door and pushed me into a swivel chair. "Who are you?"

"Jinx Ballou. My partner's Conor Doyle. We're looking for Holly Schwartz. She was kidnapped by Volkov's organization. Who the hell are you?"

"Special Agent Deborah Velasco, FBI. You're looking at several felonies, Ms. Ballou. Murder, B&E, obstruction."

"Look, Agent Velasco, I'm sorry we wrecked your undercover investigation. But we had reason to believe our fugitive was here. That gives us the right to enter. And you can't charge us with murder for defending ourselves."

Agent Velasco knitted her brow. "You're looking for the teenage girl charged with murdering her mother?"

"We have reason to believe she was kidnapped and was brought here."

"I hate to burst your bubble, but you were given bad intel. There was a disabled girl here a week ago, but it wasn't her. You just exposed a federal undercover investigation for nothing."

"Shit."

23

Conor and I were transported, still handcuffed, to the FBI's Phoenix office, then put in separate interrogation rooms. Velasco and her partner, Special Agent Danny Gleason, repeatedly questioned me over our failed rescue attempt. When I realized my explanation was getting me nowhere, I invoked my right to counsel.

By that time, the bitter coffee and stale vending machine snacks had their intended effect. My back teeth were floating when my attorney, Kirsten Pasternak, stepped into the interrogation room. Yellow-framed glasses on a chain. Gray silk jacket over a white blouse. She stood a good three inches taller than Agent Gleason. I'd met her at the transgender support group and had found her an invaluable, if expensive, resource.

"I represent Ms. Ballou and Mr. Doyle," she told the agents. "I'd like a moment to confer with my client."

I gave her a rundown of the evening's events. Apparently she had already spoken to Conor and confirmed that our stories matched. She called the agents back into the room, and the three of them sparred while I concentrated on holding my bladder.

Occasionally, I added a bit of information when Kirsten gave me the green light.

When Kirsten pressed the agents to either arrest me or release me, Velasco and Gleason agreed not to charge us for now. I made a beeline for the restroom to pee and clean the dried gore from my face and hands. My shirt and cargo pants were beyond repair.

It wasn't the first time I'd killed someone in my duties as a bounty hunter. Unfortunately, circumstances sometimes made lethal force necessary. I wouldn't lose any sleep over the deaths of a few punk-ass human smugglers.

When I trudged out of the restroom, Kirsten met me at the door.

"Am I free to go?" I asked.

"For now. Just don't leave town. There's still a chance they press charges."

"Great."

"So this Holly Schwartz you're chasing, she's the one that's been in the news, right? Charity poster girl allegedly turned killer?"

"That's her."

"Any idea who's representing her?"

"Some guy named Swearingen."

Kirsten barked a laugh. "Zach Swearingen? Last time that hack saw the inside of a courtroom, Bill Clinton was getting blow jobs in the Oval Office."

I shrugged. "Apparently he's a friend of Holly's aunt."

She handed me one of her business cards. "When you do find this girl, have her call me. Tell her I'll represent her pro bono."

"Pro bono? You don't represent *me* pro bono."

"You're a successful bounty hunter. She's a penniless orphan in a high-profile case. I could use the publicity."

I rolled my eyes but took her card. "Whatever. If she asks, I'll give her your card."

"Thanks." She patted me on the back. "Now try to stay out of trouble until we can get this matter resolved."

It was midnight by the time we got back to Conor's bunker. I headed straight for the shower to wash off the remaining blood, dirt, and the night's trauma. Only the blood and dirt came off.

I stood there letting the water wash over my body, trying to make my mind go blank. But Conor's play-acting punch had unearthed a Pandora's box of memories I'd intentionally buried more than a decade earlier.

I'd been dating Peyton Dietz at the time. He was our high school's star basketball player and had been offered a scholarship to UNLV. I was looking forward to getting gender reassignment surgery after graduation before going on to study at ASU. When he asked me out, I felt like the luckiest girl in the world. Peyton knew about my gender transition and didn't care. He accepted me for the girl I was. Peyton's father, Barclay Dietz, was a different story.

Whether Peyton told him or Mr. Dietz found out some other way, I never heard. But a few hours into a graduation party at a mutual friend's house, Peyton got a call from his father, insisting the two of us meet him outside on the street. He made it sound urgent. Fearing it might be a family emergency, we rushed outside.

We found Mr. Dietz several houses down, standing beside his Jaguar with his arms crossed. Where Peyton was tall and lanky, Mr. Dietz was massive and muscular like a bull. Peyton said he'd been a middleweight boxing champion in his day.

Mr. Dietz ordered Peyton to wait in the passenger seat, saying he wanted a private word with me. Peyton protested, but Barclay Dietz wasn't one to put up with back talk. Peyton obeyed.

Mr. Dietz started with some innocuous questions. Was I having fun that evening? How was the food and the music? He even complimented my dress, an off-the shoulder peach number full of ruffles. Back when I wore ruffles.

Then his questioning turned darker. "What kind of girl are you?" he asked with an accusatory tone.

I wasn't sure how to answer. He asked me if I had breast implants. His questions were making me uncomfortable, and I told him so. When he pressed the issue about implants, I assured him I didn't.

"What you got between them skinny little legs of yours?" Mr. Dietz stepped into my personal space, his clenched fists looking like blacksmithing hammers. "A cunt or a cock?"

"I think I should call my folks." I backed away along the sidewalk toward the house party.

He stalked toward me. "You think my son's a cocksucker?"

"What? No! Of course not."

"You must. You're not a girl. You're just a little faggot in a dress, aren't you?"

I never saw the first blow coming. I just realized I was on my back on the sidewalk with my head throbbing. A thunderstorm of punches and kicks rained down on me. Somewhere in the blackness, Peyton shouted for his dad to stop. Or maybe I imagined it. I never saw him after that to confirm.

I woke up in the hospital days later with a fractured skull, a ruptured spleen, broken ribs, bruised kidneys, and a punctured lung. Barclay Dietz, I learned, was charged with aggravated assault but had jumped bail and hadn't been seen since.

It had been years since I'd even thought about that night. I'd been in countless fights with fugitives and their associates since then. Never fazed me. But Conor's slap brought it all back and shook me to my core. So much so that I found myself shivering in the shower, the water having turned cold.

Wrapped in a towel, I stumbled out of the bathroom, trying to stop the trembling. My lip was still swollen. My jaw hurt. My chest and wrists were sore.

Conor lay on his bed in a pair of camo boxers, reading a Lawrence Block paperback. Concern shot across his face. "You all right, love?"

"I'll survive." I sat on the bed next to him. "What was I thinking? Busting into Volkov's warehouse?"

"Don't be batterin' yourself. You held your own."

"And what did we accomplish? We're no closer to finding Holly." I lay next to him, drawn to his warmth. "This crazy theory about Holly getting kidnapped. Maybe Hardin's right. Maybe she did kill her mother. Maybe someone's hiding her, trying to keep her from going to jail. I just don't know."

"Maybe the aunt. We can have another go at her tomorrow if ya'd like."

"There's something she's not telling, but I didn't get the feeling she was hiding Holly. Why would Morton risk losing her house over a girl she barely knows? She'd be better off taking her chances in court."

Fatigue was dragging me under like a powerful current. "I'm too tired to think."

Conor kissed me on my temple. "Let's get some rest, love, and reassess in the morning."

24

My head and body still ached when I woke the next morning to the sound of my phone ringing. Sunlight peeked through the vertical blinds in Conor's bedroom. I picked up my phone from the nightstand. It was a few minutes after seven. "Hi, Mom."

"Sweetie, you didn't return my call yesterday. You okay?"

"I'm fine. Sorry I didn't call back. I was busy till late last night."

"Ever since that awful newspaper outed you, I've been so worried. Your brother says it's all over the Twitter."

"I'm okay. Really." And even if I wasn't, I didn't need her worrying about me.

"The people at your work. They know?"

"I'm working for a different bail bond agent now. She knows, and she's fine with it."

"Maybe this is your chance to do something less dangerous. I don't like you chasing criminals all the time."

"Mom, relax! Most fugitives I pick up are good folks who simply forgot their court date. Nothing to be concerned about."

"But what about the dangerous criminals, sweetie? I saw on

the news there was a big shoot-out in Buckeye between bounty hunters and human smugglers."

"Really? Huh. Well, I was nowhere near that warehouse. Just out searching for a young woman. No danger whatsoever." What was I going to tell her? Yeah, Mom, I stabbed a guy in the neck, then shot two other guys while covered in the first guy's blood. So not going to happen.

"You coming over tomorrow morning for brunch?"

"Wouldn't miss it. Conor too."

"Perhaps you could come to Mass with me."

"Mom, we talked about this."

"I worry for your soul."

"My soul is fine." *Would God send me to hell for killing a murderous human smuggler? Do I even believe in God?* "I have to go, Mom. I have work to do. Love you."

"Okay, sweetie. See you tomorrow. I have some pretty dresses I'd like you to try on, so don't be late."

I rolled over and sighed. Conor leaned up on one arm, smiling at me. "Lying to your mother again?"

"What am I gonna do? Tell her I was going all Lisbeth Salander on a bunch of scumbags? She's already worried about me."

"So what's our game plan, Ms. Salander?"

"I honestly have no clue. I've been through the possible scenarios. Scenario A, she was kidnapped for ransom."

Conor nodded. "Except no one's received a ransom note as far as we know."

"True. Scenario B, she was kidnapped by human traffickers. Problem is, she wasn't at Volkov's warehouse last night. Agent Velasco said a paraplegic girl was there a week ago but assured me she wasn't Holly Schwartz."

"Which brings us to Scenario C—she's hiding voluntarily, most likely with some help."

"But help from who? And why?" I thought about it. "Maybe Detective Hardin was on to something. He claimed Holly wasn't as mentally disabled as everyone thinks she is. Her aunt hinted at the same thing. Maybe this whole thing about her being sick and disabled is just a scam."

"To what end?"

"Money. Attention. She's been on all of these telethons. Charities and individuals are sending her money."

"But according to her aunt, Holly's been sick since she was a baby. You yourself found a bunch of doctors' bills in their home, plus all those pill bottles at her aunt's house. Doesn't sound like a scam to me."

"According to Hardin, Bonnie was forcing Holly to get a feeding tube she claimed she didn't need. Maybe Mommy Dearest had that syndrome where parents make their kids sick to get attention."

"Munchausen by proxy?" Conor cocked an eyebrow. "Honestly, how could the mother fool the doctors for so long? Something would've shown up in the tests, right?"

I pondered his point. "I don't know. If she is disabled, who would take her? And why? And who killed her mother?"

"Maybe someone thought she was being abused."

"Possible. But then why not call the cops? Or report it to the Department of Child Safety?" I thought about it some more. "Unless someone did report it, and no one did anything about it."

I grabbed my phone and dialed Becca.

"Hey, Jinx! You been on social media lately?" She sounded better but concerned.

"No, why?"

"Girl, that story in *Phoenix Living* about you went viral."

"Shit. Just what I need."

"It'll pass. How's the hunt for Holly Schwartz going?"

"Not so great. Chasing a bunch of leads and coming up with zero. How are you doing?"

"Surprisingly well. Don't know how long that will last, but I'm down here at the Hub while I still have the energy to do so. By the way, I discovered something interesting."

"What's that?"

"Those donation checks that Bonnie Schwartz deposited over the past year? I took a look at the thumbnails of the checks on the bank statements. She only deposited about a third of each check's value. The rest she got in cash. Just a few thousand a month, but it struck me as odd. Not sure if that has any connection to Holly's disappearance."

"I'll look into it from my end. Maybe a substance abuse issue? Or something else she wanted to keep off the books."

"Kinda what I was thinking."

"Could you check to see if there were any abuse complaints filed against Bonnie Schwartz? Either with Phoenix PD or the Department of Child Safety."

"You think the mom was abusing Holly?"

"Just a theory I'm exploring. Right now I'm grasping at every thread to see what shakes loose."

"I'll check and call you back."

"Thanks, Becks."

"Just do yourself a favor and stay off social media for a while."

"Of course." I hung up and nervously checked Twitter. Because I was an idiot.

At the top of the trending topics list was the hashtag #TransBountyHunter. I pulled up the latest tweets. A lot of them were supportive, saying I was a hero and an inspiration. One mother of a trans teen called me a lifesaver. Others were outright vicious, misgendering me and threatening to rape and murder me. Some were creepy solicitations from men with a trans fetish, which some in the trans community called "chasers." Ugh.

I clicked to check my email and found it similarly filled with messages from grateful fans, violent haters, and nasty stalkers. Most of the hateful stuff, I deleted after reading the subject line.

One email looked like a possible job offer, with the subject line "I Want To Hire You." I opened it.

. . .

My Dearest Jinx,

Thank you for your recent visit to my warehouse. So sorry I wasn't there to greet you in person.

Despite the disruption you caused, you managed to root out a couple of rats in my organization. For this I am in your debt. I am simultaneously impressed by your fighting skills and intrigued by your background. The article in Phoenix Living *was very enlightening, though it left me with questions.*

For example, do you still have a cock? I find the idea of a beautiful, sexy woman such as yourself having a cock quite a turn-on. I long to drizzle vodka over your nubile body and lick it off. I ache to fuck you till your ears bleed. Oh the fun we could have together. The pleasure and the pain, the agony and the ecstasy.

I would very much like the opportunity to thank you in person for your assistance and perhaps offer you a position on my staff, both literally and figuratively.

Please reply and let's meet.

Warmest Regards,

Milo

Holy fuck! Fuck, fuck, fuck, fuck! That psycho piece of shit, Milo fucking Volkov, knew who I was. He knew *what* I was. And he had my email address.

Bile rose in my throat. *Is this just a creepy invitation? Or a threat?* I closed the email app and tossed the phone on the bed. I didn't need this shit distracting me from my work.

"Ya all right, love?"

I jumped at Conor's voice. "What? Oh yeah. Just some assholes posting nasty shit about me on Twitter." I couldn't bring myself to show him the email from Volkov. Just too damn humiliating.

"Don't let the cheeky bastards get to ya. They're just jealous."

"Yeah, you're right. Listen, I need to work out the kinks from last night. Thinking of going for a run. Care to come with?"

He did. I put on some workout clothes I kept in one of Conor's dresser drawers.

We jogged north on Third Avenue to St. Joseph's Hospital, then hooked a left on Thomas and again on Fifth Avenue. When we got back to his place, my body felt charged and alive. He apparently felt the same, and soon we were engaged in a more intimate workout.

The gentleness of his lips on my body and the power of his body moving with mine left me gasping with pleasure. I let my mind go blank in a whirlwind of bliss until the words from Volkov's email crept into my consciousness.

My body went rigid, and I scrambled out from under Conor and curled into a trembling ball, perched on the edge of the bed.

"What's wrong? Did I hurt you?"

I sat with my back to him, trying to clear my mind and get my shit together. "I . . . I'm fine. Just . . . I don't know."

He slid next to me but thankfully didn't put his arm on me. "Something's got ya spooked. Is this about what happened at the warehouse?"

I looked up at him, struggling to maintain eye contact. "No, that was . . . doesn't matter. I'm just in a weird space is all. Pissed off at being outed. Pissed at missing Comicon. Frustrated at not finding Holly. I'll be all right. Just need a shower."

"Ya want company?"

"Not really."

I took a shower and did some breathing exercises my father had taught me to deal with panic attacks. They seemed to help. Afterward, I got dressed and ate a bagel.

With food in my stomach and a clearer head, I printed out the docs Becca had sent me. I laid them out on the floor in Conor's spare bedroom, along with the photocopies from the murder book, and the bills and fan mail I'd picked up at the Schwartzes' house.

Conor walked in. "Feeling better?"

"A bit."

"That's a shite-load of paperwork," Conor said.

"Just trying to get an overview of the situation and figure out where she might be. My mind keeps going back to the description her lawyer gave of her mother's alleged attacker."

"Aye, it sounded familiar to me too. Hold on a sec." He disappeared down the hall and returned moments later holding a *Sports Illustrated*. "How did Swearingen say Holly described the attacker?"

"Six-eight, medium-dark skin, long hair, black wing tattoo on one arm. Gold earring and an orange shirt."

"Like a Phoenix Suns jersey?" He held the magazine open to an article. On the page was a photo of Cedric Wilson, the Suns player who'd injured himself a while back in an accident. The description matched the photo exactly.

"There was an *Arizona Republic* article on Wilson in the Schwartzes' house. Must've made up the attacker's description based on Wilson's photo."

"Interesting." Conor tossed the magazine to the side.

"Still doesn't tell us where she is or who's helping her." I studied the paperwork laid out before me.

The bank statements had thumbnails of checks deposited. As Becca had pointed out, there was a distinct difference between check values and the amounts deposited. Nothing illegal in that. But highly suspicious under the circumstances. The question was, what was she doing with all of that cash?

It was nearly lunchtime when Becca called back.

"Hey, Becks! What'd you find?"

"According to the Department of Child Safety, there've been three complaints filed against Bonnie Schwartz. All cases were closed after social workers found no abuse."

"Who filed the complaints?"

"The first one was eight years ago by a doctor. The second a couple years later by Kimberly Morton, the aunt."

"That's interesting. She didn't mention that when Conor and I talked to her. What about the last one?"

Becca chuckled. "The last complaint was filed a year ago by a George Peavey."

"Why does that name ring a bell?"

"He was on both Holly and Bonnie's call logs. That's where things get interesting. Apparently, Peavey filed a request for a paternity hearing, claiming he's Holly's biological father. But he withdrew the request after Bonnie's murder."

"Wow, this just keeps getting weirder and weirder. So what do we know about this guy?"

"He's a mechanical engineer in Mesa, no criminal record. I can keep digging if you want."

"No, just text me his address and phone number."

"Will do. I also followed up on this Richard Delgado. He's a visiting nurse working for Compassionate Care and assigned to Holly. So no real surprise there."

"Thanks. Anything else?"

"Yeah, one thing. I rechecked Bonnie's cellphone account. There have been some recent phone calls. All local."

"How's that possible? Detective Hardin has both phones in evidence. And according to the evidence report, Bonnie's was smashed beyond repair. How could anyone be using it?"

"Could have pulled the SIM card before the police arrived," Becca said.

"She's a mentally disabled girl. How would she think to do that? *I* wouldn't think of that."

"Maybe she had help."

I looked at the array of paper in front of me. "Maybe she did. Question is from who?"

"Whom," Becca corrected.

"Whatever," I said. "So who's she calling?"

"The most frequent calls appear to be to prepaid phones. Burners. Not getting names on them. The rest of the calls are mostly food delivery. Jade Palace. Sub Barn. Tony and Maria's Trattoria."

"Tratto-what?"

"It's an Italian restaurant."

"Do we know where these deliveries are going?"

"I tried to look it up but came up empty."

"Damn." I pondered what we had so far. Nothing was gelling. Nothing made sense.

"I could try to trace the phone's location."

I felt a glimmer of hope. "How long will that take?"

"Hold on a moment." There was the tapping of computer keys in the background. "No luck. I can't ping the phone. It must be off with the battery removed."

"Crap. Okay, send me the info on Peavey. If he really is her father, maybe he has her. That would explain why he dropped the paternity suit. Keep checking that phone number every so often. See if you can get a location. Whoever has the phone with Bonnie's SIM card must be connected to Holly's disappearance."

"Will do."

I hung up. Moments later, I got a text from Becca with Peavey's information.

I found Conor on the phone with his team. When he hung up, I asked, "How are Deez and the boys doing up in Salt Lake City?"

"Zeroing in on their defendant. Almost had him at one point, but he managed to sneak out before they arrived. What'd Becca say?"

I filled him in on what Becca had told me. "You up for an outing? I want to talk to Daddy Dearest."

"As long as it doesn't involve shootouts with human smugglers, I'm game."

25

Before we left, I called George Peavey's phone. I didn't want to drive all the way to Mesa only to discover he was spending his Saturday elsewhere. At the same time, I didn't want to risk spooking him.

"This George Peavey?" I asked when he answered.

"It is. To whom am I speaking?"

"Oh, hi, I'm Liz Windsor. I live a couple streets over from you," I said in an overfriendly voice. "For some reason the post office delivered a box addressed to you."

"Again? They're always misdelivering my packages. Probably a book I ordered."

I decided to play along. "Yeah, judging from the size, that'd be my guess. You gonna be home for the next hour or so? I gotta dry my hair, and then I can drop it by."

"Yeah, I'll be around."

"Great. Toodles!"

"Liz Windsor?" Conor guffawed. "So now you're the bloody queen of England?"

"Could be. Never know what a girl can accomplish when she puts her mind to it," I said with a smirk.

What would have normally taken us thirty minutes ended up taking closer to an hour because ADOT had closed Highway 60 at the I-10 interchange. After twenty grueling minutes of slow-and-go traffic, we exited onto Baseline along with everyone and their brother. The traffic eased up once we crossed over the Loop 101and turned in to the Dobson Ranch area.

George Peavey's house was a white brick two-story with brown trim, set behind a three-car garage. We geared up with vest and weapons and walked up to the front door. After two quick doorbell rings followed by a good door pounding, I yelled, "Open up! Bail Enforcement!"

The door opened. George Peavey was a dumpy guy in his late thirties with a receding hairline. But his upturned nose, large eyes, and dark hair bore a strong resemblance to Holly Schwartz. The tangerine polo shirt he wore clashed with his mustard-colored cargo shorts.

"What's all this about? Who are you?"

"You're George Peavey?" I asked. "Holly Schwartz's father?"

His eyes narrowed. "Who wants to know?"

I held up my bail enforcement badge. "Jinx Ballou. Assurity Bail Bonds hired us to return Holly Schwartz to custody after she missed her court date."

"Geez, you people! She's a little girl who's lost her mother. Why can't you leave her alone, for God's sake?"

He turned to shut the door, but Conor held it open. "If she's here, mate, or ya know where she is, ya need to tell us now, or we can arrest you for obstruction. Ya could also be charged with conspiracy to commit murder after the fact."

Conor's words did their job. Peavey looked at us, clearly frustrated with the situation. "Look, she's not here. I haven't seen her in months."

"You filed a request for a paternity test?" I asked.

"Yes, I believe she's my daughter. I saw her and her mother interviewed on TV about a year ago. She looks just like me, and Bonnie and I had a thing about eighteen, nineteen years ago. I reached out to the two of them and was starting to get to know Holly. We bonded instantly, Holly and me. Then Bonnie got killed."

His face darkened. "I feel bad about talking ill of the dead, but I believe Bonnie was hurting Holly. In the brief time I spent with them, I realized Bonnie was obsessed with taking Holly to the doctor and the hospital for one thing after another. To the point of being abusive. Holly thought her mother was poisoning her. I reported her to DCS. Not that they listened."

"So Holly wasn't really disabled?" I asked.

"Holly insisted it was all a lie."

"How could Bonnie fool the doctors? Didn't they run tests?"

"I don't understand it all myself. Holly was so skinny from malnutrition and all the drugs the doctors were prescribing. The people from the charities simply never questioned them about it. The whole thing was nothing more than a twisted scam. Bonnie was obsessed with playing the saintly mother when she was closer to the devil incarnate."

"Un-fucking-believable," I said.

"She can walk. Can you believe that? Her mother threatened that if she spent too much time out of the wheelchair, her legs would become infected and have to be amputated."

"And Holly believed her?"

"She'd been manipulated by her mother since she was an infant. She was terrified of Bonnie. That's why I wanted to establish paternity and gain custody. Holly hated living in that house."

Conor narrowed his gaze. "Yet ya dropped the paternity claim after Bonnie was murdered? Having second thoughts about keeping a murderer under your roof? Or are ya hiding her from the law?"

"I don't know who killed Bonnie. If it was Holly, then she had a damned good reason, what with all she's endured." Peavey leaned against the door and stared out past us. "But I dropped the case temporarily until this whole mess got cleared up. I've talked to Bonnie's sister, Kim. Let her know I was willing to help in any way I can. Once all of this is behind us, I intend to file for custody. Holly wants to live with me."

So Morton did know about Peavey. What else was she hiding?

"Where's Holly?" I pressed. "We need to find her now, or the court will declare the bail bond forfeited, and Ms. Morton loses her house."

"I wish I knew where Holly was. Truly." He frowned. "I hoped Kim was hiding her, but I don't think she is. I keep expecting her to turn up. Somehow."

"Look, mate," Conor said. "We'd like to believe ya. But we're gonna have to take a look inside to confirm the girl's not here."

"Fine, be my guest." He stepped aside and let us in.

The place was simple, Scandinavian modern. Peavey was clearly a man who appreciated furniture that could be assembled with an Allen wrench. An entertainment center featured a fifty-inch flat screen surrounded by models of ships from a laundry list of sci-fi franchises. A copy of *Phoenix Living* with me on the cover lay on a coffee table. I did my best to ignore it.

In the master bedroom, there was an entire wall of DVDs. Mostly sci-fi and fantasy titles, with some westerns and action flicks thrown in for balance. But nowhere was there any indication of Holly's ever having been there. No teenager-sized clothing or accessories in the spare bedroom. No meds except for a prescription bottle for statins, written for him, not Holly.

As we were leaving, Peavey stopped me. "Do I know you? You look so familiar for some reason."

My eyes instantly darted to the *Phoenix Living* on the table behind him. "I have no idea, sir."

I watched the wheels in his mind turning, then his eyes lit up. "Wait, I got it! Didn't I see you at Comicon last year? Wonder Woman, right?"

I breathed a sigh of relief. "Yeah, you caught me."

He grabbed a framed photo off the entertainment center and showed it to Conor and me. It was Peavey with his arm around me, in full superhero costumed glory. "I had no idea you were a bounty hunter. That's seriously rad!"

"Look at that, love," Conor said, chucking me on the shoulder. "You're a celebrity."

I forced a smile. Doing cosplay at Comicon was one thing. Getting recognized in my day job by grown-up fanboys felt a little surreal. My hunting his daughter made it more so. "Lucky me."

"I'd really love it if you could sign the photo." He popped it out of the frame.

"Sure. Why not?" I said as he scrambled for a permanent marker. "How should I sign it?"

"How about, 'To George, with all my love.' And your name, of course."

"Of course." *Because signing it "Your daughter's bounty hunter" would be really awkward*, I thought.

I signed it, and he put it back on the shelf. "Holly'll be thrilled to see that." His face grew somber. "Please, find her before anything bad happens to her."

I put a hand on his shoulder. "I'll do my superhero best." *Where the hell'd that come from?*

He escorted us out the front door and waved at us as we climbed into the Gray Ghost.

"See there, love," Conor said as I pulled out of Peavey's driveway. "You thought you were going to miss all those gushing fanboys at Comicon."

"I guess today's my lucky day. Let's hope we luck out and find Holly."

I was threading my way back onto the I-10 freeway, pondering Holly's possible whereabouts, when my phone rang. "Please let that be Becca with another lead!"

It wasn't. I didn't recognize the caller ID. "Jinx Ballou."

"Yeah, this is Edie Miller. You put up posters in my neighborhood, looking for Artie Renzelli."

Renzelli was one of Liberty Bail Bonds's fugitives wanted for dealing dope. I'd put up flyers asking for leads—on my dime, no less, because Big Bobby could be a real tightwad. Bobby had reassigned the case to Fiddler, but screw them both.

"Thanks so much for calling. Edie, is it? So you saw Renzelli?"

"He and Li'l Mike were out partying with some skank last night a couple doors down. I'm pretty sure they still there."

I had no idea who Li'l Mike was, nor did I care. But I took down the address Edie gave me.

"The poster didn't say nothing 'bout no reward. But I should get something for turning him in, right? I'm on a fixed income."

Nothing came free in this business. "Tell you what. If I catch him based on this tip, I'll give you twenty."

"Twenty dollars? Shit! Silent Witness pay a whole lot more than that."

"All right, I'll see what I can do. I'll be there shortly."

"You got a lead on our girl?" Conor asked.

"Nope. A tip on Artie Renzelli, one of Liberty's skips. I'm going after him."

Conor guffawed. "D'ya miss the part where Big Bobby sacked ya, love? What's the point if he's not gonna pay?"

I grinned mischievously. "Trust me. I'll make him pay, one way or another. You're down for this, right?"

"I was actually hoping we could grab lunch. I'm famished, and there's a new Irish pub near Thomas and the 51 I been meanin' to try."

"Come on! You help me bring this guy in, and I'll treat for lunch once we're done."

"Okay, fine! Let's get this guy."

"Oh, by the way, you got any more cash?" I asked.

26

———

I passed the address to Conor, who navigated us north to a neighborhood in Peoria with roundabouts and speed bumps every hundred yards. They called them traffic-calming devices, but they made me anything but calm. Maybe if I slowed down for them, but who had time for that?

We stopped in front of a small ash-gray house with wooden siding and a patchy yellowing lawn, littered with empty beer cans, liquor bottles, and a child's overturned tricycle. A line of scraggly Texas sage shrubs stood vigil in front of the iron-barred windows.

"Charming place." I switched on the walkie-talkie on my belt, slipped on my shades, and stepped out of the truck. "I'll take the front door. You take the back."

Conor pulled a shotgun loaded with beanbag rounds from the back of the Gray Ghost. "Copy that." He walked around the east side of the house, where there was a gate to the backyard.

I gave him a minute to get into position then pounded on the front door. "Bail enforcement! Open up!" I followed it up with more pounding. "Open the door now."

"I'm coming, I'm coming," an unhurried male voice said from

inside the house. A heavyset guy with a mess of wild hair opened the door, wearing a rumpled T-shirt and plaid boxers, which revealed a lot more than I wanted to see. This was not Renzelli.

"I'm looking for Arthur Renzelli. I'm told he's here."

"Arthur who?" He scratched his belly.

From the other side of the house, I heard loud barking, followed by Conor shouting and cursing. *Aw, shit!*

I keyed my walkie. "Conor, you all right?"

The belly scratcher chuckled. "That your guy trespassing in my backyard? Guess he met Bert and Ernie."

I tried to push past the guy, but he held his ground. "Get out of my way, asshole!"

"Not a chance, little lady."

I planted my heel in his instep, and he fell forward onto the porch, howling. I flipped him on his belly, one arm twisted behind his back.

A shotgun blast thundered from the backyard and then another, followed by what I guessed were Bert and Ernie whimpering after getting hit with beanbags.

"Sumbitch shot my dogs!" Bellyscratcher yelped.

"Conor!" I called again into the walkie. "What's your status?"

"Just teaching a couple of mutts who's top dog around here."

Out of the corner of my eye, I caught movement on the west side of the house. A skinny guy with long black hair and wearing only jeans and flip-flops had slipped out the side window. This was my guy, Artie Renzelli. He took off running down the street.

"Fugitive's on the run westbound out the side window!" I yelled.

I chased after him, since Conor had a handle on the dogs and their owner. Renzelli sprinted across lawns and, with his long legs, was making good time. I may have been shorter, but I was in better shape and had proper footwear. After a couple of houses, I was gaining on him. I caught snippets of Conor trying to call me on the walkie, but I was running too fast to make out what he was saying.

I was almost on Renzelli with my Taser drawn when the neighborhood street we were running down emptied onto Seventy-Fifth Avenue, thick with traffic. Renzelli charged full bore into the street, dodging vehicles amid squealing tires and angry honking.

I hesitated to follow, not wanting to get pancaked under someone's truck. When he reached the center turn lane, I decided to risk it. I didn't want to lose him. Not after chasing him for half a mile already.

With a quick glance at the oncoming vehicles, I threw myself into the street, hoping my mother's prayers for my safety would pay off. I reached the center turn lane just as Renzelli disappeared into a shopping center parking lot on the other side. I wanted to rush after him but had to wait on a dump truck to pass, followed by a slow-moving landscaper with a trailer.

When I finally reached the parking lot, I looked for Renzelli among the rows of cars. He was nowhere to be seen. I was about to tell Conor on my walkie that I'd lost him when I spotted my quarry ducking between a Corolla and a Jeep a hundred feet away. "Gotcha!"

I poured on maximum speed, angling through the maze of cars, narrowly missing a Caddy pulling out of a space. When I was almost on him, I raised the Taser and fired. A rapid whapp-whapp-whapp was followed by Renzelli howling and face-planting onto the hood of a Buick. I cuffed him and called Conor on my walkie.

"Yo, Conor!" I said between gulping breaths. "You still alive?"

"Aye! Doing better than those bloody hounds and their owner. Where the hell are ya?"

"Shopping center parking lot. In front of the Fry's Foods. Other side of Seventy-Fifth Avenue. Guess our guy wanted to do a little shopping before we hauled him back to jail. That right, Renzelli?"

"Kiss my ass!" Renzelli said.

"I'll be right over."

A few minutes later, Conor pulled up in the Gray Ghost. I secured Renzelli in the backseat, and Conor drove us toward the Peoria Police Department. I had one thing to do before returning our fugitive to custody.

I dialed the number I'd almost deleted from my contacts list. It rang four times before a familiar voice answered.

"Liberty Bail Bonds. Sara Jean speaking."

"Sara Jean, how the hell are you?" I asked.

"What do *you* want, pervert?"

"Now, Sara Jean. Don't be rude. I have something you want. Or rather someone."

"Who?"

"Your buddy Artie Renzelli. Dope peddler extraordinaire."

"That case was reassigned to Fiddler. I told you."

"So even if I turn him in and get the body receipt, you're not going to pay me?"

"I will not!" I could picture the self-righteous expression on her face.

"Huh." I turned to my prisoner in the backseat. "Hey, Renzelli, you want me to let you go?"

"Hell, yeah!" Renzelli had a confused but hopeful look.

"No!" Sara Jean shouted. "His bond comes due on Wednesday."

"But it's only Saturday," I teased. "I'm sure if I drop Artie back where he was hiding out, Fiddler'll find him in a week or three. Maybe."

"Don't you do it!"

"What's it going to be, Sara Jean? You going to pay me, or do I let this guy go?"

"Fine, I'll pay you," she grumbled.

I couldn't help smiling. "See you Monday morning around ten. Be a doll and have the check waiting for me. Wouldn't want to sully your office too much with my transgender cooties."

She hung up. I turned to the bare-chested man in my backseat. "Bad news, dude. Got to take you to Peoria PD to get this mess sorted out."

"Fuck you, bitch!"

"Aw, Renzelli darling, don't be cross. It's been kind of fun. We both got some sunshine and exercise. Almost got killed by crazy Arizona drivers. Maybe they'll reset your bail and we can do this all over again. "

He glared. Ugh, so much hostility. Oh well. At least I was getting paid. And at the end of the day, that was what really mattered as far as I was concerned.

A little while later, Renzelli was back in custody. I had my body receipt. I'd called Edie, my tipster, and sent her forty dollars via PayPal. Meanwhile, Conor and I were drinking ice-cold beers at McGowan's Pub, waiting on our lunch order.

Just as our server showed up with our food, my phone rang. It was Becca.

"What's up, Becks?" I asked between bites of my bangers and mash.

"Bonnie Schwartz's phone pinged. I got an address."

I wiped my hands on a napkin and grabbed another to write on. "Go ahead."

"The phone's at the Desert View Inn. It's off the I-17 southbound access road just past Thunderbird."

"What room?"

"The information isn't that detailed. Sorry. I did call the motel, but they don't have any rooms rented to a Holly Schwartz."

"No problem. It's a start. Thanks!" I was about to hang up when an idea occurred to me. "Oh, one more thing! Get locations on the prepaid burner phones called by Bonnie's phone."

"Gimme a sec," Becca said. "Nope. Uh, no. And . . . damn. No luck on any of them. All three burner phones must be turned off."

"I'll start with the motel. Thanks!"

I hung up and turned to Conor. "Pack it up. We gotta go."

"What? I'm still eating my bloody fish and chips." Conor gave me a what-the-hell look.

"Grab a box. We have a girl to rescue and a bounty to collect. On your feet, soldier."

Conor grunted. He tossed our lunches into a take-out box and left a couple of twenties on the table. Such a generous tipper. "Bloody hell, you're so bossy sometimes."

"Bitch, bitch, bitch," I mocked as I pushed him toward the front door.

27

As I drove us north on I-17, Conor's phone rang.

"'Ello? What? Now? I know I promised, but I'm busy at the moment." He paused with a frustrated and annoyed expression on his face. "Oy! Not *that* kind of busy." He blushed and glanced at me.

I mouthed, "Who is it?" He shook his head.

"Fine. I'll be there in half an hour." He hung up. "Sorry, love. I have an errand to run. I'll need ya to drop me off at my place."

"An errand? Who was that?"

He shook his head. "One of my mates needs my help moving a dresser." Something about his voice was off.

"Oh really?" I asked, not bothering to hide my suspicions. "Which one of your mates?"

"Jody. Not even his dresser, really. Just some girl he's shagging."

"Jody, huh? Sounds like a woman's name."

"Stop it! He's a bloke I know from work."

"Yeah, whatever," I grumbled. *Him and his damned secrets.* "But if I bag this chick without your help, I'm cutting your share in half."

"However ya want to split the bounty's fine with me. Just don't be mad." He reached for my hand, but I pulled it away. "Ah, love, I'm not runnin' 'round on ya. Ya know me better than that."

"Now you just sound guilty."

"I'm not guilty of anything 'cept wanting to help a mate."

"What about helping me? Aren't I your mate? Who knows what I could be walking into at this motel."

"You, darling, are my one true love. It's just that I owe this bloke a favor. If ya want to wait till I'm done, then wait. It won't take that long."

"Maybe I should come give you a hand?"

"What?" He shook his head vigorously. "No, that won't be necessary. You're on a deadline. Maybe Rodeo can be your backup."

"Screw Rodeo, and screw you. I can handle this myself." I rolled my eyes. "I'll drop you off at your place so you can help your so-called mate with his so-called girlfriend's so-called dresser."

We drove the rest of the way back to his place in awkward silence. I wasn't normally the jealous type. But after this thing with Levinson and now him obviously lying about this errand, I couldn't help going there.

When I pulled up in front of his house, I stared at the dash without a word.

"Jinxie, love." He lifted my hand from the steering wheel and gently placed three kisses on my knuckles. I felt my anger soften, which still kind of pissed me off. His chivalrous nature was my Achilles' heel, and he knew it. Damn him!

"I swear to the good Lord above, I've always been faithful to ya, and I always will. No one can steal my heart away."

I looked at him, fighting the angry tears pressing at the back of my eyes. My jaw felt tight, my stomach flip-flopping. I had no fear when it came to charging assholes with AK-47s. But this relationship shit could turn me into a whimpering child. "For reals?" I managed to squeak out.

"For reals."

Our eyes locked, and the tears flowed. I felt myself clinging to his words but terrified of believing them. "Go on. Help this Jody person. Call me when you're done."

He kissed me, cradling my face. My insides turned to custard. No one could kiss like that and cheat, could they?

When I opened my eyes, the passenger door was closed, and he was strolling across his yard, digging his keys out of his pocket.

I slid the Pink Trinket's album *TERF Whores* into my CD player and cranked it up to full blast before putting the Gray Ghost in Drive and slamming the accelerator.

It was one o'clock when I pulled in front of the Desert View Inn, a locally owned motel geared toward traveling families. The plaster walls outside the automatic doors showed their years, but the flowers in the planters were in full bloom in a rainbow of colors. I grabbed my paperwork and strode inside.

The woman behind the desk was fortyish and smelled of menthol cigarettes. She smiled as I approached. "Checking in?"

"Actually, I'm wondering if you've seen this person?" I showed her Holly's photo. "She might have been in a wheelchair. Or not."

She studied it for a second, then shook her head. "She doesn't look familiar. 'Course, I was off all last week. Today's my first day back."

"Anyone here who was working the past few days?"

"My coworker's on his lunch break. Should be back in an hour."

"All right, thanks." I started to walk away, then turned back. "You have security cameras?"

Her face grew less friendly and accommodating. "We're not allowed to show the security feeds to anyone without a manager present. And even then, only with a warrant."

I pulled out the authorization for me to apprehend Holly Schwartz. "I'm here on legal business. This person missed her court hearing, and I have reason to believe she may have been kidnapped."

"I'm sorry, but that's not a warrant for the security video."

"So you're just going to let this girl be raped, maybe even killed, just because I have the wrong paperwork? What kind of person are you?" I was laying the guilt on a bit thick, but I'd learned from the best—my mother.

The woman raised her eyebrows in an apologetic fashion. "Even if I wanted to, I don't have a key to that room. You'll have to talk to my head manager."

"When's your head manager get here?"

"Six tonight."

Crap! I waltzed outside and sat in the Gray Ghost to figure out the best strategy. What did I know? I knew someone had a phone with the SIM card for Bonnie Schwartz's mobile account. Maybe it was Holly or an accomplice.

It could be a kidnapper, but even then they would have to have switched the SIM card between the murder and the time the police showed up. Why would they do that and not take Holly with them? In any case, it followed that if the phone was here, Holly probably was too.

I could stake out the parking lot, but there was no guarantee Holly would leave the room anytime soon. I could go knocking on doors. There were about a hundred rooms in the motel, all of them opened to the outside rather than a central hallway. It was too freaking hot to knock on that many doors. I'd die of heat stroke before I found her.

Searching on my phone, I found a Sub Barn sandwich shop a mile west on Thunderbird. I drove over and ordered a couple of sandwiches. While I was waiting on the order, I asked the freckle-faced kid at the counter, "How much for your hat?"

He looked confused. "I don't think they're for sale."

"Aw, come on. Five bucks. Ten?" I pulled out some of the cash I got off Conor.

A middle-aged man in a white button-down shirt wandered behind the counter. I called out to him. "Excuse me, are you the manager?"

Freckles blushed as the guy in the white shirt turned. "Yes, I'm Craig. Is there a problem?"

"No problem at all." I turned on my gushing fangirl charm. "In fact, I'm a diehard Sub Barn fan. Love your sandwiches, especially the Barn Burner. So great! And that new ad with the talking horse is hilarious."

"Well, thank you. We're rather proud of it."

"I was wondering if I could purchase one of your hats." I batted my eyelashes and pushed out my chest.

His eyes dropped to my breasts. "Anything for a loyal customer."

Gushing smile turned up to eleven. "Oh, you're so sweet. How much?"

"For you, it's on the house. Call it a promotional investment."

"Aw, thanks so much, Craig."

"In fact," he said, leaning over the counter, "give me your number, and I'll throw in a shirt too. Bet you'd look hot in it."

Oh great. My flirting is working a little too well. Still, a shirt might help me get inside Holly's room. "Ya got a pen?" I replied coyly.

He popped one out of his pocket.

"Hand?" I asked with a wink.

He held out his palm, and I scribbled down the phone number for the local sex offenders' registry. Seemed appropriate.

He beamed. "I'll be right back." A moment later, he reappeared with a polo shirt and a cap, each wrapped in clear plastic. "You free for dinner?"

"I think so. Call me in an hour to confirm."

I trotted out with my bag of subs and my Sub Barn bling. A quick change in the back of the Gray Ghost, and I could have passed for a Sub Barn delivery girl.

When I pulled into the Desert View Inn's parking lot, I called the number for Bonnie's phone. A young female voice answered. "Hello?"

Was this Holly? I couldn't be sure. She didn't sound as fragile as she had on those telethons.

"Hi, someone placed a delivery order from Sub Barn. I'm here at the motel, but I don't know your room number."

"Oh, that's strange. I guess Richie ordered lunch while he was out. Okay, we're in room 278. Second floor on the back side of the motel."

"Fabulous! I'll be there shortly."

I used to think stunts like this worked only in the movies, but I'd seen Conor pull the same deal time after time. Bottom line, people were gullible. And most criminals were downright stupid. Good for me, bad for them.

I drove around to the back of the motel and parked the SUV. I pulled my snazzy new polo shirt over my ballistic vest, but it bulged too much. I could see the words Bail Enforcement Agent through the thin fabric. If they looked out the door's peephole, I'd be made before I could grab her.

Reluctantly, I ditched the vest but pulled the shirt over my Taser. It peeked out only a little. I donned the Sub Barn cap, grabbed the bag of sandwiches, and hustled up the outside stairs to room 278, paying little attention to the people coming and going along the walkway. Apparently everyone staying at the motel was either headed to lunch or coming back.

"Who is it?" the same girl asked after I knocked.

"Sub Barn delivery."

A girl who looked to be in her early teens opened the door. She stood about four foot ten with an upturned nose and eyes that were hard and dark. Her hair was dark and extremely short, as if recently buzzed.

"Holly Schwartz?"

Her gaze locked with mine for a moment, then to something behind me. I turned to see what she was staring at and caught a blur of motion and then stars.

Next thing I knew, I was lying faceup on the motel bed with

my hands cuffed to the headboard above me. Something soft had been stuffed in my mouth, with a strip of duct tape across my face. I was in trouble.

<h1 style="text-align:center">28</h1>

My head hurt with the fury of a hangover after a bender of well drinks and cheap wine. My stomach threatened to erupt like Vesuvius. I couldn't remember why I was hungover. No memories of a wild night at the bars. Nothing to explain the handcuffs or the improvised gag.

"Who the heck are you?" a male voice asked.

My vision was a bit doubled as my eyes fluttered open. I managed to make out a man with long, straight black hair and tan skin. I guessed he was Native American or Latino. He stood above me, a nervous look on his face, pointing the Taser at my chest.

"I'm sorry I hit you. But . . ." He glanced at the girl with the bristly hair who was standing beside him. "So who are you?"

I gave them an incredulous look and a muffled grunt. Like, how was I supposed to answer with a gag in my mouth?

The guy ripped off the duct tape. He must have mashed it on good because it felt as if half my face were coming off with it. He then pulled a sock out of my mouth.

"Jesus Christ on a cracker, that hurt!" I took a breath to clear my head. "I'm looking for Holly Schwartz."

The girl's gaze narrowed. "Why?"

"Holly?"

Her mouth was a thin line.

"Your aunt's worried about you. She asked me to find you. Your father too." Technically true, even if they didn't hire me.

"I'm fine."

"She's about to lose her house because of you. You missed your court date."

"Aw, crap, Holly. She's a bounty hunter."

"A bounty hunter? What do we do, Richie?"

The guy again jammed the sock in my mouth and slapped the duct tape back in place. "Look, I'm sorry, but I can't let you take her to jail. She's been through enough already."

I gave them an angry, muffled grunt through the gag. The guy pulled the trigger on my Taser, and my body convulsed in agony. Everything went black.

When I came to again, they were gone. My phone was ringing in my left back pocket. My mind was fuzzy, and the sick feeling in my stomach was worse. I steeled myself. Throwing up with a gag in my mouth could prove fatal. I wasn't going out like this. No freakin' way.

I took some slow, steadying breaths, trying to picture myself with Conor, but that made things worse as I thought about the fight we'd had. So I focused on my parents and my brother, Jake. The world was still swirling and unsettled, but I didn't feel as though I was going to puke and asphyxiate myself. By that time, my phone had quit ringing.

Okay, think, girl. You can get out of this. You have handcuff keys. I kept three keys on my person at all times. One was on my keychain in my front pocket but wasn't accessible since my hands were cuffed to a vertical metal bar attached to the headboard.

My second key was in my back jeans pocket. Also not accessible.

That left the one on a ball chain around my neck. I grabbed the chain at the back of my neck and pulled it up until I had the key in hand. Grateful laughter rumbled in my chest. I would get out of here. With a frustrating amount of effort, I released one hand, then the other.

When I sat up, the room started spinning. Bile rose in my throat. I ripped the duct tape off my raw lips and cheeks and pulled out the sock, trying not to puke. Wincing at the pain, I focused on my breathing until the vertigo lessened.

I pulled my phone out of my pocket. Three missed calls from Conor. One each from my mother and Becca. "Geez, how long have I been out?" The clock on my phone said it was nearly five o'clock. I rang Conor first.

"Jesus! Ya been dodgin' my calls? Ya treat me like a bloody tosser an' then ignore me."

"Con, listen." Another wave of nausea hit me. "I'm . . . something happened."

"Wha'? You all right, love?"

"I'm . . ." I hurled all over the floral polyester bedspread and thanked the stars I was no longer gagged. I continued heaving until nothing came up. By the time I was able to put the phone back to my ear, I was afraid he'd hung up. "You there, Conor?"

"Jinxie! Where the hell are ya?"

"I . . . I don't remember. Some motel room."

"Hang on, love. I'll track your phone. I'm on my way."

I shuffled unsteadily into the bathroom and splashed water on my face. The back of my head ached from where I'd been hit, and my hair was tacky with blood. Probably explained the nausea. I checked myself and found no other serious injuries, just chafed wrists from the cuffs and facial abrasions from the duct tape.

As for my weapons, my Ruger was locked in the Gray Ghost's glove box. I still had the revolver in my ankle holster. An expended cartridge was all that remained of my Taser. Still, it could have been worse.

I was still feeling nauseated when Conor pounded on the door.

"Jinxie, open up!"

Keeping a hand on the wall, I made my way to the door and opened it. The glaring afternoon sun and triple-digit heat hit me like a semi truck. Conor caught me before I lost my balance and helped me sit in a chair.

"What the bloody hell happened? Ya look like ya been battered."

"Holly. She's . . . not disabled. The whole thing. Must've been a con."

"She did this to you?"

"Some guy with her. Ambushed me from behind. Knocked me out. Then Tased me after I came to. Ugh, God, my head hurts so much."

Conor's hands gently touched the side of my head. "Cheeky bastards. Certainly gave you a knock, didn't they? Ya wanna call the cops?"

"No. My job's to catch Holly. Don't need the cops. How bad's it look?"

"There's a shite-load of blood, but I think ya stopped bleedin'. Oughta get ya checked out, though. Could have a concussion."

"Ugh, last thing I want to do is sit in some ER for the rest of the night."

"This yours?" Conor was pointing at the puke on the bed and floor.

I felt my face warm. "Yeah."

"Come on, love. We gotta get ya looked at. Your ma would have my arse if you up and died on me."

He helped me into his Charger and drove me to the entrance to John C. Lincoln's Emergency Department. I knew he wasn't coming in. For all his toughness and bravado, Conor had an extreme phobia of hospitals. He said it started after his sister was killed in a bombing in Northern Ireland.

I could see the ambivalence on his face as I gathered my strength to open the door. "I know. You can't go in."

"Gah! I feel like such a tosser, but . . ."

"I understand. Go grab some coffee. I'll call you when I know something. It may be a few hours, though."

"Ya want me to call someone to sit with ya?"

My eyes met his. He looked liked a wounded puppy. "I'll be okay. You got me this far."

A man in teal scrubs knocked on the door. "Are you okay, miss?"

I opened the door and pulled myself shakily to my feet. "I'll need help getting inside."

A woman in matching scrubs showed up with a wheelchair, and they whisked me inside. Four hours, one MRI, two Tylenol tablets with codeine, and a fourteen-hundred-dollar copay later, a young doctor with a South Asian name and a Brooklyn accent determined I did not have a skull fracture but did have a mild concussion. They treated my facial abrasions, cleaned out the wound on my scalp, and wrapped the top of my head with gauze.

The doctor pulled up my medical information on the hospital laptop near the bed. "It says here you take estradiol. What's that for?"

I hated answering that question. But I was too young to be menopausal and didn't feel right about lying and saying I'd had a hysterectomy. "I'm transgender," I said with all the confidence I could muster.

"I see. I suggest you stop taking the estrogen for a week or so."

"A week? Why?"

"Estradiol is a blood thinner. Because of your concussion, it puts you at risk for a brain bleed."

"Okay, you're the doc."

"We're also going to admit you for a twenty-four-hour observation. Just to be on the safe side."

"I don't think so. This job's already cost me enough. I can't afford an overnight stay. Thanks, but no thanks."

The doc looked concerned. "I hate to see money be the deciding factor on you getting proper medical care."

"You and me both. But you want to get paid, and I like to eat."

He waited with his arms crossed, perhaps expecting me to change my mind. When I didn't, he said, "I understand. I'll print out your release and some aftercare instructions, and you'll be on your way."

"Thanks for patching me up."

"No problem."

Twenty minutes later, they handed me my release papers, including a prescription for Tylenol with codeine for the headache. I texted Conor, and by the time they wheeled me outside, he was waiting for me. The nausea lingered, but I didn't think I would hurl again anytime soon.

"As if you aren't hormonal enough as it is," Conor said after I told him about going off the estrogen for a week. He meant it as a joke, trying to get me to laugh. It didn't work. Why did guys always think that was funny?

"Watch your step, buddy," I told him. "Or I may just cut off your balls with a dull knife and feed them to you. How'd you like that, funny man?"

"Aw, love, don't get your knickers in a twist. I'm sorry. Just trying to cheer you up."

"Doing a piss-poor job of it."

"I'm an arsehole. Let's get you home."

"I still need to pick up my truck."

"You sure you're okay to drive? You had quite a knock. And the doctor said you shouldn't be operating heavy machinery."

"Then I promise not to run the dishwasher when I get home." When he grimaced at my poor attempt at a joke, I continued. "I'm fine. I'm not woozy at all. You can follow me back home if you'd like."

Of course, there was another reason I wanted to go back to the motel.

29

When Conor pulled up to the Gray Ghost, I said, "There's one more thing I have to do here."

"Aw, love, you're hurt, and I'm knackered. Whaddya say we pack it in for the night?"

"I need to check with the front desk."

"Why? Ya getting a room for the night?"

"No, I want to see who rented Holly's room."

"Can't it wait till morning?"

"I'm here. I'm getting answers. Won't take long. If you don't want to stay, go on home."

He groaned as I climbed into the Gray Ghost. The codeine was taking the edge off the pain, but I still hurt. I couldn't keep this up for much longer.

I drove around to the lobby. A bald Latino dressed in a suit and tie stood behind the counter. His name tag read Miguel, Head Manager. Just the man I wanted to see.

When Miguel looked up, his professional smile was replaced with a concerned expression. "Are you okay, ma'am?" It was no doubt a reaction to my battered face and the bandage around my head.

"I'm fine, but I need your help."

Conor sidled up beside me as I handed the manager my authorization to apprehend Holly. "I've been hired by the court to rearrest Holly Schwartz, a fugitive charged with murder. She and an accomplice were staying in room 278 when they did this to me." I pointed at my head.

"A murderer's staying here?" His concern turned to panic. "Is she here now?"

"I suspect they bugged out after they ambushed me. I need to know who rented the room and to review your security footage."

"I'm sorry, but those records are private. I'd need a court order."

"Listen, mate," Conor said, leaning over the counter and tapping the paperwork. "This *is* a bloody court order. But if you'd prefer we call the cops and have them arrest ya for obstructing the apprehension of a fugitive, we can play it that way."

Most of what Conor said was bullshit, but I wasn't going to argue. "We can call the media too," I added. "I'm sure your guests would love to know they're staying in a motel with a murderer."

"That won't be necessary. Let me check our records." Miguel typed on a terminal behind the counter. "Okay, room 278 was rented to a Mr. Jablomi. Heywood Jablomi. Oh, crap."

"Heywood Jablomi?" Conor burst into laughter. "Cheeky bastard's got a sense of humor, I'll give 'im that."

I started to laugh too, but it made my head hurt, codeine or no. "Shit."

"I don't know why no one noticed this until now," Miguel mumbled.

"How did they pay?" I asked.

"They paid cash for a week, which would have brought them through next Wednesday. But we do have a credit card on file."

"What name's on the card?" Conor asked. "Ben Dover? Connie Lingus?"

"No, it belongs to Kimberly Morton."

"My fugitive's aunt." I thought about it. "Maybe Auntie Kim's helping her con-artist niece to escape."

"Unless they pinched it from her wallet," Conor suggested.

"Okay, Miguel," I said. "Let's see the security footage."

Miguel looked at me then Conor and nodded. "I really shouldn't, but considering the circumstances. Melissa!" he called.

A young woman came from the adjoining office. "You bellowed?"

"Watch the counter for me. I need to escort these people to the security room."

"I'm still on my break."

He gave her a look, and she threw up her hands. "All right. You're the boss."

He led us down a hallway, then turned left into a room the size of a broom closet. Four monitors and a keyboard were set up on a desk. Miguel sat and began typing. Conor offered me the remaining chair.

"Okay, you're looking for room 278. That's on the west side." Miguel pulled up a video showing camera footage along the walkway near the northwest stairs I'd used. He scanned backward through the footage until we got to five o'clock. I spotted Holly's companion dragging a large suitcase out of the room and toward the elevator. He was too far away to get a good look at his face, but it was definitely him.

"Can we get a closer shot?" I hoped to get a printout of his photo to show around.

Miguel pulled up a different camera, this one by the elevator. He zoomed through the footage until we spotted our guy on the feed.

"There," I said. "That's him." He was wearing shades, but at least we got the shape of his face and his overall look. "Any way we can put this on a thumb drive?"

"I'm going to have to charge you. These flash drives aren't free, you know." Miguel pulled out a small black thumb drive from the desk drawer and slipped it into the USB port.

"Bill me." I dropped my business card on the desk. "Cost you a lot more if guests found out you're renting rooms to murderers with bogus names and stolen credit cards."

"So where's our girl, Holly?" Conor asked, pointing at the security video.

"Good question," I said.

Miguel scanned more footage, going back over the past couple of days. But despite all of the cameras, Holly didn't appear in a single frame. "You sure there was a girl with him? According to our records, he was staying alone in the room."

"Trust me, she was there."

"No offense, love," Conor said, "but ya got a rather nasty knock on your noggin. Maybe your memory's a bit dodgy."

"I know what I saw, Conor. Hell, I called her phone and spoke with her. That's how I found out which room number it was."

"So where is she?" he asked.

I stared at the monitor, remembering the petite girl with the hard eyes and bristly hair. "She's in the suitcase."

"Wha?" Conor asked. "No way! How'd she fit in that trunk?"

"It'd be a tight fit," I admitted, "but I bet she could do it. It's the only explanation."

"Why not use a disguise? Gives me claustrophobia just thinking about it."

"I don't know." I rubbed my face. The codeine was making it hard to concentrate. "What about the parking lot?"

"The parking lot?" Miguel asked.

"I want to see what they're driving."

Miguel pulled up the list of camera footage files and selected one of them that gave a view of the back parking lot. He scrolled until we saw our mystery man dragging the suitcase and approaching a minivan. The camera gave us only a shot of the driver's side.

The man disappeared around the passenger side, then reappeared moments later empty handed, climbed into the driver's seat, and drove off.

"Stop!" I said.

Miguel paused the feed.

"There!" I pointed at the screen with a hazy glimpse of the inside of the minivan. A shadow was visible in the front passenger seat. "That's got to be her. She must have gotten out of the suitcase. Can we get a license plate on that vehicle?"

"Not from this angle." Miguel pulled up another camera feed and queued it up to the minivan pulling out of the parking lot.

Once the footage was enhanced, I managed to get the plate number and put it in my phone. "Gotcha, you son of a bitch."

"Come on, love." Conor put a hand on my shoulder. "Let's pack it in. You need to rest and recuperate."

I hated to admit defeat, but he was right. I was hanging on with little more than adrenaline and spite. "Okay, Miguel, put the footage on the drive, and we'll be out of your hair."

30

I was feeling no pain, thanks to the codeine, when I climbed back into the Gray Ghost. Conor followed me back to his place. I would've preferred my own bed, but Conor insisted on keeping an eye on me in case my condition worsened.

In his bedroom, I pulled off my clothes. I thought about taking a shower but was too tired. I didn't want to risk passing out and giving myself another concussion. So I stashed my gear next to his nightstand and crawled into bed. "Good night, babe," I said.

"Hey, I know you're tired, but aren't ya supposed to stay awake? You having a concussion and all?"

"Doctor said as long as I don't start puking again or go into a coma, I'll be fine."

He eyed me suspiciously. "You're not having me on, are ya?"

"Jake fell off a roof a couple years ago. The doctors told him the same thing. It's cool. Now let me go to sleep."

He didn't argue, and I drifted off.

Around two in the morning, I felt myself being shaken awake. "Jinxie, love, wake up."

"Huh? What's wrong?" My head was throbbing again.

"Wanted to make sure ya weren't in a coma."

"A coma? For fuck's sake. Let me sleep, or I'll put *you* in a coma."

"Couldn't see ya breathing. I got worried." His eyes glinted in the dim light. "How's your head?"

"Hurts."

"Ya don't feel sick?"

"Sick of these damned questions." I put a hand to my temple. "I'm not going to puke, if that's what you're worried about."

"Okay. G'night, love."

I huffed and turned my back to him. "Thanks for checking on me," I mumbled before falling back into a troubled sleep.

I woke to the sound of water running. Light filtered through the vertical blinds, and it took me a moment to realize where I was. Conor's side of the bed was empty. I sighed and took inventory of my injuries.

My head felt as if someone had been using it for a soccer ball. I thought about getting the codeine prescription filled. Damned good stuff once it kicked in. But I needed a clear head to track down Holly.

Conor emerged from the bathroom, his lower half wrapped in a towel. The sight of his ripped chest took my breath away. "Goddamn, I want you inside me."

He laughed and sat next to me on the bed. His hair was a wild mess of wet ginger curls. Beads of water on his chest glistened in the morning sunlight. "Much as I'd love a ride, I think we should take it easy till ya heal up a bit." He kissed me deep, and I felt it all the way to my groin.

I held his head in my hands, his green eyes shining like emeralds flecked with gold. "I'm fine. Really."

He stood up and pulled on a shirt. "Aren't ya supposed to be at your folks' place for brunch?"

"What time is it?"

"Ten o'clock."

"Ten? Oh shit! Why didn't you wake me sooner?" I bolted

upright and fell into a wild ride of room spins, unsettling my stomach. I nearly fell over.

"Easy there, love. This is a strict no-floor-diving zone." He held me until the vertigo passed.

"I'm all right. Shit. I gotta get to my parents' place."

"I thought you were hell-bent on finding Holly Schwartz?"

"Oh, trust me, I am. But I could use a decent meal to get my head working right. Besides, if I miss Sunday brunch, losing out on this bounty will be the least of my worries. My mother will guilt me to death."

As if on cue, my phone rang. I answered it.

"Sweetie, where are you?"

"Sorry, Mom, I overslept. Late night."

"Food's getting cold," she said. "I was worried you weren't coming."

"I'll be there shortly."

I hung up and grabbed a quick shower, careful to avoid wetting the bandage around my head. From my drawer in Conor's dresser, I pulled out a white peasant blouse and jeans to wear with a pair of dressy sandals. I tossed a T-shirt, boots, and my gear in a bag for later.

"After brunch," I said as I attempted to cover the abrasions on my face with makeup, "I'll see if Becca can get a current location for that phone again or the burners she'd called with it."

"Ya think they're still using it? If it were me, I'd've ditched it soon as I learned it was compromised."

"It's possible. But Holly's just a girl, not a brilliant criminal tactician."

"Aside from them staying somewhere while using her mother's SIM card and her aunt's stolen Visa. And this guy she's with smuggled her out of the hotel in a suitcase."

"Allegedly stolen Visa. I'm still not convinced Morton's not in on it." I sighed and tried to recall anything useful Holly and the guy had said. "What was it she called him?" I couldn't remember.

I gingerly placed my Sub Barn ball cap over my bandaged head. "Okay, let's go have some brunch."

31

The neighborhood in Mesa, where I grew up, was a mishmash of Mexican, Native American, and Anglo cultures. Brightly colored murals, old redbrick buildings, *panaderias* next to New York–style delis next to stores selling Navajo and Hopi artwork. The Usery Mountains rose up in the east, where my father would take my brother and me on hikes.

The place had a smell all its own, a mixture of chiles and sweat and hope. Mexican pop music and American classic rock echoed from passing pickup trucks in equal measure. Most everyone spoke at least some Spanish. Even my dad, a Cajun from Lake Charles, Louisiana.

Things had deteriorated since I was a kid. Street gangs had moved in, bringing with them graffiti, drugs, and violence. The sheriff's department frequently rounded up innocent residents in its relentless hunt for the undocumented. Even my mother had been picked up twice for the crime of having tan skin and black hair, despite being a second-generation Italian-American.

Nevertheless, my folks' neighborhood held a sacred place in my heart. It felt safe in a way that defied explanation. As I drove the Gray Ghost down East Broadway Road, the sights, sounds, and aromas of my childhood flooded my mind. I was home.

My parents' house was easy to spot. It was the only pink one on the block. My mother always insisted it was Mediterranean rose, not pink. But everyone in the neighborhood called it the pink house on the street.

When I stepped into the kitchen, rich aromas caused my saliva glands to kick into overdrive. The table was filled with bagels with lox and cream cheese, French toast, stacks of bacon, Cajun-style eggs Benedict, and a bowlful of shrimp and grits.

Around this mouthwatering feast sat my family. My petite mother, Gianna, was clearing empty plates while my lanky father, Edward, chatted animatedly with my brother, Jake, about football.

"Morning, everyone!" I called as we walked in. "Something smells good."

My father caught one look at my bruised face and gasped. "Jenna! What in heavens happened to you?"

My mother nearly dropped the dishes she was carrying. She rushed over and peeled off my cap to reveal the bandage around my head. "Oh, my baby girl! Who did this to you?"

Jake gave me a concerned look. "Damn, sis, you lose a fight with a bulldozer?"

"Relax, people. I'm fine."

"Is this from you chasing after criminals?" my mother asked.

I shook my head. "No, just slipped in the shower." I didn't need another lecture from my mother about my chosen profession. I took a seat next to my brother while Conor sat on my other side.

"You sure you're okay?" Jake asked with a concerned look on his face.

"I'm fine." I loaded my plate with French toast and bacon. "Just starving is all."

"I don't think you slipped in the shower," my mother said. "You've used that line too many times before."

"Just don't want you to worry, Mom. I'm okay."

She didn't look convinced. "By the way, I have some new dresses I want you to try on."

I rolled my eyes. "Maybe after breakfast."

"Hey, Jinx, think you could give me a hand this afternoon? I'm replacing an RO system on a house in Glendale, but I need someone with small hands to reach the unit."

My brother had a thriving business restoring and flipping houses. I helped out on the renovations when my schedule allowed it.

"Sorry, I got plans." I made a sympathetic face. "What about Bosco? He's a little guy."

"Unfortunately, he threw his back out last week. And Torres and his husband are at Disneyland for their honeymoon. Everyone else on my crew has big hands."

"Wish I could help, but I'm on a tight deadline."

"Lemme guess. Chasing criminals."

"A girl's got to make a living."

"You know, Jake," my mother said, "Virginia Gottlieb has long, slender fingers. Bet she could help you with your problem."

"Mom, please." Jake cast a wary glance at her. "Is this another one of your setups?"

"What setup?" She shrugged, trying to look innocent. "She's a concert pianist. Very talented. Good strong fingers. I think she could help, all I'm saying."

I laughed so hard I almost choked on my food. Our mother was always trying to set him up with girls. Problem was, Jake was gay, though he was afraid to tell our folks. Despite my urging him to come out to them, he refused, afraid of dashing their hopes for grandkids. It was a bullshit reason, and I'd told him so on numerous occasions.

"Thanks, Mom," he said. "But I'm sure she's got better things to do."

"Plus she'd probably want to get paid," I added as a playful jab.

"Hey, that's not fair. I'd pay her!" Jake insisted.

"Oh good." My mother's face split into a grin. "I'll call her mother."

"Wait a minute, I've been snookered." Jake turned to Conor. "Help me out here, man."

Conor held up his hands in surrender. "Oh no, you're not pulling me into this."

"She's a nice girl, son," my father chimed in. "Smart, beautiful, and a laugh sweet as bread pudding. You could do worse."

Jake rolled his eyes. "Whatever. Fine. Call her."

My mother finished clearing dishes with a satisfied grin on her face. "Good. 'Cause I need some grandbabies running around this house."

My father, Conor, and I guffawed, while Jake hung his head over his plate.

When I was bursting at the seams from way too much food, I got up to help clear the last of the dishes.

"Jenna," my father said. He and Mom preferred my chosen first name over the moniker Juanita had given me. "Let the others clear the table. I've got something to show you."

I gave Conor a curious look, and he said, "Go with your da. We got it handled here."

I shrugged and followed my father down the hall to my old bedroom, now used for visiting family members. Only a few framed photos on the wall and an abstract floral mural remained from my childhood.

"What's up, Dad?"

He sat on the bed and patted the quilt beside him. "Just wanted to talk is all."

Uh-oh, one of those father-daughter talks. "What about?"

He put a hand on my shoulder and met my gaze. "I know you love what you do, Jenna."

"Dad, please don't start on this again."

"Just hear me out. I've always encouraged you to follow your heart. I supported you when you came out as trans. Cheered when you graduated from the police academy. And I still want you to enjoy your current line of work."

"But . . ."

He took a deep breath and let it out slowly. "But it's killing your mother. Every time there's a violent story on the news, she frets. She wakes up with panic attacks. A few nights ago, there was a report about several people shot in a raid on a human trafficking operation."

"What's that have to do with me?" I asked, trying to act innocent. "I'm not a cop."

"The reporter mentioned a couple of bounty hunters were involved."

"Oh." Busted.

"You still going to tell me this fist-shaped bruise on your face was from a slip in the shower?" He touched my cheek, and I winced.

"I don't know what to tell you, Dad. What I do is important."

"This is because of what happened with Barclay Dietz, isn't it?"

"No!" I insisted without conviction.

He gave me a don't-bullshit-me look.

"Okay, maybe a little. But it's more than that. I love what I do. It's hard and even scary sometimes, but it makes me happy. I was miserable as a cop."

"But there's so many things you could do with your education and experience. You could still go to law school. Your mother and I would pay for it."

"I have zero interest in being a lawyer. *So* not a part of the suit-and-tie crowd."

He chuckled. "Yeah, you've got that Lafitte blood in you. You're a rebellious soul just like Grandma Marie."

Marie Lafitte, my paternal grandmother, was the great-great-great-granddaughter of Captain Jean Lafitte, a pirate who helped the American army defeat the Brits in the Battle of New Orleans. When I was a kid, Grandma Lafitte delighted me with tales of her own mischief and rebellion, which included being a rumrunner and gun smuggler during Prohibition.

"Dad, you always told me to follow my own star, not to let anyone else get in the way. I'm sorry Mom worries. But I'm a big girl. I can take care of myself."

"This is taking care of yourself?" he asked. "Bandaged head and bruised jaw?"

"When Jake fell off a roof, I didn't hear anyone demand he stop renovating houses and become an architect."

"What can I say? You're my baby girl." My father shrugged. "Maybe it's sexist to hold you to a different standard or worry about you more than Jake. But it's only because we love you."

"Yes, it *is* sexist." I kissed him on the forehead. "But I love you too."

"Any trouble from that article in *Phoenix Living*?"

"Nothing I can't handle."

"Just be careful out there. People can be so mean and ugly. And I'm here, if you ever need to talk."

"I know, Dad."

After spending more time with my family, I stepped back into my old bedroom to change into my work clothes and call Becca. The phone rang five times before she answered.

"Hey, Jinx. Wondered when you'd call back." She sounded as though she was having a rough day.

"Sorry, things got a little complicated yesterday. Listen, I need an updated location on Bonnie's phone. Also was wondering if any of those burners popped back up on the radar."

She huffed. "Okay, give me half an hour, all right? Did you not find her at that motel?"

"I did. She and some guy. Unfortunately, they got the jump on me. Get this. She's not disabled. At least not as far as I could tell."

"Some disabilities aren't as obvious as others, Jinx."

"All I know is that the 'mentally disabled girl in a wheelchair' bit was all an act. Presumably as a way to make money."

"Are you serious? I hate people who do that. Makes those of us with real issues look bad."

"I hear you. I got a plate number I need you to look up and

some surveillance footage from the motel I need facial recognition run on. You at the Hub?"

"Working from home, actually. Not up for the Hub's craziness today." Members of the Hub could be found working there around the clock. On weekends, the music and noise were often cranked up from the usual business routine.

"You mind if I drop off this thumb drive? I need to identify this dude Holly's with."

She groaned. "Yeah, I guess. The place is a mess."

"Doesn't matter to me. All I care about is finding this bitch and taking her back to lockup."

"Damn, girl. What exactly happened at that motel?"

"I'll fill you in later."

I hung up and checked my email and found another email from Volkov.

My dearest Jinx,

It saddens me I have not heard back from you. I'm not used to being ignored. Perhaps you mistook my previous correspondence as the confessions of a lovesick schoolboy. But let me assure you that my feelings for you are quite genuine. And I have an urgent need for someone like you. I am determined to make this a solid partnership. Perhaps a demonstration of my feelings will convince you.

Most sincerely,

Milo

There was an anonymized hyperlink at the bottom. I knew I shouldn't click on it. Most likely it led to some malware or porn site. But I couldn't stop myself from hitting the link. My YouTube app opened and began playing an old rock song from the 1980s —"I'll Be Watching You" by The Police. What a creepy fucking fuck!

I took a deep breath and focused on my mantra—WWWWD.

What Would Wonder Woman Do? I wasn't going to let this sick bastard get to me. So he knew my email address. Big whoop. I was always careful to keep my home address and other personal information off the web. So he could pine away to his heart's content. I wasn't going to let him live rent free in my head any longer. And if he dared cross my path in person, I'd put him in the ground the same as I did his men at the warehouse.

I stepped back into the kitchen and found Conor and Jake arguing about soccer.

"You ready to go?" I asked.

Conor nodded.

"Leaving already, sis?" Jake gave me a hug.

I kissed his cheek. "Sorry, bro, got fugitives to catch."

"Keep her out of trouble, man," Jake said.

He and Conor gave each other a fist bump. I said goodbye to my folks and Jake.

When we stepped outside the front door, a full-sized black Hummer idled on the other side of the Gray Ghost. A hissing sound came from between the trucks, like air leaking out in short bursts. "What the hell?"

I ran behind the Gray Ghost and spotted a heavyset figure in a black hoodie between the vehicles. He ducked into the Hummer and shouted, "Go, man! Go!"

The Hummer's wheels squealed as it peeled out down the road. I chased after it for half a block, but it was gone. I put my hands on my knees, sucking air into my oxygen-starved lungs. Was this Volkov? Had he tracked me down somehow? My body shook with anger and fear in equal measure.

When a hand pressed on my back, I whirled around with fists flying and caught Conor on the side of the head. I stopped myself before driving my knee into his groin.

"Oy! At ease, soldier!" he joked, rubbing his temple.

"Sorry, I . . ." I took a deep breath, trying to slow the pounding in my chest.

"It's all right. Ya get a plate number?"

"I . . . yeah, it was LZ6 . . . um . . ." I struggled to picture it, but my mind went blank. "Crap, can't remember the last three."

He put an arm around me. "Don't worry, love. You all right?"

"Just winded." And pissed. And worried. "What were they doing?"

Conor looked at me, grim faced. "You're not gonna like it."

We walked back to my folks' place, and I saw it in bloodred paint. The words Trany Faggit were spray-painted across the side of the Gray Ghost. The two driver's-side tires were flat. "What the hell? Geez!"

"So disappointing," Conor said, shaking his head. "Ya'd think if they were going to vandalize someone's ride, the silly buggers would learn how to spell."

"So not funny." I glared at him.

Jake came running out of the house. "Everything all right? I heard shouting and tires squealing."

I pointed at the side of my Pathfinder. "I'm okay. Can't say the same for my truck."

"Damn! Who did this?"

"Probably someone who read that damn article," I said. *Someone like Milo fucking Volkov.* "Not sure how they tracked me to Mom and Dad's."

"You want me to call the cops?"

I thought about it. I needed to get to Becca's. It was already Sunday afternoon. I only had another two days to find Holly. At the same time, I was worried the vandals might come back and do something serious to our folks. "Yeah, I guess so. It's just that I got someplace to be."

"Leave it with me. I got a friend with a paint-and-body shop near Fifty-Ninth Avenue and Bethany Home Road," Jake said. "I'm sure he can fix this for you. He owes me a favor for some work I did for him last year when a monsoon damaged his roof."

"What do I drive in the meantime?"

Jake held out his keys. "Take mine."

"Yours? How will you haul lumber and equipment?"

"I can handle being without it for a few days. Worse comes to worst, I'll borrow Dad's truck."

I gave him a squeeze. "Thanks, man."

"'Course, you'll owe me."

A twisted smile spread across my face. "I knew there'd be a catch. Look, I'll pay you when I get paid on this next job."

"I don't need your money. You're gonna work it off." He smirked. "By the way, what ever happened to that Diamondbacks jersey I loaned you?"

"Um, didn't I give it back to you?" I asked. If I returned it with the collar sliced open, he'd never do me another favor.

"No, you definitely did not."

"Huh, I'll check around my place." A serious concern chased away my levity. "Jake, when the cops get here, see if they can keep close watch on Mom and Dad, will ya? I'm worried whoever tagged my truck might come back."

"I'll see what I can do. Don't worry."

"Thanks, bro." I hugged him. "And for God's sake, tell them you're gay. Before they set up poor Virginia Gottlieb, whoever she is, on a date that leads to nowhere land."

"I'll think about it."

"Don't think. Just do."

"Let me get my stuff out of my truck, and you two can head out." He hustled off toward his Dodge Ram pickup. I grabbed my gear from the Gray Ghost.

Moments later we swapped keys, and Conor and I drove to Becca's.

Becca answered the door a moment before I touched the doorbell. "Wow! Somebody really did a number on you." Her energy level sounded low.

"Yeah, you could say that. How'd you know we were here?"

Becca offered a weak grin and pointed at a small white device mounted above the door. "Camera sends a feed to my tablet when the motion sensors are tripped."

"I should get something like that for my folks."

"They having problems with prowlers?" She led Conor and me to her dining room table on which sat three computer screens surrounded by a debris field of computer parts, empty cardboard boxes, dirty dishes, and discarded snack wrappers.

I cleared off a chair and handed her the surveillance video thumb drive from the motel. "Just some asshole stalking me and spray-painting bigoted graffiti on my truck. I'm worried they may go after my folks."

"Boy, you pissed someone off."

"Tell me something I don't know. Say, listen, you think you can run these plate numbers for me?"

"Plate numbers, plural?"

"One for the van Holly's riding in. Another for the asshole who vandalized my truck."

"Sure." She opened an app on her computer and went through a series of mouse clicks and keystrokes. "Damn."

"What's wrong?"

"Motor Vehicle's server is down for maintenance right now. I'll try them later."

I gave her the license plate information I had for the two vehicles. "Any luck with the phones?"

"I tried pinging Bonnie's phone, but it's off the grid for now. But not before calling one of those burners, which popped back up." She pulled up a map on her computer, showing a red blinking dot at the Burton Barr Central Library , north of downtown Phoenix.

"Is it near the library or in the library?" I asked. The last thing I needed was to have to go scouting around five floors.

Becca zoomed in. "Hard to tell. Here, give me your phone."

"My phone?" I unlocked the screen and handed it to her.

She clicked away, then handed it back to me. "It's installing a locator app."

"Like the one you put on Conor's and my phones before?"

"The one I put on before will let you track each other's phones. This new app will locate any phone based on a number. It's accurate to within about five feet."

"Damn, I'm glad you're on my team."

"Don't get caught with that on your phone. Its legality is questionable."

"Good to know. Can we take a look at the surveillance footage?"

Becca inserted the thumb drive into her desktop and pulled up a listing of six video files Miguel had saved on it. "Which one should I start with?"

"The one called Elevator," I replied.

She opened the file, and the video began playing.

"Go to sixteen hundred hours."

She zoomed ahead, and there was our guy, staring up into the camera in his shades. "Hello, Moto!" Becca said with a tired grin. "He's kinda cute."

"Any chance you can run facial recognition on this bloke?" Conor asked.

"The sunglasses don't help, but we might get some partial matches that could narrow it down. It'll take some time." She did a screen capture and uploaded the image to an online app.

"How much time?" I asked.

"This app compares the image against the major federal databases and Interpol. Should have results by tonight or tomorrow."

I sighed. "Becks, I need it right away."

"What do you want me to do, Jinx? Pull the answers out of my ass? It'll take as long as it takes. I should be in bed. I really don't have the spoons for this."

"Sorry. Get me what you can when you can. I'm sorry I got upset."

"No worries. I'll call you when I have something else."

"Thanks, Becks! You're the best." I hugged her and turned to Conor. "All right, let's go track down that burner at the library. See what we can find out."

33

It was a short hop from Becca's house to the Burton Barr library, a five-story building of glass and steel. The parking lot was filled with vehicles, as it often was on weekends. I breathed a sigh of relief when I spotted someone pulling out of a space. The truck's dash said it was a hundred and five degrees outside. The less I had to walk in this heat, the better.

I checked the app Becca had installed on my phone. "The burner shows as being on the library's east side. Guess we'll have to go floor by floor until we find it. Let's gear up."

"Just leave the weapons behind," Conor said.

"Aw, you're no fun," I said with a smirk. I pulled the revolver from my ankle holster and locked it in the glove box along with my Ruger.

When we reached the courtyard in front of the library's entrance, I checked the locator app again. According to the map, the burner phone wasn't in the building but about ten feet from it in the courtyard.

"It's right here," I whispered to Conor, comparing the map to my surroundings.

A dozen or so people sat on the low retaining walls on either side of the front door—a mixture of homeless people, college students, and skaters. Behind them, lantana, cacti, and other desert-tolerant plants grew in a xeriscape garden.

"So where is it?" Conor asked, looking over my shoulder.

I zoomed in as much as possible, then glanced at the people sitting along the north wall. "It appears to be one of them." I nodded in that direction.

We approached cautiously. Several people looked up, including one guy in his twenties with a hipster haircut, wearing a torn black hoodie. How he wasn't melting from the heat in that hoodie, I'd never know.

As soon as my gaze met his, he charged us and knocked me on my butt, sending my phone clattering to the ground. I regained my feet and hauled ass after the hipster. I had no idea who this wiseass was, but clearly he was involved. I wasn't going to let him get away.

He ran east past the employee lot and cut south toward Margaret T. Hance Park. I chased him over a small decorative wall lined with shrubs, then over a field of sun-scorched grass, turned west, and followed a paved walk toward the Central Avenue overpass.

I was starting to lose steam when he tripped and tumbled onto the hard surface. I grabbed hold of his hoodie, pinned him on his stomach, and cuffed him. "Gotcha!" I said between gulps of air.

"Get off me, you bitch. I ain't done nothing." He struggled to escape.

"Where's Holly?"

"Jinx! Jinxie, stop!" Conor came up panting.

"I don't know anyone named Holly."

"Jinx, let the lad go. He's not our guy." He held up my phone. There was no red dot where we were. The red dot was still back by the library's entrance.

"Aw, crap." I uncuffed the guy. "How come you ran?"

"None of your damn business." He stood up, examining a bloody hole in the elbow of his hoodie. "Shit. See what you did?"

"Sorry." *God, I hate being wrong.*

The kid flipped me a double bird as he backed away. "Kiss my ass, you stupid bitch."

"Well, that could have gone better." I fanned my face on our walk to the library. "Geez Louise, could it get any damn hotter?" My head was throbbing again.

Conor handed me my phone when we reached the library courtyard. The people sitting on the walls had cleared out. I guessed our little stunt was too much drama for them. But the burner phone was still showing here. "This doesn't make any sense. Where's the goddamned burner? No one's here."

I looked on the other side of the north wall into the flower bed and caught a reflection of something shiny. I reached down and picked up a black-and-silver flip phone.

"Clever girl!" Conor clapped me on the back.

"Yeah, but who had it?" I tried to recall the faces of the people sitting on the wall, but it was a blur.

"No tellin'."

I opened the phone and pulled up the call history. I recognized Bonnie's phone number on some earlier calls, but there were different numbers on the more recent ones. I was tempted to punch the numbers in the locator app, but I had no idea who they might belong to. Wouldn't do us any good to go chasing after dead ends. "Maybe Becca can get something off the call history that can point us in the right direction."

We returned to my brother's pickup, and I cranked up the AC full blast. As I put the truck in gear, my phone rang. I put it back in Park and checked the caller ID, hoping it was Becca with more leads.

Instead, it was my friend Izzie Quiñones, owner of a women's bar called L Street on Camelback, just east of Twelfth Street. Izzie's wife, Chelsea, was a friend of mine from the Phoenix Gender Alliance.

"What's up, Izzie?"

"Remember those flyers you dropped off a week or so ago, looking for Mandy Tipton?"

Another one of Liberty's fugitives. She'd jumped bail on charges of theft and trafficking in stolen property. "You know where she is?"

"Sitting at my bar, throwing back tequila shots, and getting uglier by the minute. You want this chick, come get her. Otherwise I'm cutting her off and calling her a cab."

"I'll be there in fifteen."

"Good, 'cause she's chasing away all my regulars. Sunday afternoons are slow enough as is."

"Be right there. And thanks for calling." I hung up and tossed the phone to Conor. "Change in plans, babe. One of Liberty's fugitives is getting shit-faced at my friend Izzie's bar."

Conor chuckled. "That makes two so far. Big Bobby's going to have a shite fit. Ya sure he'll pay ya?"

"He better. Even if he doesn't, I doubt he'll pay Fiddler, and that's its own reward. Because screw Fiddler."

"Aye! Screw Fiddler!"

34

I pulled up to L Street's front door. "Wait here," I told Conor. "I'll be right back."

"Ya don't want me to come in with ya?"

"Izzie's not too fond of men in her bar." I shrugged. "Besides, I think I can handle a drunk. You can cuff her once we get outside, if you like."

"Yeah, yeah."

I walked inside past a rack of queer-friendly magazines by the door. The Pink Trinket's "Singing Mammogram" played on the sound system, and the hoppy scent of beer filled the air.

Izzie stood behind the bar with a blond mullet haircut showing darker roots, particularly on the shaved sides. Her black cutoff T-shirt read I Kiss Girls in lavender letters. I figured she was in her mid-to-late forties.

"'Sup?" she asked.

"Someone called for an Uber ride?"

Izzie grinned. We'd played this game before. She pointed at the hunched-over brunette a couple of seats over. "Hey, Mandy, your ride's here."

Mandy raised her head. She had a drawn face and track

marks on the inside of both elbows. She opened her eyes to a squint. "I didn't call for no ride."

"Sorry, chica," Izzie said. "Gotta cut you off, and you're too drunk to drive. I want you to get home safe."

"Cut me off? Shit! I ain't drunk. Goddamn, bulldagger." She started to slide off her barstool.

I caught her. "Easy there, princess. Let me get you home. I won't even charge you for the ride."

Her face was inches from mine. She looked up at me and smiled. "You won't? You're kinda cute, you know it?"

I forced a smile despite the wave of tequila breath and the cigarette smoke assaulting my nostrils. "Thanks. Come on. I'll help you into my truck." I gave a quick glance to Izzie and mouthed "Thank you."

I pushed open the door, and the furious summer heat rushed us like a flash fire.

"Damn!" Mandy flinched and almost slipped out of my grip. "So hot."

"Don't worry. I left the AC running."

She turned to me, giving me a drunken seductive look. "No, I mean you, sweetie. You're hot. I wanna take you to bed." She put an arm on my shoulder and leaned in, or fell, to kiss me.

"Sorry, sweet cheeks, I'm taken." I spun her around and opened the back door of Jake's pickup truck. Conor slipped behind her and snapped the cuffs on.

"What the hell?"

"Mandy Tipton, you failed to appear at your court date. Your bail bond agent hired me to return you to custody." I tried to help her into the truck, but she started to buck and kick away at the step.

"I ain't going back to jail. You said you were taking me home." She snapped her head back and caught me on the nose. I once again saw stars as a shock wave of pain traveled through my skull.

"Fuck!" I grabbed a fistful of her hair and slammed her face against the side of the truck.

"Ow! You're burning me."

I pulled her away from the hot metal, slightly, but kept my grip on her. "Settle down, or I'll put you face-first on the pavement. You understand me?"

She stopped struggling and hung her head and sobbed. "Please don't send me back to jail. I didn't do nothing. I just needed money."

"Not for me to decide. You missed your court date, you go back to jail. That's the rules. But if you're nice on the way back, maybe you can get your bail reset. Okay?"

She nodded without saying anything. Just sniffling and ugly crying.

Conor and I helped her into the truck and got her seat belted in without any problems. I handed Conor my keys. "You drive."

I hopped into the passenger seat and used a packet of tissues to stop my nose from bleeding. I didn't think it was broken, but it wasn't helping my headache.

"It was all a misunderstanding," Mandy mumbled from the backseat. "My girlfriend just overreacted. Next thing I know, cops show up at my door."

"You steal her stuff?" I asked.

"Technically it was her grandma's. But I told her I'd pay her back."

"Uh-huh." *That's what they all say,* I thought as I dabbed at my nose with the bloody tissue.

"My public defender ain't done shit for me. Fucking loser!"

I ignored her and punched Sara Jean's number on my phone's contacts list.

"Gosh darn it, Jinx. Now what do you want? It's Sunday afternoon for crying out loud. I'm at a church picnic."

I wanted to taunt her, but my head hurt too much to be cute. "Just wanted to get a verbal acknowledgment that you'll pay me for Mandy Tipton."

"Mandy Tipton? I told you Renzelli was the last one. I'm not paying you for Tipton. That case belongs to Fiddler."

"And yet I have her and Fiddler doesn't. Found her in one of the valley's many gay bars. Guess it pays sometimes to be a part of the queer community after all. If I let her go, Fiddler will never find her. I guarantee that. Liberty will be on the hook for the entire amount of her bail. What was it? Twenty grand?"

"You think you're so smart, don'tcha?"

"Five seconds, girlfriend. Four. Three. Two."

"Oh, all right! I'll pay you for Tipton too."

"Pleasure doing business with you." I hung up.

"You can still let me go." Mandy looked like a puppy begging for table scraps.

"Yeah, right. I'd rather get paid."

When we turned south on Central, Tipton groaned. "I don't feel so good."

I turned around in my seat and looked at her. "Aw, crap. Conor, pull over. She's going to puke."

"Hold on. I'm in the left lane. Gotta let this bloke on my arse get past me."

"Hurry, she's—"

The woman leaned forward and unleashed what looked like gallons of vomit all over the back of Conor's seat and the floor.

"Aw, shit." The smell hit my nose and made me gag.

By the time Conor pulled into the parking lot of the Park Central shopping center, Tipton was down to dry heaving and spitting into the mess on the floor of my brother's truck. He was going to kill me.

"I . . . I feel better now," Tipton said.

35

A fter turning Tipton over to the fine folks at the Madison Street Jail's intake, we stopped at a do-it-yourself car wash on McDowell and rinsed out the backseat of the truck as best we could. Still, the stink of vomit lingered. I figured I could get the truck detailed in the next day or so before I returned it to Jake.

It was dark when I dropped off Conor at his place.

"Ya coming in?" he asked as he handed me the truck keys by the driver's door.

"I feel like sleeping in my own bed tonight."

"Ya don't look well, love. Ya okay to drive?"

"Just got a headache, and my nose hurts. I'll survive." I hugged him and gave him a peck on the lips.

"I could follow ya back to your place."

"Up to you. I won't be much company."

When we walked in my front door, I made a beeline to my kitchen for a couple of acetaminophen. I chased them down with a cold beer Conor handed me as I flopped down in a chair and rested my head on the table.

"You all right, love? Ya look like shite warmed over."

I pressed the bottle against my temple. "Should've stopped to fill that pain meds prescription."

"Ya want me to go fill it for ya?"

"No, thanks."

"Ya want something to eat?"

"No!" The thought of food turned my stomach.

"Ya feelin' nauseous? Should I take ya back to hospital?"

"The word's nauseated. Even if I were, I'm not spending another night in the ER."

"Nauseous, nauseated. Same difference to me."

"Just leave me alone."

"Feelin' hormonal, huh?"

I raised my head and gave him a death stare. "First of all, fuck you. Second, I only missed one dose, so no, I'm not hormonal. I've got a busted nose and a headache, a fugitive that I can't find, and your endless questions are annoying the hell out of me. So for the love of all things holy, shut the fuck up."

"Sorry, love. I'm a tosser for saying you're hormonal," he said in an appeasing tone. "Whaddya say we go back into your bedroom for a ride, eh? Get your mind off work stuff."

"What fucking part of 'I've got a fucking headache' did you fucking not under-fucking-stand?"

"Fine. Then what do you want?"

"I want you to shut the fuck up."

He folded his arms and glared at me. "Look, love, I'm sorry ya've got a headache. And I'm sorry you're in a pissy mood. And I'm sorry ya haven't caught your fugitive. But I'll not be treated like a bloody bastard when I'm tryin' to help ya feel better. I'm outta here."

He stormed out and slammed the front door so hard the windows rattled. I buried my head in my arms. "Fuck."

An hour later, the acetaminophen had taken the edge off my headache. I called up Becca, hoping for some help and more than a little BFF sympathy.

"Hello?" She sounded worse than I felt.

"I need you to research some phone numbers for me."

"It'll have to wait until morning, Jinx. I'm not able to handle anything tonight."

"Crap." I was tempted to press her, but even in my mood, I knew it would be wrong. "All right. Hope you feel better tomorrow." I hung up.

I made myself a bowl of cereal just to have something in my stomach. I felt like shit. I no doubt looked like shit. Shit. Shit. Shit.

I pulled out the burner phone we found and grabbed a yellow legal pad and a pen. I created a written log of the recent calls, then started dialing the numbers I didn't recognize. Three were no longer in service. One rang at the motel where I'd found Holly and her boy toy. And two more had a male voice saying, "I'm not here. Leave a message." No names. I wasn't sure if it was the same voice on both numbers.

I dialed the first number again and forced myself to sound chipper but professional, which in my condition took considerable effort.

"Hi, my name's Liz Windsor with the Arizona Foundation for People with Disabilities. I'm not sure if I have the right number, but I'm looking for either Holly or Bonnie Schwartz. I have a check made out to them for nine thousand dollars. Please call me back so I can send you your money." I left my phone number and hung up, then did the same on the other mystery number.

I poured myself a hot bubble bath and played one of Selena's albums on my old iPod. When I was a teenager longing to be a girl, listening to her music always made me feel better. I popped in my earbuds as I eased into the water. My phone was on the floor within arm's reach, in case Holly called looking for her imaginary check.

I had only a couple of days left to locate Holly Schwartz and very few leads. If I didn't find her in time, chances were Sadie Levinson wouldn't hire me to locate any more of her skips. And then what would I do? No one else wanted to hire me. What would I do for income? Working a nine-to-five was not an option. Not for a pirate girl like me. Too much Lafitte blood coursing through my veins.

Selena's song "Dreaming of You" got me thinking about how I treated Conor. I was a bitch. Totally. Sure, I was off my hormones, and my body felt like shit. My head still hadn't completely stopped hurting. But those were just excuses. If he'd treated me that way, I would've walked away too. I felt awful.

I turned off the music and called him. It went straight to voicemail.

"Uh, hi, Conor. Sorry I was such a bitch tonight. I, uh, call me when you get this. Thanks."

Did I apologize enough? Should I call him back and apologize some more? Have I already screwed up everything beyond repair? Is he avoiding my calls? Is he talking to someone else? Is he cheating on me?

Pressure built up behind my eyes. Tears streaked down my face until I was full-on ugly crying in the tub. *Just soap in my eyes,* I told myself. That and I felt utterly alone, worthless, and miserable.

36

─────────

s I was drying off, my phone pinged. I prayed it was Conor sending me a text saying he was sorry too and he would be over to make everything okay. Underneath all the badass was a princess who sometimes just wanted to be taken care of.

I picked up the phone. It was a text but from an unfamiliar number.

I'm hoping the gift I left on your doorstep will convey my true feelings for you.

Was this Volkov again? And what the hell was left on my doorstep?

I pulled on some shorts and a shirt, flung open my front door, and gasped. A six-foot-long bundle of clear plastic stretched on the floor of my front porch. I didn't have to unwrap it to know it was a body. I could see smears of blood on the inside of the plastic. What I didn't know was whose body it was or who had left it.

Panic blazed in my mind as I rushed to unwrap the body. *Please don't be Conor!* My hands grew slick with blood from pulling at the slippery plastic in my furtive attempts to reveal the body in front of me. *Please, please, no!*

When the last layer of plastic was peeled away, I didn't immediately recognize the body. The face was a battered, pulpy mess. I dug into the victim's pockets and pulled out a wallet. The driver's license read Thom Hensley.

I barked out a laugh of relief as I realized it wasn't Conor. One laugh turned into a series of guffaws that abruptly devolved into uncontrollable sobs. My mind struggled to make sense of the situation. I hated Thom Hensley for what he did to me, but I never wished him dead.

Under the golden glow of my porch light, I sat on the wooden bench, staring at the carnage. An envelope underneath the layers of plastic caught my eye. I snatched it up and tore it open, smearing it with blood. A computer-printed note read:

My dearest Jinx,

I'm told this man outed you without your permission. Truly a tawdry, cruel, and invasive thing to do to such a lovely and gifted woman as yourself. A man like that does not deserve to live. Please take this gift as a token of my affection.

Warmest regards,

Milo

I felt numb. Why was this sick fucker so obsessed with me? Was this revenge for raiding his warehouse? Or did he really have a twisted crush on me? I'd hoped if I ignored him, he'd give up and leave me alone. Clearly, that wasn't working. And now he knew where I lived.

I was in way over my head. It was time to bring in reinforcements. I called Conor, my hand shaking as I held the phone. The call again went to voicemail. "C-Conor, please call me. It's . . . it's an emergency."

Why wasn't he answering? Was he punishing me? Or had something happened to him too? I tried not to think about it. I punched his number into the locator app on my phone. It showed his phone was at his house. I was tempted to drive over, but I couldn't leave Hensley's body on my porch. Sooner or later the cops would show up. It would look worse for me if it was someone else who called them.

I made one more call before bringing in my former brothers in blue.

"Somebody better be dead or on fire," Kirsten Pasternak's groggy voice said.

"S-Someone's dead."

"Jinx? What happened?"

I took a deep breath to get a hold on my emotions. "Someone killed Thom Hensley. Dumped his body at my place."

"Thom Hensley, the reporter?"

"Yeah."

"Where are you?"

"At home. On my front porch with the body."

"Are the cops there?"

"No."

"Call 911, but do not answer any questions until I get there. You hear me? Just tell them you found a body on your porch. Nothing else."

"Copy that."

Within minutes of my call to 911, patrol cars had cordoned off the street. Curious neighbors stood outside their homes and peeked from windows, drawn like moths to the flashing lights. When the first officer on the scene, an Officer McAfee, started his battery of questions, I told him I'd found the body and would answer the rest of his questions when my attorney arrived.

By the time Kirsten walked up my driveway, yellow crime scene tape stretched across the wrought-iron supports holding up the roof of my porch. Crime scene techs scoured the scene for evidence, including Volkov's note.

I breathed a sigh of relief. "Thank God you're here."

"What happened to your face?" she asked.

"Drunk fugitive head butted me. Nothing to do with this mess."

She eyed me suspiciously. "If you say so. Let's step inside, and you tell me what happened."

I led her to my kitchen table, afraid I'd get blood from my clothes on anything else. I gave her a complete rundown of events, showing her the emails and text I'd received from Volkov. "Will I have to surrender my phone as evidence?" I asked. "I rely on this for work." Also, I still had that locator app that I didn't want them to find.

"We'll see what we can work out."

I heard a knock on my front door, followed by a familiar voice. "Hello? Anyone home?"

"In here." I gave Kirsten a look.

Detective Hardin shuffled into my kitchen. "Gotta say, Ballou, you're the last person I expected to be talking to this evening."

"Feeling's mutual."

"Then again, bounty hunters do like to push legal boundaries." He nodded at Kirsten and pulled out a pen and a notepad. "Good evening, Counselor."

"Evening, Detective."

"I didn't do this, Hardin, if that's what you're thinking."

"If you say so. Why don't we start with a statement."

I provided a brief explanation of my infiltration of the warehouse, leaving out the part about Conor and me killing Volkov's men. I brought up the disruption of the FBI sting and the release of the kidnapped women being held at the warehouse, giving retaliation as a possible motive for Volkov. Finally, I mentioned the note left with the body.

"If Volkov's mad at you for disrupting his human trafficking operation, why would he murder Hensley?"

"How should I know? I've never met Volkov. But judging from the note he left, he seems to have some weird fascination with me."

Hardin nodded, taking notes. "When's the last time you saw Hensley?"

I took a breath and shared a glance with Kirsten. She nodded. "The day that article came out. He and I had a heated discussion about it after he outed me without my permission. But it was just an argument. I let it go."

"So you were angry at him."

"Yeah, but not enough to kill him. He's an asshole. But so what? The world's full of assholes."

"You never threatened him?"

I tried to remember what I'd said to him in his office. "I threatened to sue him. That's it."

"Tell me, Jinx, why's your face all black and blue? You and the victim get in a fight?"

"No, a drunken fugitive head butted me this afternoon."

"Really? Where were you earlier this evening?"

"Conor and I dropped a fugitive off at the Madison Street Jail around seven. Got back here around eight o'clock. Been home alone ever since."

"Last time I checked, it didn't take an hour to get from the jail to here. Maybe fifteen minutes in heavy traffic."

"We had to rinse out the backseat of my truck after a fugitive got sick." I ignored Hardin's chuckles and continued. "Then I dropped off Conor at his place and came home."

"And the body wasn't here when you got home?"

"Sure, it was here," I said sardonically. "I thought I'd wait until the middle of the night to call you guys. What, do you think I'm crazy?"

"You didn't ask Volkov to kill him?"

"I have never talked to Volkov. Nor do I ever want to." I just wanted to put a few bullets into the sleazeball's skull.

"We're going to need your clothes for evidence. And we'll need to swab your hands for GSR."

"Fine, whatever."

37

Hardin promised to have Patrol keep an eye on the house in case Volkov or one of his goons showed up. He made me swear to let his team handle it. I was too tired to argue. It was nearly dawn by the time the last of the officers left.

When I was finally alone, I showered and collapsed in my bed, only to wake what felt like minutes later to the sound of my phone ringing. "Conor?"

"Sorry, girl, no. It's Becca."

It took a second for my brain to focus. Right. Becca. Plate numbers. "Hey, Becks, what's up? What time is it?"

"Eight twenty-one. Too early?"

"Late night. Someone murdered Thom Hensley and dumped his body on my doorstep."

"Seriously? Holy crap! Are you okay?"

"I'm fine. Just exhausted."

"Any idea who did it?"

"Milo Volkov."

I heard her gasp. "Are you serious? Girl, you should get someplace safe till they catch him."

"I'm not worried, just pissed off." I swung out of bed and shuffled into the kitchen. I'd forgotten to put coffee grounds in the coffeemaker, so there was a lovely carafe of hot water waiting for me. Shit. I popped in a fresh filter and some grounds, dumped the water into the reservoir, and pressed the brew button.

While it ran, I grabbed my file on the Holly Schwartz case. "What've you got for me on those license plates?"

"The one from the hotel is a rental from Cheap Ride Rentals."

It was a national chain. "Do you know which office?" I asked.

"Northwest corner of Tatum and Shea."

I wrote down the address, which wasn't far from Kim Morton's house. "That's a start. What about the Hummer that tagged the Gray Ghost?"

"You only gave me a partial plate, so I was able to narrow it down to three vehicles. One belongs to a Dmitri Gorkov."

"Never heard of him." I wondered if he was an associate of Volkov's.

"The other two possible matches are Yvonne McKinley and Robert Dixon."

"Wait, did you say Robert Dixon?"

"Yeah, full name is Robert Lee Dixon. You know him?"

I sighed. "Fiddler. It was motherfuckin' Fiddler. I swear, next time I see him, I'll kick his ass."

"You know him?"

"Old bounty hunter for Liberty Bail Bonds who was on my team until a few days ago. The one Big Bobby gave my outstanding cases to." I managed a smile. "He also was looking for Holly Schwartz, until Sadie Levinson turned the case over to me. Thanks for the 411."

"Glad I could help."

"Do me a favor, though. Don't tell Conor it was Fiddler, if you happen to talk to him."

"Why not?"

"I want to handle it myself."

"You got it. Anything else?"

I thought about it. I hadn't heard back from my charity check scam on those two phone numbers. "Yeah, I located that burner that had been calling Bonnie Schwartz's number. Got some other phone numbers I want you to reach." I gave them to her.

"I'll run them and let you know what I find out."

I poured myself a cup of coffee. Despite my lack of sleep, I actually felt better than I had the day before. My nose was still tender, but my headache was gone. After some eggs and coffee, I was actually feeling almost human. I still felt a bit emotional, especially when I thought about Conor. *Why the hell hasn't he called me back?*

After throwing on some clothes, I decided it was time to get paid. I hopped into Jake's truck, which still stank faintly of vomit, and zipped downtown to Liberty Bail Bonds with body receipts in hand.

Big Bobby was talking with Sara Jean when I walked in through their glass doors. They did not look happy to see me, which made the situation all the sweeter. Assuming I actually got paid, that was.

"Good morning, assholes! How the hell are you?" I said with a smug grin.

Big Bobby stood up tall and crossed his arms. Damn, he was a big man. "What the hell you doing here? We fired you last week."

"Maybe so, but you still owe me for these two." I waved the body receipts.

Sara Jean looked as if she'd just eaten a cockroach. Big Bobby got a confused look on his face.

"We ain't paying you for those!" Big Bobby insisted. "We gave your cases to Fiddler." He reached for the body receipts, but I pulled them out of his grasp.

"Au contraire, monsieur. Sara Jean and I already discussed it. I even recorded our conversation."

"What?" He turned to Sara Jean. "What the hell's she yammering about?"

Sara Jean harrumphed. "What was I supposed to do, Bobby? We were running out of time on those two. She grabbed Renzelli on Saturday. Said she'd release him if we didn't agree to pay her."

"What about the other one?"

"Mandy Tipton?" I asked with a smirk. "Grabbed her yesterday."

"She was at one of them lezzie bars," Sara Jean said with a sneer. "Fiddler never woulda found her."

"Aw, why all the sour faces? This is good news. I found your skips, turned them in, and saved you good people a ton of money and hassle."

Big Bobby still didn't seem grateful. Oh well, not my problem.

"Enough chitchat." I set the body receipts on Sara Jean's desk. "Time to pay for services rendered."

"I don't care what Sara Jean told you." Big Bobby stepped between me and Sara Jean's desk. "I'm the owner of this here outfit. And I say, I ain't paying you nothin', ya little pervert."

"Seriously? I'm the pervert?" This was getting old. Time for a change of tactics. "From what Fiddler told me, Bobby, you've been spending a lot of time with a young thing you met at Chasing Tails, that strip club near Grand Avenue and Indian School. The one that dresses up like a Catholic schoolgirl? Not that I judge."

"You what?" Sara Jean glared at him.

Big Bobby muttered incoherently, no doubt trying to come up with an explanation. "I, uh, she don't know what she's talking about."

"Big Bobby, are you seriously going to deny it? You want me to show Sara Jean your credit card receipts? I mean, seriously, who puts lap dances on a credit card? Honestly, I think you wanted to get caught."

Sara Jean slapped him. "You filthy pig. You said you was on a stakeout."

"I was, sugar pie, honest."

"Don't get so high and mighty, Miss Sara Jean."

Sara Jean turned back to me with a confused look on her face. "Me? What did I do?"

"Gee, let me think. How about the money you've been slipping some of the defense attorneys under the table. I wonder what the Department of Insurance would say to that if they found out you were paying referrals to lawyers. They could shut you down."

Her fleshy face turned a lovely shade of fuchsia. "You wouldn't?"

"Hey, I understand. Cost of doing business. And as long as I get paid for these body receipts, it'll just be our little secret."

"That's extortion," Big Bobby exclaimed.

"Naw, extortion would be if I demanded another ten grand to keep my mouth shut. I just want what I would have earned if you two weren't such backwoods bigots."

"All right, all right. Pay the woman, Sara Jean!" Big Bobby glared at me. "But this is it, ya hear? All your other cases have been reassigned."

Sara Jean scribbled out a check and handed it to me without a word.

"Thanks!" I said, slipping the check in my back pocket. "You two hypocrites have yourselves a fabulous fucking day."

The office door squeaked open behind me. I turned, and Fiddler was walking in. The image of my spray-painted truck popped into my head. My blood boiled. "There you are!"

Fiddler's eyes went wide. "Aw, shit!" He turned tail and dashed out the door with me on his heels. I maneuvered through a trail of toppled pedestrians left in Fiddler's wake as he barreled down the sidewalk. He didn't get more than half a block before I grabbed him and threw him against a building.

"Whatcha running from, Fiddler?"

He was gasping, trying to catch his breath. "I . . . I don't know .

.. what . . . you're talking 'bout," he huffed. "Just seemed . . . nice day for . . . a run."

"Cut the shit, Fiddler. I know you vandalized my ride." I popped open my phone and showed him the photo.

"Not me."

"Had a friend of mine trace your license plate, douchebag." A small crowd of people started to gather around us, holding up their phones, no doubt recording the excitement.

"So what?" He got a smug look on his face. "You *are* a faggot, right? Heard you even got your dick cut off. Fucking tranny faggot."

Suddenly Fiddler was on the ground, moaning. Blood dribbled from his nose and a cut below his left eye. I didn't remember hitting him, despite the throbbing in my fist.

"Stay away from me, Fiddler, or I will kick the ever-loving shit out of you. Got it?" I turned away, cradling my hand. I glared at the lookie-loos recording me. "What are you looking at?"

As I was on the way back to the parking garage, my phone rang. "Yeah?"

"Jinxie? You okay?"

I felt all the bluster go out of me like a deflating balloon. "Conor."

I collapsed onto a nearby bus stop bench. Memories of the night before flooded my mind. The acrid smell of blood, death, and plastic. Hardin's never-ending questions.

"Hensley's dead."

"Aye. Heard about that on the news. Recognized your house on the telly."

"It's Volkov. He's . . . " I wasn't sure how to explain it. "He's been stalking me. Sending creepy emails. Then this."

"Jesus Christ, I'll kill the fucker before he lays a hand on ya."

"Honestly, I think he's got a creepy crush on me. I promised to let Hardin's guys handle it. I need to focus on finding Holly Schwartz."

"Where are ya?"

"Downtown. Just picked up a check from Liberty. Had a run-in with Fiddler."

"Fiddler? What about?"

"He's the one who vandalized the Gray Ghost."

"That bloody wanker! Ya give him what for?"

"I punched him in the face." I actually felt bad about it, which made me wonder what the hell was wrong with me. Was I going soft?

"Good for you, lass." I heard him chuckle.

"Conor, I'm sorry for getting all pissy with you yesterday."

"Aw, Jinxie, I understand. Been a rough couple of days."

"Thanks, you're the best."

"So ya want some company?"

"Yeah. I'm heading to a rental car place at Tatum and Shea. Seems our girl and her boyfriend rented that minivan from Cheap Rides."

"Cheap Rides?" Conor guffawed. "Sounds like a low-cost hooker."

"Yeah, yeah. Very funny. You in?"

"Aye! I'll meet ya there."

38

———————

Conor was already sitting in his Charger in the parking lot when I pulled in. I parked and stepped out into the heat, wearing my gear. He hugged me, and it honestly felt good to be held.

"I'm sorry for yelling at you," I said, trying not to tear up. If I had to go much longer without my hormones, I was going to fucking kill someone. I only hoped it wasn't him.

"Don't give it a second thought, love." He kissed me on the forehead. "You doing okay?"

I shrugged. "I'll feel better once we apprehend Schwartz."

"You said Volkov's been stalking you?"

I showed him the emails and the text.

"Jesus, Mary, and Joseph! Why didn't ya mention this earlier? He could've killed ya."

"Hoped he'd give up when I didn't respond."

"Bloody good that did."

"So this is my fault?" I glared at him incredulously.

"Not saying that. This is all on him. But we have to watch our backs."

"Fuck Volkov! I hope Hardin kills him," I said, getting control of my runaway emotions. "I have more important things to worry about than some twisted, lovesick Chechen gangster."

"Aye. Let's go see what the good folks at Cheap Rides can tell us about who rented that vehicle."

We stepped into the small office with cheap carpeting and even cheaper-looking cubicles on the other side of the scratched-up counter. A clean-cut man a few years younger than me, wearing a clip-on tie and a white dress shirt, stepped up to the counter with a car salesman smile. "Hi, my name is Chad. How can I help you folks?"

I flashed my Bail Enforcement Agent badge. "One of our fugitives was seen with a man who rented a car from your office. We need to find out who he is and where he lives."

"I'm sorry, but I can't give that information out to just anyone."

Conor pointed at my bruised and battered face. "See this, lad? The people we're looking for did that. Nearly killed her. They're wanted for murder."

"Trust me," I said, "you want us to get them off the streets. We might even get your minivan back for you."

"You don't think they'll return our van?"

I raised an eyebrow. "They're wanted for murdering a woman and jumping bail. You think they're worried about stealing your van?"

Chad went pale and stepped up to one of the computer terminals at the counter. "What are their names?"

"I'm not sure what name they rented under. Here's the license plate." I slid him the paper I'd written the plate number on.

He did his magic on the computer. "That car was rented a month or so ago by a Richard Delgado."

Holly's nurse. "He got an address, mate?" Conor asked.

"Komatke, Arizona. Diamondback Drive." Chad wrote down the exact address.

"Where's Komatke?" Conor gave me a quizzical look.

"Down on the Gila River Indian Reservation south of town. You have a phone number for him?" I asked the guy.

"I'll print out the file for you."

He tapped on the keyboard, and a nearby laser printer spit out a few pages. Chad handed them to Conor, who passed them to me. "He look familiar?"

The printout had a copy of Delgado's driver's license picture. "Yeah, that's the guy who roughed me up. The one with Holly."

"Anything else?" Chad asked.

"No, that'll do. Thanks." I gave him a smile and turned to leave. "Guess we're taking a trip south of the city."

"You will call, won't you?" he said as Conor and I walked out. "Let us know if you find the van."

"Sure," I lied.

~

I climbed into Jake's truck with Conor following behind in his Charger. On the way to Komatke, I called Becca.

"The guy who rented the car's named Richard Delgado."

"Delgado? Holly's nurse."

"Conor and I are headed to his house in Komatke now. Pull up everything you can on him. Phone logs, bank records, the works."

"Will do."

"Thanks, Becks."

I hung up and breathed a sigh of relief. I was back in the hunt. With a little luck, we'd find Holly hiding out at Delgado's place, and with Conor there, I wasn't going to get ambushed like before. Maybe I'd even get my Taser back.

Still, something nagged me. Why hadn't Conor answered his phone when I called to apologize last night? Did he not feel like talking to me after I'd been so awful to him? I couldn't shake the feeling that something else was going on.

He'd disappeared a couple of times the past few days without explanation. When I'd pressed him, he lied. Or maybe the lack of hormones was making me paranoid. Ugh. I hated this.

I decided when I got home, I'd take a double dose of estradiol. I didn't care what that doctor at the ER said. The mood swings and the fucking crying was worse than dying. If I didn't get relief soon, I'd be the one going on a murderous rampage. Could I plead temporary insanity?

39

Komatke was a sparsely populated town in the Gila River Indian Community, in the open desert south of Phoenix. I'd occasionally passed through Komatke in an attempt to bypass rush hour traffic when I had to get from west Phoenix to the southeast valley and beyond.

We parked on the street in front of Delgado's place, a small wooden frame house coated in a layer of desert dust so thick it was difficult to tell what color it'd been painted. The yard was natural desert. No lawn. No crushed rock. Just bare ground littered with wild grass, creosote, brittlebush, and other plants I saw all the time but didn't know the names of. One of them might have been a Mormon tea bush. But what did I know? I was no botanist. I wasn't Mormon. And I didn't even like tea all that much.

No cars were parked in front in Delgado's dirt driveway. The curtains were drawn. Not a sign of life anywhere. The nearest house was a quarter mile away.

"Think they're in there?" I asked Conor as we met between our vehicles. I donned my shades and racked the slide of my

Ruger. If Delgado tried to ambush me again, he'd find me rather unforgiving.

"No vehicles, but those tire tracks in the driveway look recent."

"Maybe they had someone drop them off so it would look like no one was home."

It was flimsy, and we both knew it. Technically, we could force our way in only if we had reason to believe our fugitive was inside. It was a gray area. If we were right, we were golden. If we were wrong, we could be in a whole lot of trouble, especially on the reservation.

Several years back, a team of bounty hunters was given bogus information. They stormed a house while looking for a fugitive, only to discover the address they'd been given belonged to the Phoenix chief of police. Several innocent people were hurt in the process. The bounty hunters were sentenced to serious time in federal prison.

I didn't want to face the same fate. Trans people didn't do well in prison. But I wasn't going to let Holly slip through my fingers again. This was about more than the fifty-thousand-dollar bounty. I had a grudge to settle.

I looked around. The street was empty in all directions. "Let's do it."

Conor nodded. "Suits me, love. Ya want the front or the back?"

"I'll take the back this time. I'll wait for your signal." I turned on my walkie.

"Suits me fine."

I hustled around to the back. Under a small porch, a ceramic chiminea sat next to a couple of dust-covered plastic lawn chairs. The back door looked weathered, the outer laminate peeling at the bottom. I put my back against the wall next to the door, my Ruger ready.

Conor pounded on the front. "Open up! Bail enforcement." He pounded again. There was no response.

"Looks like no one's home," Conor said over the walkie.

A crash came from inside, like a box of something being knocked over. "Someone's in there. I'm going in."

"Jinx, hold on."

I gave the back door a good kick with my boot. The frame shattered, and the door snapped inward. I rushed in, pivoting right and left as I advanced into a dark room. A flurry of dust motes swirled in the air lit up by the midafternoon sun pouring through the back windows. I whipped off my shades to better assess my surroundings. I was in the kitchen. The scent of cooking oil hung in the air.

I checked under the small kitchen table and opened every cabinet. I'd had fugitives hide on closet shelves and even in a chimney once. After Delgado spirited Schwartz away in the suitcase, I wasn't making any assumptions. But after a thorough search of the kitchen, I'd turned up nothing but a drying rack full of dishes.

I continued into the living room, modestly furnished with an aging Barcalounger and a bulky TV that looked about twenty years old. An entertainment center held a stereo, turntable, and a stack of LPs. Photos of Delgado and lots of family members covered the wall. On another hung several awards from the Komatke High School Rifle Club recognizing Richie Delgado as their top marksman. Unopened mail lay in a basket on an end table.

Warily, I unlocked the front door and let Conor in.

"A tribal police car drove past but didn't stop. I think we're in the clear," he said.

"Good to know."

We continued down a short hallway and verified that the two cozy bedrooms and only bathroom were unoccupied, as was a utility room with a stacked washer and dryer.

"I swear, I heard somebody knock something over," I said, rechecking one of the bedrooms. "Wait a minute."

I found a bowl of kibble on the floor.

"Looks like Delgado has a cat," Conor called from the bathroom. "Found a litter box."

I rechecked under the bed and noticed a pair of eyes, like glowing coals. "Hello, kitty."

I met Conor in the hallway.

"Also found this," he said, holding up my Taser.

I holstered my Ruger and tucked the Taser into my waistband. "So they were here."

"Aye, but it looks like they bugged out."

"Now what?"

"Nothing of interest here," he replied. "We could conduct a stakeout."

"Doesn't seem promising. Let me see if Becca's got anything else on Delgado."

I called and updated her on our situation. From the noise in the background, I could tell she was working at the Hub today.

"I've done some digging around. He goes by Richie. He posts a lot on Facebook and Twitter, but nothing significant. He's got a brother named Christopher Delgado. Nothing of interest on his bank statements. The only recent transaction on his bank card was an authorization for a car rental. No recent activity on his cell phone account."

My phone buzzed. "I got another call coming in, Becks. Let me know what else you find out."

"Will do."

I clicked over to the other call, hoping my little phishing expedition from the night before was finally paying off. "Hello?"

"Ms. Ballou? This is Sadie Levinson. Where are you on the Schwartz case?"

"Sadie! How the hell are you? Good news, I'm closing in, hoping to have her in custody by the end of the day."

"Really?" She didn't sound convinced. "Sounds like one of Fiddler's cock-and-bull stories."

"Ouch! Sadie, you wound me."

"Cut the theatrics, Ms. Ballou. Schwartz's bond goes up for

summary judgment first thing Wednesday. I can't afford to lose this. I'll be out of business, and so will you."

I sighed. "We'll find her. Don't worry."

"Hold on, love. Looks like we got company." Conor spun me around and lifted the corner of the living room curtain. A tribal police patrol car had pulled up behind Conor's Charger.

"Who's we?" Sadie asked. "Is that Conor Doyle I hear?"

Aw, shit. Shit, shit, shit. "Oh, that? Naw, just the TV."

"That was Conor. I'd know that Irish brogue anywhere."

I made crackling sounds with my mouth. "What's that? Can't . . . hear . . . breaking up."

"You're not fooling me. I told you that I specifically did not—"

"Gotta go . . . fugitives to catch." I ended the call. Because apparently I was an eight-year-old in a twenty-nine-year-old's body.

"Sadie?" Conor asked.

"Yeah," I said, keeping my eye on the police cruiser outside. "One of these days you're going to tell me what the hell happened between you two."

He grimaced. "Another time. Right now, we have more immediate concerns."

The officer stepped out of his cruiser and circled our vehicles, then turned toward us peering out the window. "Aw, crap."

40

———

There was a solid knock on the front door. I pushed Conor aside. "Let me handle it. People like me."

Conor cough-laughed. "Oh really? I've met sandpaper less abrasive than you."

I gave him an eat-shit look. "Don't push me, Doyle." I pulled off my ballistic vest and tactical belt, tossed them to the side, and opened the door.

Officer Quiroz, whose name was on a brass name tag, was slender with a smallish face, wary eyes, and a pleasant smile, which I tried to return as convincingly as I could.

"Hi," I said. "What's up?" Mentally, I kicked myself. Could I sound more like a vapid teenager?

"Afternoon, ma'am. Are you the owner of the house?"

I thought about saying yes but didn't figure I could pull it off. "No, I'm afraid the owner of the house isn't here right now. I'm house-sitting. Is something wrong?"

"When will the owner be back?"

I shrugged. "Hard to say. He's out of town on family business." Sounded vague enough to be reasonable.

"The owner is Richie Delgado, is that correct?" He took out his notepad and started writing.

My stomach sank. Conor approached as if to "handle the situation," but I was in no mood. I gave him a back-off glare. "Oh yeah, good ol' Richie. We go way back."

"Really? That's interesting. Is he up at his brother's cabin in Payson?" Clearly, Officer Quiroz knew more than he was letting on. How long before this guy was slapping the cuffs on me for B&E?

"You know, I think he did mention Payson. Yeah."

"That so? Because his brother's cabin is in Prescott."

Crap. "Prescott. Payson. I get them confused sometimes."

"Tell me something, ma'am. What happened to your face?"

Conor stepped between us and held up his bail enforcement agent shield. "Look, Officer Quiroz, the truth is we're looking for a fugitive named Holly Schwartz who is charged with the murder of her mother. Mr. Delgado has been actively interfering in her recapture."

"Really? You have any paperwork backing up these claims?"

"In my truck." I led him out to Jake's truck, with Conor shutting the front door behind us. I showed Quiroz the paperwork authorizing me to apprehend Holly Schwartz.

"You have proof that Richie is involved in this?"

I was done playing nice. "I found him hiding Schwartz in a Phoenix motel room under an assumed name and using a stolen credit card. When I attempted to apprehend my fugitive, Delgado assaulted me. I had reason to believe he might have brought her back here."

"You know," Quiroz said, gazing out at the very blue horizon, "Richie's my cousin. Known him my whole life. Sweetest, most gentle soul I've met. Can't imagine him doing anything like what you claim."

"Don't believe me? Call the Desert View Inn on Black Canyon Highway. Ask for the head manager."

Quiroz stared at me, then Conor for a few moments before saying, "I should charge you both with trespassing."

"We are authorized to . . ." I was about to launch into my speech about the historic court case authorizing bounty hunters to enter, when Quiroz held up his hand.

"But I'll let you go with a warning. And the warning is this. If I ever catch either of you in this community, breaking into a home without the owner's permission, I will run you in. If you so much as drive one mile an hour over the speed limit, I will hit you with every violation I can. You understand?"

I considered our options. Clearly Schwartz wasn't here. Time to move on. "Yes, sir," I said.

"Now get out of my sight before I change my mind."

I climbed into Jake's truck, and Conor hopped into his Charger. I turned north on Fifty-First Avenue headed back to Phoenix and talked into my walkie. "Hey, Conor. You copy?"

"I copy, love. What's the plan?"

"I think we need to find this cabin in Prescott Officer Quiroz was talking about."

"Be a brilliant place to hide someone."

"Let's stop by the Hub and see if Becca can give us a location."

"Roger that."

As I turned east onto I-10, my phone rang again. "Jinx Ballou."

"Good news, sis," Jake said. "Your Pathfinder looks good as new. My friend squeezed you in right away."

"So soon? It's barely been a day." I took a sniff and was sure I could smell a hint of Mandy Tipton's vomit.

"Looks better than new, actually. Tell me where you are, and we can swap vehicles."

"You know, I should really get your truck detailed. It's the least I can do."

"Forget it. I use it for construction. Doesn't need to be clean. Just functional. Besides, how dirty could it be?"

"Okay." I sighed. Maybe he wouldn't notice. "I'm on my way to the Hub."

"I can be there in half an hour. Will that work?"

"Yeah, I guess so."

"Something wrong?"

"Not at all. I'll see you at the Hub." I took another sniff. It definitely still smelled like puke.

41

The Hub was located at the three-way intersection of Grand Avenue, Roosevelt Street, and Fifteenth Avenue. The old building reminded me of an inverted boat, with a keel that rose into the sky. It started out as a car dealership, later converted to a bank, then became the home for the Phoenix Council on the Arts.

For the past few years, it had served as a coworking space for solo entrepreneurs. Most members were in the tech industry, a few were artists, and then there was me, a bounty hunter.

The parking lot was small, but Conor and I managed to grab the last two spaces and hustled inside the glass doors to get out of the heat.

The interior was an open grungy industrial space with a cracked cement slab for a floor, pockmarked with divots from where they'd pulled out the walls. Dozens of collapsible tables served as desks with a wild assortment of secondhand chairs, from fancy super adjustable executive-style thrones to flimsy plastic folding numbers.

The hypnotic beat of electronic dance music thrummed from

unseen speakers. Overhead lighting was subdued. Conor and I strolled across the room to where Becca stared vacantly at a pair of flat screens. "S'up?" Becca asked without a glance.

"I have a lead on where Delgado may have taken Holly Schwartz. His brother has a cabin up in Prescott somewhere."

"Interesting. I've done more digging on Delgado. No criminal record. Good credit. Worked as a nurse for much of his adult life. First at the Gila River Medical Center, then as a visiting nurse for Compassionate Care. As far as I can see, he's clean as a whistle."

"So why is he helping hide Schwartz?"

"Beats me." Becca went through a series of mouse clicks and keystrokes. "Christopher Delgado, age forty-two. Real estate developer. Owner of Stardust Properties Corporation. Makes good money too."

"Great. Where's the cabin?"

"Let me take a look." She cycled through a number of screens. "Aha! Yes, he owns a property in Prescott." She typed the address into a map. "Looks like it's down off of Senator Highway south of Prescott."

"Gotcha, you son of a bitch!" I shouted a little too loud. A half dozen people around us looked up. I flushed. "Sorry."

I returned to the task at hand. "So how exactly do we get there?"

"I'll print you out a map. You'll be taking some forest service roads, most of which aren't paved. Not all intersections are well marked, either."

"Thanks. I'm sure between Conor and me, we can figure it out."

My brother walked up. Becca sat up straighter, beaming at him. She'd never admit it, but she'd always had a crush on him, even when we were in high school. She was disappointed when she learned he was gay. Not that it stopped her from embarrassing herself whenever he was around.

"Hi, Jake," she said, gushing like a schoolgirl.

"Hi, Becca. Conor." He gave me a hug and handed me my keys. "Hey, sis. I parked your Gray Ghost on Thirteenth Avenue. Couldn't find a closer parking space."

"I'll manage. Thanks for doing this so quickly."

"You owe me big-time. And I intend to collect."

"How?" I asked warily.

"Just closed on a house near Northern and Thirty-Ninth. Needs some serious demo work. You're going to help me this coming Saturday."

"Fine. Just tell me the house has AC."

"Power's turned off, but I've got some portable swamp coolers I can bring in."

I sighed. "Fine. Fair's fair." I pulled his keys out of my pocket, hoping again he didn't notice the puke smell in his truck. "Thanks for the quick turnaround."

He gave me a mischievous grin. "See you Saturday. Bring lots of Gatorade."

What have I gotten myself into? I wondered. As he turned to leave, I asked, "You tell Mom and Dad about you know what?"

He sighed. "I'm working up to it. Talk to you later."

I turned to Conor when Jake left. "I don't think your Charger will do so well on the back roads of Prescott National Forest."

"Aye. I've been up there a few times. Lots of tranny rocks."

I raised an eyebrow. "Tranny rocks?"

"Aye, tranny rocks. They're rocks that stick up out of the road, waiting for some dumb bloke in a car. When he drives over the rock, it rips the tranny right out from the undercarriage."

I rolled my eyes. "Tranny as in transmission. Got it."

Conor flushed. "Oh, sorry. Didn't think about the other meaning."

"Let's just go before I decide to rip out your undercarriage." I pushed him toward the door. "Thanks for the info, Becks," I said over my shoulder.

"Hey, wait!" she called. "You need to see this."

"What? We're losing daylight." I returned to her desk. She had some news articles on her screen.

"There are rumors floating around that Christopher Delgado may be laundering money for the Sinaloa cartel. Watch your ass, Jinx."

"Thanks for the warning."

42

Conor drove me to where the Gray Ghost was parked on Thirteenth Avenue. My brother was right. On the outside, it looked like a brand-new vehicle. The dented, scraped-up, dull-gray side panels were now gleaming silver, like a newly minted coin. Maybe a little too new. Not nearly as invisible as before. But at least Fiddler's spray-painted epithets were gone.

When we stopped at Conor's, we loaded up on a little extra firepower—his assault rifle, a shotgun, boxes of ammo, my trusty battering ram, plus a few flash bangs for good measure. We had no idea what we were walking into, so I wanted to be prepared.

The drive up Black Canyon Highway to Prescott took a few hours. I started out driving, then at Cortes Junction, we switched places. From there, we took Highway 69 through Prescott Valley and grabbed a quick bite to eat at a Tastee Freez.

My phone rang. It was my lawyer. "What's up, Kirsten?"

"Bad news. The FBI is looking like they want to press charges for your interference in their sting operation at Volkov's warehouse."

"We had every right to be there. We had good intel."

"If it was good intel, we wouldn't be talking, would we?"

I sighed. "Crap. So what do we do?"

"They want you in their office for further questioning tomorrow morning. I gave them my word you'd be there."

"Are they going to arrest us?"

"Possibly. Unless you can think of something to offer them. Intel on Volkov they don't have. Like where he's hiding out. He has been contacting you, right?"

"He's a sick chaser, but I have no idea where he is, nor do I want to."

"Be at their offices tomorrow at nine a.m. Dress professional. That goes for Conor too."

"I'm busy on a case. I'm almost out of time."

"You'll be cooling your heels in federal lockup if you don't show, Jinx."

I sighed. "Fine. We'll be there."

"What's up?" Conor asked. I filled him in. He was almost as overjoyed as I was. Damn feds!

The shadows were getting long and the sun was sitting on the mountains to the west when we pulled onto Gurley Street in Prescott and finally turned left onto South Senator Highway.

I'd always loved this part of Prescott. Older homes, some dating back to when Arizona was still a territory, were crowded on tiny lots under stately oaks and ponderosa pines.

I rolled down the windows and was treated to the cool mountain air scented with juniper and pine. The drone of cicadas brought back memories of childhood camping trips. The effect was hypnotic. I started to wish we could forget about chasing Holly and grab a room in one of the old hotels off Prescott's Courthouse Square.

"So where the hell are we going?" Conor asked as the road went from paved to gravel on the outskirts of town.

"Looks like stay on this road for another couple of miles, then bear sort of left onto Stone Mill Road." I flicked on the light from the visor's vanity mirror to get a better look at the map. "After that, the road winds around for about five miles and then we take another left—no, wait." I rotated the printout, trying to make sense of the twisty road. "No, it's a right onto Davis Homestead Trail. David or Davis, I'm not sure which. Can't read it in this light."

"Let me see that." Conor grabbed the map, and we hit a deep divot in the road. "Damn it!"

"Keep your eyes on the road, will you? Last thing we need to do is blow a tire or run off the side of a mountain."

The farther we went, the harder it became to negotiate. The last glimmers of twilight were fading. Deep ruts and large rocks troubled the road. Conor slowed to a snail's pace, making me all the more tense.

"There, turn there!" I pointed at a gap in the trees off to the left.

"Bloody hell! Is that even a road?"

I wasn't entirely convinced, but there appeared to be a parallel set of wheel ruts with tall weeds growing between them. "I think so," I replied. "Maybe."

We turned, and the road smoothed out for a mile before growing considerably more rocky and uneven. My headache was back, pounding out a primal beat of pain that ran from the top of my skull down my spine. I felt at any minute we'd blow the shocks.

Finally, we came to a clearing. Two trails branched off to our right, a third off to the left. I studied the map and surveyed the dark trails leading off into the night. I pointed at the one on the right that wasn't as sharp a turn.

"I think it's that way." I held up my crossed fingers as we inched our way along. Gullies appeared on either side of the trail.

"Christ, I hope you're right," Conor replied. "It'd be a bloody nightmare to turn around here."

"According to the map, the cabin should be a mile ahead on the left." Tree branches scraped the side of the Gray Ghost, like fingernails on a chalkboard. So much for my new paint job.

The trail grew narrower as it turned sharply uphill. Every

bump sent a new shock wave of pain through my skull. I tried not to show how I was feeling, but after a glance in my direction, Conor asked, "You all right, love?"

"I'll survive. Just get us there in one piece."

I caught a glimpse of a light up in the distance on the left. "Hold on. Cut the lights."

Conor turned off the ignition. Darkness rushed in.

"That's gotta be it." I pointed at a cluster of lights, soft amber glowing in the pitch black of the forest. My pulse sped up as I anticipated catching my quarry.

Conor started the engine again and crept forward without the headlights until we reached a makeshift driveway where a large 4x4 pickup truck sat parked. No sign of the rented minivan. "I'm going to turn us around so we can make an easy getaway if we need to."

"Okay."

It took some maneuvering, but Conor managed to get the Gray Ghost turned around the way we came and pulled to the side. The truck lurched to the right, and the passenger-side tires dipped into the gully.

"Conor!" I yelled, holding on to the oh-shit handle above the door as the truck listed sharply.

Conor growled and turned the wheel. One of the wheels whined as it spun freely. "Bollocks!"

He put it in reverse and gave it a little gas. We slipped farther into the gulley.

"We're never gonna get out of here, with or without Holly."

"Shut it. I got this." He turned the wheel again and eased on a little acceleration. Finally the truck lurched level again onto the trail.

I breathed a sigh of relief. "Thank God! Much as I wouldn't mind spending a night under the stars with you, this isn't exactly what I had in mind."

"No worries. Let's gear up and grab our girl."

43

When we stepped out of the Gray Ghost, my eyes were drawn to the sky. Stars blazed as if someone had scattered glitter across the black expanse of space. The full moon crested the tops of the trees. "Wow."

"Aye, it's a pretty sight. But we've got a job to do."

We opened up the back of the truck and put on our vests and walkie-talkies. Conor racked the slide on his Glock. I snagged the shotgun loaded with beanbag rounds. My Ruger was on my right hip, my revolver on my ankle, in case things went badly.

"You ready?" Conor whispered.

"Ready as I'll ever be. Let's go rock their world."

In the silver moonlight, I spotted a wooden sign along the gravel walk leading up to the cabin. The name Delgado was carved on it. At least we had the right place. Last thing I wanted to do was burst in on Ma and Pa Kettle and have them both drop dead of a heart attack. It'd look very bad on my report.

The two-story log cabin was sixty feet wide and solidly built. Three steps led up to a wraparound porch. We scouted the perimeter, making note of windows and the back door. Muffled voices drifted from inside, both male.

When we circled back to the front, Conor gestured that he'd cover the back door. A moment later his voice crackled in on the walkie. "Ready when you are."

"Roger that."

I checked the door. It was unlocked. I burst into a room the length of the building, filled with rustic furniture and with a large kitchen on my left. I leveled my shotgun at two men playing cards at a rough-hewn wooden table. One was Richie. The other man was older with similar facial features but a broader jaw and cropped hair—his brother, Christopher, no doubt, the one with ties to the Sinaloa cartel.

"Bail enforcement!" I shouted. "On the ground! On the ground now! Hands above your heads."

"What the hell's this?" Christopher remained sitting even as his brother complied with my commands. "This is a private residence."

Conor charged through the back door, his pistol trained on Christopher. "Bail enforcement. Get on the ground, or I'll put a hole in ya."

Christopher glared at Conor but lay on the floor next to Richie.

"Where's Holly Schwartz?" I demanded.

"We don't know anyone by that name," Christopher said matter-of-factly.

"This one does. He took her from her aunt's house." I kicked Richie hard in the ribs, and he cried out in pain. "You gave me a concussion, asshole."

"I'm sorry," Richie whimpered. "I was just trying to protect Holly."

"Where is she, ya little shite?" Conor asked.

Richie shook his head. "She's not here."

"Where. Is. She?" I pressed my boot into his side, making him wince.

He turned his head and shot daggers at me with his stare. "I'm not telling you. Holly's mother tortured her for years with countless unnecessary medical procedures. I'm not letting you or anyone else hurt her again."

"She murdered her mother, Richie," I said. "She has to answer for that."

"She did what she had to do to survive."

"Then she can plead self-defense. You have to tell me where she is, or you're guilty after the fact."

"We won't tell you shit," Christopher piped in.

Conor kicked Christopher. "Either ya start talking, or we'll beat it outta ya."

A gunshot shook the cabin. Conor doubled over, groaning and holding his chest. I whipped around to see where the shot came from. Perched on the rail of the second-floor loft, Holly glared down at us, a deer rifle in hand. I fired a beanbag round at her, which hit her in the gut. She fell back, howling in pain.

Before I could race up the stairs after her, Christopher growled behind me. "Drop the shotgun, or I kill your boyfriend."

I turned. Christopher stood using Conor as a shield, with the Glock to my boyfriend's head. I couldn't get a clean shot. And even if I did, a beanbag round wouldn't prevent Christopher from pulling the trigger.

"You don't want to do this," I said, keeping the shotgun trained on him.

"You came into my home, assaulted me and my brother, and shot his friend. Don't tell me what I want."

"She'll be okay. It was just a beanbag round. Everyone can still walk away. Just put down the pistol."

Above us, Holly continued crying. Richie got to his feet, holding his side, and hobbled up the stairs. "Hang on, kiddo. I'm coming."

"The only way you're getting out of here alive is if you drop that shotgun." Christopher's eyes were cold. He wouldn't hesitate to pull the trigger.

"Not going to happen." I caught Conor's eyes. He was in pain, but there was no blood. His vest had stopped the bullet. "If it makes you feel better, you can point your gun at me, since I'm the one who shot Holly." It was a gamble, but it was the only move I had.

Christopher followed my suggestion, and I stared down that cavernous .40-caliber barrel. I gave Conor the smallest of nods, and he drove his elbow into Christopher's rib cage. Pain exploded in my lower chest an instant before I heard the gunshot.

I dropped to one knee, struggling to bring in air. Pain engulfed my body, and it felt as though a rib was broken. I steeled myself and rose to my feet. Conor now had Christopher back on the ground, hands cuffed behind his back.

I tossed the shotgun on the kitchen table, drew my Ruger, and aimed it up at the loft. The top of Richie's head peeked above the loft floor with his eye to the scope of the deer rifle, now aimed at me. Distracted by the searing pain in my chest and struggling to breathe, I found my aim wobbling uncontrollably. I had no shot.

"Drop your weapons, both of you." Richie's voice was shaky, but that didn't mean he wouldn't pull the trigger, especially to defend his brother. I recalled the rifle club awards in his house. "Or I put a bullet through her head."

"Take it easy, man," I said, gritting my teeth against the pain. "We're not here to hurt anyone."

"Drop your guns."

I was tempted to shoot, but with so little of him exposed, the odds of me hitting my target were slim. If I missed, he wouldn't. Our best chance of getting out alive, much less with Holly in custody, was to de-escalate the situation. I laid my pistol on the table and raised my hands. Conor did the same.

"Happy now?" I asked.

"Uncuff my brother."

Conor huffed but obeyed. The elder Delgado brother got to his feet and snapped the cuffs on Conor. He then grabbed Conor's Glock as well as my Ruger. This night was so not going as planned.

"You busted into my home." Christopher pressed a pistol against my temple. "You shot Holly."

"With a beanbag round," I reiterated.

"You white trash bounty hunters are going to pay."

"Oy! We did what ya asked, lads," Conor said. "Let us go, and we'll be on our way."

"You think we're stupid?" Christopher asked. "You won't stop till you drag this poor girl back to jail, and us along with her. Time we ended this here and now."

If my chest hadn't been hurting so much, I could've disarmed Christopher and taken him out along with Richie. But every breath was a new experience in pain. I didn't have the speed or the strength required.

"Chris, don't." Richie and Holly gingerly descended the stairs. He looked a lot less threatening without the rifle. "Not in front of Holly."

"Fine, we take them outside and shoot them."

"Don't do this, guys. We can help Holly straighten things out. Get her bail reset." I locked gazes with Holly. "You want your aunt to lose her house? She paid your bail. Took you in. Paid for your lawyer. Is that how you repay her?"

"I'm not going back," she said, tears streaming down her face. "That lawyer was a joke, wanted me to pretend like I'm crazy. My mother was the crazy one! Not me. I did what I had to."

She wiped her face and pulled closer to Richie. "Richie and Chris are the only ones who care about me."

"Ya can't run away from it, lass," Conor said. "Sooner or later, someone'll track ya down. And now ya've got your mates involved too. Come along now, and we won't charge them."

"What do we do, Richie?" Holly begged. "I can't go to jail."

Richie took the Ruger from his brother. "Chris, you and Holly put our gear in the truck. I'll take our guests outside."

My heart thundered as I searched for a way out of the situation.

44

———

Conor and I shuffled ahead of Richie out the front door into the yellow glow of the porch light. I bent down, reaching for the revolver in my ankle holster, and instantly felt Richie's foot kicking me in the same place I'd been shot. Stars exploded in my vision as I tumbled down the steps, rolling down the hill until I collided with a tree. I struggled to breathe, despite dizziness and chest-crushing pain.

"Jinxie, you okay, love?" Conor sounded as though he was next to me.

I reached out but felt only the bark of the pine tree I'd collided with. "Oh . . . okay." I dug deep and pulled myself shakily to my feet.

"Just don't know when to quit, do you?" Richie stood five feet away in the darkness.

"Yeah, I'm funny that way."

"Not so funny when you're dead." Richie pulled the cuffs out of the pouch on my tactical belt and snapped them around my wrists.

"Richie, ya don't have to do this, lad. You're a nurse. Ya have a duty to protect life, not take it."

"Shut up. Where are your keys?"

"My front pocket," Conor said.

Richie fished into Conor's jeans, pulled out the keys, and pitched them into the inky night.

"Bloody wanker."

"You rather I shot you?"

Is he going to let us live? I couldn't figure out his play. "Now what?"

"Keep walking down the hill."

Conor and I trudged down the hillside, past the road, trying not to trip over a root and pitch headlong into darkness. As the ground leveled out, I heard the gurgle of a stream. Moonlight flickered off the moving water.

"Sit down, back-to-back, against this tree," Richie said.

I could barely make out a foot-wide tree near the edge of the stream. I knelt down next to it, lost my balance on the uneven ground, and slammed my back into the trunk. "Fuck!"

By the time the pain and shock of the impact subsided, Richie had recuffed Conor and me to each other on opposite sides of the tree trunk. Richie stood silhouetted against the dim light of the cabin up the hill. He raised the Ruger. I glared at him, refusing to look away.

But instead of shooting us, he fired two shots straight up into the air, then tossed the pistol at my feet. Without a word, he disappeared up the hill.

"You okay, love?" Conor asked.

I groaned, wishing I had some of those pain pills from the ER. "I've had better days."

"Are ya hurt?" He sounded concerned.

"Cracked rib, I think. You?"

"Nothing that won't heal. Maybe we should call Richie back. He can do his nursing thing for your rib," Conor said with a chuckle.

I started to laugh and felt a sharp jab of pain. "Ow! Fuck! Don't make me laugh."

"Sorry, love."

"How the hell'd this happen? We're professionals."

Conor sighed. "We were outnumbered. It's why I prefer working in a team of three or more."

"I underestimated them. Again." I reached into my back pocket for the handcuff key I kept there and went to work finding the keyhole in one of the pairs of cuffs. It was trickier doing it one-handed with the tree in the way.

By the time the first pair of handcuffs ratcheted open, I heard the roar of a truck pulling away.

"At least they're gone," Conor said as I twisted around to release the other pair of cuffs.

"Yeah, but so is our bounty." Using the tree as support, I pulled myself to my feet. "I'm really tired of them getting the best of us."

"It's a pisser, no doubt. But we're alive to fight another day." He picked up my Ruger and handed it to me. I slipped it into my holster.

As we climbed the hill, he turned on the flashlight app on his phone. It cast harsh, dancing shadows among the underbrush along the hillside.

"What're you doing?" I mumbled as I plodded toward the cabin.

"Tryin' to find the keys to your lorry so we can get the hell out of here."

"You'll never find them in the dark."

"I can bloody well try. Maybe if ya helped, it'd go quicker."

I pulled mine out. "I got five percent power left. And no signal. We really are in the ass end of nowhere."

I left Conor searching the bushes and continued up the hill. When I reached the cabin, I tried to open the front door, but the knob didn't turn. "Fuck." I plopped down on the top step of the porch, wrapping my arms around my rib cage, trying not to breathe too deeply despite being winded from the climb.

Twenty minutes later, the step creaked beside me, and I felt Conor's presence.

"Jinxie?"

"Find the keys?" I didn't look up at him.

"'Fraid not. What say we go inside and grab some sleep."

"Door's locked."

"Oy! Bloody bastards." I heard him slam against the door a few times. "Jesus fuckin' Christ."

The clomp of his boots faded around the corner of the building. The muffled crack of shattering wood made me wince. Moments later, the front door creaked open. "Wankers made off with my shooter. But we have a place to sleep, at least. Back door wasn't nearly as solid."

"I hurt too much to sleep. I just want to kill those fucking guys and drag Holly's skinny white ass to jail."

His hand rested on my shoulder. I almost shrugged it off but didn't. "Jinxie, love, I know you're hurting."

"And pissed."

"And pissed. I am too. But we're not getting out of here till morning, and we need rest. Let's gets some ice on that cracked rib of yours. Maybe we can find something to wrap it with too."

"Whatever." He helped me up and led me inside, where I sat at the kitchen table while Conor rifled through the cabinets.

A few minutes later, I gasped as something cold pressed against my side. I took hold of the ice pack he offered. "Thanks."

"Found some ibuprofen and a wrap in the loo and a six-pack in the fridge." He deposited a rolled-up ACE bandage, two white pills, and an open beer bottle on the table.

Drops of condensation glistened on the brown glass. It was some microbrew whose name I didn't recognize. I popped the pills in my mouth and took a long pull on the beer to wash them down. It tasted rich and earthy with a hint of citrus. "Thanks, hon. Why do you put up with me?"

"Because you're hot as hell, wicked smart, and can kick ass with the best of them. And when I see ya in your Wonder Woman costume, it's all I can do not to jump your bones." He sat next to me.

"You're too good for me, you know that?" I clasped his hands and soon found myself kissing that sweet Irish face of his.

"Whaddya say we drink all their beer. Then I'll wrap your chest and we can catch some shut-eye."

"Works for me."

Midway through our third beer, Conor's face darkened. "I want to tell you about what happened between Sadie and me."

45

———

I stared at him, not really interested in hearing the ugly details about his previous relationship with Sadie. "Look, you two had a bad breakup. I get it. Ancient history. No big deal."

"That's not it. We didn't have a bad breakup. In fact, we never dated."

"Then what?"

"For starters, my name wasn't always Conor Doyle."

"What was it?"

"Liam Patrick O'Callaghan."

"I don't understand. Why—"

"Because when I was seventeen, I did something stupid."

"We all do stupid shit when we're seventeen."

"Not like this."

I set down my beer and took his hand. "Conor . . . er, Liam . . . what should I call you?"

"Conor."

"Conor, what happened?"

Waves of anger and grief radiated from him so intensely I

braced myself for what he might say or do. His hand was trembling so much I thought he'd drop his beer bottle.

I put my hand on his. "Does this have something to do with when your sister was killed?"

His eyes pricked with tears. His mouth opened, but no sound came out at first. "Yes." It was more of a croak than a word.

"Oh, sweetie, I'm so sorry."

"I was five when my da moved our family from Dublin to a small village in Northern Ireland called Gillygooley. He was a member of the Provisional IRA, using his skills as an electrician to wire bombs."

"Holy shit." My chest tightened. "Why?"

"Most people in the States think the Troubles were about claiming Northern Ireland for the Republic. But that was only a small part of it. Catholics in Northern Ireland faced a lot of brutality and oppression, much like trans people do today in this country. Bad enough the government treated us like second-class citizens, limiting our rights to vote. But loyalist paramilitary organizations like the UVF often attacked Catholics' homes, businesses, and individuals. Several of my childhood friends were murdered."

"Jesus! Couldn't the police do anything to stop the violence?"

"The RUC, which was the police force there, usually turned a blind eye to it. Sometimes they were behind it." He picked at a knot in the wooden table. "That was why the IRA turned to violence themselves. We were fighting for our survival."

"I had no idea."

"I was thirteen when I learned my da worked for the IRA. I wanted to get involved myself, to do my part to protect Catholics. But my father refused. Didn't want me getting hurt or going to prison."

"But you did, anyway."

"Eventually. In 1998, it was looking like the Troubles were coming to an end. The Provisional IRA signed an agreement with the Brits early that year ending discrimination against Catholics in Northern Ireland."

"That's good, right?"

"It was. But that summer, the Orange Order, an organization with loyalist paramilitary ties, staged one of their 'marches' through Catholic neighborhoods," he said with air quotes. "They weren't really marches. More like terrorist attacks on innocent people. The government tried to ban the march, but the Order rallied thousands of loyalist thugs armed with guns and petrol bombs. Three children were burned alive by loyalist bombs."

"Oh God."

"Many members of the Provisional IRA, including my da, broke off to form a new organization, the Real IRA. If the loyalists weren't going to abide by the cease-fire, neither would they. They stole a car, and my da wired it with five hundred pounds of explosives. Another volunteer drove it to Omagh, a town not far from where we lived. It was a Sunday afternoon, and there were a lot of people shopping along Market Street where the bomb car was parked."

His eyes grew distant, lost in the horror of his youth. My heart was breaking. I didn't want to hear more, but I had to know. And at some level, he needed to confess.

"Since I was seventeen, my da allowed me to get involved. My job was to call the media and give them a general location where the bomb was, supposedly to minimize civilian casualties. But somehow I was told the wrong intersection. As a result, the RUC unknowingly herded people toward the bomb car instead of away from it."

I instinctively released his hand and covered my mouth in shock. "Oh my God."

Like a piece of paper set alight, his face disintegrated into a knot of agony. "I showed up at the scene moments later, expecting a glorious victory. Instead, it was a bloody nightmare. Body parts strewn everywhere. The air was filled with screams and sirens. It was no victory. It was an abomination. And it was my fault. I had made this happen."

I didn't know how to respond. This was a man whom I loved, and yet I was repulsed by what he had done.

"As I walked through the carnage, I got a call from my mum telling me to come quick to the hospital. My sister, Bernie, had been in town, shopping for a friend who was ill."

He began bawling. "When I got there . . . God almighty . . . the floors were slick with blood. They were so overcapacity, people lay dying in hallways. And Bernadette, my sweet, generous big sister, who had a heart big as the moon . . . they'd tried to save her, but she'd lost too much blood. Her face was so mangled, I barely recognized her."

He buried his head in his arms and sobbed uncontrollably. I laid my head on his shoulders.

Over the next hour, he confessed that a friend of his father's had helped him get papers under the name Conor Doyle and get the money to travel to the States, where he started a new life.

"Sadie knew about this?"

Conor sighed. "I used to work for Aaron Levinson, Sadie's father. She was working as his office manager at the time. I learned he was giving kickbacks to attorneys who hired him to bail out their clients, which is, of course, illegal. When I confronted Aaron about it, he told me they knew about my past."

"How'd he find out?" I asked.

"Some documentary the BBC did on the bombing. Aaron recognized me in one of the photos they showed of potential suspects. He made it clear that if I turned him in over the kickbacks, he'd notify INS and have me deported. I would've been turned over to Scotland Yard to face charges. We made a pact to keep quiet about each other's crimes. I quit working for Aaron. A few days later, Sadie called and asked why I quit. I told her to ask her father. That was the last time I spoke to them."

I found myself wrestling with feelings of betrayal. And yet it was obvious he had suffered for his crimes. I didn't know whether to scream at him or comfort him. "So you and Sadie were never a couple, huh?"

"We shagged a few times. But she's a wee bit posh for my tastes."

"Why are you only telling me now after we've been dating a year? I told you I was trans before we were ever romantic."

"I should have. I'm sorry. I'd like to think I'm not that same person anymore. Liam O'Callaghan died the day I saw my sister's body in the hospital. He was a naïve kid, in the middle of a war he didn't understand."

"I don't know who you are," I confessed. "I thought I did, but this..."

"I've worked hard to become a good man, the man who loves you." His gaze met mine. Our fingers intertwined.

"I love you too," I whispered, though the words felt empty. My mind struggled to wrap itself around the horrors of Conor's past and the fact that he'd waited until now to tell me. Could I love such a man? If I had grown up as he did, would I have done the same thing? I couldn't count the number of times I'd wanted to plant a bomb in some transphobic politician's office. But to kill innocent civilians? It was all so much to take in.

"Let's go to bed," I suggested when I'd drained the last drops of my beer. I wasn't feeling much pain. The ice in the pack was melted.

"I'll help ya up the stairs."

"That's okay. I can manage on my own."

I hobbled up to the loft, with Conor behind me, where we found a double bed. I stripped off my vest, wincing. The mushroomed .40-caliber slug was still embedded in the layers of Kevlar. I dug it out and pitched it across the room.

When Conor helped me off with my shirt, I found a bull's-eye-like bruise the size of a grapefruit under my left breast—a swirl of dark crimson around a black, fingernail-sized spot of dried blood.

"Oy, that's a nasty bruise," Conor said, kneeling down shirtless in front of me. A similar bruise darkened his upper chest. "How's mine?"

"Ugly. How's it feel?"

"Hurts, but don't think it broke anything. A twenty-two doesn't do near the damage of a forty cal at point-blank range."

"Tell me about it."

He held out the rolled ACE bandage. "Ya want me to wrap your chest?"

I shook my head. "Rather not."

"Suit yourself." He set it on a nearby table. "If ya change your mind, let me know."

"Good thing it was a twenty-two rifle," I mumbled, remembering my shock when he'd been shot. "Most hunting rounds go through Kevlar like butter."

"Aye! Suppose we should count our lucky stars."

"Too tired to count. Just want sleep." I lay on the bed, my head swimming with the beer. Our confrontation with Holly and the Delgados played on a loop in my mind, mixed with horrific scenes from Conor's confession. I tried to will it all to turn out differently. It never did. Somewhere in the early hours, I drifted into a restless sleep.

46

———————

I woke around nine the next morning to the aroma of fresh coffee drifting up from the kitchen. It took me a few minutes to get my bearings. Log cabin. Middle of fucking nowhere. I hated waking up in a strange bed.

My mouth was dry as cotton. My head felt achy and hungover. My rib cage burned, but breathing seemed easier. Maybe I hadn't broken a rib after all. Still, it was another morning without my hormones. God help whoever got in my way. I was out for blood.

I pulled myself into a seated position. My clothes and gear lay in a pile in the corner of the dimly lit loft. I had only the vaguest memory of taking them off. Too much beer, no doubt. I remembered Conor's confession, and the empty, unsettled feelings returned.

I shuffled down the stairs, wearing only my shirt and underwear, following the savory aromas of breakfast. Conor stood over the stove, cooking.

"Morning, love. How ya feeling?"

"Like I lost a fight to a heavyweight champion." I leaned my head on his shoulder, clinging to the memory of the man I thought I knew.

"Hungry? Managed to scrounge some eggs and bacon. Coffee's by the sink."

"That'd be great. Thanks." I didn't have much of an appetite, but I needed the fuel if we were going to catch Holly. I kissed him on the ear and sat at the table. "Any ideas on getting out of this little prison in paradise?"

"Now that the sun's up, I'm hoping we can locate your keys. If not, we can break the window and hot-wire your lorry."

"It has a chipped key. Makes hot-wiring it a bit difficult."

"Ah, yeah. Not like the good old days, huh? When I was a lad in Ireland . . . never mind."

He brought over a plate with a couple of over-easy eggs, their yolks a pale pink. The bacon wasn't as crisp as I liked it, but I didn't complain. The coffee was strong and helped pull me out of my funk.

"After breakfast, I'll climb the hill," I said. "Try to get a phone signal."

He nodded as he lay into his own breakfast. "Sounds like a plan."

Fifteen minutes later, I pulled on my gear and stepped outside. The air was chilly and damp with the scent of evergreens. It felt good. Climbing the hill helped warm me up.

By the time I reached the summit, my heart was hammering in my chest, and I was gasping for breath as if I had just run a sprint. At six thousand feet above sea level, the air was quite a bit thinner than the low desert in Phoenix. My rib cage burned as I tried to avoid breathing too deeply.

I checked my phone. I had one bar of connectivity. The battery was at two percent, enough for one call. I was about to dial Becca when the phone rang. I tried to push it off to voicemail but hit the answer button by mistake. "Hello?"

"Ms. Ballou, I need an update," a very stern Sadie Levinson said. "We're down to the wire here. Do you have Holly Schwartz in custody?"

"Not exactly. We had her, but she gave us the slip."

"Again? I thought you were better than Fiddler."

"We are. I mean, I am. Unfortunately, she's got two guys helping her. But we'll bring her in. I swear it." I had no idea where Holly was, but I wasn't going to tell Sadie that.

"You keep saying 'we.' You're working with Conor, aren't you?"

"Yes, I'm working with Conor."

"After I specifically told you not to."

"Look, lady, you want this girl brought in or not?"

"Yes."

"Then let me do my job and leave my personnel choices to me."

"You want to split your bounty with Mr. Doyle, so be it. But unless Ms. Schwartz is in custody by the end of the day, I will no longer require your services. Are we cl—?"

The call ended. My phone was powering down. Out of juice. I hoped Conor hadn't used up all of his phone's battery while looking for the keys last night. I slogged back down the hill, shivering from the chill. If we couldn't find my keys, it would be a long-ass walk back to civilization.

I found Conor sitting on the cabin's front steps, my keys dangling from his index finger.

"Where'd you find them?" I asked.

"They landed in a patch of prickly pear. Managed to fish them out with a twig."

"Thank God! Now for the love of Xena, can we get the hell out of here? We have a fugitive to catch and not a helluva lot of time to do it. Sadie's about to have kittens over us not having Holly in custody."

"She called?"

"Just as I got to the top of the hill. My phone died in the middle of the conversation."

"No worries, love. I think I know where Holly may be headed."

47

———

"So where are we going?" I asked once I was again behind the wheel of the Gray Ghost, my phone plugged into the charger. The narrow, rutted dirt road was much easier to navigate in the daylight.

"When I was walking around to the back door before we made entry, I caught bits of the Delgados' conversation. They were talking about getting new IDs."

"They mention where from?"

"Picardo." Conor beamed.

Picardo was the top producer of fake IDs in Phoenix. No matter what the state or federal governments did to try to make passports, drivers' licenses, and other identification hack proof, Picardo somehow had a way to duplicate them.

Over the years, Conor had developed an arrangement with Picardo. He'd help us track down our fugitives who used his services, and we wouldn't turn him in to the law. So far it had worked well for everyone involved except our bail jumpers.

When we got back into Prescott and within range of cell towers, my phone rang. Kirsten. Shit! The meeting with the FBI. I sent it to voicemail and looked over at Conor. "We're going to be in big shit, dude."

Conor nodded and placed a call of his own. When he hung up, he said, "Good news. Picardo says a woman and a man matching Holly and Richie's description showed up at his place this morning, asking for two complete sets of IDs. Passports, credit cards, birth certificates, drivers' licenses, and a digital paper trail to boot. New names are David and Olivia García. They're due to pick up the new IDs day after tomorrow."

"Day after tomorrow? That's no good. We need them today, or the bond defaults."

"That's what I told Picardo. He'll see if he can get them in this afternoon."

I stared out at the serene hilly grassland around us, which contrasted with the maelstrom of concerns and emotions battering my psyche. Losing out on this bounty now seemed the least of our worries. Missing this meeting with the feds could mean charges and prison. For a trans woman, that could easily be a death sentence. It could also mean they'd discover Conor's true identity and deport him overseas. While I was still wrestling with my thoughts on his past, I wasn't ready to lose him.

By one o'clock, we were hitting the outskirts of metro Phoenix. Conor's phone rang. He spoke to the caller for a few minutes and hung up.

"Picardo talked to Richie. Told them he bumped them up on the schedule. They'll be at Picardo's at three."

"Think they'll suspect a setup?"

Conor shrugged. "With these people, I don't know what to think. Holly's a clever girl, no doubt. But they're desperate. Ya heard them in the cabin."

I glanced at the clock. "Three o'clock gives us two hours. I could really use a shower and a change of clothes."

"You and me both."

Traffic was light coming down the Black Canyon Freeway, though it slowed when we reached Glendale Avenue. I turned off onto Thomas Road a few exits later. When I pulled up in front of my house, my phone rang. It was Becca.

"You get your fugitive?" she asked.

"Not yet," I replied. "But we're closing in."

"I've been tracking credit cards belonging to your buddy, Christopher Delgado."

"And?"

"He just bought a bunch of tickets."

"What kind of tickets?"

"Multiple plane tickets, train tickets, and bus tickets. Nearly twenty total. All in pairs in the name of David and Olivia García, each leaving from Phoenix but going to different destinations."

"Why different destinations?" I thought about it a second. "He's trying to throw us off the trail."

"That would be my guess. They're harder to catch if you don't know where they're going."

"What are the destinations?"

"Plane flights are headed to Honduras, New York, and Toronto. Train tickets show destinations as Dallas, Philly, and DC. Buses are headed to El Paso, Salt Lake City, and San Ysidro, California."

"Clever, but not clever enough. They're planning to pick up fake IDs at Picardo's at three. Conor and I will be there when they do."

"So my search was a waste of time."

"Not at all. It just confirms my suspicions. I was afraid they'd be on to us. But since they put the tickets in their fake names, it tells me that everything's going according to plan. Our plan, that is, not theirs. I'll be in touch soon."

After a shower, my head felt clearer than it had in days. Conor wrapped an ACE bandage around my chest after the pain worsened. As I watched him stretch the bandage around me, I decided that knowing his past didn't change anything for me. We were two imperfect people with past lives we'd rather forget. Sometimes we treated each other kinda shitty, even taking the other for granted. But I, for one, still wanted him in my life.

"That too tight?"

I took a breath and grimaced as my rib cage pressed against the bandage. "No, that's good. Thanks."

"We good?" He gave me that wounded-puppy-dog look.

I took him in my arms and kissed him. "We're good."

From my place, we headed over to Conor's bunker so he could replace the Glock he'd lost in Prescott. From the mini-arsenal in his walk-in closet, he opted for a Smith & Wesson .44 Magnum. He was always a Dirty Harry fan, and we were both in a Dirty Harry kind of mood. We then hit the road toward Picardo's.

Picardo lived in a nice house in east Phoenix, not far from the Papago Buttes, a cluster of wind-carved sandstone hills. We ran into a wall of traffic on the I-10 between the Deck Park Tunnel and the Loop 202 turnoff thanks to a four-car pileup blocking two lanes. It was three thirty by the time I parked the Gray Ghost a couple of doors down from Picardo's.

I grabbed the sawed-off shotgun, Conor the TEC-9, and we charged down the street, hoping not to draw too much attention from neighbors. I pounded on the door only to find it unlatched.

"That can't be good," I said.

"Picardo?" Conor pushed past me and stepped inside, his TEC-9 raised. I followed, ready for anything.

Picardo, a skinny Latino, lay on the dining room floor. The side of his face was smeared with blood. His bottle-thick glasses were askew.

Conor checked his pulse. "He's alive." Conor shook him. "Hey, Picardo. Wakey, wakey!"

The skinny man groaned and winced, straining his eyes to open. "What? Where am I?"

"You're at your place, mate. What happened?"

We helped Picardo into a chair. "Y'all are late." He glared at us.

"We got delayed," I said. "Major accident on the highway. Where's our fugitive?"

"Gone."

"Shit!" I grabbed a small towel from his kitchen and handed it to him. "How long ago did they leave?"

"I dunno." He pressed the towel to his head and glanced at his watch. "Maybe twenty minutes ago. When I told them their IDs weren't finished, they demanded their money back. They weren't thrilled about my no-refund policy. That was when the chick punched me. I swear, for a little thing, she packs a wallop."

"Any idea where they went from here?" I asked.

"How the hell should I know? You know, not being able to deliver as promised isn't good for business."

"Relax, mate. You got paid fifty percent on a job you didn't even have to deliver on. That's something."

Picardo didn't look pleased. He patted his back pocket. "Shit! Wallet's gone. I had nearly a grand in there. Dammit to hell."

My phone rang. It was Becca. "One of the phones you have me tracking? Just made a call to Tijuana."

"Any idea who in TJ they were calling?" I asked. "Or where they were when they called?"

"No idea who was on the other end. At the time of the call, they were on McDowell and Fifty-Second Street heading east, but then the phone went offline again."

"No worries. I know where they're heading. Thanks for the update, Becks!"

I hung up and grabbed Conor. "We got to get to the bus station."

"Hey, wait a minute!" Picardo grumbled. "What about me?"

"Oh, you want to come too?" Conor asked with a smirk as he and I rushed to the front door.

"I did y'all a solid, and your fugitives beat me up and robbed me. I think some compensation's in order."

"Have to settle up later, mate." Conor slammed the door behind him.

I could still hear Picardo shouting from inside his house as we scrambled into the Gray Ghost.

I had to hand it to the Delgados. Booking multiple tickets going to multiple destinations via multiple forms of transportation was clever. But calling someone down in Tijuana gave them away. One of the bus tickets was for San Ysidro, California, just this side of the border from Tijuana. If we could catch them at the Greyhound station before the bus left, we could grab Holly.

48

The Greyhound station was just the other side of Sky Harbor International Airport, which wasn't far from Picardo's. Unfortunately, when we reached the station, the parking lot was near capacity.

I pulled up to the passenger drop-off area and turned to Conor. "I'm running in. You find a parking space." I removed the Glocks and the shoulder rig as well as my Ruger and the Rossi revolver, as weapons were banned inside the bus station.

Conor didn't look pleased that I was leaving him with the job of finding a parking space, but he didn't argue, either. By the time he pulled away from the curb, I'd stepped inside the glass doors and surveyed the bustling terminal.

People swarmed in all directions, like ants after someone kicked their nest. Many wore sports jerseys I didn't recognize. I wondered if a soccer tournament was in town. I wasn't a fan myself, but the sport was very popular in the Latino community. Just my luck that Holly picked this time to get the hell out of Dodge.

I hustled to where an overhead schedule of departures was displayed near the ticket counter. The bus bound for San Ysidro was due to leave in ten minutes from Gate Four. Great. So where the hell was Gate Four?

As I glanced around looking for signs directing me to the right gate, I spotted a familiar petite figure with bristly dark hair walking down the corridor, dragging two large suitcases. I pushed my way through the press of people, getting angry glances and obscenities muttered in Spanish and English.

When she was in reach, I grabbed her by the back of the collar and drove her hard to the floor. "Gotcha this time. Holly Schwartz, you're under arrest."

She yelled and squirmed under me. "*¡Ayudeme!* Security! Help!"

As I reached for my handcuffs, I realized the voice was deeper and strongly accented. I turned her over. It wasn't Holly. The woman was Latina, probably in her midforties.

"Aw, shit." I was tempted to help her up, but two Phoenix police officers were working their way through the crowd, headed in my direction.

"Sorry," I muttered and took off running toward the gate.

I was just passing Gate Five when I spotted Chris Delgado leaning against the wall, talking on a cellphone. I grabbed him by the front of the collar. "Where is she, asshole?"

His eyes grew wide. "You're alive?"

I leaned into him. "Tell me where Holly is, or you won't be."

He pushed me away and straightened his shirt. "Gone where you can't reach her."

"She's a fugitive, wanted for murder. You realize helping a fugitive is a felony, right?"

"What are you going to do? Arrest me? You're not a cop. You're just a pathetic little bounty hunter."

Over the PA system came the announcement, "Last call for Bus Number 534 for San Ysidro, California, Gate Four."

The sign for Gate Four caught my eye. I was about to rush toward it when a hand gripped my shoulder. "Excuse me, ma'am."

I turned to see one of the uniforms with a stern expression on his face. "Did you assault this woman?"

The other uniform was standing with the woman I had mistaken for Holly. The two of them blocked my access to Gate Four.

Meanwhile, Chris Delgado nonchalantly disappeared into the crowd, giving me a little fuck-you wave and blowing me a kiss. I didn't have time for this. I had a skip to catch.

I pivoted out of the one cop's grip and bolted back toward the terminal's main entrance, ignoring all commands to stop. I bobbed and weaved through the swarm of people, using all of my parkour skills.

I vaulted over benches and leapt through the narrowest gaps between clusters of impatient passengers. Unfortunately, I was getting farther and farther from the gate. I dodged a heavyset man gazing at a map. Bounded over a cluster of toddlers herded by a frazzled-looking woman. Zipped down the railing of a short flight of stairs. Leapt atop a bank of pay phones and grabbed hold of the overhead sign to swing over a dozen or so people. Skidded underneath the zigzag queue lines of passengers waiting at the ticket counter and jumped over it, ricocheted off the back wall, then rolled to my right and into the back personnel area.

Uniformed employees gave me quizzical looks as I raced past offices, pushed through a door, and burst into the bright sunlight. I looked around. To my left were a string of buses side-by-side in various stages of boarding and unboarding. To my immediate right was a large green dumpster. Beyond that stood the fueling bays for the buses.

From the other side of the door came the sounds of shouting and leather soles slapping tile. I heaved the dumpster in front of the door, its wheels squealing in protest, then took off running toward the buses, in hopes of catching the one bound for San Ysidro.

I pushed past people waiting to board while also glancing at the digital destination signs on the front of the buses. Tucson. Los

Angeles. Albuquerque. A bus slowly backed away from the building. It had to be the San Ysidro bus. Crap!

Behind me, I heard the cops shouting for me to stop. The dumpster must not have been much of an obstacle after all. I grabbed the side mirror of the nearest bus and swung onto its roof. From there, I vaulted across to the bus next to it and the two next to that one.

The San Ysidro bus was still pulling away from the gate. I poured on speed, sprinting the length of the bus I was on, and leapt with all my might across the twenty-foot gap. For an instant, I was soaring. And then the roof of the San Ysidro bus flew at me with blinding speed.

I landed hard on the roof, my legs smacking the side windows. My chest exploded in pain. I felt myself starting to slide off. I slapped my hands flat on the scorching-hot sheet metal. Somehow I got purchase in a ridge, while my boots pushed off the top edge of a window. Ignoring the agony of my torso, I dragged my body onto the roof, even as the bus itself maneuvered out of the terminal lot and onto the surface streets.

As the wind speed blowing across my face increased, my eyes began to water. I shimmied to one of the roof hatches that served as both an emergency exit and a vent. Try as I might, I couldn't open it from the outside. I had nothing to use as a pry bar. What the hell was I thinking?

With one hand clinging to the hatch, I pulled out my phone with the other and called Conor.

"Where are ya, love? Ya sound like you're in a wind tunnel."

"On the San Ysidro bus," I said through clenched teeth, doing my best to ignore the pain.

"Ya got her in custody?"

"No, I'm on top of the bus. Pulling onto the I-10 as we speak."

"Did you say you're on top of the bus?"

"Yes. For the moment, anyway."

"Hold on, Jinxie! I'm on my way."

I put away my phone and began pounding on the roof with

my free hand. Cars around me were honking. When the I-10 turned west near the Loop 202 interchange, my legs began to swing right toward the edge of the roof. I white-knuckled my two-handed grip on the roof hatch, desperately hoping not to slide off into early rush hour traffic.

When the bus straightened again, I resumed my pounding with my last remaining strength. As we approached the Deck Park Tunnel, I pressed myself flat against the roof of the bus, terrified I'd get swept off by the roof of the tunnel. I heard the whoosh of cross supports breezing past just above my head.

When we reemerged into daylight, the bus moved left into the carpool lane and began picking up speed. The wind became a roar in my ears. I wanted to continue pounding, but it was all I could do to hang on.

After what felt like an eternity, I heard the shrill scream of police sirens. At first I thought it might be just the wind whistling in my ears. But then the bus began to slow, changing lanes to the right until we pulled off onto the shoulder. In the distance I could see the signs for the Verrado Way exit. We were at the far reaches of the west valley, a few miles outside the Loop 303.

My heart thundered in my heaving chest. Sweat dripped down my forehead and burned my eyes. I was in a daze. I struggled to figure out a next move.

"What the hell you think you're doing, lady?" called a voice on the right side of the bus.

I crawled to the edge of the roof and swung down using the side mirror. The driver was an African-American woman with a name tag that read Flo.

"Trying to stop a murderer," I said between gulps of air. "My name is Jinx Ballou. Bail enforcement agent."

She raised an eyebrow. "A murderer? On my bus?"

I nodded. Flashing lights caught my eye. Two Phoenix PD cruisers had parked behind the bus. The unis emerged, weapons drawn. Flo pointed at me.

"Aw, shit."

I was grabbed by an officer a few years older than me with a cheesy Magnum PI mustache. He threw me to the ground and cuffed me. "You're under arrest for trespassing and assault."

"Get off me! I'm a bail enforcement agent! I have a fugitive who skipped bail on a murder charge on that bus." I pointed my head in the direction of the bus. "You really want to let a murderer escape justice?"

Officer Magnum lifted me to my feet and glanced at my Kevlar vest. "Do you have proof to back up your story?"

"If you uncuff me." I twisted around and held out my cuffed hands.

Magnum removed the handcuffs. I showed him my ID as a licensed bail enforcement agent.

"Who's your fugitive?"

"Holly Schwartz. Murdered her mother. She has an accomplice on board too—a guy named Richie Delgado."

Another uniform showed up just as I noticed the Gray Ghost pulling off behind the farthest patrol car.

49
———

"You know what she looks like?" Magnum asked.

I pulled out my phone and showed her photo. "Her hair's been buzzed short since this photo."

Conor walked up, and I introduced him to the two officers. Once we'd established our bona fides, the driver escorted us on board.

I'd never been on a cross-country bus before, and I was honestly impressed. It was a lot nicer than the rattling hunk of junk that used to take my classmates and me to elementary school.

I crept down the aisle, scanning the faces, but didn't see Holly or Richie. Had they actually boarded, or was this whole thing another ruse by Christopher to throw us off the trail? I was almost to the back of the bus when I noticed a couple of empty seats in the otherwise filled bus. I ducked down and spotted Holly trying to hide under the bench seat.

She darted out, quick as a bunny, slamming into the rear emergency exit. She was still fumbling with the mechanism to open it when I grabbed her.

"No!" she said, twisting and swinging and punching like a maniac. "No, you're not taking me back. No, no, no!"

There wasn't a lot of room to grapple. In the struggle, she kicked the back door open, and an alarm sounded. I wrapped her in a bear hug. She tried to bite me, and I spun her around, pinned her to the floor in the aisle, and cuffed her.

"Stop it, Holly. I don't want to hurt you."

"No, I can't go back to jail. Please don't do this to me."

I nearly lost my grip on Holly when someone grabbed my ponytail and started pulling. I turned and ducked just in time to dodge a blow from Richie. Conor grabbed him and tackled him to the floor, then turned him over to one of the officers.

Richie cried out as the cop dragged him to the front of the bus. "Leave her alone! It's not her fault."

"Get him out of here." I turned my attention back to Holly, who continued to scream and struggle. "Settle down!"

"Please, please don't send me back to jail. I'm just a kid. She was killing me." She bawled and howled like a toddler who'd been told that her beloved kitten was dead.

As mad as I was for all the shit she'd put me through, it got to me. She might have been almost eighteen, but in so many ways she was still a frightened kid, robbed of her childhood by a deranged mother.

"Settle down. I know you don't want to go back to jail. But maybe I can help you if you cooperate."

She stopped struggling. "How?"

"I got a really good lawyer. She's offered to help you. Maybe she'll let you plead self-defense." Hell, the girl had convinced me. Who was to say she couldn't sway a jury?

"I ain't got no money. Spent all I had on the fake IDs we never got."

"That the money that was stashed in your mom's bathroom?" I asked, remembering the money machine.

"How'd you know about that?"

"Call it an educated guess."

"She had about ten thousand. But it's gone now."

"Well, you're in luck. My lawyer's agreed to take your case pro bono." She certainly never did that with mine, unfortunately.

"What's that mean?"

"Means you don't have to pay. But only if you come along quietly back to jail."

She let out a deep breath, like a punctured tire. "All right. What about Richie?"

"I'm afraid Richie's got problems of his own. At the very least, for assaulting me in that hotel room. Possibly for harboring a fugitive."

"He was just trying to help me." She started bawling again.

"Hey! Enough with the waterworks. Nothing I can do. Now you coming along peacefully or not?"

She nodded.

I helped her to her feet while the passengers looked on among whispers of "Who is she?" "What'd she do?" and "She one of them illegals?"

Conor was waiting for me outside along with a cluster of Phoenix PD officers.

"Come on," I told her, nudging her toward the Gray Ghost. "It'll all work out."

I thanked the officers and got Holly buckled into the backseat of the Gray Ghost. I climbed behind the wheel with Conor in the passenger seat next to me and pulled onto the Verrado Way exit to get turned around toward Phoenix. Rush hour traffic was starting to pick up. Fortunately, the majority of vehicles were going the other way.

A few miles before we reached the Loop 101, I heard some honking and a roaring engine behind us. I noticed a familiar Hummer in my rearview mirror, bearing down on us and driving aggressively.

"What the hell?" At first I thought it was a typical aggressive Phoenix driver. Then it clicked. "Shit! It's Fiddler."

Conor whipped around and looked. "How the hell'd he find us?"

"Beats the hell out of me, and I don't intend to ask him." I pressed harder on the accelerator.

"Who's Fiddler?" a very nervous Holly asked.

"The bounty hunter originally assigned to pick you up."

"Him?" she whimpered. "He's a psycho."

"Won't argue with you on that." I spared a glance in the mirror. He was barreling into us from behind, apparently trying to ram us. "Everybody hold on."

I jammed the accelerator to the floor and started weaving through the traffic as best I could without rolling the Ghost. We had a lot of power but not the wide wheelbase that Fiddler's Hummer had. Our best chance was to outrun him. But even with the lighter inbound traffic, there were enough cars to make maneuvering around them tricky.

I got caught behind a slow-moving Caddy. All the other cars were maneuvering around it, making it impossible for me to pass. The Hummer slammed into the Gray Ghost's rear bumper. My seat belt grabbed hard, making me wince in pain.

"Fuck!" I cut off a Corvette trying to pass the Caddy. The Corvette driver flipped me off. I didn't care.

I squeezed through narrow gaps between vehicles until I reached the HOV lane, which was clear for the next mile or so. I slammed on the gas, and the speedometer rose. Ninety. A hundred. One ten. I prayed that no one in the lane to our right pulled in front of us. I continued to floor it. One twenty. One thirty. We were in the redline now, but the Hummer stayed on our tail.

We were rapidly closing in on a cluster of cars driving at a reasonable rate of speed.

"Jinx, you got cars coming up."

"I see them." I didn't slow down, too busy looking for a gap on the right to maneuver around them. But there wasn't one.

"Jinxie . . ."

"Yeah, yeah." At the last second, I jerked the Gray Ghost onto the shoulder, sending up a cloud of gravel and dust behind us, nearly tipping us. The right wheels slammed down again as we blew past the slower cars. When the HOV lane was clear again, I pulled back onto the road.

"Good God, woman, this isn't NASCAR."

"No, I call it survival. He still behind us?" I studied the traffic ahead. We were approaching the I-17 interchange and an impenetrable wall of cars.

"Don't see him," Conor said.

I breathed a sigh of relief, mentally patting myself on my back for my fast and furious mad skills.

"No, wait. Shite! The bugger's still on our tail."

I spotted a gap in the cars in the regular lanes and pulled in, then I continued to push my way to the right, hoping he'd lose track of us. In the process of squeezing between cars, I swapped paint with a few of them.

We were in the center lane when the Hummer pulled alongside of us and rolled down the passenger window. I caught the black dot of a gun barrel and a flash just as I was showered in broken glass. I instinctively jerked the wheel right, then slammed on the brakes to avoid colliding with a semi stopped in front of us.

"Everybody okay?" I asked. I took a quick inventory of myself. I was in shock from the blast but wasn't shot. I glanced around us and didn't see the Hummer.

"I'm okay," Conor said. "You're bleeding on the side of your face."

I wiped my face, and my hand came away wet with blood. "It's from the glass. I'll live."

"Holly? You still with us?" I looked in the backseat. Holly was bent over at the waist, not making any sounds. "You okay?"

She didn't move or say anything. Since I had my seat belt on, I couldn't reach her. With the traffic at a standstill and no sign of

Fiddler's Hummer, I hopped out and opened the back door. I shook Holly.

She groaned and sat up. "What happened?" Her eyes were dilated.

"Fiddler shot out my window. But he's gone." I searched her for signs of injury but didn't find any.

"She okay?" Conor asked, looking back at her.

"I think she may be in shock."

"We'll deal with it at the jail, love. Traffic's moving again."

A car honked and slipped past me. I closed Holly's door and found myself face-to-face with Fiddler pointing a .38-caliber revolver at me. "Give 'er to me, you goddamned freak."

50

———————

"Oy! Ya bloody wanker!" Conor called from the passenger seat. "You hurt her, I'll fuckin' end ya!"

Fiddler pulled out a compact semiautomatic with his left hand and aimed it at Conor. "Keep talking, smart-ass! I'll put a hole in her head and then yours."

"You really are an asshole, Fiddler," I said, staring past the gaping barrel in my face, my pulse racing. I thought about trying to disarm him, but he was far enough away that he would pull the trigger before I reached him.

"Just want what's rightfully mine. This was my case."

"We apprehended her. She's ours."

His trigger finger tightened.

"Whoa!" I held up my hands. "Fine. You can have her."

"No funny business, Ballou."

I reopened Holly's door. "What's going on?" she asked in a terror-filled voice.

I released her seat belt and grimaced. "Sorry, kiddo, but looks like you're going with Fiddler."

"What? No."

"Don't worry. You'll be okay. He'll take you down to the jail instead of us. He won't hurt you." I hoped. At this point, anything was possible. But if Fiddler wanted to get paid, he'd have to get Holly checked into custody unharmed.

I helped Holly out of the truck and handed her over to Fiddler. He holstered one of the pistols and grabbed her by the back of the collar.

I glared at him. "You're going to regret this, douchebag."

"Oooh, I'm trembling," he said with a sneer. "You two faggots think you're so clever. But no one beats Fiddler. Where's her paperwork?"

"It's in the console."

"Well, fucking hand it over. And so help me, if you try anything . . . "

"Just keep your pants on." I leaned inside the front seat. As I did, Conor showed me the gun in his hand. He offered it to me grip first.

"Not worth the risk," I whispered. "Best just to let him have her."

I grabbed the folder and handed it to Fiddler. "Holly, do as he says, and everything'll be fine. I'll call my lawyer and let her know where you are."

He aimed the compact pistol at the Gray Ghost's left front tire and fired off two rounds. Holly screamed and dropped to her knees.

Fiddler kicked her. "Get up, you little cunt."

Holly obeyed, giving me a final glance, as if she were going to her execution. The two of them disappeared into a shifting tableau of cars driven by rage-filled drivers.

"Jesus, Mary, and Joseph, I swear I'm gonna wreck that guy," Conor said as I climbed back into the driver's seat.

"Going to have to get in line behind me."

I started the engine and pulled off onto the shoulder. The front tire hissed as the last of the air escaped.

A half hour later, I had the spare on. It would've been too easy to forget about Holly and let her take her chances with the legal system and the lawyer her aunt hired, but I felt responsible for her. Maybe it was my lack of hormones. I would call Kirsten when I got home to let her know Holly was in custody.

Conor agreed to drive us back to his place, while I used the first aid kit in the glove box to treat the cuts on my face and arm from the broken glass. On the outside I appeared calm, but on the inside, a tempest was brewing. I was counting on that bounty.

What would Sadie say when she learned what happened? Would she believe me or Fiddler? Who would she hire in the future? Maybe it was time to get my PI license and expand my options. But the thought of taking photos of cheating spouses for a living was as appealing as eating a bowl of cat turds.

My father was always telling me to trust the process, but I never understood what he meant by that. Whenever I pressed him, he gave me a lot of abstract nonsense answers. What process? The process by which the rich and powerful screwed the rest of us?

As we pulled onto the Seventh Avenue exit into downtown Phoenix, my phone dinged from a text. I opened it.

Oh, my dearest Jinx,

I have a lovely surprise for you! One I know you will appreciate. More soon.

Warmest regards,

Milo

Chills ran down my spine. "Fuck!"

"What's wrong, love?" Conor shot me a concerned look.

"Fucking Volkov's sending me messages again."

"Jesus Christ! Why doesn't that bloke just bugger off! What'd he say this time?"

"He's got another surprise for me." I noticed my hand was

trembling as a chill ran down my spine. Holly! "Drive to the Madison Street Jail!"

"What? Why? You can't get a body receipt if Fiddler's returning her to custody."

"I have a bad feeling."

Conor turned around and drove to the garage next to the jail. We walked in and showed our identification to Sergeant O'Brien, an old friend who was working the intake desk.

"Evening, Ms. Ballou, Mr. Doyle. How can I help you two this sultry summer evening?" the desk sergeant asked.

"I want to make sure Holly Schwartz was returned to custody. Fiddler . . ." I resisted the urge to spit. "Fiddler should have brought her a little while ago."

He crinkled his brow and began typing on his computer keyboard. "I'm sorry. No Holly Schwartz here. And haven't seen Fiddler today."

My heart sank. "Are you sure?" *Why would Fiddler take her to Volkov instead of here? Would Volkov pay him more than the bounty was worth?*

"Sorry, Jinx. Maybe he took her to the detention facility up on Dunlap by mistake." O'Brien clicked a few times with his mouse. "Nope. Not there, either. Honestly, I think that Fiddler fella is starting to slip."

"Bollocks! I knew that bastard was up to no good," Conor said. "Ya shoulda plugged 'im when ya had the chance, love."

"Maybe he stopped for a bite on the way," O'Brien suggested.

"Thanks anyway, O'Brien."

"Y'all have a good night."

As we were crossing over the street to the parking garage, my phone rang. The number wasn't one I recognized. "This is Jinx Ballou. Can I help you?"

"Ah, Ms. Ballou. What a pleasure to hear your voice at last." The caller was male, his voice resonant and slightly accented. Eastern Europe by way of London, perhaps?

"Who the fuck is this?" But I knew the answer before I even asked.

"Someone who has a lovely surprise for you."

My heart leapt into my throat. "What the hell do you want, Volkov?"

51

———

"**I** believe you are acquainted with one of my associates. A gentleman who goes by the moniker Fiddler."

"Fiddler works for you?" I could have spit nails. Was this how he tracked me down? None of this was making sense.

"Over the years he's performed a number of tasks. But between you and me, I've been less than impressed with his performance of late. So unreliable. He takes that medical marijuana for his cancer. I think it has made his mind mush."

"Is there a fucking point to this phone call?"

"Why, yes, there is." He chuckled. The sound of it made my skin crawl. "I'd like to offer you a job."

"A job? Doing what? Working as one of your sex slaves? No, thanks!"

"Oh heavens, no! You are far too talented in other areas, though I do think you and I could have so much fun pleasuring each other. Tell me, do you still have your cock? You never did say."

"Fuck you! I'm hanging up now."

"Oh, I wouldn't if I were you." His voice became cold steel.

"What do you want?"

"By busting into my facility some nights ago, you exposed an FBI sting attempting to infiltrate my organization. For this, I am immensely grateful. I'm also impressed with how well you handle yourself. I could use someone with your skill set to handle certain tasks for me."

"What makes you think that I would consider working for a fucking flesh peddler like you?"

"A fair question. In a word, leverage. I understand you apprehended a fugitive by the name of Holly Schwartz earlier today."

"Yeah, what of it?" I grew from being annoyed to genuinely concerned.

"Except Fiddler took her from you. Such a dishonorable thing to do. Was your truck damaged much?"

"Never you mind."

"Since Fiddler works for me and I am very interested in meeting with you, I picked them both up. So now I have her for you to pick up and take to the jail and collect your bounty. Pretty hefty one, so I've heard. What was it? Fifty grand?"

"Yeah." My heart thundered in my chest.

"So here's my generous offer to you. You come to work for me, for which I will compensate you generously. And I turn this poor girl over to you, and you collect the fifty grand. And you're still free to do your bounty hunting so long as it doesn't interfere with any of my operations. It's a win-win."

"Not interested. And if you dare hurt one hair on Holly's head—"

"I'll even throw in a little signing bonus," he continued. "I understand those FBI agents who infiltrated my outfit are causing you some trouble. Something about interfering with a federal investigation or some nonsense."

"What about it?"

"Those charges hinge on the testimony of those two agents, yes?"

"Maybe. Why do you care?"

I heard muffled voices on the other end of the line, followed by two gunshots that nearly shattered my eardrum. "No more charges."

My jaw dropped. "What the fuck did you do?"

"I made your problem go away. See how generous I can be?"

Bile rose in my throat. I didn't want to believe he'd just executed those agents, but in my gut I knew he had. Still, I was not going to let his violence turn me into one of his goons. "You're a sick fuck, you know that?"

"Oh, my dearest Jinx, can't you see I did you a favor?"

"I will never work for you. I will make it my mission to hunt you down and bury you in a hole where no one will ever find you."

I heard a girl's pleading voice in the background. It was Holly's. "You really do not want to test my temper." His voice turned icy once again. "If you won't work for me, then I must make you reconsider."

"Come and get me, motherfucker. Meaner assholes than you have tried to kill me and failed."

"Oh, I will not kill you. But I will kill everyone you love. Your boyfriend. Your family. And every one of your friends. Also I certainly won't have need to keep this poor girl Holly alive any longer." Holly's screams intensified.

"Wait. Stop!" I begged.

"Yes? I'm listening."

"Can we meet to discuss this further?"

"But of course, my dear." Once again the delightful entrepreneur. "Nothing would give me more pleasure. But just you. Your friend, what's his name, Doyle? I have no interest in him. I just want you, my delicious tranny."

"The word's transgender, you goddamned piece of shit."

"Apologies. I don't care what you call yourself, so long as you are working for me."

Every cell in my body told me to tell him no. But I couldn't. I couldn't put my family or Conor or Becca or even Holly at risk. I had to find a way out of this. And in order to do that, I had to stall for time. "Fine. Where are you?"

"I'll have a driver pick you up from the corner of Central and Thomas. Next to the Indian statue. Thirty minutes"

"I'll be there."

"And Jinxie dear, I want you there alone. If my driver sees your man Doyle anywhere around or attempting to follow, he has orders to shoot you. Is that understood?"

"I understand."

"Excellent. I so look forward to meeting you."

52

———

I hung up, and Conor was giving me looks. "What the bloody hell was that about?"

"Volkov wants me to work for him."

"Fucking mother of Christ, Jinxie, you're not seriously considering working for that gobshite, are ya?"

"Not in a million years."

Relief washed over his face. "Thank the heavens above for that. I thought you'd lost your mind."

"But I am meeting with him."

"You what? Are you daft?"

"He's got Holly. And he just killed those two feds while I was on the phone with him."

"I don't care if he's about to shoot the bloody pope, you're not meeting with him. He'll put a bullet in you too. Or worse. The man's a complete nutter. I'm not letting you walk into that mess."

"If I don't at least meet with him, he'll go after my family and after you. I can't risk that." I sighed as I tried to formulate a strategy, but I had no idea where Volkov's driver would take me. "Maybe I'll get lucky and put him out of everyone's misery."

"Maybe ya hadn't noticed, love, but luck ain't been on our side lately."

"What do you expect me to do, Conor? Walk away? Pretend everything's hunky-dory? What happens when he goes after my family?"

"Why you?"

"Who knows? He's a sick fuck who apparently has a fetish for trans women. He also likes how I fight, supposedly. He thinks he's got me cowed. But he doesn't know the shit I've been through. I won't let him win."

"I can't let you walk into this shitstorm alone."

"His guy's picking me up from the corner of Thomas and Indian School by the code talker statue. If you try to tail him, he has orders to shoot me. But I've got a plan."

"What?"

"Track my phone. At a distance, so there's no way he can spot you. Stay at least a mile behind."

Conor and I stood there, our eyes locked. I understood his need to protect. But I couldn't let this go any further. I would save Holly if I could. I wouldn't give this asshole a chance to hurt my family.

"I don't like this, love. Too many things can go wrong."

"I know."

"But you're gonna do what you're gonna do regardless of what I say."

"Damn straight I am."

"Then I'll follow your plan, because I don't know what else to do. Just stay alive long enough for me to show up."

"So you can come riding up on your white horse and rescue me?" A sad grin curled the corners of my mouth. I patted his chest. "You're cute when you're trying to be noble."

Conor dropped me off at the corner of Thomas and Indian School with five minutes to spare. I was grateful the sun had gone down, but even at seven o'clock in the evening, the temperature was still in the triple digits and would be until almost midnight.

Especially around the center of town. The day's heat clung to the concrete jungle like water to a sponge.

Conor had wanted me to at least wear a ballistic vest, but I chose not to. Odds were Volkov or his driver would force me to remove it, anyway. It also made it tougher to move around as freely as I liked. I needed the flexibility if I was going to survive.

Right at seven, a black Escalade pulled up and stopped at the curb, much to the frustration of the drivers behind it. The back door opened, and a burly meathead of a guy stepped out.

"You Jinx Ballou?" he asked.

"Yeah."

He patted me down, getting a little friskier than I liked around my breasts and between my legs. I guess he couldn't be too careful. Surprisingly, he let me keep my phone and wallet. "Get in."

I did so and found myself wedged between him and another guy. They were all dressed in black suits. All sporting shoulder rigs with large pistols.

As soon as the Escalade was in motion again, the slab of beef on my right slapped a black hood over my head. I protested, but they insisted it was Volkov's orders.

"Dude, we're on the same team."

They didn't answer.

I sat back and tried to follow where we were based on the sensations of movement and the muffled sounds outside. Despite my best efforts, I soon had no idea where we were, much less where we were headed. We could have been in north Phoenix or still downtown, or we could have been in one of the outlying suburbs. I hoped Conor was keeping enough distance so as not to be noticed.

When the truck finally stopped, I expected the hood to be removed. No such luck.

"Get out," Meathead One said.

"Can I at least take this stupid bag off my head? It's embarrassing."

"No."

I started to take it off, anyway. A strong grip crushed my upper arm. Something hard and metallic pressed against my temple.

"Don't," Meathead One said.

I raised my hand in surrender. "Fine. No need to get physical."

I was pulled out of the vehicle and struggled to gain my footing on the concrete slab beneath my feet. From the echoey sounds, I guessed we were in an underground garage.

We stopped walking. A moment later, a ding sounded, followed by the whoosh of an elevator door opening. I was pushed forward, then spun around as the doors closed. Unlike some elevators, there was no audible indication of the floors we were passing. Even if Conor found the building, his chances of finding where I was in the building were slim to none. As were my chances of surviving without agreeing to be Volkov's new play toy.

Another ding, and the doors whooshed open. Meathead One led me out.

We traipsed down a carpeted hallway. One of the meatheads knocked on a very solid-sounding door. It squeaked open, and I was led through a series of turns. Another door opened, and the bag was removed.

The meatheads walked out and closed the door as my eyes adjusted to the brightly lit office.

Volkov sat behind an antique wooden desk with his hands tented as we assessed each other. He looked to be in his sixties, though rather physically fit. He had a certain Hollywood-leading-actor look about him. He was clean shaven and dressed in a coal-gray suit with his tie loosened and the top button of his shirt undone.

An automatic pistol fixed with a silencer lay on one side of the desktop, a stack of folders and a laptop on the other. A familiar metallic scent hung in the air—the smell of blood. Either Volkov had peculiar taste in cologne, or this was where he'd shot special agents Gleeson and Velasco.

Behind him, a wide collection of books, framed photos, and knickknacks occupied a floor-to-ceiling bookshelf. On the opposite side of the room was another door with a sign that read Private.

A floor-to-ceiling window revealed a view of the Central corridor with the red lights atop South Mountain twinkling in the distance. I judged we must be about seven or eight floors up.

"We meet at last, Jinx Ballou," Volkov said, a wicked grin curling the corners of his mouth.

53

———————

"Funny, I thought you'd be taller." My mind was busy formulating a strategy. Assessing potential weapons, defenses, and tactics.

"Did you? And here I thought our first meeting would be more civil."

"Happy to disappoint."

A wry smile split his face. "My sweet, sweet Jinx, we could exchange barbs all evening. But I'd rather get down to business. And then later perhaps we can have some fun." The sudden zeal in his eyes unsettled me.

"Fine, let's talk business."

"You don't seem enthusiastic about my offer. Why?"

"For one, I don't like being threatened. Two, I don't like men who treat women like property. And three, I don't like your ugly face."

"Ah, back to exchanging insults. How droll." He picked up a folder from his desk. "Tell me, are you familiar with the name Liam Patrick O'Callaghan?"

I shrugged. "Should I be?" I wondered how much Volkov knew.

"I didn't think you were." He flipped through papers in the folder. "You see, you're not the only one I checked up on. I researched your Irish-born boyfriend as well. Very interesting history. Tragic, even. I think you'd be surprised."

I folded my arms. "If you brought me down here to annoy me with vague innuendos and boring conversation, maybe I should leave."

He slapped down the folder and picked up the pistol, aiming at me. "And how far do you think you'd get?"

I glared at him but held my tongue.

"I realize you think I'm a monster. But despite what you may have heard, the sex workers I bring into my employ are given a much better life than the abject poverty from whence they came."

"Oh really? So being endlessly raped and abused is better than being poor?"

"They are provided with excellent healthcare, for starters. Better than most laborers in this country of yours. Not to mention decent housing, fine clothing, and other niceties. All in all, it's a good life."

His tone and demeanor might have been convincing if I hadn't already known he was a lying sack of shit. But I played along, vying for my chance to turn the tables and successfully get Holly and myself to safety.

"So what exactly do you need me to do? What's the job?"

"For starters, I want you to help train my existing security personnel in some of those fancy moves you do. What is it? Taekwondo? Jujitsu?"

"Aikido and krav maga, actually. But I'm not an instructor."

"Considering what I'll be paying you, I'm sure you can come up with a training program. I also want you to consult with my director of security on how to better harden our holding locations. Like the one you and your colleague infiltrated. Clearly changes need to be made, and you are the ideal candidate."

I sat there holding his gaze, trying to appear to consider his offer. "Fine. I'm in."

He beamed. "Excellent. That's what I like to hear." He pressed a button on the phone. "Mr. Richardson, please bring in our other two guests."

The office door opened, and the meatheads shoved Holly and Fiddler into the room. Both had their hands bound behind them. The meatheads stood next to the door, their hands folded in front of them, clearly awaiting their boss's next order.

Holly's face was bruised and swollen. Her eyes were wild with fear. Fiddler just looked pissed.

"I assume you know these two people."

"Yeah."

"Then now is where the rubber meets the road." Volkov offered me the pistol grip-first. "If you are truly on the team, I want you to shoot Fiddler here. I know there's no love lost between the two of you. And honestly, he has outserved his usefulness."

Fiddler stepped forward. "Hey, now, I can still—"

"Silence!" Volkov barked.

"If I do as you ask, what happens to Holly?"

"Jinx, please, don't listen to him," Fiddler pleaded. Meathead One belted him in the gut. He doubled over, groaning.

"Holly will be put to work. Don't worry. No sex work. You have my word on that." An indulgent grin creased his face as he leered at her. "I wrote to you a while back. Saw you on the television with your mother. Everybody so inspired by this poor little crippled girl with the voice of an angel. But you were nothing but a fraud, weren't you? A fraud and now a murderer."

Holly just sobbed.

"Leave her alone."

"What? I'm just saying she has skills maybe we can put to use. Maybe she could be your apprentice, Ms. Ballou. Wouldn't that be a helluva thing. Two female assassins, taking out my enemies. Very sexy."

"I don't think so," I muttered. "Holly goes free to live her own life away from you."

"Your other option is to shoot Holly and let Fiddler live. But then if I keep him, I won't have much use for you, now will I?"

I held his gaze as I considered the pieces on the board. Moves. Countermoves. Risks. Sacrifices. I waited a breath, hoping Conor would come busting through the door with an army of cops. Didn't happen. Not that I was a Prince-Charming-saving-the-day kind of girl. And I was no Cinderella. More leather boots than glass slipper.

I took the offered pistol and immediately confirmed what I suspected. It felt light. I pressed the magazine release, caught the magazine, and slapped it on his desk. I then racked the slide, which locked back, revealing no round in the chamber, either. "What game are you playing, Volkov?"

Volkov burst out laughing. "Clever girl. See that, Richardson? This girl knows her stuff."

Meathead One, aka Richardson, shrugged, apparently unimpressed.

As Volkov launched into some self-indulgent monologue, I spun around and nailed Richardson in the head with the butt of the pistol. As he fell like a domino onto Meathead Two, I snagged the pistol from Richardson's shoulder rig. Meathead Two got off a shot that zinged past my ear. I put a round under his left eye and a second one just above it.

Holly screamed, but it was in the background of my consciousness. I turned toward Volkov, ducking behind the desk. I caught a glimpse of a gun barrel an instant before a shock of white-hot pain erupted in my left arm. I fell back against the wall, raised my pistol, and fired twice but only hit the desk and the laptop.

A section of the bookshelf swung inward then slid back into place.

"What the . . .?" I raced around the desk, forcing myself to ignore the pain in my arm. Volkov was gone. Asshole had a secret passage out of his office.

"Look out!" Holly screamed behind me. I turned and caught

Richardson raising a gun toward me. I put two in his chest and a third in his forehead.

I looked around the room. Fiddler was on the floor, blood pouring from a neck wound. His eyes were wide and glassy, his face pale. He wasn't moving or making any sounds. I turned to Holly, who was curled in a ball on the floor, shivering.

"Are you hit?" I searched her but saw no obvious wounds.

"I . . . I . . ." She dissolved into a sobbing mess.

I hugged her. "It's all right. You're safe."

I heard feet pounding on carpet, getting closer by the second. I was torn between fighting off these goons and going after Volkov. I stood up and opened the wooden door marked Private. It was a bathroom with a lock on it. "Holly, get in there and hide."

She remained on the floor, her arms wrapped around her legs, shaking like a leaf and moaning.

"Holly! Snap the hell out of it. Get in the goddamned bathroom!"

She looked up at me. "Why?"

I didn't have time to explain. I picked her up by the arm and practically tossed her inside the bathroom. When she reached for the light switch, I batted her hand away. "Leave it off. Lock the door. Don't open it until I come for you. Got it?"

She stood there shivering. Footsteps and voices were getting louder.

"Do you understand?"

She nodded. I closed the door and rushed across the room. I pushed against the concealed door in the bookshelf. It was stiff, but it gave way. I wedged it open with a book. Better to have the goons chasing after me than looking in the bathroom for Holly.

I entered the dimly lit corridor lined with metal studs holding up the drywall for the rooms on the other side. I had no idea where this passage went. For all I knew, Volkov was waiting to ambush me somewhere around a corner. But I was not going to let him get away.

54

I raced down the corridor, looking for exits, but didn't see any as it turned right, then left and came to a dead end. "What the hell?"

Had I missed something? I felt along the walls, looking for a hidden panel or release. Nothing. "Where the hell'd you go?"

The pain in my left arm grew more intense. I jammed the pistol I stole from Richardson in my waistband and looked at my arm. The flesh was torn. Blood dripped down the length of my arm onto the floor. But the wound appeared superficial. I looked around for something to put over the wound, but there was nothing.

My right hand pressed on the wound as my gaze drifted to a spattering of blood on the floor. I noticed an odd seam near my foot. A trapdoor. "Son of a bitch."

I found a hinged handle and pulled it up. A metal ladder disappeared into inky darkness. "In for a penny . . ." I kneeled down, trying not to put too much weight on my left arm. Not easy to do when descending a ladder.

My foot had reached a concrete slab floor when a bullet ricocheted off the metal rung just above my head. I dropped, rolled, and came up with the gun raised. I couldn't see shit. Another shot rang out and impacted the wall behind me. I fired two rounds in the direction of the muzzle flash and was rewarded with screams of pain.

I duckwalked toward Volkov, my eyes slowly adjusting to the dark. The light from the trapdoor above framed objects in the room. I bumped into a wall with my left shoulder and cursed as lightning bolts of pain shot through me, making me see stars.

"We could have been a hell of a team, Ms. Ballou," Volkov said, his voice gravelly and strained. He was wheezing.

Keeping my gun trained on my adversary, I flipped a light switch on the wall. "Happy to disappoint you."

I'd hit him on the left side of his chest. Probably penetrated his lung. Not his heart. I fixed that problem with two more bullets. He stopped wheezing. No use getting chatty with a piece of shit like him.

The numerous insulated pipes running down one side of the room told me I was in some type of mechanical room. A first aid kit mounted on the wall caught my eye. I popped it open, slapped a large nonstick pad on the wound, wrapped it in gauze, then tied it as best as I could with my teeth and one hand. I turned back to the ladder. I needed to get Holly safely out of the building.

I forced myself back up the ladder, grunting and grinding my teeth every time I had to use my left arm. As I raised my head through the floor above, a man in a Polo shirt and with a high-and-tight haircut trained his gun on me. I ducked just in time to avoid two shots that hit the trapdoor behind me. I drew my gun and blindly fired off a couple of shots. I was rewarded with return fire that nearly took off my hand. I pulled the trigger again and realized my gun was empty.

Grabbing Volkov's gun from his dead hand, I dropped to the floor and raced across the room. I killed the lights, trained my gun at the top of the ladder, and slowly approached the opening, peering up at the floor above. The goon appeared in the opening.

I put a round right up his nostril, splattering brains on the ceiling upstairs. He fell with a thud.

I hobbled up the ladder, grabbed his pistol, and raced down the passageway, reemerging into Volkov's office. It was empty. The bathroom door was ajar and riddled with bullet holes. Holly was gone. "Shit!"

A distant scream caught my attention. I hustled out of the office into a large room filled with a labyrinth of cubicles. On the far side of the room, a door was closing. Holly's screams continued until the door shut completely. I flew across the room, swung open the door, and found myself in a stairwell. Holly's cries echoed from below. I caught a glimpse of the man hustling Holly down the stairs a few floors below me.

When I raced after them, the man turned and fired a couple of rounds that ricocheted off the concrete walls. I kept along the outer wall as much as possible, but doing so slowed my pace. A sign at a landing revealed I was on the fourth floor. I'd never catch him at this rate. Time for something crazy. Or stupid. Whatever.

I launched myself at the center railing and began a controlled fall, bouncing from one rail across to another, screaming as jolts of pain shot through my left arm. The guy holding Holly came into view. He had a confused look on his face as I vaulted over the rail toward him. Before he could raise his weapon, I drove the heel of my right hand into his nose and used his body to cushion my landing. The back of his head smacked into the concrete wall with a sickening thud, leaving a smear of blood. I caught Holly as she started to tumble down the stairs. My left arm quivered with pain from the effort.

"You okay?" I asked Holly.

She looked at the dead guy beneath me. "He dead?"

I nodded. "Yeah. Are you hurt?"

"I don't think so." Her voice was small and fragile. She looked again like the girl on the telethons but without the big grin. "You going to send me back to jail?"

"Yeah."

She gazed absently at the man whose life force dripped onto the concrete steps. "Figures. Guess it can't be much worse than what I already been through."

"Hopefully my lawyer can help you get the charges dropped. Now let's see if we can find a way out of here."

We descended the stairs and emerged out a fire door marked with a warning that an alarm would sound if the door opened. It didn't. We found ourselves in a small parking lot. The Gray Ghost was parked in a handicapped parking space about twenty feet away. Conor stepped out.

Tempting as it was to rush Holly to jail and leave the carnage behind for someone else to discover, Conor and I opted to do the right thing and call 911 and then Kirsten. Within fifteen minutes, the surface parking lot was ablaze with flashing red, white, and blue lights. The Fourth of July had come early, though the real fireworks were thankfully over.

When Kirsten arrived, I gave an initial statement to the first officer on the scene, then again to Detective Hardin when he showed up a little while later. Holly was turned over, and I eventually got a body receipt. Kirsten seemed convinced she could get Holly's bail reset in the morning and return her to her aunt's custody.

At Conor's insistence, I agreed to let the EMTs transport me to the hospital to be treated for my gunshot wound and checked for broken ribs. To my surprise, he managed to overcome his hospital phobia and showed up at my bedside shortly after I was wheeled in. He looked agitated, as if he'd start climbing the walls any second.

"Damn, dude, you look as bad as I feel," I whispered, trying to keep my mind off everything that hurt.

"Well, I figured you'd taken on Milo Volkov all by your lonesome. Least I can do is show up at your hospital room."

The X-rays showed no broken bones, only bruised ribs. The gunshot wound would leave a nasty scar but would otherwise heal okay. By the time Conor and I arrived back at my place, it was after two in the morning.

55

At six the next morning, I called Becca and filled her in on everything—catching Holly, killing Volkov, and Conor's dark confession. She had been my confidante since middle school, so I knew she wouldn't tell anyone else about Conor's history. She was as shocked as I was.

"I don't know what to tell you, Jinx. It's a lot to digest."

"Tell me about it. I love him, but I'm still struggling with what he did. All those people."

"I hear ya. But as long as we've known him, he's been an upstanding guy. And he loves you with all his heart. That's not nothing."

"True, though I never thought I'd be dating a former terrorist wanted by British intelligence."

"It's a tough call. If it were me, I'd keep him. But you have to decide what you can live with."

"Thanks, Becks. I have a lot of thinking to do."

Conor and I didn't talk much after he got up. Just a polite but minimal greeting, swimming in a cesspool of awkwardness. I figured he was giving me time to process, for which I was grateful.

At nine, Conor and I showed up at Assurity Bail Bonds. When

we walked in Sadie's office, she didn't look happy to see us. Not even when I held up the body receipt time-stamped for the previous night at 11:50 p.m.

"I suppose you expect to get paid, even after I expressly forbid you from involving this no-good son of a bitch." She didn't so much as glance at Conor.

"Okay, flag on the play!" I leaned over Sadie's desk. "First of all, I would never have been able to apprehend Holly Schwartz had it not been for Conor."

"Oh, is that a fact?"

"Yes, it is. Secondly, I know about his involvement in the Omagh bombing."

Conor stared at his shoes.

"And you're okay with him murdering innocent civilians?"

"Hell no, I'm not okay with it. Just as I'm not okay with your father giving kickbacks to attorneys back when he ran your company."

Sadie fidgeted in her chair but said nothing.

I took a deep breath. "I'm trying to live in the present, let the past be the past, and give everybody a fresh start. And considering he helped me save you half a million dollars, maybe you can too."

Sadie sighed, straightened her blouse, and looked at Conor. "Very well, Ms. Ballou. A fresh start. I'm willing to give it a try."

"Thank you," Conor said quietly.

I held up the body receipt for Holly. "Excellent! Time to pay up. Fifty large. Cash, check, or charge."

Sadie pulled out her checkbook and began filling it out. "I must admit I wasn't sure you'd pull it off—apprehending Schwartz."

"It was touch and go for awhile. Especially when Volkov got involved."

Sadie's pen froze in midstroke. "Milo Volkov? The Russian gangster?"

"Chechen, technically, but he's not a problem. He's dead."

"Do I want to know the details?"

"You really don't." I took the check and slipped it into my pocket. "So what else have you got for us?"

"Us?" Sadie looked at Conor.

"Hey! Fresh start, remember?" I said.

"Very well." She opened a drawer and pulled out a few files. "These three have missed their court dates in the past week."

56

―――――

We left Assurity and dropped by the bank to deposit the check. I then did a bank transfer to Conor and to Becca for their cut of the bounty. Shortly afterward, I got a text from Becca thanking me and telling me she'd see me soon. But despite it being the middle of the week, I needed a day of some serious downtime.

Conor and I spent the next few hours at my place, catching up on some badly needed sleep and some serious couple time. After our second round of sex, I got up and made some margaritas, and we sat at my kitchen table.

"You still attracted to her?"

"Who? Sadie?" Conor scoffed. "Don't be daft!"

I couldn't help feeling insecure. It was always the comparison thing. "But she's cisgender, right? All original equipment?"

"Jesus, Mary, and Joseph, cisgender, transgender. It doesn't bloody mean a damn thing to me. I fell in love with you. I don't care what parts you used to have. I've only known you as Jinx. You're all girl as far as I'm concerned. As far as Sadie, she's part of my past. She doesn't hold a candle to ya. Ya got nothing to worry about."

"You think she's sexier than I am?"

"Are ya bloody kidding me? Even if she were, which she's not, it wouldn't make a damn bit of difference. You're my girl, Jinxie. There's no one I love more than you."

"Fair enough."

I spent the rest of the day reading up on the three cases Sadie had assigned me. None of them were the big money that Holly Schwartz was, and they weren't anywhere close to going into default. The charges were for minor offenses like possession and passing bad checks.

When dinnertime approached, Conor suggested getting dressed up to go out someplace to celebrate.

"Where we going?"

"It's a surprise."

"A surprise?" I cocked an eyebrow. "Not really a big fan of surprises."

"You'll like this one, I swear on the bloody Virgin Mary."

"This have anything to do with the reasons why you've been disappearing a lot the past week or so?"

His face opened into a mischievous grin. "Maybe."

"All right, mister, out with it." I started to act as though I was going to tickle him. He hated that. And he was extremely ticklish. I, on the other hand, wasn't, one of the few areas in which I had a distinct advantage over him.

"Oh for fuck's sake, Jinxie. It's just a celebration. Okay?"

"Celebrating what?"

"Catching Holly Schwartz, for one."

"And . . .? What aren't you telling me, Conor Doyle?"

"You'll see soon enough, I swear." I considered tickling him some more, but I figured I'd let him enjoy his surprise.

We piled into his car, and I spent the ride trying to guess where we were going, but he refused to confirm or deny any of my guesses. We were headed into the East Valley, and that was all I knew.

My phone rang as we passed the Loop 202 interchange. Caller ID said it was Kirsten.

"Good news," she said. "No charges pertaining to your showdown with Volkov and his men last night."

"That's good to hear."

"Also the FBI has dropped all charges against you from the warehouse incident."

I breathed a sigh of relief. "Glad to hear it. Federal prison would really interfere with my lifestyle. How's Holly?"

"She's had her bail reset, and her aunt has agreed to let her stay with her biological father."

"George Peavey."

"How'd you know?"

"Let's just say he's a fan."

"I see. Well, I'll send you my invoice."

"Great." More of my bounty money gone. "Hey, what about the Delgados?"

"They're facing charges of kidnapping, obstruction, and aggravated assault unless you choose to drop the charges."

I thought about it. "What if we agreed to drop the charges in exchange for them paying for my legal and medical expenses associated with this case? Is that possible?"

"I'll talk to their attorney and get back with you."

I hung up and noticed Conor exiting onto Broadway Road. "We're going to my parents'? Are they in on this?"

He whistled along with the radio.

When we reached my parents' street, I noticed a string of cars parked along the road. Conor pulled into my folks' driveway and led me up to the house.

My father opened the door and gave me a big hug. "So happy to see you, honey."

"What's going on, Dad?"

He gave me his cheesiest of grins. "You'll see."

The two of them led me outside into the backyard, where a

crowd of friends and family from all areas of my life greeted me with cheers. Jake and Rodeo were there getting awfully chummy. Becca, who looked great in a flowing blue dress, waved from across the yard. Members of my cosplay group and the Phoenix Gender Alliance mingled with neighbors and family friends. Somewhere in the crowd, I could hear Juanita's raucous laugh as she "terrorized the straights." This collision of different aspects of my life felt surreal.

Conor and Jake had installed a misting system overhead to keep things cool. Tables stretched across the yard, decorated with pink tablecloths and covered with a spread of dishes that smelled spicy and wonderful. Finally my mother appeared from the kitchen, holding a large rectangular cake.

I kissed her on the cheek before examining the cake. Drawn in icing was a stick-figure girl in a pink dress and the words "It's a Girl!" I blushed and had the strong urge to disappear.

I looked at my mother. "Mom, what is this?"

"The anniversary of you getting your surgery. My baby girl was reborn eleven years ago today."

"Oh my God! I am so embarrassed. Now everyone knows."

"Oh, baby girl," my father said, "don't blame your mother. This was my idea."

"Dad! Why?"

"Because after what that reporter did, everyone knows, anyway. You needed to know that none of your friends care. We all love you and are here to celebrate you and your journey."

I turned to Conor. "And this is why you kept disappearing?"

"I was helping to arrange things. Ordering the cake and such." He leaned in close. "I wanted them to decorate it with a picture of a big furry—"

"Stop! Don't even say that."

"Fortunately, your father vetoed that idea."

"Thank the gods for that." I looked around the crowd and got some waves from my friends around the yard. "You had to invite everybody?"

"Here ya go, sis. Maybe this will help." Jake handed me a Corona with a squeezed lime already in the bottle. It tasted good.

"Thanks." I noticed his arm was around Rodeo's shoulders. "I see the two of you have met."

Rodeo blushed. "I wasn't even sure I should come since things got awkward."

"It's good to see ya, mate." Conor raised a glass of whiskey.

I gave Rodeo a hug. "I'm glad you came. I missed you."

"Missed you too. Did you hear about Fiddler?"

I grimaced. "Yeah, unfortunate."

"The offer still open to rejoin your team?"

"What's wrong?" Conor chuckled. "Trouble with Big Bobby?"

"Bennies were great, but Big Bobby and Sara Jean have become insufferable now that you're gone."

"Then Conor and I'd love to have you," I said.

"Thanks!" Rodeo raised his beer bottle. "And happy vagina-versary, by the way!"

"Ugh!" I recoiled and punched him in the shoulder. "You're so gross."

"My bad," Jake said. "I bet him ten bucks he wouldn't say that to you."

"Geez! Men! Can't live with him, but you bet your ass I can shoot 'em when the situation calls for it."

"Hey, serves you right for returning my truck stinking of puke!"

Someone in the crowd started shouting, "Speech! Speech!" Everyone joined in the chorus until they formed a mob around me.

There were a lot of things worse than being loved and accepted just as I was. Still, I felt naked. My gender stuff had always been a private thing. And now I was as out as a trans girl could be. But I decided to embrace it. Happy vagina-versary to me!

EXTREME PREJUDICE

JINX BALLOU SERIES - BOOK 2

1

———————

I don't typically show up at a fugitive's door dressed as Wonder Woman. I'm a professional bounty hunter licensed by the State of Arizona, for fuck's sake. And yet there I was knocking on a bail jumper's hotel suite, dressed in a homemade foam-and-leather Wonder Woman costume. Maybe it's true what they say—dress for the job you want, not the one you have.

I was armed with a rubber sword and a Lasso of Truth made from electroluminescent wire. All of my real weapons and my handcuffs were at home. If things went sideways, I'd be in deep shit.

Earlier that morning, I'd been enjoying the Winter Con comic book convention, meeting my favorite celebrities, hanging with fellow cosplayers, taking selfies with fans. Sure as hell beat fighting the crowds at the mall less than three weeks before Christmas.

A teenage Wonder Woman fan was about to take a selfie with me when my phone rang. "Hold on a moment," I told her.

The *Game of Thrones* ringtone indicated the caller was Becca Alvarez. We'd been best friends since junior high, having met soon after I began my gender transition. These days she worked as an IT security consultant while doing electronic skip tracing for me on the side.

I pulled my phone out of my gold-lamé fanny pack. "What's up, Becks?"

"Sorry to interrupt your fangirl weekend, Jinxie, but I believe I've located Danny Warren."

Daniel Warren was the sixty-year-old star of *Danny & Friends*, a local sci-fi children's TV show that ran in the 1980s and '90s. Recently, the aging role model's squeaky-clean façade was shattered when several former child stars came forward making tearful accusations against him. Scottsdale police had charged him with multiple accounts of sexual assault on minors.

When he failed to appear for trial, his bail bond agent, Sadie Levinson, assigned me to go after him. He'd dodged me for weeks, and time was running out. If I didn't apprehend him soon, Sadie would have to pay the court Warren's full bail amount. I had conflicting feelings about arresting a childhood hero. But after Warren had harmed so many people, I wasn't letting the creepy fucker escape justice.

"Where's the old perv hiding out?"

"You're still at Winter Con, right?"

"Yup."

"He's there at the Calderwood Hotel."

"He's here? Why?"

"Winter Con invited him as a guest speaker. Apparently, he's got lots of adult fans who grew up watching the show. Or did before he was indicted."

"The con didn't ban him?"

"The convention organizers did, but the hotel didn't. I accessed the Calderwood Hotel database and confirmed his sister checked into suite 623 a couple weeks ago. And yet the same credit card was just used at a Walgreens near her house in Fountain Hills. I think he's there at the con."

"That sneaky little shit. I knew his sister was lying to me." I scanned the crowd, wondering whether he'd snuck into the convention. "Thanks for the 411, Becks. I'll be in touch."

I hung up and turned to my young fan, who was looking rather impatient. "Sorry, girl. One more quick photo, and then I have to go catch a bad guy."

The girl's eyes widened. "You're a real superhero?"

I grinned. "No superpowers, but I do bring bad guys to justice."

After the girl took a final selfie with me, she hugged me and moved on to someone cosplaying Rey from *Star Wars: The Force Awakens*.

I considered running to my vehicle to retrieve my weapons, handcuffs, and body armor. I didn't like apprehending fugitives when I was unarmed. But with the convention going on, there was no way security would let me in carrying a Taser, much less a revolver. Then again, Warren was a skinny old guy. How much trouble could he be?

But first I had to find him. I figured there was a fair chance he would be on the convention floor, even if he'd been banned. Celebrities thrived on attention, even if it was negative. Why else would he be here?

Security guards stood at all of the entrances, but they were looking for people with dangerous weapons or without the proper badges. Not sixty-year-old pedophiles.

For fifteen minutes, I wandered the crowded convention floor past comic book dealers, prop vendors, and T-shirt booths. But unless Warren was disguised in a costume, I didn't see him.

I approached one of the security guards at the convention floor entrance and pulled up Warren's photo on my phone. "Excuse me, have you seen this man?" I asked. "I've been assigned to return him to custody."

The guard glanced at my costume and gave me a bemused look. "This is a joke, right?"

I flipped out my state-issued bail enforcement license and

badge. "No joke. I'm a bail enforcement agent. Have you seen him?"

He studied the photo. "That's the guy who molested kids from his TV show."

"Yeah, Daniel Warren. You seen him around the con?"

"No, they banned his sorry ass."

"My sources tell me he checked in to the hotel after missing his court date."

The security guard shrugged. "Sorry, haven't seen him."

"If he shows up, call me." I handed him my business card and walked into the lobby.

I considered going directly up to the sixth floor and forcing my way into his room, but that could lead to problems of its own. Better to have an employee with a key let me in. So I approached the registration desk.

"Welcome to Calderwood Hotel and Convention Center. How may I help you?" asked a pleasant fortyish woman with chestnut hair and a name badge that read Nancy.

I held up my ID. "Jinx Ballou, bail enforcement agent working for Assurity Bail Bonds. One of my fugitives, Daniel Warren, is checked in to suite 623. I need someone here to let me into his room."

Nancy looked at my ID, then began typing at her computer. "I'm sorry, we don't have a Daniel Warren checked in to any room."

"He's registered under his sister's name."

"What name would that be?"

Shit, I forgot to ask Becca. "I don't know. But he's the one in suite 623. I need to get in there to arrest him."

She glanced down at my costume and gave me a snooty look. "I'm sorry, but I can't help you. Our high-profile guests value their privacy. Fans go to great lengths to sneak into their rooms. I can't let you in unless you have a warrant or something."

"Look, lady, you have a serial child molester staying in your hotel. As a licensed bounty hunter, I'm allowed to enter any location where I believe my fugitive is hiding. I don't need a warrant. Supreme Court said so."

"I'm sorry, ma'am, but you don't exactly look like a bounty hunter to me."

"I'm here for Winter Con. Not my fault you let fugitive sexual predators stay in your hotel."

"Do you have any paperwork showing he's your fugitive?"

I sighed. "Not on me. I wasn't expecting Warren to be here."

"Then I'm sorry. Come back when you have a warrant."

I rolled my eyes and turned away. "Bitch," I said under my breath as I strode to the elevators.

If I couldn't go through official channels, I'd have to do things the fun way. I rode the elevator to the sixth floor and followed the signs to suite 623. I was about to knock when a stern voice caught my attention.

"Can I help you, miss?" The voice belonged to a hulking security guard who outweighed me by a hundred pounds.

"Nope, I'm good. Thanks!"

"I'm gonna have to ask you to come with me." This guy was getting on my nerves.

I approached him. "Look, I'm here to arrest a child molester who's jumped bail. Now let me do my job, and you can go back to harassing people at the convention."

He grabbed my arm. Bad move. No one touches me without my permission.

In the span of a heartbeat, I twisted back his wrist and drove him to his knees. Keeping his wrist pinned, I pivoted and locked my arm around his thick neck in a chokehold. Guys this big are tough to choke out, but I've had a lot of practice. He struggled for ten seconds, frantically reaching for the Taser on his belt before going limp.

He wouldn't be unconscious long, so I rushed back to Warren's door and knocked, keeping an eye on the guard.

A familiar but tired voice asked, "Who is it?"

"Mr. Warren, I was hoping to get an autograph." It was a

stupid cover story, but then I was dressed as Wonder Woman. The doors to the hotel rooms were solid and would be hard to kick in.

The door inched open with the security latch engaged. "I'm sorry, but I'm not up for signing autographs at this time."

"Please, I've been a fan since I was three." My voice was urgent. "I've been waiting my whole life for this chance."

"How'd you know I was here?"

I fake blushed. "Girlfriend of mine works the front desk. She knows I'm a die-hard fan."

Warren sighed. "Okay, but please make it quick."

He closed the door and released the security latch. Down the hall, the guard was starting to stir.

The door opened, revealing Warren in a white undershirt and a pair of blue gym shorts. I flashed my bail enforcement ID and badge. "Daniel Warren, you're under arrest for failure to appear at your court date."

For an old guy, he was fast. The dude turned on his heel and hauled ass through the suite's spacious living room. He tried to shut the bedroom door, but I put my weight against it before he could latch it. He stumbled back and picked up a nickel-plated Colt 1911 from the nightstand. It trembled in his hand as he pointed it at me.

"I...I'm not going back to jail. Y-You know what they do to people who've molested kids?"

In situations like this, I asked myself WWWWD—What would Wonder Woman do? I held up my hand in a de-escalating gesture, trying to ignore the .45-caliber barrel pointed at my chest. "Whoa, take it easy, Danny."

"I'm not going back."

"Calm down. No one believes the charges." I was lying out my ass because I couldn't deflect bullets as Gal Gadot did on screen. "We can work this out, but you gotta put down the gun. You don't see me with a gun, do ya?"

"I didn't mean to hurt nobody." His face colored and tightened like a fist. "I loved those kids."

"I know you did. And you don't want to hurt me either, do you? I really am a lifelong fan." I started humming the show's theme song.

The gun lowered a bit. "I just...I can't go back to jail."

"Look, we can get your bail reset and your court date rescheduled. No big deal. You can beat this rap but not if you shoot me."

He looked up at me. Sorrow and a disturbing resolve haunted his eyes. "I'm sorry." He raised the pistol again.

I rushed him, reaching for the gun as his finger squeezed the trigger.

2

The hammer clicked without firing. I snatched the Colt out of his hand and tackled him to the floor.

"Try chambering a round next time you try shooting someone, dumb ass." I reached for my handcuffs only to find the loops of my homemade Lasso of Truth. *Oh well. When necessary, improvise.*

I unsnapped the lasso and lashed Warren's wrists together behind his back.

"Please don't do this," he whimpered. "I never meant to hurt nobody."

"Like you didn't mean to shoot me just now?" I applied more pressure on his arm until he yelped in pain.

"I'm...I'm sorry. I just...I panicked."

"Shut the fuck up, perv." I yanked him to his feet. "To think you were once my hero. Makes me wanna puke. Or kick the shit out of you."

"Just kill me and get it over with," Warren whined.

"Kill you? Ha! Like I'd throw away my future over filth like you. Au contraire, I want you to spend the rest of your miserable life in some hellhole bent over as someone's prison bitch."

I'm not a fan of prison rape, but in his case, I'd make an exception.

I stashed his pistol in my fanny pack and pushed him toward the living room. "Okay, perv. Let's move."

"I'm not even dressed."

"I'm sure the corrections officers in Scottsdale will be happy to hook you up with a fancy orange jumpsuit."

"It's cold outside. I'll freeze to death."

"Ask me if I care?"

Warren hung his head like a scolded child.

I sighed as my conscience got the best of me. "Fine. You got a coat?"

"In the closet. There's a pair of loafers in there too."

I helped him on with the loafers and draped the heavy winter coat over his shoulders. "There. Now let's go."

A loud pounding shook the front door. "Security!" said a familiar baritone voice.

"Shit," I grumbled.

The lock clicked, and in rushed the hulking security guard I'd choked out. Next to him was a smaller, squatter guard with a buzz cut. Both stood with Tasers trained on me.

"Hands up!" they shouted in unison.

I kept my grip on Warren in case he tried to bolt. "Easy, boys. I'm a licensed bail enforcement agent hired to apprehend this scumbag, who failed to appear in court. Now get out of my way, or I'll charge you both with interference in the apprehension of a fugitive." It was a made-up charge, but they didn't know that.

"Get those hands up, or I will light you up, lady," said Hulk.

"Hey, big guy. I already kicked your ass once this morning. You want a rematch?"

Buzz Cut peered up at his taller cohort. "She kicked your ass?"

Hulk's face screwed up in anger. Hulk's Taser shot two metal darts into my thick leather costume, but they didn't penetrate enough to affect me. I smacked them away with the braces covering my forearms.

Hulk tossed his Taser and swung at me. I grabbed his arm and twisted him around into an elbow lock. His buddy got a panicked look in his eye and drew down on me. I used Hulk as a shield. Buzz Cut's Taser darts hit Hulk in the back. He bellowed as his muscles constricted at once, dropping him to the floor like a felled tree.

I drew Warren's pistol and aimed it at Buzz Cut. "Drop the Taser!"

"Crap." Buzz Cut tossed his weapon and held up his hands in surrender.

Hulk groaned but stayed down.

"Now listen up, boys! All I want is to return my prisoner to custody. So if you two are quite done playing Keystone Kops, I'll be on my way."

Buzz Cut eyed me warily. Hulk managed to utter a muffled "Cunt." My work here was done.

"Come on, perv. Let's take you back to lockup."

I kept a firm grip on Warren's arm as we rode the elevator to the lobby. From his drooping posture, I gathered he'd resolved himself to his fate.

I caught my reflection in the polished steel doors. My hair was mussed, making me look less like a demigod superhero and more like a wild woman raised by wolves. I did what I could to finger comb it back into place, but it didn't help much.

"Could you loosen the rope? I've lost feeling in my hands," Warren muttered quietly between the third and second floors.

"Shut up, perv, or I'll make it tighter." Never let it be said that I'm one of those TV bounty hunters who gets all touchy-feely once a perp was apprehended.

"I could lose my hands if I don't get the blood flowing."

"Oh, wouldn't that be a shame," I said with dripping sarcasm. "How would you ever fondle little kids without your hands?"

The elevator doors opened to a lobby filled with the costumed masses of my fellow comic book geeks. Several of them noticed me perp walking Warren toward the hotel entrance and started applauding. Others held up their phones to capture the Kodak moment. I had to admit, getting cheered on by my fellow cosplayers kinda rocked.

Outside, the early December air was cool but not cold.

Phoenix doesn't have the same four seasons most places do. Autumn doesn't begin until mid-October and lasts until New Year's. Winter is a myth. Spring starts in January. By mid-April, summer arrives with temps climbing into the triple digits. In July, the dry heat of summer cranks up into the muggy hell of monsoon season, with spectacular thunderstorms, widespread flooding, and nightmarish dust storms called haboobs.

For now, I savored the all-too-brief cool weather as I guided Warren down the street, while the sapphire sky played peekaboo between the glass-and-steel buildings. A few blocks away, we reached the parking garage.

Warren froze as I tried to lead him up the outside staircase. "I can't climb stairs with my hands behind my back."

"Move, asshole! I'm only parked on the third floor. You can make it."

"Untie my hands first so I can hold the rail."

"Fat chance."

He leaned away from the concrete steps as if they were made of lava. "I'll fall and break my hip." His voice trembled.

"Fine, we'll take the elevator." I punched the call button with my fist. "Big baby."

On the third floor, I pressed the key fob to unlock my SUV. Nicknamed the Gray Ghost, the seven-year-old Nissan Pathfinder was pockmarked with scrapes, dents, and broken trim, rendering it virtually invisible in most Phoenix neighborhoods.

I shoved Warren into the back seat and secured him with the seat belt. "Comfy?" I asked with a sneer.

"You know what they'll do to me in prison."

"Maybe you should've thought of that before you molested those kids."

"I'll pay you double whatever the bounty is just to let me go." His face looked deathly pale under the dim glow of the Gray Ghost's dome light.

"So you can hurt more kids? I don't fucking think so."

His gaze fell. "It's not my fault. I have a problem."

"Oh, is that what you call it?" I chuckled darkly. "Alcoholism is a problem. Missing your court date is a problem. Molesting children is an abomination."

"I get urges I can't control."

"Maybe your fellow inmates can help you with those urges." I slammed the side door shut and climbed into the driver's seat.

"Can't we make some sort of deal?" he whined as I started the engine.

"The only deal I'm interested in involves returning your sorry ass to jail. Now pipe down, or I'll strap you to the bumper. You got me, perv?"

He stayed silent for the remainder of the trip.

I drove north to I-10, then transitioned onto the Loop 202 before taking the McDowell exit. As I waited for the light to change, my phone rang. Becca again.

"Jinxie, did you seriously just arrest Daniel Warren while dressed as Wonder Woman?" She sounded excited and tired at the same time.

"Yeah, why?" I asked nervously.

"It's trending all over social media with the hashtag #WonderWomanPerpWalk. Hold on. I'm clicking on a video."

"There's video?" I felt a lump in my throat.

"Wow! That's seriously badass. No wonder the local news stations are all over it."

"The news stations? Seriously? Shit." I've had an aversion to the press ever since the *Phoenix Living* weekly newspaper outed me as transgender. Bail bond agents around town blackballed me when they read it.

"Don't worry. Your name's not mentioned. But folks are wondering who this mystery Wonder Woman is. Most think you're a cop."

"Let them keep thinking that. You at the Hub today?" The Hub was a coworking space near Fifteenth Avenue and Grand, where we both worked.

"Yeah, but about to call it a day. Chronic fatigue's kicking in. I'm done out of spoons."

"That's why I keep telling you to switch to knives. They're much more fun."

"Ha ha."

"You need me to pick up anything for you?" I often helped her out whenever her chronic fatigue flared up.

"A friend of mine already did some shopping for me."

I scoffed. "Hey! That's *my* job."

"You were at Winter Con. I didn't want to bother you. But you're still my bestie."

"Damn straight! I'm headed to Scottsdale lockup to drop off Warren. You need anything else, you call me. Got that?"

"Will do."

I'd dealt with the correction officers at the Scottsdale Jail for years. All in all, they were good folks. But they weren't above catcalling, whistling, and otherwise giving me shit when I walked in.

CO Bennett, a woman with a coppery ponytail and freckles, smirked while she pulled up Warren's records. "Damn, Ballou, you can arrest me in that costume anytime," she teased.

My face warmed as I untied Warren. "Thanks, Bennett, but I prefer guys."

"Oh well, a girl can dream." She gave me a coy wink.

I had to admit I felt a little physical attraction when she handed me Warren's body receipt.

"See you around, superhero," she said.

I waved and walked out the door, hoping she didn't see my face turning red. Things were getting way too hot in there.

3

———

With paperwork in hand, I pointed the Gray Ghost toward Phoenix. I debated whether to return to Winter Con or turn in Daniel Warren's paperwork and get paid. The last few days, Sadie Levinson had been having a cow over Warren's defaulted bail bond. I decided to drop off the body receipt and put her fears to rest.

The con would continue into the weekend, so I could go back tomorrow and with more money to spend on rare comics and maybe some Funko Pop figures. I'd had my eye on a Funko version of Negasonic Teenage Warhead from *Deadpool*.

But first, a change in attire was called for. I was not showing up at Assurity Bail Bonds in costume. Sadie already had a stick up her butt. I didn't need her giving me shit about being dressed as Wonder Woman when I captured Warren. So I pulled off the highway at Seventh Avenue and headed home.

I lived in a cozy house in Phoenix's trendy Willo District, north of downtown along the Central Corridor. The neighborhood dated back to the 1930s. The homes were small but solid and tended to be on the pricey side.

My brother, Jake, who remodeled and flipped houses for a

living, had acquired the two-bedroom, two-bath on the cheap after the housing bubble burst. He'd restored the hardwood floors, brought the wiring up to code, and installed Saltillo tile in the kitchen and dining area. I converted the spare room into workout space with an exercise station for strength training and a human-shaped punching bag for combat practice.

My decor could best be described as millennial Bohemian meets sci-fi/fantasy fangirl. Lots of bright colors and different textures throughout the house. Roy Lichtenstein prints and movie posters covered the walls, including one autographed by Gal Gadot. A bamboo bookshelf in the living room was filled with comics in plastic sleeves. A breakfront in the dining room displayed a carefully curated collection of action figures. It wasn't the tidiest place, but it was clean. Mostly.

The best thing was that my boyfriend, Conor Doyle, lived only a few streets south of me. We alternated spending the night at each other's houses, so the proximity was a real time-saver.

Once in my bedroom, I shimmied out of the Wonder Woman outfit and pulled on a Pink Trinkets concert T-shirt, cargo pants, and a well-worn pair of black Doc Martens—my preferred business attire.

For safety, I strapped on a ballistic vest emblazoned with the words "Bail Enforcement." A tactical belt around my waist held my Taser in a holster on my right side, and a snub-nosed Rossi .357 revolver for backup nestled in an ankle holster. I hooked a walkie-talkie on the belt and slipped two sets of handcuffs in a thigh pocket.

A pair of my wraparound shades, fingerless leather gloves, and a black ball cap embroidered with the words Ballou Fugitive Recovery completed the ensemble. Time to rock and roll.

I opened the fridge to grab a bottle of water for the road, only to find there weren't any left. I would've sworn there'd been at least a few last time I checked. I made a note to pick up another case on the way home.

As I walked out the door, my phone began playing a Flogging Molly's "Drunken Lullabies"—Conor's ringtone.

"Heard ya nicked that pedo Danny Warren," he said in his Irish brogue. "Nice catch, love."

"Thanks," I said, feeling a flush of embarrassment. Maybe Conor hadn't heard how I was dressed.

"By the way, ya looked mighty deadly in your Super Girl getup."

I chuckled. He was intentionally tweaking me with the misreference. "It's Wonder Woman, ya dodgy bloke," I replied in a poor imitation of his accent.

"So ya say, love. Wear it tonight, or I'll remain unconvinced."

I felt myself getting aroused thinking about getting him in bed, with or without the costume. Mostly without. "You're on, mister," I replied.

"We at your place or mine tonight?"

"Mine, if that's all right. I've got paperwork and stuff to catch up on."

"Ya know, this would be a lot easier if ya just moved in with me already. All this back and forth between houses is driving me mad."

And with that, the passion escaped like air from a balloon. "We talked about this, Conor." It came out more sternly than I intended.

"We've been dating for two and a half years. Don't ya think it's time we stop this sleepover madness and live together like normal people?"

"Normal?" I scoffed, trying to lighten the mood. "When've you *ever* known me to be normal?"

"You're dodging the issue, love." His voice stiffened. "Been wondering if ya really fancy me or if ya just want me for the occasional shag."

Ouch! That one hurt. "I love you, Conor. Really, I do. It's just... I like having my own space."

"Ya want to hold on to your bungalow, fine. But for Christ's sake, can't we live under a single roof? After what that fucker Milo Volkov did last year—"

"Volkov's dead. I killed him. Remember?"

"Aye, but not before he left that reporter's body wrapped up in plastic on your doorstep."

"I can take care of myself."

"That ya can." The silence between us stretched. "Maybe you're just scared."

"Scared? What've I got to be scared of?" I made sure my voice didn't shake, even though he was hitting a little close to the mark.

"Scared of commitment, maybe. Not sure exactly."

"I have to go. Sadie's been shitting kittens over Daniel Warren. I have to bring her the body receipt."

"Fine. I'll see ya tonight." He sounded hurt, which piled onto the guilt I was already feeling.

"See you then." I felt like a heel. He was a sweet guy who treated me with respect and was great in the sack. So why did I resist moving in with him? Hell if I knew. But my gut was telling me not to, and I'd learned to trust it.

I hopped in the Gray Ghost and floored down Central Avenue with the windows open and Le Tigre playing full blast on the stereo.

Assurity Bail Bonds was wedged between an accounting firm and a temp staffing office on the second floor of the Arizona Center. Sadie Levinson had opened it a few years back when the touristy outdoor shopping mall was rebranding itself as a corporate business center downtown. Lately, management had been opening stores that catered more to year-round residents.

I parked in the adjacent garage and hustled along the sidewalk, past a smorgasbord of restaurants, clothing shops, and kiosks. Mothers at outdoor tables monitored their toddlers playing around a fountain that randomly shot streams of water from jets in the sidewalk. I jogged up the grand staircase near the movie theater, vaulting the steps two at a time.

A string of bells attached to Assurity's doorframe jingled as I entered. The office consisted of a twenty-by-thirty-foot room with two stained oak desks, one on each side of the cream-colored room. Vertical filing cabinets lined the back wall. The other walls featured framed prints of paintings by Monet, Picasso, and Gaugin. The decor was professional if a bit sterile, making it feel more like an art gallery than a bail bond office.

Sadie Levinson sat at the desk to my left with two faux leather guest chairs in front. She was a slender woman in her forties with a short wedge haircut, red metallic frame glasses, and a no-nonsense expression on her face.

"You got Warren," she said without looking up.

"Told you I would." I unfolded the body receipt and handed it to her. She frowned and flattened out the folds as best she could.

"Is there a reason you were dressed up like a caped crusader?"

"Where'd you hear that?" *When in doubt, play dumb.*

Sadie shot me a don't-bullshit-me look. "Word gets around."

"Technically speaking, 'caped crusader' refers to Batman. I was cosplaying as Wonder Woman."

Not even a chuckle. Tough crowd.

"I was at Winter Con when my skip tracer tracked him to the hotel." I gave her a rundown of my impromptu capture of her prodigal client. "So what else do you have for me?" I asked as she wrote out a check for Warren's bounty.

She pulled some files from the stack on the left side of her desk and handed them to me. "I got two more skips for you."

"Just two? Come on, Sadie! How am I supposed to pay my team with two measly jobs? You giving jobs to other bounty hunters?"

She cocked her head with a look of superiority. "I pride myself on properly underwriting my clients so I don't have to pay you to pick them up for failing to appear. If you need more work, go someplace else."

We both knew she was one of the few bail bond agents who would hire me after my trans status was made public. I let the matter drop and thumbed through the files. "Tell me about these deadbeat clients of yours."

"First one's Robert Rossellini. You've picked him up before."

I chuckled. "Conspiracy Bob! I love him. What's our uber-paranoid buddy done now?"

"Charges are trespassing, causing a disturbance, and violating an order of protection by the office of the Arizona State Mine Inspector. Bail's set at ten thousand dollars."

"The mining inspector has a restraining order against Conspiracy Bob? What in the world for?"

Levinson shook her head. "Mr. Rossellini's been haranguing the mine inspector's staff. Some nonsense about mole people plotting the end of the world."

My chuckle turned into an all-out belly laugh. "Jesus Christ on a surfboard, where's he get this stuff?"

"I couldn't begin to tell you. Just pick him up."

"Bob's bounty is chump change, but I'll take him just for entertainment value." I pulled up the next file. "Who's this Pratt fellow?"

"Rudy Pratt. Charged with murder in the first degree in the death of a coworker. Bail's set at two hundred fifty thousand dollars."

"Now we're talking. I can use twenty-five grand." My bounty rate was ten percent of the bail amount. I flipped through the defendant's application. "What's your take on him?"

"No priors. His demeanor was rather subdued when I met with him. His wife has a bit of a mouth on her. He missed his evidentiary hearing yesterday. Judge wants him picked up and held until trial. I've left messages on his phone, with his wife, and his attorney but haven't heard back."

I stood up. "Okay, I'll track him down."

Sadie leveled her eyes to my chest. "Try not to take so long this time, okay? I want Pratt back in custody pronto. I prefer not to play Russian roulette with my business."

"I'll do my best."

"Oh, and do it dressed in street clothes and not as"—she made a hand gesture as she struggled for the words—"one of the Avengers."

"The Avengers are from the Marvel universe. Wonder Wom—"

"Goodbye, Ms. Ballou." She turned back to her computer and resumed typing.

I saluted with the client folders and walked out.

One of these days, I was going to get that woman to loosen up. Maybe take her out for drinks at Grumpy's and help her get laid.

On second thought, who knew what she'd be like if she loosened up. Might be worse than she was now.

4

It was after one o'clock, so I scarfed down a couple of Chicago hot dogs in Arizona Center's food court while I perused the files for the two fugitives. Conspiracy Bob, I could handle on my own. This Rudy Pratt fellow might be a different story.

Pratt's lack of priors was a good sign he wasn't a hardened criminal. Then again, the man was charged with first-degree murder, and now the judge wanted him remanded. He might not be so keen on going back to jail willingly. So once I took care of Conspiracy Bob, I'd contact my crew for backup on Pratt.

After lunch, I hopped on I-10 to the Loop 101 North and exited west onto Bell Road. Sun City was a retirement community northwest of Phoenix, where golf carts were a common form of transportation and turning left from the right-hand lane was considered going with the flow of traffic.

Conspiracy Bob lived in a small yellow house. A low wall cordoned off a front patio littered with dusty old watering cans and garden gnomes his late wife had collected before she died a few years back. A forest of weeds, some at least two feet tall, poked up from the layer of crushed rock in the front yard.

Bob's forest-green Subaru, a relic from the 1980s, baked in the sunny driveway. From the back, I could hardly tell what color it was painted with all of the conspiracy-themed bumper stickers.

Behind the house, a shortwave antenna rose forty feet into the air. Bob used an elaborate radio set to communicate surreptitiously with his fellow conspiracy theorists.

I blocked the driveway with the Gray Ghost in case Bob got any ideas of making a run for it. He'd done so once or twice out of the dozen times I'd picked him up. What he lacked in rational thought, he made up for in determination.

My knock at the door triggered a series of barks from inside. Sounded like a big dog and might have been convincing if it hadn't deteriorated into a fit of very human coughing. Conspiracy Bob was up to his usual shenanigans.

"Bob, it's Jinx Ballou!" I hollered loud enough for him to hear me. "You missed your court date."

The barking continued, although with less enthusiasm.

"Sure is a nice door you have here. What is it? Oak? Be a shame if I had to knock it in with my battering ram."

"Bob's not here right now," said a rattly tenor voice, "but if you leave a message at the beep—"

"I'm getting my battering ram."

"Wait! Wait!" Several locks clicked free, and the door opened to a dour little man in his seventies standing on the tile floor in leather Jesus sandals. He stood six inches shorter than me and had a gray beard that hung down to his chest. He wore tattered jeans and a pale-green shirt that read Everything You Know is a Lie.

"We really have to do this?" he asked with hands on his hips.

"'Fraid so. You wouldn't want to lose this, uh, lovely house of yours."

"None of this would've happened if they'd just listened to me." He sighed. "All right. Let me get my coat."

I followed him into his house, past half-empty cardboard boxes, computers in various states of assembly, stacks of newspapers, dirty dishes, and heaps of clothing. Aluminum foil lined the walls and windows.

"You know, you'd save yourself a lot of money and trouble if you just showed up to court." I trailed him into his bedroom. A bookshelf stuffed with yellowing paperbacks stood next to a bed that reeked of urine.

"Where's the fun in that?" He picked through the crammed wall closet until he found a faded Grateful Dead hoodie. "I'm trying to make people understand what's happening before it's too late."

"And what's going on?" I asked casually, not interested in hearing his latest conspiracy theories.

"The mole people are planning to take over the city, possibly the world." He pulled on the hoodie and held my gaze with fervor in his eyes. "They're planning to detonate bombs at strategic places around the city. The first one's set to go off in a few days near the state government buildings."

I gestured toward the front door, and he led the way outside.

"Have you actually seen these mole people?" I asked.

"You think I'm crazy, don't ya?" He pointed at me as we stopped next to the Gray Ghost.

"Well, Bob, the thought crossed my mind." I unlocked the passenger door, and he climbed in. I hopped in behind the wheel and cruised out of the neighborhood.

"They've been living in the abandoned mines north of the valley and communicating via shortwave," he explained. "I started picking up their transmissions a couple months ago."

"So mole people have shortwave radios, huh?"

"Oh, they've adopted much of our technology. Radios, gene splicing, even video games."

"How do you know they're mole people? Maybe they're just, well, people."

"For starters, they use code names like Lodestar, Grays Gulch, and Crizaba—all names from abandoned mines in the area."

"That doesn't necessarily mean they're mole people."

He got a gleam in his eye. "When you've been listening as long as I have, you can tell. They have a certain way of speaking. And one thing I heard is that the days of tolerance are over. They refer to us as the immigrants because they were here first. They're tired of how we're polluting the planet. All the drugs and violence and corruption."

"They speak English?"

"Oh yeah, they've been studying us for a long time. Listening in."

"And what do they look like?"

He pulled up a photo on his cell phone. I glanced at it as we waited at a red light. "Isn't that a character from a *Star Wars* movie?"

"That's what they *want* you to think. But they're real. And when they start blowing up buildings in Phoenix, everyone's going to be sorry they ignored me."

"If that happens, you are welcome to tell me you told me so."

Suddenly his glee vanished, replaced with profound sadness. "We'll all be dead or enslaved by then. So what would be the point?"

Conspiracy Bob got quiet for the rest of the trip to the North Phoenix Jail.

As the officer was processing him in, I told Bob I'd put in a good word with Sadie for him and hoped his lawyer could get his bail reset.

I felt bad for the guy. Yeah, he was brainwashed by the talking heads spreading absurd ideas, faulty logic, and outright lies to the gullible masses. But all in all, Conspiracy Bob seemed to have a good heart and never gave me any trouble.

After Bob was back in custody, I sat in the Gray Ghost and studied Rudy Pratt's file in depth. Pratt lived in a single-family residence, not far from Metrocenter mall in Phoenix. He was married with two kids and had worked for ten years as an electronics engineer on rocket systems at SpaceJet America.

More recently, Pratt had worked as a salesclerk at Hardware

SuperCenter, where the murder in question occurred. From rocket scientist to cashier to murder suspect to bail jumper. Helluva fall from grace.

No prior convictions. His credit report showed some medical bills that had gone ninety days before being paid, but whose hadn't these days? He owned three pistols, a revolver, and a shotgun registered in his name. Not unusual for Arizona, but as a bounty hunter, I didn't like taking any chances.

I called my friend Rodeo, who worked for me part-time. His real name was Nathaniel Kwan, but he'd earned the nickname Rodeo during his time in the army due to his fondness for cowboy hats. More recently, he'd developed a fondness for my brother, Jake, who was newly out of the closet.

"Hey, Rodeo, I need your help with a case."

"Copy that. Who's our FTA?" Shorthand for *failed to appear*.

"Rudy Pratt, a former rocket scientist charged with first-degree murder."

"Interesting. You want me to meet you somewhere?"

"The guy lives near Metrocenter. I'll text you the address."

"Meet you there in a couple hours."

"Couple of hours? Come on, dude. Time's money. Whatever it is can wait."

"Sorry. I'm dropping Gwyneth off at her dance studio as we speak. They're rehearsing their Christmas recital."

"Ugh, I'm so tired of this Christmas nonsense."

"Come on, girl. Don't be such a Scrooge."

"Charles Dickens can kiss my skinny white ass." I sighed. "Go do the daddy thing then get your butt over to our fugitive's house. I want to get this job done so I can go back to Winter Con tomorrow."

"Aha! The real motive for urgency emerges."

"Screw you."

"I'll see you in two, boss."

I disconnected and hit another number on speed dial.

"This is Caden." His voice was a youthful tenor, growing deeper each month he was on testosterone therapy.

I'd known Caden Morrow for a few years, having met him at Phoenix Gender Alliance, a local transgender support group. At the time, he was working as a CO at the women's prison in Tonopah. When his employer, Rehabilitation Systems of America, fired him for transitioning on the job, he came to me looking for work. Turned out he was a good fit for the job.

"We got another case, dude. Need you to meet Rodeo and me near Metrocenter in a couple hours."

"Sounds good. Hey, d'you hear someone dressed as Wonder Woman arrested Daniel Warren at a comic book festival?"

"Really? Imagine that," I replied with feigned surprise. "I'll text you the address."

"Oh my God, was that—"

I ended the call and started the Gray Ghost.

Caden's cobalt-blue Audi roadster was parked in front of Rudy Pratt's driveway when I pulled up behind him. The setting sun had smeared the western sky with a palette of fuchsia, blood orange, and lavender.

As I climbed out of the Gray Ghost, wind gusts tugged at my ponytail and whipped the bougainvillea bushes in the Pratts' front yard like a flag, sending scarlet petals tumbling down the street.

I hugged Caden as he got out of his roadster. He had a sparse but scraggly beard and wore his hair in a well-gelled fauxhawk. Though a few inches shorter than me, he was ripped from an intense bodybuilding regimen he'd been on lately.

On his left hip, he carried a Taser pistol, similar to mine, as his primary weapon. A twenty-six-inch collapsible baton sat in a holster on his right. I knew he also had a SIG Sauer P229 .40-caliber concealed inside his waistband at the small of his back.

"How's it going, bro?" I asked.

"Kicking ass and taking names. So that was you with Warren?" he asked with a wry smile.

I shrugged and glanced down the street. "Where the hell's Rodeo?"

"Come on, Jinxie. It's cool." He chucked me on the shoulder. "You're a badass. Who else could pull off something like that?"

"Yeah, a badass who prefers to stay out of the limelight if I can help it."

"You going to Juanita's fundraiser next week?"

Juanita Valdez was a trans woman who mentored me when I came out. She currently owned the Main Drag, the most popular queer bar in the city.

"What fundraiser?" I asked.

"The Barbra Shop Quartet. Four queens performing Barbra Streisand songs in a barbershop quartet style."

I shuddered at the thought. "Good fucking grief! That's insane."

"Yeah, but they're raising money to rebuild the Queer Youth Shelter after some asshole torched it last month."

"If it's to support a good cause, I'll be there. Besides, Juanita would have my ass if I missed it."

Caden laughed. "Yeah, she can be scary when she's pissed."

Rodeo's turquoise Mazda Miata turned onto the street and rolled to a stop behind my SUV.

"'Bout damn time," I said as he got out of his car. "Is it New Year's already?"

Rodeo was clean-shaven with an athletic build. He wore mirrored aviators and a Stetson that arched over his head.

"Very funny." From his trunk, he pulled a shotgun loaded with beanbag rounds. "Just wait till you have kids."

"No, thanks."

"Oh, come on," Rodeo teased. "Just a matter of time before you and Conor adopt a few of your own. Gwyneth would love some cousins to play with."

"I can just see Jinx now," replied Caden, "carrying a baby on her hip in a little Kevlar onesie."

"You two are seriously delusional. Let's bag this deadbeat already."

I gave Rodeo and Caden the 411 on Pratt. "He's charged with murder. No priors, but he has multiple weapons registered in his name, so stay frosty."

Rodeo asked, "What's the plan?"

"Standard procedure for now. I'll hit the front door. Rodeo, you cover the back. Caden, stay here by the vehicles and keep an eye out in case Pratt sneaks out the garage or side window."

Caden sighed dejectedly. "Why do I always have to stay by the vehicles? I want to be where the action is."

I patted him on the back. "I need a lookout. You up to the task, or you gonna bitch?"

"I'm up for it." He crossed his arms. "Sometime I'd like to cover the back door and let Rodeo keep lookout."

Rodeo clapped him on the shoulder. "Hang in there, little man. I used to be the newbie. Now it's your turn."

Pratt's house was a combination of white siding and tan brick. A red sign reading "Christ Is Born" stood in the yard, next to an inflatable snowman, currently deflated.

A white Toyota Camry sat parked in front of the two-car garage. The license plate matched the one listed on Pratt's bail application. Between our three vehicles, we had the driveway blocked, but some FTAs weren't above plowing across their own yard to avoid going to jail.

Rodeo scooted around the side of the house.

"Let's get this party started." I strode to the front door. "You ready, Rodeo?" I asked into the walkie.

"Ready and waiting."

"Caden?"

"As ready as I'll ever be."

My pulse quickened. This was the scariest and most exciting part of the job. Anything could happen and usually did.

I drew my Taser and pounded on the screen door. "Open up! Bail enforcement!"

After a minute or so with no answer, I pounded again. "Open the door, Mr. Pratt, or we'll force our way in."

I heard hushed voices inside. I had no way to tell if one of them was our guy or not.

"Last chance!" I shouted. "If we come in by force, you'll wish you'd surrendered voluntarily."

6

———

The door opened. A woman in an orange cotton dress glared at me through the security screen door. Her face was bony, with eyes the color of steel and every bit as cold. "Can I help you?" she snarled.

"You Mrs. Pratt?"

"Yes, I'm Linda Pratt."

I recognized her name from the application. "Your husband missed his court date. He needs to come with me. Now."

"He ain't here."

"Bullshit. His car's in the driveway."

"My son's borrowing it. My husband's in our minivan."

"And where is your husband?"

"Why should I tell you?"

"Because if the bond is forfeited, Assurity Bail Bonds takes your house and kicks you out on the street."

"This is all such bullshit. My husband was defending himself after that wetback assaulted him."

"Ma'am, I'm not here to try him. He and his lawyer can do that when he shows up in court. So unless he wants to spend the duration of his trial in jail, he needs to come with me."

"They're railroading my husband because he's white. The goddamn Mexicans and blacks and faggots all got more rights than a good white Christian man does."

I so wanted to slap the stupid out of her racist, Fox-News-watching ass. But the last thing I needed was to be charged with assault. "Tell me where Rudy is, or I'll run you in for aiding and abetting a fugitive."

"Fuck you, lady. My husband doesn't tell me where he's going. I'm not one of them shrill femi-Nazi types who has to monitor their husband's every move. You can tell that Jew lady at Assurity Bail Bonds he's not guilty. And if she tries to take our house, she'll regret it." She slammed the door shut. The dead bolt clicked in place.

I heard Rodeo laughing over the walkie. "Wow, she's a piece of work, huh?"

"You can say that again." I holstered my Taser.

"You think he's in there?" asked Caden.

"Hard to tell." We had the right to force our way in provided we had reason to believe he was inside. His truck in the driveway constituted enough reason for me, no matter what his wife said. "Bring me the battering ram!" I shouted to Caden loudly enough for everyone inside to hear.

"Battering ram coming up!" Caden yelled for similar effect.

The front door reopened. Linda Pratt glared at me. Her mouth squeezed tight like a sphincter.

"You break in here, I'm calling the cops."

I put my hand on my cheek and feigned horror. "Oh my, not the cops!"

"You think I won't?"

"Call them, lady. Your husband murdered someone and jumped bail. Now you're hiding him. Who you think they'll side with?"

"I'm telling you, he ain't here."

Caden trudged up the walk while hefting the thirty-pound

battering ram, the strain showing on his face. He set the ram on the concrete with a clunk. "Battering ram as requested."

"What the hell you gonna do with that?" Some of the iron was draining from her voice.

"Unless you let us in, I will use this ram to tear your door off its hinges. And then me and my team will search your house room by room, cabinet by cabinet until we find your loser of a husband or determine for ourselves that he's not here. Could take us a few hours." I turned to Caden and nodded.

"At least." He hefted the ram and drew it back for his first hit. "Here goes!"

"Wait! Stop! Stop!" Mrs. Pratt hurriedly unlocked the screen door.

Caden stopped just in time. "Damn."

"Stay outside in case our guy tries to sneak out," I whispered to him.

"Yeah, yeah."

I stepped into the living room as Mrs. Pratt backed up with her arms folded. The room was filled with a combination of antique wingback chairs, a glass coffee table, and an IKEA entertainment center. Walls were decorated with an assortment of religious Christmas decorations, family photos, a picture of white Jesus, and Bible verses stitched in needlepoint.

From my vantage point, I could see through to the kitchen at the rear of the house. Rodeo stood outside the French doors, his shotgun at the ready. A hallway led off to my left.

"Happy now?" she asked.

"Overjoyed. Where's your husband hiding?"

"I. Don't. Know."

"I'm just going to verify that. Open the back door and let my associate in," I ordered.

"Do it yourself, lady."

Movement in the hallway caught my eye. I turned to see a shirtless boy in his late teens holding a Japanese katana one-handed, as if it was a fencing foil. He bore a strong resemblance to the photo of Rudy Pratt but was a couple of decades younger.

I stepped back, keeping both mother and son in my line of sight, and drew my Taser. I was tempted to juice the little juvenile delinquent with a nice jolt of electricity but wasn't sure which direction the katana would fly when his muscles contracted.

"Drop the katana, kid. No one needs to get hurt."

"Leave us alone!" he bellowed as he entered the living room. "Our family's got enough problems right now."

"The sooner I locate your dad, the sooner me and my team will be outta here."

"Fuck you, you goddamn spic!"

"Spic? Seriously?" I rolled my eyes.

Because of my dark hair and tan skin, people often assumed my family was from south of the border. However, my mother's side of the family was Italian, my father's Cajun. Not that I minded being mistaken for Latina. I did, however, object to people using racist slurs.

"Let me rephrase. Drop the katana, or I'll light you up with my Taser and jam that blade right up your ass."

"You don't scare me." He raised the katana as if to strike.

The sound of breaking glass caught the boy's attention as Rodeo busted through the French doors. I kicked the boy's wrist, knocked the katana from his grip, and pulled the trigger on the Taser. The boy shrieked as his muscles seized, and he collapsed to the floor, gasping for air.

"I warned you."

While Mrs. Pratt rushed to her son, I examined the katana. It was a cheap Filipino knockoff, probably bought at a local swap meet. I jammed the tip of the blade into the floor and snapped it in half with my boot.

"Now if you two are quite done with the theatrics, my associate and I will check the house for dear old Dad. Any more bullshit from you two, and I will handcuff you both. Do I make myself clear?"

The two of them huddled on the couch. The kid was still moaning while his mother consoled him.

Rodeo reached through the broken pane on the French door and let himself in. I replaced the Taser cartridge in case mother and son got any other bright ideas.

"Thanks for the distraction." I fist-bumped Rodeo when he walked into the living room.

He grinned. "Hate to see you sliced into steak tartare."

"Ha! Blade was so dull it probably couldn't cut rotten bananas."

We systematically searched the house for Rudy Pratt and didn't bother to be neat about it. We flipped over beds and cleared out closets, cabinets, and any nook where a person could hide. We sifted through drawers for clues that might lead us to Pratt.

In the master bedroom, we found a bookcase filled with Bibles and books by Glenn Beck, Alex Jones, and other ultraconservatives.

A Confederate flag hung from the second bedroom wall. Underneath one of the dresser drawers, I discovered a stack of porn magazines, a box of condoms, and a bag of weed. The Holy Trinity of being an all-American teenage boy.

The third bedroom was decorated in every imaginable shade of pink. A menagerie of plushy animals huddled together at the head of the four-poster bed.

When the main part of the house turned up nothing, I hoisted Rodeo up to check out the attic while I searched the garage. Only thing I found was a workbench with a soldering station and cabinets filled with wires, circuit boards, and other electronic parts.

"Well, what now?" Rodeo asked when we reconvened in the kitchen.

I picked a piece of dusty fiberglass out of his hair. "Let's talk to the wife again." We returned to the living room.

"Didn't find him, did you? Told you he ain't here," the wife said with a sneer.

"Where is he?" I demanded.

She shrugged with feigned ignorance. "How should I know?"

"You're not doing yourself any favors by hiding him."

She crossed her arms and glowered. "If your husband was being framed, you'd do the same damned thing."

"Fine." I pulled out a pair of handcuffs. "But tell me. How can you protect him when you're in jail?" I snapped the cuffs on one of her wrists.

Her son moved to intervene, and Rodeo stepped toward him with the shotgun aimed at the boy's chest. "Sit."

"He's at work, all right!" said the boy.

"Rusty!" his mom scolded.

"I ain't letting them take you to jail too." Rusty's eyes burned into me. "You got the information you wanted. Now leave us alone."

"He's at the Hardware SuperCenter?"

"Yes," he mumbled.

"They didn't fire him?"

"Like I said," the wife piped in, "it was self-defense, and they know it. That beaner attacked him. Rudy said he caught the guy selling drugs. You know how they are. Nothing but drug dealers, rapists, and murderers."

I resisted the urge to give her a jolt from the Taser. "You two have a nice fucking day." I unlocked the cuffs. "Come on, Rodeo."

"Yeah, y'all get out of here, you fucking spic and goddamn chink!" the kid called. "Go back to your own countries."

Rodeo wheeled around and aimed the shotgun at him. Mrs. Pratt shrieked, shielding her son with her body.

I put a hand on Rodeo's arm. "Don't. They're not worth it, dude."

We hustled out of the house and met Caden near the street. "What was all that yelling?"

"Nothing," I said.

"Just putting a little fear into a couple of racist assholes," Rodeo said with a chuckle.

"How come I always get stuck outside while you two have all the fun?" Caden whined.

Rodeo mussed Caden's fauxhawk. "'Cause you're the new guy, little man."

"Cut it out." Caden tried to reshape his fauxhawk, leaving it a bit lopsided.

"Okay, folks, we still have to find Pratt. Wife says he's at work. Next stop, Hardware SuperCenter on Peoria. Let's move!"

7

———

Hardware SuperCenter was a sprawling big-box store composed of ten-foot-tall shelves stocked with hardware, tools, pool supplies, appliances, and a garden center. And not a helpful hardware person in sight. I'd once accompanied my brother, Jake, to the location near my house. Big mistake. He was like a kid in a candy store. Seriously, how many hammers or saw blades does one person need?

Caden, Rodeo, and I strolled in through the automatic doors, drawing stares from customers and employees alike. Between our ballistic vests, walkie-talkies, and weapons, they probably figured we were a SWAT team.

"Caden, head over to the garden center and cover that exit," I said. "Pratt's file says that's where he works."

"Finally a chance to get in on the action." Caden hustled away past the pool supplies toward another set of automatic doors separating the garden center from the rest of the store.

"Where you want me, Jinx?" Rodeo asked.

"Circle around outside to the back door. Don't need him slipping out through an employee exit."

"Copy that."

I approached the customer service desk. A woman in her midforties wearing a brown employee vest looked up as I came near. Her name tag read "Sylvia" and indicated she was a shift manager. A concerned expression emerged on her face.

"Can I help you?" she asked.

"I'm Jinx Ballou." I held up my badge and ID. "I'm looking for Rudy Pratt, one of your employees."

She shook her head. "What now?"

"He missed his court date. I'm authorized to return him to jail."

"Let me see if he's clocked in." Her mouth was a thin line as she typed on a computer keyboard. "Should be in the landscaping tools section."

"In the garden center?"

"Not quite. I'll show you."

I followed her past bins of Christmas lights and yard decorations. "I'm surprised you didn't fire him."

"We did initially," she said through gritted teeth.

"But what? You thought, 'What the hell, he's only charged with murdering one of our employees?'"

"I got an email from corporate insisting we reinstate him pending the outcome of his trial."

"Corporate office wants an accused murderer working here? Sounds like a lawsuit waiting to happen."

She turned and met my gaze. "I don't disagree."

"What's he like as an employee?"

"All I'm allowed to say is that he works here. For now, at least."

We arrived at an aisle stocked with shovels, pickaxes, machetes, and other implements of destruction. A wiry man with close-cropped hair and a brown vest walked past the other end of the aisle.

"That's him," she said, pointing. "Hey, Rudy! Someone to see you!"

He poked his head back down the aisle. His eyes widened. He took off toward the middle of the store.

"Shit!" I took off after him, dodging customers, carts, and product displays. The guy was fast. It was all I could do to keep up with him. I drew my Taser, but too many people wandering through the aisles made it impossible to get a clean shot.

He cut to the right into the hand tools section. I rounded the corner and just missed getting beaned with a claw hammer he'd thrown. I raised the Taser. "Stop, Pratt!"

He ducked behind a Dremel tool display and took off back toward the garden center.

"Dammit!" I poured on speed, trying to catch him, and spoke into my walkie. "Caden," I said through gasping breaths. "Pratt's headed...your way."

"Copy that."

I gained on him as we blazed through the Christmas decorations area. I aimed the Taser squarely at his back. As my finger squeezed the trigger, a shopping cart appeared out of nowhere. I tumbled headlong over it, ducked into a roll on the bare concrete floor, landed on my feet. A box of icicle lights flickered from the jolt of electricity from the Taser darts embedded in the package.

"You people should watch where you're going!" A pudgy African-American woman with a crown of white hair gave me the stink eye while a store employee helped her to her feet. A load of plastic Santas, artificial garland, and gold Christmas balls lay scattered on the floor next to her overturned cart.

"Sorry." I took off again after Pratt, replacing the Taser cartridge as I ran.

In the garden center, I scrambled down aisles of potted plants, searching for my quarry. My nose filled with the scent of soil and growing things.

I turned in time to see Pratt charge toward Caden with a shopping cart loaded with potted citrus trees.

Caden hunkered down in an attempt to stop the cart and grab Pratt, but the momentum of the cart was too much for him. He fell hard into a row of concrete statuaries. The cart overturned, and Pratt raced out the entrance.

By the time I reached the doorway, Pratt had vanished into the parking lot. "Damn it!"

I returned to check on Caden. He was pulling himself to his feet. He felt the back of his head and winced. "Mother puss bucket."

"You okay?" I asked.

"Just a bump on the head. Can't believe I let him get past me."

"Don't worry about it. We'll get him."

"What happened to your knee?" he asked.

My jeans were torn and stained with a quarter-sized spot of blood. "I tried vaulting over a shopping cart. Failed to stick the landing, I guess."

"Shopping carts are dangerous," Caden said with a smirk. "They should be banned."

Despite the ache in my leg and my frustration at losing Pratt, I couldn't help chuckling. "Damn straight."

I called Rodeo on the walkie. He showed up along with Sylvia, the shift manager.

"How'd he get past you?" Rodeo asked.

I shrugged. "Home field advantage." I turned to Sylvia. "No offense, lady, but your corporate office was stupid to keep him on."

She looked embarrassed. "I just called HR corporate about Rudy jumping bail. They denied advising me to rehire him after his arrest. Turns out the email was a fake."

"Do yourself a favor and don't take him back." I handed her a business card. "If he shows up again, call me."

"Don't have to tell me twice." She walked away and assisted a fellow employee cleaning up the toppled trees and statuaries.

I led my team out into the parking lot. The sun was below the horizon, and the reds and oranges of the Phoenix sunset were fading to pink and gray. The air had grown chilly.

"Let's check to see if Pratt went home to the wife and kids. I suspect he's in the wind, but since he's a first-timer, you never know."

We piled into our vehicles and returned to the Pratt residence. Nearby street lamps flickered on, and houses glowed from within like a cheesy Thomas Kinkade painting. Except for the Pratt house. It remained dark. The car in the driveway was gone.

I sent Rodeo around one side, Caden around the other, while I crept to the front door, peeking through the side windows. No movement from inside as far as I could tell and no sounds. I pounded on the door and rang the doorbell a few times. "Open up! Bail enforcement!"

I waited a few minutes, but there was no sign of life inside.

"You guys see anything?" I asked over the walkie.

"No lights in any of the bedrooms," replied Caden.

"They put a piece of plywood over the broken door," Rodeo said. "Kitchen and living room are dark. Looks like they bugged out."

"What now?" Caden asked.

I pulled out my phone and called the cell phone number listed in Pratt's file. It went straight to voicemail. "No answer."

"Can you use that tracking app?"

The previous year, Becca had installed an app on my phone that let me instantly track the location of another phone by entering the number. She'd also warned me that the app's legality was questionable.

"I deleted it after Becca said the feds were tracking installations of the app. I'll have her do some skip tracing on Pratt and see where he might be holed up. Let's canvass his neighbors, then call it a day."

Even in this day of internet searches and virtual paper trails, 90 percent of apprehending FTAs was knocking on doors and making phone calls. In short, talking to people who knew the person I was looking for.

I sent Caden east. I took the neighbors to the west. Rodeo

knocked on doors across the street. Since it was early evening, I figured people would be home from work and might know where Pratt was hiding out.

A Latina woman with tired eyes and graying hair opened the first door I knocked on. She looked frail and all of five foot two if she were standing on her tiptoes. The pale-pink-and-gray sweater she wore looked as if it had been knitted sometime before the color television was invented.

"Hi! I'm looking for your neighbor, Rudy Pratt. Would you know where he is by chance?"

"*No hablo ingles.*" She started to shut the door.

"Wait!" I repeated my question in Spanish. The neighbor replied that she didn't know her neighbors well. Just noted that they were rude. She wasn't surprised he was arrested for murdering a Mexican immigrant.

Got no argument from me, sister, I thought.

I gave her my business card and told her I was there to take Mr. Pratt to jail.

"Call me if you see him," I said in Spanish.

The twinkle in her eye told me she'd be happy to help if she could. "Is there a reward?" she asked.

"If you help me catch him, I'll pay you twenty dollars."

"*Cinquenta dollares,*" she insisted. Fifty bucks.

"*¡Demasiado!*" Too much. "*Trenta.*"

She harrumphed and started shutting the door.

"Fine. *Cuarenta,*" I said. Forty.

"Okay. I call you if I see him," she said in English and shut the door.

I continued to the next neighbor but with similar luck. No one knew the Pratts by name, but a lot of people, both Latino and Anglo, held a dim view of the family. Most had seen his picture on the news and weren't surprised he'd been arrested.

When I reached the end of the block, I backtracked and met Caden and Rodeo by the vehicles.

"Any luck?" I asked, trying not to shiver. I was a hot weather girl, so anything below sixty degrees felt like freezing.

They both shook their heads.

"Not exactly a popular guy," said Caden. "I don't think even Mr. Rogers would want to be his neighbor."

"Can't imagine why," I said with dripping sarcasm. "Just because he's a racist charged with murdering a Latino coworker."

"Where to now?" Rodeo rubbed his arms to keep warm.

"Let's call it a day. I'll phone the references on his bail application. See if anyone knows where he might be."

"Okay, catch y'all later," said Caden.

Rodeo fist-bumped him. "Later, dude."

"Take care, Caden." I waved as he climbed into his car.

I turned to walk to the Gray Ghost when Rodeo asked, "Jinx, can we talk?"

He had a pained expression on his face, exaggerated by the shadows cast by the overhead streetlights.

"What's up?"

"I'm planning on breaking up with your brother."

"Why?" I asked. "You two make such a cute couple."

He folded his arms and stared at the pavement. "He's embarrassed to be seen with me."

"Bullshit! Why would he be embarrassed to be seen with you? You're fucking hot."

Rodeo's face colored. "Thanks, but I think he's dealing with some lingering internal homophobia. Absolutely refuses to hold my hand in public. And God forbid anyone sees me give him a peck on the cheek. I'm getting tired of it."

"Have you talked to him about it?"

"Many times. He keeps begging me to give him time, but it's been a year." He adjusted his Stetson. "I know Arizona's not the most gay-friendly state, but dude, come on. We're two tough, masculine guys. No one's going to mess with us. And if they do, fuck 'em."

I sighed. "I don't know what to say. I wish you'd give him

another chance, but I get where you're coming from. Do what you feel's right. It doesn't affect you and me."

Rodeo put a hand on my shoulder. "Thanks, girl. I didn't want things to get weird between us."

"Would it help if I talked to him?" I asked.

"I don't want it to seem like I'm airing our dirty laundry with you."

"Well, you kinda are."

"I know, but for now, let me handle it."

"You got it." I gave him a hug and a pat on the back. "I hope you two work things out. I like having you as family."

8

———

I called Becca on the way home. "How are you feeling?" I asked.

"Managing."

"Good. When you're up to it, I need you to do some digging for us on an asshole named Rudy Pratt. Phone logs, bank records, credit report, the works."

"I'll run it in the morning if I'm feeling better."

"Great. I'll send you the info I have on him." My phone beeped, showing an incoming call. "That's probably Conor. I gotta go. Take it easy, Becks."

"Say hello to lover boy for me."

"Will do."

I clicked over to the incoming call. "This is Jinx Ballou."

"Where are ya, love?" he asked in his Irish brogue.

"On the way home. Where are you?"

"At your place. Cooking dinner."

"You're cooking?" This was new. He could cook up a decent breakfast, but dinner was a new twist for him. "What's on the menu?"

"Potato leek soup. My grandmother's recipe."

"Sounds delish. I'll be there in ten." I hung up and drove the rest of the way home.

Before we started dating two years ago, Conor had been my boss at Viper Fugitive Recovery. But mixing business with pleasure turned out to be more problematic than I'd expected. So I quit and started my own bounty hunting crew.

I walked through the front door and was immediately drawn to the wonderful aroma in the air. "Smells good."

"Hope ya like it," he replied.

I stopped in the bedroom to pull off my gear. I was tempted to slip into my Wonder Woman costume since he'd mentioned it earlier. But I was too tired and stuck with my T-shirt, jeans, and bare feet.

The kitchen looked as if a monsoon had blown through. Cooking utensils, mixers, dirty bowls, and vegetable scraps were scattered everywhere, including the floor. Conor was wearing a lacy cooking apron over his tan Viper Fugitive Recovery polo shirt. His coppery curls were mussed. "Should be ready shortly. Just needs to simmer a bit more."

I hugged him from behind and was about to kiss him on the back of the neck when he jerked to the side. "Oi! Watch out!"

"What's wrong?" I asked.

"Nothing serious. Things got a wee bit rough when me and the boys nabbed this bloke." Conor tried to put on a brave face, but I could tell from his eyes he was hurting. "How was your day?"

"Two out of three for the day. Captured Daniel Warren, as you noted earlier." A flush of warmth ran up my neck as I thought about images of me in costume all over the news and internet. "Also picked up Conspiracy Bob."

A big grin split Conor's face. "How's our mate Bob doing these days?"

"Convinced that mole people are living in abandoned mines and planning acts of terrorism."

"God love the silly bugger! He's entertaining if nothing else."

He scooped up a spoonful of soup from the pot, blew on it, and ate it gingerly. "I think that's bloody well right."

He tossed the apron on the counter. I grabbed a couple of bowls from the cabinet, and we sat down at the kitchen table to eat. I caught him wincing as he settled into the chair next to me. A dark spot on his shirt glistened under his left arm.

"Con, you're bleeding."

Conor looked down at the growing stain. "Jesus bloody Christ!"

I peeled up the bottom of his shirt. A folded piece of gauze was taped to his skin and oozing blood. "Doesn't look good, babe. What happened?"

"Some wanker came at me with a broken bottle to keep me from dragging his mate back to lockup. It's nothing."

"Nothing, my ass. I'm not letting you bleed out on my kitchen floor." I tugged off the tape and revealed an ugly gouge, crusted with dried blood but still seeping quite a bit. "Shit, this needs to be stitched up, hon. We gotta take you to the ER."

"Bollocks! I'm not going to bloody hospital for a wee scratch. All it needs is a little superglue. That's what they'd use at the ER, anyway. Why hand over a few thousand dollars to those greedy fucks when I can do the same job for a buck ninety-nine?"

His aversion to going to the ER wasn't about money. It was fear. I'd seen the man stare down the barrel of guns, tangle with large dogs, and go at it with some seriously scary dudes. He was no wilting flower. But a brutal experience twenty years earlier had left him with a phobia of hospitals.

He and his father had been involved with a car bombing in the shopping village of Omagh. Shortly before the blast, Conor made a call to the media to warn people away from where the bomb would be detonated. But he was given the wrong location. Local police ended up steering people toward the danger zone. Conor's sister, Bernadette, was among those killed in the blast. When he found her shattered body in the hospital, along with dozens of other casualties, it left a deep and lasting scar of guilt and trauma on his psyche.

"Fine. But just so you know, this isn't how I prefer to 'play doctor.'"

I tried to squeeze the edges of the wound closed, and he yelped. "Bloody fucking Christ!"

"I don't think superglue's going to close this, Conor. This cut looks deep, and it could get infected. It's not worth the risk. I'm taking you to the ER."

"I'm not going to bloody hospital." His freckled face turned flame red. His eyes grew large, no doubt from a mix of anger and deep terror. "I...I can't."

Our eyes locked. I caught a glimpse of the frightened seventeen-year-old embroiled in the insanity and violence of the Troubles in Ireland. "Oh, come on. You took me to the hospital last year when I got hurt."

He shook his head. "That was for you, love, when ya had a major concussion. I'm not going through all that..."

"Trauma?"

"Whatever ya want to call it, over a fucking scratch. Just put some of that disinfectant on it and pull it shut with a couple of plasters."

I sighed. Nothing I said would convince him to get proper medical treatment. "Fine. I'll do what I can. But I'm telling you now, if it gets infected, I'm going to roofie you, throw you over my shoulder, and drag your freckled Irish ass to the ER." I retrieved my first aid kit from the guest bathroom.

"Before you do anything, can ya give me a little whiskey first?"

I grabbed a sterile pad and pressed it to the wound. He winced. "Hold this in place so my kitchen floor doesn't end up looking like a crime scene."

I grabbed the bottle of Jameson from the pantry. He took it from me and made a face. "Ya trying to be funny, love?"

I glanced at the bottle. It was empty. "Guess you finished it off last time you were here."

"Don't be daft. There was at least a third of a bottle left last Thursday."

"Don't look at me." I shrugged. "I rarely touch the stuff. I'm more of a tequila girl."

"Must've been the dog, then," he said with a half smile.

"I don't have a dog." I playfully chucked him on the shoulder. "Guess you're gonna have to grit your teeth while I deal with this barroom battle wound. You want a wooden spoon to bite down on?"

He harrumphed. "Just bloody do it."

I donned a pair of latex gloves and squeezed antibiotic gel into the wound. He growled when I pulled the wound closed.

"Huh," I said, grinning. "I guess I have a dog after all." I secured the wound with four Steri-Strips.

"Ya done?" His forehead glistened with sweat.

I covered the wound with a sterile pad and taped it in place. "For now. Try not to twist around too much."

"Now what fun is that?" he asked with a mischievous grin. "No need to stop playing doctor now."

9

After dinner, as I was cleaning up the mess Conor had made, he came up behind me and wrapped his arms around me. He planted kisses on the back of my neck, sending jolts of excitement down my spine and an intense heat to my groin. My breath quickened, and my ass curled into hardness. "Oh...sweet mother of bliss..." I hissed with pleasure.

"Now where's this super suit I saw ya wearing on the telly?"

"Silly boy." My head swam as he pinched the hardened buds of my nipples while pressing my hips against the kitchen counter. My body ached to feel him inside me. "You've...you've seen me wear it...a hundred times. Oh fuck, that feels so good."

"What? You'll dress for your geeky mates but not for me?" he teased, pulling my T-shirt up and off and turning me around to face him.

Those emerald eyes coupled with his cheesy grin took my breath away every bit as much as his firm but gentle touch.

"Oh, baby...I'd do anything for you."

He kneeled down, grunting, and began teasing my nipples with his tongue. "Would ya now?"

"Anything, just please don't stop." My hands reached into his ginger curls, pressing him to my chest. Waves of passion, plea-sure, and gratitude tossed me around like a ship in a storm.

Slowly he rose to his feet, leaving a trail of kisses up my neck until I kissed him deeply. When I finally came up for air a moment later, I managed to ask, "You want me in my costume?"

He grinned and shook his head. "Naw, I'd rather us just get naked."

Despite my wobbly knees and the headiness of hormones raging through my system, I managed to lead him to the bedroom, where I peeled off my jeans, then helped him off with his shirt. His torso was pockmarked with scars acquired from his experiences as a security specialist in Afghanistan and Iraq and a few from his work as a bounty hunter. But these marks only turned me on more, reminders of his strength and endurance.

I glanced down at his most recent injury. The Steri-Strips seemed to be holding because no more blood was seeping from his wound.

"You okay to do this?" I asked as I sat on the bed and pulled a bottle of lubricant from my nightstand. "Maybe I should be on top this time."

He studied me for a moment, the wheels clearly turning in his head. His smile deepened. "I think I'd like that."

He lay on his back on the bed, wincing. I helped him off with his jeans and boxers. The sight of his hard cock rising from a nest of coppery hair sent a new wave of chills through me.

I bent down and wrapped my lips around the head of his cock, eliciting a throaty groan from Conor. "Bloody hell, that feels good."

I continued to suck, taking him into my throat as deeply as I could, stroking his shaft with my hand. More groans told me he wasn't feeling too much pain. His hands guided my head in a rhythm with his hips. I would have let him come in my mouth, but my own need to feel him in me grew irresistible.

I sat up and rubbed a spot of lubricant on his cock.

"Oh yeah, love, come here," he murmured.

Gingerly I mounted him, trying not to bump his side with my knee. I rubbed my labia up and down the length of his cock, the head rubbing the nub of my clit. Shock waves of pleasure caused me to gasp. When I could take no more, I let him slip inside me. I gritted my teeth as his cock throbbed and filled me. "Conor, yessss..." I purred.

He leaned up and suckled the bud of my breast as we fell into a natural rhythm, creating our own music of sighs and moans. My pulse raced as I neared climax. We thrust harder, slamming into each other with such force that each beat nearly took my breath away.

His hands tightened around my waist as he neared orgasm. "Oh, Jinxie. I'm so close."

"Yes, yes, yes!" I gasped. A flash of lightning rippled through my brain, sending shock waves of orgasm through every nerve ending in my body. An instant later, a blast of warmth exploded inside of me as he came. I pressed him as deep as he could go.

He eased me on the bed beside him, cradling me in his arm. Waves of ecstasy continued to crash on the shores of my mind, like the aftermath of a storm.

"That was fucking brilliant, love," he whispered into my ear.

"I didn't hurt you?" I asked.

"Don't see me complaining, do ya?"

I pulled him close, breathing in his scent. We'd been together more than two years, and it still amazed me that a guy as sexy and sweet and masculine as Conor could be interested in a trans gal like me—the niggling remnants of internalized transphobia.

"Oh, Jinxie," he said, laying gentle kisses on my shoulder. "Now don't ya think life would be easier without worrying whose house we're sleeping at on any given night?"

I groaned and not from pleasure. "Let's not spoil the evening."

"Just sell your place and move in with me. Make everything loads simpler."

"Or you could move in with me. I've got more square footage.

How am I supposed to squeeze all my shit into that matchbox you call a home?"

He made a face. "I'm still paying for the renovations I had done a few years ago. You've got all that equity in your place. Think of what ya could do with all that money."

I met his gaze. "I'm sorry, but your place is empty and...sterile. It feels like a bunker."

"No one's saying ya couldn't gussy it up a bit, love."

"I've grown really attached to this house. It was the first place that was mine, you know? Besides, where would I put my workout equipment? And my action figures. And my comic books? Also, your kitchen's so tiny, you can't cook a decent meal there."

He shrugged. "I've been eating there quite fine for several years."

"Frozen dinners and mac 'n cheese from a box don't count."

"Oi, I can cook more than that. Didn't ya like the soup?"

Now I felt guilty. I kissed him. "The soup was wonderful."

"This is about your ex-boyfriend, isn't it? Willie Steinwhats-it?"

"His name was Wilson Stametz. And how do you know about him?"

"Your brother mentioned him a couple weeks ago at your parents'."

"Where was I?" It felt weird that Conor and Jake were talking about me behind my back.

"Helping your ma with something in the kitchen, I think. We were talking about his business renovating houses. He mentioned he renovated your place."

"What's that got to do with Wilson?"

"He thought that might be the reason ya didn't want to shack up with me."

"Jesus, fuck!" I rolled over and faced the wall. "Why can't Jake mind his own fucking business?"

"What's the big deal, Jinxie?" He started to massage my shoulder. I shrugged off his hands. "And how come ya never mentioned this bloke before?"

"Because he's ancient history, that's why. I was in the process of moving in with him when I caught him sticking his dick into some bitch from work. In what would've been our bed." I wanted to throttle Jake so bad I could almost feel his pulse underneath my grip.

"Is that it? Ya think I'm gonna shag some other girl? 'Cause ya know I'd never do that to ya."

"I'm just not ready, okay? Besides, what would my mother think of the two of us living together?"

"You don't think she knows we're shagging?"

"I try not to think about it."

"Is this a backhanded way to get me to marry ya?"

I turned around to see a big grin on his face. "Marriage? What? No...I'm..." My face grew hot.

"I'm just messing with ya, love. We got no need to rush anything." He cradled my head in his hands and kissed me gently on the lips. "Jenna Christina Ballou, I love ya with all my Irish heart. Even if you don't want to marry me."

"I love you too. With all my Italian-Cajun-whatever heart. I just... I never thought of myself as being someone's wife. Sounds so..."

"Normal?" he said with a chuckle. "You're anything but, that's for sure."

"What?" I asked, playing along. "Just because I'm a transgender woman who works as a bounty hunter and dresses like Wonder Woman when I'm not practicing parkour or krav maga? You're saying that's not normal?"

"I think the proper term would be uniquely brilliant." He kissed me. "Besides, normal girls bore the shite outta me."

"Do you hate me for not wanting to give up my little Bohemian bungalow?"

"'Course not. If you're not ready, you're not ready. I just think life'd be simpler if we both lived at my place. And safer."

"Safer? Why?"

"Those renovations I did? Well, I actually did turn it into a bit of a bunker."

I sat up. "What do you mean?"

"The walls are a foot-thick solid brick. The windows are one-inch polycarbonate instead of glass. Steel-reinforced doors. No one's getting in unless I want them to."

"Was this because of that drive-by a few years back?"

"Aye! When I captured a member of the Nineteenth Avenue Jaguars after he jumped bail, some of his mates decided to use their TEC-9s to send me a message. Luckily I was out with you that night."

"Why haven't you told me about these renovations before?"

Conor blushed. "You already called it a bunker. I was embarrassed to admit you were right."

"You think I should do the same to my house?"

"No, I think ya should move in with me. Trust me, love, we can sort out all the details. And if ya decide ya wanna get hitched, then I'm happy to oblige."

"Let me think about it." The afterglow of sex was morphing into fatigue. "It's been a long, weird day. I'm exhausted."

"Sweet dreams, love." He kissed me again on the lips. Passion rekindled, but I was too exhausted to go another round, even with someone as sexy as Conor.

10

I took the next two days to enjoy Winter Con and give Becca time to see what she could dig up on Rudy Pratt. On my way home from the convention each evening, I drove past the Pratts' residence, but the place remained dark and deserted.

On Monday morning, I woke to the sound of someone laying on my doorbell at quarter to six. I usually got up at six, anyway, but those extra fifteen minutes of sleep could make all the difference. Whoever was at my door was going to meet a slow and painful death, unless they had a good reason for being there.

Conor had spent the night on a stakeout for one of his fugitives. I chambered a round in my Ruger and shuffled out of bed in my pajamas. Overly cautious? Maybe. But after finding the body of a dead journalist on my doorstep the previous year, I'd been wary of unexpected visitors.

"Who the hell is it?" I mumbled, too bleary-eyed to make sense of anything through the peephole in my front door.

"Morning, sunshine. It's your favorite brother, Jake," he replied in a tone way too cheerful for that time of morning.

"Oh for fuck's sake. You're my only brother."

I set the Ruger on a side table and opened the door. It was still dark outside and damned near freezing. My brother stood there in a ratty denim jacket over a Stone Temple Pilots T-shirt. His gelled hair was tossed in a devil-may-care style.

"Dude, you're lucky I didn't shoot your ass. You got any idea what time it is?"

"You missed Sunday brunch yesterday. Mom was worried. Didn't you get her voicemail messages?"

Sunday brunch at my parents' house was a big deal in my family. Missing it without a good excuse was a mortal sin in my mother's eyes, especially after I quit accompanying her to Mass several years ago.

A good daughter wouldn't blow off Sunday brunch to cosplay at Winter Con, especially without telling her mother ahead of time. A good daughter would return her mother's calls to keep her from worrying. I was not a good daughter.

But to be fair, several cast members from *Black Panther* had appeared on a panel Sunday morning. I figured it was easier to beg forgiveness than ask permission.

"I was busy. Work stuff." And now I'd lied to cover my ass. I was a bad daughter.

"You couldn't call? Mom's been freaking out. Bad enough you chase bad guys for a living."

"Look, I'm sorry, all right? Things have been crazy lately." I regretted upsetting my mom more than she already was. But sometimes her incessant worrying felt oppressive, dripping with Catholic guilt.

"You're going to be there tomorrow night for her birthday, right?"

Shit. I totally spaced it. "I...uh...yeah, of course."

"You forgot, didn't you?"

"No," I insisted. "I just, well, I'm a little groggy from being woken up early."

"You forgot." He shook his head. "Sometimes I wonder—"

"I'll be there, all right? You want to play the Catholic guilt game, let's talk about..." I stopped myself, remembering that Rodeo had told me to let him handle their situation.

"Talk about what?" His face darkened.

"Nothing." I stared at his dusty work boots as the tension between us grew. "I'll call Mom in a little while and tell her I'm sorry for worrying her. I'll see you tomorrow night, okay?"

"Yeah," he said without enthusiasm. "See ya." He stormed back to his truck. His tires squealed as he drove off.

I stood there feeling like shit. I was a horrible daughter, a lousy sister, and a rotten girlfriend afraid of commitment. I just felt so smothered by everyone wanting something from me. Maybe that was what family was supposed to be.

A couple of hours later, I called my mom and apologized for missing brunch and not calling. I even admitted that it was to attend Winter Con. Catholic guilt was a powerful weapon, and my mother was a true master.

After a quick shower, I pulled on my bounty hunter gear, determined to track down Rudy Pratt. At eight thirty, I arrived at the Hub, near Grand Avenue and Roosevelt Street.

The old building reminded me of an inverted boat hull, with a broad metal beam that jutted out like a ram bow. A twenty-foot-tall wall of paned glass served as the front of the building, a carry-over from its days as a car dealership in the 1940s.

I shuffled across the parking lot, still weary from my early wake-up call. I carried a tray of two coffees from Tres Leches Café in my left hand, with my computer bag slung over my shoulder. I stopped short when a flyer taped to a lamppost caught my eye. Across the top, the words "White Nation" were printed in large block letters with swastikas on either side. "What the hell?"

White Nation was a militant white separatist group that had held rallies across the country, particularly in conservative-leaning states. These rallies often ended in violence. A few people had been killed. And yet somehow these people still managed to get permits to protest.

The text of the flyer announced an upcoming protest at Wesley Bolin Plaza near the Arizona State Capitol complex. It called on "white citizens to show up and take back their city from all the undesirables." It decried the planned removal of the Confederate Troops Memorial in the plaza as symbolic of "the liberal elite's systematic agenda to extinguish the white race and imperil Christianity."

Bile rose in my throat. Since Republicans had taken the presidency and both houses of Congress, white nationalists of all stripes had been emboldened to spew their hate without fear of reprisal. Violence against women, queer people, and people of color was on the rise.

I ripped the flyer from the post and crumpled it in my hand. I was tempted to toss it on the ground, but I tried to avoid littering. Also I didn't want some alt-right neo-Nazi to put it back up either. I stuffed it in my pocket and trudged inside the building.

The Hub's interior was a grungy, open industrial space with a cracked cement slab for a floor, pockmarked with divots from where they'd pulled out the walls. Dozens of collapsible tables served as desks with a wild assortment of secondhand seating ranging from uber-adjustable Herman Miller knockoffs to flimsy plastic folding chairs.

Like Becca, most members of the Hub worked in the tech industry. A few were online entrepreneurs. And then there was me, bounty hunter extraordinaire. As I walked in the door, the hypnotic beat of electronic dance music thrummed from unseen speakers. Overhead lighting was subdued.

Becca sat at the table we shared, staring intently at a trio of flat screens. I set a large latte with almond milk in front of her.

"Good to see you up and about," I said.

"Yay, coffee!" she exclaimed, her eyes suddenly coming alive. "You are a goddess."

"You're welcome." I pulled the crumpled flyer from my pocket and handed it to her. "Can you believe this shit?"

She took a sip of her coffee and uncrumpled the flyer. Her upper lip curled in disgust. "Jeez Louise, what is it with these people? That buffoon gets elected, and suddenly every bigot thinks it's open season on marginalized people. If I weren't so opposed to guns and violence, I'd have half a mind to get a machine gun and mow them all down."

"Good thing I'm not opposed to guns and violence," I said with a smirk.

"Don't! The last thing we need is you in prison. I just get so sick of these assholes."

I sat down next to her. "Speaking of bigoted assholes, what'd you find out about my latest fugitive, Rudy Pratt?"

She took another sip of her coffee and rattled away on her keyboard. "Rudy Pratt. Rudy Tootie Fresh and Fruity. The Rudester. Quite a bit, actually."

"Yeah?"

"He was originally from Houston. Got a track scholarship to Texas A&M, where he earned a degree in electrical engineering. Worked at SpaceJet—"

"I know all that. I'm not writing his memoir. I need to know where he is. Who's he been talking to?"

"Most of the recent calls to his cell phone are to his immediate family—wife, son—and to his attorney at the law firm Longstreet, Bragg, and Jackson. I'll send the log to your cloud drive."

"What about social media?"

"He has accounts on Facebook, Reddit, and Twitter. Not very active. He follows a lot of extreme right-wing political and religious groups. The guy's a bigot from the word go. Racist. Homophobe. Transphobe."

"His family's the same way. Any indication where he might be hiding out?"

"No. As I said, he's not real active. Lurks mostly."

"Financial records?"

"He has a checking account and a small savings. He makes small but regular donations to ultraconservative organizations like the Christian Heritage PAC, the Patriots of Liberty Caucus, and the Divine Truth Full Gospel Church. But get this, he has numerous debit card charges from the Pink Pearl Gentleman's Club and Maggie's Cabaret. Both strip clubs. The guy likes the ladies, despite being married."

"Maybe he's going there to spread the gospel of Jesus," I said in an exaggerated Southern accent.

"Praise Jesus!" Becca said with a chuckle.

"Also a bar called Dixie's but no more than once a month or so."

"Not a lot to go on, but it'll have to do. Thanks."

I opened up the file Becca sent me and perused the most frequently called phone numbers.

"Oh, Jinx. There is something else."

"More info on Pratt?" I looked up, hoping for a clue to track down my quarry.

"I'm afraid not." Her face had an unsettled expression on it. "It's bad, but you need to see it."

11

On one of Becca's screens, a grainy surveillance video began playing. In the video, a burly white guy was holding up a bank while wearing a rubber Halloween monster mask. A tattoo peeked above the collar of his coat, but I couldn't make it out.

"This was taken a week ago at a bank in Casper, Wyoming," she said.

"Why are you showing me this?"

"You'll see."

She pulled up a second video over the first, this one from an exterior camera. "This was taken in the bank parking lot." The same guy was pulling off his mask. The video was less grainy than the first, but I still couldn't make out any details.

"He looks vaguely familiar, but I can't place him. That tattoo on his neck looks like a cartoon. Can you boost the resolution?" I asked.

She enhanced it enough that my subconscious started sending up red flags. The hand holding my coffee trembled. Something I had buried deep in my memory was struggling to surface. Something about that tattoo.

She pulled up a third video. "Another robbery a few days later in Grand Junction, Colorado. Same guy, same mask, same tattoo."

My stomach twisted like a rope. "Becca, I—"

"And this from last Friday at a bank in Kayenta, Arizona." This time it was clear enough for me to make out the ink—Woody Woodpecker with boxing gloves.

My coffee cup slipped from my hand and hit the floor, but I barely noticed. My whole body was shaking, my eyes fixed on the screen. I knew why.

Someone was calling my name. Someone else was repeating the word "no" like a broken record. I realized the latter voice was mine.

I was no longer the thirty-year-old bounty hunter who could take down fugitives twice my size. I was back to being a shy seventeen-year-old trans girl being bludgeoned in the street by former middleweight boxing champion Barclay "The Beast" Dietz, who happened to be my high school boyfriend's father.

Police arrested Dietz that night, then released him on $200,000 bail. He never showed up to court. He simply vanished without a trace after emptying the bank account he shared with his wife.

Dietz's family lost their house. His son, Peyton, lost his football scholarship to UNLV. All because Barclay Dietz couldn't deal with the fact that Peyton and I were dating. Didn't matter that Peyton knew I was trans and didn't care. His father was terrified I'd turn his son gay.

"Jinxie! Look at me, girl." Becca held the sides of my head in her hands, forcing me to look away from the screen and into her eyes. "I'm so sorry. You're safe. You're with me."

"No, no, I...I'm not safe. He's coming. He...he...he's coming after me."

"What the hell's wrong with her, Becca?" asked Troy Reid, a game developer at the next desk.

"Jinx, listen to me. He's not coming after you. He's probably coming back to see Peyton."

I took a deep breath and tried to stuff all of the fear into the furthest reaches of my mind. "How...how do you know?"

"A hunch. It's been what? Ten years?"

"Th-Thirteen."

"He doesn't know anything about you. What you look like. Where you live. For all he knows, you moved clear across the country."

"He might've seen that article in *Phoenix Living*."

"That article was published over a year ago, and he's been living up in Wyoming or North Dakota somewhere."

"Peyton could've sent it to him."

"Why would Peyton do that? He probably hates the guy. The man ruined Peyton's college career."

"Peyton never came to see me in the hospital. You know that? I spent a month in the ICU and not one word from him. Not even a text. He blames me for ruining his family. I just know it."

"Don't be stupid. Peyton probably feels guilty about what happened to you."

I turned away from her and stared at the floor. My pulse was still racing. I felt the need to be very, very violent. "I should go. I've got a fugitive to catch." I stood unsteadily from my chair.

Becca stood up and hugged me. Her arms helped steady me.

"You've got this, girl," she said as she pulled back. "Don't let that piece of shit fuck with your head. Go splash some water on your face in the restroom. Get yourself centered. You're gonna need your head in the game when you go after Pratt."

"You're right." I took a deep breath and walked toward the restrooms at the back of the building.

"And grab some paper towels to clean up the coffee while you're at it," Becca teased.

The two restrooms at the Hub each had four stalls, but they were no longer marked as men's and women's. Both were designated as unisex. It had felt weird the first time I walked in and saw a guy washing his hands at the sink. But since the stalls all had locking doors on them, I figured what the hell. It wasn't that big of a deal. Everyone else adjusted, as well.

I stood for a moment, staring at my reflection in the mirror. My heart thundered in my chest as I tried to stop the loop of memories playing in my throbbing head.

Someone put a hand on my shoulder. Instinctively, I wheeled around with a palm heel strike. The blow landed on Troy's chin, cushioned by his bushy hipster beard. I stopped myself an instant before years of training drove my other fist into his solar plexus.

"What the hell, Jinx?" he said, rubbing his chin. "Just checking if you're okay. Shit."

"I-I'm sorry. I thought you were...doesn't matter what I thought. You okay?"

He eyed me warily. "Remind me not to pick a fight with you. Damn!"

"Sorry." I couldn't think of anything else to say. He walked out without another word.

"Shit." I turned back to my reflection. One thing I was sure of. Somehow, I was going to track down Barclay Dietz. And I was going to make him wish he'd never laid a hand on me.

12

I sat down at my desk, and Becca gave me a strange look. "You okay?"

"I accidentally punched Troy," I said, staring blankly at Pratt's file.

"What?" She chuckled. "Seriously?"

I shrugged.

"Considering all the times he tried to mansplain IT security shit to me, I'd say he had it coming. What'd he do this time?"

"Put his hand on my shoulder." When Becca raised an eyebrow, I continued. "Not in a sexual way. I think he was checking if I was all right."

"That'll teach him. Seriously, though, you going to be okay?"

"I'll be fine. Especially once I track down Barclay Dietz."

"And then what? You going to arrest him or..." She let it hang, as if uncertain where to go with it. She knew me well.

"I'll decide that when I find him. Would I kill him in cold blood? I can't tell you how many times I've wanted to."

"It might be a tad illegal. I'd hate to see that beautiful bod of yours in a pair of Department of Corrections coveralls. Do they still make prisoners wear pink boxers?"

"Just the guys." I caught her staring at me. "Okay, I wouldn't kill him in cold blood. But you know, a guy like that might easily get provoked. And if I let him throw the first punch…"

"Don't be crazy. The man's a former boxer. Even though he's older now, he could still knock you out. And then who knows what?"

"I'm not saying he'd *land* the first punch. I've learned a thing or two since high school graduation. I can take him. The fact that he's a boxer plays in my favor. I could claim I was in fear for my life, especially since he nearly killed me the first time."

"I'm not hearing this." She put her fingers in her ears. "Lalalalalala…"

I balled up the White Nation flyer and threw it at her. "Fine. I won't kill him. I'd much rather get the reward money for dragging his ass back to jail."

"That's more like it."

"How'd you put all of this together?" I asked her.

"Back when I was a fledgling hacker, I was experimenting with search algorithms. I used what you'd told me about Barclay Dietz as search criteria to scour the web. Never thought it'd locate him for real."

"Well, it worked."

"How you plan on finding him?"

"As you said, he's probably here to see Peyton. If we track down my ex, maybe we'll find the Beast."

"You want me to skip trace your ex-boyfriend?"

"If you don't mind."

"Will do."

"Now I just need to track down this Pratt fellow." I opened Pratt's file. He'd listed several personal references on his bail application. Always a good place to start. The first name on the list was Jack Stagg, so I called the number.

On the third ring, a gruff voice asked, "Yeah?"

"Oh, hi. Is this Jack?" I cranked up my voice to bubble-headed babydoll stripper.

"Yeah, who the hell's this?"

"My name's Amethyst. I'm a dancer down at the Pink Pearl."

Becca glanced up from her computer and gave me a bemused look.

"How'd you get this number?" asked Jack.

"Well, here's the thing. Last night, this guy Rudy came into the club and asked me for a lap dance. Believe me, I give the best lap dances. Afterward, I discovered he'd left his wallet. Total bummer, right? So I looked through it and found his address. I went by his house, but no one was home. Then I noticed this little piece of paper with your name and number on it. So I figured, like, I'd call, you know, hoping I could get him his wallet back."

Becca started cracking up. I put my finger to my lips so she'd keep quiet.

"Why'd he have my number in his wallet?"

"Honestly, sir, I got no idea. I'm just trying to get it back to him. Especially after he gave me such a generous tip."

"Try his cell." He rattled off the cell number listed on the bail application. No help there.

"Thanks, but do you know where he is? Don't want the missus answering the phone when I call, if ya know what I mean?" I snort-laughed.

Becca turned purple trying to keep quiet.

"Look, lady, I got no idea where he's at."

"Well, if you see him, can you have him call me?" I gave him my number. I'd have to be careful how I answered so as not to tip him off when he called.

"Not planning on seeing him anytime soon. But if I do, I'll have him call you." He hung up.

The moment I put down the phone, Becca burst into a raucous fit of laughter. The other people in the Hub stared at the outburst. "Oh, shit. I gotta say, Jinx, that was the best one yet. When you snorted, I about peed my pants."

"Unfortunately, the dude didn't know where Pratt is and seemed awfully suspicious."

"I know you. You'll track him down one way or another."

"Let's hope." My mind drifted to the events of the night before. "Hey, I meant to tell you. Conor asked me to move in with him. Again."

"It's about damn time you two shack up."

"I like having my own place."

"So have him move in with you."

"He doesn't want to sell his house. Still owes a lot on those renovations he had done." I rubbed my face with my hands, trying to clear my head. "And then he sort of asked me to marry him."

"He proposed?"

"Not exactly. He asked me if I was asking *him* if I wanted to get married."

She shook her head. "Doesn't sound very romantic."

"Speaking of relationships, who's this new friend of yours?"

Her face turned a rosy tan. "Easton. They're nonbinary."

"Yeah? That's cool. And when do I get to meet this Easton?"

"Soon. We're taking things slow for now," she said.

"But they've been helping out when your chronic fatigue flares up?"

"Yeah. They moved in next door a couple months ago. We got to talking and learned we're both ace," she said, meaning asexual. "We've been doing a lot of cuddling but no decisions on whether this is a long-term committed thing."

"Well, I'm happy for you."

"Thanks. Me too."

"Just know that if Easton's ever not available during a flare-up, I'm still here for you." I put a hand on her shoulder.

"Thanks. We're still besties, right?" she asked shyly.

"Absolutely! And if Easton breaks your heart, I'll break their fucking legs."

Becca laughed. "Thanks. Let's hope it doesn't come to that."

I called Pratt's other references and left a few generic voice-mails saying I was a friend of Pratt's and was having trouble getting ahold of him.

From there, I flipped randomly through the documents I had on him. Nothing jumped out at me as an obvious lead.

Using a word processing program, I created a Fugitive Wanted poster with Pratt's photo and details on it, along with my phone number and a promise of a reward for tips leading to an arrest. The promise of a reward usually generates leads. Most turn out to be bogus, but every once in a while, I get a vital tip when all other leads have been exhausted.

When I was satisfied with the poster, I emailed the file to the GraphX print shop on McDowell Boulevard, requesting a hundred copies.

That was when an idea came to me, and I picked up my phone. "Amber?" I asked when she answered. "It's Jinx."

13

"**O**h my goodness! Jinxie!" Amber said in a velvety voice I'd always been envious of. "How the hell are you? I haven't seen you in forever!"

"I'm doing well. And you?"

"School's kicking my butt, but doing well otherwise."

"You still dancing?" I asked.

"How else could I afford ASU? You should drop by sometime. I'll give you a complimentary lap dance."

I laughed nervously. "I think I'll pass on the lap dance, but I would like to get together."

"Aw, what's wrong? You shy? Afraid you might like titties and pussy instead of dick?"

"Funny. No, I need your help with a case I'm working."

"Ooh, color me intrigued. I'm on my way to work, but you're free to stop by. You know where the Arizona Bush Market is?"

"I'm sure I've passed it a time or two, but can't say I've ever been in."

"It's south of Indian School Road on Thirty-Ninth Avenue. I'd love to see you."

"I'll meet you there in about an hour."

Call me a prude, but strip clubs don't interest me. Yeah, the women are hot. But hanging out in a room full of creepy men drooling over the dancers? Yuck! I have better things to do with my time.

Not that I have anything against the women who work there. We all gotta do what we gotta do to pay the rent. And when it came to sizable expenses like gender reassignment surgery and college tuition, sometimes a less conventional approach is necessary.

I hugged Becca and stopped at GraphX to pick up my Fugitive Wanted posters before heading west to the Arizona Bush Company.

The building had an all-wood façade, like a trading post from Arizona's pioneer days. I walked inside and found it wasn't as sleazy as I thought it'd be. I had pictured a smoke-filled room that stank of stale beer and piss. Instead, it smelled more like pine cleaner and reminded me of the Grand Palace Saloon in Old Tucson.

The music was a bit loud and clangy. One of the speakers was buzzing. The girl dancing on the main stage pole moved as though she'd had some serious gymnastic training. The small clusters of men in the audience seemed more interested in their conversations than the female entertainment.

I was scanning the room for Amber when a burly guy with a bad haircut and a tomato for a nose approached me. "Look, Officer, we don't need no trouble."

I realized I was still geared up in my ballistic vest, with my Taser and Ruger holstered at my waist. "No trouble. Just came to talk to a friend."

"Yeah, well, you can take your business outside. Don't need no dyke cops scaring off paying clients."

"Lay off, Lou! She's with me." Amber sauntered over in a see-through top and a sequined thong. A part of me was jealous of her sexy body. I reminded myself that the Barbie-doll figure was a patriarchal fantasy. But still, whew! If anyone could get me to switch to the all-girls team, it'd be her.

"This ain't some kinda sting, is it?" Lou blustered. "I run a legit business. No drugs. No prostitution. So unless you got a warrant—"

Amber slapped him on the shoulder. "Relax, big man. She's a friend. It's all good."

He gave me a stern look and turned on his heel.

"He seems charming," I said.

"Aw, Lou acts all tough, but he's just protective of us girls. But enough about him. How the fuck are you?" She hugged me, and I felt myself getting aroused. What the hell was wrong with me?

"I'm good. You're looking...hot." Embarrassment colored my face.

"You're sweet." She flashed a seductive smile. "Let's go where we can have some privacy." She led me through a door to the left of the stage. We passed through a dressing room and a couple of closed doors until we emerged out the back.

"So what's this case you think I can help you with?"

"I've got a skip that likes to frequent topless bars. Hoping maybe you've seen him." I pulled out my phone and showed her Pratt's photo.

"Doesn't look familiar. He come here often?"

"Mostly at the Pink Pearl and Maggie's Cabaret, according to his bank statements. You ever dance there?"

"Never danced at the Pearl. That place is a real shit hole. Lots of drugs and sleazebag customers. Run by a family of Russian gangsters named Volkov."

"As in Milo Volkov?" I asked.

"Milo ran things till someone killed him last year. His brother Sergei's in charge now. Total psycho. I was warned early on to stay clear of that place." She shivered. "As for Maggie's, I quit there a few months before my surgery. Money's better here at Arizona Bush Company. But I still know some gals working there. You want me to ask around?"

"That'd be great." A thought occurred to me, though it was a long shot. I pulled up an old publicity photo of Barclay Dietz. "How about this guy? He may be a bit older now."

"Looks vaguely familiar. He one of them MMA fighters?"

"Retired boxer. Jumped bail on aggravated assault a while back."

"Haven't seen him in here, but I can check with some of the other girls."

"Thanks! I'll text you their photos. I'm offering a reward if a tip leads to their capture."

"Nice. You sure I can't interest you in a lap dance?" she asked with a wicked twinkle in her eye. "Bring that boyfriend of yours, I'll give you a two-for-one."

My face warmed. "You don't have to."

Her expression grew somber, her voice choked with emotion. "It's the least I can do after you helped me out when I, uh, you know."

"Amber, you're not the first trans girl to attempt suicide. I tried it when I was eleven. We stick together and help each other through." I hugged her again. "Good luck in school."

"Go kick some ass, girl." She kissed my cheek.

From there, I drove by Pratt's house again and pounded on the door. No sign of life inside. No surprise.

I distributed Fugitive Wanted posters in his neighbors' mailboxes and taped them to light poles. I even handed a few to people walking the neighborhood. They grew concerned when I mentioned Pratt was wanted for murder, and promised to keep an eye out.

Clouds were rolling in, threatening a downpour, so I retreated to the Gray Ghost and contemplated my next move. There was one last source of information that might give me a lead I didn't already have. I put the Pathfinder in gear and headed south to downtown Phoenix.

14

———

efore I was a bounty hunter, I was an officer with the Phoenix PD. I quit after a year because I couldn't take all the regulations and paperwork. Also, not a big fan of uniforms.

Because the desk sergeant was a buddy of mine back in the day, he let me through unescorted with my visitor's badge attached to my shirt. I took the elevator to the third floor and pushed through the glass doors of the Homicide Unit.

My chest tensed as I approached the cubicle belonging to Detective Pierce Hardin, my former training officer. He held rookies to such a high standard that he earned the nickname Officer Hard Ass. On a good day, he'd ream me over the minutest detail on how I handled a call-out. The bad days felt as if I'd showered in hydrochloric acid.

When I left the force to become a bounty hunter, he didn't hold back from expressing his disappointment. "You had potential, Ballou. Would've made a top-notch detective and could've paved the way for other transgender officers. But no, you'd rather play Dog the Bounty Hunter with some limey hotshot you met in a bar." What hurt was the thought he might be right.

Cutting to the present, I found Hardin talking on the phone. His shirt was rumpled and his tie loosened. A pale line on his ring finger told me that his years on the force had taken their toll on his marriage.

"Yes, if you'd come down and tell us what you know, that'd be a real help. Oh, I realize that, but people often remember more than they think they do. If you'd rather, I can send a uniformed officer to pick you—what? Oh, okay, then I'll see you here at one o'clock. Thanks a lot, Mrs. Reynolds."

"Morning, Detective," I said, peering over the partition of his cubicle.

He leaned back in his chair and put his hands behind his head. "Well, look who it is." He was a dark-skinned black man in his late fifties. His hair was frosted with gray, especially around the temples. His brow hung low over his eyes from years of glaring at witnesses and perps. "Heard you picked up Danny Warren while dressed as Wonder Woman. That's some messed-up shit right there."

"Got the little perv off the street, didn't I? Wonder Woman saves the day." I figured what the hell, might as well embrace it.

Hardin didn't crack even the faintest of smiles. "What do you need, Ballou? I got real cases to solve."

"Rudy Pratt."

He scoffed and looked at whatever paperwork was in front of him. "Can't help you."

"Bullshit. Bail application shows you were lead detective on the case."

"Operative word being *were*. Even if I wanted to, which I don't, I can't help you."

"Why not? Some new Phoenix PD policy?" I snarled. "Or you shaking me down for some spending money?"

"Don't insult me by insinuating I take bribes. I can't help you because we no longer have the case."

"Who does?"

"FBI. Came in a week ago and grabbed all our files and evidence."

"What do the feds want with a simple murder case?"

"Have to ask them. They had a court order. I followed it. End of story."

"Crap." The last thing I wanted to do was talk to the feds. Bad enough having to deal with Hardin. "Surely there's got to be something in your system about known associates, aliases, anything to help me find him."

"We had him dead to rights on video, committing the murder behind the store where he worked. We found him at home. No priors. Not a lot in our system. Sorry, Ballou."

"Anyone in particular at the FBI I should talk to?"

"Special Agent Tabitha Lovelace served us the paperwork. Start there."

"All right. Thanks."

As I left the precinct, the dark clouds started to unleash their bounty into a steady drizzle. Usually, I cherish the rain since we get so little of it in Phoenix. But I prefer to appreciate it from the dry safety of indoors. Driving in it sucks rocks.

My wiper blades, which I'd used only once since I'd replaced them, had dried out and split into black rubber spaghetti. They turned my windshield into a smear of wet and grime that was impossible to see through.

Between the weather, the ever-present construction zones, and the countless fender benders I squeezed past, it took me nearly an hour to reach the FBI headquarters in north Phoenix. The blocky redbrick building with tall narrow windows over-looked labyrinthine piles of rocks arranged like the loops and whorls of a giant human fingerprint.

In the building's atrium, I passed through security and approached the information desk. "I'm here to see Special Agent Lovelace about a case she's working." I held up my bail enforcement agent badge and ID.

"Is she expecting you?" asked the woman behind the counter.

"I'm a little early, but I hope so." I flashed my most endearing smile but to no effect.

"Just a moment." She picked up the phone in front of her. "Hi, I have a bail agent named Jenna Ballou to see you. Okay." She hung up and gave me a suspicious look. "Special Agent Lovelace will be down momentarily."

I glanced around the lobby for a place to sit, but there wasn't one. Along one wall was a display recounting the history of the FBI in Phoenix, highlighting major cases and agents of note.

Next to that, the FBI's most wanted fugitives glared out from a collection of black-and-white photos. Under each photo was the fugitive's full name, physical description, alleged crimes, and the reward offered. Barclay Dietz was fourth on the list. The reward was two hundred thousand dollars for tips leading to his arrest.

"Ms. Ballou?"

A slender woman with a head of curly sandy-brown hair approached. She was dressed in a gray suit and a pink blouse. With her was a man with a baby face and a pear-shaped body.

"You Lovelace?" I asked.

"Special Agent Lovelace. This is Special Agent Bender." She shook my hand. "I wasn't aware we had an appointment."

"We don't. I've been assigned to apprehend a fugitive murder suspect. The FBI recently took over his case from Phoenix PD."

"I see. Please come this way and let's talk."

I followed them through a secured door, down a corridor, and into an interview room. It was nicer than the ones in the Phoenix PD. I guessed it was designed to put interview subjects at ease rather than on edge, to get them talking.

"Which case is this involving?" Lovelace asked as she and Bender sat on the opposite side of a table from me.

"Rudy Pratt."

Lovelace nodded. "Yes, I'm familiar with it. It's part of a larger operation. What can you tell me about him?"

"I was hoping you could provide some insights as to his current whereabouts. He and his family appear to have vanished.

I've canvassed his neighbors. Spoken to his former employer. Called the references on his bail application but haven't turned up much."

"So you are looking for information, rather than providing it?" Bender asked.

"I prefer to see it as us having common goals. I'm here to make sure this mutual suspect is returned to custody so he can stand trial. Wouldn't want him killing anyone else, now would we?" I forced a polite smile, which wasn't returned.

Lovelace crossed her arms. "As I recall, Ms. Ballou, last year, you and a male associate exposed a sting op we were conducting on Milo Volkov's human trafficking enterprise."

"My partner and I were tracking down a young female fugitive we believed Volkov had kidnapped. We had no idea about your sting operation."

"And did you find your fugitive in Volkov's warehouse?" I got the impression she already knew the answer. She was toying with me, and I couldn't do shit about it.

Sweat beaded under my chest. "No, but—"

"Meanwhile, the two agents who arrested you were later murdered in Volkov's corporate office downtown," she pressed. "Is that correct?"

"Volkov killed them. I wasn't there when it happened."

"Were you working for him?" asked Bender.

"No. Look, this was all resolved a year and a half ago. I was cleared."

"Were you?" he asked. "Because we turned up some interesting texts Volkov sent you. Got the impression you two were intimate."

My stomach turned as I recalled his creepy emails. The man was what we in the trans community called a chaser—someone who fetishized trans women as sex objects. "Volkov had some twisted, stalker crush on me. He murdered a reporter and later your two agents, thinking this would somehow get me into his bed. It just made me sick. I killed Volkov and several of his men while rescuing my fugitive. I would think that would put me in the FBI's good graces, not on your shit list."

Lovelace and Bender exchanged a look, but neither responded. The silence in the room became a presence in and of itself.

This was a familiar tactic. People today have a strong aversion to silence and boredom. Give a suspect the silent treatment, and they're more likely to talk.

I wouldn't have played along, but I had a fugitive to find and didn't have all day to play mind games with some fed with a vendetta.

"All I'm asking is for a little help returning one of your suspects to custody. Whatever info you have on possible places he could be hiding out. Other known associates I might not have reached out to. I have no intention of interfering in your larger investigation, whatever the hell it is."

"I'm sorry, Ms. Ballou, but we can't discuss an ongoing investigation. You're simply too much of a liability." She stood and opened the door to the room. I was at once relieved by the inflow of fresh air and frustrated by their lack of cooperation.

"Do you already have Pratt in custody?" I asked. It wouldn't be the first time they'd scooped someone up without notifying the courts or the bail bond agent.

"I'm afraid we can't share that information," replied Bender.

"Fine." I stormed out the door into the corridor. "But if he kills again, it's on you people." I snatched off my visitor's badge and tossed it on the floor on my way out to the lobby.

As I passed the lineup of the Most Wanted list, I thought about Barclay Dietz. I was sure Lovelace and Bender would love to know he was back in town. But fuck them. I'd take him down myself. I deserved that much satisfaction. But first I needed to deal with Pratt before Sadie started breathing down my neck.

15

———————

Frustrated by my lack of progress, I returned to the Hub and resumed looking through Pratt's paperwork. As I thumbed through recent bank statements, I noticed a charge for Arizona Dialysis Solutions. I checked his phone logs, but there weren't any calls to any doctors or medical offices that I could see.

"Hey, Becks? You think you could run call logs for Pratt's wife?"

"Sure. What's the phone number?"

I gave it to her, and she tapped away on her computer keyboard. "Got it."

"Anything for medical offices?"

"Yeah, a shitload. Arizona Dialysis. Thunderbird Nephrology. Mayo Clinic Hospital. Camelback Children's Hospital. Lots of doctors' offices. I'm guessing someone in the family has kidney problems."

I checked Pratt's bail application. Under family, he listed his wife, his son, and his daughter. "I think it's his daughter, Bethany. She wasn't at the house yesterday, and his son looked fairly healthy." Stupid and bigoted but healthy.

I had a hunch and dialed the number for the Mayo Clinic Hospital. When the person on the other end answered, I asked, "Can you tell me which room Bethany Pratt is staying in, please."

"Hold on, let me check. Is that Pratt with two *t*'s?"

"Yes."

"I'm sorry, I'm not showing anyone with the last name Pratt with two *t*'s as a hospital patient."

"Okay, thanks." I looked up the number for Camelback Children's Hospital and dialed it. "Yes, I need to know which room Bethany Pratt's staying in."

"Certainly, let me pull that up." She paused a moment. "Okay, I just need her PIN code."

"Oh, hold on." My mind raced as I scanned his application for possible numbers that they would have used as a PIN code. "Dang it, Linda gave it to me, and I can't find where I put it," I lied. "Can you just put me through?"

"Not without the PIN. I'm sorry. Because we treat children..."

"Yeah, I understand." I hung up. "Becks, Pratt's daughter is at Camelback Children's Hospital. I think he may be hiding out in her room. Think you could locate which one it is?"

"Hold on. I'm trying to hack into one of my new clients' database servers to test the security protocols. I'm on a time crunch."

Her fingers raced on the keyboard, interrupted by the occasional spout of profanity. Her face twisted through a range of emotions from frustrated to determined to angry to sly until she, at last, did a fist pump. "Yes! Broke it!"

"This is a good thing?" I asked.

"I wanted to show them that their previous IT consultant had left some vulnerabilities. And now I can patch them."

"Great. Now, Camelback Children's Hospital."

"Oh, right. What was the name?"

"Bethany Pratt."

She typed away. "Wow, they have a good system. Let me try... nope, that didn't work. How about this little code injection. Aha! I'm in. Now, Bethany Pratt. Pratt Sprat could eat no... here she is.

Room 481. What else did you need?" She beamed with triumph. I loved my hacker bestie.

"That's it. By the way, did you get anything on Peyton or Barclay Dietz?"

She handed me a stack of printouts. "I ran a comprehensive search on Peyton Dietz. He's working at a liquor shop on Baseline in Mesa. Lives in an apartment just off Country Club Drive. No criminal history. Pays most of his bills, though he's sometimes a month slow. MVD shows he drives an eight-year-old Honda Accord. No outstanding traffic tickets. I'm still going through his latest phone bill and social media."

"Thanks," I said as she pulled out another couple of pages.

"As for Barclay Dietz, it's like you said. After June 2005, he dropped off the grid. Emptied his bank accounts, cashed out a CD, and left his family high and dry. His wife, Gloria, who divorced him in absentia a year later, died in 2010 from pancreatic cancer."

"Interesting. Thanks for the info." I pulled out my phone and called Rodeo. It rang four times before he answered. "Hey! You busy?"

"Yeah. Just a bit. Why?" He sounded out of breath.

"I think I know where Pratt might be hanging out."

"Oh yeah? Where's that?"

"Camelback Children's Hospital. Looks like his daughter has kidney problems."

"Ah. Makes sense."

I heard him take a deep breath.

"Unfortunately, I'm with Conor and his team tracking a meth dealer in Queen Creek. May be a couple hours before I can meet you."

"Don't worry about it. Give my love to Conor."

"Copy that. Check with you later."

I hung up and called Caden. "Hey, man. I need your help."

"Please tell me I'm not going to be hanging out by the cars, missing out on all the action."

"Well, if you'd stopped Pratt the first time..." I teased.

"Hey, I tried, but the guy—"

"I'm kidding, Caden. He got away from me too. And this time, you're my main backup. Rodeo's tied up at the moment."

"That's what I'm talking about. Where are we meeting?"

"Camelback Children's Hospital."

"Hospital? Someone hurt?"

"Pratt's daughter. I think that's where he may be hiding out."

"I'll be there."

I hung up.

16

I walked into the lobby of Camelback Children's Hospital in full Bail Enforcement gear minus my weapons. The last thing we needed was to turn this place into a shooting gallery. I could only hope Pratt was similarly unarmed.

Brightly colored murals of flowers and happy children decorated the walls. Christmas lights and greenery hung from the front of the information desk, with a miniature Christmas tree, a menorah, and a Kwanzaa kinara on the counter between the two workstations. Everything about the decor conveyed a sense of hope and holiday cheer. And yet for all the bright colors and happy images, there was no denying the dark truth—children here faced the unimaginable horrors of cancer and other brutal diseases.

Caden walked up and acknowledged me with a nod. He was also decked out in his vest and tactical belt.

"You think he's here?" he asked.

"I hope so."

I studied a sign on the wall to locate the elevator. A woman in business attire approached me. "Excuse me, can I help you two?"

I pulled out my ID and a folded copy of Pratt's bail application. "Bail enforcement. We suspect a fugitive may be on the premises."

"Here? This is a children's hospital."

"His daughter's a patient on the fourth floor."

"Be that as it may, I can't allow you to disturb our other patients and their families."

"We'll do our best not to disturb anyone. But the man we seek is wanted for murder. I'd hate for him to put your patients, their families, or your staff in danger."

She put a hand to her mouth. "A murderer? Here?"

I handed her the bail application. "See for yourself."

She unfolded the paper. "Goodness. Okay, well, please resolve this as quietly as possible. We have some very sick children here."

"You won't even know we're here." I signaled to Caden to head toward the elevators. "Let's find our guy."

"You think he'll come along quietly?" Caden asked as we rode up the elevator.

"Maybe. But be ready for anything."

The elevator door opened. I scanned the hallway. The chilly air held the scent of alcohol gel and floor cleaner. We followed the signs listing room numbers to the ward where Bethany Pratt was being treated. Memories and emotions from the weeks I spent in the ICU as a teen pressed against my mind.

We strolled past a nurses' break room and a cluster of empty wheelchairs lined against the wall. The corridor widened into a circular ward with a nurses' station in the center with rooms like spokes in a wheel along the outer wall. Somewhere, a couple of vital monitor machines beeped incessantly out of sync with each other.

In front of one room, a woman with a Great Dane in a service animal harness stood next to a bald girl in a wheelchair. The girl beamed with excitement as she petted the enormous dog.

"Which way?" Caden asked.

"Looks like Bethany's room is at two o'clock. Stay out here by the nurses' station while I check out the room." I pointed in that direction. "Keep your head on a swivel in case he's out grabbing a cup of coffee."

"Copy that. I got your six."

I cautiously approached the room, keeping an eye out for movement. By the door, the name "Pratt" was written on a whiteboard decorated with shells and starfish. I peered into the room. A lone figure sat hunched over a bed. It had to be Pratt. I tried to ignore the tightness settling in my throat as I got a view of the pale, emaciated child in the bed.

"Rudy Pratt?" I asked in a quiet voice.

He turned. His eyes were red and deeply set in his tear-strewn face. In an instant, his expression turned from sorrow to rage. He wasn't a big guy. But there was an animus about him, a threatening energy that I could only assume stemmed from his daughter's suffering.

"Leave me alone." His voice was both high-pitched and malevolent.

"I'm sorry, but you missed your court date. You need to come with me to get it rescheduled and your bail reset."

"I'm not going anywhere with you. My daughter is dying because those idiots put a bunch of Negroes and illegals ahead of her on the kidney recipient list."

Compassion for his kid tempered my anger at the racist epithets. "I'm sorry about your daughter, but you missed your court date. Don't make this harder than it has to be."

"Daddy?"asked a fragile voice.

"It's all right, darlin'." He patted her arm and picked up a Styrofoam cup from the bedside table. "Daddy has to step outside the room a moment. I'll be right back."

He turned to me. "I'll come along quietly. Just don't cuff me in front of my kid."

I followed him out of the room. He turned. I recognized the fire in his eyes an instant before he tossed the scalding coffee in my face. I shielded my eyes, but my forearm, cheek, and neck started burning. I steeled myself against the pain and took off after him around the nurses' station.

"Caden, cut him off!" I shouted.

When Caden cut off his escape, Pratt pulled a revolver from his waistband and fired. The entire ward erupted in screams and shouting. Caden fell to one knee, still reaching for our fugitive. Pratt fired again and took off down the corridor.

I wanted to follow Pratt, but I had to check on Caden. "You hit?"

Caden was on the ground, moaning. I found two slugs embedded in the fibers of his vest. Even with the Kevlar, the impact of point-blank gunshots could break ribs and cause internal bleeding.

"I...I'm okay," Caden replied through gritted teeth pressing on his chest. "Fuck that hurts."

I reached to the back of his waistband. Sure enough, he had a SIG Sauer in a concealment holster. "Hang tight. I'm going after Pratt." I took off hoping I could stop our quarry without anyone else getting hurt.

I arrived at the elevator lobby with corridors going off in multiple directions. The call buttons were lit, but Pratt was nowhere in sight. The sounds of a child's screams echoed from down one corridor. I charged full speed, narrowly missing a gurney emerging from a room.

Inside the room where the screams were coming from, I found only a family and a nurse huddled around a child's bed. No sign of Pratt.

"Shit!"

The nurse glared at me, then glanced down at the pistol in my hand. "What are you doing with that?"

"Sorry, wrong room."

I tucked the SIG Sauer in my waistband and retraced my steps. Caden sat in a wheelchair by a nurse in blue scrubs. His Kevlar vest was on the floor and his shirt pulled halfway up, exposing his chest binder underneath.

"You okay?" I asked, kneeling beside him.

He nodded. "Started having trouble breathing, but I seem to be in one piece. Did you catch him?"

"Afraid not," I replied. "You okay to head out?"

"You can't leave. Police are on their way," the nurse said. "They'll want to know what happened."

Not wanting to spend the next hour talking to the cops, I pointed at Bethany Pratt's room. "Her father jumped bail after being charged with first-degree murder. We were here to take him back to jail. When we tried to arrest him, he shot my associate here and took off. That's what happened."

Alarm electrified her face. "Murder? Well, what if he shows up again? What do I do?"

I handed her a business card and said, "Call me."

She nodded. I helped Caden to his feet, picked up his vest, and started to walk away.

"Hey," said the nurse. "You look familiar. You with that superheroes group that comes by now and again to visit the kids?"

I stopped and turned back to her. "I'm usually dressed as Wonder Woman."

"Thought so." She glanced at my business card, then back at me. "I'll call you if he shows again. Go on before the cops get here."

I followed Caden trudging out of the ward toward the elevators.

"I can't believe I let him get away again." Caden's shoulders slumped.

"Yeah, what the hell's wrong with you, man? Aren't bullets supposed to bounce right off you?" My comment managed to get him to smile. "Look, we'll get that asshole. Don't worry. You sure you're okay?"

"No, but I'll be better once I get this binder off."

"We just passed a public restroom. You could take it off in there."

He shook his head and put an arm across his chest. "Not here. I'll be okay till I get home."

I understood. Dysphoria could be a bitch. "Suit yourself."

"What happened to your face?" he asked as we rode the elevator down to the first floor.

In the adrenaline rush, I'd blocked out the burning sensation in my face and arm. I felt it now and winced. "The coffee here doesn't agree with me."

He chuckled and grimaced. "Ow! Don't make me laugh."

"Sorry."

"Where to now?"

I had no idea where Pratt would go. "He's probably holed up in a motel room somewhere, maybe with a friend. Becca's tracking his bank card. If he uses it, she'll let us know. I've been putting out feelers with associates and with some of his hangouts. You should head home and get that binder off."

Caden nodded. "What about you?"

"I have a lead on another case I'm working on."

"Who is it? I'd love to help out."

The elevator doors opened, and we walked out. "Just a personal thing. I can handle it."

Wrinkles creased his forehead. "Is this because I screwed up?"

I handed him his vest. "You didn't screw up. This...it's something I have to take care of on my own."

We entered the lobby just as two uniformed guards approached the information desk. Caden and I slipped past and hustled out the doors.

In the parking lot by his car, I handed him back his SIG. "Thanks for the loaner."

"Probably shouldn't have taken it in there, but I feel naked without it."

"No worries. Go take care of yourself. I'll be in touch about Pratt." I hugged him gingerly.

"Be safe, girl. Keep your head on a swivel."

"Always."

"And if you need me, don't hesitate to call."

I forced a smile. "Thanks."

Caden drove off.

I treated myself to a *pollo asado* burrito at Filiberto's and perused Peyton's paperwork—credit reports, bank statements, emails, social media posts, and phone texts.

I discovered he'd recently broken up with his latest girlfriend, was a frequent customer of local dance clubs, and hated his roommate, Hughie, who made their apartment smell like weed. But no indication his father had been in touch. Would Barclay the Beast drive all this way and not reconnect with his son?

After dinner, I headed east toward Peyton's apartment complex in Mesa. As I sat in afternoon rush hour traffic, I wondered if and when I did track down the Beast, I could best him and put an end to my nightmares.

17

—————

A few stars were twinkling above me as I reached the Orange Blossom Apartments, where Peyton lived. The community was gated except for a small lot in front of the office. Not that it presented much of a barrier to anyone determined to get in. It didn't take a genius to realize you could park and wait until a resident opened the gate and follow them in.

I didn't wait long before a green Hyundai drove up and someone punched a code into the keypad. The gate rattled open like a sideways portcullis. The Hyundai drove through. I followed, my rear bumper barely clearing the gate as it closed. Easy peasy lemon squeezy.

The parking lot inside the fence encircled a block of three-story stucco buildings centered around a grassy courtyard. I pulled into an uncovered visitor's spot and geared up with my Ruger on my right hip and the backup revolver in my ankle holster. If Barclay Dietz was here, he was leaving either in my custody or in a body bag. I didn't care which.

According to Becca's research, Peyton lived in building 5, apartment 109. I scanned the sides of the apartment buildings but didn't see any signs. The street lamps were hooded and cast light only along the concrete walkways that ran through the courtyard.

Outside the truck, I aimed an LED flashlight at the nearest building. A sign near the roof indicated it was building 3. I was close.

I crept through the courtyard, passing only a few people, none of whom were my quarry. With a hand on the grip of my Ruger, I searched the shadows for the monster who still haunted my dreams.

"Building 5." I shined the flashlight's beam at apartment doors, circling the building until I found number 109. My pulse quickened. I pocketed the flashlight and drew my Ruger.

I pounded hard on the door and stepped to the side. Sometimes an FTA's response to a knock at the door was to let their firearm do the talking. I preferred to be out of the line of fire.

When there was no response, I knocked a second time, harder. "Fugitive Recovery! Open the door. Now!"

From inside the apartment, a male voice said, "All right, dammit, I'm coming." Was it Peyton or his father? I couldn't tell. It had been too many years since I'd heard either. My grip tightened, and I readied myself to spring into action.

"Who is it?" asked the same voice, just the other side of the door. Too young to be Barclay. Most likely Peyton.

"Jinx Ballou. I'm looking for Peyton Dietz."

"Why?"

I rolled my eyes. *Just open the fucking door, Peyton,* I wanted to shout. Instead, I played it cool. "We dated in high school."

The door squeaked open. I stepped out of the shadows. The man inside the apartment looked glassy-eyed, with about three-days' worth of beard growth. He was thin and wore a plain white T-shirt and frayed jeans. He smelled of weed and french fry grease. I studied his face, looking for the young man I had once given my heart to. "You're not Peyton," I said.

"Naw, man, I'm his roommate, Hughie." He glanced at my vest, and his eyes popped open wide. "Oh shit, you're a cop." He scrambled clumsily to shut the door, but I held it open with my boot.

"Relax, Hughie. I'm not a cop."

He looked confused. "You sure?"

I nodded. "Unless you've jumped bail, you've got nothing to worry about from me."

"Did I jump bail? I don't think so." He scratched his stubbly beard, as the wheels turned unsteadily in that head of his. "Whew! That was close, huh."

"Where's Peyton?"

"Oh yeah. You're looking for him, right?"

"Yes. Now, where is he?"

"Um..." More beard scratching. "I think he's, like, at work, ya know?"

"San Tan Convenience Liquors?"

"Yeah, how did you know?" Hughie asked. "Are you a psychic? 'Cause that would be too cool. You could, like—"

"When do you expect Peyton back?" I pressed. "I need to speak with him."

"Not till late. But I'll tell him you stopped by."

"Thanks for nothing." I started to turn away but stopped myself. "Hey, has he been in touch with his dad lately?"

"His dad? Not that I know of. Wait, there was that one guy who called. I think he said he was Peyton's dad. Or was that my dad? I can't remember. I forget a lot of stuff. Not sure why. Kinda weird, ya know?"

"Yeah, whatever. Have a nice night."

Hughie closed the door.

I holstered my weapon and slogged back toward the truck. Before I reached the parking lot, I was intercepted by a petite woman in a floral skirt and a fuchsia top, teetering on four-inch heels. Her heart-shaped face wore a stern expression.

"Excuse me. Who are you?"

Aw crap. "Just visiting a friend." I gave her my most charming smile, but she didn't seem to be buying it.

"I'm the property manager. A resident saw your van follow them through the gate. You're not allowed to tailgate someone inside the fence. Who are you here to see?"

"Not important. I was just leaving." I tried to step around her, but Ms. Busybody Property Manager blocked my path.

"If you don't tell me who you're here to see, I'm calling the cops and reporting you for trespassing. Mesa PD has a substation in the strip mall next door." She pointed in the direction of the shopping center next to the apartment complex.

I pointed at the words "Bail Enforcement" printed in yellow across my vest. "Look, lady, I'm tracking a fugitive wanted by the FBI for armed robbery, aggravated assault, and fleeing the jurisdiction. You want to call the local LEOs, be my guest."

"You're with the FBI?"

I smiled but said nothing. Impersonating a federal agent was illegal. Letting someone else make their own assumptions wasn't.

"Why would you be looking for them here? We run background checks on all our residents."

"He's the father of one of your residents."

"Which resident?"

"Peyton Dietz," I said.

"That nice boy? I can hardly believe that." Ms. Busybody looked at me, as if deciding whether I was pulling her leg. "Well, okay. But next time, check in with the office before you go traipsing around the property. We've had some recent break-ins and are trying to clamp down on the situation."

"Office was closed, lady." I pushed past her to the parking lot. It was time to head to the liquor store. I needed to pick up some Jameson for Conor, anyway.

18

S an Tan Convenience Liquors was only a few miles away, just off the Loop 202. The store was decently stocked with three long main aisles. Nothing froufrou. No cutesy chalkboard signs advertising the latest microbrew. Just shelves of booze for the not-so-discriminating connoisseur.

The guy behind the counter was ringing someone up when I walked in, so I went searching for a replacement for Conor's mysteriously empty bottle of whiskey. Four other customers cruised the aisles with me, two of them dressed in pajama bottoms and bedroom slippers. In short order, I found the whiskey section and grabbed a bottle of Jameson. A few steps away, I picked up a bottle of Cuervo Gold for myself.

The cashier looked up as I approached the counter. A mix of emotions tore through me as I recognized him. The years had softened his athletic build and widened his face, but it was Peyton Dietz all right. The first boy who said he loved me. The one I believed would be my Prince Charming. The one who never once visited me in the hospital, who didn't so much as text me, who broke my fucking heart after his father shattered my body. It was payback time.

"Hello, Peyton." I slammed the bottles on the counter hard enough to make him jump.

His eyes narrowed as he tried to place me.

"It's me, Jinx Ballou. Remember?"

He stumbled backward into a shelf of high-priced liquor. "Holy shit! Jinx? That really you?"

"It's me, Pey."

"You . . . you look . . . different."

"Maybe because doctors had to rebuild my face after . . ." Hurt and sorrow mixed with the anger. I struggled to keep my composure. This was more awkward than I thought it'd be. What would happen when I confronted Barclay?

"Yeah . . . I'm . . . I'm so sorry. My father wouldn't let me see you. I was afraid to . . . "

"No need to explain." I took a deep breath and stared at the counter. "Your dad was a scary guy. What happened wasn't your fault."

"I should have at least called."

I looked up at him, and our eyes met. "Yeah, you should've."

"So, you're a cop now?" He glanced at my vest.

"Was a cop. Now I'm a bounty hunter." My fury once again surged. "Your dad's a wanted man in several states. Tell me where he is and all's forgiven."

Peyton gasped as if I'd punched him in the solar plexus. "I...I haven't seen him in years. Not since he took off."

"Bullshit! He's in Arizona and was last seen headed toward Phoenix. Don't tell me he hasn't reached out."

Peyton held up his hands in surrender. "He hasn't. I swear."

"You sure? No phone calls? Christmas cards?"

"No," he said firmly, appearing to get a handle on his awkwardness. "Bastard left me and my mom to fend for ourselves. We lost everything 'cause of him." A fire blazed in his eyes. "I never should've asked you out, knowing what you were...are."

"You knew who and what I was before you ever asked me out.

You said you didn't care, that I was a girl as far as you were concerned. He's the son of a bitch who tried to kill me and then jumped bail. His actions and his alone cost you your basketball scholarship and your house. So don't you dare put that shit on me, Peyton."

Peyton crossed his arms and dropped his gaze. "You're right. I'm sorry."

"So where is he?"

"I told you, I don't know. I haven't seen him. Nor do I want to."

I slapped my business card on the counter along with a couple of twenties for the booze. "Call me if you hear from him. And don't wimp out like last time."

Peyton stared at the card, his face a palette of concern and remorse. "Yeah."

"And FYI, if you don't, that's called aiding and abetting. A felony. I'll take you both in. You two can catch up on old times in a cell in Perryville." I walked toward the door.

"Hey, Jinx!"

I turned. "Yeah?"

"You look good, by the way. Even better than before."

His compliment caught me off guard. For a moment, I was once again that lovesick teenager doped up on estradiol and high school romance. "Thanks, Peyton. You look good too."

All of the memories and emotions swirling round my head left me dizzy. I couldn't tell if he was still covering for his dad or if I was wrong about his father's return to the valley. The only way to know for sure was to watch him.

I drove next door to a QT convenience store and parked so that I had a clear view of the liquor store. Peyton would get off work in a few hours, so I'd hang out until then. Becca had a program monitoring Peyton's phone activity. If anything interesting came up, she'd forward it to me.

Stakeouts are long and boring, so I stepped inside the QT and bought a large cup of coffee, a bag of Sriracha beef jerky, and a bag of hot 'n spicy *chicharrones*. It's hard to fall asleep when your mouth's on fire.

As I settled back in the Gray Ghost, Conor called.

"Hello, love! Ya coming over?" he asked. "I got the new Charlie Hunnam action flick recorded on the telly."

"Can't. I'm on a stakeout." My face still throbbed from the coffee burn Pratt had given me earlier.

"Shite! I already ordered a pizza for us. Barbecue chicken, your favorite."

"No, Conor, that's *your* favorite."

"That's right. You're more the pepperoni and Italian sausage type."

"Actually, I'm more the Irish sausage type," I teased, suddenly feeling frisky. Seeing Peyton again had whammied me good. My emotions were all over the place.

"Irish sausage?" He paused a moment. "Aren't you a cheeky girl! How about some company on this stakeout of yours?"

The last time we did a stakeout together, we ended up making out in the back seat. Our fugitive drove off without us. "Tempting, but I'm way out in Mesa. Besides, I'd hate to get between you and Charlie Hunnam. I know you two have that whole bromance thing going."

"I'm not gonna dignify that bloody remark with a comment."

"'Cause you know it's true," I said with a giggle.

"So who are ya staking out? Anyone interesting?"

I didn't want to tell him I was stalking my ex-boyfriend. Or that I was hunting Barclay the Beast. Not that Conor was the jealous type, but I knew he'd insist on coming out to protect me. I needed to do this for myself. "Just an old assault case. Pretty routine, actually."

"How long you expect this stakeout to go?"

"Late. I'll crash at my place when I'm done."

"This is why we need to combine lots and move in together."

"I'm not doing this, Conor."

"Doing what? I want a real relationship, love. The shagging is lovely, but I need more than that."

"You're such a girl," I said. "You want marriage and children and a fucking white picket fence. Well, news flash! I can't have kids and don't want them even if I could."

"Don't be daft. I never said nothing about kids."

"I...I don't want to talk about it."

"Jinxie, I know you've had some dodgy relationships in the past. I can't blame ya for being squeamish. But ya know I'm not like that. I'd never so much as look at another girl. You know that."

We'd been over this enough, and I fell silent.

"Ya still there?"

"My mother's birthday's tomorrow night. Party over at my folks' place. You in?"

There was a long pause that seemed to stretch for hours. "I don't know. Got a lot to do."

"Fine." I hung up.

A few minutes later, my phone pinged. I expected it to be a text from Conor, sending an apology. It was from Becca instead.

Jinx, this just came over. Thought it might be relevant.

She'd attached a screenshot showing a brief conversation. Peyton had received a message from a nonlocal number.

Hey, I'm in town. You want to meet?

Peyton responded, *Meet me at Vybe at 930pm.*

"Now we're getting somewhere," I said.

Vybe was a dance club a few miles away. I ran a reverse-lookup search for the phone number but found no identifying information associated with it. Possibly a burner phone. The 801 area code, however, was from Salt Lake City, where Barclay had recently robbed a bank.

While tearing into the sriracha beef jerky, I added the phone number to a file I'd been keeping on Barclay Dietz for the past several years—bits and pieces of information that, until now, had never led anywhere. I was finally gonna get this son of a bitch after all these years.

19

I used the time to apply a little makeup and pull on a lacy black blouse I kept in a bag in the back of my SUV for situations where I preferred a stealthy ambush over my usual badass approach. If I was going to take down the Beast, I was going to have to get close before I pounced.

Ten minutes after nine, Peyton turned off the interior lights, locked up the liquor store, and shuffled to a burgundy Honda Accord.

I trailed him as he drove, keeping at least two or three cars between us. I didn't need him getting suspicious, and since I knew where he was going, I wasn't afraid of losing him.

When I reached Vybe's half-empty parking lot, Peyton was approaching the club's front door. After parking the Gray Ghost, I tucked my revolver into a concealment holster at the small of my back and a couple of pairs of handcuffs in my back pocket.

Thirteen years of revenge fantasies flashed through my mind as I walked to the door. I wanted Barclay Dietz to suffer as I had suffered. I wanted him begging me to stop the way I had begged him to stop. I wanted to humiliate him and see the arrogance fade from his beady eyes.

At the door, I handed my ID to a guy with a goat beard and granny glasses. I could feel the steady thrum of the electronic dance music inside.

Goat Boy checked my license and handed it back to me. "Cover charge is ten bucks."

"Kinda steep for a Monday night."

He shrugged. "Go home, then."

I reached into my purse and pulled a ten out of my wallet.

"Have fun," he said.

When I opened the door, a tidal wave of sound washed over me. The entryway was pitch-black. I followed a series of LED lights up a ramp that wobbled like plywood stretched between too few studs, and I emerged on the perimeter of the dance floor.

Across the room to my right, the bar glowed with purple neon. Lights backlit the glass shelves and the bottles behind it. On the far wall, the DJ booth towered above the dance floor. A girl with blue and scarlet hair head-bobbed to the beat with a set of headphones over one ear as she queued up the next song.

I scanned the dance floor for Peyton and his dad. They were both over six feet and should be easy to spot. But I didn't see them among the small, glow-stick-clad group gyrating on the dance floor. I slipped into the shadows, stalking around the perimeter like a panther. But neither were anywhere to be seen.

Does Peyton already have a set meeting spot here? Could they be in the men's room? Are they out back?

I sent a text to Becca asking if there were any other texts from Peyton's phone. She replied there hadn't been.

I was about to give up when a lanky figure emerged from the men's room. Peyton. I sank deeper into the shadows. He stopped near the DJ booth and looked around the dance floor. *Will he spot me? Can he recognize me across the dark room?*

Peyton nodded to someone. A man emerged from the crowd on the dance floor and gave him a bro hug and a pat on the back. The stranger was a white guy, average height, midtwenties. Longish hair. Not Barclay. But maybe the Beast would show yet.

The pair made their way across the room and back toward the entrance. I gave them a few seconds' head start and followed.

When I stepped outside, the sudden silence felt as if I'd gone deaf. The lights over the parking lot seemed almost blinding compared to the club's dark interior. It took me a moment to spot Peyton and his buddy walking between cars in the lot.

"Didn't like the music?" Goat Boy asked with a sarcastic tone.

I gave him a withering stare. "I prefer punk to EDM." When I looked back out at the lot, Peyton and his buddy had disappeared. "Shit."

I wandered through the lines of cars, looking for movement and straining to hear sounds above the thrum-thrum-thrumming still in my ears from the club.

"Don't turn around," said a deep male voice with a Texas accent. Something hard pressed against the back of my head. I caught a glimpse of my attacker in the side-view mirror of a pickup truck next to me. The guy Peyton met inside the club.

I whipped around and caught his gun hand in an arm lock. I drove the heel of my other palm into his nose. The gun went off, shattering glass in a car behind me. I plunged my boot into his instep and my knee into his crotch.

As he collapsed into a moaning heap on the ground, I recovered his gun—a Smith & Wesson .38 revolver. I also picked up a plastic bag that had fallen out of his pocket. It contained a multicolored assortment of pills stamped with little pictures—ecstasy.

I pointed the revolver at my attacker. "What's your name, asshole?"

"Mahoney." It was more of a wheeze than a word.

"You shouldn't go sneaking up behind women and putting a gun in their back, Mahoney. Someone could get hurt." I kicked him in the ass. "Where's Peyton?"

"Jinx?" Peyton emerged from the passenger side of a car with dark tinted windows. "What are you doing here?"

"You know this bitch?" asked Mahoney, wiping his nose and leaving a smear of red across his face.

"We dated in high school," Peyton added, a guilty look playing across his face.

Mahoney pulled himself to his feet and put some distance between us. "Shit, the way she was looking inside the cars, I thought she was a cop trying to bust us."

"Why are you following me, Jinx?" asked Peyton.

"You know why."

Peyton stepped toward me, his mouth a thin line. "Look, I told you, if my dad shows up, I'll call you."

"You wouldn't be the first person to cover for a fugitive family member."

"Fugitive? So she *is* a cop." Mahoney pointed an accusatory finger at me.

"What's wrong, Mahoney? I interrupt your little drug deal?" I emptied the baggie on the ground and crushed the pills into dust with my boot heel.

"Fuck you, Five-O!"

"Relax, dipshit. If I were a cop, you'd be handcuffed and in the back of my patrol car by now."

"You ain't a cop, then what the hell are you?"

"Bail enforcement."

"What?"

"She's a bounty hunter," said Peyton. "She's looking for my dad."

"Then you owe me four hundred bucks for that ecstasy you just ruined." Mahoney held out his hand. "And I want my gun back too, bitch."

I studied the revolver. "It is a nice gun. I think I'll keep it."

"Like hell, you will."

"You gonna take it from me, big man?" I aimed the revolver at Mahoney. He wilted like a dying flower in the summer sun.

"I will catch your father, Peyton," I said. "And until I do, expect to see a lot of me."

I turned on my heel and drove home.

20

It was nearly eleven when I walked in my front door. I thought about calling Conor, then decided against it. He'd want me to come over, and I didn't feel like going anywhere. Not after our argument. A restless energy that I couldn't shake flowed through me. I needed some time to process the evening's events.

After stashing Mahoney's Smith & Wesson next to Daniel Warren's Colt in my gun safe, I put on a pair of shorts and a tank top and went into my workout room, where I had a Bodyman II, a man-sized electronic punching bag. I put on the Pink Trinkets' *Orange, You Stupid*—a protest album against the current president—and proceeded to kick, punch, and slam the shit out of the Bodyman.

I pictured Barclay Dietz's beefy face with its misshapen nose on the head of the mannequin. Fury crackled through every nerve in my body. I punched with all the energy I could muster. I kicked so hard every metatarsal in my foot throbbed from the repeated blows.

Faster, harder, drawing on every ounce of strength, my anger exploded onto the rubberized plastic dummy until I was so exhausted that one of my roundhouse kicks missed its target and spun me hard into a workout bench. I landed in a heap and sobbed. Sweat poured off my body despite the coolness of the room. Eventually, I pulled myself to my feet, stepped into the shower, and cranked up the water as hot as I could stand it.

I should've gotten over all this shit years ago. My love for Peyton. His father's brutality. And the deep wounds they both had caused me. It was so pathetic. I thanked the stars Conor wasn't there to see it.

A part of me wanted Conor to hold me. To reassure me that I'd get through this. That I was tough. And yet the thought of moving in with him triggered feelings of claustrophobia. His place wasn't just a house, it was a bunker. A real bunker. A place of hiding. A place where he was hiding. And what was I hiding from?

Why didn't I want to move in with him? Was I worried he'd cheat on me as Wilson had? It made sense, but deep in my gut, it didn't ring true. So why did the thought of moving in with him make me feel as if the walls—those cold, stark walls of his—were closing in on me?

My body trembled. The water had gone cold. I turned it off, pulled a towel over me, and sat on the toilet, letting my mind go blank. I needed to focus on capturing Pratt and Dietz.

As far as Dietz was concerned, I had no hard evidence he was in the valley. Sure, he'd robbed a bank in Kayenta, but for all I knew, he'd continued on to Los Angeles or Mexico or who knew where. It was only my gut that told me he was here. I could feel it in my bones. And when I'd confronted Peyton about it, I could sense he felt the same way. Sooner or later, Dietz would make contact.

I ambled into my kitchen and made myself a bowl of Lucky Charms. It's true what they say—they are magically delicious. But that got me thinking about Conor all over again. My appetite soured, and I dumped the cereal, magical marshmallows and all, down the food disposal.

I was about to turn on the television to watch the latest season of *Jessica Jones* when something went thump.

I told myself it was nothing. A stupid bird crashing into a window. The ice maker dumping a load of cubes in the freezer. The wooden beams in the roof contracting with the evening chill. A furry critter seeking a warm place in my attic. Santa Claus showing up two weeks early to tell me I was on his naughty list again.

Or someone trying to break into my house, said the paranoid voice in the back of my mind.

My experience as a bounty hunter had taught me that a strong sense of caution was a survival skill, not a neurosis. The people I sent back to jail often held a grudge. It wouldn't be the first time someone with ill intent got out and tracked me to my home.

I grabbed my Ruger and a flashlight and crept outside, looking for anything or anyone that shouldn't be there. The street was quiet. No late-night parties. Not surprising for a Monday. I circled the house, checking the roof. But other than a few missing tiles on the back of the house, nothing seemed out of place.

I stepped inside. Room by room, I searched the house. When a thorough canvassing turned up nothing, I put away the Ruger and returned to watching *Jessica Jones*. But I couldn't shake the feeling that I wasn't alone. Or that someone was watching me.

This Barclay crap had me jumpy. Caution was one thing, but this was turning into outright paranoia. I was physically and emotionally exhausted. Perhaps some sleep would get my head right.

I climbed into bed and read the latest Isabella Maldonado novel until I drifted off to sleep.

I woke a few hours later from a nightmare, the details of which eluded my conscious memory. But the sense I was not alone in the house had only grown stronger. I tried to tell myself it was my paranoia kicking up again, but I couldn't shake the feeling.

I opened my eyes and scanned the room without moving a muscle, in case my intruder was in the room with me. I had excellent night vision and could make out the shapes of my dresser, my closet, and the door to the hallway. But no intruder.

I pulled the Ruger out of my nightstand and slipped out of bed. Keeping the lights off, I covertly searched the house again. The voices in my head argued over my state of mind. Was I crazy, or was I in danger?

As before, the search turned up nothing. All doors were locked. All windows intact and secure.

"What the fuck is wrong with you, girl?" I asked myself in the dim glow of my kitchen.

Perhaps a little Mexican sleeping medicine would help. I opened the cabinet and pulled out the bottle of Cuervo Gold I'd bought. Anything to quiet the voices in my head. I stopped short when I saw that the tax label on the cap was already torn and the level was down a bit. I didn't remember opening it.

In my mind, I could hear Conor's voice saying, "Don't be daft, girl."

I must have opened it. No one would break into my house and take a drink of tequila and nothing else. My computer and electronics were all accounted for. The money on my dresser was still there. Clearly, I was losing my fucking mind. I took a long draught of alcohol, enjoying the burning in my throat, and left the bottle on the counter.

I shuffled back to bed, read another chapter in the Isabella Maldonado novel, and was soon in a dreamless sleep.

21

———

The *Game of Thrones* ringtone woke me at eight o'clock. I must have slept through the alarm I'd set for six. I fumbled for my phone. "Yellow," I mumbled.

"Jinx, I could use some help." The exhaustion in Becca's voice was telling.

"Ye olde chronic fatigue kicking up again?" I asked.

"Yeah. And Easton flew out this morning for Denver on a two-day business trip."

"I'll be right there."

"Sorry to impose."

"Don't be sorry. We're there for each other, goofball. You need me to pick up anything for you?"

"Just a few basics. I'll text you a list."

I poured myself a cup of coffee to shake off the weariness of the night before. The sense that I was not alone persisted despite my getting a few hours of restless sleep. I didn't want to move in with Conor, and now being in my own home had me on high alert. *What the fuck is going on with me?*

I packed up my vest, weapons, and other gear in a duffel and set it on the passenger seat of the Gray Ghost. I didn't need to be shopping at Fry's Foods dressed as if I were ready to take down a drug-dealing bail jumper. Along with the groceries Becca asked for, I picked up some flowers to cheer her up a bit.

When I reached her front door, I let myself in with the key she'd given me years earlier. The kitchen was cluttered with dirty dishes on the counters, pans stacked up on the stove, and floors that looked as if they'd been dusted with crumbs. She'd never been much of a cleaner, and I never judged her for it. She jokingly called her decorating style "post-disaster." Apparently, Easton wasn't a neatnik either.

"Yo! Becks! You up?" I dumped some empty TV dinner trays and a half-opened pizza box into a garbage bag to make room on the counter for the groceries.

"In here," she said in a voice as thin as paper.

I walked into the living room, where the six-seat dining table was covered with two laptops, three screens, empty food wrappers, and a wide assortment of computer parts I couldn't begin to identify. Becca sat at one of the computers, heavy-lidded, hair mussed, and looking as if she'd been poured into the chair. Her hands alternated between short fits of typing and mouse clicks.

"I figured you'd be in bed."

She took a deep, halting breath and let it out. "I know, but I've got to install this patch for a client by the end of the day."

"You need some downtime. I feel bad for texting you about Peyton last night."

"You find his father?"

"Not yet. Have you eaten this morning?"

"Not hungry." She held up a coffee cup, the outside rim crusted with gunk. "Get me a one-more-please?" Our silly term for another cup of coffee after I'd given her a mug with the words "One More Please" painted inside the bottom of the cup.

I took the cup and set it down on the table. "You're going to bed, Ms. Alvarez."

She leaned back and stuck out her bottom lip in a pout.

I pulled a pair of cuffs from my back pocket. "Look, lady, we can do this the easy way or the hard way."

A wicked yet weary grin creased her face. "Oooh, promises, promises."

"Or I could just tell your mother to drive down from Flagstaff."

"You wouldn't."

"Try me."

Becca's mischievous grin dissolved into an eye roll. "Fine. I'll go to bed."

I helped her to her feet. When she grabbed the laptop in front of her, I shook my head. "Put down the laptop. That's an order."

"You're so damned bossy," she said.

I shadowed her down the hall to her bedroom. Clothes cluttered the floor. The head of her adjustable bed was raised in a reclining position. She rolled into it, slipped under the covers, and clicked on the TV with a remote from the nightstand. She patted the other side of her bed. "Come lay with me."

I was torn. I needed to be out looking for Rudy Pratt and Barclay Dietz, but I had no active leads at the moment. Besides, Becca was the closest thing I had to a sister. "Let me put the groceries away and then I'll hang with you a bit."

A smile reappeared on her face. "You're the best, Jinxie."

Ten minutes later, I climbed into bed next to her. "What are we watching?"

"*Stranger Things*, season two. You watch it?" Becca switched on the television. Eerie music began to play as shimmering red lines of the opening title slid across the screen. It looked like some old sci-fi movie from the 1980s.

"Not so far."

"It's freakin' awesome. You want me to back it up to season one?"

"That's okay. I'm sure I'll catch on."

I tried to follow the story with Becca filling in bits of plot I had missed. It probably would have made more sense if I had watched the previous season, but I was less concerned with the show and more with just spending time with my bestie. Between episodes, I said, "I saw Peyton last night."

Her face got a slow burst of energy. "Seriously? What was that like?"

"Weird. More than a little awkward."

"He still hot looking or has he flabbed out?"

"Still pretty hot. Followed him to a club in Mesa and caught him buying a bag of ecstasy."

"Ugh. What a loser."

"I kinda feel bad for him. He had such potential in high school."

"Not your fault his dad turned out to be a transphobic, psycho bank robber."

"I know. But it wasn't Peyton's fault either."

"So is he in touch with his dad?"

"Didn't claim to be."

"You believe him?"

"Maybe."

She perked up for a moment. "Oh, are you still looking for Rudy Pratt?"

"Yeah. Why? You got something?"

Becca reached over to her nightstand and grabbed her phone. She tapped on the screen and handed it to me. "This might help."

On the screen was an email about a planning meeting for the upcoming protest by White Nation. Among the list of email recipients was one Rudy Pratt. The meeting was scheduled for three this afternoon at Dixie's, a bar Pratt patronized once or twice a month.

"So Rudy's involved with White Nation, huh?" I said. "Why am I not surprised."

"Be careful, girl. Bring lots of backup. Maybe Conor and his crew can help you out."

"I'll call Rodeo and Caden and see if they can help."

"How is Conor, by the way?"

I sighed. "Conor's...Conor."

A chuckle escaped her throat. "What's that mean?"

"We got into an argument last night about me moving in with him."

"Oh, Jinxie, take the plunge already."

"Every time I think about living with him..." I sighed as a wave of emotion washed over me. "I swear I feel the walls closing in."

"Not afraid of commitment, are you?"

"It's not that."

"Afraid he's going to hurt you like Wilson did?"

"Maybe. I don't know. It just doesn't feel like the right time."

"You gotta do what you feel's right."

"There's something else. Last night when I was home, I kept getting this creepy feeling like someone was in the house with me. Then I went to have a drink of tequila from a bottle I'd just bought and found the seal cracked. Becks, I don't remember opening it. I'm seriously losing it."

"You don't have another stalker again, do you? Leaving dead bodies on your doorstep?"

"Nothing like that."

"Maybe it's a poltergeist," she said matter-of-factly.

"Poltergeist?" I scoffed. "Yeah, right. I don't think so. I think this whole Barclay Dietz thing's got my head spinning around in all directions."

"Speaking of which, I've been looking into the bank jobs Dietz pulled on his way south," she said. "In all cases, local police were already responding to an explosion or fire in the immediate area."

"You're kidding!"

"In Wyoming, a cattle feed plant exploded. In Salt Lake City, a plant that prepares emergency rations caught fire. Kayenta, it was a car bomb."

"That's a little disconcerting."

"There's more." Becca continued, "Before Barclay was a boxer, he served in Operation Desert Storm. As a demolitions expert. He knows his way around things that go boom."

"Shit."

"I'm thinking we should tell the FBI what we've found out. Just too risky for you to take on by yourself."

"And tell them what? We know who's setting off bombs and robbing banks based on a Woody Woodpecker tattoo? Maybe it's not even him. Or maybe these explosions and fires aren't connected to the bank robberies."

"Jinx, you know it's him, and they *are* connected."

"Thing is, me and the feds aren't exactly on speaking terms. Not after what happened last year with Volkov. Sooner or later, Dietz is going to contact Peyton. And when he does, I'm going to be there."

"Oh, Jinxie. He nearly killed you last time. And now he's blowing shit up."

"Things have changed. I've changed. If I can handle Volkov, I can handle this."

An awkward silence settled in. Her eyes started to droop. I kissed her on the forehead. "Get some sleep, girl."

"Love you."

"You too. Call me if you need anything else, sister girl."

I walked out to the Gray Ghost and called Caden and Rodeo, giving them the 411 on the White Nation meeting. Both agreed to meet me at Dixie's. But first, I had another stop to make.

22

I passed under an arch of climbing vines and knocked on the front door of an elegant four-bedroom home a stone's throw from North Mountain in Phoenix. The residents of the house tended to be night owls. My watch read one o'clock in the afternoon, so I hoped I wasn't waking anyone up.

The door opened a moment later revealing a dark-skinned, slender, sixty-something woman draped in colorful silk that accentuated her curves in all the right places. If Tina Turner had been transgender and Puerto Rican, she would have been Juanita Valdez.

"Oh my Godiva," Juanita exclaimed when she saw me. "Come here this instant and give your *tía* Juana a hug!"

Juanita had started out as a drag queen back in the day, performing under the name Tía Juana. She later came out as transgender and transitioned to living full-time as a woman. These days she owned and operated the Main Drag, the biggest queer bar in the valley.

We'd met twenty years earlier at the Phoenix Gender Alliance support group. A firestorm of attitude and wisdom, Juanita immediately took me under her wing and declared herself my fairy drag mother. She also bestowed upon me the nickname Jinx, a mash-up of my first and middle names, Jenna Christina.

"How're you doing, *tía*?" I asked as I released her from the hug.

"If I were any better, I'd give birth to myself. Come on in, *mi'ja!*" I followed her down a dark hallway to a large airy kitchen with a great view of the lush courtyard out back. She poured us coffee, and we sat across from each other at her breakfast bar.

"It's been ages since you called," she said sternly. "Shame on you! You know how I worry about my little ones. Especially you, chasing down all those criminal types."

"Sorry. I've been busy."

"Too busy you can't pick up the damned phone, Miss Thang?" She pointed a well-manicured nail at me. "You should treat your elders with more respect."

"I will, I promise." I grinned.

"To what do I owe this unexpected but much overdue visit?"

"Can't a girl visit her auntie without having an agenda?"

She cocked an eyebrow but said nothing. It wasn't exactly the first time I'd shown up asking for her assistance.

I sighed. "Okay, fine. I need your help."

"More fairy drag mother wisdom?"

"Actually, I need to disguise my appearance."

"A disguise? Color me intrigued."

"The fugitive I'm pursuing is expected at a White Nation meeting this afternoon."

"White Nation?" Her posture stiffened. "You're tangling with those *pendejos*? Bitch, are you loco?"

"I don't even know for sure he'll be there, but I don't have any better leads at the moment. He killed someone, and now he's in the wind, most likely holed up with one of his White Nation buddies. I'm hoping to grab him at this meeting."

Juanita shook her head. "You're a braver girl than me."

I shrugged. "Just doing my job."

"Job like that can get you killed," she continued. "No wonder your mama worries about you."

"Problem is, he's seen me before. He's fast and smart. Used to literally be a rocket scientist. So I have to get close to him without him realizing it's me. Thus the need for a disguise."

"To get a racist peckerwood off the street, you can count on my help." She put a hand to my chin and studied my appearance. "Question is how best to disguise you."

After a moment, she said, "I've got an idea, but you probably won't like it."

"If it helps me nail this guy, I'm in."

She met my gaze and said, "We disguise you as a guy."

I nearly fell off my stool. "Oh hell no!"

"Oh, come on, Miss Thang! What's wrong with a little boy drag now and then? Are you so insecure in your femininity that you can't stand to look like a boy again?"

"I tried to be a boy for eleven years. I hated it."

"Bitch, please! I did it for twice that. The point of this is illusion, make-believe. It's an act so you can catch a murderer, right? You dress up as Wonder Woman all the time. Hell, I saw you the other day on TV, arresting a guy in your superhero drag. Just think of it as a little cross-play."

"But I transitioned before puberty. My voice never dropped."

"Oh, well, aren't you the little *princesa*," she said snottily. "Oops, did your tiara fall off? Let me pick that up for you."

"*Tía*, stop. Even if I wanted to, there's no way I could pull it off."

Juanita sighed and lifted up strands of my hair. "There gonna be a lot of fighting?"

"Not if I do it right." I lied as honestly as I could.

"Fine. Come with me."

I followed Juanita past a few closed bedroom doors to her boudoir, which always looked like a set from *Moulin Rouge*. Imperial-red wallpaper accented with gold flourishes covered the walls. A canopy bed with dark wood posts and a plum satin comforter dominated the room. Along one wall stood a vintage vanity table in front of a large mirror bordered with lights. The only modern accommodation was a flat-screen and sound system in an entertainment center opposite the bed.

Juanita led me into her walk-in closet. Shelf upon shelf of wigs on Styrofoam heads stretched the length of one side. They came in all colors, styles, and lengths. Most were natural colors, though a few were on the wilder side—electric blue or rainbow.

"Put your hair up," she told me, handing me some bobby pins.

I tied my long dark hair into a tight bun while Juanita studied her collection of wigs. After a moment, she took down a short bleached-blond wig from a stand someone had drawn blue eyes on.

"How about Miss Norma Jean here?" She offered it to me.

"A little too fifties, don't you think?"

She huffed and snatched it from me and set it carefully back on its stand. "So goddamned picky! Let's see, how about this one. I call her Ginger Rose." She handed me a strawberry-blond wig.

I tried it on and looked at myself in a mirror on the back of the door.

Before I could say anything, she snatched it off my head. "Nope! Wrong coloring. No one would believe a redhead with tan skin and brown eyes." She was right about that.

"How about that one?" I asked, pointing at a long blond wig with wispy wings.

"Ah, Farrah." She sighed, holding a hand over her heart. "I always wanted to be her."

"Who?"

"Farrah Fawcett! Please tell me you've heard of *Charlie's Angels.*"

"The one with Drew Barrymore? Never saw it."

I thought she was going to give birth to kittens right then and there. "Not that ridiculous movie! The original series from the seventies. I have failed as a mentor and fairy drag mother."

"I promise I'll look it up on Netflix when I get a chance." I held up a three-fingered salute.

"See that you do. Farrah was a goddess." She lifted the wig from its stand and fixed it onto my head with more bobby pins and teased it here and there. "You know, this one just might work."

"What's that one called?" I asked, pointing at a super-campy wig on the high shelf.

"That, my dear, is Hedwig. From *Hedwig and the Angry Inch*."

"Never heard of it," I said with a shrug.

Her eyes widened. "Are you fucking kidding me? I swear, queer kids today have no sense of their own culture."

I broke into a grin. "Relax, *tía*. I'm messing with you. I've seen it. A few times, in fact. A bit campy for my taste, but a good flick."

"*Pendeja*," she muttered under her breath.

She reached onto a shelf full of accessories and pulled out a pair of large rose-tinted glasses and slipped them on my face. "There! With the right makeup, even your own mama won't recognize you. Now, follow me." She led me into another room filled with racks of outfits.

"Damn! I haven't seen so many clothes outside of a department store."

"A performer needs to have the proper costume." She pulled out a lacy top and a pair of cut-off jeans. "Try these on."

"Right here?" I asked, suddenly feeling a little embarrassed. "Can I have a little privacy?"

"You afraid you got something I ain't never seen before? Bitch, please!"

I took a deep breath and released it. "Fine." I pulled off my T-shirt and jeans. As soon as I did, Juanita guffawed.

"What the hell are those? Granny panties?"

My face flushed. "They're comfortable." I snatched the Daisy Dukes from her and slipped into them. "They're a little loose."

"'Cause you got them skinny boy hips."

"Juanita! That's mean!"

"Oh, please. Just put a belt on them. They'll be okay."

I pulled on the lacy top. "Well?"

She handed me a pair of strappy leather sandals with two-inch heels. I slipped them on, hoping I wouldn't have to run in them.

Juanita nodded. "Close, but we need one more thing. Follow me."

She led me to her vanity, where I sat down on the padded bench.

"We need to recontour your face so that redneck rocket man doesn't recognize you."

Juanita set to work like a master artist with me as her canvas. It had been so long since I'd gotten a makeover, it felt weird for someone else to be doing my makeup. But I followed her instructions to look up or open my mouth in an O, so she could achieve the desired effect.

She applied a lot more makeup than I ever did. I favored the minimalist look, especially in the summer. Didn't need makeup melting across my sweaty face after chasing down FTAs. But in this case, I trusted her judgment to get me close enough to Pratt to slap the cuffs on him.

She finished and stepped back. "Well, what do you think?"

I studied my reflection in the mirror. "I barely recognize myself. This might work."

"You look totally fish. Those redneck boys' dicks will be so hard, they won't know what hit them."

"Thanks for your help." I hugged her and kissed her cheek.

"What's a fairy drag mother for?"

"I'll get the wig and the clothes back to you in a little while."

"In the next day or so is fine. And I best see your skinny white ass at my show tomorrow night."

"The Barbra Shop Quartet? Sounds very campy."

"In the very *best* of ways."

"I'll be there."

"Your little boy toy, Conor, too, I hope."

A wave of sadness passed through me. "Absolutely." *Assuming he's still speaking to me.*

"Be careful, *mi'ja*." She shot me a concerned look.

"Always, *tía*."

23

A t a quarter to three, I met Caden and Rodeo outside Dixie's. An image of a buxom woman carrying a Confederate flag was painted on the bar's plate glass window, with stars and bars decorating the name above her. Vehicles sporting pro-gun, Confederate, and far right-wing political and religious bumper stickers filled the parking lot.

Rodeo guffawed when he saw me. "Holy shit, girl! Who the hell are you supposed to be?"

I flipped him the one-finger salute. "Pratt's seen me before. I need to get in close without him recognizing me. My friend Juanita helped me out."

Caden joined in the laughter at my expense. "You look like that woman from that poster back in the seventies. I forget her name."

"Farrah Fawcett?" I asked.

"Yeah, that's it. She was on some show, wasn't she?"

I ignored the question. "Look, is it too over-the-top? I was trying for inconspicuous."

Rodeo took a deep breath and regained his composure, but a

couple of persistent giggles crept out. "Inconspicuous? Not a chance. More like fuckably hot!"

"Shit." Maybe going to Juanita was a mistake.

"Don't worry." Caden put a hand on my shoulder. "You look sexy but convincing. Pratt won't know what hit him until it's too late."

"So what's the plan?" asked Rodeo.

"Pratt is supposed to be attending a meeting here for White Nation. The plan is I go in like I'm looking to join. When Pratt shows up, I'll figure a way to lure him outside, slap the cuffs on, and away we go."

They both shook their heads.

"A honeypot lure? Spectacularly bad idea, Jinx," Rodeo said. "That same tactic nearly got us both killed last year when you tried it with Freddie Colton."

"As I recall, we caught Colton," I said confidently.

"While also drawing a mob of armed thugs from the bar you lured him out of."

"Hey, I handled it."

Rodeo glared at me.

"Fine," I conceded. "We handled it, even when Fiddler bailed on us. And now we have Caden. We've got our bases covered."

Caden looked a little nervous. "Sounds pretty sketchy, Jinxie. No offense. Maybe we should stake the place out and follow him when he leaves."

"And then what? He's probably staying with a bunch of White Nation thugs. So whether we take him here or somewhere else, the risk's the same."

"You think he's in there?" Rodeo asked.

I scanned the parking lot and noticed a white Camry, like the one listed on Pratt's bail application. I circled around to the rear of the vehicle. "Shit. Plates don't match."

"Could've switched plates," Caden suggested.

"Anything's possible with these guys." I racked the slide of my Ruger and slipped it into the concealment holster at the small of my back. "Rodeo, guard the back door. Caden, you watch the front. I'll draw him out into the parking lot. I won't have my radio with me, obviously, so if I'm not out in thirty minutes, come and get me."

Rodeo nodded. "Copy that." He slung his beanbag shotgun over his shoulder and strolled around to the back of the building.

Caden drew his SIG. "Watch your ass in there."

"I intend to."

I approached the door of the bar. A sign on the outside read "Libtards Will Not Be Served." *Great.*

Inside, the place was empty except for a bartender and one old man who looked as if he had melted into his bar stool.

"Can I help you?" asked the bartender, a beefy guy with a flattop.

"I'm looking for the White Nation meeting."

The bartender fixed me with a look that said he wasn't sure I was the right type. Was there a password or something to indicate I was with the in crowd? If there was, I was shit out of luck. I flashed my sexiest smile.

"To your right and in the back room past the pool tables." He gestured with his thumb and continued wiping down the bar.

"Is Rudy Pratt here yet? He asked me to meet him here."

"Dunno. I stepped out for a cigarette a bit ago. He mighta come in when I wasn't up here."

"Okay, thanks!"

I felt his eyes follow me as I rounded the corner and followed the sound of male voices laughing and shouting, past a room with two pool tables to a wooden door. My heart pounded in my chest, partly from fear, partly from the thrill of the hunt.

I opened the door and found a dozen people gathered around a wooden table topped with pitchers of beer and stacks of flyers for the upcoming rally. A few were women, but most were men. None of them Rudy Pratt.

I expected a room full of stereotypical white supremacists— militant skinheads, neo-Nazis, and good ol' boy, South-will-rise-again types in wifebeaters. But the people here looked like ordinary suburbanites, most in collared shirts and dad jeans.

"Can I help you?" asked a man with an angular face and a distinct air of authority. He wore a white button-down dress shirt. A leather notebook lay in front of him at the head of the table.

I took a few cautious steps into the room. "Hi! I'm looking for Rudy."

"And you are?"

"Liz Windsor." It was an alias I often used. "He asked me to meet him here. Said y'all could use my organizing skills to help with the rally."

"Well, Rudy isn't here right now, Miss Liz Windsor." His gaze made my skin crawl, like a rattlesnake staring down a potential meal. "You look familiar to me. Have we met?"

A shiver ran down my spine. For the millionth time, I kicked myself for having been interviewed by *Phoenix Living* the previous year. Conor had warned me not to do it, saying bounty hunters should keep a low profile. And now people recognized me as the cover girl for the local trans community.

"Naw, I just have one of those faces," I replied nervously.

"Of course." He didn't look convinced but stalked over and extended a hand. "A pleasure to meet you, Miss Windsor. The name's Eric Freytag. I'm the chairman of the local White Nation chapter."

"Likewise," I said. "Is Rudy expected?"

"Hard to say. A lot going on with his family these days, I'm afraid."

I nodded. "His daughter. I know, he told me. Truly heartbreaking." My survival instincts were screaming at me to get the hell out of there.

Pull your shit together, girl, I told myself. *Act like you belong here.* I took a deep breath.

"How long have you known Rudy?" Freytag asked.

"We met a few months ago at the hardware store where he

works. He helped me pick out some shrubs for my front yard. We got to talking politics and things."

"Well, do come join us." Freytag shut the door, put his arm around me, and led me to a seat on the opposite side of the room. *"Come into my parlor," said the spider to the fly. And I'm in a room crawling with spiders. I fucking hate spiders. But I'm no fly, I reminded myself. I'm a tarantula wasp.*

"Why don't we get down to business," Freytag said. "We have a few stragglers, but I'm sure they'll be along momentarily. Until then, Miss Windsor, perhaps you'd care to tell us about yourself and why you chose to join us."

Ugh, this plan is totally going off the rails. Bad enough being in the same room as these people, and now I have to pretend to think like them.

"Well, I, uh…I love America and Jesus, and I just want our country great again, the way it used to be. Where good Christian people have freedom of religion and being white isn't considered a crime." The words tasted like ashes in my mouth. I couldn't believe I was saying this shit. On the bright side, my rambling white nationalist drivel drew cheers from the other attendees.

"Well said, Miss Windsor. You are certainly among friends." Freytag's expression was hard to read. I wanted to believe I was giving a convincing performance, but I wasn't sure I'd succeeded.

"Now, everyone, I have very high hopes for the rally this Saturday. Our website and social media campaigns have been getting a great response. The conservative media has been helpful in promoting the event. If all goes as planned, our protest will make Charlottesville look like a lonely man's funeral. I believe this will be the biggest rally for white pride this country has seen in over a century."

I wanted to punch this guy in the face so hard, my fists were balled up like hammers.

"And there'll be none of that college boy, tiki-torch nonsense. We will have real people. Families. Hardworking men and women who embody the heart and soul of this country, a soul that for decades has been strangled by liberal PC brainwashing. It was white men who made this country what it is, and for all us white men and women, it is long past time we reclaim our rightful place."

A knock interrupted his speech. "Come in."

The door to the room opened. I expected it to be Pratt, so I readied my body to spring into action.

A figure came into view. My heart thundered in my chest. It wasn't Pratt. The face was familiar, though aged since I'd last seen it in person. But the Woody Woodpecker tattoo was unmistakable. The imposing presence of Barclay "The Beast" Dietz entered the room.

24

———

The Beast sauntered through the doorway as if he owned the place. The years had reduced his eyes to deep-set slits, but he still carried himself with the threatening presence of a rogue bull.

"Sorry I'm late," he said, or something similar, as Freytag stood and shook his hand. It was hard to hear over the roaring of blood in my ears. Deep inside me, a long-dormant fury rumbled forth like magma gushing up the throat of a volcano, erupting into a cataclysm of emotion and violence.

In an instant, I vaulted onto the table and launched myself at Dietz, swinging, kicking, and pummeling. The world spun around the two of us. I drove hard with elbows, knees, and the heel of my palm at every potentially vulnerable spot on the man.

My arms were twisted behind me as I was pulled off of Dietz.

"Miss Windsor, what is the meaning of this nonsense?" asked Freytag.

My chest heaved. I gulped ragged breaths as the fury of adrenaline burned through my bloodstream. The right side of my face throbbed, and my vision in that eye blurred.

Dietz staggered to his feet. His nose dripped blood, and one of

Dietz's eyes was red and swelling. "Crazy bitch! What the hell's wrong with you?"

I struggled to free my arms from the men who held me, but they held fast. I drove a heel into the instep of the man to my right. He released my arm, and I drove it into the nose of the guy holding my other arm. I drew my Ruger and backed toward the door. Unfortunately, several others drew guns, as well.

With my free hand, I flashed my bail enforcement badge and ID. "My name is Jinx Ballou. I'm a bail enforcement agent. I'm here to arrest Barclay Dietz for failing to appear on aggravated assault and attempted murder charges."

"Mr. Dietz, is this true?" Freytag asked.

Dietz cocked his head, and his eyes opened wide in recognition. "You filthy piece of garbage!" His face burned dark red, and he pointed a finger at me. "This *he-she* seduced my son when he was in high school, pretending to be a girl. But it ain't nothing but a faggot in a dress!"

Freytag crossed his arms and grinned. "Jinx Ballou! I thought I recognized you. You were on the cover of that liberal rag of a newspaper last year. Well, I am sorry to disappoint you, but this gentleman here is our guest. He's not leaving with you."

"Like hell, he isn't."

"Mr. Quinton," Freytag said with venom in his voice.

"Yes, sir." A man pointing a snub-nosed .38 at me stepped forward. He had the look of a retired cop.

"Would you and Mr. Overcash please escort this intruder off the premises?"

"Gladly." Something in Quinton's gaze suggested he planned to do more than escort me outside.

Overcash, a skinny guy with a .44 Magnum, edged around the table with him. The large-barreled revolver looked as if it weighed as much as he did.

"Not without my fugitive," I insisted.

"Fuck this bullshit!" Dietz thundered. "Shoot that bitch!"

Overcash raised his hand cannon and fired. I put two in his

chest and ducked out of the room before slamming the door shut. Several bullets ripped through the door around me as I braced it closed with a chair.

"You okay?" a voice behind me asked.

I spun around and came just short of putting a nine-millimeter hole in Caden.

"I heard shouting. Figured you could use an assist." He stood by one of the pool tables, his SIG Sauer in hand.

The door shuddered as if someone had slammed into it from the other side. The chair gave an inch.

"Let's get out of here," I said.

"What the hell y'all doing?" The bartender appeared in the doorway between us and the main barroom, holding a rifle.

I smiled and pointed over his shoulder. "Ask the guy behind you."

"Seriously, you expect me to—"

Rodeo pressed the muzzle of his shotgun into the bartender's back. At point-blank range, even a beanbag round could be lethal. The bartender laid the rifle on the floor and held up his hands. Rodeo tossed it to me. I was acquiring quite a collection of other people's guns.

Again someone slammed into the meeting room door. On the third attempt, the chair buckled, and the door flew open. The air exploded with gunfire.

"Out!" I shouted.

Caden, Rodeo, and I charged out the front door. My left calf burned with a sharp stinging sensation. I ignored it as we raced through the lot and took up positions behind a Hummer. I kept my Ruger trained on the bar's front door. Caden and Rodeo did the same.

"Anyone hit?" My body trembled in pain, mostly in my head and leg.

"I'm in one piece," replied Rodeo. "Caden?"

"I'm good."

"Jinx, you're bleeding." Rodeo pointed. My left calf was covered in blood.

I gritted my teeth as the sharp pain intensified. "Fuck."

Rodeo crouched down, took out a bandana, and wiped away some of the blood.

"Shhhhiiittt," I hissed.

"Hold still." He snapped open a jackknife.

"Wait! What are you doing?"

I looked down to see Rodeo insert the blade a half inch into the wound and flick out a piece of something I hoped wasn't flesh. I almost bit off my tongue from the pain. "Jesus fucking Christ!" My arms trembled as I held myself up.

"It's okay." He tied the bandana across the wound. "Just caught a piece of a ricochet." He stood up and showed me a bloody bit of metal. "Put a little alcohol on the wound when you get home."

"What happened to your face, Jinx?" asked Caden.

"I'm in fucking pain," I grunted. "This is my fucking-pain face."

"No, your eyes are all dark and swelling."

I felt my face and temple, and a bobby pin came loose in my hand. If it was possible for me to feel worse, I did. "Aw fuck. The wig came off in there."

Caden shook his head. "Juanita's going to kill you."

I took a deep breath, struggling to get a handle on the pain. "She'll have to get in line behind these other fucks." I glanced toward the bar's front door. "This plan went to shit."

"So Pratt's still in there?" asked Rodeo.

I shook my head. "Pratt didn't show."

"Who were you trying to arrest in there?" Caden gave me a confused look. "I heard you say, 'Not without my fugitive.'"

"Barclay Dietz."

Rodeo did a double take. "Barclay 'The Beast' Dietz? The boxer?"

"Damn, girl. Miracle you're still alive," Caden added.

I looked over at my teammates. "Don't tell Conor about Dietz, all right? I don't want him to worry."

"You got it," Caden replied.

"He's bound to find out sooner or later, especially with your face looking like that," said Rodeo.

"Barclay Dietz is gonna have a lot worse before I'm done with him."

We fell silent. Rodeo was right, and Conor would find out eventually. I just hoped I could put Dietz behind bars first.

"Doesn't look like your buddies are coming out any time soon," said Rodeo. "What now?"

Before I could formulate an answer, the wail of multiple police sirens pierced the air. Two Phoenix PD patrol cars pulled into the parking lot. Two more pulled in a moment later and effectively blocked off the exit. The officers got out and approached us with their weapons drawn.

25

"Drop your weapons and get down on the ground, hands behind your head," two of the officers shouted in unison, one man and one woman. Rodeo, Caden, and I complied.

Why didn't I keep my cool in there? I scolded myself. *If I had, maybe I could have somehow lured Dietz outside, and no one would have been shot.* Not that I would have admitted it to the cops.

"I'm a former cop, now a bail enforcement agent," I told the female officer who approached and cuffed me. "I was here to apprehend two fugitives. My ID's in my back pocket."

"Someone will be along to take your statement shortly." She pulled me to my feet and escorted me to a waiting patrol car.

As I sat and stewed in the back seat, resisting the temptation to release the handcuffs using one of the keys I had kept on me, an ambulance arrived, and a medical team charged into the bar. A little while later they exited carrying a draped body on a gurney. Overcash, I assumed.

I should have been worried about getting arrested and possibly facing charges for killing Overcash. I should have been worried about the shit I was going to get from Juanita for losing her precious wig. But what worried me most as I sat in the cramped back seat of the patrol car was the massive guilt trip I was going to get if I missed my mother's birthday party, especially after blowing off family brunch last weekend.

The car door opened. A familiar face beckoned me out.

"Damn, Ballou. What'd you get messed up in this time?" Officer Mitch Evans had been in my squad for the year that I served on the force. He'd hit on me relentlessly until word got around the precinct that I was trans. All of a sudden, all the sexual innuendoes ended. But so did any sense that I was part of the team. I left the force not long after that.

A couple of years ago, Evans had been suspended after shooting an unarmed black man. Six months later, an all-white jury exonerated him, and he returned to active duty.

"Nice to see you too, Evans."

He pointed at my leg. "You need medical attention?"

I looked down at my calf. The bandana was weeping blood. "Yeah."

He pulled me out of the patrol car and called over an EMT who wore her hair in a French braid. "Looks like we got a GSW," he said.

"Hi, I'm Angie. Can you walk?"

I nodded and followed her to an ambulance, where she examined the wound. "What happened here?"

"Not sure, but I think I caught a ricochet."

She poked around the wound. I did my best not to bite my tongue as I tried not to scream.

"I don't see any fragments. I think you got lucky with just a flesh wound. I don't think you need a trip to the ER, but it's your call."

"I'd rather not." I decided not to mention that Rodeo had already dug out the fragment.

She cleaned it with saline, applied some ointment, and bandaged it up. "Keep it clean and dry for the next week and apply an antibiotic ointment a few times a day. If it gets infected, call your primary or go to the ER."

"Thanks."

"If you'd like, I can give you an ice pack for that black eye."

I shook my head. "Naw, I'm good."

"If you start to feel nauseated or dizzy, get yourself checked for a concussion."

"Will do."

I hopped out of the ambulance and was intercepted by Evans. "How 'bout you tell me what the hell happened here?"

"My team and I are currently pursuing two fugitives—Rudy Pratt and Barclay Dietz—both of whom were expected at a White Nation meeting at this bar."

"White Nation, huh?" He wrote it down in a notebook he pulled out of his pocket.

"Pratt was a no-show. When I tried to arrest Dietz, he fought back. Some of his White Nation buddies also intervened. Some skinny guy shot at me with a large-caliber revolver, looked like a .44 Magnum. I was in fear for my life and returned fire in self-defense." Wording was everything if I was to stay out of jail.

"They carried a guy out with two in the chest. That your handiwork?"

"I don't know. It was rather chaotic."

"Then what happened?"

"When it became apparent my team couldn't safely appre-hend our fugitive, we retreated to the safety of the parking lot." I might have left out a few things, but it was basically the truth as I saw it.

"Barclay Dietz. Why does that name ring a bell?"

"He used to be a boxer. Jumped bail some years ago on an aggravated assault charge."

"That's right. That was a while ago. How come you're tracking him now?"

"Got a tip he was in town. The FBI's offering a nice reward for his capture. This is what I do."

"Okay, stay put. I'm going to check out a few things. I'll be back in a bit." Evans again escorted me to the back of the squad car. He returned twenty minutes later. "No one by the name of Barclay Dietz is in the bar."

"Well, duh. He's been on the lam for more than a decade. Probably has a fake ID with an alias. He's a big guy, over six feet and built like a side of beef. You can't miss him."

"No one fitting that description either."

"What?" He must have slipped out the back somehow before the cops showed up. "Damnit. I almost had him."

"Everybody in the bar's saying you assaulted one of their guests. When Mr. Overcash tried to intervene, you pulled your weapon and shot Mr. Overcash. Sounds like second-degree murder."

"That's bullshit, and you know it. I used to be a cop myself, in case you've forgotten. I know what the law is. These people are nothing but a bunch of racist neo-Nazis harboring at least one, possibly two fugitives. They have every reason to lie."

"I follow the evidence." His voice was cold as he recuffed me and read me my Miranda rights.

"You're a real piece of shit, you know that, Evans?"

After I spent an hour counting cockroaches in my holding cell, an officer called my name and escorted me to a room smaller than my walk-in closet. Not the first time I'd been in this interrogation room. Probably not the last.

My attorney, Kirsten Pasternak, sat on the far side of a table mounted to the floor. She was taller than me by a few inches, dressed in a near-black tailored suit and a beige blouse. Yellow-framed glasses brought out the golden highlights in her chestnut hair. Her fingers were long and delicate, and her voice was deep but sultry enough that most people didn't know she was trans unless she told them.

"What did you get yourself into now?" she asked.

I gave her the rundown of the events at Dixie's. She asked a few pointed questions and made suggestions on framing my version of the story so as not to implicate myself. When we were satisfied with our game plan, she knocked on the door. Moments later, Detective Brent Loughlin and Detective Emma Skoglund walked in carrying folders and notebooks.

Back when I was on the force, I had a crush on Detective Loughlin. Square jaw, broad shoulders, and ice-blue eyes. Just the sound of his laugh made me ache to feel him inside me. We'd met only a few times at crime scenes, though I doubted he ever knew my name. If I hadn't been dating Wilson at the time, I might've done something about that.

I'd run into Detective Skoglund a few times over the years. She'd always seemed a bit twitchy to me and hard to read. The overhead lights on her pale skin made her look jaundiced. She wore a pale-pink cardigan over her ballet-dancer frame.

Loughlin gave me a stern look that crushed any lingering feelings of romantic attraction. This guy meant business. He slid a picture of Overcash to my side of the table. It looked like a mug shot. "Just so we're all on the same page, this man, James Robert Overcash, was fatally shot twice in the chest. I'd like to know why."

I glanced at Kirsten. She gave me a nod to proceed as planned.

"I arrived at Dixie's Bar around three looking for one of my fugitives, who was expected at a White Nation meeting being held here. When Barclay Dietz arrived..." A repetitive clacking derailed my train of thought.

"Yes, keep going," Skoglund said in a monotone voice. A vibration in her jacket clued me in that she was bouncing the heel of one foot. From her poker face, I couldn't tell whether she was doing it intentionally to throw me off-balance. Either way, it was unnerving.

"I, uh, I was attempting to arrest Dietz when Overcash and several White Nation members grabbed me. I pulled away. That's when they drew weapons and fired on me. Out of fear for my life, I returned fire in self-defense."

Loughlin gave Skoglund an annoyed glance and shuffled through the papers in his folder. "Barclay Dietz, the former boxer?"

"Yes." I faced off with Loughlin, trying to tune out the clack, clack, clack of Skoglund's shoe heel. "He jumped bail thirteen years ago on aggravated assault charges. He's also involved in several armed robberies across the country."

"Who hired you to apprehend Mr. Dietz?" asked Detective Skoglund. *Clack, clack, clack, clack.*

"No one."

"Barclay Dietz is wanted by the FBI for numerous violent crimes," Kirsten interjected. "My client was acting within her capacity as a bail enforcement agent as she attempted to return a dangerous fugitive to custody."

"How'd you know Dietz would be there?" Loughlin made a move under the table, and the clacking stopped.

"I didn't. I showed up at Dixie's looking for Rudy Pratt, who jumped bail on a murder charge."

Loughlin nodded. "Must have been quite a shock, seeing your childhood bully after all these years."

Shit. How long had he known? "My intel indicated Dietz was in the area. So no, not a complete shock."

Skoglund sorted through her paperwork. "We have witnesses who deny Dietz was ever there. They say you showed up uninvited, assaulted one of their members unprovoked, and then opened fire." The heel clacking started up again.

"That's bullshit. Check the surveillance recordings."

"Unfortunately, the bar doesn't have any interior cameras," said Loughlin. "What footage we do have shows you and your fellow bounty hunters exiting the building while exchanging gunfire with those inside. That leaves us with the statements from witnesses, all of whom point to you as initiating the confrontation."

"What about the statements from my guys? Caden Morrow and Nathaniel Kwan?"

Skoglund's finger trailed a line across a report in front of her. "Per their statements, neither Mr. Morrow nor Mr. Kwan were in the room at the time the shooting began." *Clack, clack, clack.*

"Would you quit clicking your heels?" I snapped.

Skoglund met my gaze for a second and stopped. "Sorry."

"Bottom line, Ms. Ballou," said Loughlin, "no one's corroborating your story."

"Come on, Loughlin," I replied. "I used to be a cop myself. I wouldn't do anything like that."

He tapped the paperwork in front of him. "What I know is that in the years since you left the force and signed up to play bounty hunter, you've been involved in multiple violent incidents, including the deaths of two FBI agents just last year."

"I did not kill those agents. That piece of shit Milo Volkov killed them in cold blood. I did everything I could to save them. When that failed, I took down Volkov and several of his men, getting them off the streets."

"In other words, you killed them."

"Detectives, you have nothing. My client clearly acted in self-defense. And if you think a jury is going to believe the lies of a white nationalist hate group over a former police officer..."

Loughlin turned to her. "Key word being *former*. She hasn't been a police officer for quite some time. Now she's just a vigilante with a fake badge, pursuing her own idea of justice on my streets."

"I'm not a vigilante, you ass—" I took a breath. "I was there to apprehend a fugitive. That's all."

"Unfortunately, Ms. Ballou, the evidence is not in your favor," Loughlin replied.

We went round and round. In the end, Loughlin and Skoglund charged me with aggravated manslaughter, acting as if they were doing me a favor and not charging me with murder one.

I spent another hour being processed and was eventually released on seventy-five thousand dollars bond via Assurity Bail

Bonds. Sadie Levinson wasn't thrilled to be posting bail for her own bounty hunter. In short, I was on everyone's shit list.

It was after six before I was released. The Gray Ghost was still parked in front of Dixie's. As Kirsten gave me a ride back, I checked in with Caden and Rodeo. Neither were charged. Thank goodness for small favors.

When we arrived in the bar's parking lot, she turned to me. "I'm assuming you're not interested in a plea if they offer one."

"You got that right, sister. I stand by my story. I was just there to do my job. They're the ones who turned it into a gunfight."

"I'll get ahold of the witness statements, as well as the ballistics and autopsy reports, as soon as they're available. Hopefully, we can find something in there to clear you. If nothing else, I'm guessing we can dig up enough dirt on these good ol' boys to impeach their testimony."

"I hope so. I don't intend to spend the next decade behind bars." I thought about Conor and his vanishing act after the Omagh bombing. Would I give up my family and friends, my whole life, to avoid going to prison? It felt odd entertaining these thoughts when my job had me chasing after people making the same decision.

26

I was pulling out of the bar's parking lot when I remembered my mother's birthday party. *Shit! Fuck!*

I wanted to go home, put some ice on my swollen eye, and chase some ibuprofen down with a few belts of tequila. But I'd promised Jake, and by extension my mother, I'd be there. Bad enough I was late. But if I ghosted again, there'd be hell to pay. Italian Catholic guilt was nothing to sneeze at.

I pulled up in front of my parents' place around seven o'clock. Jake's truck was in their driveway, and Conor's Dodge Charger was parked on the street. My hair and makeup were a wreck. I was still dressed in the revealing blouse and cutoff jeans I'd borrowed from Juanita. I had several messages on my phone from Conor and my family asking where I was. I slipped on a jacket from the go bag I kept in the SUV.

"Sorry I'm late," I hollered as I walked into my parents' house. The dimly lit living room was filled with comfy furniture and a conglomeration of Cajun, Native American, and Mexican artwork. Family photos in brightly colored frames covered the walls. Conor appeared in the doorway to the kitchen as the warm aroma of Italian spices hit my senses.

"Where've ya been, love? We expected ya an hour ago." His face was a mask of concern and anger. "And what the bloody hell happened to your face? Looks like someone's been using you for a punching bag."

I sighed, trying not to react with the anger that boiled just beneath the surface. "Don't start with me, Conor. I've had a shitty day."

He paused for a moment and put a hand on my shoulder. "I'm sorry, love. It's just we've all been worried since ya missed dinner."

"Things sorta went off the rails. I'll fill you in with the gory details later. Right now I just want to eat, if there's anything left."

We joined my family in the kitchen. My mother sat at the table, surrounded by Jake and my dad. Her face was red and puffy.

"About damn time you showed up!" snapped Jake. "What's your excuse this time? Abducted by aliens?"

I ignored him and embraced my mother from behind. "Sorry I'm late, Mom. Happy birthday." I handed her a greeting card I'd picked up on the way over.

She stood and hugged me tightly. "Oh, punkin, I was so worried something happened to you." Her voice was thick with emotion. Guilt welled up in me. I was a horrible daughter.

"Everything's fine." Except for me facing five to twelve years in prison, every trans woman's dream.

"You should have called." She pulled away and held me with her gaze. "And your face. What happened to you?" She touched my swollen eye socket. I tried hard not to wince.

"Just part of the job, Mom. Nothing I can't handle."

"Your job?" She studied my outfit and shook her head.

"Maybe her pimp beat her up," Jake added with a self-indulgent chuckle. "You working as a hooker now, sis? Couldn't cut it as a bounty hunter or a cop?"

"What the hell's wrong with you?" I glared at him. He and I usually got along.

"You're the one dressed like a beat-up crack whore, and you want to know what's wrong with me? That's rich."

I stepped toward my brother, the fire in my gut curling my hands into fists. "You wanna go, big man? Let's go."

"You think you can take me?" Jake shot to his feet and knocked his chair onto its side.

"Someone who doesn't have guts enough to hold his boyfriend's hand in public? You're goddamned right I can." As soon as I mentioned Rodeo, a sharp pang of guilt stabbed me in the gut. I'd promised I wouldn't bring it up. Whoops.

"Stop this right now. Both of you!" My father rose with a stern expression. He was a tall, lanky man who usually had the demeanor of Mr. Rogers. It took a lot to piss him off.

"Sorry, Daddy." I took the seat between him and Conor.

"That's better. I don't know what's gotten into y'all, but it stops now. You hear me?"

Jake and I both nodded, but the heat between us continued to simmer.

"Now, *cher*, there's leftover lasagna in the fridge, if you still want dinner. Although, I was about to serve up the bread pudding and coffee," my dad said.

"Grandma Marie's recipe? With Southern Comfort sauce?"

"It is."

"I'll have some of that, please."

"Very well, then." He sauntered over to the stove and stirred a small saucepot.

The silence thrummed with tension. The antique clock on the wall ticked like a time bomb in an Alfred Hitchcock flick. Just when I felt as if I'd be the one to explode, my father walked in carrying plates of bread pudding on a tray.

"So, Jenna," my mother said softly between bites, "I understand the two of you are moving in together."

I gave Conor the evil eye and clenched my jaw. "We've discussed it. That's all."

"I think it's a grand idea," said my father. "'Bout time y'all got yourselves married."

I choked on a mouthful of bread pudding. "Married? Who said anything about getting married?"

Conor shifted in his seat. "Just speculating about the future, love. That's all."

"Would you wear a white or off-white Kevlar dress?" asked my brother, a snide smile creeping onto his face. "And will you exchange rings or handcuffs?"

"Bite me, asshole," I whispered.

"Language!" my mother scolded.

My father put a hand on my shoulder. "I think you'll be a lovely bride no matter what you wear."

I tossed down my fork, my appetite gone. "We're not getting married, okay? I'm not even sure I want to move in together." I gave Conor a look that said, *See what you started?* "What's next? You going to ask me when we're gonna adopt kids?"

"Oh, punkin." My mother cupped my chin, making me feel like a five-year-old. "No one's saying you have to do anything right away."

I bore holes into the table as I tried to keep my shit together. My head and leg throbbed. I needed to get out of there before I said something I regretted.

"Happy birthday, Mom. But I need to head home."

"But you just got here."

"I'm sorry. It's just my eye hurts, and I'm not very good company right now."

She put her hand on mine. It was warm and brought back a lot of happy feelings from my childhood. "Maybe you should take some time off, punkin. You and Conor could take a trip to San Diego or down to Rocky Point. Spend some time together."

"I'll think about it." I kissed her cheek.

My father stood when I did. "Be careful out there, *cher*." He kissed the top of my head.

"I will."

"Walk ya out, love?" Conor asked.

I stiffened. "Yeah, I guess."

I followed him out to the street. Even with the jacket, I was shivering. The air was damp and misty, creating halos around the streetlights.

"Come home with me, love. I'll put something on that shiner of yours to bring down the swelling. Take your mind off your troubles."

"Conor, you told them we were moving in together and that we were thinking about getting married."

"I just figured with your mum being Catholic and all, she wouldn't want her little girl living in sin."

"My point is I don't need you airing our dirty laundry with my folks and using them to pressure me. I'm a grown woman. I get to decide who I live with. And when, and *if*, I ever get married. You going behind my back pisses me the hell off."

"Aw, love, I'm not trying to go behind your back. It just slipped out."

"I...I just need some space. Things are crazy now."

"You said ya'd tell me what happened to your face."

I took a deep breath. "Remember me telling you what happened the night of my high school graduation?"

"Aye, your boyfriend's da battered ya near to death."

"Barclay Dietz. Well, he's back in town."

"Jesus fuckin' Christ! He did this to ya? Tell me where he is, and I'll put an end to him straightaway."

"Not that simple. He's mixed up with White Nation." I filled him in on the day's events.

"The bloody cops charged ya with manslaughter? Are ya fuckin' kidding me? This is madness. Can't have ya going to prison for defending yourself against a bunch of racist mother-fuckers. How long have ya known this bastard was in town?"

"A couple days."

"A couple days? And you're just telling me now?"

"It's my problem to deal with. Not yours."

"He's a fucking monster. And his mates are right-wing militants. Ya can't go after them alone."

"I had Caden and Rodeo with me."

"You need someone with more experience, love. Someone like me."

"See? And this is why I didn't tell you. I knew you'd want to take charge. I've been a bounty hunter for nearly ten years, most of it working with you. I've learned a thing or two in that time. I can handle myself."

"And yet here ya are with a battered face, a hole in your leg, and charged with murder."

"Manslaughter. But I'll deal with it. Kirsten's good. She'll get the case dismissed." I hoped.

After an awkward moment, Conor took my hand and met my eyes. "Fine. You're a big girl who can handle herself. I won't try to butt in. Just know that I'm here for ya, love."

"I know. That means a lot. It really does."

"Then just for tonight, give yourself a break and let me take care of ya at my place."

It was tempting. "I don't feel like being around anyone right now. Nothing against you, but I need time to process all the shit going round in my head."

He looked like a wounded puppy I'd just kicked. "Are we breakin' up? Is that what this is?"

"What? No. I still love you, you big lunk." I kissed him. "I'll see you tomorrow, okay?"

"All right. Get outta here, ya crazy lass. Before I throw ya over my shoulder and drag ya back to my man cave."

I pulled away from him. I felt torn, longing for his embrace and feeling smothered by it at the same time. I climbed into the Gray Ghost and gave him a finger wave as I drove off.

27

I drove past multicolored constellations of Christmas lights and turned on the radio only to be assaulted by cheesy Christmas songs. I switched the stereo to a playlist I'd created called Bad Girls. Meredith Brooks's song "Bitch" came on —an oldie but a goodie. I cranked it up and scream-sang the lyrics.

Where the fuck does Conor get off telling my family that we're moving in together, much less getting married? As if! Not that I have anything against marriage, but I am so not ready, even though I'm now thirty. Why can't things just stay the way they are?

Gin Wigmore's "Devil in Me" came on as I turned onto my street. But I didn't pull into my driveway. I didn't even stop in front of my house.

Instead, I cruised on past, turned north onto Central, then east on Camelback until I found myself in the parking lot for L Street, a women's bar run by my friends Chelsea and Izzie Quiñones.

If I'd been smart, I would've called a friend, met them for dinner somewhere, talked out the shit in my head, and gone home. But I wasn't always that smart. Besides, Becca was dealing with her chronic fatigue. And most of the other people in my life were men. Except for Chelsea and Izzie. So what better place to be but at their bar, right? Drinking on a mostly empty stomach. What could go wrong?

There was only one couple sitting at a table when I walked in. Not surprising, considering it was eight o'clock on a Tuesday. Most of the regulars were probably out Christmas shopping.

Chelsea sat on a stool behind the bar watching a football game. Prominent brow, broad shoulders, and a baritone voice made it hard for her to hide the fact that she was trans. But rather than complain, she just did her own thing. Purple and blue hair, gothy makeup, multiple facial piercings, and a corset wrapped around a billowy, burgundy split-sleeve dress made her a sight to behold. "I don't do subtle," she had told me on more than one occasion.

Behind her, a printed sign mounted on the wall read, "All women are welcome here, regardless of orientation or assigned sex at birth." Someone had written "and nonbinary people" in permanent marker above the word "women."

Chelsea's face lit up when she saw me. "Hey, girl. Didn't expect to see you this evening. How's it going?"

"Don't ask. Gimme a margarita."

She mixed up the drink with the efficiency of an expert bartender. The tequila wasn't top shelf, but I didn't care. "Where'd you get that shiner?"

"Long story."

"Wasn't Conor, was it?"

"No."

She placed the drink on the bar. "What brings you out to L Street tonight?"

"Does a girl need a reason to drink?" I downed the drink in a few quick swallows. It burned, and I liked it.

"You and Conor have a fight?"

"Nope." I pushed the glass toward her. "Hit me again."

"What's wrong, Jinxie? You seem wound up."

"Oh, for the love of fuck, why's everyone wanna play armchair psychologist? I just wanna throw back a few without being interrogated. All right?"

She filled my glass without another word and returned to the game. Deep down, a part of me felt terrible for being rude to her. But I was in a pissy mood, and I was fucking going to let myself be pissy.

I had her refill the glass a few more times. On the fourth request, she said, "Slow down there, sweets. How about some soda or coffee?"

"Fuck that shit. Just gimme another goddamned margarita." The world was starting to feel a little wobbly, but I didn't care.

"I'll give you another, but you'll have to give me your keys. I'm not letting you drive home shit-faced."

"I am not shit-faced. I am comforbly...comfortububbuly...I'm fine, okay. Fine."

Our gazes met. She had gorgeous eyes. Soulful eyes. No wonder her wife, Izzie, was into her. Not that I was attracted to women. But she was adorable. Her lips looked so kissable with the sapphire-blue lipstick. Maybe I was bisexual or pan or whatever. *You never know until you try, right?*

"I'm sorry for being such a bee-atch, Chels! I've had a really, really, *really* shitty day. You forgive me?"

"I forgive you, sweets. Which is why I can't have you driving home in your condition. So fork over them keys." She held out her hand expectantly.

I fished the keys out of my pocket and dangled them next to my face, then beckoned her with a finger. "C'mere. I wanna tell you a little, itty bitty, little shecret...um, I mean, a secret."

She smirked and raised an eyebrow. "What?"

"You gotta come close. I'll whisper it to you."

She bent down. I leaned forward, my lips extended. Her lips were a lot firmer than I thought they'd be and smelled of furniture polish. As she pulled the set of keys out of my hand, I realized she'd backed away. I'd kissed the bar instead.

"Look, Jinxie. I think you're a beautiful woman. And while Izzie and me are poly, I know you and Conor are exclusive. Not gonna let you mess that up over a few drinks. Besides, I've been tending bar far too long to fall for the old 'tell you a secret' trick." Her voice sounded distorted, as if someone had cranked up the reverb or something.

"What? I didn't try to kish you." I kept my hands firmly on the bar as the room gently swayed. "I was just playing around. Gah! You know, that must hurt."

"What must hurt?"

"Having that pool cue stuck up your ass. Seriously, loooshen up."

The jukebox started playing some tired old angsty Melissa Etheridge song. Fuck that shit. "Fuck that shit!" I repeated in my outside voice. "Sappy, pathetic leshbian...shit. That...that's what that shit ish. Where's my drink?"

"Jinx, you've already had six. You don't need any more."

"Shix? Don't you think how shtupid you think I am? I think. I can count, you know. I only had floor of them. Four. Four of them."

"Hello, love." Conor magically appeared in front of me. *How's he do that? Must be some kind of Irish faerie leprechaun magic shit.*

"Heeeeyyy, babeee... What're you doing here? Don't you know boys aren't allowed in here?" I reached out to him and felt myself topple into his arms. His powerful arms. Goddamn, I loved that man. Fuck women, I got me a real man's man.

"Come on, love. Let's get ya home. I'll even hold your hair when ya hurl."

"No, no, no, no. I doan wanna go home. It's haunted."

"Thanks." Conor winked at me. No, not at me. He winked at Chelsea.

"Doan you go winking at her, Mr. Man! She's a married woman." My body was moving, but the room felt as if gravity kept pulling at odd angles. "Ugh, she gave me some bad liquor, I think. Fucking cheap tequila. Tastes like horsh pisses and fire. Maybe she gave me a roofie. Trying to get me in bed with her. Oh, fuck, I think I'm gonna be sick."

No sooner did the icy December night air hit my face than I was puking my guts up outside the front door. My throat closed up, and I struggled to get air. *Oh fucking shit. I can't breathe. Oh shit. I'm gonna die.*

"Just relax, love. You're hyperventilating." His hand on my back felt good. I pushed against the panic. Air seeped into my burning lungs.

"Breathe, Jinxie. Breathe."

I breathed and stood up. I wobbled only a little bit with Conor holding me up. Damn, he smelled so good. I wanted to feel his warm body against mine.

Puke was splattered all over the rainbow welcome mat by the bar's front door. Served them right for selling such shitty booze. Mexicans didn't know shit about liquor. But the Irish, though, they knew whiskey. Irish. Like my Irish honey.

"Ya gonna be okay, love?"

"Yeah, I think so." My stomach felt better. But the taste of bile remained burning in my mouth.

"Let's get ya home." He opened a car door and was manhandling me into the front seat.

"Keep your man hands off of me, mister. I'm not a child, you know." I bumped my head and tumbled into the bucket seat.

"You're bloody acting like a toddler. Now put on your seat belt, or do ya need help with that too?" He was sitting in the driver's seat already. *Holy shit, how'd he fucking do that?*

"I can do it." I yanked on the seat belt, and it jammed. I yanked it again, but it wouldn't pull. "If it wasn't fucking stuck."

Conor sighed. "Ya got to be gentle with it." He took the buckle from my hand and pulled it out and clicked it shut.

"Yeah, works for you." I folded my arms and stared out at the cars driving past on Camelback Road. In the distance, a siren wailed. Red and blue flashing lights blew past. "Uh-oh."

"What's wrong?" asked Conor, pulling onto the street in the

same direction the police cruiser went. "You're not gonna be sick again, are ya?"

"No! Gah!" I sneered at him and pointed at the disappearing lights of the ambulance. "Someone's having a bad night." It was something my father always said any time he heard sirens or saw flashing lights.

"Yeah," said Conor. "That someone is me."

28

"**W**ake up, sleepyhead! Time to catch bad guys."

I opened my eyes to a Conor-shaped silhouette in front of a window. His eyes burned like lasers into my skull. Or maybe that was just the sunlight coming through. My mouth tasted of cotton flavored with tequila and cat shit. My body felt as if I'd somersaulted off the top of the Papago Buttes. My hair smelled like puke.

"I...whuh?" My mouth didn't seem to want to kick into gear.

Conor stepped away from the window, pulling a shirt over his ripped body. "Come on, love. We both got people to track down."

I pulled myself into a seated position on the bed and stared at the floor until the room quit spinning. I could tell from the tile we were at Conor's bunker. "What the hell happened last night?"

"I picked ya up at L Street after Chelsea called me."

"Why would Chelsea call you?"

"Prolly 'cause ya were shite-faced, and she didn't want to deal with your drunken nonsense any longer."

I sneered at him. "Rude."

"Aye. That you were." He wasn't smiling much. So not like him.

"Well, thanks for that, I guess."

"Come on. We gotta go."

"Just go on. I've got a key. I'll head out when I'm feeling a little more human."

"Yer lorry's still at the bar."

Vague memories of being at the bar flitted in and out of reach. A deep desire to kiss Chelsea's pillowy blue lips bubbled up, as well. "Oh yeah. Damn, I hope I didn't do anything stupid."

"Aside from dancing naked on the bar while cry-singing 'Total Eclipse of the Heart'—"

"What?" My jaw hit the floor.

"Just funnin' with ya. Ya weren't naked. At least not in the video posted on L Street's Facebook page."

"Fuck." I pulled on my clothes and shoes. My phone showed that Sadie had texted me, asking if I'd caught Pratt yet. *Shit.*

"Let's pick up the Gray Ghost before some wanker takes it for a joyride or uses it as a canvas for a spray-painted public art project." Conor tossed me my keys. "Then ya can go home and make yerself presentable."

"I'm presentable," I protested, trying to finger comb the knots out of my hair.

"Aye! I forgot 'homeless hipster' is the popular new look these days. That shiner ya got makes quite the fashion statement. Purple's a good color on ya."

I flipped him off and followed him out to his Dodge Charger. *Men and their muscle cars.*

A while later, we pulled into the L Street parking lot. Thankfully, the Gray Ghost was still there with all four tires and no custom paint jobs. A piece of paper under the windshield wipers warned me of hellfire and damnation unless I repented of my perverted lifestyle and surrendered to white Jesus. I crumpled it and tossed it into a dumpster.

Conor walked with me to the door of my SUV. "I'm sorry I've been so pushy about moving in together. I know you're working through a lot, especially with that gobshite of a boxer being back in town. But I want ya to know I'm here for ya. I love ya." His voice grew hoarse with emotion. "I don't want anything to happen to ya. So watch your arse."

"I know. I love you too. Once I bring Barclay Dietz to justice, I'll be in a better headspace to figure out this moving-in-together business."

"I'm happy to help ya out with Dietz. Caden and Rodeo only have a couple years of experience between them. You're going to need more than that to handle this bloke."

"I'll take it under advisement. By the way, Juanita's having her Barbra Streisand fundraiser tonight at eight. Will you come with me?"

"If you want me there, I'm there, love. Want me to pick you up? Or will that also be cramping your style?"

I wasn't sure if he was joking or serious. I wasn't sure of much of anything anymore. "Pick me up around seven fifteen."

We kissed, lightly at first and then more intensely.

"Thanks," I said as I pulled away, more than a little breathless. "For picking me up last night. And for being patient with me."

"You're most welcome, love."

I climbed into the Gray Ghost and dove into the morning rush hour traffic clogging Camelback Road. It took me nearly thirty minutes to go four miles. By the time I pulled into my driveway, I was so frustrated with slow, inattentive drivers that I was ready to strangle a small child.

I started the coffeepot, choked down two ibuprofen, and hopped in the shower to wash off a night of shame.

When I reemerged smelling less like a sewer than I did when I went in, I poured a cup of hot bitterness into my favorite Bitch with a Big Ass Gun mug. I opened my laptop at the kitchen table and studied the files Becca had sent me on Pratt's credit card statements, phone logs, and social media activity. There was nothing since he jumped bail, but maybe there was something from the past few months that would point to his current whereabouts.

As my eyes began to cross, I turned to his past emails. Plenty of forwarded cartoons and jokes rife with racist and homophobic stereotypes. No shortage of newsletters from extremist right-wing organizations.

Becca had also uncovered a subreddit titled Pure Gardening where Pratt posted under the handle Crizaba. The posts seemed to have an aggressive, almost militaristic tone, especially toward weeds and invasive plant species. I guessed some people got rather passionate about their hobbies.

None of the documentation gave me a clue where Pratt might be hiding out.

I was about to pour another cup of coffee when the roof creaked. I nearly jumped out of my skin. Once again, I got a strong feeling I was being watched. Driven by a deep sense of paranoia and a need to figure out what the hell was going on, I scoured the kitchen, looking for hidden cameras or bugs. It wouldn't be the first time a violent criminal had tried to turn the tables on me.

But after two hours of disassembling toasters, light fixtures, and outlets, sifting through flour and sugar canisters, and checking behind the refrigerator and dishwasher, I turned up exactly squat. Clearly, my instincts had gone haywire, probably induced by a combination of past traumas, legal troubles, and a lack of sleep.

If my dad had been there, he'd have told me to spend the day resting. But I couldn't. Not while Pratt and Dietz were walking the streets free as a bird. And not while my own freedom was in jeopardy thanks to the White Nation pricks.

So instead of a nap, I grabbed my gear and did what bounty hunters do. I drove by Pratt's house. When there was still no sign of life in the house, I recanvassed his neighbors, then spoke with Pratt's former coworkers. I called the contacts on his bail application, trying every trick in the book. The contest winner scheme. The lost wallet scheme. Even a promise that an organ donor had been found for his daughter. Not a goddamn thing worked.

Around one o'clock, I stopped by Peyton's apartment. His roomie, Hughie, was unexpectedly coherent but hadn't seen Peyton for the past day or so. The manager at San Tan Liquors said the same thing and was pissed off that Peyton had missed a shift without calling in. Had Barclay reached out to his son? Or had something happened to him?

A call to Becca yielded nothing new on either Pratt or the Dietzes. I reconnected with the nurse at Camelback Children's Hospital, where his daughter was being treated. She told me Pratt was now banned from the hospital. If he showed up, they had instructions to call me, then the police.

By four o'clock, I decided I'd struck out for the day. Such is the life of a bounty hunter. Just as fishing isn't necessarily catching, searching isn't always finding. Some days were spent going through the motions, shaking the trees, hoping something would eventually shake loose.

29

───────

I got home and took a shower, spending way too long trying to style my hair. It refused to hold a curl or do anything but hang stick straight. As a last resort, I put it up into a French braid.

The swelling in my face had gone down a bit, but no amount of makeup would hide the black eye. Instead, I went heavy on the eyeliner and some dark-purple eye shadow to even things out.

With that done, I stared blankly at my closet. I couldn't remember the last time I'd worn anything even close to formal. I don't usually hang with the evening gown crowd. Galas, fundraisers, and holiday soirees aren't my scene. I prefer to be low-maintenance and casual, for which Juanita gives me no end of grief.

After twenty minutes, I settled on an indigo dress that hadn't seen the light of day for years. I used a lint brush to remove the layer of dust on the shoulders. The collar was cut low and fringed with lace. The bodice was shaped to give the illusion that I had hips. The hem came to midcalf with a slit up one side. I paired it with a cute pair of filigree tights to hide the large bandage on my calf.

I accessorized with midnight-blue three-inch heels, a pair of diamond stud earrings my mother had given me, and a small skull cameo pendant on a white gold choker.

I studied my reflection in the full-length mirror. I was a dimestore diva at best. Oh well. If Conor or Juanita didn't like it, tough. I was there to enjoy myself and to donate two hundred bucks for a rubber chicken dinner and a campy performance of Barbra Streisand numbers by a foursome in drag.

"Don't *you* look deadly," said a deep voice behind me.

I whirled around, grabbed a plaster statue of Wonder Woman from my dresser, and prepared to throw it at my intruder.

Conor stood in my bedroom doorway looking like James Bond in a tailored tuxedo. That is, if James Bond had red curls and freckles. Suddenly I felt very underdressed.

"You think so?" I gave him an insecure smile.

"Absolutely smashing, love." He kissed me. "Ya gonna bludgeon me with that Wonder Woman doll?"

"What?" I looked at the statue in my hand and set it down. "Sorry, I've been a bit jumpy today."

"Didn't get much rest after I left, eh?"

"You look great." I gave him a hug. "Smell great too. I have half a mind to throw you down on my bed and have my way with you."

"Not that I would object, love, but I think we best get going or we're gonna be late."

I was tempted to say screw the event, but I was already going to be in hot water when Juanita learned the wig she'd loaned me was now in Phoenix PD's property room. I grabbed my clutch purse and followed Conor to his car.

When we arrived at the club, a large sign at the entrance of the parking lot read "Lot Full."

"Damn, I had no idea this was going to be so popular," I said.

Conor pulled into the small shopping center on the other side of the club and found a spot. I stepped out and felt exposed and vulnerable, in part because of the dress and heels but mostly because I was unarmed. I'd considered stashing a subcompact semiauto in my clutch, but it would have been too heavy and just felt wrong. I wasn't on the job, hunting some scumbag bail jumper. I was here to celebrate queer culture and raise money for the youth community center.

The speakers outside the club were playing high-energy, EDM versions of Barbra Streisand's more upbeat songs like "The Main Event" and "No More Tears." At the door, a familiar burly man in a white tux and glittery eye shadow stood collecting tickets. His face lit up when he spotted me.

"Oh my Gloria Estefan! Could it be? The one and only Jinx Ballou? How the hell are you?" He hugged me so hard I swore I felt ribs cracking.

"Good to see you too, Mace." I gasped as he released me.

"And in a dress? I never thought I'd see the day."

"Yeah, well, it's kinda hard to chase down fugitives in a ball gown and heels." I gave his bushy beard a playful tug. "Nice man-moss, by the way."

"You like it? My boyfriend says I look like a hipster wannabe. Though he doesn't complain when I go down on him. He likes the way it tickles his jubblies."

"Ew, TMI!" I said with a smirk.

Conor cleared his throat and gave me the side-eye. "Sorry! Mace, this is my boyfriend, Conor. Babe, Mace here is one of the Main Drag's top performers."

"My, my, my!" crooned Mace, sidling up next to Conor, who blushed bright red. "You are one fine hunk of man meat."

I put up a hand between them. "Hands off, bitch," I teased. "He's mine, and he's straight."

"Ha! That's what they all say."

"Pleasure to meet ya, Mace." Conor offered his hand to shake.

Mace took it and kissed Conor's knuckles. "Oh my, what an accent. I'm verklempt. Is it hot out here or is it you?"

"Yo, Mace!" called someone behind me. "You taking tickets or staging your own sex show? We're freezing our nuts off out here."

"Shut it, bitch!" Mace replied while taking our tickets.

"These young queens are so rude. Y'all have a good time at the show. And thank you for supporting the Phoenix Queer Youth Center."

"Thanks, sweetie."

Conor's face was still glowing red as we walked into the nightclub. "Well, he...or she was interesting."

"Yeah, he can be a bit of a cliché, but he's a sweetheart. He and his boyfriend, Chad, let me crash on their couch for a while after I caught Wilson fucking around on me."

We stepped through the lobby into the main hall. I'd been to the Main Drag dozens of times and almost didn't recognize the place. The mismatched garage sale tables were now draped in elegant white cloths and set with candles and holiday greenery. The scent of pine and pumpkin spice replaced the usual reek of cheap cologne and beer.

"Wow, you'd never know what a shit hole it usually looks like," I whispered to Conor, who chuckled in response. "And if you ever tell Juanita I said that, I will kill you in your sleep."

"Duly noted, love."

We threaded our way through the candlelit tables until we found Rodeo sitting with an Asian-American woman I didn't recognize. He wore a lavender tux with a matching cummerbund and a white ruffled shirt. Her dress glittered as if woven of diamonds.

"Mind if we join you?" I asked.

"Not at all. Guys, this is Nicole." Rodeo gestured toward us as we sat. "Jinx and Conor are fellow bounty hunters."

I was surprised to see Rodeo with a date so soon after dumping my brother. Of course, considering what an asshole my brother had been lately, it'd serve him right to see Rodeo hook up with someone else so fast.

"Pleasure to meet you." Nicole's eyes sparkled in the flickering candlelight.

"Likewise," I replied.

Caden and Kirsten walked up holding drinks. Caden's face

brightened when he caught my eye. "Look who I found by the bar."

"Hey, I'm an attorney. Where else would I be?" Kirsten snorted at her own joke. She and Caden took the two remaining chairs at the table. "Seriously, though, since getting surgery a few years ago, I've drifted away from the queer community. Figured it was time I show up and give something back."

Nicole started to say something, but half the lights overhead blinked off. "Ladies, gentlemen, and the rest of us," came Mace's voice over the sound system, "please take your seats. Tonight's entertainment is about to begin."

A moment later, the remaining lights went out, replaced by a spotlight blazing on the center of the stage. The crowd hushed in a rustle of people finding their seats. The clack of high heels echoed in the large room, and Juanita stepped into the light in full Tía Juana regalia. "Hello, bitches!"

"Hello, bitch!" the drag bar's well-trained regulars replied in unison.

"Damn straight!" Juanita strutted across the stage. "For those who don't already know me, my name's Tía Juana, and I will be your Monster of Ceremonies."

"You better work, bitch!" yelled someone from the audience.

Without missing a beat, she snapped her fingers and said with a wry grin, "I always work, motherfucker!"

The crowd roared with laughter.

"However, this is a special occasion. Tonight we are here to help fund the rebuilding of the Phoenix Queer Youth Center that was damaged in a recent fire. And I want to thank each and every one of you bitches for your generous support."

The crowd erupted again in applause so thunderous I feared the roof would collapse.

"So without any further ado, I want to introduce four fabulous ladies who have taken the musical stylings of Saint Barbra of Streisand to a place no one ever dared. And Goddess willing, no one will again. I give you, the Barbra Shop Quartet."

The spotlight vanished. The opening notes from *Yentl*'s "Papa, Can You Hear Me?" began amid a final surge of cheers. When the spotlight returned, a façade of a barbershop had been lowered to stage. Four of the campiest Barbra ever impersonators appeared in skimpy barbershop quartet costumes.

As bizarre as it was to hear Streisand tunes performed in four-part harmonies, I had to admit the performers were remarkably talented. I found myself entranced in this mishmash of genres. Songs from my childhood were transformed into something oddly mesmerizing.

Just as the quartet finished singing "Somewhere" from *West Side Story*, a man shouted, "Fucking fairies!"

I turned to see three dark figures standing in the aisle fifteen feet away. The place erupted in automatic gunfire.

30

The four drag queens fell, their bodies ripped apart in sprays of blood and gore. Audience members screamed and ran in all directions.

I dropped to the floor, peering above the table toward the thunder of the automatic weapons. I counted muzzle flashes from three automatic weapons held by the strangers in the aisle. I reached for my sidearm only to find the fabric of my dress and nothing more. *Shit!*

I slipped off my heels and gripped one of them like a weapon. Whoever these fuckers were, I wasn't going to let them hurt my friends without a fight.

Keeping low, I hustled between the tables and toward the gunmen. Conor and Rodeo appeared next to me amid the strobe light of muzzle flashes.

I paused a few feet from the shooters. When the rifle of the gunman nearest me ran empty, I pounced before he could reload. I drove the three-inch heel into the back of the attacker's head. When he stumbled, I reached for his rifle and blistered my left hand on the barrel.

The gunman struggled to his feet. I adjusted my grip and

drove the butt of the rifle into his head and torso repeatedly, driven by pent-up rage.

Overhead lights blazed on, blinding me for an instant. I squinted, adjusting to the glare.

A hand clasped my shoulder. "Jinxie, ya can stop now. It's over."

Instinctively, I whipped around and nearly took off Conor's head before I recognized him.

"Shit." I lowered the AR-15 in my hand.

Conor was holding the Walther PPX he usually carried on one of the other gunmen, who lay cuffed facedown on the floor. Like the other two gunmen, he was dressed all in black with a balaclava over his face. When Conor unmasked him, I recognized him as Quinton, one of the guys from Dixie's.

I turned back to the gunman I'd disarmed. I pulled the balaclava from his head and felt my gorge rise. His face had been reduced to a pulpy mess.

Spent bullet casings, empty magazines, and two other AR-15s littered the floor. As my ears recovered from the deafening roar of the gunfire, I noticed the dozens of people crying and screaming in agony. The air was sharp with the taste of spent gunpowder and spilled blood.

"Are ya hit, love?" Conor stepped in front of me, inspecting me for wounds.

My legs and dress were splattered with blood. Angry blisters bulged on my palm from grabbing the hot rifle barrel, but that was the worst of it. "No, no, I don't think so. You okay?"

"Nary a scratch."

"What happened to the third shooter?"

He grimaced. "Bloody wanker got away."

"Jinx." A strained voice caught my attention.

Rodeo lay on the floor, his face twisted in pain. A woman in an emerald gown knelt over him, using his cummerbund as a makeshift compress on his shoulder. His once bone-white shirt was now a study in scarlet.

I crouched down next to them. "Shit! How bad is it?"

"This?" He scrunched his face, trying to smile. "Just a skeeter bite. Had hickeys worse than this."

"Liar," said the woman treating him. "Looks like he took a small-caliber round to the shoulder. Doesn't appear to have hit a major artery. But the slug's still in there."

"You a doc?" I asked, hoping.

"Trauma nurse. Maricopa Medical. Treated more than my fair share of GSWs."

"What happened?" I asked Rodeo.

"One of the shooters dropped his AR-15. Jammed or something. I thought I had him, but he pulled out a pistol. Shot someone on stage and then nailed me."

"Well, sounds like you're in good hands, Rodeo. I'm going to check on the other wounded."

"Find Nicole," he grunted. "My aunt'll kill me if something happened to her."

"Your aunt?"

"She's my cousin. Came out last summer." He took a deep breath, obviously trying to control the pain. "Begged me to come to this shindig."

"I'll keep an eye out for her."

I took a deep breath myself and tried to clear my head from the jumble of sharp emotions. I surveyed the chaotic scene around me. Numerous tables and chairs lay on their sides. A nearby tablecloth had caught fire from a capsized candle.

Broken bodies lay scattered across the room like carcasses in an unruly slaughterhouse. Survivors struggled to save the injured, while others trembled under the imagined safety of their tables and chairs. Across the aisle, Mace sobbed and pleaded on the phone with a 911 operator.

I turned toward the carnage onstage. Caden was kneeling over someone. I pushed people out of my way and vaulted onto the stage to where Juanita lay on the floor near the other drag queens. Caden's hand pressed against her blood-smeared forehead. My knees buckled, and I knelt on the other side of her.

"Juanita! Shit! What happened?"

"They...they shot her," he said in a choking voice. "They fucking shot her."

Panic threatened to undo me. I channeled the rush of adrenaline to keep my anguish in check and focus on the situation. "Is there an exit wound?"

Caden shook his head. "Don't think so."

"Keep the pressure on," I told Caden. "Don't let her bleed out."

I turned to the other drag queens. Three of the Barbras were dead from multiple gunshots that left baseball-sized exit wounds. High-velocity rounds tended to have that effect.

A nearby whimpering caught my attention. Behind the barbershop façade, I found the fourth Barbra—a short African-American drag queen named Blake Washington—in a fetal position, clutching his wig, mascara streaming down his gore-splattered face.

"Blake, are you hit?" I knelt and put a hand on his trembling arm. There was blood on his bare shoulders and his dress, but no visible wounds.

"Why?" he squeaked in a trembling tenor voice. "Why'd they do this?"

"Blake, look at me. Are you hurt anywhere?"

His face was that of a terrified child. His pupils were as wide as saucers. He was in shock. I examined him as best I could. No physical wounds that I could find. Just emotional trauma. I sat next to him and held him close. "Hang in there, Blake. We're going to get through this."

31

By the time the police secured the area and medical personnel arrived, I had counted at least fifteen people dead. Dozens of others were severely wounded and traumatized. Rodeo had been transported to the hospital, with his cousin Nicole trailing after the ambulance. Those of us with noncritical injuries were herded into the club's lobby to await questioning.

Conor, Caden, Kirsten, and I huddled together in a far corner. An EMT had treated my burned hand and loosely wrapped it in gauze. Despite Conor's jacket draped over my shoulders, I shivered from adrenaline withdrawal and the chill of the December night air blowing through the lobby's open doors.

As we waited, I consulted privately with Kirsten, giving her my account of events. She made some suggestions on wording and on specific questions she didn't want me to answer.

When my father called, having seen the reports on the ten o'clock news, I assured him I was okay and would talk to him in the morning.

Around midnight, a familiar figure stepped through the front doors, carrying a case file. Detective Hardin looked grim and exhausted. "Ballou." He beckoned me with a finger.

"Detective." I pushed myself to my feet. My legs felt unsteady, my mind a scorched wasteland of exhaustion, sorrow, and anger.

Kirsten stood. "I'll join you two, if you don't mind. I'm her attorney."

"I know who you are, Ms. Pasternak. You're also a witness."

"While I was in the audience when the events transpired, I'm afraid I wasn't close enough to see the assailants. When the shooting began, I helped people nearby take shelter behind one of the tables. That is the entirety of my statement."

Hardin regarded her for a second. "Very well." He led us out the front door and into a small room in a Tactical Command Center van parked on the street.

"Can I get either of you anything? Coffee? A snack?" Hardin asked as if we'd just dropped in for a casual chat.

I shook my head as we sat. "No, thanks."

Hardin set down the case file and opened a notebook, with pen at the ready. "What can you tell me about this evening's events?"

Kirsten nodded before I spoke. "During the performance, three men entered the club dressed in all-black and wearing balaclavas. Each carried an assault rifle full-auto. At least two were white, average height and weight. I didn't get a good look at the third. He escaped before the lights went up."

"And what happened?"

"One shouted the words 'Fucking fairies' right before they opened fire. First at the performers on stage, then spraying the audience."

"What did you do when the shooting started?"

"My crew and I disarmed two of them. One got away."

"Your bounty hunter crew?"

"Yes."

"Were any of you armed?"

"I was not armed, no."

"How about your crew?"

"You would have to ask them."

"What happened to your hand?"

"Burned it on the barrel of one of the attackers' rifles when I attempted to disarm him."

"Did you recognize these men?"

"The two we captured are members of White Nation. I recognized them when I crashed one of their meetings looking for two fugitives."

"That when you shot the guy at Dixie's?"

"In self-defense."

"Is that why they attacked the club? Retribution?"

Pangs of guilt constricted my chest as I thought about the shootout at Dixie's. *Was this retaliation?* "Have to ask them."

"One of the suspected shooters suffered a massive head wound." Hardin held out his phone with a photo of my guy's bashed-in head. "What can you tell me about this?"

I resisted the urge to glance at Kirsten. We'd discussed this. "All I know is that my crew and I acted to disarm the assailants in an attempt to save lives. It was dark, and everything happened fast. I don't recall a lot of details."

Hardin eyed me warily. If he persisted in this line of questioning, Kirsten would step in.

"After the suspects were, uh, disarmed, what did you do?"

"I assisted in helping the injured and the traumatized."

Officer Evans popped his head in the room, gave me a quick look, and whispered something to Hardin while handing him a piece of paper.

Hardin thanked him, and Evans stepped out again with a sneer. *What the fuck was that about?* I wondered.

"Ballou, do we have some sort of gang war going on?"

"Detective, my client is not a member of any gang," said Kirsten. "Her actions at Dixie's Bar were well within her lawful duties as a licensed bail enforcement agent. The fact that your department is charging her with manslaughter for defending herself from a room of armed racist militants is a travesty of justice."

"Counselor, your client—"

"I'm not finished, Detective. If the violent nationalists of White Nation are seeking payback for my client's attempt to return to custody a fugitive whom they are illegally harboring, then that is on them."

Go, Kirsten! I was so wiped out emotionally and physically, I almost stood up and gave her a woop-woop!

Hardin flipped a page in his notebook. "Anything else you can tell me about this evening's events?"

"No."

Hardin reviewed his notes and scribbled a few more as if we weren't there. If he was hoping to get me talking to fill the silence, it wasn't working.

"Detective Hardin," said Kirsten. "Unless you have further questions for either myself or my client, we will be going."

Hardin leaned back and crossed his arms. "Whatever's going on between your *crew* and White Nation, it stops now. You got me, Ballou?"

"I'm merely tracking down fugitives and returning them to custody. I got no interest in anything else White Nation or anyone else has going on."

"I don't want any more bodies dropping on my streets because of this." Hardin closed his case folder. "Call me if either of you remembers anything else to assist us in our investigation."

"Yeah," I said. "I'll do that."

After thanking Kirsten for her help, I found Conor standing alone inside the lobby. He looked like I felt. His eyes held the haunted look of past traumas. "How ya holding up, love?"

I hugged him. "I've had better days."

"Aye. It's a bloody pisser. At least we stopped the bastards when we did."

"I want to go to the hospital," I said. "Need to check on Juanita and Rodeo."

"Jinx..." Conor's face darkened. "I...I can't."

"Dude, seriously, it's been, what, twenty years? You need to get over your phobia of hospitals."

"It's not that simple. Bernie...she was my fucking sister."

"Yes, and Juanita is my family. So's Rodeo." My voice choked with emotion. I couldn't get the image of Juanita's bloody face out of my mind. "I know you were traumatized by your sister's death. And I know you blame yourself. But that was a lifetime ago."

"It's gonna be a madhouse, love. We'd just be in the way."

"Being there for family isn't being in the way. But if you're too chickenshit to help me..." I pulled off his jacket and threw it at him.

"Jinx!"

"Go home, Conor." I slipped off my heels and started fast-walking barefoot down the ice-cold sidewalk in the direction of the hospital.

"Jinxie, stop!" He grabbed my arm and wheeled me around.

"What?" My eyes burned into him. My head felt as if it would explode.

"I can..."

"You can what?"

He took a deep breath and released it. "I can at least give you a ride."

"Oh gee, thanks! Don't do me any favors!" I pulled away, but he held on.

"Don't be daft. Ya can't walk all the way to hospital in your bare feet. Look, I..." His eyes closed and jaw tensed. "I will come in with you. And when it gets too much, I'll...step outside for some air or something. Do you know where they took Juanita? All these casualties, they probably took people to several different hospitals."

"I got a text from Rodeo. He and Caden are at John C. Lincoln, where Juanita's in surgery."

In an awkward silence, we drove to the hospital in Conor's Charger and parked in the nearby garage. I led him through the glass doors of the ER. "Fuck me," I muttered under my breath.

32

───────

The waiting room was wall-to-wall people. Interspersed among the usual crowd of flu sufferers, home accident casualties, and car crash victims were the survivors from the Main Drag shooting in bloodstained formal wear.

People squeezed onto crowded waiting room benches and huddled together on the floor. The more severely injured lay on gurneys stacked two deep against the walls. Medical personnel hurried about, leaving shoe prints on the blood-speckled linoleum.

The sounds of sobbing melded with muffled voices from the televisions mounted on the wall. The tension and trauma was so palpable I could literally taste it—a metallic, bitter flavor that cut through me like a Japanese blade.

Conor stopped abruptly, as if his feet were cemented to the floor. He looked like a man walking to his execution. "I'm sorry, love. I...I thought I could stay here, but I can't." He backed away toward the door, and I followed.

"Why not? You did when I got hurt last year. And when Deez was shot the year before that."

"I know." He swallowed hard, his chest heaving. "But it wasn't like this. This...this is Omagh all over again. Bodies and blood everywhere."

I held his trembling, tear-strewn face in my hands. Instead of a badass bounty hunter, I saw a terrified boy, haunted by shame for a crime he could never make right. I wanted to sympathize, to tell him I understood. But I didn't. People I loved were here, clinging to life if they weren't already dead. I couldn't be there for them and play nursemaid to Conor as well.

"Look, I get this is hard for you. But our friends need us. And I need you. I can't do this alone."

"I'm sorry. I just can't." He started to pull away, and I grabbed his arm.

"Conor, stop! Yes, you can."

He shook his head like a dog shaking off water. "I can't. I just. Fucking. Can't! Every time I walk into a hospital, I keep seeing Bernie's blood-splattered face. Her broken body. And I know it's my fault. I never should have made that phone call. I never should have...I don't know."

I thought of Juanita, lying on the stage. Caden desperately pressing against the head wound. A flood of memories filled my mind. Juanita teaching me how to walk like a girl, how to do makeup, even all the times she teased and taunted me in her sassy, drag queen way. She was my fairy drag mother. Anger, sorrow, and abandonment wrapped together into a single, raw emotion, which I directed at Conor.

"Do whatever the hell you want." I stormed away and searched the waiting room for Caden and Rodeo.

I found them sitting on a bench underneath one of the televisions. Caden scooted over and let me squeeze in. Rodeo's arm was in a sling. A large bandage was wrapped around his shoulder and upper arm. His eyes were glassy, and he had a dopey grin on his face. Clearly not feeling any pain.

"Hey," I whispered. "How's the shoulder?"

"Fucking awesome," said Rodeo.

"Aside from the painkillers they gave you."

His smile cooled. "They say the bullet tore through my upper arm. Nicked the humerus, but no damage to the shoulder joint. They patched me up, told me to take it easy for the next six weeks, and wrote me a script for some good drugs."

"I'm surprised the hospital didn't admit you."

"Short on beds. I was noncritical."

"Where's your cousin? What's her name? Natalie?"

"Nicole. I gave her the keys to my Mazda and told her to go home. This shit messed her up bad."

I hugged him and turned to Caden. "Any word on Juanita?"

Caden's eyes bubbled with tears. He still had dried blood on his arm. "Still in surgery. It's not good, Jinx. Even if she lives, there's a good chance she could become a vegetable."

I didn't want to hear this. "Yeah, well, she's tougher than ten-year-old beef jerky. She'll pull through," I said as much to convince myself as anyone else.

"Where's Conor?" asked Rodeo.

"Doesn't matter."

Rodeo nodded. He'd worked with Conor enough to know about his deep-seated fear of hospitals. "This must've really freaked him out."

"We're all freaked. The important thing is you guys are here."

"Any IDs on the shooters?" asked Caden.

"I recognized two of them from Dixie's," I said.

"Shit," said Caden. "You think it was retaliation?"

I didn't want to admit it, but I feared it was. Guilt twisted my insides like a corkscrew.

I should have kept my cool and waited to grab Dietz when he wasn't surrounded by a room full of allies. I could have tailed him to wherever he was staying. But no, I had to act like an impulsive teenager. And now my lack of self-control had cost the lives of more than a dozen members of my own community.

I shook my head. "I don't know. White Nation's planning a rally on Saturday to protest the city removing the Confederate

Troops Memorial in Wesley Bolin Plaza. Got a feeling it's going to be bigger than the Charlottesville protest. And possibly deadlier."

"We gotta do something to teach them a lesson." Caden's voice crackled with anger.

I put a hand on his shoulder. "No. We do our job. When we get a lead on Pratt or Dietz, we go after them. But that's it. They already charged me with manslaughter. Don't need you two getting in trouble too."

The conversation dwindled. I tried to catch some z's while sitting on the bench, but after a couple of hours, my butt ached. I wandered outside for some fresh air and called Conor. I was pissed at him for leaving, and at the same time, I still needed him.

"How is everyone?" he asked.

I wanted to get snarky with him, but I held my tongue. "Rodeo'll survive, but he's out of commission for a month or so."

"And Juanita?"

"Still in surgery last I heard."

"Tell everyone I'm pulling for her."

"Yeah, yeah, thoughts and prayers and all that shit."

"Even if I was there, there's not shite I could do for her, love."

"No, but you could be here for me."

"I wish I could, love. I thought I'd have a heart attack in that waiting room. Bodies lining the wall. Blood on the floor. Smelling like a goddamned slaughterhouse. It was just like hospital in Omagh."

"You can't run from the past forever, Conor. Sooner or later, you gotta face it and move on."

"I'm trying, love. Truly I am. I'm at home, trying not to watch the telly. But I can't stop myself."

"Oh, so you can watch it on the news, but you can't be here for me? That's such bullshit, Conor." I hung up and walked back inside.

"Is Juanita Valdez's family here?" called a pear-shaped white guy in forest-green scrubs and a matching surgical cap.

"I'm her family." I rushed over to him with Caden and Rodeo right behind me.

"And you are?"

"I'm her daughter, Jenna." Close enough to the damned truth.

He gave me a disbelieving look. "But he's—"

"She!" I corrected.

"She's black and you're..."

"Adopted. How is she?"

"I'm Dr. Linden. I'm one of the neurosurgeons on the team. She came in with a gunshot wound to the right frontal lobe." He pointed at the right side of his forehead. "We managed to remove the slug, but we've had to temporarily remove a portion of the skull to alleviate the pressure on the brain caused by swelling."

"Fuck." Caden covered his mouth with his hand.

I felt sick to my stomach, but I had to be strong for Juanita. "What's her prognosis?"

"There are a lot of variables that can affect both short-term and long-term outcomes. On the one hand, the slug appears to be a small-caliber bullet from a handgun. Much less damage than from the high-velocity rounds we've seen a lot of this evening."

"Thank the stars for small favors," I muttered.

"Also, the bullet only penetrated about three millimeters from the entry wound, confining the injury to a single lobe in the right hemisphere. The human brain can often compensate when the damage isn't too extensive."

"So she'll recover?" asked Caden.

The doctor's expression darkened. "Maybe. She lost a lot of blood. Her being HIV positive also complicates matters. While her viral load is very low, her compromised immune system means the risk of infection is high."

Just when I was starting to have hope.

"A neurosurgeon by the name of Dr. Lisa Wolfe is en route from Seattle. She specializes in this type of traumatic head injury with patients who are HIV positive. When she gets here, we'll assess Ms. Valdez's condition and formulate a game plan."

"What're her chances?" I asked, trying to ignore my heart going full throttle in my chest. I couldn't get the image of Juanita's blood-smeared face out of my head.

"Best-case scenario, once she's stabilized, we'll transfer her to a rehab facility where she'll receive physical, speech, and occupational therapy. The part of the brain in question handles certain types of memory, spatial reasoning, and some motor functions, including speech. We won't know how significantly she's been affected until she regains consciousness. If she does."

"You're saying she might not wake up?" Caden asked, his voice breaking.

"We simply have to wait and see. We'll know more once Dr. Wolfe has had a chance to evaluate her."

Caden looked as though he was about to collapse. Rodeo and I put our arms around him. If I couldn't have Conor with me, at least I had my crew.

"I want to see her," I said.

"We're transferring her to the critical care unit right now. She'll be in room 524. Family only at this time." He said it as though he doubted my veracity.

I looked him dead in the eye. "Like I said, she's our mom."

"Thanks for your help, Doc," Rodeo said.

"You're welcome. Now if you'll excuse me, I have other patients waiting." Linden walked away.

"Fuck," I cursed under my breath. "Let's go up and see her."

We followed the signs to the main elevators and rode up to the fifth floor. In the critical care unit, Rodeo pointed at the small CCU waiting room. "I don't really know her. You two go on in. I'll be in here when you're done."

"Go home, if you want," I replied. "Get some rest."

"I would, but Nicole's got my car."

"Conor dropped me off." I slapped Caden on the back. "Guess you're our ride, bro."

Caden and I strolled into the ward and made a beeline to the room, avoiding anyone who might try to keep us from seeing Juanita.

At first I wondered if we were in the wrong room. Her face was so pale and waxy, I mistook her for a white person. A thick crown of bandages encircled her head. She had more wires and tubes coming out of her than a Borg queen.

Anger, sorrow, and guilt constricted my chest. I collapsed into a wood-framed chair, struggling to suck in enough air so I wouldn't pass out. One thought dominated all others. I wasn't going to let these bastards win.

Caden and I sat staring at Juanita's broken body for what felt like days. Only the wheezing from the ventilator and an occasional alarm from the vitals monitor disturbed the grave silence.

I caught myself starting to fall asleep and scolded myself for being so insensitive when one of the most important people in my life was so close to dying.

Caden must have noticed, because he said, "Why don't I take you home? We could all use some rest."

I wanted to argue, but I knew he was right. I wasn't any good to anyone like this.

We picked up Rodeo on the way out. "How is she?" he asked.

"She..." I didn't know how to finish the sentence.

Rodeo put an arm around me.

33

I woke to a garbage truck rumbling through the neighborhood at nine the next morning. The blisters on my left hand looked red and angry. Possibly infected. But I was too numb to care.

I was halfway through a dreary-eyed breakfast when my phone rang.

"Good news," said Kirsten when I answered it. "The Maricopa County Attorney's Office has dropped the charges against you."

"Really? Why?"

"Honestly, I'm not sure. Deputy County Attorney Perkins was unusually abrupt. He said the charges had been dropped and hung up. Maybe he thought it'd look bad to be prosecuting one of the heroes of the Main Drag shooting."

"Heroes! Like hell." I scoffed. "Suppose I should take good news wherever I can find it. When will I get my pistol back?"

"I'll look into it, but considering it was seized as evidence in a homicide case, I wouldn't hold your breath."

"Crap." Considering I'd picked up a Colt M1911 from Danny Warren and a Smith & Wesson revolver from that punk Mahoney,

I guessed it was a net plus. Still, I hated losing the Ruger. A good firearm cost money.

"How's your friend Juanita?"

"Alive but still critical."

"I'll keep her in my prayers."

"Thanks." Not that I put much stock in prayers.

"And just so you know, last night's legal representation was on the house."

That woke me up a little. "Dare I ask why?"

"You and your friends saved a lot of lives taking down those shooters. Least I could do."

"Thanks."

"Take it easy, Jinx."

I hung up and decided to go for a parkour run along McDowell Road—shimmying up walls, leaping trash cans, and somersaulting across bus stop shelters. Anything to generate endorphins to help me cope with the current shitstorm and figure out what my next move should be.

While I bounced and ricocheted off of various structures, my subconscious sorted out issues I was struggling with. How to track down Pratt and Dietz, ideally without getting anyone else killed or injured. What to do about Conor. And trying not to think about Juanita being at death's door.

When I was a block from home, my phone rang. To my surprise, it was my brother, Jake.

"Calling to yell at me again?" I slowed my run so that I could maintain a conversation.

"Jinx, I'm sorry. I know I've been an asshole lately."

"Yeah, you have."

"I heard what happened at the Main Drag. You okay?"

"Physically, yeah, more or less. Emotionally, I...shit, I don't know."

"Rodeo called, told me about Juanita. I'm so sorry. I know she's been your mentor and all."

"Thanks." Grief wrapped its tentacles around my chest.

"If you got time, I'd like to buy you lunch."

"Wow. To what do I owe this sudden generosity?"

"I could use your advice."

"Damn, bro. You must be desperate. You usually go to Dad for advice."

"If you don't want to meet…"

"No, that's fine. Where and when?"

"Firebird Cantina at Desert Ridge. Say around one."

"You're on."

At home, I took a shower, went back over everything I had on Rudy Pratt, and made some more phone calls. So far the nurse at Camelback Children's Hospital hadn't called. Neither had any of his neighbors or the references on Pratt's bail application, despite all the messages I'd left.

It didn't help that I couldn't get Juanita's deathly pale face out of my mind or the images of the carnage at the nightclub. *This is what Conor's dealing with*, said a little voice in my head. *Only more so.*

I hated to admit it, but it was true. He was no doubt reliving the trauma of the Omagh bombing and the death of his sister. And in response, I took my frustrations and anger out on him. I owed him an apology. But it would have to wait.

My phone had several text messages from Sadie Levinson asking where I was on the Pratt case. I ignored them and called Becca after I got dressed. I filled her in on the previous evening's chaos.

"Listen, Becks, I need to see if there's been any activity on Pratt. Credit cards, phone calls. Him or his wife."

"Hold on a minute." A voice in the background said something I couldn't make out. A door closed. "Okay, let me take a look. Nope, no recent activity. Wherever he is, he's laying low."

"Damn. Was that Easton I heard?"

"Yeah, just got back from their trip. Said they froze their ass off in Denver."

"Glad they're back." An idea popped into my head. It was a

long shot, but at this point, long shots were all I had left. "Who's been paying Pratt's daughter's medical bills?"

"Do you have a provider name?"

"Start with Camelback Children's Hospital."

The clicking of her fingers on the keyboard was so fast it almost sounded like static over the phone. "Bills paid by someone named Eric Freytag. Wow, to the tune of about four hundred thousand dollars. Must be nice to have a sugar daddy like that. The name's familiar, though I can't place it."

"He's in charge of the local White Nation chapter. A real snake. I met him briefly a couple days ago at that White Nation bar."

"Sounds like a real charmer. Think he's hiding Pratt?"

"Possibly. Pratt's case has been taken over by the feds, so something big's going on."

"I'll see what I can dig up on Freytag and let you know."

"Okay, thanks."

"Be careful, Jinxie. I mean it."

"Always."

I hung up and checked my watch. "Shit!" I was going to be late.

I pulled on my body armor, slipped the Glock into a holster on my hip, and raced the Gray Ghost north up I-17 to the Loop 101 until I reached Desert Ridge Marketplace on Tatum. The parking lot was packed with snowbirds, holiday shoppers, and the late lunchtime crowd. I snatched a parking space just as someone pulled out.

As I closed my door, I came face-to-face with a forty-something white guy in a polo shirt and Titleist ball cap. He held himself like a frat boy turned corporate executive. "I was waiting for that spot, lady!"

I flipped out my badge, rested a hand on the Glock, and tilted my head. "We gonna have a problem?"

His jaw tightened visibly. "You bitches think you're so smart!"

He hopped back into his Tesla roadster and flipped me off as he burned rubber down the lane.

I hustled across the parking lot and into a sprawling outdoor mall filled with overpriced shops and trendy restaurants. Good thing I knew where I was going. Last time I was there, the maps lacked those You Are Here markers, rendering them all but useless.

I charged into the Firebird Cantina, scanned the room for Jake, and joined him six tables in with a morose look on his face.

"Sorry I'm late. Parking's a bitch."

Jake sighed and picked disinterestedly at his focaccia sandwich. "No big deal."

The server came, and I ordered a burger bloody and fries.

"So you gonna tell me what the hell's going on with you these days?"

He looked up. My ordinarily too-cool-for-school brother looked like a whipped puppy. His eyes were bloodshot and rimmed with tears. "Rodeo dumped me."

I tried to act surprised. "Why would he do that?"

"He was always pushing me to hold hands and stuff. In public. I wouldn't."

"Holding hands? In public? What a perv!" I couldn't hold back the sarcasm any longer.

Jake threw a bit of sandwich at me. "I'm serious. I told him it was going to take time."

"And to think you've only been going out with him for a year and a half. What's his rush?"

"Hey! I'm hurting here. If you're just going to make fun of me..."

I held up my hands in apology. "Sorry. I know it hurts."

The server brought my lunch, and I dove into it with gusto. The run earlier had fueled my appetite.

"I loved him, Jinxie." A tear dripped onto his plate. "I thought he loved me."

I clasped Jake's hand. "I'm sure he did. You two were great

together. I guess you're just at different levels of...outness? Is that a word?"

"He says I've got internal homophobia."

"Ooh, sounds serious. Have you seen a doctor about that?"

He glared at me, and I apologized for making light of the situation.

"Maybe I do have some issues, but I'll work through them eventually." He surreptitiously wiped his face with a napkin, clearly trying to make it look as though he was wiping sauce from his mouth instead of tears from his cheek.

"Why won't you hold Rodeo's hand, Jake?"

"I do. Just not when there's people around."

"Why not?"

"I don't want anyone thinking, 'Hey, there go a couple of faggots.'"

"Why do you care what anyone thinks? The whole town knows I'm trans, thanks to that *Phoenix Living* article last year. Yeah, I got some shit for it, but I'm still living my life."

"You were always the strong one."

"Oh, please. Says the guy who can bench-press a Toyota."

"You know what I mean."

"Here's what I know. You're a fucking idiot."

"What?"

"You heard me. Jake, you're prioritizing the imaginary opinions of faceless strangers over the one man who truly loves you. He wants to show you affection, and you're rebuffing him."

"I have the right to determine when and how I'm touched."

"Yes, but this isn't about consent, and you know it. You're worried about people finding out you're gay. You're riding on your perceived straight privilege. Well, guess what? That shit's over."

I stood up and turned to the restaurant. "Attention, everyone!"

The place grew quiet.

"Jinx, don't do this," Jake muttered.

"I would like to inform you all that my big brother is gay. He's a big ol' fairy with six-pack abs and a heart of gold. And I think he's awesome, and I love him."

To my surprise, about half of the patrons and servers in the crowded restaurant applauded. I sat down, supremely satisfied with myself.

Jake was covering his face. "I truly hate you."

"Oh, come on, you big baby. Did you hear that applause? They love you."

"Bullshit, they love *you*. The saintly sister who loves her queer brother."

"You want me to tell them that I'm transgender?"

"No!" He grabbed my hands to keep me from standing up again.

"Hiding is no way to live."

"You sound like Dad."

"Dad's right. I tried to hide who I was when I was a kid, and it nearly killed me. I was always worried people would figure out I was trans, and about what would happen when they did. It's like a fucking cancer that eats at you all the time. Sound familiar?"

"Maybe."

"Fuck all the haters. Just be your own goddamned gay self. And if anyone gives you shit, call me. I'll kick their ass."

He laughed. "Just what I need—my baby sister fighting my battles for me."

"On the other hand, if you continue this bullshit of pretending to be straight when you're not, refusing to hold the hand of the man who's crazy about you, I swear to fucking God I will kick you into next Tuesday."

I held his gaze for a moment before he looked away. "You're right. I've been a wimp."

"Yeah, but you can change that. Find some *cajones*, man. Go fight for the man you love."

"It's too late. He broke up with me."

"Then call him up, tell him you've seen the error of your ways, and beg him to give you another chance."

"You think he will?"

"Never know until you try."

"Thanks, sis. I can always count on you not to sugarcoat it for me. How are things with you and Conor?"

It was so much more fun bagging on his love life. Why'd he have to bring up mine?

"Complicated."

"'Cause you don't want to move in with him?"

"Among other things."

"See, that's what I don't get. You two are crazy about each other. Why not move in together?"

"I like having my own place. Besides, you worked so hard to renovate my house. Why would I give it up to live in that reinforced bunker of his?"

Jake held my gaze until I looked away, distracted by someone or something or whatever. "Is that what it is?"

"What else would it be?"

"I think you're commitment-phobic."

"Bullshit." I sat back and crossed my arms.

"Ever since things went bad between you and your high school boyfriend, you've never gotten serious with a guy."

"That's not true."

"No? When your ex-boyfriend Wilson invited you to move in with him, you dumped him."

"I dumped Wilson because I caught him in bed with some skank." I rolled my eyes. "And when I asked him why, he said there was no spark between us anymore."

"Shit, that must've hurt. What'd you do?"

"What any self-respecting woman would do. I Tasered his ass and said, 'Here's your fucking spark, asshole!'"

We both burst out laughing. Holy hell, that felt good. It rippled through my body, shaking loose all of the crap I'd been feeling.

"Is that why you don't want to move in with Conor? You think he's going to cheat on you?"

It was an easy excuse, but it wasn't the whole story. Before I could answer, my phone rang. "I gotta get this. It's Becks."

"I found your guy Freytag. He lives in a gated community north of Scottsdale. Very tight security."

"Damn, how's a weasel like that get all this money?"

"He's the CEO at Suma Financial, an investment firm in north Scottsdale. The guy's got money all over the place. I've turned up numerous offshore accounts. Major shareholder in beaucoup businesses in high tech, aerospace, and advanced weapons manufacturing. Makes a lot of donations to far-right organizations and politicians. His phone records are extensive, but nothing connected to either your guy Pratt or to...uh...you-know-who."

"Barclay Dietz."

"Yeah, him. Not that I have a number for Dietz, but his name doesn't show up anywhere."

"Thanks, Becks. Text me Freytag's work info. I'm going to pay him a visit. Email the rest to me."

"You're not going there alone, are you?"

"Listen to you. You're as bad as my mother. I'll be fine."

"Be careful."

"Yes, mother." I hung up. "Well, bro, duty calls."

"What's going on?" Jake looked worried.

"What do you mean? Becca's just getting me information on one of my skips."

"You mentioned Barclay Dietz just now."

"He's in town. I almost bagged him the other day. Feds are offering a big reward for his return."

"Damn. After all these years. And this Freytag? He involved with Dietz?"

"Maybe. It's just a lead for now."

"You need me to tag along? Since Rodeo's out of commission for a while."

"No, I need you to go play nursemaid to Rodeo and have some hot makeup sex."

He blushed. "You sure? Barclay Dietz nearly killed you way back when. He could still be dangerous."

"My job's all about the dangerous. If it wasn't, I'd be in danger of falling asleep on the job." I stood up and hugged him. "Now quit being such a pussy and tell the world that you're here, you're queer, and anyone who doesn't like it can just fuck off."

I pulled out my wallet and dropped a ten on the table. Jake snatched it up and stuffed it back in my hand. "No, this is my treat."

"Wow! You *have* turned a corner. See ya soon."

I left him at the table to settle up the bill. When I reached the front door, Jake shouted, "I'm here, I'm queer, and anyone who doesn't like it can fuck off!"

The restaurant responded with another round of applause. I gave him a thumbs-up and hurried out of the restaurant and back to the Gray Ghost. After punching Freytag's business address into the GPS, I headed out.

34

Suma Financial was located on the top floor of a three-story glass building on Northsight Boulevard north of Raintree. As I parked, I thought about how to play this. Freytag had already seen me, so there was no point trying to pretend I was anything other than what I was—a bail enforcement officer pursuing fugitives wanted on multiple violent criminal charges.

I strolled into the building in full gear. I wanted Freytag to know I was all business and that if he stood in my way, he would be hurt. White-collar bigots like Freytag were always pussies, anyway, getting their underlings to do the dirty work. With enough pressure, they always folded like a lawn chair.

The elevator opened to a glass-enclosed office with the company logo etched on the door. I stepped inside. The receptionist looked like a seasoned gatekeeper, fiftyish with a helmet of dark hair and a shrewd expression.

"I'm here to see Eric Freytag." I flipped my badge and ID.

"You got a warrant?" she asked without breaking her professional façade.

"Odd question. I'm not here to arrest him. Just have a few questions."

"Is he expecting you?"

"He'll know what it's about."

"Your name?"

"Jinx Ballou."

She picked up the phone handset and dialed an extension. "Mr. Freytag, there is a Jinx Ballou here to see you. Yes, sir."

Without a glance at me, she turned back to her work. "He'll be up momentarily. You can have a seat."

"I'll stand, thank you very much."

"Suit yourself." She tuned me out.

"Momentarily" apparently meant thirty minutes. No doubt a power move intended to intimidate me. Freytag opened the door to the back offices. His aquiline features were so snakelike, I half expected him to flick his tongue.

"Ah, Ms. Windsor, isn't it? No, wait. It's Ballou now. That's right. How can I help you this afternoon?"

"I'm looking for Rudy Pratt. He skipped bail on a murder charge. I believe you know where he is."

"I see. Why don't you and I discuss this in my office."

Into the serpent's den, I thought, as he led me to a roomy, well-appointed office. Everything looked very corporate. No signs of his connections to White Nation. No swastikas. No Confederate flags.

He coiled up behind his desk with a look on his face that told me he wasn't intimidated at all. I'd have to do something about that.

"So tell me the name again of this person you're seeking?"

"Rudy Pratt. He was scheduled to be at that meeting at Dixie's. It's why I was there."

"Huh, well the name does ring a bell, but I can't say I know the man. White Nation's such a large organization. Thousands of members in the Grand Canyon chapter alone."

"Really? You don't know him? And yet you've been paying his

daughter's medical expenses to the tune of hundreds of thousands of dollars." I pulled out Pratt's photo and set it on his desk. "This refresh your memory?"

He gave it the briefest of glances and returned it. "Not really. No. I donate to numerous charitable causes, you see. My way of giving back to white society."

"The man's a murderer and a fugitive. Your protecting him makes you an accessory after the fact. Ever been to prison, Mr. Freytag?"

"Can't say I have. And your little threats do not intimidate me. Should you display the same type of uncontrolled behavior you did the other day, I will have you arrested. *Again.* I am a busy man with important matters to attend to."

"Like rallying your violent little band of neo-Nazi white nationalists?"

"Violent? You're the only one I've seen use violence. You attacked one of our out-of-town guests without any provocation."

"I attempted to capture a man wanted by the FBI for aggravated assault and armed robbery. And in retaliation, you sent your thugs to murder people in a gay club last night."

"That is a slanderous accusation. We are not thugs, Miss Ballou. White Nation is a peaceful organization fighting for the rights of God-loving white Americans. Right now illegals, Negroes, and homosexuals have more rights than we do. It's a disgrace. And if someone did shoot up one of your queer sex clubs, well, then, it must be God's will."

It took all of my self-control to keep from putting a nine-millimeter hole in Freytag's skull. "You're so full of shit. Poor persecuted white men." I stood and leaned over his desk. "You have no idea what persecution feels like. But before this is all over, you will. I guarantee it."

"Is that a threat?"

I smiled. "Take it however you want, asshole. I will drag both Rudy Pratt and Barclay Dietz back to jail. And then I'll take you down for protecting them."

I turned on my heel and slammed open his office door so hard it smacked the wall. I stormed past the receptionist and charged down the staircase rather than waiting for an elevator.

When I reached the Gray Ghost, I put Freytag's home address in my GPS and drove northeast to where the posh golf-centric communities of Scottsdale embedded themselves in the desert foothills. Clouds were rolling in, giving the desert landscape a dreary, desolate feel.

Becca wasn't kidding about the security at the gated community. Multiple surveillance cameras mounted around the entrance left no square inch unmonitored. Two security guards stood in a guard shack alongside a wrought-iron gate that connected to an eight-foot border wall that I assumed ran around the entire property.

I pulled up to the gate. A man who carried himself like a military veteran, complete with a high and tight haircut, approached the Gray Ghost. "Can I help you, ma'am?"

I flashed him my badge and handed him photos of Pratt and Dietz. "I'm looking for these two violent fugitives. Rudy Pratt and Barclay Dietz. I have reason to believe they are holed up in a house on the grounds."

"What are they wanted for?" asked the guard as he studied the photos.

"Murder, aggravated assault, and armed robbery." I pointed at my black eye. "Dietz did this to my face when I tried to arrest him at a local bar. Believe me, you don't want them going after any of your residents."

"They don't look familiar to me." He showed the photos to his associate, who shook his head. "We haven't seen them. Do you know which house they're supposedly in?"

"The one belonging to Eric Freytag." I gave them the street address.

"Mr. Freytag *is* a resident here. Do you have a warrant?"

"I don't need a warrant. I'm a bail enforcement officer. By law, I can enter any home where I believe my fugitives are hiding."

"Well, I'm sorry, but I can't let you inside the gate without a warrant."

I considered pushing it, but I didn't get the impression he would budge on the issue. And honestly, I had no proof they were staying at Freytag's house.

After taking back the photos, I handed him one of my business cards. "Call me if you see them. Hopefully, they won't murder any of your residents before then."

I turned around and headed down the two-lane side street that bordered the complex. The eight-foot block wall might intimidate the casual intruders. I was not giving up so easily, however.

As I parked the truck on the street, I scanned the area. No security cameras and very little traffic as far as I could see in the late-afternoon gloom. I made a running jump at the wall. I grasped the top and used my momentum to propel me up and over.

The homes in the community, at least those I could see, were five thousand square feet or more, set on sprawling lots that butted up against a golf course. The lawns were mostly crushed rock planted with a variety of palm and citrus trees, cacti of all types, and heat-tolerant shrubs.

Using the maps app on my phone, I followed the directions to Freytag's place a mile and a half away. With my body armor and holstered weapons, I stuck out in this refuge of wealth and tranquility. But most residents were either at work or safely tucked inside their desert castles.

Thirty minutes later, I was standing in front of Freytag's mansion. A wide driveway led up a slight hill to a four-car garage. A blue light on a security camera above the garage flickered to life when I came within range of its sensor. I suspected all the entryways were similarly monitored.

With the darkening overcast skies, I could see through the windows with relative ease. Rooms were lit, and there was movement within. I decided to try a little social engineering.

I stashed my body armor and sidearms under a large oleander bush and rang the doorbell.

A moment later, a towheaded boy about seven years old opened the door, followed by a frazzled-looking woman with long dark hair. "Leonard, how many times I tell you," she said in a thick Latina accent. "Don't open the doors to strangers."

I didn't know if she was the housekeeper, nanny, or both. Couldn't be the wife, could it? Still, it surprised me that Freytag would have an immigrant working in his home. Or that this woman would willingly work for a scumbag like Freytag. The world was weird.

"*Buenas tardes, señora,*" I said.

"*Buena tarde,*" she replied. From the way she used the singular, I guessed she was from Chile or Argentina.

"I apologize for disturbing you," I continued in Spanish. "Señor Freytag asked me to deliver an important message to his guests."

"His guests?"

"Yes, Señor Pratt and Señor Dietz. Are they here?"

She got a confused look on her face. "I'm sorry, but you are mistaken. No one is here by those names. Señor Freytag's guests usually stay at the ranch."

I popped my forehead with the heel of my hand. "Of course. Silly me! Do you have the address? I seem to have misplaced it."

Her eyes narrowed with suspicion. "Who are you?"

"Liz Windsor. I work with Señor Freytag at Suma Financial. Do you have the address for the ranch?"

"Maybe I should call Señor Freytag."

"Wait, you know what? I remembered I have the address in my phone. No need to bother him. You have a nice day, señora."

I hurried away and picked up my gear once I was out of sight of the front door. So much for social engineering.

I retraced my steps and hopped the wall, the wind gusts tugging at my hair and clothes. The Gray Ghost was farther down than I remembered. I must have crossed one house early. And mine was no longer the only vehicle parked on the street. A dark-blue Caprice sat a half block behind me.

I'd had enough unproductive fun for the day. I turned the key and pointed the Gray Ghost toward home.

As I drove toward the main road, the Caprice's headlights blazed to life behind me. The car followed me at a distance through three turns. When it remained behind me after I completely circled the block, I knew I had a tail.

I suspected the driver was one of Freytag's goons. He wasn't hiding the fact that he was tailing me, so I figured he was trying to intimidate me into backing off. But I didn't scare easily. I'd gone toe-to-toe with crazed meth dealers, serial rapists, and sadistic Chechen mobsters. An investment banker with a Hitler complex barely moved the needle.

He changed lanes whenever I did, never more than a car or two behind me. At times, he crept so close to my rear bumper I thought he was going to ram me. Traffic was getting heavier as the afternoon rush hour began. Losing my shadow was going to be a challenge. I'd taken strategic driving courses designed to lose a tail. But I was in a top-heavy SUV, not a supercharged sports car. Another tactic was needed.

I turned south on the Piestewa Freeway and worked my way over to the carpool lane. Driving solo in that lane was illegal after three. If I got pulled over by a cop, it could earn me a hefty fine. But it might also shake loose my pursuer.

The Caprice joined me in the HOV lane, staying hot on my bumper, as I whizzed past the slower lanes. Ahead of me, a Prius nosed into my path. I swerved to avoid it. The Gray Ghost lifted onto two wheels and slammed down hard enough to rattle my teeth. Behind me, tires squealed. I glanced back, hoping for a collision. No such luck! The Caprice whipped around the Prius and once again bore down on me. I had no hope of outrunning him.

I dashed into a gap in the lane next to me and forced my way back across the interstate until I cut off the gore point at the Cactus Drive exit and screeched to a stop in the pullout lane designed for minor accidents.

I scrambled out of the truck, drew my Glock, and squatted behind the Ghost's front grill. Icy, fat droplets of rain fell, hitting the pavement with a smack-smack and sending a chill down my back. The wind whipped up, blowing wisps of hair in my face.

A moment later, a Caprice cruised up the exit ramp. I caught Special Agent Bender glaring at me as he drove past and turned right onto Cactus. *Goddamned feds.*

My hands trembled as the cold rain came down harder. I hopped back into the Gray Ghost. Since I was already on the east side of town, I decided to reach out again to Peyton, see if he'd heard from dear old Dad. Along the way, I kept a wary eye on my rearview mirror in case anyone else decided to play follow the leader.

35

It was early evening when I pulled into parking lot of San Tan Liquors. Rush hour traffic had made the drive all the more unpleasant. Even listening to the Pink Trinkets' *Singing Mammogram* album couldn't free me from my worries. It felt as if the world was coming to an end. Everything was so fucking upside down. I was determined to make it right again if it killed me.

The bell over the door jingled as I walked in. A hulking guy in a red flannel shirt stood at the counter, ringing up a couple of college kids in ASU sweatshirts. Maybe Peyton was stocking the shelves or in the back somewhere.

I wandered aimlessly through the aisles. I needed to call Conor and apologize for getting angry at him. But with everything going on, I couldn't bring myself to do it. I didn't even know what to say to him. I still didn't want to move in with him and wasn't sure why. Not wanting to give up my house and old baggage from an ex-boyfriend sounded like legit excuses, but there was something deeper. I just didn't know what.

"Let me know if you need any help," called the lumberjack behind the counter. There was a warning in his voice, as if he thought I planned to slip out without paying. Last time I shoplifted, I was a closeted eleven-year-old and got caught stealing a dress for my secret stash.

I wandered over to the cooler, grabbed a six-pack of Four Peaks Ale, and carried it to the counter. "Peyton here?" I asked as the lumberjack rang up my purchase.

Lumberjack shot me a look. "Why?"

"He's a friend of mine."

"Your *friend* stopped showing up for his shifts. I fired him."

"Any idea where he might be?"

"Don't know. Don't care."

I paid for the beer and cruised over to Peyton's apartment, where I nabbed a visitor spot outside the gate. When a resident drove through, I slipped inside the rattling gate on foot, keeping an eye out for the property manager.

I pounded on Peyton's door. When there was no response after a few minutes, I knocked again. Still no response. Where was he? It was only a little after six. Too early to hit the clubs. *Could he be hiding out with his father somewhere? Or just out running errands?*

I weighed my options and decided to let myself inside to look for clues to Peyton's whereabouts. After a quick glance around for possible witnesses, I pulled out a set of lockpicks and went to work on the door lock. It took me a few minutes and a few false starts before I defeated the security pins in the dead bolt. As soon as the cylinder turned, I was inside in a flash.

The sweet haze of weed hung in the air. A wooden trunk with circular watermarks served as a coffee table between a floral upholstered couch and the flat-screen TV. The blue glass of a bong glinted in the dim light next to a PlayStation controller.

I pulled out a flashlight and thumbed through a loose stack of papers on a side table. Just a few unpaid bills, a postcard advertising solar panels, and a *High Times* magazine for Hughie.

I moved on to the bedrooms, bypassing the one with the sour smell of smoked ganja in favor of one that was relatively tidy. I searched through the drawers of a black laminate desk. I found the usual bank statements, appliance warranties, and health insurance statements. A ream of printer paper and a stack of blank envelopes. An external hard drive and a Bluetooth keyboard lay on the edge of the desk, but there was a blank spot where a laptop might go.

I dug through the wastebasket, finding mostly crushed beer cans, used tissues, and the remains of a padded mailing envelope with no return address. Further digging turned up a handwritten note that read, *Meet me at Lodestar Ranch. Address in the phone. I'll explain everything.* It was signed "Dad."

I was about to search a little further when I heard voices and laughter outside the apartment. I glanced out the bedroom window but couldn't see anyone. Time to get out.

I crept to the front room again and checked the window there. A straight couple shuffled drunkenly along one of the paved walks. It wasn't Peyton or his roomie. But it was time I cleared out.

I slipped out the front door, leaving the dead bolt unlocked, and shuffled past the couple, who were too wrapped up in each other's affections to pay me any mind.

It was only seven thirty when I got home, but I was exhausted. I called the hospital to check on Juanita only to learn she was still in a coma with no change in condition. The texts from Sadie asking for an update were piling up, so I told her I was close. Of course, I felt closer to having a complete mental breakdown than finding Pratt, but she didn't need to know that.

Something about Barclay Dietz's note to his son was pricking the back of my mind, but I couldn't fit the pieces together. Maybe a little libation would take the edge off enough for me to sort it out. I opened one of the bottles of Four Peaks and took a long pull. I was putting the rest of the six-pack in the fridge when I heard a thunk and a muffled voice say, "Damn it to hell."

"What the fuck?" I hunched down and drew my Glock. Someone was in my house.

I listened further. Shuffling sounds in the attic. The feeling of being watched rushed back. I wasn't crazy. Someone had been watching me. And whoever it was, was still here.

I crept to the hallway and gingerly pulled down the trapdoor to the attic. The ladder creaked as I unfolded it and placed my foot on the first step. More shuffling from above. Go time!

I vaulted up the ladder and turned on the light. The bare bulb threw harsh shadows across the stacks of my stored possessions. I scanned my surroundings, finger on the trigger of my Glock, but didn't see anyone or anything out of place. "I know you're here. Whoever you are, you best surrender now. Or so help me, I will end you," I said in my most threatening voice.

On the far side of the attic, from behind a stack of old suitcases, a pair of dark arms rose. "Please, ma'am. Don't shoot me. I don't mean no harm." The voice was male and frightened.

"Come on outta there. I won't shoot as long as you do as I say."

A gaunt figure stood unsteadily. He wore a green US Marine Corps utility jacket. His hair was an untidy nest of silver, matching his scraggly beard. His skin looked like dark leather.

"Who are you?" I eased my finger off the trigger but kept the gun trained on my intruder. "And what the hell are you doing in my attic?"

"Reginald Campbell, ma'am. Just needed a warm place to stay. I'll be on my way. Won't be no more bother."

"How'd you get up here, Mr. Campbell?"

He stared at the floor. "There was a loose board under the eaves. I climbed up your air conditioner and shimmied up inside. I'm real sorry."

Once my sense of alarm had subsided, I found myself feeling sorry for the man. He looked to be in his sixties. From the condition of his clothes, I guessed he'd been homeless a while. "You hungry?" I tucked the pistol into my waistband.

He looked at me with lifeless eyes. "A little."

"Come on, then. I'll fix you something."

"Don't wanna be no bother. I just get my gear and go."

"No bother. Long as you don't do anything crazy."

"Won't have no trouble from me."

I stepped down the ladder, and a moment later, he followed suit. In the full light, his face had a skull-like quality, his eyes deep-set and sunken. His cheekbones poked out like knives.

I folded up the ladder and nudged the trapdoor closed. He looked up at it worriedly.

"Don't worry," I said. "I'm not going to steal your stuff."

I led him to the kitchen. He sat down at the heavy wooden table my grandmother, Marie Lafitte, had given me a few years back. She claimed it was originally from the ship captained by our ancestor, the pirate Captain Jean Lafitte.

"You allergic to anything, Reginald?" I asked. Last thing I needed was poor Reginald going into anaphylactic shock from something I gave him.

"Not that I know of. And my friends call me Reggie."

"All right, Reggie. My friends call me Jinx."

"Mighty odd name."

"Well, I'm a mighty odd woman."

He smiled as I cooked up some scrambled eggs and bacon.

When I served his plate, I asked how he came to be homeless. Reggie explained he was originally from Snellville, Georgia, just outside Atlanta. "Weren't much of a town when I grew up there. Last time I was back, though, it was so growed up I didn't recognize the place. Atlanta done swallowed it whole. Cut down all the forests to put up Starbucks and Costcos and office parks. Never went back."

He'd served as a corpsman in the Marine Corps during Vietnam. When he returned to the states after the war, he moved to

New York and struggled to find his footing. A drug problem kept him from becoming a paramedic.

He kicked the habit after a few years and worked as a super for a while, then got his hack license and started driving a taxi. After ten brutal New York winters, he moved to Arizona and continued to drive a taxi for twenty years. When Uber and Lyft got in the game, the taxi company he was with folded.

Eventually, he lost his house and spent a few months living out of a twelve-year-old Lincoln Town Car parked in a vacant lot. Then his car disappeared. Whether stolen or towed, he never found out. He'd been on the streets ever since. Until a week ago when a cold snap led him to crawl into my attic.

"You been drinking my whiskey and eating my food this past week?"

He looked humiliated. "Yes, ma'am."

"You haven't been spying on me, have you?"

A wounded look crossed his face. "No, ma'am. Wouldn't never do nothing like that."

I believed him. "Well, what're we gonna do, Reggie?"

He was wiping his face with a napkin after finishing the last of the eggs. "I'll gather my belongings and be on my way. I thank you for the hospitality."

"No, you don't have to go. It's Christmas, for fuck's sake. Not that I'm all that religious. But it don't feel right to kick you out with it being cold as it is." I thought about my options. I didn't want to be taken advantage of, but at the same time, I couldn't turn him away. "For tonight, you can sleep on my couch. We can figure out the rest tomorrow."

"I ain't got no money to pay you back, understand. Don't qualify for social security for a few years yet."

"Maybe you can do some chores around the house, starting with the loose boards around the eaves."

"I can do that."

After dinner, Reggie went to the attic to retrieve his belongings. I called Conor. The call went straight to voicemail.

"Hey, babe. Sorry for getting upset at you last night. Give me a call when you can."

I got Reggie settled on the couch, showed him how to use the remote, and reminded him that I tracked down and arrested people for a living, just in case he got any ideas about pawning any of my belongings.

After that, I turned in for a fitful night of disturbing dreams.

36

When I stumbled out of bed the next morning, I noticed a Caprice parked in front of the house. No sooner had I thrown on a T-shirt and sweatpants than three people emerged. Agents Lovelace and Bender marched toward my front porch. Trailing them was a grim-faced man with a bad combover and wearing a long, black woolen coat. They pounded on my door a moment later.

I walked into the living room. Reggie looked worried.

"Relax, I don't think this is about you," I said.

He nodded warily and made tracks to my guest bathroom before I opened the door and crossed my arms.

"First you refuse to help me track down wanted fugitives, then Tweedle Dee here starts tailing me. What gives?"

"Ms. Ballou, we need to speak with you," said Lovelace.

"I'm kinda busy at the moment," I replied. "So unless you two have a warrant—" I started to shut the door.

"Ma'am, if you please," said Black Coat in an Irish accent with a hint of British posh. He held out a photo. "We need to speak with you about this man. Do you know him?"

The photo was of Conor. He was a teenager in the photo, but I'd recognize his face anywhere. "Who the hell are you?"

"Detective Chief Inspector Matthew Collier of the Police Service of Northern Ireland, ma'am. I'm following up on a cold case."

"What's this about?" In my gut, I already knew the answer.

"Can we come in?" asked Lovelace. "Or do we have to freeze to death on your doorstep?"

My instinct told me to tell them to take a hike, but I doubted it would do much good. "Yeah, come on in."

I led them to the kitchen and started a pot of coffee. Reggie poked his head in as my guests sat down. "Everything okay, Miss Jinx?"

"For now. Thanks."

"Would you mind too terribly if I used your shower?" Reggie looked embarrassed to ask.

"I'd mind if you didn't. Towels are in the linen closet in the hall."

He shuffled off to the bathroom. I poured myself a cup of coffee and sat at the table. "I'd offer you all some coffee but you won't be staying long. Now, what's this about?"

"You're still dating Conor Doyle, are you not?" asked Lovelace.

"Yeah, why?"

"When did you last speak with him?"

"Night before last at the Main Drag. He and I helped take down the shooters. Why?"

Lovelace pulled out a notebook and flipped it open. "Where did you go afterward?"

"To the hospital. John C. Lincoln on Dunlap. A friend of mine was shot in the head."

She scribbled some notes in her notebook. "And Mr. Doyle was with you?"

"Why? What's going on?"

"Answer the question, Ms. Ballou," said Bender. Despite his

baby-face look, his voice had some steel to it. Maybe he wasn't quite the doofus I'd originally taken him for.

"Conor dropped me off at the hospital. From there he went home."

"He didn't go in with you to the hospital? Seems odd," Bender pressed.

"I'm not answering any more questions until you people tell me what the hell's going on." I glared at Lovelace.

"Miss Ballou, are you familiar with the name Liam O'Callaghan?" asked Collier.

Fuck. It was Conor's birth name. "Don't know anyone named Liam."

Collier continued. "Liam O'Callaghan was involved in a bombing that took place twenty years ago in Northern Ireland. Nearly thirty people were killed. Countless others severely injured."

"What's this got to do with Conor?"

"We believe Conor Doyle is an alias O'Callaghan assumed after the bombing."

"Conor's not a terrorist. He's a bounty hunter. He puts criminals away for chrissakes." Suddenly I sounded like the family members of the bail jumpers I went after.

"I'm sure this is all just a misunderstanding. As soon as we can speak to him, I'm sure we can clear it up in no time." Lovelace patted my hand, as if to reassure me. It didn't work. How many times had I said those same words to coerce someone connected to one of my skips?

"I don't know where Conor is. I left him a message last night. He hasn't called back."

"So he's not here?" pressed Lovelace.

"Why would he be here?"

"Don't bullshit us, Ballou." Bender was looking less like a man-baby and more like a schoolyard bully.

"He lives a few streets south of here on Almeria. I suggest you try there."

"We have," said Bender. "He's not there."

"Then I don't know what to tell you."

"Does the word 'Freebird' mean anything to you?" asked Collier.

"Freebird? As in the song?"

Collier nodded. "Someone sent your Mr. Doyle a text at one o'clock this morning that said 'Freebird.' Nothing else. We were hoping you could tell us what it means."

"How the hell should I know? That someone's a fan of moldy oldies? Who sent the message?"

"The sender is as yet unidentified," Collier said. "It was sent from a prepaid phone."

"You have no idea what it means?" Lovelace tilted her head, giving me a disbelieving look.

"Not a clue." I shrugged. "You'll have to ask Conor or whoever sent the message."

Bender leaned toward me and growled. "Where is Conor?"

"Aww, having trouble following the grown-ups' conversation, Bender? Let me use small words so you can catch up. I. Don't. Know."

"So you don't mind us looking around?" Lovelace asked.

"Show me a search warrant, and the place is yours. Until then, the answer is no. You may not look around." I drained the last of my coffee.

"Miss Ballou, if you're harboring Mr. Doyle..." warned Collier.

"I'm not. And this discussion is over."

"You mind if I use your restroom?" asked Bender.

"Nice try, Bender. Either hold it or go in your diaper." I pointed toward the front door. "All three of you, out! Now."

"We'll be watching this house," Bender replied as the three of them stood.

"Good. I've heard there've been a few break-ins in the neighborhood. Nice to know you'll be here keeping an eye on things when I'm out."

When they left, I locked the door behind them and leaned my back against it. *Jeezus, Conor, what've you got me into?*

I stepped back into the kitchen, needing something to settle my nerves.

"They gone?" asked Reggie. I poured him a cup of coffee and a second for myself. I resisted the temptation to add a little Jameson to it.

"For now."

"You in some sorta trouble, Miss Jinx?"

"When am I not in trouble?"

Reggie raised an eyebrow.

"I'm fine. It's my boyfriend, Conor, I'm worried about. Brits and the feds have him confused with someone else. I'm sure it'll work out." I just had no idea how.

I grabbed my phone and called him. Again it went straight to voicemail. "Conor, call me. We need to talk."

I made breakfast for Reggie and myself and told him he could use my washer and dryer to clean his clothes. He thanked me and agreed to do some repairs and other chores around the house that I'd been putting off for a while. The drip from the shower-head. Dusting. Trimming the hedges. Pulling weeds. Replacing several light bulbs that had gone out in the house, including the one in the fridge. And of course, the loose boards that had allowed him entry in the first place.

After breakfast, I showered, put some burn cream on my left hand, gathered my gear, including my laptop and files, and headed over to the Hub. I picked up a couple of coffees from Tres Leches along the way.

Becca was already hard at work. I set her quad shot vanilla latte in front of her.

"How's Juanita?" she asked.

"Caden's hanging out in her hospital room, reading her trashy romances while she lies in a coma. We're still hoping she comes out of it soon."

"And how are you doing?"

"Managing." I didn't want to discuss Conor's legal troubles in the open room of the Hub. Too many nosy people.

"D'you get anything from that Freytag guy?"

"Nada. Claims not to know Pratt. My gut's telling me differently. I think something big's going down. Maybe this weekend at the rally White Nation has planned." I pulled out the note I'd found in Peyton's trash can and handed it to her. "What do you make of this? Ever hear of a Lodestar Ranch?"

She studied the note. "Doesn't ring any bells."

I opened my laptop and did a search for Lodestar Ranch. The only significant results were for a couple of horse ranches —one in British Columbia, one in Zimbabwe. Nothing in Arizona. I refined my search and added the word "Arizona" to it.

Top result was the Lodestar Mine, an abandoned copper mine north of Cave Creek. Something triggered in my brain. I pulled up the subreddit I had found that Rudy Pratt had been on, talking about gardening. He'd used the handle Crizaba. I ran an online search for that word. It too came up as an abandoned mine in Arizona.

"Holy shit!" Fear crackled down my spine. I pulled out Agent Lovelace's card and dialed the number.

"You calling to tell us where your boyfriend's hiding, Ms. Ballou?"

"I have no idea where he is."

"Then we have nothing to talk about."

"Wait! I've stumbled on something I think you should know about White Nation."

"Oh? And what is that?"

"I think they're planning to set off a bomb at their protest on Saturday."

"And what makes you think that?"

"A fugitive I know has intercepted shortwave radio transmissions from people planning to detonate bombs in Phoenix. He thought they were mole people, but I think it's White Nation."

"Mole people?" Lovelace laughed. "Are you calling to mess with me, Ballou?"

"He's a bit of a conspiracy nut, but I think he may have stumbled onto something real."

"Fine, who is this conspiracy nut of yours?"

"Robert Rossellini." I gave her Conspiracy Bob's contact information. "I returned him to custody a few days ago, but he may have renewed his bail bond."

"I'll look into it."

"You do that." I hung up. Becca was staring at me.

"What?" I asked.

"You think White Nation's going to set off a bomb at the rally?" She looked worried.

"Maybe not at the rally itself. But think about it, what better time to set off a bomb than when a significant portion of the police force is trying to maintain order between a bunch of neo-Nazis and counter-protesters."

"No offense, Jinx, but you're starting to sound like your buddy, Conspiracy Bob."

"I know it sounds crazy. But Bob claims he's intercepted radio transmissions from people using the names of abandoned local mines. Several people on that subreddit we found were using handles that are also the names of abandoned mines. Then in that note that Barclay Dietz wrote to his son, he mentions Lodestar Ranch. Lodestar is an abandoned copper mine near Cave Creek, not far from Freytag's home. It can't all be a coincidence."

"Seems a bit of a stretch. Like Conspiracy Bob's theory that jackalopes and chupacabras were extraterrestrial beings that built ancient stone temples in Latin America."

"Maybe you're right." But I wasn't going to let it go. There was a connection here. I just had to find it.

I went through the information that Becca had dug up on Freytag. His business, Suma Financial, held a number of assets, but they were all commercial properties, including payday loan businesses, nail salons, shopping centers, and a small timeshare resort. Nothing residential.

I dug deeper and found he was on the board of several other businesses, but still nothing that might be this Lodestar Ranch. At times I felt like a rat running through a virtual maze of nested shell companies, many of them based in the Caymans, Turks and Caicos, or some other ridiculous tax haven.

From time to time, I called Conor. Same results. Didn't bother leaving a message, though I was getting seriously worried. Was he laying low to avoid the feds? Or had something happened to him?

Around four o'clock, I packed it in and drove north to the hospital. Juanita's condition hadn't changed. Caden was looking and smelling awful. The staff had allowed him to remain after visitors' hours. I told him to go home and take a shower while I kept an eye on Juanita. He resisted, but I threatened to fire him if he didn't.

"Doc says her vitals are improving," he said on his way out the door. "Mild infection, but the antibiotics appear to be working."

"Best news I've heard all day. Now get the hell outa here, Stinky! And get some fucking rest."

With Caden gone, I sat listening to the wheezing of the respirator. I wanted to believe Juanita was looking less ashen than when I saw her last, but in the dim light of the room, it was hard to tell. Her hands were cooler to the touch than they usually were.

Memories of the shooting flashed in my mind. I kept hearing the one shooter shout "Fucking fairies" before the turmoil began. His voice sounded familiar. I'd heard it before and recently. I just couldn't place it.

Caden returned around eleven. I was struggling to stay awake when he walked in looking more like his old self.

"Any change?" he asked.

I shook my head and hugged him. "'Fraid not, bro. You get any sleep?"

"A little. Thanks for spotting me."

"I'm sorry I haven't been here more," I said. "But time's running out on getting Pratt."

"Keep your head on a swivel, girl." Caden sat down in the chair next to Juanita. "And if you need me, call. I'll be there."

"I will."

The cold air outside woke me up enough that I wouldn't fall asleep on the drive home. The strings of holiday lights decorating homes and businesses didn't help my mood. I couldn't shake this chilling sense of foreboding. Maybe it was just lingering trauma from the shooting. Or unresolved anxiety from my bitter history with Barclay Dietz.

I walked in my living room and nearly jumped out of my skin when I flicked on the lights and found Reggie lying on my couch. I'd completely forgotten about my houseguest.

"Didn't mean to scare you, Miss Jinx," he said as I sat and let my heart rate return to normal.

"It's okay. I'm actually glad to have a little company." Especially since Conor was incommunicado.

Reggie and I talked for a while. I should have been uncomfortable having a complete stranger sleeping under my roof, but he'd been doing it for a week, and nothing bad had happened.

I woke the next morning to the smells of breakfast. Coffee. Bacon. Eggs. My first thought was that Conor had returned and was making me breakfast. I walked out in a tank top and a pair of his boxers only to find Reggie at the stove. He wore a faded Rolling Stones T-shirt and a ragged pair of jeans.

"Morning," I said, feeling a bit awkward.

"Morning, Miss Jinx. You hungry?"

"Starving. What's cooking?"

"Eggs, grits, and bacon. You like grits?"

"My father's from Louisiana. It's one of the major food groups there."

"Here you go." He dished us each a plate and poured cups of coffee to go with it. "Been a while since I cooked, but it shouldn't be too bad."

"Looks great." I dug in. It was.

"Got the drip in your showerhead done and the boards under the eaves. Won't nobody be sneaking in that way no more. However, while I was up there, I noticed some roof shingles missing. I can fix that too, if you like."

"Happened during the monsoons last August. If you think you can repair it, I'd appreciate it, Reggie. I'll give you the cash for the replacement shingles."

"My pleasure, Miss Jinx."

"There's a ladder in the garage. If you need anything else, let me know. You have a phone?"

Reggie pulled a silver flip phone from his pocket. "Got a prepaid. Not sure how many minutes left on it, though."

I opened his phone and put my info in his directory. "Now you got my number. Call if you need anything."

"'Preciate that. Where you headed today?"

"That big protest that White Nation's got going."

Reggie stopped with a forkful of grits halfway to his mouth and gave me a look. "You with White Nation?"

"No! I'm not *with* them. But the fugitives I'm chasing are. I'm going on the slim chance that they'll show up."

Reggie shook his head. "Them's some bad folks, hating on people for being different."

"Tell me about it. My gut tells me they were behind the shooting at the Main Drag."

"Main Drag? Whassat?"

"You didn't hear about it on the news?" I asked.

He shook his head.

It had completely escaped me that Reggie didn't know about me being queer. And despite being out to my friends and family for most of my life, coming out to someone new never got easier. "It's a club where drag queens perform."

"Like men in dresses?"

"Pretty much. Friend of mine owns the club. She was shot in the head."

I could see the wheels turning in his head, but I wasn't sure which way. "Sorry to hear 'bout your friend. She gonna be okay?"

"Not sure. She's in a coma."

"Terrible thing to happen during the holidays. Your friend, she a girl, right?"

"Yes. She's transgender. I am too."

"Transgender? What's that?"

"Started out as a boy on the outside, but on the inside I was a girl. When I was eleven, I transitioned to living as a girl."

He studied me for a moment. "You look like a girl."

I couldn't help laughing. "Well, yeah. That's 'cause I am one."

"You got girl parts? Down there I mean?"

"That's an awfully personal question to ask a relative stranger, don't you think?"

"Welp, I suppose it is. But since you're—"

"A human being," I said. "Just like you. Just because I let you stay doesn't mean I don't value my privacy."

He was quiet for a moment. "You're right. Ain't none of my business what you got between your legs."

"Now you're catching on."

"That boyfriend of yours. The one the feds are looking for. He a gay man?"

"Nope. He's straight as they come. Strictly attracted to women."

"And you a woman."

"Bingo!"

"You shore gave me a lot to think about, Miss Jinx. I ain't never met a transgender before."

"That you know of. There's a lot more of us than most people realize."

"I suppose you're right." He finished his coffee. "You best be careful at that rally. Them White Nation folks be crazy and fulla hate."

I gave him a wink. "I'm tougher than I look." I took my plate to the sink, went to my bedroom, and geared up. When I walked out in my Bail Enforcement body armor and tactical belt, Glock at my hip, and wraparound shades tucked into the collar of my shirt, Reggie gave me a whistle. "You look like you mean business, Miss Jinx."

I smiled. "See you after a while, Reggie."

An hour later, I parked in a surface lot on Adams and Twelfth Avenue and walked a few blocks to Wesley Bolin Memorial Plaza between the Arizona state legislative buildings and the state supreme court. The usually empty plaza was now a roiling mass of humanity. Streets were cordoned off for a half mile in every direction.

The plaza contained a dozen different memorials, ranging from an enormous anchor from the USS *Arizona* to a recent memorial for the Granite Mountain hotshots, nineteen fire-fighters who lost their lives fighting a blaze up near Yarnell.

The White Nation crowd was easy to spot with their Confederate and Nazi flags as well as a few flags I didn't recognize. I estimated the group size to be about a hundred, holding their ground around the main circle of memorials. A large portion of them wore black uniform shirts with white nationalist patches, assault rifles slung over their shoulders. Others were skinhead biker types with bomber jackets and chains. Klan-type hoods in a variety of colors poked up among the crowd. Some members stood with shields and helmets similar to those carried by police working riot control. Ninety percent of their ranks were men between the ages of thirty and fifty.

A sea of counter-protestors surrounded them, holding banners supporting diversity and denouncing racism. Uniformed patrol officers manned barricades that created a twenty-foot gap between the opposing sides. The air vibrated with the beating of drums, chants, and random shouts rife with profanity and threats.

The news media also got in on the excitement. Armed with video cameras and large microphones, they wandered the crowd to capture the dark carnival-like atmosphere to be repackaged as infotainment for hungry viewers.

My chances of finding either Pratt or Dietz in this angry sea of humanity were low. I didn't have either the time or energy to waste on this. I turned on my heels and pushed my way through the park.

Under the shadow of the colossal USS *Arizona* anchor on the east end of the plaza, I spotted a familiar figure. "Peyton!"

He turned as I rushed toward him. "Jinx! Wh-What are you doing here?"

"Oh, you know, fighting bigots. Punching Nazis. The usual. Where the hell's your dad?"

"I...uh...dunno."

"Bullshit! I know he reached out to you. Staying at the Lodestar Ranch, right? Where is that?"

His expression hardened into a warning. "Jinx, you should go."

"Why? Whose side are you on?"

"Doesn't matter. Get outta here. It's not safe. I-I don't want you to get hurt, okay?" The tone of his voice triggered a sense of foreboding.

"What's going to happen, Peyton? What's White Nation planning?"

His face turned to stone. "My father was right. I never should have dated you. You ruined my life."

"The fuck I did. You knew about my history before we ever dated. You told me it didn't matter."

"I was young and impressionable. You seduced me."

"I what?" I almost laughed at the absurdity. "You asked me out, remember? Everything was fine until your father tried to kill me."

"My father only tried to protect me from your depravity. You were nothing but a trap."

His vicious words cut me to my core. I felt as if I'd been sucker punched. "You're a piece of shit, you know that? Just like your dad. I'm going to put him behind bars if it's the last thing I do. And if you don't tell me now where he is, I'll send you there too."

"Go home, Jinx. Last warning."

I grabbed him and threw him against the base of the platform on which the giant anchor rested. Despite him being several inches taller than me, I had him off-balance. "This is your last warning. Tell me where he is right now or—"

Someone seized the back of my collar and yanked me away from Peyton. I whirled around, pinwheeling my arms to break my attacker's grip. I was about to go at him when I recognized Officer Evans—the same one who'd arrested me for shooting the guy at Dixie's.

"What the hell you doing, Ballou? How many times I gotta arrest you this week?"

I pointed at Peyton. "This man is protecting two wanted fugitives. It's my job to return them to custody."

"You lay one more hand on him, I'm arresting you for aggravated assault."

"Oh, so you *want* violent criminals walking the streets of Phoenix. Good to know! Fine cop you turned out to be, Evans."

"I'm warning you, Ballou. Walk away or I'll drag your faggoty little ass back to jail."

I glared at him. I needed to locate Pratt and Dietz, but I couldn't do it from a holding cell. I turned to Peyton and pointed at him. "You're gonna wish you talked."

"Come on, Peyton." Evans put his arm over his shoulder. "Don't know what you ever saw in that fucking fairy."

I stopped in my tracks, feeling as if someone had struck my chest with a hammer. *Fuck me. Evans was the third shooter at the Main Drag.*

I pushed my way through the raucous crowd, trailing Evans and Peyton and unsure of my next move. At the barricades for the counter-protest, Evans flashed his badge to an officer keeping the two sides separated. Evans and Peyton continued into the White Nation area.

If I reported what I knew to Detective Skoglund, would they do anything? I had no proof other than a vague memory of Evans's voice that night. And eyewitness accounts were unreliable. For all I knew, my mind could be filling in details just because Evans and the shooter both said, "Fucking fairies."

"Jinx! Jinx!"

I turned around, looking for who had called my name. Chelsea and Izzie from the L Street bar were pushing their way through the crowd.

"Hey!" I hugged them. "Crazy scene, huh!"

"I know, right?" Izzie's head was shaved on the left side, while the right side flowed in shoulder-length purple locks. "D'you hear what happened at the Main Drag last night?"

"I was there."

"Shit," said Chelsea. "You all right?"

"Better than most who were there. I..." I couldn't finish my sentence. And judging from their faces, I didn't need to. "Hey, sorry for getting trashed at the bar a few nights ago."

"No worries." Chelsea winked at me. "Lotta people in a funk this time of year."

Someone in the White Nation crowd began launching smoking canisters into the air.

"What the hell?" shouted Izzie.

One landed at my feet, spewing white smoke. The acrid scent of tear gas stung my eyes. I covered my nose with the inside of my arm and looked toward the source of the projectiles. Most of the counter-protesters backed away from the barricades. A few others picked up the canisters and threw them back at White Nation.

"Let's get out of here," I yelled to Izzie and Chelsea over the din, pointing toward the *Arizona* anchor. Coughing and wiping their eyes, they nodded.

Before we could take two steps, an explosion shook the air, nearly knocking me off my feet. Screams erupted as dark smoke rose from the now blackened and shattered USS *Arizona* anchor. Caught between the tear gas and the explosion, the crowd flowed north like a powerful ocean current. I moved with them to keep from getting trampled, losing Izzie and Chelsea in the process.

My mind raced with questions as I tried to make sense of what was going on. Was this what Peyton was warning me about? What had his father gotten him mixed up in? Conor's face appeared in my mind. Was this how he'd gotten involved with the IRA?

And why hadn't the feds believed me when I tried to warn them? Yes, my evidence was flimsy, but now people were dead. I took no joy in being right. Instead, I just felt sick and angry.

The panicked crowd snaked between buildings and began to thin around Monroe Avenue. I hustled east and crossed back to Adams on Fifteenth Avenue, where I'd parked.

I sat in the Gray Ghost, staring at the black column of smoke rising over the downtown area. Police sirens screamed like a chorus of coyotes.

What the hell was this world coming to? All the hope I'd once had of a kinder, safer world during the Obama administration had been crushed with the new politics of cruelty, apathy, and bigotry. Outright lies and absurd conspiracies were trotted out as truth. Stalwarts of journalism had abandoned investigation and objective reporting for an endless parade of political consultants and biased talking heads.

And now my high school boyfriend blamed me for his father's brutality. My current boyfriend was being hunted by the Northern Ireland police for the crimes of his youth. The world was upside down. I didn't know how to turn it right side up. But that didn't mean I wasn't going to try.

38

Too numb and shaken to drive, I dialed Detective Hardin's cell phone.

"Not now, Ballou," he said sharply. "Shit just hit the fan downtown."

"I was there, Hardin. That's why I'm calling."

"Where are you?"

"In a parking lot. Monroe and Fifteenth Avenue."

"Stay put. I'll send a uni to pick you up."

As I waited, I texted Becca and my brother to let them know I was okay.

Thirty minutes later, I was sitting in an interview room in the Phoenix PD Homicide Unit with Hardin after a patrol officer picked me up. He pulled out his notebook and asked me what I saw.

"When I was at the protest, I ran into an old friend. Peyton Dietz."

"Why's that name sound familiar?" Hardin asked.

"His father's Barclay Dietz."

He paused a moment, then nodded. "Barclay the Beast. He's

the one who assaulted you when you were a teen. Peyton was his kid, whom you were dating."

"I'm surprised you remember."

"I remember you had a lot of potential when you were a boot. I was disappointed when you quit the force." He looked up from his notes. "Is this Peyton kid connected to the bombing?"

"He told me to leave the protest, said he didn't want me getting hurt. When I pressed him why, your buddy Officer Mitch Evans intervened. Threatened to arrest me for assaulting Peyton."

"Had you assaulted him?"

"No. But Evans and Peyton seemed awful chummy. The two of them went over to where White Nation was staging their white nationalist temper tantrum."

"Seems a little thin, Ballou."

"There's something else. As the two of them were leaving, I heard Evans call me a 'fucking fairy.' It was his voice I heard the night of the Main Drag shooting. He was also first on scene when I tried to apprehend Barclay Dietz at that meeting at Dixie's Bar, where a White Nation meeting was being held."

"You're saying Evans was involved in both this bombing and the shooting? Those are some serious accusations with very little proof."

"Hey, I'm trying to help you out, doing my civic duty and all. If you don't want the info, fine by me." I stood up to leave.

"Hold on, Ballou. I'm not saying I don't believe you. But if you're going to be pointing fingers at a law enforcement officer—"

"An officer who's already shot an unarmed black man."

He held my gaze for a few minutes. The wheels were turning in his head.

"Look, Hardin, you know him better than I do. Is it really a stretch to believe he's involved with White Nation? I've given you a few leads you might not get anywhere else. Do with them what you want."

He called after me as I walked out. I didn't care. I'd done what I felt was right. Now it was on him.

I barely noticed the cold as I walked the mile back to where the Gray Ghost was parked. I was about to call Caden for a status update on Juanita when my phone rang. It was Becca with what I hoped was a new lead on either Pratt or Dietz.

"Becks, what've you got for me?"

"Jinx, you need to get home now."

"Why? What's going on?" Had Reggie fallen off the ladder trying to fix my roof? Would my homeowner's insurance cover that?

"I can't say over the phone." Her voice had an odd quality to it.

"You're freaking me out here. I barely survived that explosion downtown. Just tell me what the hell's going on." I had a flashback to when Milo Volkov had left the body of a dead journalist on my porch in a sick attempt to woo me. "Is my house on fire? Was there a burglary? What?"

"I...I can't say. Just trust me. Get home now."

A sick feeling spread through my body. Whatever it was, it sounded bad. But why couldn't she tell me? "Fine. I'm on my way. Are you there now?"

"No, but someone else is."

"Who?"

"Go."

I hung up and raced the Gray Ghost north along Seventh Avenue. No sooner had I crossed Fillmore Street than I noticed that damned Caprice tailing me again.

"Mother-goddamn-fucker, can't those feds leave me alone for once?" I swerved into a convenience store parking lot, tired of playing these silly games. The Caprice followed suit before parking a few spaces to my left.

I jumped out of the Gray Ghost and slammed the door shut. Time to give Special Agent Baby Face a piece of my mind.

As I approached, the Caprice's passenger window lowered. The barrel of a gun emerged from the dark interior. I ducked behind an ice machine as two rounds ripped through the air.

"What the fuck?" *When does the FBI shoot at people they're tailing? Answer: they don't.*

I drew my Glock, peeked around the ice machine, and unleashed a barrage of nine-millimeter rounds into my attacker's car. The Caprice's wheels smoked as it whipped around in reverse. I had enough time to put another two rounds into the trunk and read the license plate before it peeled out and disappeared down the street, tires screaming, engine roaring.

I looked around to see where the shooter's bullets had gone. Clouds of steam billowed from under the hood of a nearby Toyota.

A black man jumped out of the car. "What the hell? I just bought this car."

I wrote the Caprice's license plate on one of my business cards and handed it to the guy. "Call the cops. Tell them this is the car that the shooter was in. I'm going to go try to catch them."

"Hey, wait a minute, lady," he called as I hopped in the Gray Ghost.

There was no way I was going to catch the Caprice. It was long gone. But I still had an unknown emergency at home to deal with. So I floored it, honking for the slower cars to get out of my way. What the hell was going on? A house fire? Had White Nation attacked my house and hurt Reggie?

When I pulled onto my street, I looked for emergency vehicles, but there weren't any. No crowd of onlookers gathered in their yards. In fact, the street was as quiet as it usually was on a Saturday afternoon.

I pulled into my driveway and rushed in my front door to the sound of raised voices.

"For the last time, Miss Jinx's letting me stay here while I do a little repair work around the house." This was Reggie.

"If she needed repairs done, she woulda hired her brother to do it." *Fuck me.* Conor'd shown up finally. "So put down that whiskey bottle or I'll put a hole in ya."

"What the hell's going on?"

"Finally!" Conor said, holding a gun on Reggie. "Took yer bloody time gettin' here."

"I had stuff to deal with. Now what the fuck's going on, Conor?"

"Found this creepy bloke lurking in your yard, helping himself to my whiskey."

"Miss Jinx, would you tell this gentleman you asked me to fix your roof and that I could help myself?"

Good grief. Men. As if I didn't have enough shit to deal with.

I pointed at Conor. "You! Put away the gun." I turned to Reggie. "As for you, I said help yourself to food, not booze." I grabbed the bottle from him.

To Conor, I said, "You and me need to have a serious talk, mister."

Reggie guffawed, and both Conor and I told him to shut the hell up. I led Conor down to my bedroom and slammed the door shut.

39

———

"What the bloody hell's going on, Jinxie? Ya taking in strays and lodgers now? When I said you should get a pet, I didn't mean a scraggly git like that dodgy bloke."

I took a breath. "First of all, my house, my rules."

"The guy's a drunk."

"The guy has a name. It's Reggie. And just because he takes a drink doesn't make him a drunk."

"Oh yeah? And who's Reggie when he's at home? Or your home, I should say."

"I found him camping out in my attic. He's homeless." I held up a hand before Conor could interrupt. "He's been living here for a week already with no harm done."

"'Cept drinking my whiskey."

"For the record, it's my whiskey. I bought it just the other day. And I asked him to do some repair work on my house."

"And how long is he staying?"

"I don't know. But enough about Reggie. Let's address the real elephant in the room. Where the hell have you been? I haven't seen you since the shooting at the club."

His demeanor changed. In an instant, he looked like a deflated balloon. "They're onto me. PSNI and the feds."

"Yeah, I know. They showed up earlier this morning asking where you were. I didn't tell them shit."

"I'm so bloody sorry, love." He hugged me. It felt so good to be in his arms again.

"Any idea who tipped them off? It wasn't Sadie, was it?"

Conor shook his head. "I talked to one of my mates from Dark Horse Security. Apparently PSNI's working cold cases. Something to do with Brexit and wild rumors of Irish unification. Somehow they got hold of surveillance footage with me in it. Face recognition pulled up a possible match."

"After all these years? Damn." I shook my head. "So what's your plan?"

I didn't like the idea that I was harboring a fugitive wanted for an act of terrorism.

"Been staying with someone from way back who happens to be local."

"Who?"

"Best ya didn't know, in case they question ya again."

"Maybe you should come clean. You've been running for most of your life. Explain you never meant for anyone to get hurt. That you were told the wrong information. Besides, you were just a teenager at the time."

"I was seventeen, love. And they don't care what I was trying to do. That bloody phone call..." His words caught in his throat. "On the other hand, I don't want you gettin' messed up in this nonsense. I just...I hate to think I'd never see yer gorgeous face again."

"I could visit you in prison, maybe. They have bounty hunters in the UK?" It was a feeble attempt at humor, but it beat crying, which was what I felt like doing.

Conor's face turned deadly serious. "Traitors and terrorists aren't exactly greeted with open arms over there. Assuming they don't execute me, I probably won't last long in prison. But maybe that's what I deserve."

"No," I said, choking back tears. "I'm not going to let anyone hurt you. But you shouldn't be here. They've been watching the house. They've been tailing me."

"I know, but I had to see ya. I've been shite without ya, love."

"I've missed you too." He smelled of body odor and sweat. Nothing ever smelled so good to me. "I'm sorry for all the crap I said to you about not coming into the hospital."

"How's your mate, Juanita?"

"Not good. Still in a coma."

"I'm so sorry."

"Sometimes I wish I could just chuck it all and move away. Like to Canada or the UK. Some place where people aren't trying to kill each other all the time. Maybe Scandinavia. But I'd probably miss the sun too much. And I don't do real well in the cold."

"What about Spain?"

"Spain?" I looked to see whether he was kidding. But his face was serious, if a bit earnest.

"It's a warm, relatively dry climate, not that different from Arizona."

"You serious? Just pack up and leave?"

And that was when it hit me—why I didn't want to move in with him. We were bounty hunters, bound to return fugitives to custody. And yet he was a fugitive. If I moved in with him, I'd be no different than the people hiding their bail-jumping loved ones. I couldn't live with myself.

"Why not pack up and leave? It'll be an adventure."

"Adventure, my ass. Conor, that's crazy. What's to keep the Northern Ireland police from coming after you there?"

"Picardo can set us up with new identities. A whole new start." Picardo was a document forger who sometimes helped us with fugitives trying to leave the country. In exchange, we didn't turn him in to the cops.

"What will we live on?"

Now he grinned. "I have a sizable nest egg I set aside a while back in case I had to run."

"Like how big a nest egg?"

He shrugged. "Three, four hundred grand. Maybe a little more now. Been a while since I checked the balance."

"Three or four hundred grand? For doing what?"

"Combination of things. I made some good investments early on. I did some private bodyguard work for some Arab royalty after Iraq. They pay rather well, it turns out, especially when you're watching their kids."

"You're just telling me this now. I feel like I don't even know you."

"I'm someone who wants to live the rest of his life with the woman he loves."

"Conor...What about my family? My friends?"

His enthusiasm waivered. "Unfortunately, ya wouldn't be able to contact them. Not ever."

"Fuck." I sat on the bed, my head spinning.

"I realize it's a tough choice, love. I know how close ya are with your folks. But I can't stay now that they're onto me."

"I'm going to have to give this some thought." I looked into his eyes, as green as the first buds of spring. I felt I was being torn apart, forced to choose between the people I loved the most. "How long do I have to decide?"

"A couple days at the most."

"That's it?"

"I'll need some time to arrange documents, transport, and lodging, so the sooner you decide, the better. I don't know how long I can keep dodging that inspector from PSNI."

"I love you so much, Conor. But this is the hardest decision I've ever had to make."

"Maybe this will make it easier." He reached into his pocket and got down on one knee. "This isn't how I meant to do this, but now's as good a time as any."

He held a black velvet box that he opened to reveal an 18-karat-gold ring with a large diamond bordered by two emeralds.

"Holy fuck, Conor!"

"Jenna Christine Ballou, would ya do me the honor of becoming my wife?"

I struggled to suck in enough air to speak. "Conor, I...I...uh..."

"I know, it's last minute. But we've been dating a couple years. Your mother's been nagging ya about getting married for a while. If you're gonna run away with me, the least I can do is make an honest woman out of ya."

"Conor, I...this...fuck." My stomach knotted. "I want to say yes. You know I do. But it means giving up everything else."

"I know, but honestly, I can't live without ya." He put his hands on either side of my head and kissed me so deeply all I wanted to do was fuck his ever-loving brains out.

"I feel the same way."

My heart was hammering away like a piston. Could I give up my whole life for a man? I had reinvented myself once before when I became a girl at age eleven. But I had a lot of support then.

Here I was at thirty, looking at reinventing my world once more, assuming a new identity, and at the same time giving up all that support. It was insane. And yet one look into Conor's eyes and it felt as though it just might be worth it.

As my mind considered the possibilities, I imagined a completely new life and what that would do to my family. Before I could reply, my phone rang. It was Caden.

"Juanita's awake!" His voice rattled with a combination of exhaustion and joy.

"Seriously? What are the doctors saying?"

"She's really confused, but she can move her hands and feet. They have the infection under control. She's having trouble speaking and walking, but the neurologist said she might recover with therapy. Jinx, she's alive!"

Before I could stop myself, I was bawling from a combination of gratitude, guilt, fear, and who knew what else. Conor put a hand on my shoulder.

When I was finally able to speak, I said, "Caden, that's great. I...I can't believe it."

"You think you can come by this afternoon?"

"Yeah, give me about an hour or so, but I'll be there."

I hung up and shared the good news with Conor.

"I'm happy for her. I know how much she means to ya."

"I have to go see her, Conor."

He nodded. "I understand."

"Ask me again."

"Ask what—oh! That!" He knelt down again. Jenna Christine—"

"Yes! Yes! I will fucking marry you!" Maybe it was gratitude that Juanita was on the mend. Or maybe it was a reaction to the trauma of the past few days. Or maybe I'd gone completely insane. But all at once, I had no doubt about who I wanted to spend the rest of my life with.

He slipped the ring on my finger. It fit perfectly. Seeing it glitter in the light made me feel so girly, a feeling I could only describe as gender euphoria. Like the time my mother took me shopping for my first bra. I was going to get married. How weird was that? Me married. It didn't seem real.

"You think it's okay for me to wear? What if the feds and that inspector from Northern Ireland want to question me?"

"If they ask about the ring, tell them I proposed a few days ago. But if you think it will cause too much trouble, you can take it off until we're ready to leave."

I looked at it. "I'll leave it on."

"That's my girl. I'll reach out to Picardo and my other contacts to make the arrangements. And darlin', you're gonna love Spain."

40

———————

Conor slipped out the back door, and I found Reggie sitting in the corner of the living room, watching the news coverage of the bombing. Much of it was speculation and updates of body counts. So far, eight were confirmed dead.

"Hey, sorry about the confusion earlier," I said. "Conor's a bit protective with all the craziness going on."

"Man nearly kilt me. Pointed a gun at me."

"I'm sorry. It won't happen again. Last year, I had someone stalking me. People died. So when he found a stranger in my house, he went a little overboard."

"I'll say." He stared at the TV as a reporter interviewed someone. "You down there when that explosion went off?"

"I was." The euphoria I'd been riding evaporated as memories of the chaos returned. "White Nation set off the bomb after driving the crowd toward it with tear gas."

"You still in one piece, though, right?"

"I am." I sat down next to him. "My friend who's in the hospital just came out of the coma. I need to go spend some time with her."

"What about your man?" Reggie looked a little concerned.

"He has to run some errands, but he understands you're staying here for the time being. Shouldn't be a problem anymore."

"Well, let's hope not. I don't mind fixing your roof to help pay for my lodging and food, but ain't nothing worth getting shot at."

I caught myself looking at the ring. The emeralds reminded me of the green of Conor's eyes. I took off my ballistic vest and my utility belt, then secured the Glock in the small gun locker in my closet. I kept the revolver in my ankle holster just in case.

An hour later, I walked into Juanita's hospital room. The ventilator was out. White bandages peeked out from under the scarf on her head. Her face was blank as she stared at the television mounted across the room.

"Hey, look who it is!" Caden smelled of BO and looked as though he hadn't slept since the last time I was there.

Juanita turned to me. Her eyes narrowed for a moment, as if she were trying to remember who I was, then she gave me a faint smile. "*¡Mi'ja!*"

I blubbered up right away and gently hugged her.

"I'm so glad to see you, *tía*." I wiped my eyes and sat on my haunches, my head level with hers. "You had us all worried."

She nodded. "I worry."

The tears kept coming. It broke my heart to see her like this. I missed my sassy, sarcastic fairy drag mother. I hoped I would get to see her again before I left for Spain.

"They treating you all right here?"

She made a face. "Nurse *puta*. Kept waking me up."

"I'm sorry. They tend to do that in places like this."

"Doctor good, though. Knows her shit. Kept me alive." She turned to Caden and pinched her nose. "*Apesta.* Caden stinky."

Just like that, I burst out laughing. Caden covered his face in embarrassment, but I caught a hint of a smile.

"Yeah, he's a bit ripe. But considering he's been by your bedside nonstop for days, maybe we'll cut him a little slack."

One side of her mouth curled up in a grin. "Maybe slack."

I spent the next few hours with her while Caden ran home to grab a shower and a change of clothes. Someone brought in dinner, which consisted of chicken broth, Jell-O, and weak tea. Juanita drank half of the broth, turned her nose up at the Jell-O, and took a few sips of the tea. Not bad for a first meal.

When Caden returned, he noticed the ring on my finger. "Hey! Is that what I think it is?"

I blushed, a mix of embarrassment and guilt. "Conor asked me to marry him."

"Congrats, girl!" Caden hugged me. "Isn't that something, Juanita?"

"'Bout damn time," she whispered. Maybe she was in there after all.

"Speaking of time, I better be heading home. But I'll stop by tomorrow, okay?" I hugged her again, then Caden.

"You better, *mi'ja*."

I stepped out of the room and found myself getting choked up again. At this point, I didn't know what the hell I was feeling. The only word that came to mind was *overwhelmed*. I needed to put some cream on my burned hand and could use a few beers for the pain.

As I walked outside into the chilly early evening, my phone rang. No name came up on the caller ID, but it was a local number. "Hello?"

"Jinx?" asked a familiar voice.

"Who is this?"

"Peyton. Peyton Dietz." He was speaking in hushed tones.

"Well, well, Peyton Dietz. How's life as a Nazi terrorist?"

~

"I didn't know it was going to happen like that. I didn't think...I didn't realize people would be hurt."

"Then you're dumber than you look, Peyton. Bombs tend to have that effect."

"I tried to warn you. You should thank me for saving your life."

"Oh yeah, and what about the people you killed? Doesn't exactly make you a hero in my book."

"Jinx, we need to talk."

"You want someone to talk to? Try the cops or maybe the feds. I know an Agent Lovelace who'd love to chat with you."

"I need to talk with you, Jinx. Those things I said earlier, I didn't mean them. I was just trying to piss you off enough to get you to leave. Remember in high school, you and me watched that *Lassie* marathon on TV. That one episode where the ranger's coming to take Lassie away, so the kid tells Lassie he hates her."

"So in this scenario, I'm the dumb dog. Yeah, that makes things *so* much better."

There were voices in the background on his end of the line. He started whispering. "I still care about you, Jinx. I know my father's done some awful things. That's why I wanted to talk with you."

"Fine, so talk."

"Not on the phone. In person."

"In person? How stupid do you think I am? First you have no idea your father's in town. Next thing I know, you're planting a bomb that killed ten people. And now you want me to meet you? I know a setup when I see one."

"It's not a setup. And I wasn't the one that set the bomb."

The voices in the background got louder. Peyton spoke to whoever it was. The phone got bumped around until finally he came back on the line. "They're planning something big. I need your help to stop it. Please. I'll even help you bring my father in."

"Fine, where do you want to meet?"

"Take Carefree Highway and turn south on Fifty-First Avenue. It's basically a dirt road, but there's a sign. Go about a mile and it dead-ends at an old abandoned ranch."

A ranch, huh? The ranch. "When?"

"Tomorrow around eleven o'clock."

"I'll be there. But if this is an ambush, you *will* regret it, I promise you."

"It's not, I swear." The line went dead.

"Shit." I had every reason not to believe him, but in my gut, I felt Peyton was on the level. Still, who was I to stop White Nation's next act of terrorism? This was something better suited to the cops.

I dialed Hardin's number in Homicide. It rang twice before a male voice answered. "Detective Hardin's desk."

"I need to speak with Hardin."

"He's not available at the moment. Could I take a message?"

"Who is this?"

"Detective Loughlin. Who is this?"

I hung up. Last person I wanted to leave a message with was Loughlin after he'd arrested me for shooting Overcash. Chances were he was clean, if a bit too eager to arrest people for defending themselves. On the off chance that he, too, was in with White Nation, I didn't want to tip them off that Peyton had turned on them.

I called Hardin's cell number. After three rings, it went to voicemail.

"This is Ballou. Call me when you can. It's important."

It might still be a trap, but this proposed meeting with Peyton was now my best chance at catching his dad and possibly Rudy Pratt. But I didn't want to risk it alone. Safety in numbers and all that shit.

I called Rodeo first, though I knew it was a long shot. "What's up, Jinx?"

"How's the arm?"

"Not bad. Only hurts when I move it. Or when I think about it. Or when I'm sleeping. Basically all the damn time. How's your friend, Juanita?"

"She's awake. Docs are optimistic." I wanted his help meeting with Peyton, but if things got rough, he'd be more of a liability than an asset.

"Good to hear. Incidentally, Jake called, begging me to take him back and promising to work on his internal homophobia."

"Is that so? Who knew my brother had it in him."

"Seems someone gave him a good talking-to."

"Huh. I wonder who that could've been."

"I told him I'd give him another chance. So I guess we're un-broken up."

"I'm happy for you two."

"Thanks, Jinx. Jake's lucky to have you as a sister. I owe you one."

"You take care of that arm, Rodeo."

"Roger that."

I hung up and called Caden.

"Everything all right?" he asked.

"I got a call from Barclay Dietz's kid. He's offering to help bag his father. Wants to meet at an abandoned ranch off Carefree Highway and Fifty-First Avenue."

"Sounds like a trap."

"I thought so too. But my gut's telling me he's legit. You think you can step away from Juanita for a little bit tomorrow?"

"I think I can manage that. What time?"

"Meet me in the parking lot of the Ben Avery Shooting Range at twelve thirty. The meet's not until one, but I want to get there early. Just in case."

"Smart. I'll see you there."

A calm came over me as I drove home. I even caught myself humming Christmas tunes, which never fucking happened. I had no idea what I might face in my meeting tomorrow with Peyton. But with Juanita on the mend and this crazy ring on my finger, I couldn't help feeling hopeful, even cheerful.

When I walked in the door of my house, I found Reggie watching *A Christmas Carol*, the one with the guy who played Patton as Scrooge.

"I hope you don't mind, but I made a meatloaf for dinner. There's plenty left over if you hungry."

"Wow! You can fix roofs and you can cook? How come you're not already married?"

He laughed. "Yeah, who wouldn't want a homeless junkie for a husband?"

"Ex-junkie. You seem all right to me. Lot of people ended up homeless during the recession. Shit happens. Hell, if I wasn't already"—I almost said "engaged"—"dating someone."

"Girl, I'm old enough to be your grandfather."

"Father. Maybe. Look, we all got a past. Doesn't have to define us."

"Maybe you right."

"Conor around?"

"He snuck in the back door while back."

"Didn't give you any more trouble, did he?"

"Naw, not so far."

"Good. I'm going to freshen up a bit, and then I'll grab some dinner."

I walked into my bedroom and found Conor on the floor in the dark, typing away on a laptop.

"Peyton wants to meet tomorrow. Possibly a trap, but it may be my last chance to grab his dad. You in or are you still laying low?"

"You know I've always got your back. I'm in."

"Thanks. What are you working on?" I sat on the floor next to him and leaned my head on his shoulder.

"Plane tickets from Puerto Peñasco, Mexico, to Valencia, Spain. We should get our new passports in two days. What do you think of the name Eileen Anne Crawford?"

"Hmmm, I'm not sure it suits you."

He shoved me playfully. "Not for me, ya daft girl. For you."

"Sounds very British. Eileen Anne Crawford," I repeated in a posh British accent.

"Well, technically, you're Canadian."

"Am I?"

"At least according to your new passport."

The reality hit me like a clue-by-four. "Shit, this is really happening? Tomorrow may be the last time I see my folks." The excitement mixed with a deep sadness and guilt.

"It is. Having second thoughts?"

"A few. But I want to be with you. I just hope they'll understand."

"When I was a wee lad, my da told me about the American wakes."

"American wakes?"

"When someone in Ireland decided to venture to the New World, his family knew they'd not likely see them again. So they'd throw a wake, as if they were dying."

"Sounds very sad."

"Aye, a bit. But also happy for the lad or lass going on to new adventures in America."

"Did your family throw an American wake for you?"

"Not sure. They didn't know I was leaving."

"Are we going to have to keep doing this? Building lives, then running away?"

He kissed my forehead. "I bloody well hope not. From now on, I'll try to keep a lower profile than I have."

"Where will we live?"

"My mate Tuckey's working on securing us a villa in Valencia. You like the ocean?"

"I've been to the beaches in San Diego a bunch of times. It's okay. Water's too cold to swim in."

"Valencia is nothing like San Diego. Mediterranean is warm and beautiful. Not cold and clogged with kelp like the Pacific. Great music. Great food. Hot wom...well, that last part's not important anymore."

"Damn straight! You're gonna be a married man, Mister, uh, what is your name going to be?"

"Damien Ellsworth Crawford. Also Canadian."

"Yeah, well, you're going to need to do something about that Dubliner accent of yours."

"Hey, I can talk with a Canadian accent, eh?" The result sounded like a Southerner faking a bad Minnesota accent.

I burst out laughing. "That is the worst Canadian accent."

"Where's my tuk? Did I leave it in the washroom? How about some poutine?"

I laughed so hard I could barely breathe. "Oh...oh, shit, that's fucking horrible." Another spasm of giggles took hold of me until I was snorting. "I suppose I can't go wrong with a man who makes me laugh like that."

41

———————

The next morning, I showed up at my parents' place for Sunday brunch. Conor wanted to come, knowing this would be hard for me. But we decided that with him on PSNI's Most Wanted List, he should stay put.

Jake and Rodeo were already there when I arrived, looking like two teenage lovebirds who couldn't keep their eyes off each other. My mother doted on Rodeo because of his injured arm. My dad was busy cooking strawberry crepes, which were being eaten as fast as he could make them. When they asked about Conor, I told them he was on a stakeout that ran long.

Christmas music was playing on a radio on the kitchen counter, and the whole place was decked out for the holidays. The twelve-year-old artificial Christmas tree gleamed in the corner, covered in lights and decorations that dated back to my childhood and before. Some of the glass ornaments were at least a century old.

And while I tried to join in with the holiday spirit, an emptiness gnawed at me. Never again would I groan at my father's corny jokes or roll my eyes at my mother's nudges to have a family of my own. Jake would no longer ask me to help him reno-

vate a run-down house he was planning to flip. I wouldn't even be
spending Christmas with them, which was only ten days away.

After breakfast, I helped my father with the dishes. Despite
having a dishwasher, he preferred the "zen of washing them by
hand," whatever that meant.

"Dad, you know I love you, right?"

"Course I do, *cher*. Why would you ask?"

"Just wanted to make sure. Mom and Jake too."

He set down a glass and held my gaze. "Something wrong,
sweetie?"

"After what happened to Juanita, it got me thinking about
how quickly things can happen. I just wanted to make sure you
all know."

"You know we all love you, too, don't you?"

Tears pricked behind my eyes. "Yeah, I do."

"How's Miss Juanita doing, by the way?"

"She's out of the coma. Got a long recovery ahead of her, but it
looks hopeful. I think the worst is over."

"That's so good to hear. When you came out, we weren't sure
how best to help you. That girl, she really stepped up and became
a mentor for you. Your mom's been lighting a whole lotta candles
for her."

"Huh. I didn't think Mom liked her."

"I'll admit, your mother wasn't sure what to make of her. That
whole intense drag queen act and all. I think Juanita scared her a
bit."

"She can be a bit scary at times."

"But your mother saw how much Juanita helped, especially
with matters your mother and I didn't know much about—the
dysphoria, the misgendering, things that only a trans person
understands."

"Yeah." It made me sad all over again, thinking how much I
would miss Juanita. "She's something special."

The silence between us grew until my father said, "We

received a visit from the FBI the other day. A gentleman from Northern Irish police was with them, looking for Conor."

Shit. "Really?"

"Conor in some kind of trouble?"

"They have him confused with someone else," I said as convincingly as I could. "Kirsten, my attorney, is helping to straighten it out."

"Are you in some kind of trouble?"

He cupped my head in his hands. Worry troubled his eyes.

"I'm okay, Dad." He didn't look convinced. I hugged him. "I love you so much."

At eleven o'clock, I hugged them all again. I tried to act normal, as though I would be seeing them all again within the next week, if not sooner. But my heart felt like lead.

I cried all the way back to my place. I wiped my face before I walked in the house. Conor pulled on one of my spare Kevlar vests, with his Walther tucked in his waistband. I grabbed the Colt 1911 I'd taken off Daniel Warren. If things went sideways, I'd rather not have any spent rounds traced back to me.

Before we left, I checked outside to make sure there weren't any suspicious cars on the street. It was clear. No sign of the feds. Still, Conor kept low as I drove the Gray Ghost north to meet Caden at Ben Avery.

42

———————

Conor and I pulled into the Ben Avery Shooting Range parking lot a few minutes before Caden, who arrived decked out in his body armor and gear.

"How's Juanita this morning?" I asked as he approached the Gray Ghost.

"Pissed that she's on a clear liquid diet. Pissed that I had to leave. Pissed that you're not there."

"So pretty much her usual self."

He shrugged. "For the most part. Still having problems with speaking, walking, and some fine motor skills, but the doctors are optimistic that will come back with therapy."

"Good to hear." The fact that she was improving eased the guilt of my impending departure but only a little.

I pulled out a printed map of the area. "On to the business at hand. Peyton's only expecting me. He's supposed to come alone himself. However, I don't trust him. So Caden, I need you to be our lookout. I want you here, concealed if possible." I pointed at a spot on the dirt road for the ranch, just off Carefree Highway. "Give us a heads-up on the walkie-talkies when you see vehicles headed our direction."

"Roger that."

I turned to Conor. "You'll be with me down by the abandoned ranch. I suggest we leave Caden's car here in the shooting range parking lot so Peyton doesn't get spooked when he sees it. Any questions?"

We climbed into the Gray Ghost and drove the half mile down the road until we came to the turnoff. A short ways down the road, I stopped. Caden turned on his walkie-talkie, stepped out of the Gray Ghost, and took cover behind a cluster of palo verde trees.

Closer to the ranch, the gravel road deteriorated into a seldom-used Jeep trail riddled with ruts and creosote bushes. Other trails intersected it here and there, but we continued south until the trail dead-ended at the remains of an adobe building. Nearby, cracked wooden posts dangled from rusted barbed wire clinging to ocotillo plants in the corners of the corrals.

I backed up the Gray Ghost next to the ranch house. If things went south, I didn't want to waste time making a three-point turn.

Conor and I got out and inspected our surroundings. The roof of the ranch house was gone. The adobe walls were worn and crumbling from the brutal heat of countless summers and the intense storms of the monsoon seasons. A cracked wooden door hung from one hinge, squeaking in the slight breeze. Only fragments of glass remained in the windows.

"Why does this feel like high noon in some spaghetti western?" Conor asked.

"You've watched too many Clint Eastwood movies." But I felt it too. A sense of impending doom.

The radio squawked. "One bogie headed your way," called Caden. "Dark-red Honda sedan. Driver is a white male, no passengers visible."

"Thanks, Caden. That'd be our guy. Keep an eye out in case we have any unexpected company."

"Roger that. Over and out."

A dust cloud rose, and I spotted Peyton's Accord. I had my hand on the Colt. Conor drew his Walther and held it at his side.

Peyton pulled alongside the Gray Ghost and got out. He shuffled up to us, his eyes wary. "I wanted this to be just the two of us," he said to me. "Who the hell's this?"

I was tempted to say he was my fiancé. "Fellow bounty hunter. I needed to be sure you were on the level. And I wanted help bringing in your father. Where is he?"

"At a ranch near Cave Creek."

"He alone?"

Peyton stared at the dirt, kicking around a stone. "No. There are others there."

"So what's the plan, boyo?" Conor took a step toward Peyton. "Ya setting Jinxie up like ya did the other day with the bombing?"

"No!" Peyton backed away. "I never meant for anyone to get hurt! You have to believe me."

"Oh?" I approached him, my fists clenching. "And what did you expect would happen when you set off that bomb?"

"It wasn't me!"

"Then who the bloody hell was it, ya fucking wanker?"

I stepped into his personal space, forcing him to look up at me. "It was Evans, wasn't it?"

"Yeah, he's the one that left it by the anchor." His face colored. "They're planning another one. Bigger."

"Where?" I pressed.

"I don't know yet. They always speak in code. Site A. Site B. But wherever it is, I get the impression they plan to kill a lot of people. They said it'd be bigger than Oklahoma City. Maybe bigger than 9/11."

"When, ya little shit?" growled Conor.

"I don't know. But soon."

I shook my head. "You need to be telling this to the cops, Peyton."

He chuckled darkly. "The cops? Who do I tell? Evans *is* a cop. If they find out I talked, I'm a dead man."

"And yet you're talking to us," replied Conor.

"Because I thought I could trust you, Jinx. And you were always smart. I hoped you could stop them somehow."

"We're just bounty hunters, Pey. We're not the bomb squad or SWAT."

"Fine." He turned on his heel and shuffled back to his car.

I hustled after him. "Peyton, wait!"

He stopped and stood with his car door open.

"You help us arrest your dad, we'll see what we can do to stop this other bomb." I glanced at Conor. He had a disapproving look on his face.

"Can you bring him in alive? I know he's done a lot of bad things, but he's still my dad. I'm afraid if I went to the feds, they'd kill him." He looked as though he were about to cry.

I put a hand on his shoulder. "I don't think he'll come along quietly no matter who tries to bring him in. After what he did to me, I'd fantasized about killing him a gazillion times."

"I can't blame you. But I'm asking as a favor to me. If you promise not to kill him, I'll set it up so you can bring him in."

My radio crackled. "Jinx, we got two bogies inbound. A red pickup truck and a black sedan. Both coming in fast."

"You expecting anyone else?" I asked Peyton.

"No!"

"You're a fucking liar." Conor rushed him, putting his Walther to Peyton's temple.

"I swear I didn't tell anyone I was coming."

The staccato beats of automatic gunfire caught my attention.

"I'm taking fire," Caden shouted.

The gunfire ceased, replaced by the roar of engines.

"Caden!" I shouted into my walkie. "Caden, do you read me?"

No response.

Conor grabbed my arm and pulled me toward the ranch house. "Jinxie, we got to get to cover."

I followed him into the ruined adobe building and crouched

at a broken window, my Colt pointed at the rising column of dust. Conor took a position standing inside the door.

Movement caught my eye. Peyton was still out there.

"Peyton, get in here!"

He ignored me and instead walked past his car toward the approaching vehicles, waving his arms in the air. What the hell? Had he set us up? Or had he been followed?

A red pickup truck crested a small hill. In the bed of the truck stood a man armed with a large assault rifle.

"Peyton, get your ass in here!"

The guy in the back of the truck opened fire. Peyton's body exploded in a blast of red.

Conor and I returned fire. The gunman turned to us. The ground shook as bullets peppered the adobe wall. I fired until the gunman's chest blossomed red and he collapsed in the truck bed. The pickup veered off and turned back the way it had come, then passed the black sedan roaring down the trail.

The sedan skidded to a stop. It looked like the Caprice that had opened fire on me the day before. The dust became a wall, engulfing the cars and the old ranch house. Everything outside the building became an eerie tan shadowland. Gunshots pinged off the side of the building. I raised my pistol to return fire only to realize the slide was locked back. I was empty.

As I ducked behind the wall to reload, Conor yelped and fell. I rushed to his side. He lay in the doorway, gripping his chest. I pulled him out of the line of fire as the bullets hit all around me.

"You okay?" I gasped, not finding any blood.

"Aye. Bloody bastard got me in the vest." He pulled himself to his feet.

Voices outside caught my attention. "Shit." I peeked out the doorway. Two figures emerged from the car as the dust thinned. I fired at the taller of the two. The other figure fired and dove back into the driver's seat. His shots went wide. I continued firing, but the Caprice whipped around and sent a shower of dirt and rocks in my direction as it charged back down the trail.

43

I approached the figure I had shot and immediately recognized him as Officer Evans. Blood pooled around his body. My first two shots had hit dead center, the third in his throat. My ears rang from the sudden silence and from the realization that I had killed a cop. A dirty, murdering, racist cop but a cop nevertheless. I was in a shitload of trouble unless I could prove he was dirty and that I had acted in self-defense.

Conor came up from behind me. "Looks like ya got the fucker. Good shooting, love."

"He's the cop who set off the bomb at Wesley Bolin Plaza."

"Shite! Bloody wanker. Glad ya got him." He kicked the body.

"We need to check on Caden and...and Peyton."

Conor gave me a look. "I'll see to Caden. You check on your boyfriend."

"Ex-boyfriend!" I shouted as he hustled off the Jeep trail.

I found what was left of Peyton lying on his back, his blood soaking into the sand. I checked for a pulse but knew there wouldn't be one. He was already cool to the touch.

"Fuck, Peyton. What'd you get yourself mixed up in?"

I didn't want to cry. I shouldn't be crying. He hadn't been my boyfriend in over a decade. I tried to tell myself I was just wiping sweat and dust from my eyes. My heart ached as I squeezed his pale, cold hand.

After a while, the rational part of my brain kicked in. I needed to find his dad and Rudy Pratt. I rummaged through his pockets and found a phone, a set of keys, and his wallet. I kept the phone, hoping it might help me track down my fugitives. The rest I stuffed back into his pockets.

"Jinx? Ya there?" Conor called on the radio.

I wiped my face again. "I'm here. How's Caden?"

"He has a through-and-through on his right thigh. It's bad. Using a belt to stop the bleeding, but he needs medical attention now. How's the ex-boyfriend?"

"Dead. I'm coming to you." I took a final glance at Peyton. I hated leaving him for the vultures and the ravens, but there was nothing else to do.

A couple of bullets had torn through the Gray Ghost's rear seat but hadn't hit anything mechanical. I raced up the dirt road, passing another body I assumed was the shooter from the truck.

I skidded to a stop by the palo verde trees, where Conor was tending to Caden, and hopped out to assist. Caden was groaning and gritting his teeth. His skin was pale. Conor had pulled off his vest and was using his shirt and belt as a makeshift tourniquet to stop the bleeding from Caden's leg.

I tossed Conor's vest into the Gray Ghost. "How's he doing?"

Conor looked worried. "Lost a lot of blood from the exit wound. We gotta get him to hospital fast."

"Nearest one's Deer Valley. Let's get him in the truck."

"How you holding up, Caden?" I asked as we set him into the back seat of the SUV.

"Fucking goddamn hurts," he whimpered, draping his arm over his face. Conor knelt on the floor and snapped the seat belts to hold Caden in place.

I jumped behind the wheel. "We'll get you to the hospital soon, okay?"

"No." He gulped air, trying to get a grip on the pain. "Last time, they kept calling me ma'am. Treated me like a freak."

"Look, mate," said Conor. "You'll die if ya don't get proper medical attention."

"Mika from the support group," Caden grunted. "She's a doc."

"She's a fucking psychiatrist, Cade. You need a trauma surgeon." I jammed my foot hard on the accelerator, fishtailing onto Carefree Highway and hoping I didn't get pulled over by a cop. My mind raced for ideas. "Reggie served as a corpsman in the Marines back in the day."

"Are ya daft? You're gonna trust Caden's life to that free-loading bum?"

"You got any better ideas?" I shot him a look.

"All due respect, love, I spent enough time in Afghanistan and Iraq to know corpsmen just bandage people up long enough to get 'em to a proper surgeon. That's what we're doing. Your mate Reggie can't fix this."

"Fine. Deer Valley it is."

"No! Please," Caden yelled, his voice hoarse and ragged. "I'd rather die than get treated like that again."

I understood how he felt. Most medical personnel were cool, but some were so judgmental and shaming they made you want to slit your own wrists.

"Don't worry, Caden," I said. "We won't let them treat you like that again."

"Just hope he doesn't bleed out before we get there," snapped Conor.

At the on-ramp for the Black Canyon Highway, we passed two county sheriff's cars with lights and sirens, racing back the way we came. Neither turned and came after us, thank the stars, because I wasn't stopping and didn't want to turn this into a wild police chase.

I screeched to a halt in the ER pass-through, and Conor and I carried Caden through the sliding glass doors. As soon as medical personnel had Caden on a gurney, a woman in business attire approached asking questions about Caden and what had happened. Before long, police officers would be there asking the same questions and more. I wasn't prepared to answer questions that would connect us to their dead racist colleague a few miles away.

I told her I needed to park the truck in the lot and we'd be right in to provide her with answers.

We hustled to the Gray Ghost, tears running down my face. Once behind the wheel, I got back on the southbound Black Canyon Highway.

Guilt felt like a millstone on my chest. I hated myself for abandoning Caden to the care of strangers. First thing, they'd cut off his pants and shorts, only to discover he was trans. I could only hope they'd treat him with more dignity than they had the last time. I needed to focus on finding my fugitives and getting the hell out of town.

"Where we headed, Jinxie?"

"Home."

"Not a good idea, love. There were security cameras at the entrance to the ER. Won't take the cops long to connect Caden getting shot with what went down at that old ranch. And then to me and you."

"Suppose you're right."

"I'm sorry, love."

"Not your fault."

"Ya all right?"

"No." Tears made it hard to see the road.

"I'm sure he'll make it. He's a tough lad."

"Hope so."

"You want me to see if Picardo's got our new docs ready a day early?"

"I gotta find these fuckers and take them down." Sorrow squeezed my heart.

Conor put a hand on my leg. "You've done all ya can. Meeting with Peyton didn't accomplish anything. Maybe it's time to throw in the towel on this one."

"After what they did to Juanita, Rodeo, and now Caden and Peyton, I'm not gonna stop until I bring the whole lot of them down."

"Jinxie, I understand you're pissed, but we're not equipped to take on all of White Nation. It's not our bloody fight anymore. It's bigger than just the two of us."

"Then call Deez and the rest of your crew."

"I can't put anyone else in danger."

"People are already in danger. Didn't you hear..." My voice choked. "Peyton. Bigger than Oklahoma City."

"I understand, but that's for the FBI to handle. And ATF and all those other three-letter organizations. You and me just need to get outta town."

"That's always your answer, huh? When the heat gets too much, just cut bait and run."

"Maybe it is. But I'm only thinking of you."

I pulled off at the Camelback Road exit, sat at a red light, and stared down at the blood on my hands and clothes. Peyton's phone felt like a lump in my pocket. I pulled it out. It was a flip phone, the kind often sold as a burner.

I grabbed my own phone and called Becca, hoping she could somehow use Peyton's burner to lead us to this Lodestar Ranch. The call went to voicemail, and I left a message for her to call me. The light turned green, and I turned left onto Camelback.

"What's the plan, love?" asked Conor.

"No idea."

"Where are we headed?"

"No idea."

He put his hand on mine. I resisted the urge to push it away. My phone dinged. I glanced at it, hoping it was Becca. Instead, Reggie had texted, "Cops looking for you. Didn't tell them nothing."

"Shit. Cops are at my house."

"That's it. Turn south on Central when you come to it. There's a tattoo parlor on McDowell, across the street from Grumpy's Bar and Grill."

"Tattoo parlor?"

"You'll see."

44

———————

It was about five thirty when we pulled the Gray Ghost into the parking lot of the Prowling Tiger tattoo studio on McDowell, one street south of Conor's place.

"I wasn't aware getting new ink was part of the escape plan."

"We're not getting any new ink," he said with a grin.

"Then what?"

I followed him into the tattoo studio. In one of the chairs, a man with long hair, multiple piercings, and a full tableau of ink across his body was working on a female client.

"Weevil!" said Conor in greeting.

"Danny boy! How's it going?" The two of them went through a series of handshakes, grips, and a fist bump.

"Good."

"Who's the pretty lady?" Weevil cast a smile in my direction, and I felt undressed.

"Weevil, this is my old lady, Jinx!"

"Nice to meet you, uh, Weevil." I reached to shake his hand.

"Pleasure's all mine, Miss Jinx." He kissed my knuckles.

"Need to use the back door, mate." Conor pointed at the back of the shop.

Weevil raised an eyebrow. "Expecting company?"

"Yeah, but it bloody hell ain't Father Christmas."

"You need backup?"

"Naw, we got it covered, but thanks."

"Keep it real, man." Weevil went back to work.

I followed Conor through a curtain and past a storage room full of ink and other supplies. "Danny Boy?" I asked with a chuckle.

Conor shrugged. "It's what he calls me." He moved aside a mop bucket to reveal a metal plate in the floor with a keyhole. He pulled out a set of keys, inserted one in the lock, and lifted the plate to reveal a three-foot-wide hole in the floor. A ladder disappeared into the pitch-black hole.

"Are you shitting me?"

Conor climbed down into the darkness and switched on a light. "Come on. It's safe."

I followed him down. Ten feet below the tattoo studio, a tunnel led off to the north, lit by bare bulbs set in the solid concrete wall. "This tunnel leads to your place?"

"Clever girl. When I was a teen working with the IRA, a bloke named Gerry McFadden told me that rabbits always have multiple entrances to their burrows. In case one gets blocked, there's always a way out. Or *in,* as the case may be."

I gazed in amazement down the length of the tunnel. "Doesn't it flood during monsoon season?" I asked.

"It's fairly watertight." He beamed. "Brilliant, eh?"

"How the hell'd you build this without anyone finding out?"

"One of my mates from Dark Horse Security knows a lad who builds these things. I did him some favors."

"Do I want to know what kind of favors?" I asked hesitantly.

"Just some security work. Nothing black ops or anything."

"And why am I just learning about all of this? I thought you'd told me all of your secrets."

Conor stared at his feet for a moment then up at me. "I hate keeping secrets from ya, love. But a few things like this are on a need to know. And you didn't. Least not at first."

"We've been dating for two years!" My voice echoed along the corridor.

"Aye, we have. It just never came up."

"Anything else you haven't told me?"

He shook his head. "That's the last of my secrets, love."

We reached the end of the tunnel. A series of rungs built into the wall rose to another trapdoor. Conor inserted a key into the lock and pushed it open. He vanished for a moment and flicked on a light.

I followed him up and found myself in his coat closet. "Okay, I admit this is kinda cool."

"Thought you'd like it, seeing as how you're into superheroes."

We stepped out into the hallway to his bedroom. The windows were covered with his security shutters, leaving the place dark. He turned on a bedside lamp. Without thinking about it, I pulled off my vest and utility belt and curled into a fetal position on the bed. Conor snuggled in behind me, cradling me in his arms.

"I wish I could make it all better for ya, love."

"I know. But you can't. Maybe no one can."

I opened myself up to a storm of emotions I'd been struggling to contain for the past few days and sobbed uncontrollably for ten minutes. My whole world felt as if it was coming apart and me with it. But for the first time in days, I felt safe.

When I was cried out, I turned around and faced Conor. He wiped my face and kissed me. He became the light at the end of a very dark tunnel, the fragile strand connecting me to what was left of my sanity. He reached under my shirt as his kisses drifted to my throat. I pulled off my shirt and bra. Conor slipped out of his clothes, then teased my hardened nipples with his tongue, sending me into the stratosphere of ecstasy. My mind swirled as I shimmied out of my pants.

The firmness of his body coupled with the soft ginger curls covering his chest washed away the last of my worries. I ached to feel him inside me. But Conor took his time, leaving a trail of kisses down my stomach to the inside of my thigh. I gripped the hair on his head tightly, knowing if I didn't, I might go spinning off the earth into space.

He parted my labia with his tongue, teasing my clit, while squeezing my ass with his strong hands. My breath grew ragged. I pressed my pelvis into his face. I wanted to beg him to fuck me, but I couldn't form words.

As if he read my mind, he squeezed on some lubricant and pressed himself inside me. His face was next to mine again, and I kissed him hard as we thrust toward one another. He tasted like me.

I squeezed him hard and pressed his ass to drive him deeper into me. I was so close. His face contorted in pleasure, and I knew he was too.

"Oh, baby, yes," I whispered. A couple more hard thrusts and my brain short-circuited, as if it had been Tasered. My entire body contracted in orgasm so hard it almost hurt. I felt him release inside me. My heart raced like a hummingbird's. I felt at once as light as a feather and at one with the earth below me. "Thank you."

He peppered my face with gentle kisses. "You will always be my love."

The next thing, I knew my eyes fluttered open. We had fallen asleep. A small clock told me it was after five in the afternoon.

The sorrow, guilt, and anger raged like a storm that was miles away. For the moment, I floated on a cloud of bliss and gratitude. And for the first time in a week, I felt hopeful. I would find a way to stop White Nation from detonating another bomb. And I would bring both Rudy Pratt and Barclay Dietz to justice.

A while later, we got up and fixed a light dinner. I sent a text to Becca with a list of numbers on Peyton's burner phone, asking if she could narrow down a location, ideally in the Cave Creek area. She replied that she would get back with me as soon as she had something.

I wanted to do more research, but my printouts were back at my place. Only a few streets north of me, and they might as well have been across the country for all the good they did. I tried to study a few of the documents Becca had sent me over the past week on my phone, but they proved useless.

When I was at my wit's end trying to locate this mysterious Lodestar Ranch, I dared a phone call to Deer Valley Medical Center. I told the person on the other end of the line that I was Caden's mother and that I'd just heard he'd been injured. I was transferred.

"Hello?" asked a weak voice.

"Caden, it's Jinx."

"Where are you guys?"

"Sorry, man. But we couldn't stay. Too much heat on both of us. How's the leg?"

"Hurts like a fucker. Broken femur. Damage to several major blood vessels, which I can't remember the names of. Femoral artery was okay, though. Got so much metal holding my leg together I could open a Hardware SuperCenter."

"Glad you're alive, at least. How's the staff been?"

He actually giggled. "I think a couple of the nurses have the hots for me."

"Ever the ladies' man." I managed to smile. Damn, I was gonna miss him. "What'd you tell the cops?"

"Told them I don't remember much. Last thing I remember, I was out hiking near the Ben Avery Shooting Range, since that's where my car was. They asked me about the shooting by the abandoned ranch. I told them I didn't know anything about that. I think they bought it, but don't know for sure."

"Okay, man. You get better. We'll see you soon."

"Thanks, Jinx, for saving my life."

A lump formed in my throat. "Any time."

It was only eight o'clock, but Conor and I crashed not long

after my call to Caden. A few hours later, my phone rang. Caller ID revealed it was my friend Amber.

"Sorry to call so late, Jinx, but I have some information on those two guys you're looking for. My friend Chloë says they and a couple other guys came in earlier this evening. That ex-boxer invited her to come up to some ranch near Cave Creek. Lodestone or something like that."

"Lodestar?"

"Yeah, that's it. Lodestar. She went up there with them and partied for a bit. But then she got real creeped out when she recognized them from the photos I'd shown her. She made an excuse to use the bathroom and got the hell out of there."

"She get an address?"

"Yeah." She gave it to me and sighed. "Jinx, from the way she talked, these are some freaky guys. And not the fun kinda freaky. More like crazy, dangerous freaky."

"Don't worry. This is what I do. Thanks for the tip. Tell your friend Chloë to keep a low profile for the time being. Especially since they know where she works."

"Thanks, Jinx. Be careful, sweetie. I want you in one piece when I give you your lap dance."

I hung up and woke Conor. "We got an address."

45

I used Conor's laptop to locate the ranch on Google Maps. The ranch was a few miles northwest of the town of Cave Creek.

The satellite photo revealed a large main house, roughly three thousand square feet, if I had to guess. A second building that looked like a garage stood about fifty feet away. A dirt parking lot separated the two. Both buildings sat at the base of a small hill.

I printed out a copy of the map and stuffed it in a pocket in my ballistic vest. "Let's do this," I told Conor.

Conor opened his walk-in closet to reveal his personal arsenal of pistols, rifles, knives, and box after box of ammunition. My own arsenal wasn't nearly as impressive, but then, I didn't usually take some of the bigger jobs he did.

"For the record, I'm still pissed off you didn't tell me about your secret tunnel until now," I said as I loaded two spare magazines for my Glock. "We've been dating for two years, for fuck's sake."

"Aye, we have, love. But if the feds or the Brits ever interrogated you about my past, the less ya knew, the better." He pulled out a green duffel and loaded it with weapons, ammo, and related gear.

"Conor, they did interrogate me. I told them nothing. I can't believe you couldn't trust me."

He stopped what he was doing and turned to me, clearly crestfallen. "I hate ya had to go through that for me. If I had to do it over again, I never woulda gotten involved with the bloody IRA." He shook his head. "I've been working my whole life to make up for it. To make the world a better place than I found it."

I took him in my arms. "You're a good man, Conor Doyle. I wouldn't have agreed to marry you otherwise."

A loud rumble outside caught my attention. At first I thought it was one of those new jets from Luke Air Force Base, but the rumble intensified.

"What the hell's going on outside?"

Conor opened the laptop on his desk and pulled up his security feed. Several black trucks with "FBI" on the sides had pulled up in front of the house, choking the street. Blue lights were blazing.

"Holy shit! How'd they know we were here?" I asked.

"My guess is your phone."

My stomach sank. "Shit. Can they do that?"

"They're here, aren't they?" Conor replied, grim-faced.

A woman in a ball cap and body armor stepped between the vehicles, holding a bullhorn. It took me a moment to recognize her. Lovelace.

"Liam O'Callaghan and Jenna Ballou, we know you're in there. Come out with your hands behind your head. No one needs to get hurt."

"Not gonna fucking happen." Conor went back to loading his duffel bag.

The reality of our situation sank in as it never had before. I was in love with a wanted man. And if I ran away with him, I too would be a wanted fugitive. We were Butch Cassidy and the

Sundance Kid. Or Thelma and Louise. It hadn't worked out well for any of them.

"What's the plan?" I asked, feeling my pulse quicken.

He zipped the duffel closed. "Go out the way we came. Then you and me are going to grab your fugitives. You're going to take them down to lockup. If you get stopped by the feds, tell them you haven't seen me. That you only stopped by to feed my fish."

"You don't have any fish."

"They don't know that."

Just as he said that, my phone rang. There was no caller ID.

"Don't answer that," he warned, but it was too late. I'd already pressed Accept.

"Yeah," I said.

"Ms. Ballou, this is Special Agent Lovelace. You and your boyfriend need to surrender right now. Or we will come in there and get you."

"What are you talking about, Lovelace?" When in doubt, play dumb. "I just stopped by Conor's place to feed his fish."

"Don't fuck around with me, Ballou."

"You've got the wrong man, Lovelace. Conor's from Dublin. He didn't set off that bomb in Northern Ireland."

"He's welcome to tell that to DCI Collier. I'm giving the two of you one minute to come out. After that, we're coming in."

I met Conor's gaze. He had slung the duffel over his shoulder. "Hang up," he mouthed silently.

"Fine, Lovelace. Just give us a few minutes. This may be the last time I get to see my boyfriend." I hung up and pulled the battery out of my phone.

"Let's go," I said.

"I'm not surrendering." His face was firm.

"No," I replied. "*We're* not."

46

———

We returned to the coat closet. The top of the trapdoor was covered with a square of carpeting that matched its surroundings. No wonder I'd never noticed it before.

He reached into his pocket, then patted himself all over. "Shite! Where's my bloody keys?"

"They must be in the bedroom. Hang on, I'll get them." I hurried to the bedroom and scanned everywhere for the keys. Outside, a SWAT team was moving into place, armed with assault rifles, a very heavy-looking battering ram, and what appeared to be some sort of launcher, most likely for teargas. Lovelace was making more demands over the bullhorn, but I ignored her.

"I can't find them, Conor." I searched the bed, the closet, the bathroom.

The pounding of the battering ram on the front door rattled my teeth. These guys were serious.

Conor rushed into the room. "They've got to be here somewhere."

"We got no time."

"The door's reinforced with steel rods that go into the floor and ceiling. It'll hold for a little while."

I checked behind the nightstand. How could he lose his keys in a room with so few furnishings? I bent down and looked under the bed. "Bingo!" I handed him the keys just as something smacked hard against the window. Concentric fractures appeared in the Plexi, but the window didn't shatter. Outside, clouds of smoke billowed from a teargas canister that had failed to penetrate.

"That'll teach 'em," Conor said with a chuckle.

He unlocked the trapdoor and sent me down first. I descended into the tunnel, then helped him lower the duffel bag. It weighed a ton. He shimmied down the ladder in a flash.

"Do you need to lock it?" I asked.

"It relocks automatically. Now let's move before they breach the front door."

Moments later, we emerged from the tattoo studio, giving Weevil a wave. The acrid scent of teargas drifted across the parking lot from Conor's place. We hopped in the Gray Ghost and drove east to the I-17. It was after midnight, so traffic was light.

"I'm worried about my family," I said as I cut around a slow-moving Kia Sportage. "What are they going to think when I just disappear without saying goodbye?"

But I knew what they'd think. They'd assume I'd been killed or kidnapped or something worse. The image of my mother grieving my loss cut me deeply.

Even if the feds told them I'd run away with a wanted fugitive, would my folks believe them? The situation sounded like a rock ballad from the 1980s that my dad listened to sometimes. Styx or Queen or one of those groups.

"When we get to where we're going, you can write them a letter. I can make arrangements to have it delivered in a way that won't be traced back to us."

I felt a glimmer of hope. "I can write to them?"

"Once. Maybe twice. Any more than that, you risk exposing us, and we'd have to relocate all over again."

"I understand."

He took a deep breath. "If ya'd rather stay, I'd understand. I'd miss ya like hell, but I'd understand."

"You still want to get married?" I didn't know why I asked. The question just pushed its way out.

From his expression, my question clearly caught him by surprise. "Wha? Are ya daft? Of course I want to marry ya. Ya still want to marry me?"

"I do. I just never imagined it'd be like this. I don't even know what brides wear in Spain. Do you?"

A smile crept across his face. "Got no bloody idea, love. But whatever you wear, you'll look smashing."

It was almost one in the morning by the time we reached Cave Creek, where large homes gave way to the desert foothills with little but creosote bushes, cactuses, and large outcroppings of rocks stained black by the weather. Out here, coyotes, bobcat, and javelina roamed freely, largely unmolested by humans.

The landscape was dark in a way that Phoenix never was. Homes were spread out. Much of the glow of the city was blocked out by rolling terrain. What little light there was came from the moon rising in the east.

We parked on a side road a mile from Lodestar Ranch. Our first goal was to surveil the area from the top of the hill to get a feel for who was there.

Conor hefted the duffel onto his back like a pack and led us around the perimeter of the property, navigating by GPS to the top of the hill. The buildings lay quiet below us. Three vehicles sat in the parking lot, including the dark-blue Caprice and the pickup truck from our failed meeting with Peyton. A dirt driveway stretched into the darkness toward the main road.

Above us, Orion the Hunter hung from the heavens, searching for his quarry. I wasn't much of an astronomer, but Orion was one of the few constellations I could recognize. And being a hunter of sorts, I took its presence in the sky as a good omen. Not that I was superstitious or anything.

"Wish I'd packed a sweater," I said as the night's chill sent goose bumps on my arms.

"There's a windbreaker in the duffel," Conor said.

I pulled out a windbreaker with the logo of Conor's company, Viper Fugitive Recovery, printed on the left breast. It wasn't much, but it cut the chill to bearable levels.

Moonlight glinted off the stones of my engagement ring. *Am I ready to walk away from everything and everyone in order to live a life on the run with the man I love? A man with layers and layers of secrets?*

I felt so strongly pulled in opposite directions I thought I'd rip in two. "Ambivalence" was what my father called it. Not apathy but rather being torn apart by powerful yet opposing needs.

My father would no doubt accept whatever I did. My leaving would crush my mother. And Jake, I honestly didn't know how he'd react. Becca would be pissed off, as would Juanita. Could I survive without the safety net of people who'd supported me through so much? My transition, breakups, and career changes?

I studied Conor's moonlit figure as he watched the ranch through binoculars. He had rebuilt his life a time or two. If he could do it, perhaps I could too.

47

We watched the place in silence for about fifteen minutes. A few interior lights were on at the front of the house. The back of the building was dark. No one walked outside. No one drove up. The place was quiet.

At one point, a pack of coyotes starting yipping, no doubt over a kill. A rabbit or such. Their chorus would rise to a crescendo and suddenly drop off to a few random yips until the whole thing started over again.

There was something primal in their cries, something terrifying, though I knew we were in no danger. It haunted me and called to the darkness in my own soul. Something in my hunter brain awoke. A need to hunt, to subdue, to kill. A need for blood.

When the pack of canines finally ended their feral symphony, I stood up. My butt was cold and numb from sitting on a rock. I put away the binoculars and stuffed them in Conor's duffel.

"I'm going down there for a closer look," I announced. The moon was high overhead. It was bright enough that I could negotiate down the mountain without tumbling off a boulder or walking into a cholla cactus. At least I hoped so.

"I'll join you," he replied. "I wonder what's in that garage." He zipped up the duffel and heaved it onto his back.

"The garage? Why?"

"Your boyo said White Nation's planning to detonate another bomb. Something bigger. If it were me, that garage would be the ideal place to put it together."

"Why?"

"It's away from the main house, for one. When my da and his mates were putting together bombs for the IRA, that's the kinda place they'd use."

"I'm not here for the bombs. I'm here for Pratt and Dietz."

"Jinx, if those bombs are in there and they go off, killing God knows how many, how are ya gonna feel if ya done nothing to stop 'em?"

I wanted to tell him he was wrong. But he wasn't. I might not have been a cop anymore, but protecting innocent people was a strong part of my moral compass. Making a buck by bringing in fugitives came second to that.

"Fine, we'll see what's in the garage. If there are bombs, then what?"

"I'll try to disarm the bloody things."

"Disarm them? Since when are you in the disarming-bombs business? You could get yourself killed and me along with you."

"I learned a lot watching my da. Also did a wee bit of bomb disposal when I worked with Dark Horse in Iraq and Afghanistan."

"I thought you worked as a bodyguard with Dark Horse."

"Aye, that was the official line. But our duties were often a bit more involved. They trained us to handle all kinds of situations we might face in our protection duties. And let me tell ya, it came in handy more than once. IEDs were as thick as scorpions over there."

"Fine. Let's go see what's down there. But once you've disarmed the bombs, if there are any, I'm going next door to find my fugitives."

The climb down toward the buildings was steeper than our approach around the outside of the property. At one point, I was a step away from a ten-foot drop. It wouldn't have killed me, but a broken ankle would have seriously wrecked our plans.

It was two thirty by the time we reached the garage. The large overhead doors were closed with no way to open them from the outside. Our only way in was a side door, which was also locked.

"Shite! Left my picklocks at home." Conor shook his head in disgust.

"No worries," I said with a smile. "I've got mine."

I retrieved the leather pouch from my tactical belt and unzipped it. Conor held out his hands expectantly.

I shook my head. "I can handle it, big boy."

He chuckled and turned toward the main house, drawing his Walther. "Aye, that ya can, love."

It took me a couple of minutes to defeat the seven-pin lock. As soon as I opened the door, Conor shuffled in behind me. I looked around for signs of an alarm system or a surveillance camera but didn't see one.

The place reeked of a deadly combination of fertilizer and diesel fuel. I flipped on a light switch. The place lit up, revealing two large stakebed trucks, similar to the kind landscapers sometimes used. Each held a dozen fifty-five-gallon drums. The cabs were painted with the words "Stewart's Non-Hazardous Transport" along with an address and phone number.

"Holy Mother of Christ," Conor said with a whistle. "These lads are fucking serious."

"No kidding. How big an explosion would this create?"

"Twice what brought down the Murrah Building in Oklahoma City," he said. "You could bring down a city block with just one of these trucks."

"So now what?"

Conor climbed into the bed of the nearest truck and atop the steel drums. "Eeny meeny miny moe. Catch a piggy by the toe."

"Enough with the nursery rhymes."

"Hold your horses, love." He removed the lid of a drum near the center of the truck bed and examined what was inside. What little humor remained in his face drained away.

"What is it?"

"An explosive package. Just a small one. But add the barrels of diesel and fertilizer and suddenly ya've got a weapon of massive fucking destruction."

"How'd you know where it was?"

"Lid had a white sticker on it. Others didn't. And it was in the middle of the stack for maximum effect."

My pulse quickened as he pulled out a jackknife and dug at the contents of the barrel.

"Looks like it's booby-trapped. Multiple redundancies. Charged capacitors will blow it if I try to remove the battery. Got a cell phone wired in to detonate it. Gotta give these lads credit, they know what they're doing."

My heart hammered like a piston. "Great, I'll be sure to nominate them for Terrorists of the Year. Now for the real question. Can you disarm it?"

Conor grunted, eyeing the explosive package from different angles. "Maybe. Good chance I could blow myself to kingdom come."

"Well, we wouldn't want you to do that."

"On the other hand, if I don't at least try, dozens of people could die. Possibly hundreds."

"Oh, that makes me feel a whole lot better."

"On the upside, if it blows now, we'll be dead before I can even say 'Oops.'"

"Conor!"

"Don't get your bloomers in a twist. Tell ya what, love. Go scope out the house. See if you can find a way in and who may be in there. I'll join you shortly once I disarm these buggers."

"Try not to blow yourself up, all right? I'd hate to miss my wedding night on account of you splattering yourself trying to play the hero."

"I'll do my best."

Conor was whistling to himself as I walked out. I was glad he was so confident. I sure as hell wasn't.

48

My walkie-talkie squawked from local radio traffic, so I turned it off. Didn't need it giving away my location.

I crept around to the back of the house and peered into the windows at a dark kitchen. I paused and listened for any sounds of activity. I had no idea how many people were inside. Didn't want to walk into an ambush if I could help it.

After several minutes of hearing nothing but the sounds of the desert, I figured I had the advantage of surprise. I pulled out my lockpicks and set to work on the back door. Both the door handle lock and the dead bolt were set. The main lock yielded in just a few minutes with little bother. Just a run-of-the-mill five-pin lock. The dead bolt, on the other hand, was a whole other story.

The security pins refused to cooperate. Just when I thought I had them all aligned, I'd put pressure on the tensioner only to learn one or more of them was still out of place. It didn't help that my hands were growing numb and achy from the cold. A snow bunny I was not. Give me the triple-digit heat over bitter cold any day.

Eventually, I was forced to pull my hands inside the windbreaker and stuff them under my armpits to warm up. My body was shivering. My knees aching. And it was all I could do to keep my teeth from chattering.

I looked at the kitchen window, hoping I could make entry there. Unfortunately, it was a solid pane of glass that didn't open. I could break it, but that would instantly alert anyone inside. Not an option.

There were four other windows on the back side of the house. A small high window farther down had a frosted pane. A bathroom window, no doubt. The three remaining windows appeared to be located in the bedrooms. Super risky, especially if occupied.

I opted to try the bathroom window first. It would be awkward climbing in a small window set at chest height, but it seemed safer than climbing into an occupied bedroom. I studied the frame and looked for the telltale signs of an alarm but didn't see any. The window consisted of two panes, one of which slid horizontally on a track. I tried pulling on one of the two panes. It didn't move. I tried the other but with the same results.

I turned on my phone and activated the flashlight. If it drew the feds, so be it. But I needed to see, goddammit! I pressed my face against the icy pane, looking for a latch. As I did, I caught movement inside. I dropped to the ground as the bathroom light flickered on. *Shit, shit, shit! Did he see me?* My heart pounded so hard against my chest I thought it'd break a rib.

Someone hummed tunelessly inside as he did his business on the commode, accompanied by some award-winning farts. A moment later, the toilet flushed. After what felt like an eternity, the light from the bathroom window winked out. I took a deep breath to clear my head.

I waited another ten minutes before I once again peeked into the dark bathroom. I could just make out the outline of a hinged latch. If I had the right tool, a slim jim, perhaps, I might be able to squeeze it between the two panes and release the latch. I recalled seeing Conor slipping a survival knife onto his belt. Maybe that would work.

I shuffled through the shadows to the garage and slipped silently through the door. Conor wasn't atop the barrels any more. But the explosive package he had found remained in place.

"Conor?" I whispered.

"Over here, love."

I found him sitting at a workbench covered with bits of wiring and an assortment of screwdrivers, pliers, and wire cutters. A small electric kettle rested next to bricks of C-4. Conor sipped a steaming liquid from a tin cup.

"What the hell, Conor?"

"Sorry, love. Needed to warm up with a cuppa."

"Great time for a coffee break. I'm freezing my ass out there trying to find a way into the house."

"Tea."

"What?"

"Not a coffee break. It's tea. I woulda called ya on the radio, love, but didn't want to break radio silence. But since you're here, would ya like a cup? Ya look like a frozen fish finger."

I wanted to grab Pratt and Dietz and get the hell outa there. But as cold as I was, I would've drunk hot piss if it would warm me up. "Yeah, I suppose."

He pulled another tin cup from his duffel, poured some tea, and handed it to me. I wrapped my hands around it and let the warmth seep into my frozen fingers. "Any luck with the explosives?"

Conor shrugged. "Whoever wired up the fucker knew what they were doing. Multiple redundancies. Bloody nightmare to disarm without a schematic."

"So can you disarm it?" I took a sip of the tea. It was strong for tea but didn't have the level of kick I preferred from coffee.

Conor stared over at the trucks with their lethal cargo. "I'm sure I can. It'll just take time. What'd ya find at the house?"

"No luck at the back door. I think I can get through the bathroom window if I can borrow your knife."

He pulled it out of the sheath. The black blade was narrow with a saw blade on the back side. "Try not to damage it. It was a gift from a friend when I was in the sandbox," he said, referring to Iraq. "Saved my arse on more than one occasion."

"I'll be careful. You gonna join me, or am I supposed to apprehend two violent fugitives on my own?" My tone had a bit more grit in it than I anticipated. "I didn't invite you along to play Bomb Squad."

"I'll be along. See what ya can do with the window and wait for me before making entry. Don't want those blokes getting the jump on ya."

"Hurry it up, then." I set down the cup and rose to my feet.

To my surprise, he stood up and hugged me. His body heat felt delicious. "I love ya, Miss Jinxie Ballou." Something troubled me about the tone of his voice and the smile that didn't quite meet his eyes. I saw a sadness that sent chills down my spine.

I returned to the bathroom window and wedged the blade of Conor's knife through the rubber seal between the panes of frosted glass. With a little maneuvering, I used the teeth of the saw blade to catch onto the latch.

I twisted and pulled up on the blade to release the latch, but it slipped loose. I tried again, with more pressure, but it wouldn't budge. With my frustration rising, I put my body weight into it. The latch started to pull away from the track of the window. *Just a little more. Just a little more.*

The crack of the knife snapping sounded like a gunshot. The blade bit into my hand. I pulled out the handle and pressed my back against the wall. Conor was going to kill me if Pratt or Dietz didn't.

I waited another five minutes, listening for sounds of alarm from within, looking for any lights being turned on. But all remained quiet in the house.

Blood seeped from the cut on my hand. I was so cold I hardly felt it. What hurt more was the fact that these assholes were sleeping soundly while planning to kill who knew how many people.

I cast a glance toward the garage. Conor was no doubt still fucking around trying to defuse the damned bombs. Fuck him. I was going to bring these assholes down if it was the last thing I did.

I peeked through the bedroom windows, hoping to find one of the rooms unoccupied. The bedroom on the far side of the house had a bed that appeared empty. By luck, the window was open just a smidge. Guess one of the idiots forgot to close it all the way.

The crack between the window and the sill was enough for me to wedge the broken remains of Conor's knife into. I used it as a lever to nudge the window open a bit more. Then I inserted my fingertips and pulled, ignoring the throbbing in my injured hand. The window squeaked open.

"Why's it so fucking cold in this house?" asked a voice from inside. I suspected it belonged to Pratt.

I pivoted to the side, out of view of the window. *Fuck, fuck, fuck, fuck.*

"Thermostat's set at sixty-five," replied someone who sounded like Freytag. "If that's too cold for you, Mr. Pratt, you're welcome to find lodging elsewhere. But seeing as how we are only a couple hours from showtime, I suggest you take another comforter from the linen closet and shut the hell up."

"Whatever."

I stood there, trying to keep my teeth from chattering, and waited. After several minutes of silence, I peered through the open window. The bed was still unoccupied. Time to make something happen.

I put my left boot on the sill and pulled myself up to a crouch. As I stepped down on the floor, movement to my left caught my eye. Then everything went black.

49

____

Pain in my jaw and the taste of blood caught my attention as I came to. I squinted in the glare of a brightly lit room at the misshapen face of Barclay Dietz staring down at me with a cruel grin. Next to him stood Rudy Pratt, Eric Freytag, and a short guy with a mullet.

I was sitting on the floor in the front room with my back to the wall. My shoulder ached, and the steel of my own handcuffs bit into my wrists. My Rossi revolver lay next to a large green glass ashtray on a nearby rough-hewn wood table. No sign of my Glock. I was seriously up shit creek.

"Sleep well, ya little freak?" asked Dietz.

There were a lot of things I wanted to say to this asshole. Things I'd waited more than a decade to say. But I figured my chances of survival would be improved if I refrained from sharing them with the class just yet.

"Where's my son, faggot?"

I blinked, not expecting that question.

"They didn't tell you?" I glanced over at Freytag, then back at Dietz. My right hand fished into my back pocket, where I always kept a spare handcuff key. "One of your buddies shot him. He's dead."

"You're lying." Dietz kicked me in the knee, sending a shock of pain up my spine.

"Actually, she's telling the truth," said Freytag with a look of arrogance. "Your son betrayed us to our guest here. We were forced to deal with the situation."

Any hopes that this would create a conflict between them were quickly dashed. Dietz's anger was directed only at me. He leaned over and grabbed me by the collar, his eyes burning with murderous intent. "You seduced him with your filthy perversions. It's your fault my son is dead."

"He betrayed you because he saw you all for what you are—racist ammosexuals with nothing better to do than kill innocent people. Not to mention a sleazebag father who likes to beat up teenage girls."

He slammed me against the wall so hard I saw spots. *Note to self, don't piss off the assholes until you're ready to defend yourself.*

"I'm gonna enjoy killing you!" growled Dietz. He reached behind his back and pulled out a Glock. Mine, most likely.

Shit. Time for plan B. Or plan C. My brain was still fuzzy, so I wasn't sure where I was on the list. I locked my gaze on Freytag. "You realize Barclay here's working with the feds, too, right? Like father, like son. Or vice versa in this case."

All eyes turned to Barclay, who had a who-me look on his face that quickly morphed into anger. "She's lying. I ain't no rat."

"He's a CI for Special Agent Lovelace. Peyton told me before your goons showed up. They recognized the tattoo on his neck from security footage when he robbed banks on his way down from Canada. Busted him shortly before our little tête-à-tête at Dixie's. They made a deal, Freytag. He'd flip on you and your organization in exchange for a lighter sentence."

"You're a fucking liar!" He rushed at me, shoving the Glock in my face.

"Barclay!" said Freytag in a firm, cool tone. "Stand down."

"She's a fucking liar. I ain't no snitch."

"Regardless, put away the gun."

I inserted the key into the cuffs and released one hand then the other while the attention was on Barclay.

"You ain't gonna trust him for the deliveries, are you?" asked Mullet. "He could blow the whole operation."

Barclay turned the gun on Mullet. "Listen, you pipsqueak, I ain't never talked to no feds."

The two of them started shouting at each other, throwing shade and innuendos. Finally, something was working.

"Silence!" Freytag shouted as the two men were about to come to blows.

"Mr. Shepard," Freytag said, turning to Mullet. "You deliver the package to Site A. Go give those liberal snowflakes a convention they'll never forget. Pratt, you're still delivering the package to Site B."

"Now wait a minute here," Barclay started in, but Freytag cut him off.

"I'm in charge of this operation, Mr. Dietz. Not you. I'm not taking any chances. Mr. Shepard's making the drop. Since your son led this girl here, you're responsible for disposing of her."

"It," said Barclay with a sneer in my direction. "It ain't a she. It's an it."

"Whatever. Pratt, Shepard, you two get a move on. Rush hour traffic will be starting up soon." He locked eyes with Pratt. "I need that package delivered to that specific parking space in the City Hall garage to bring down the building."

"Will do," said Pratt.

"See ya later, traitor," Mullet said to Barclay, whose face turned dark red.

"This ain't right, Freytag. I drove all the way from Canada to help you guys out. Hell, I formulated the damned explosives for God's sake," bellowed Barclay.

"My decision is final. Now go outside and dispose of our guest. There's a trail out back that leads to a cave that pumas use as a food cache. Save you the trouble of burying the body. I have to retrieve Mr. Pratt and Mr. Shepard after they make their drops. See that this matter is taken care of before I get back."

Freytag turned to me. "Ms. Ballou, I must say I've been impressed with your determination and resourcefulness. Sad we have to part. Better luck in your next life."

Fuck, fuck, fuck. Outside, engines roared to life. I wondered where Conor was and if he'd had any success disabling the bombs.

Barclay stood over me, holding the gun. My hands were free, but I needed to get to the Rossi revolver.

He pulled me to my feet. I reached for the revolver. Before I could get a solid grip on it, I caught a jab to the chest. I stumbled back, and the Rossi fell to the floor.

Dietz aimed the Glock at my head, and time slowed. I stared down the barrel, watching his finger tighten on the trigger.

In that instant, I was no longer that frail, frightened teenager facing off against a monstrous bull. I was Jinx Ballou, bounty hunter. I was a survivor, a scrapper trained in krav maga. For eleven years, I'd longed for this moment. Fire rose in my belly. Adrenaline blazed through my body. I was no longer human. I was a force of nature as powerful and unrelenting as the monsoons that tore through the valley every summer.

I pivoted right as the gunshot thundered in the room. A bullet buzzed past my left ear. Running on pure instinct, I twisted his gun arm. Dietz bellowed in pain, dropping the pistol.

A left hook barreled toward my temple. I turned my head in time so that it grazed only my forehead. The blow was enough that I tumbled against an end table and knocked it on its side. Blood dripped into my right eye, partially blinding me.

He came at me again. I pulled myself to my feet and drove him back with a barrage of punches and kicks. He stepped back in a pugilist's pose, mallet-like fists at the ready. I fell into the fighting stance I'd learned from years of krav maga training.

He advanced with a couple of jabs, which I blocked and

followed up with an elbow to his chin and a heel to his instep. He stumbled but quickly regained his balance and charged at me like an enraged bull.

I tried to sidestep, but he managed a couple of blows to my abdomen. I doubled over in pain, gasping for air. An uppercut knocked me on my ass. Before I knew what was happening, the Beast was on top of me with his hands around my throat. I tried using the techniques I'd learned to break free, but his grip was like steel.

Out of the corner of my eye, I noticed a green glass object. The ashtray. My fingers clutched it, and I slammed it against Dietz's head with all of my remaining strength. The air filled with fluttering bits of ash. Dietz tumbled over, losing his grip on my neck. I swung again, but he grabbed my arm, forcing me to drop it.

With both of us struggling to stand, I rotated my arm inward, breaking his grip, and caught his left arm in a lock. He reared back for another punch, but I twisted till I heard the satisfying crackle of his radius and ulna snapping. He dropped to one knee, cradling his broken arm. I pressed my advantage with a couple of elbow strikes to his face. He fell back against the hardwood floor, coughing and spitting blood, his chest heaving.

I snatched up the Glock and stood over him with the gun aimed at his god-ugly face. My finger slipped into the trigger guard.

He glared at me. "Do it," he growled. "Or don't you got the balls?" He coughed as he tried to laugh at his own joke.

"I dreamed of this day for thirteen years. The day I got my revenge on Barclay 'The Beast' Dietz. The day I got to blow his fucking brains out. And you know what I realized? You aren't worth it. I'd rather you live a very long life knowing you got your ass handed to you by a trans woman."

"Fucking bitch," grumbled Dietz.

"Now get on your belly so I can cuff you."

"Kiss my ass, you goddamned freak. You broke my fucking arm."

I aimed the Glock at his crotch. "I might not kill you, but I have no problem blowing your goddamned dick off. Now roll over like a good dog."

He glared at me but slowly turned over, cursing at the pain. I snapped the cuffs on him. As I contemplated my next move, my phone rang. It was Conor.

50

"Where are you?" I asked Conor.

"In the Caprice that was parked by the garage. I'm pursuing one of the lorries south on the 51. The other was headed west on the Loop 101 along with a chase car when they split up."

"Did you disable the bombs?"

I heard him sigh. "Afraid not, love. That's why I at least gotta stop this one lorry. Shot at the wheels, but the bastard's got dual tires in back. Trying for the front, but traffic's bloody thick. Hard to get a clear shot. Oh shite!"

I heard tires squealing and Conor grunting and cursing.

"Conor, are you there?"

"The wanker tried to push me off the road. Just passed the Glendale exit. If I can—"

I heard an exchange of gunfire. An engine roared followed by crunching metal. More shots, then the clunk of a car door being slammed.

"Conor? Are you there?"

Conor was yelling at someone to get out of the truck. I couldn't hear the response.

Outside the house, the wail of police sirens approached, accompanied by the chut-chut-chut of helicopters. The cavalry had arrived. Late as usual.

"Conor, can you hear me?"

I heard more urgent shouting over the phone followed by a deep thump and dead silence. "Conor?" My phone beeped. The call had dropped. "Shit."

The front door burst open in a shower of splintered wood. Men in assault gear and automatic weapons flooded into the room.

"Down on the ground. Get down on the ground now!"

I put my hands behind my head and got down on my knees. It was all I could do to keep my shit together while wondering what was happening to Conor. "There are two trucks delivering explosives—"

"Get on the ground now! Or we will shoot you!" One of the SWAT team members bore down on me, holding the barrel of his rifle a foot from my head.

"I'm on the ground. Now, listen to me!" I pleaded. "I'm a bail enforcement agent. This man is my fugitive. His cohorts are driving two trucks full of explosives."

He cuffed my hands, hoisted me up, and escorted me outside. The eastern sky was a pale yellow with the coming dawn.

"That truck already exploded, lady," he said.

Tears pricked my eyes, and I gasped for breath. "Conor." I struggled to control my emotions. More lives were on the line. "There's another one. My fugitive knows where it's headed."

They hauled me inside a large black FBI mobile command vehicle and stuffed me in a small room with a table mounted to the floor. The cuffs chafed, but I barely noticed. My body shivered from adrenaline withdrawal, cold, and despair.

"Please be okay, please be okay," I muttered repeatedly.

After what felt like hours, Special Agent Lovelace and another agent walked in with a couple of case folders. "You can uncuff her."

The agent did so and left. It was just Lovelace and me.

"What's happening out there?" I asked.

"I'm asking the questions here." Her tone was assertive but not mean. "You're shivering. You need a blanket?"

"I need to know what's happening with Con—with the trucks."

Her eyes narrowed. "Was Conor Doyle driving one of the trucks?"

"No! He tried to stop them. And now..." Tears ran down my face. I'd hit my limit.

"Miss Ballou." She put a gentle hand on my arm. "Jenna, I'm sorry. We have reports from Phoenix PD of a large explosion on the 51 just south of the Glendale exit. The blast zone is the size of a city block. I don't know how many casualties there are, but last count there are at least thirty-three dead and countless injuries. I expect those numbers to rise dramatically. If Mr. Doyle was anywhere near that truck...well, you have my sincere condolences."

Even though I was expecting it, the news hit me like a ton of bricks. I sobbed uncontrollably. At some point, a blanket was put around me, and I felt Lovelace's arm on my shoulder.

"I...I need to see him," I choked out.

"Who?" asked Lovelace.

"Conor."

"Jenna, you won't be able to get anywhere near the site. It's a massive crime scene. It's going to take some time to identify remains."

I wanted to believe that somehow he had survived. But he'd been right there. There would be little left to identify.

"Now I hate to do this, but I need some answers from you. What are you doing here?"

I reminded her of my attempts to locate Pratt and Dietz. She asked about the shooting off Carefree Highway, and I filled her in on how our meeting with Peyton had gone off the rails. Apparently, she and her team had been on to Officer Evans for some time.

Pratt, as it turned out, was driving the truck that blew up. So no bounty for me. The other truck was intercepted before it could be detonated at the Gila River Arena. The driver, Bennie the Mullet, apparently got pulled over for speeding and was promptly arrested.

Lovelace had me write out a statement. When I was done, I slid it over to her.

"Now what happens?"

"DCI Collier wanted to charge you with harboring a fugitive. And you're on my shit list for interfering with a federal investigation. Again."

I said nothing. I no longer cared what she did.

"However, in light of recent events, Collier has agreed to return to the UK empty-handed, and the FBI will not be filing charges against you."

"Thank you."

"I know you have a job to do, Ms. Ballou. But in the future, stay out of our way. Do I make myself clear?"

"Crystal."

I walked out into a bright-blue morning that left me dead inside. The ride home was a blur. I remembered turning off the radio and driving in silence. I slogged through traffic on I-17, which was no doubt a result of the closure of Highway 51 following the explosion.

The next thing I knew, I was walking into my front door. In the pantry, I found the bottle of Jameson I had bought for Conor. I drank a few glasses. At some point, Reggie walked in and put me to bed.

51

———

I spent the next week staying at Becca's, being waited on by her and her new cuddle-buddy. Easton was cute with long blue bangs, freckles, and a fondness for bow ties and suspenders. Both Becca and Easton seemed to tiptoe around me as though I was apt to fall apart any second. And maybe I did that a few times.

My parents and Jake stopped by several times bearing food, including a ton of holiday sweets. My folks begged me to stay with them for the holidays, but I declined. I wasn't in the mood to be psychoanalyzed by my father. Neither did I feel like being in a house filled with nativity scenes and heralding angels and all that Christmas shit.

Caden called, and we talked for a while. He was expected to be released from the hospital soon but would be out of commission for a while. His sister had come in from Santa Fe to help him while his leg healed. He was thinking about applying to law school at ASU. I told him I'd miss him but supported whatever he decided.

I referred the few bail-jumper jobs Sadie Levinson had over to Deez, who was now in charge of Conor's bounty-hunting team.

He and the boys dropped by to bring me flowers along with their condolences.

"Whenever you're ready to get back to work, you're welcome back with the old team," Deez said in his deep bass voice. I told him I'd think about it.

Despite everyone's hospitality, nothing could fill the gnawing emptiness inside me. I caught myself sniping at anyone who got near me.

"You know what you need?" said Becca one morning over coffee.

"A frontal lobotomy?" I joked darkly.

"A dog."

"Yeah, right."

"No, I'm serious," she insisted. "You need someone to take care of. Someone who will love you and shower you with kisses no matter what."

"Becks, I know you mean well, but a dog won't replace Conor."

"Not replace. But a dog might help you through the grief. Sometimes having someone to take care of can get your mind off your own troubles."

"You sound like my dad. He keeps pushing me to join a grief support group."

"Might not be a bad idea."

I scoffed. "Yeah, right. Don't see me sitting around a circle singing 'Kumbaya.' 'Hi, my name's Jinx, and I used to date an Irish terrorist who got himself blown up by a white nationalist.' Not gonna happen."

"We're all just trying to help, Jinx. We love you and hate to see you suffering."

"I know. Nothing anyone can do. I just feel dead inside."

"But you're not dead. I know Conor is, and it fucking sucks. But dammit, Jinx. Life goes on."

I pushed away my untouched cup. "I think it's time I move

back home." I stood up and walked to the guest bedroom where I'd been staying.

Becca followed me. "Don't leave mad."

"I'm not mad. I'm just...I just have to figure this shit out for myself." I turned and hugged her. "You're the best bestie a girl could have. But I've been crashing here long enough. I know Easton's tired of me hanging around."

"Easton adores you. They just think you're a little..."

"Scary?" I asked.

"Intense. I mean, it's Christmas in a few days. Easton's used to everything being all cheerful and merry. They don't know what to say after what you've been through."

I made the bed, threw my clothes in my bag, gathered my toiletries, and tossed them in, too. "All the more reason to give you two some space. I don't want to be harshing anyone's holiday spirit."

She held my gaze as I shouldered my bag. "You gonna be okay?" She had the look of a worried puppy.

I nodded. "I'll be okay. I think I need some time to think. Sort through some feelings. Maybe I'll even show up to one of those grief support meetings."

"I'm always just a phone call or a text away. You're welcome back as long as you need."

"I know." I gave her another hug, and she walked me to the door. "Thanks, Becks. Thanks for being there for me all these years."

At home, I gathered up my pile of mail and spent the better part of an hour sorting it, tossing out the junk, and creating a pile for bills to be paid and another for Christmas cards. One serious-looking letter was from the Federal Bureau of Investigation. "Shit."

I opened it, expecting some sort of summons or threats of legal action. Instead, I found a check for two hundred grand for apprehending Barclay Dietz. Considering I lost out on the bounty for Pratt and had missed a week's worth of work, I could use the dinero. In fact, I could probably take the next few months off if I wanted.

As I pondered what else I could do with the money, my phone rang. I didn't recognize the number.

"Ms. Ballou, this is Harvey Mashburn with the law firm of Mashburn, Steele, and Wallace. Is now a good time to talk?"

Ugh, lawyers. "Not really. What's this about, Mr. Mashburn?"

"I understand. I represent the estate of Conor Doyle. He has named you as the sole beneficiary of his trust."

"His trust?"

"His property and other belongings. It's like a will but avoids all of the problems of probate. At any rate, I'd like to schedule a time to meet with you so that I can go through all of this with you."

"Can we do this after the holidays? I'm...I'm not ready to deal with all this right now."

"I certainly understand. You take your time." He gave me his phone number, even though it was on the caller ID. "You get in touch whenever you're ready. And I am truly sorry for your loss. Merry Christmas."

I hung up. "Merry fucking Christmas."

For two days, I stayed at home, not going out for anything. Reggie, who had started working for Jake remodeling houses, wasn't around as much. I did manage to move aside my workout equipment and set up the spare bedroom for Reggie so he wouldn't have to crash on my couch anymore.

For the most part, I just ate kids' cereal, binge-watched British crime serials on Netflix, finished off the bottle of Jameson, and let my body steep in its own juices.

Try as I might, I couldn't keep from thinking about Conor. The feel of his arms around me, the exhilaration of making love to him, even his proclivity for getting under my skin. I missed it all.

At eleven o'clock one night, I climbed in the Gray Ghost and started driving. Traffic was all but nonexistent. I had no destination in mind. I just needed to be in motion, to get out of the stinking, stifling house.

To my surprise, the holiday lights and other decorations through town started to cheer me up despite the fact that I hadn't much cared for Christmas since I was a kid. Sure, I bought a few token gifts for immediate family and the closest of friends, but I avoided parties and serious shopping expeditions in search of the perfect gift.

I found myself sitting in a parking lot at the corner of Glendale Avenue and Sixteenth Street, a block away from the highway that was still cordoned off due to the bomb blast. I wrapped my coat around me and wandered off with a flashlight in hand.

A makeshift memorial of flowers, candles, and stuffed animals lay at the barricades to the highway's on-ramp. I stepped past them, paying them no mind, and shuffled down the ramp until I reached another set of barricades that marked the edge of a crater. To my right, the water in the Arizona Canal glimmered in the moonlight.

I stood there. This was where he'd died. The man I loved. A man who'd been caught up in violence of one sort or another his whole life. And this was how it ended. Dozens of people had died here on the 51, but Conor had saved thousands at City Hall. And now I didn't have anyone.

A patrol officer startled me as I walked back up the ramp. "Ma'am, this area is off-limits."

"Sorry. I just needed to see it."

"I'm sure you can find better things to do on Christmas Eve than wandering out here in the dark."

"Is tonight Christmas Eve?" I'd lost track.

"Yes, ma'am. You lose someone in the blast?"

I fingered the ring that now hung from a chain around my neck. "My fiancé."

"I'm sorry for your loss, ma'am, but you need to be on your way."

"Yes, Officer."

I wandered back to the Gray Ghost and started driving again. Thirty minutes later, I found myself at Juanita's hospital room.

"*Ay, ay, ay!* It's Wonder Woman," she said as I stepped into the room. I'd forgotten I was wearing a Wonder Woman T-shirt.

Juanita was propped on her bed with a scarf wrapped around her head. *It's a Wonderful Life* was playing on the TV. She muted it.

"No superheroes tonight, I'm afraid, *tía*. Just little old me."

Juanita patted her bedside. "Don't stand there like an IV pole. Come here, *mi'ja*, and snuggle next to me."

She winced as she scooted over and made room for me. I carefully slid in next to her, afraid of hurting her. But it felt good to be near her.

"You sound more like your old self." I asked, "How you feeling?"

"I feel like fuck on stale toast," she said with a chuckle. "Staff can't wait to get rid of me. Moving me to rehab in a few days to help me walk again."

I nodded quietly. Even though she was improving, it hurt to see her like this.

"How you holding up, Miss Thang?" she asked.

"Everything feels wrong with Conor gone. I feel like I'm ruining everyone's Christmas."

"Fuck them, *mi'ja*. You been through hell and back."

"I don't know how to get on with my life. It's hard to explain."

"Ain't nothing to explain, *chica*. Back in the eighties, all my friends were dying. That *pendejo* Reagan called it the gay plague. Like it was God's judgment on us queers."

"I've heard the stories."

"My boyfriend, Esteban, got this spot on his face." She shook her head. "After the clinic confirmed he had AIDS, he admitted he fooled around on me. Got infected by some *pinche* white boy."

I shook my head, not knowing what to say.

"For weeks I refused to get tested. Couldn't face it. Then he got real sick. I go down to the clinic. Sure as shit, Esteban had infected me too."

"What happened to him?"

"Sorry motherfucker died on me. I was devastated. Wanted to die myself."

"Oh, Juanita, I'm so sorry." I leaned my head on her shoulder.

"But then I realized, no! I was not gonna die. And you know why?"

"Why?"

"Because fuck them. Fuck them all. Fuck Reagan. Fuck them haters. Fuck them cheating *maricones* getting everyone sick. I was gonna live just to spite them."

She took a few breaths as she started to get winded. "Don't get me wrong. It was touch and go for a while. I earned some frequent flier miles in the hospital. But thanks to my friends and medical science, I pulled through."

"I'm glad you did, *tía*."

"I ain't telling you this for some bedtime story, *mi'ja*. Your man is gone. And it fucking sucks. Unlike my Esteban, Conor died doing right. Going after them White Nation *hijos de puta*. He gave his life trying to save people. Best thing you can do is say 'fuck you' to them racist assholes by living your life."

"I suppose you're right."

"Tía Juana is always right."

Fatigue was seeping into my bones as the movie dragged on. Juanita needed her rest too.

I pulled myself to my feet as she started to drift off to sleep. I kissed her cheek, wished her a *Feliz Navidad*, and drove home.

52

I woke the next morning to my doorbell ringing. I ignored it, hoping whoever it was would go away. It rang again. I continued to ignore it. A moment later, someone was knocking on my bedroom door. Instinctively, I rolled out of bed and drew a pistol I kept next to my nightstand.

"Don't shoot! It's me." Jake stood in the doorway, holding a golden retriever puppy on a leash. Rodeo stood next to him.

I put away the gun and ran a hand through my hair. "What are you two doing in my house? With a dog?"

Rodeo beckoned me with his hand. "Come on. You'll see."

I followed them into my living room. My parents were arranging stacks of wrapped presents around a hastily set up Christmas tree. Rodeo's seven-year-old daughter, Gwyneth, and Reggie were helping decorating the tree with lights and ornaments.

"Merry Christmas," my parents said in unison.

"What's all this?"

"You didn't show up for Christmas breakfast, so we brought Christmas to you," said my mother. "We even brought panettones to make Italian French toast." She held up the odd-shaped yellow boxes. It was a weird family tradition, but Italian French toast had always been my favorite part of Christmas morning.

"You guys, you shouldn't have." I caught myself feeling emotional.

My father reached out and hugged me. "I've been worried about you, kiddo."

"I'm actually feeling a little better." And I meant it. Juanita's talk was starting to sink in.

"So what's the dog's name?" I asked Gwyneth.

"I don't know," she replied with a coy smile. "Whatever you name it, I guess."

"Huh? Jake, whose dog is this?"

Jake grinned. "Yours."

"What?" I looked at my brother, then each of my parents. I bent down and petted the dog, who was all waggly tail and lapping tongue. "You're giving me a dog?"

"Becca suggested it," explained Jake. "Dad seconded the idea. Thought it'd do you good. They'll be over later, by the way."

"Who?"

"Becca and Easton." Jake rolled his eyes. I guess my brain wasn't fully functioning yet.

After a few rich pieces of my mother's Italian French toast and opening presents, we were sitting around my living room playing with the dog and semi-watching *A Christmas Story*.

I was feeling more alive than I had since the explosion. I even decided on the name Diana for the dog, which was Wonder Woman's cover name.

Just as Ralphie was getting his mouth washed out with soap on the television, my doorbell rang.

"About time." I figured it had to be Becca. "Great idea about the dog," I said as I opened the door. Except it wasn't Becca but a large white man with a buzzed head standing at my door. He was dressed in fatigues. "Sorry. Guess you're not Becca, huh?"

"No, ma'am," he said with a thick Southern accent. "The

name's Tuckey. I was asked to deliver this to you." He handed me a small cardboard box.

As a bounty hunter, I'm suspicious of any hand-delivered packages. "Asked by whom?"

"Your fiancé, ma'am. He and I served in the sandbox a while back."

My legs felt like jelly. Gravity pulled at odd angles. I grabbed the doorframe to steady myself. *Is this a joke? Or a threat?*

"When'd he ask you to deliver this? And what the hell's in it?"

"Received it by mail just yesterday. Postmarked from Spain four days ago. As to the contents, I could not say."

"Spain?" I took a deep breath to clear out the gremlins. Suddenly things started to coalesce. "Thank you, Tuckey."

"Merry Christmas, ma'am." He turned and disappeared into a pickup truck on the street and drove off.

"Who's that at the door, honey?" asked my father.

"Just a delivery man," I said, closing the door before shuffling to the kitchen.

"On Christmas morning?"

I grabbed a knife and opened the package. Out slipped a flip phone with one number in its memory. My heart beat so fast in my chest that I wondered if I was having a heart attack. *It can't be. It can't be.*

I dialed the number.

"Feliz Navidad, love," said Conor. "You should see the view of the Pacific from this villa. Had no idea Ensenada, Mexico, was this gorgeous."

Conor and I sat on the sand at Playa Hermosa, drinking a local wine, while Diana the wonder pup chased after shorebirds. The cry of gulls and the pounding of the surf helped to untie the knots in my soul that had built up since early December.

I drove down just after New Year's, telling my family I needed time to think and heal. I made no mention that Conor was still alive. We had spent the past week exploring Ensenada, living on street tacos and fresh fish, and fucking like rabbits.

All the while, I wrestled with what to do about Conor. When I arrived at his villa, he explained that he'd realized Pratt was about to set off the explosive. Conor jumped into the canal and dragged himself out a mile downstream. He hooked up with Picardo the document forger and headed south of the border.

Diana came running up to us and shook her fur, showering the two of us in salt spray and sand. I would have been upset if she weren't so cute.

"Never took ya for a dog person." Conor chuckled.

"Me neither. I guess people can change."

"Does that mean you're ready to become Mrs. Eileen Crawford?"

I took a deep breath, remembering what I went through when I thought he was dead. The soul-crushing grief would have consumed me if it hadn't been for Becca, Juanita, and my family.

"Don't suppose there's any way you could return to Phoenix now that the Northern Ireland police think you're dead."

"Afraid not, love. Too risky. Besides, the weather's better down here. And what's not to love about the beach? It's paradise." He sighed. "Or would be if you were with me."

I turned to him, gazing deep into his emerald eyes. "I love you, Conor. No one has made me feel the way you do. But my life is back in Phoenix." I slipped the engagement ring off my finger and put it in his palm. "I'm sorry."

He kissed away the tears. "Nothing to be sorry for, Jinxie. I should never have saddled you with my past. But do me a favor. Keep the ring. Remember me with love."

I took the ring back and hugged him. "Always."

A month later on a Saturday night, L Street was packed and rocking to the beats of the Pink Trinkets' latest album, *#MeThree*, a tribute to the #MeToo movement. It was only Groundhog's Day, but the bar was already decked out with rainbow-striped hearts in anticipation of Valentine's Day.

I'd had a couple of beers and was feeling relaxed, enjoying the Pink Trinkets' driving beats and searing vocals. Becca and Easton sat across the small table, chatting with me about some video game Easton was reviewing for a podcast they hosted. I was only half listening.

"I think it's a great improvement over the previous version of the game, but—" Easton waved to someone behind me.

I turned, and a shiver ran up my spine. This was such foreign territory for me. But if I could learn to be a dog person, perhaps I could learn other things.

CO Toni Bennett looked sexy in her uniform but a helluva lot sexier in her civvies. My heart went full hummingbird as she put her arms around me and kissed me. "Hey, gorgeous. Sorry I'm late."

A BROKEN WOMAN

JINX BALLOU SERIES - BOOK 3

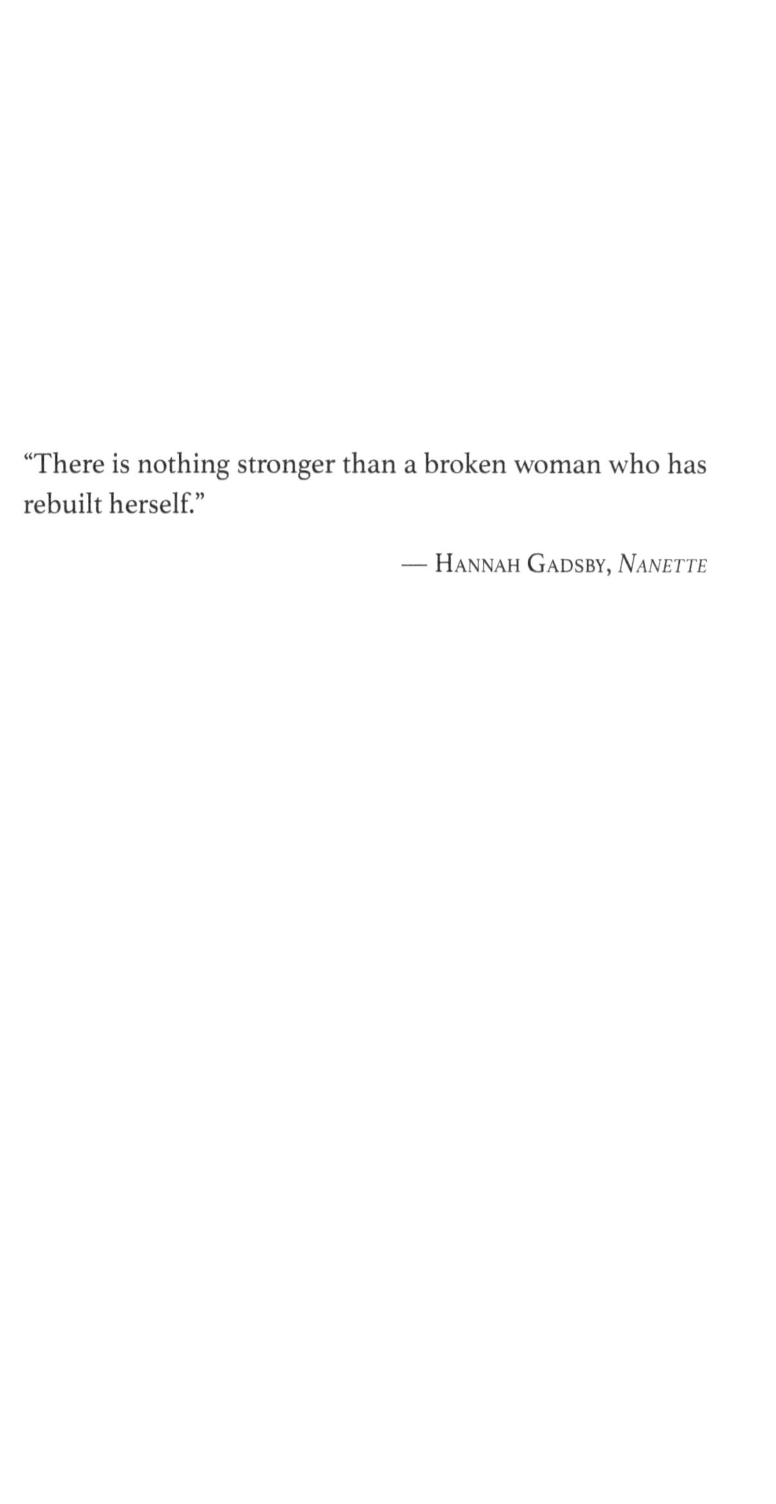

"There is nothing stronger than a broken woman who has rebuilt herself."

— HANNAH GADSBY, *Nanette*

1

The metal railing on the concrete staircase groaned when I fell against it. A bottle of Cuervo Gold dangled precariously from my unsteady hand. I shivered while a shrill chorus of coyotes pierced the cool night air. One cried out the plaintive melody. The others harmonized, raising it to a crescendo, fading to silence for a heartbeat before the cycle started again.

A lot of people hated coyotes, but their cries resonated deep in my soul. Hunter. Trickster. Solitary and yet still reaching out to connect with others of their kind. I'd been solitary too long. I needed some connection.

I pulled my body up two flights, stumbled along the walk to room 319, and pounded on the door. "Willie, man. Let me in."

"Who the hell is it?"

"Liz. Liz Windsor." Not my real name, but he'd find that out soon enough.

"Never hearda you."

"Frank sent me. Thought we could party a little."

I was trying to keep my mind on my business, but part of me just wanted to play the role of the drunken whore for a night. Drinking on the job, especially on an empty stomach, was never a good idea, but what the hell. I was a solitary hunter, but I needed to connect. Lately, the nights had been awful lonely.

The door breezed open so fast I almost fell into the room.

"Whoa," I said with a laugh, steadying myself with the doorframe.

The bare-chested man before me looked worse than his mug shot. Three days' worth of beard growth extended halfway down his throat. He smelled of sweat, musk, and weed. A few weeks on the lam will do that to a person.

His name was Wilhelm Penzler. He'd been charged with money laundering and fraud. When he failed to appear at his court hearing, his bail bond agent hired me to pick him up and take his stinky ass back to jail.

"Hey, Willie!" I held up the bottle of tequila and shot Penzler my most seductive smile. "Ya wanna party?"

"It's Wilhelm." His gaze slid down to where my tube top barely covered my breasts. He grabbed the bottle and took a long pull. "Come on in."

I should've cuffed him right then. But I'd been in a funk for the past week. Okay, more like the past few months. Hadn't been laid in forever. I deserved a little fun.

A porno played on the television. Open boxes of Chinese takeout sat on the nightstand next to green glass pipe and a mirror dusted with a white powder. Clothes were strewn across a wood-framed chair, the bed, and the floor. A small trash can by the dresser overflowed with fast-food bags and an empty Entenmann's pastry box.

"Nice place," I said playfully.

"The maid hates me. So Frankie sent ya, huh? Gotta say, you're better lookin' than most of the skanks he has in his stable. How'd he know where I was, anyway?"

I shrugged. "Didn't say."

Penzler came up behind me and grabbed my crotch. Under

normal circumstances, I would've given him a nose job with my elbow and twisted his wrist until the bones popped.

Instead, I moaned with feigned pleasure. Well, somewhat feigned. It felt damn good to be touched. Penzler's hands migrated up to my breasts, squeezing and massaging. *Oh, Conor*, I almost said out loud, remembering my ex-fiancé.

I sat on Penzler's bed, eyeing the glass pipe that lay next to a box of Mongolian beef. "You smoking a bowl?"

"Yeah. Wanna hit?"

"Definitely."

He handed me a lighter, and I indulged myself a little further. The smoke burned my throat, but it helped silence the voice in my head asking me what the hell I thought I was doing. *Yeah, I got a fucking job to do. So what?*

"Shit." I lay back on the bed, releasing a billowy cloud of sweet white magic. My brain felt like an old barnstorming biplane doing loop the loops. I passed the pipe and lighter back to Penzler.

He lay next to me and took a hit. "I know, right? Good shit."

My phone pinged. "Dammit."

I glanced at it. A text from Assurity Bail Bonds' Sadie Levinson read, *You find Penzler yet?*

"Fuck."

"What's wrong?" Penzler asked.

"My asshole boss."

"Frankie?"

"Not exactly." I took the pipe and lighter from him and set them on the nightstand.

"Whaddya mean, 'not exactly'? You're one of his girls, right?" He slipped a leg over mine and started massaging my breast.

I rolled my eyes. I wanted to just lie there and let Penzler fuck me. Instead, I sat up and twirled my finger in the air. "Turn around."

"Why?"

"Just do it," I insisted.

He guffawed but obeyed. "You ain't gonna do nothing kinky, are you?"

"Not kinky."

I took a deep breath to clear my head. Didn't help. I pulled the handcuffs out of my back pocket and snapped them onto his wrists.

"What the fuck?" he yelled.

"Wilhelm Penzler, you missed your court date and violated your bail agreement." I'd repeated these words so many times that, even high as a kite, I could repeat them without missing a syllable. "I've been hired to return you to custody."

"Bitch, take these off me, or I'll fucking kill you. You know who I work for?" He began to buck. I tried to pull him off the bed, but in my impaired state, I lost my balance. I fell on my ass, banging my head on the nightstand.

"Fuck, that hurt."

A loud thud shook the room. I pulled myself up enough to see Penzler slam the door with his shoulder a second time. The doorjamb cracked.

"Dude, chill." I rubbed the goose egg forming on the side of my head.

He charged again. The door smashed open. I heard a metallic clang and a yelp of fear followed by a sickening thud.

My head cleared with a rush of adrenaline. "Awww...shit!"

I rushed out the door after him and stopped at the metal railing. Penzler lay in a heap on the pavement two stories below. "Shit, shit, shit, shit!"

I raced along the walkway, vaulted down the staircase with moves that'd make Jackie Chan jealous, and rushed over to Penzler's body. In the dim overhead light, I could make out a dark liquid puddling around his head. "Goddamn motherfucker shit."

My official title is bail enforcement agent, but that's just a fancy term for a bounty hunter. Unfortunately, the days of "Bring 'em back dead or alive" were long gone. I don't get paid when my fugitive is in the morgue.

I can just walk away. Or call 911 from the burner phone in the glove box of my car. Then when I've sobered up, I can tell Sadie I found Penzler dead in the parking lot, with no idea how he got that way. Yeah, that might work.

"Hey!" A woman in a flowery dress and flip-flops ran toward me with an ice bucket in her hand. "What happened?"

Fuckity fuck fuck fuck!

"Not sure." My heart thudded in my chest. "He...he pitched himself over the rail."

"He dead?" She pulled out her phone, no doubt dialing 911.

"I think so." I was so fucked.

While Ice Bucket Lady called emergency services, I raced back to Penzler's room and tried to figure out what to tell the cops. Between the booze, the weed, and the adrenaline, my mind was having trouble focusing.

Okay, I was never here. Wait, my handcuffs are still on his wrists. Shit. Even if I remove them without anyone seeing, the autopsy will show his wrists were bound. See, I may be drunk and half baked, but at least I remember shit like that.

Okay, so I was here, and I...I knocked on the door, and he ran out of the room and pitched over the rail. No, that doesn't make sense. Why would he do that?

How about, he opened the door. When I told him who I was, he ran back inside. I chased after him and cuffed him. But he knocked me off balance and busted through the door to escape, only he pitched over the railing instead. Okay, we'll go with that. Wait, who is this we? Shit, I'm so fucked up.

With a ratty towel from the bathroom, I wiped down the tequila bottle, the pipe, and every surface I thought I'd touched. Didn't want anybody to know I was high when I showed up to arrest Penzler. Finally, I called my attorney, Kirsten Pasternak. The phone rang four times before she picked up.

"Jinx? What's up?"

My teeth chattered from a combination of nervousness and the cold. "I'm...in a bit of a situation."

"Can it wait? I'm at the movies with this really charming man. I think he likes me."

I didn't say anything. I just felt stupid for letting something like this happen.

She sighed on her end of the line. "Okay, where are you?"

I gave her the details. She promised she'd be there as soon as she could. "Don't say anything to anyone until I get there."

"I know the drill."

Sirens alerted me that the police had arrived. I hated leaving the bottle of tequila behind. I was going to need it after dealing with this shit. But best to leave the wiped bottle for the crime scene techs. I took a deep breath and wandered downstairs to face the music.

As a general rule, the local cops weren't fond of people in my profession, especially after a team of bounty hunters mistakenly stormed the home of the Phoenix chief of police a few years back. I wasn't involved, but it didn't boost our reputation among those sworn to protect and serve.

When a uniformed officer showed up and asked me for an initial statement, I followed Kirsten's instructions and said, "I'm not saying anything until my attorney gets here." Statements like that naturally drew suspicion, but in my impaired state, it would have been way too easy to slip up and say something incriminating. I didn't need to give the cops a win tonight.

I was sitting on a wooden bench outside the motel when Kirsten's silver-blue Mercedes pulled up. We had met years earlier at the Phoenix Gender Alliance. She stood an inch over six feet and wore a black blazer over a revealing white blouse.

"Jiminy Christmas, Jinx. You look like the walking dead," Kirsten said in her deep, sultry voice.

"Gee, thanks," I replied sarcastically. I couldn't stop the shivering, even after I'd grabbed a jacket from my car.

"Look, I'm not trying to be mean. I'm worried about you. You're skinnier than a runway model, and you smell like a frat house after a kegger. You been smoking pot?"

"No!"

She glared at me over her yellow-framed glasses.

"Okay, maybe. Lately, things have just been so...I don't know."

She put a hand on my arm. "You know you're more than a client to me, right? You're my friend. What's gotten into you? Is this because of what happened with Conor?"

Five months earlier, my fiancé, Conor Doyle, had attempted to stop a white nationalist with a truckload of explosives bound for Phoenix City Hall. Conor forced the truck off the highway several miles away from its destination. The driver triggered the bomb, killing forty-three people and injuring two hundred more.

Conor was lauded as a hero until the media learned that the Police Service of Northern Ireland had an outstanding warrant for him, dating back to his teenage years. Reporters hounded me at my house and followed me when I went out, making it impossible to do my job. By the time they had scavenged the last tasty morsel of gossip, I was a broken woman—traumatized, alone, and struggling to reassemble the shrapnel of my life.

"I don't want to talk about Conor," I told Kirsten. "Or about Toni."

"Oh yeah, that corrections officer you were dating. Toni Bennett. Helluva name. I'd forgotten about her."

I snickered darkly. "Wish I could."

She put a hand on my arm. "I'm sorry. But if it's any consolation, Conor died a hero. Had the driver reached City Hall, the death toll would have exceeded a thousand."

It wasn't any consolation. Nor was Conor dead as everyone thought.

"Back to the matter at hand. What happened this evening?" Kirsten asked.

"Wilhelm Penzler skipped on a money-laundering charge. I tracked him here and talked my way into his room. When I cuffed him, he freaked. Busted through the door so hard that he flipped over the railing and fell two stories."

"Were you inside the motel room?"

"Yeah."

"Where'd you get the pot?"

"He was already smoking it when I arrived. Looked like he'd also done some lines of coke before I got there."

"So rather than arrest him right away, the two of you had a little party. How very Hunter S. Thompson of you."

I shrugged. What could I say? Guilty as charged.

"What a mess." She shook her head. "Do you have any drugs on you?"

"Sorry. No. You'll have to get your own." I burst out giggling. Couldn't help it. This was all so absurd.

"Jinx, this is serious. You could be charged with involuntary manslaughter."

That sobered me up a bit. "I didn't bring any drugs other than a bottle of tequila."

"Did he drink any?"

I tried to remember. So many of the details were muddled. "I don't think so."

"Well," said Kirsten, "time to face the music."

Detective Pierce Hardin was speaking with two other detectives near the staircase, then wandered in our direction when Kirsten waved him over.

Hardin's graying hair contrasted with his dark skin. He'd started growing a beard since the last time I'd seen him. Ten years earlier, when I joined the Phoenix PD, Hardin had been my field-training officer. He was so tough and by the book, he'd earned the nickname Detective Hardass.

My pulse quickened as Hardin approached. I assured myself I

wasn't responsible for Penzler's swan dive, but I still felt guilty.

"Detective Hardin," said Kirsten.

"Evening, Counselor." He gave her a brief, polite smile, which vanished the instant he looked at me. "Jesus, Ballou! What the hell's going on with you? You look like shit on a cracker. And you smell worse."

"Pleasure to see you, too, Detective," I said as soberly as I could.

"You mind telling me why this guy Penzler took a header onto the pavement? And why he's wearing a pair of handcuffs, which I'd bet my left nut belong to you?"

Kirsten gave me a nod.

"He failed to appear in court. I tried to arrest him. He went berserk. Charged out of the room like an enraged bull on steroids, hit the rail, and belly-flopped onto the asphalt. If only he'd stuck the landing." A guffaw threatened to surface. I covered my mouth to suppress it.

Hardin's nostrils flared. "You think this shit is funny? A man is dead, Ballou."

"I know. Sorry." I clamped down hard on the urge to laugh, but it felt like riding a bucking bronco. This whole thing was so absurd, it was hard not to laugh at it.

"You realize who Penzler worked for, right?"

I tried to remember, but the details were fuzzy. "Shit, some bar in Scottsdale, I think."

This time, it was Hardin's turn to scoff. "Some bar? Is that all you got? Used to be you'd know an FTA's shoe size and their third-grade teacher's maiden name. Now all you know is he worked at some bar?"

"Why? What's the big deal?"

"That bar is a strip club run by the Volkov crime family." The Volkovs were Chechen gangsters with ties to the Russian mafia.

"Volkov? Volkov's dead. I—" I stopped when Kirsten gave me a red-light look.

"Yeah, Ballou, you killed Milo Volkov. I know all about it. But here's the rub. Milo had a brother, Sergei, who now runs the organization. The tittie bars, the sex trafficking, money laundering, and probably a whole host of other shit we don't even know about. And Penzler was in the middle of all of it. His attorneys had been in talks with the feds and the county attorney's office about a plea deal."

The fog in my mind burned away. Milo Volkov had been a ruthless Chechen mobster running a human trafficking organization. I'd landed in the son of a bitch's crosshairs while pursuing a teenage murder suspect he had kidnapped. When the smoke cleared, Volkov, several of his men, two federal agents, and a fellow bounty hunter were dead.

"Penzler had a plea deal? To testify against Volkov, I suppose."

"So I'm told," replied Hardin.

"Shit, that'd be suicide. Wait, maybe that's why Penzler jumped. If Sergei's anything like his sadistic brother, jumping off a balcony'd be a helluva lot less painful than what awaited Penzler if he testified."

"You're saying he committed suicide?" Hardin didn't look convinced.

"You have any proof he didn't?" Kirsten countered.

Hardin shook his head. "You realize this was one of Special Agent Lovelace's cases? I know you two have a history of butting heads. When she hears you wrecked their case against Sergei, she's going to go ballistic."

"Detective, do not threaten my client. She has had a rough few months. And yet, she's here doing her job. It is not her fault Mr. Penzler skipped his hearing. Nor is it her fault he fell over a railing, whether accidentally or intentionally."

"Unless you're working for Volkov." Hardin's gaze landed on me.

Daggers flew from my eyes. "You know me better than that. I might bend the rules here and there. And I'll admit, I've been in a funk the past few months, but I would never, ever work for the Volkov organization."

Hardin didn't look happy, but the fire in his eyes tempered a bit. "Anything else I should know about what happened here?"

"Nope. But I would like my handcuffs back."

"Too bad. They're evidence." Hardin glared at me. "Now get the hell off my crime scene."

"Gladly." I turned and walked away, with Kirsten beside me.

"And get your act together!" he shouted at my back. "Because if shit like this happens again, I will lock your skinny white ass up and throw away the key. You got me?"

I ignored him. When we reached my car, Kirsten put a hand on my arm. Her face showed concern. "You okay to drive?"

"Yeah, I'm fine. Thanks for tonight."

"Jinx, I'm seriously worried about you."

I yanked my arm out of her grip. "I said I'm fine."

"You look anorexic."

"Oh, so you're going to body-shame me for being slender."

"That's not it, and you know it. I'm concerned. You're not slender; you're emaciated. You're clearly not eating. You're driving and working while under the influence. And if you don't get help soon, situations like tonight or worse are going to happen again. And I may not be able to keep you out of jail. Or the morgue."

"If I wanted someone to play armchair therapist, I'd call up my dad. At least he's the real deal."

"Jinx, I'm only saying this because I care."

I turned away, irritated. "Maybe you shouldn't care so much. Conor cared, and look where it got him." I climbed behind the wheel of the Dodge Charger.

Kirsten started to say something, but I revved the engine.

"What's that? I can't hear you!"

"I said—"

I revved the engine louder and roared out of the parking lot, leaving twin trails of rubber on the pavement. I was a total bitch, and I knew it. But I didn't need anyone feeling sorry for me. Especially her.

3

———

I arrived home around eleven o'clock to the boundless energy of Diana, my nine-month-old golden retriever. She jumped and yipped with excitement as I closed the front door. Her paws were covered in dirt from digging in the backyard, but I didn't care. With all the shit going on in my life, Diana was my one source of happiness. I'd never thought of myself as a dog person before my brother, Jake, gave her to me as a Christmas present. But now I couldn't imagine my life without her.

"Hey, baby girl." I lay on the floor and let her slather me with slobbery puppy kisses. "How you doing?"

I went to hug her, and she bolted to the kitchen. "Fine. Be that way."

She returned a moment later with her empty food bowl in her mouth. *Shit. I forgot to fill it before I left this morning.* "I'm sorry, baby. Mama was out later than expected."

I grabbed the bag of gourmet kibble from the pantry and filled her bowl. She dug in, tail wagging like a high-speed metronome.

I tried to remember if I'd eaten that day and couldn't recall anything. The dishes in my sink were at least a couple of days old.

The fridge was empty except for a gallon of milk that was turning lumpy. I checked the pantry. A package of ramen, a few dusty cans of tuna, and a box of Rice-A-Roni. I looked at the instructions on the Rice-A-Roni box. It required butter, which I didn't have, unless the sour milk counted. I settled for the ramen dusted with the contents of the "oriental-flavor" seasoning packet. I concluded that if oriental really was a flavor, it shouldn't be.

The old me would have had plenty of healthy food in the kitchen. And it wasn't like I was short of funds. End of last year, I'd brought in two hundred grand for capturing one of the FBI's most wanted. My fiancé, Conor Doyle, had listed me as his beneficiary on his life insurance policy, so when he was declared dead, I'd inherited a sizable sum.

If anything, I was short on motivation. The thought of wandering the grocery store aisles, dodging idiots who paid no attention to where they were going, set my teeth on edge. Last time I was there, I was two seconds away from bludgeoning an old man who'd been blocking the aisle with his cart for five minutes, trying to decide between two brands of canned peas. They were canned peas, for fuck's sake. They all taste like green mush, so just pick one!

Using the wall for balance, I zombie-shuffled down the hall to my bedroom with Diana trailing me. I lay on sheets that hadn't been washed in weeks and stared at the popcorn ceiling. My body craved sleep, but my mind wouldn't shut off.

As Diana snuggled her warm body next to me, I kept thinking about Wilhelm Penzler. Was it an accident? Was it suicide? Either way, he'd still be alive if not for me. A lot of people would still be alive if not for me. In nine years as a bounty hunter, I'd killed nearly a dozen people. Granted, the world was a better place without most of them—drug dealers, human traffickers, rapists, murderers, and a few terrorists.

But each one came with a cost. What made me better than any of them? I didn't solve crimes. I just tracked down people who didn't show up for court and took them to jail. Before you knew it, most were bailed out again. I was useless. A drain on society. A drain with a mail-order badge and a gun.

At some point, I drifted off because the next thing I heard was the garbage truck rumbling down the street. Diana dangled a slobbery leash in my face.

"Hey, puppy." I gave her a head scratch. "What's up?" As if I didn't know.

She dropped the leash beside me on the bed and gave an impatient whine.

"Okay, let's go for a run."

I dragged myself to the bathroom, emptied my bladder, and stared at my reflection in the mirror. Gaunt didn't describe it. Aside from the limp black hair, the pale woman staring back at me looked like a White Walker from *Game of Thrones*.

"Bitch, get your shit together," I muttered.

My phone rang. I glanced at the screen. *Ugh.* Sadie Fucking Levinson of Assurity Bail Bonds. I sent the call to voice mail. She was going to have a shit fit when I told her dear old Wilhelm Penzler failed his first flying lesson.

A text appeared on the screen. "Ms. Ballou, get your tuchus in here."

I was in no mood to deal with her attitude. *It's Saturday*, I replied.

Don't care what day it is. Get here now. Not a request.

I pulled on a mostly clean T-shirt and a pair of shorts, grabbed a Wonder Woman baseball cap, snapped a leash to Diana's collar, and we went for a run through the neighborhood.

I lived in Phoenix's historic Willo District, near Third Avenue and McDowell Road. The neighborhood was a labyrinth of streets lined with small but pricey brick houses sheltered by maturing shade trees. The area attracted quirky Gen Xers and millennials who sported a lot of ink and had a live-and-let-live attitude.

Up until last December, I'd lived a couple of streets north in a house that my brother had renovated and sold to me for a song after the housing bubble burst.

After Conor was declared dead, I inherited his house, which I'd nicknamed the Bunker. It had twelve-inch-thick brick outer walls, bullet-resistant polycarbonate windows, and steel-reinforced doors. Oh, and there was the underground tunnel that led from the coat closet to the back room of a tattoo shop on McDowell Road. Conor had hardened the place's defenses after a drug dealer he'd returned to jail sent his crew to retaliate.

I'd offered my old house rent free to a few transgender friends who needed a safe place to transition and rebuild their lives. Not everyone had a supportive family like mine.

The cool air buzzed with the droning of leaf blowers, their modulating pitches going in and out of phase with each other. Despite the high temperature hitting the triple-digit mark just days ago, a cool front had settled in, giving the city a temporary reprieve before summer blazed into full fury.

Fellow residents walking with their canine companions waved as we passed. I knew faces and dogs but not names. The petite Korean woman with the Shiba Inu. The older white guy with the pug. The muscular Latino with the Belgian Malinois.

Just as well we never spoke. Who in their right mind would want to know me? I was a drunken loser who'd been engaged to a man wanted for terrorism. Didn't exactly make for pleasant small talk.

How was your day?

It was great! I got wasted and let a fugitive take a twenty-foot nosedive into a parking lot. How was yours?

Diana stopped to lift a leg next to the tire of a pickup decorated with MAGA and NRA bumper stickers.

"Good dog," I said before rounding the corner back toward home.

After our run, I hopped into the shower to wash off the previous night's shame, got dressed, and pulled my hair into a ponytail without bothering to blow it dry. This was Arizona. It'd be dry in thirty minutes, anyway.

For breakfast, I poured coffee into a travel mug and flavored it with a dash of coconut rum. Or more than a dash. I needed a little liquid courage before I told Sadie about Penzler's recent demise, assuming she didn't already know.

I strapped my ballistic vest over my T-shirt. I hooked my utility belt around my waist and slipped a Taser in the holster on my right hip, a Ruger nine-mil in a cross-draw on my left. Pouches in back held two pairs of handcuffs, a spare Taser cartridge, and a spare magazine of ammo. I hung my bail enforcement agent badge around my neck and slipped on a pair of wraparound shades, followed by a pair of fingerless gloves. Ready for action.

"Okay, Diana. Be good while I'm gone." I topped off her food bowl and filled her water bowl from the RO spout. "Try not to terrorize the feral cats too much."

She responded with a bark, which I took to mean, "Yeah, who are you kidding?"

I hopped into the Charger and cruised downtown for my meeting with Sadie.

4

I drove south a few miles to the Arizona Center, an open-air shopping center that was a mix of trendy restaurants, touristy shops, and small business offices. Assurity Bail Bonds was tucked away on the second floor in the corner of the L-shaped complex. A string of bells jingled as I walked in.

Unlike most bail bond shops, which had all the charm and elegance of a check-cashing joint, Assurity looked more like a cross between a law office and an art gallery. Plush carpeting. Framed prints on the wall. Leather armchairs for clients. Two cherrywood desks separated the waiting area from the rest of the office. One of them was occupied by Sadie, who did not look pleased to see me, despite her urgent texts.

Her wedge-cut helmet of hair was immaculate as always. Her makeup understated and professional. And the scowl on her face all too familiar.

I plopped down in one of the chairs in front of her desk. "Whassup?"

The creases in the corners of her eyes deepened. "Whassup?" she echoed in a mocking tone. "Are you genuinely asking me that? Where is Mr. Penzler?"

"Well, you see, there was an incident."

She pulled a folded newspaper from the side of her desk and slapped it down between us. The headline read "Mob Informant Leaps to Death."

"Would this be the 'incident' in question?" Her mouth was an ugly slash across her face.

I shifted in my seat. Maybe I should've brought Diana with me. Or that bottle of rum. "Yeah, poor Penzler, huh? Maybe the Volkovs got to him."

"Don't give me any of that mishegas, Ms. Ballou. It's beneath even you. Tell me what happened."

"Look, I tracked him to a motel off I-17 and Northern. Talked my way inside, but when I cuffed him, he busted through the doorway so hard he flipped over the railing. Totally not my fault."

"And were you drunk like you are this morning?"

"Drunk? Who's drunk?" I stood in protest.

"Don't even try! You smell like a tiki bar."

"My point is Wilhelm Penzler either fell by accident or he jumped. Cops said so. At least you don't have to pay out the full bail amount."

"I have a business to run, and Mr. Penzler was a client. In the past three months, I've had more than a dozen complaints against you. Harassment. Assault. Abusive language. One gentleman claimed you broke his wrist."

"That asshole broke his own wrist trying to squeeze out of the cuffs."

"Not what he said." She turned her attention to her computer screen.

"Who you gonna believe? Me or your criminal clients? Besides, a little rough play makes them more likely to show up to court."

"You've got chutzpah. I'll give you that."

"Thank you. I think."

"You're fired."

The words hit me like a gunshot from a sniper. "What?"

"You heard me." Her gaze met mine. "I have no need for someone who lacks a single iota of professionalism. I'm reassigning your remaining cases to Viper Fugitive Recovery."

"What about me? Where am I supposed to go? No one else will hire me."

"Not my problem." She tossed the newspaper in the trash and turned back to her computer.

"I've recovered a ton of fugitives, including some that no one else could locate. Paul Russo. Doug Chang. Shelly Reid. Steve Shaw." I counted each one off on my hand. "Remember Holly Schwartz? Not even Fiddler could track her down. I did."

Sadie leaned back and crossed her arms. "Yes, you used to be an ace bounty hunter. And you'll recall I hired you when no one else would. I didn't care if you were transgender. All I cared about was results. Right now, your results are bupkis. Time you get over Conor Doyle's death and ..."

The mention of Conor's name sent a bright blade of rage slicing through me. "Leave Conor out of this!" I slammed my fist on the desk so hard she jumped. "I bet you're the one who snitched on him to the Northern Ireland police."

"I did nothing of the kind." Her face became a wall of stone.

"Only three people knew about Conor's past. Conor, me, and you. And I sure as fuck didn't turn him in."

"Ms. Ballou...Jinx." She took a breath, and her expression softened. "I apologize for what I said. While I did not care for the man, I kept my knowledge of Conor's past to myself. And I am sorry for your loss."

"I don't need your pity, lady."

"Jinx, listen to me."

Were those tears in her eyes?

She put a hand on my arm. "I respect you. You have the potential to be a top-notch bail enforcement professional. But since Conor's passing, you've fallen apart. Understandable. Grief hits us hard. I struggled after my father passed. But you need to get help. Until you do, you're a liability."

I stepped away from the desk, even as my own eyes threatened to water. I was not gonna let her see me cry. "Fuck you, bitch! I don't need this shit, anyway. I got money. Maybe I'll just hang out at coffee shops and write a novel."

"Do what you like, Ms. Ballou. But for your own sake, get some help. Your father's a psychologist, isn't he? I'm sure he can recommend someone."

I flipped her a single-finger salute with each hand, turned on my heels, and marched out of the door.

On the way home, I stopped at a liquor store and picked up a couple of bottles of tequila. Back in the car, I poured some into a travel cup. Fuel for the road.

Despite my simmering rage, I kept to the speed limit as I drove north up Seventh Street. Not hard to do since there were so many stoplights.

"Go, you fucking idiot!" I shouted at the Ford Explorer ahead of me, going five miles under the speed limit. When I finally passed him, I noticed the Phoenix Police decal on the side of the car. *Fuck!*

I kept pace with the patrol vehicle until it turned west on McDowell, then I floored it. *Fucking slow cop.*

I was feeling better when I pulled into my driveway. Grabbed the paper bag with the two bottles along with my travel cup and shuffled to the front door. Took me a moment to figure out the right key to open the door. When I finally stumbled inside, I collapsed on the couch and turned on the TV.

For the record, daytime television sucks ass. Seriously, it's all talk shows with the worst sorts of people on. And the commercials. Holy fuck me with a spoon! Nothing but ambulance chasers, substandard insurance, and pharmaceutical ads with a mile-long list of horrific side effects. I finally found a punk-rock music channel and cranked it up while I vegged to ponder what a shithole my life had become.

"Hey! Can you turn it down? Some of us are trying to sleep."

I looked up to see an androgynous person in a wifebeater and boxers standing over me.

"Who the fuck are you?" I asked.

"I'm Max, and I live here. Who the hell are you?"

"This is my fucking house!" I tried to stand up, but the room wobbled, so I sank back down on the couch.

"Like hell it is. I've never seen you before. I'm getting Ciara."

Ciara. The name was familiar. Ciara. Ciara Mountains. No, that was the Sierra-something Mountains. Who was Ciara again?

Next thing I knew, a woman with a familiar yet asymmetrical face was standing next to the asshole, telling me to get out of my own goddamn house. Ciara. Now I remembered. I drained my travel cup.

"Jinx, what are you doing here?"

"I'm sitting here listening to music in my house. What are you doing here?"

"I was trying to do some bookkeeping until Max interrupted me."

Max. The asshole giving me shit. "Tell Max to get the hell out of my house, then."

"Jinx, Max lives here. And while yes, technically you still own this house, you live in Conor's old place now. Remember?"

Thoughts flitted against the current of booze lubricating my brain. Shit. I was at my old house. Ciara was...was something...oh yeah, she was the resident manager. Fuck.

I took a deep breath and looked at the asshole. Max. Not an asshole. Or maybe an asshole. Wasn't sure. "Look, man, I'm sorry. I got a little confused."

"Like I don't have enough shit to deal with." Max crossed his arms.

I rolled my eyes. "Whatever. Just sorry." I pulled myself to my feet. The room spun, but I managed to stay upright and hold onto the bottle of tequila. "I'm outta here."

Ciara put a flat hand on my chest. "Whoa. You can't drive

home like this. Come on. There's an empty bed in my room. Sleep it off."

I looked at her. Or tried to. Everything was so goddamn swirly and hard to focus on. I was tired. "Yeah, okay."

5

———

I woke with my mouth tasting of coconut-flavored bile. The bedsheets didn't feel right, though the room was vaguely familiar. The front of my shirt was damp.

"Diana?" I called. Where was she?

"Feeling better?" Ciara stepped in and flicked on the overhead lamp, sending steely shards of light through my eye sockets.

I squinted in the glare. "Oh fuck. Tell me I didn't do anything too stupid."

"You mean like yelling at our newest resident and puking in the bathtub? Yeah, a little."

"Shit. I'm sorry." I rubbed my temples, trying to get the explosions of pain to stop.

"No worries." Ciara sat next to me on the bed and offered a glass filled with something red. "Here, have some of my hangover remedy."

I took a sip. It was thicker than it looked, but it didn't taste bad. "What's in it?"

"Spicy V8, raw egg, parsley, and a dash of lemon juice. You'll want to drink a lot of water too. That much alcohol will dehydrate you."

"Thanks. You're a good friend."

"You're a good friend, too, usually."

"But not lately."

She shrugged. "You've been in a slump. I get it."

"I...I haven't been myself since Conor..." I was surprised by my openness. I hadn't exactly been forthcoming with my feelings of late, other than rage.

"Can't blame you there. After I was attacked a couple years ago, I had a lot of PTSD. Even now, sometimes I feel triggered looking at my misshapen eye and jaw. The doctors saved my life, but I couldn't afford a reconstructive surgeon."

I felt guilty. I'd experienced a similar attack on my high school graduation night. But I had supportive parents with good insurance. Ciara didn't have anybody but her friends in the trans community.

"You look good, Ciara. Really."

She blushed. "I don't, but thanks."

We sat there as the silence grew awkward. "I should head back to my place. My real place. Thanks for helping me out." I gave her a hug and handed her the empty glass.

"That's what family's for. And if you need to talk, you got my number."

"I do. And I know where you live."

She laughed, and it sounded like sunshine. "You off to capture more bad guys?"

I let out a deep sigh. "I got fired this morning. So, no."

"For being trans?"

"No, for being a drunken bitch."

"You need money?"

I shook my head. "No, I'm good. Just need to get my shit together."

I grabbed my utility belt and vest and followed Ciara to the front door. The sun was riding the horizon, painting the clouds with red, orange, and lavender. How long had I been asleep?

"Take care of yourself, Jinx. Maybe you should look into getting some—"

I cut her off with a gesture. "Don't say it. I know. I need help. When I'm ready, I'll...I don't know. I guess I'll talk to someone."

After a final hug, I walked wearily to the Charger and drove up two streets to the Bunker. A black SUV sat parked in front of the house. With the light bar on top, it looked like a police vehicle. But the gold lettering on the side read Viper Fugitive Recovery.

"Shit." I pulled under my carport and walked down the driveway toward my visitor.

A white guy I recognized as Paul "Deez" Dzundza climbed out of the SUV. I had a vague memory of a recent text conversation with him, though the details escaped me.

Deez stood six-eight, a walking wall of muscle. Even in the fading light, I could see the scar on his neck from when he'd taken a bullet for me three years earlier when we worked together on Conor's crew.

"I's getting worried." His voice was a gentle rumble. "I thought we said seven."

I glanced at my watch. It was seven thirty-five. "Sorry. Traffic."

"No worries." A wave of sadness washed over me when he wrapped me in a tender bear hug. I hadn't seen him since Conor's funeral.

"How's it going, Deez?"

He released me and met my gaze. "Good. How you holding up, girl?"

I shrugged. "Same shit. Different day. How's Tommy Boy?"

"That kid of mine won't quit growing. Just turned twenty-five. He's an inch taller than me now."

"Twenty-five? Shit. Guess that makes you..."

"Old as the hills." His eyes watered. "We've missed you, kid."

"Yeah, me too."

"Sorry about Assurity. That wasn't my doing. I'd never steal work from you. You know that, right?"

"I know." My headache started hammering a little harder behind my eyes.

"I'd love to have you on the team again."

Memories of the day he got shot gutted me with guilt. "Thanks for the offer, but you know, I got my own thing going."

"Well, listen, I have a job I think might be right up your alley."

"Deez, Sadie gave me the boot. She doesn't want me anywhere near her cases."

"This isn't Assurity. It's Pima Bail Bonds in Scottsdale."

"Pima? They didn't want anything to do with me after I got outed a few years ago."

"I know, but this case is different. I've already talked to Maurice about it. He's cool with you taking it."

I narrowed my gaze at him. "Why?"

"It's the James Fitzgerald murder case. You familiar with it?"

"That preacher? The one that got his dick cut off in the sleazy motel? Why does Maurice want me to take the case?"

Deez hesitated a moment. "The client's transgender like you."

I eye-rolled hard. "Oh, I get it. Maurice will hire me if I'm putting away one of my own. Is that it? Well, you can tell Maurice Begay that I won't be his Judas, all right?"

Deez put a hand on my shoulder. "It's not like that. From what I'm told, this client got roughed up pretty bad in lockup before she was bailed out. Put her in with the men."

My stomach turned. Recent changes in DOC policy dictated that transgender prisoners be housed based on their assigned sex at birth, even those who had had gender confirmation surgery. Many had been assaulted as a result, and one had died. Lawsuits had been filed, but so far, DOC hadn't blinked.

"Shit, Deez, and you want me to put her back in that hellhole?"

"No, but who better to safely return this woman to custody and get her bail reset but someone like you?"

"What'd she do?"

"Charged with first-degree murder for allegedly killing Brother James Fitzgerald."

I shook my head. "That fucking street preacher who showed up at schools, saying women deserved to be raped and calling for queer people to be put to death? We should give her a medal, not lock her up."

"I don't disagree. Nevertheless, she jumped bail. I had Tommy Boy and Rodeo on it, but they hit a brick wall. Pearson's a member of an all-girl biker gang up north. They're not giving her up."

"Not my problem."

"Think about it, Jinx. If you don't take it, Maurice will assign the job to someone else, someone who isn't afraid to get rough."

"How long before the bond is forfeit?"

"Little over a week. You could ask for double the standard rate. Maurice'll pay it. Bail's at three hundred thousand. That'd be a sweet sixty grand for you."

I thought about it, then shook my head. "I appreciate you thinking of me, man, but I can't do it. Maurice had his chance to hire me a few years ago. If the only reason he wants me now is to go after one of my own, he can go to hell."

"I understand." Deez shook my hand and clapped me on the back. "If you change your mind, let me know."

"Yeah, whatever."

"Take care of yourself, Jinx. You're family to Tommy and me."

"Likewise." I trudged back down my driveway.

"Hey!" he called from inside his SUV.

I turned. "Yeah?"

"Let's get a drink sometime."

"Yeah. I'll call you." I wouldn't. Too many fucked-up memories.

Inside the house, Diana jumped up and nearly bowled me over. "Hey, baby! How's my girl?"

I filled her bowls with kibble and water, then plopped down

in front of the TV, looking for something on Netflix to help me unplug. Nothing looked interesting.

I pulled out my phone. My best friend, Becca Alvarez, had left a message asking me to call her. No doubt she was worried about me too. Like I needed anyone else's pity.

I tossed the phone aside, opened the other bottle of tequila, and settled in to binge-watch *Dexter*. Something satisfying about watching assholes get what they deserve.

6

———

I didn't know how long I had been staring at my ceiling—
minutes, hours, weeks. Diana lay beside me, her head on
my chest. I would have stayed there, but my bladder was so
full my back teeth were floating.

I padded to the bathroom and sat on the toilet. The golden
glow of morning shone through the window. A clock on the wall
told me it was nine o'clock.

What the hell am I going to do now? I had liked working for
Sadie Levinson. Sure, she had a stick up her ass, but after I was
publicly outed by a local newspaper, she'd given me a chance
when no one else would. And now I'd screwed that up.

The thought of taking the job with Pima Bail Bonds turned my
stomach. Tracking down a transgender woman to throw her back in
jail? I don't think so. Jail's bad enough for cisgender people. For trans
people, it's a fucking nightmare. No way would I be a part of that.

I felt lost with nothing to do, nothing to look forward to. Like
a sailboat adrift in the doldrums.

I was shambling into the kitchen when the doorbell rang. I
glanced at a video monitor on the wall that showed my bestie,

Becca Alvarez, and her nonbinary partner, Easton St. Claire, at my front door.

Becca and I had been thick as thieves since we first met in middle school. She now worked as a freelance IT security consultant, whom I frequently hired for skip tracing.

Becca was dressed in a shirt emblazoned with a portrait of Frida Kahlo made up like a sugar skull. Easton wore a cornflower-blue button-down with a yellow tie and matching suspenders.

I pressed the call button. "Hold on a sec."

I ran to the bedroom and pulled on a clean shirt and jeans. Diana started whining, clearly wanting to go for her morning run.

"Gonna have to wait, girl."

She shot me a look of disappointment.

"Hey." I opened the door and welcomed Becca and Easton inside. They each gave me a lukewarm hug and greeted Diana enthusiastically. "Want some coffee?"

"Sure," said Becca in a curt tone she often took when she was upset about something.

They followed me into the kitchen and sat at the antique wooden table that my grandmother Marie Lafitte had given me. She claimed it once belonged to our ancestor, the legendary pirate Jean Lafitte. I filled three mugs with coffee. "How you want your coffee?"

"A little cream," Becca answered.

"Black's fine for me," Easton replied.

I added a dash of cream in Becca's and brought all three mugs to the table.

"What's up?" I said in my most convincing "everything's great" tone.

Becca stared daggers at me. "You don't answer my calls. Don't reply to my texts. Your hair looks like a rat's nest, and you look and smell like something Diana threw up."

Diana glanced up at the mention of her name, her tail wagging excitedly.

"Becks, I've been busy."

"Bullshit! In the years we've known each other, you've never shut me out like this. You didn't go to Pride. You haven't shown up at the Hub since Goddess knows when."

The Hub was a coworking space downtown where we shared a table for our respective businesses.

"I called you to get a location for Wilhelm Penzler," I pointed out.

"And then hung up on me before I could say anything else. Are you even signed up for Phoenix Fan Fusion? Or have you given up cosplaying too?"

"I'm dealing with enough shit without you getting all up in my grill."

Easton put a hand on mine. Flecks of glitter in their nail polish sparkled in the morning light. "Jinx, we're not here to guilt-trip you. We're concerned about you. You look depressed."

"And anorexic," Becca added.

"Don't body-shame me!" I wrapped my arms around my chest.

"I'm not body-shaming you, Jinxie. I'm worried." The angles of Becca's face softened. "You and me, we've had each other's backs since forever. Part of that meant speaking up if the other was self-destructing."

Words caught in my throat. I hated that she was right.

"Remember what I went through when my mom got sick?" she asked. "Between the grief from her death and my chronic fatigue flaring up, I felt like a zombie. You were there for me, even when I tried to shut out the whole world. You helped me get back into my groove. You were at my apartment so much my dad thought we were a couple."

I chuckled in spite of the immense pressure inside me. "I remember."

"With Conor gone, it's understandable what you're going

through. There's no set timeline on grieving. But it's easy to let grief turn into something more toxic. Like alcoholism. Anorexia. If this keeps up, you could get fired."

"Too late. Sadie fired me yesterday."

"I'm sorry, babe."

Becca laid her head on my shoulder. Easton side-hugged my other shoulder. I liked being in the middle of this cuddle puddle.

"Guess it's time to quit feeling sorry for myself."

"You have any prospects for work?" asked Becca.

"Deez dropped by yesterday with a job. Not sure I want it, though."

Becca turned and met my aimless gaze. "Why not?"

"The FTA is transgender."

"What's an FTA?" asked Easton.

"Failure to appear," I replied. "She didn't show up to court. She's allegedly the one who killed that douchebag Brother James."

"Holy sugar!" Easton covered their mouth in surprise. "You're talking about Zia Pearson, aren't you? I heard what happened to her in jail. It was horrible."

"Didn't look at the file, but the name sounds familiar."

"She's been on the news," they added. "Apparently, she and Brother James got into a shoving match at a biker festival in Scottsdale. That same night, he turned up dead in a skeevy motel room. Police found her partying at a strip club next door. She said she didn't do it, but even if she did, he deserved it."

"You should take the job," Becca said matter-of-factly.

"What?" I pulled away and stared at her. "Why?"

"Sooner or later, someone will. And maybe they won't be as understanding as you."

I barked a laugh. Unlike the bounty hunters portrayed on TV, I wasn't the type to get all touchy-feely with my fugitives once they were in my custody. "Understanding as I drag her ass back to jail where God knows what will happen to her, whether she's guilty or not."

"And then you can help her get her bail reset," Easton added. "Becca told me you do that sometimes."

"I don't know." The whole idea turned my stomach. "I'd feel like a traitor to the community."

"Doesn't Zia deserve her day in court?" asked Becca.

"Of course. I'm not stopping her. She's the one who failed to appear."

"But by bringing her back," said Becca, "you're giving her the opportunity to clear her name."

My head was swimming. "Let's say I bring her back. What if she's innocent, and they convict her anyway?"

Becca shook her head. "That's not on you. That's on the legal system."

"It doesn't feel right." I buried my face in my arms.

"Fine, don't take the job," said Becca. "What *are* you going to do?"

"About what?"

"Your life."

"I don't know. I don't feel like doing anything. What's the point? Between the reward I got for capturing Barclay Dietz and Conor's life insurance, I'm not exactly hurting for cash."

"This isn't about money, sweetie." Becca cradled my face in her hands, forcing me to meet her gaze. "But you know that."

I saw in her eyes the friend who'd stood up for me when I was bullied in school for being transgender. "You're right."

"Uh, hon," said Easton. "We gotta get to the airport."

Becca glanced at her watch. "Shit. You're right."

"I'm updating some backup servers in Denver," Easton said to me.

I gave them a smile that I actually felt. "Enjoy the freezing weather."

"Thanks!"

I looked at Becca then Easton. "I love you guys, people, whatever."

Easton chuckled. "Right back atcha."

"Love you, girl." Becca gave me a tight squeeze.

I led them to the door. As she was walking out, Becca turned and said, "And for the love of garbanzos, return my calls and texts next time. Maybe show up at the Hub once in a while."

"I will." And I meant it. "Let me know if you need any help while Easton's out of town."

"Will do. See you soon, I hope."

After they drove off, I grabbed Diana's leash, and the two of us went for a run. The exertion felt good, energizing me both mentally and physically, sweating out all the alcohol from the day before. I hadn't yet decided whether to take the job from Pima Bail Bonds, but I needed to get my ass in gear and do something. This pity party had gone on long enough.

I was rounding the corner back onto my street when my phone rang. Caller ID told me it was Deez.

"If you're calling to pressure me on the Pima job, I'm considering it, okay?"

"This isn't about that. It's Conor. He's..." His voice choked on emotion. "He's alive."

I just missed colliding with a palm tree. "What?"

"And he's been arrested."

7
____

"Jinx? You still there?" Deez's voice sounded like it was in a tunnel.

I leaned my back against the tree as my heart thundered in my chest. "Arrested? I...I don't understand."

"He survived the explosion. Don't ask me how. But the news is saying he ran away to Mexico before turning himself in to the police in Northern Ireland. They're convinced he's really Liam O'Callaghan, a terrorist who was involved with a bombing two decades ago. It's insane."

"I...I can't believe it."

"I know this must be a shock. Here we all thought he was dead."

Guilt and shame pressed down on me with all the crushing weight of an SUV. He turned himself in because I refused to run away with him. Thoughts swirled through my mind so fast it left me dizzy. "I need to talk to him."

"I don't know how. Though I guess he must have a lawyer...or a solicitor or barrister or whatever they call them there. I can have our investigator try to find out."

"That'd be great. And Deez, thanks for letting me know."

"You going to be all right, Jinxie?" The concern in Deez's voice threatened to rip me in two.

"Yeah, look, I gotta go, okay? I'll be in touch about the Pima job."

I hung up. Diana was tugging on her leash. "Come on, girl." I ran home at top speed.

When I got inside, I dug through the junk drawer in the kitchen until I found the old burner phone. I dialed the number saved in the Favorites. It rang three times before a recorded voice said the number was no longer in use. I threw the phone across the room.

An idea came to me. I scrambled through my home office, digging out bits of paper from my center desk drawer until I came across a business card with nothing but an email address and a single name—Tuckey.

Using an anonymizer app on my laptop, I tapped out a quick email and waited. For ten minutes, I stared at the computer screen, waiting for an instant reply. But there was nothing. "Shit."

I flipped on the TV in the living room, and there he was. Conor Doyle being hurried by police officers through a crowd and to a waiting car. The headlines read "American Hero An Irish Terrorist?" and "Piestewa Freeway Hero Faked Own Death."

My stomach convulsed. I made it to the kitchen sink and heaved until I was too weak to stand. I sank onto the cool tile floor. Diana walked in, her claws clicking on the tile, and licked my face. I held on to her and bawled.

My phone rang in the other room. I pulled myself to my feet and shambled into the living room, banging my leg against an end table. I snatched up the phone.

"Conor?" I asked breathlessly.

"Um, no. Ms. Ballou?" asked an unfamiliar male voice.

"Yeah, who the hell is this?"

"Pete Stansfield. I was the claims adjuster for Mr. Doyle's life insurance policy."

Shit. "Yeah? What do you want?"

"It has come to my attention that our payout to you of three hundred thousand dollars was…well, premature. Mr. Doyle, as it turns out, is still alive. I hate to say this, but I'm afraid you will need to return the money."

I hung up without a word and tossed the phone onto the couch.

My insides felt like a colony of ferrets were conducting an MMA free-for-all. I crawled to the pantry and grabbed a bottle of tequila, then stumbled back into the living room, where some news guy in heavy pancake makeup and overly pink lips was asking a panel of talking heads their opinions about the situation, speculating on facts they knew nothing about.

"Fuck you assholes!" I chugged what remained in the bottle. Laying my head on the couch, I spotted the handle of the Smith & Wesson .44 Magnum I kept mounted underneath my coffee table. The empty bottle clanked to the floor, and I slid the revolver from the holster.

The weight of it felt solid, almost reassuringly so. I had said goodbye to Conor twice. The first time, when I thought he was dead. A week later, on Christmas morning, Conor's buddy, Tuckey, hand delivered the burner phone with Conor's new number in it. He had survived the blast with only a broken leg and escaped to Ensenada, Mexico.

When I visited him a few weeks later, he begged me to join him. But I couldn't walk away from my friends and family. Letting him go ripped out what was left of my soul. Was I the reason he turned himself in?

Guilt and sorrow coiled around my chest, smothering me like a python. I ached to feel him in my arms, his hands on my body, to hear his Irish brogue teasing me about my cosplaying as Wonder Woman at comic book conventions.

I stared down the barrel of the revolver, the long dark tunnel drawing me in. My thumb curled over the trigger. *I'm such a waste of space. A black hole sucking joy and happiness from the good people around me. Maybe it's time I join those I've killed—all of the murderers and rapists and drug dealers and human traffickers. Am I any better than them? I've killed. I've lied. I've broken into places. I've even protected a man wanted for terrorism.*

I squeezed harder on the trigger. *What waits on the other side? Sweet oblivion or hellfire?* I pressed my forehead against the barrel. *Just squeeze and find out.*

A cold, wet nose stuck in my ear, followed by a doggy tongue. My thumb slipped out of the trigger guard, and the revolver clattered to the floor, unfired. The noise was still enough to send Diana dashing away down the hall.

"Fuck." Some angels have fur instead of wings.

"This is what happens when transsexuals are allowed to run free on our streets." I looked up to see some scumbag in a MAGA hat talking to a reporter on the TV. "They should all be rounded up and shot. They're a menace to decent society. Bad enough they're allowed to invade ladies' rooms. Now they're killing men of God? Is nothing sacred in this country? What happened to the Constitution?"

The video footage cut to a woman in shades holding a baby on her hip. "I don't really know. I mean, that preacher was telling people to rape women. That's just wrong. I don't really agree with her lifestyle, but I hope she's proven innocent."

Cut to the anchor in the studio with a photo insert of a black woman with a headful of braids. "Thanks, Mike, for that report. As of right now, Ms. Pearson's whereabouts remain unknown. The courts consider her a fugitive from justice. If you see this woman, do not approach her. She is considered dangerous and possibly armed. Instead, you are advised to call the authorities immediately."

Once I saw Zia Pearson's face, something in me shifted. *Considered dangerous and possibly armed.* They were practically telling all good ol' boys with a gun that it was open season on trans women of color.

Deep in my soul, a small flame ignited. A need. A calling to get back into the fight.

I returned the revolver to its holster under the table and shuffled to the kitchen. My refrigerator was near empty. My freezer was a wasteland of unknown objects coated in a thick layer of frost. With a little digging, I located a Marie Callender's chicken potpie, only two years out of date. Close enough.

I stuck it in the microwave. While it cooked, I filled Diana's food and water bowls. A few minutes later, I was testing my molars on hardtack piecrust and burning the roof of my mouth with magma-hot gravy. It was the best meal I'd eaten in days.

An hour later, I was showered and dressed in a clean collared shirt and cargo pants. My long black hair was braided. My breath smelled only a little like alcohol. I was mostly sober.

The TV news program was still on, this time talking about a professional photographer found stabbed to death in his studio, possibly linked to a serial killer dubbed the Valley Slasher.

I pulled out my phone and called Deez. "Tell Maurice I'll take the job. For twenty percent, not ten."

"I'll make the call. You learn any more about Conor?"

"Not yet," I said. "But I've put out some feelers."

"Keep in touch. I'm worried about our boy."

"Will do."

I hung up and checked my laptop. A reply from Tuckey. "Conor being held without bail in Belfast. Has legal team on board. Will try to learn more soon but security is tight."

"That's it?" I said out loud.

My phone rang. "Yeah?"

"Maurice has agreed to twenty percent. Head on over there, and he'll get you set up with the paperwork. When you've got it, give me a call. I'll give you a rundown of what we've already learned so you don't cover the same ground."

"Thanks, Deez."

I hung up and looked at Diana's face. "You saved my life."

Her tail wags seemed to say, "You're welcome."

"Time to rebuild."

8

———

I drove the Charger east on I-10 to Scottsdale. Pima Bail Bonds was a block away from the Scottsdale City Jail on Pima just south of Thomas. The office was an old renovated house with faded-yellow wood siding. The letters on the sign out front were peeling from decades of brutal heat.

Last time I'd been here was after the *Phoenix Living* weekly newspaper outed me as transgender and got me fired from the bail bond agency I'd worked for. Maurice was one of the many agents who'd agreed to keep my resume on file but never called. Conor later confirmed I'd been blackballed.

The cluttered office showed the years. Faded pictures, recognitions, and framed thank-you letters competed for space on the scuffed walls. The corners on the wood furniture had been worn smooth in spots. The scent of pine oil hung in the air.

Short, dark hair framed Maurice Begay's round face. He spoke in soothing tones to a frail woman who sat clutching a tissue. "Don't worry, Ms. Lewis. We'll get your son bailed out and home with you. Okay?"

She nodded wordlessly.

He handed her a stack of papers stapled together. "Take this to the Scottsdale City Jail, and they will get him processed out."

Another nod. "Thank you." She stood, and he walked her to the door.

When she was gone, Maurice turned to me. "Jinx Ballou, am I right?"

"So they tell me."

"Come on over." He led me to his desk.

"You were working for Assurity, were you not?" he asked.

Oh, brother. Here we go. "Yeah. About two years now."

"Word on the street is she fired you and hired Viper Fugitive Recovery instead."

"Sadie and I had some...creative differences."

"Creative differences?" He gave me a disbelieving look. "Those creative differences wouldn't be named Wilhelm Penzler, would they?"

"Penzler's death was an unfortunate accident. Maybe a suicide. I understand he had agreed to testify against Sergei Volkov. God knows what Volkov would've done to him if he caught him."

"And you're working for Volkov, are you? Maybe a little wet work on the side?"

"Are you kidding me?" I shot to my feet, sending the wheeled chair spinning away behind me. "Is that what you think? That I'm a hit man working undercover as a bail enforcement agent?"

"I heard you had some involvement with Sergei's brother a while back."

"Milo Volkov was a psycho dirtbag who murdered two feds and kidnapped a teenage fugitive I was tracking. I didn't work for him. I put him in the ground. Or did your research not uncover that little tidbit?"

"Relax. I wanted to see how you'd react." He leaned back and gestured toward the chair I'd vacated. "Sit down."

I did but was not cool with the way things were going. "Look, slick, you need somebody to find your wayward defendant. I'm your gal. If you'd rather play head games, I got better things to do."

"Deez recommended you for this job. Though to be honest, I wasn't expecting someone so...scrawny. This defendant, she's a member of a women's biker gang. You sure you're up to the task?"

"I get the job done. I've taken on drug dealers, murderers, sex traffickers, and domestic terrorists. A few women on motorcycles don't scare me."

He shuffled through some files and pulled out a folder and opened it facing me. "Defendant's name is Zia Pearson. She's a transgender woman who lives up in Ironwood with her wife. Bail's set at three hundred thousand. Deez thought since you're trans yourself, you might have an in he doesn't."

"How long before the bond is declared forfeit?" I asked.

His tan face darkened. "A week, I'm afraid."

"Not much time. I'm gonna have to demand twenty percent."

He gave me a shrewd look. "Deez mentioned you were looking for that. Sure you can't do it for fifteen?"

"With only a week to bring her back? I charge double for rush jobs. Deez already tried and failed. I can get her back."

I let the silence hang between us. He twiddled the pen in his hand. "Very well. Twenty percent." He held out his hand, and I shook it. "Just be sure you deliver Ms. Pearson on time."

"I'll get her." I took the folder from him and headed toward the door before turning back around. "And thanks for the opportunity."

"You can thank Deez for that."

It was getting on to two o'clock when I called Deez from my car. "I got the job. You still available to meet?"

"Absolutely. What's your twenty?"

"Still at Pima Bail Bonds."

"Meet me at Abuela's Cucina in thirty. Corner of Hayden and Indian Bend Road. Byrd and I are dropping off an FTA at the Scottsdale jail."

I found the Mexican restaurant easily enough. The lunch crowd had largely dissipated. No sign of Deez or Byrd.

I grabbed a table and ordered a couple of fish tacos. A small sign on the table advertised their top-shelf tequila. Tempted as I was for a victory celebration, I didn't want Deez to think I was a drunk. Especially after what happened to Penzler. I settled for a Dos Equis instead.

I was finishing off the tacos and my second Dos Equis when Deez and Byrd, a light-skinned African American man, strolled in the door. Byrd had joined Viper Fugitive Recovery after I left to run my own company. I waved them over.

"Jinx, you remember Byrd, right?" asked Deez.

I nodded. "We've met a couple of times."

Byrd shook my hand. "Sorry about Conor."

"Thanks." The mention of Conor's name intensified my craving for tequila. I took a deep breath, pulled out a small notepad, and opened the folder Maurice had given me. "What can you tell me about Zia Pearson?"

Deez snagged a chip from the basket on the table. "Honestly, I'm disappointed Tommy Boy and Rodeo couldn't find her."

Nathaniel "Rodeo" Kwan had been a member of my team until I got blackballed. Despite his loyalty to me, he needed paying work and joined the Viper crew.

"Tommy and Rodeo are good hunters. Some people are just harder to find," I replied.

"And to be fair," added Byrd, "they got close. Missed her by minutes one time. Pearson's got a lot of people trying to keep her out of jail."

"Interesting."

Deez opened up a notebook of his own. "Zia Dominique Pearson, goes by the nickname Indigo. Two prior arrests, one for solicitation, another for possession. Charges dropped on the solicitation, probation on the possession charge. She works for the Lambda Resource Center, an LGBTQ support organization up in Ironwood."

I flipped through the file. "What does she do for Lambda?"

"Serves as community relations with the Cortes County Sheriff's Office. Her boss told Rodeo and Tommy Boy she's on temporary leave. No intel on her current whereabouts."

"Maurice mentioned Pearson belongs to a biker gang. What can you tell me about them?"

"The Athena Sisterhood Motorcycle Club," said Byrd with a dark chuckle. "Some seriously scary chicks."

"Pearson and her wife, Chelsea Tucker, are both patched members," added Deez. "The club's based in Cortes County, though it's not unusual to see them here in the valley. Not technically an outlaw club like the Confederate Thunder or Hell's Angels but still pretty hardcore from what I hear. Had a few run-ins with the law over the years."

I jotted notes as they talked. "Tell me about Pearson's wife."

Deez nodded. "Chelsea Tucker works as an EMT. Former military medic. Goes by the nickname Savage. Tommy Boy and Rodeo searched their house. Looked like Pearson had pulled up stakes and left."

"Who is this Shea Stevens? The one who put up the bond. Used her house and a fleet of motorcycles she owns as collateral."

"One of her biker buddies," Byrd replied. "Ex-con who did time for grand theft auto a while back."

"She's the co-owner of Iron Goddess Custom Cycles," said Deez. "It's a motorcycle shop in Sycamore Springs that hires a lot of second-chancers."

"Second-chancers?"

"Ex-cons, recovering addicts, and the like," Deez explained.

"Stevens sounds like a real peach," I joked. "Think she's single?"

"Oh, it gets better," Byrd added. "This chick's father was president of the Confederate Thunder biker gang until he murdered Shea's mom about twenty years ago. In 2016, Shea and the Thunder teamed up against a Latino drug gang after Stevens's niece got kidnapped. Things got bloody."

"Shit. Starting to sound like a real FUBAR job."

"You think you can handle it?" asked Deez.

"Oh, I can handle it." I had no idea how, but that never stopped me. "Though I could use a little backup. My guy, Caden, quit the business after he got shot last year. And Conor, well...you know. Maybe you could spare Rodeo, since he used to work for me."

"Rodeo's currently working another case." Deez glanced at Byrd, who nodded. "But my man here can give you a hand, if you need it."

Working with someone new was always awkward. But Byrd was a veteran bounty hunter who knew how to pull his weight or he wouldn't have been working for Viper as long as he had.

"That'd be great." I locked eyes with Byrd. "I appreciate the help."

The server laid down another bowl of chips as I stared at the paperwork. "I'm thinking maybe the best approach is to do this low-key. No show of force."

Deez nodded. "Maybe you being a woman, and a transgender one at that, will yield better results."

"How amenable you think Maurice will be to recommending her bail be reset?"

"I've worked a number of Maurice's cases. He's a reasonable guy. As long as a defendant wasn't violent when we recovered them, Maurice was usually able to get bail reset."

"Good, because that may be my only bargaining chip. Convincing a trans woman to sit in a men's jail through her trial would be impossible. I wouldn't even attempt it."

"Under the circumstances, I'm sure Maurice would consider it."

"Any idea where Pearson's hanging out?"

"Tommy Boy and Rodeo seemed to think Stevens was hiding her. But they weren't willing to risk a shoot-out on a hunch."

The more I thought about the job, the more a feeling of dread crept over me, like I was walking into a deep, dark cave without a light. I felt a strong desire to just get fucked up again. Tequila therapy.

I set down a few bills to pay my check. "Thanks, Deez. I'll let you know how it turns out."

"Good to see you again, girl." As we stood to leave, Deez drew me into a hug. "You hear any more about Conor?"

I shook my head. "Just that he's being held without bail in Belfast."

"Still can't believe the fucker's still alive and didn't reach out. This whole mess about a bombing in Northern Ireland just floors me. The man I knew would never do something like that."

I didn't know how to respond. To Byrd, I said, "Meet me at my place tomorrow morning at eight. Pack a bag in case it takes us a few days. We'll head up to Cortes County in the Gray Ghost."

"That beat-up old SUV that looks like it belongs to a soccer mom?" Byrd laughed.

"She may not be pretty, but she blends in. Perfect for sneaking up on fugitives. Driving around in one of those shiny new SUVs you guys at Viper drive—all decked out with light bars and decals that practically scream 'cop'—I'm surprised you catch anything more than a cold."

"Touché, girl. Touché." Byrd clapped me on the shoulder. "I'll see you at eight."

9

I returned to central Phoenix and cruised into the Hub's parking lot, near Roosevelt Street and Grand Avenue. The large, glass-sided building dated back to the 1940s when it served as a car dealership. It resembled an inverted boat hull with a broad metal beam that jutted from the roof, piercing the sky like a ram bow.

The Hub's interior was raw and industrial. Steel beams rose like spires from the concrete slab floor to the cavernous ceiling. Krewella's song "Alive" thrummed from speakers in the back, the volume turned up just enough to make it recognizable.

Once my eyes adjusted to the dim lighting, I navigated through the maze of folding tables where entrepreneurs—from tech startups to accountants to Realtors—had created a home base for their businesses.

"Hey." I sat in my chair across from Becca.

Mock surprise bloomed across her face. "I don't believe it. Could it be? No way! Not the one and only Jinx Ballou, bounty hunter extraordinaire. She hasn't been seen in these here parts in almost forever."

I smirked. "Funny. And for your information, I took that job I told you about."

"Really?" She rushed over and hugged me. "So good to have my bestie back from the dead."

"Good to be back."

She sniffed. "You been drinking?"

I gave her a look. "Becks, don't start."

"Fine." She pulled her chair around next to me. Her face grew serious. "Speaking of being back from the dead, did you hear about...?"

"Conor? Yeah."

"Did you know he was still alive?"

I held her gaze and knew I couldn't lie anymore to her about it. "Not at first. On Christmas morning, he had a burner phone delivered to me. When I called him, it felt like talking to a ghost."

She punched my arm. "And you didn't tell me? What happened to sisters before misters?"

"I'm sorry. I...I didn't know what to do. For a week, I thought he was dead and then...it was so fucked up. I was fucked up."

"That's why you took that trip right after New Year's. You went down to see him in Mexico."

I nodded. "He wanted me to run away with him. But I couldn't walk away from you and everyone I cared about, not even for Conor. And I loved him so much." Sorrow gripped my throat, choking off my words.

She squeezed me tight. "I'm sorry. But I'm glad you stayed."

"Me too."

"But now he's been arrested for that bombing in Northern Ireland?" Becca was the only other person I'd told about Conor's past. "He was a teenager when it happened, and all he did was phone the local media."

"I know." I took a deep breath. "You forgive me for not telling you he was alive?"

She sighed as she thought it over. "Yes. But no more secrets, all right?"

"No more secrets."

I pulled out the notebook where I had stashed the Pearson folder. "Now, I need you to do your magic and see what you can find out on Zia Pearson. Also her wife, Chelsea Tucker, and Shea Stevens, the one who put up the collateral for the bail bond."

Becca took the folder from me. "Will do."

10

____

The next morning, Byrd showed up in a red Chevy Malibu at quarter to eight. Diana greeted him at the door with a wagging tail and a few friendly barks. Byrd looked a little wary. "He bite?"

"She," I corrected. I grabbed her by the collar and pulled her back as I let him inside. "And in answer to your question, no. Diana's friendly."

Byrd walked in carrying a gear bag over his shoulder. He wore a heavy leather jacket over a navy-blue T-shirt. "She's cute. My pittie, Peaches, loves people. Not so good around other dogs, though."

"Thanks. She keeps me sane or as close to it as I come." I pointed toward the hallway. "Diana, go lay down." She trotted back to my bedroom.

"You want some coffee?" I offered.

"Naw, just ready to get this show on the road."

I flicked off the coffeepot. "Sounds good to me."

I pulled on the wool-blend winter coat that I'd dug out of the back of my closet. I hadn't worn it in two years, and the shoulders had a layer of dust on them.

I stuffed the Pearson file, filled with printouts of the background info Becca had dug up, into my notebook and tucked it under one arm. With my other hand, I grabbed my canvas go bag, which contained my Kevlar vest, my weapons, extra ammo, clothes, and other essentials. "Okay, let's do this thing."

We threw our gear into the back of the Gray Ghost, an eight-year-old Nissan Pathfinder covered in scratches, swapped paint, and a few spots of missing trim.

I hopped behind the wheel. Byrd slid in beside me. I started up the Ghost and pressed Play on the sound system. The Pink Trinkets' *TERF Whores* album filled the truck with screaming guitars and feminist vocals.

"So this stuff about Conor is something else, huh? First he's alive. Now it comes out he was a terrorist in his teenage years?"

"He wasn't a terrorist. His father was a member of the IRA. Conor was just a kid who got caught up in the conflict." I wasn't one to open my heart to strangers. But Byrd had worked with Conor for a while now.

"He was a good man. Is...is a good man. A miracle he survived the Piestewa bombing. I saw photos of the carnage. Somebody upstairs was looking out for him that day."

"Yeah." I wasn't much of a believer myself. I'd seen too much.

"You talk to him?"

"Not recently." It was as close to the truth as I wanted to go.

The miles dragged on as the silence between us grew awkward. We left the city for the long, lonely stretches of scrub desert. Towering saguaros and scraggly chollas eked out an existence among aromatic creosote and brittlebush. Clusters of green-barked palo verde trees huddled along the washes. Rugged mountains rose in the hazy distance on all sides.

An hour later, the road twisted up in the rocky switchbacks of Sycamore Mountain. Clusters of yucca clung to the craggy mountainside, white blooms rising on stalks above the prickly leaves. Spiny lizards darted from their sunny perches as we passed.

The air was chilly at the top, just barely in the forties,

according to my dashboard. A wooden sign welcomed us to Olde Towne Sycamore Springs, a mile-long string of family-owned cafés, antique shops, and a real estate office or two.

"Iron Goddess Custom Cycles" was painted on the plate glass window of a storefront to my right. Five motorcycles sat out front in half-width spaces. Women in full biker leathers, their faces covered with bandanas, stood out front chatting despite the cold.

I pulled into the first full-sized space and surveyed the area.

"Looks like Shea Stevens is doing all right for herself, running a place like this," Byrd said.

"I've been meaning to stop here for some time. Been thinking of learning to ride. I hear Iron Goddess makes some kick-ass bikes."

Byrd shot me a grin. "You're going to take Stevens's friend back to jail and then ask her to sell you a bike? Girl, that is bold."

"You think she'd rather lose her house for defaulting on the bond? You ask me, we're doing her a favor."

"So how you want to play this?"

"Low-key. No weapons, except concealed. No vests. No badges. I'll introduce ourselves, explain we just want to help Pearson get her bail reset so she can stay out of jail until she gets her name cleared."

"You think that'll work with these hard-core biker chicks?"

"Rodeo and Tommy Boy tried the tough-guy approach. Figured it's worth a shot."

"I'll follow your lead, then."

We hopped out of the Ghost and stepped into the shop. The place was bigger than I expected. To our right, motorcycle jackets and leather chaps hung from racks in front of a wall display of helmets. To our left, T-shirts, hoodies, and clothing featured the Iron Goddess logo. Several customers, mostly women, wandered aisles.

On the other side of the sales counter, a dozen or so motorcycles gleamed on the showroom floor. The adrenaline junkie in me gazed longingly at the mechanical beasts, a perfect blend of artistry, engineering, and raw horsepower.

A stick of a woman in her forties with long bottle-blond hair and leathery tan skin sat behind the sales counter, flipping through a magazine. She reminded me of an aging pinup girl. "Can I help y'all find anything?" she asked.

"We're looking for Shea Stevens."

"And you are?"

"Jinx Ballou. This is my partner...Byrd." I realized I didn't know his first name.

The woman behind the counter regarded the two of us for a moment. "Wait here." She sauntered to the back of the showroom and down a hallway.

I caught Byrd staring at her waggling ass, and I nudged him. "Cut it out."

"What? A man can't appreciate God's fine craftsmanship?"

"Oh, please."

"Fine, I'm gonna check out these leather jackets over here."

While Byrd explored the jackets, I wandered among the motorcycles. One look at the price tags and my jaw dropped. These were not cheap bikes. Some were the price of full-size cars. Not that I was hurting for cash at the moment, but still. These two-wheeled beauties were a serious financial commitment.

A display stand showing off several helmets with black, white, and pink designs caught my eye. The top of the display held a photo of Maria "Wicked" Wickham, Victoria "Vicious" Ruiz, and Natasha "Nasty" Johnston from the Pink Trinkets standing behind three pink and black motorcycles. Each helmet on the stand featured a band member's name as part of the design.

"You listen to the Trinks?" Shea Stevens stood a few inches shorter than me, wearing a sleeveless denim shirt. Her sinewy arms, dark-blond pixie cut, and deep, irregular scars crisscrossing her face gave her an intense look that suggested she knew how to handle herself.

"Only all the time." I gestured toward the photo. "You build these bikes for them?"

A flush of pride spread across her disfigured face. "They wanted some bikes to kick off their Singing Mammogram tour."

"Great album. Beautiful bikes. I'm Jinx Ballou, by the way." I offered my hand, and she shook it.

"Shea Stevens. What do ya ride?"

"I don't yet," I said. "But I've been wanting to learn."

I would have liked to shoot the shit with this woman. She had good energy and reminded me a little of my ex-girlfriend, Toni. I caught Byrd's eye, and he wandered over to where Shea and I were standing. "Look, we're here on a more serious matter."

"Oh? And what matter is that?"

"Zia Pearson's bail bond."

Shea Stevens's face turned to cold steel in the span of a heartbeat.

My pulse quickened. *Here we go.*

11

———

"Shea, we want to help her," I said as pleasantly as I could.

"Bullshit. Y'all wanna send her back to that men's jail. Like I told them other guys, Indigo ain't going back to that hellhole. Not for one fucking minute. Not while I still draw breath."

"I get it. I'm transgender as well. I heard what happened at the jail, but—"

Stevens stepped into my space with fire in her eyes. "But nothing. She ain't going back 'cause she didn't kill that son of a bitch no matter how much he deserved it."

"I'm not doubting you. The last thing I want to do is put a member of my community in harm's way. I can promise you, if she comes along without a fuss, we can get her bail reset, get her court date rescheduled, she'll be home for dinner."

"What chance you think a black transgender woman has with a conservative white Scottsdale jury? Hell, they already got some fabricated DNA evidence against her. Do I really gotta explain what'll happen? One way or another, this is a death sentence against an innocent woman."

Byrd and I exchanged a brief glance. She wasn't entirely

wrong. All too often, white cisgender men got a pass for rape and other violent crimes, while women and minorities faced maximum sentences, even when acting in self-defense.

"As a black man, I hear what you're saying, Ms. Stevens. My family's experienced our share of the ugly side of the legal system," Byrd said. "But this case against Zia isn't going away. Don't she deserve her day in court? The chance to put this whole mess behind her?"

"She deserves to be left alone."

Byrd opened his hands in a pleading gesture. "Believe me, if it were within our power to get these charges dropped, we would. None of us wants to send an innocent woman to prison. But we can't do that. But we can improve her chances of beating this by getting her trial back on track."

"Otherwise, the judge'll issue a bench warrant and remand her without bail," I added. "She could spend the next few years in jail enduring hell knows what while her trial drags on."

Stevens sneered at us. "Only if she gets caught."

"You're willing to lose your house and your personal fleet of motorcycles to protect her?" asked Byrd.

"My house. My bikes. My money. My life, too, if need be." Not a hint of hesitation in her voice. "Now you two get outta my shop!" She pointed toward the door as her shout echoed off the walls. Customers stopped their browsing and stared at us.

Clearly the low-key approach wasn't working. "I admire your loyalty, Shea," I said. "But we *will* find her, whether you help us or not. And we *will* return her to custody."

"You can try, but you'll fail just like them other knuckleheads. Don't matter how many bounty hunters Pima Bail Bonds sends. You'll walk away empty-handed or wish you had."

I laughed. "Are you trying to scare me, Ms. Stevens? We've dealt with people a lot bigger and scarier than you and your biker gang. If Indigo doesn't come willingly...if you or your buddies try to interfere, I will recommend she be remanded. You know what that means?"

"Yeah, it means you're a pawn for the prison industrial complex. You'll have her innocent blood on your hand when she gets murdered in prison for a crime she didn't commit. Now get the hell outta here!"

A bearded black man in an Iron Goddess polo shirt and a Native American woman wearing grease-stained coveralls and swinging a large wrench walked in from the back of the shop and stood on either side of Stevens. Shea lifted her shirt enough to reveal the grip of a pistol tucked in the front of her jeans.

Byrd put a hand on my shoulder and whispered in my ear, "What say we mosey on out of here?"

"Fine," I said to Stevens. "You win. If we can't locate Ms. Pearson, she'll stay out of jail. For now."

"Glad we came to an agreement," replied Stevens.

"Consequently, Pima Bail Bonds will take your house, all your fancy motorcycles, which you won't need anyway since you'll be in prison."

Anger amplified on Shea's face. "What the hell you talking about?"

"After I file my report, the Maricopa County Attorney's Office will charge you with hindering prosecution and with conspiracy to commit murder after the fact. Both major felonies with serious prison time. But hey, I'm sure it's no big deal for you. You being an ex-con and all, it'll be like homecoming. Am I right?"

The black man shot Stevens a nervous glance, but all three held their ground. Time for a tactical retreat.

"Come on, Byrd." I gave Stevens a confident smile I didn't feel and backed away. "Enjoy prison, Ms. Stevens."

They followed us out of the store, shooting daggers with their eyes as we hopped into the Gray Ghost.

"That went well," said Byrd.

I started the engine. "No worries. We'll find her." I peeled out of the parking lot and headed down Sycamore Mountain the way we had come.

"If we're not giving up, then why are we headed back to the valley?"

"Stevens lives at the base of Sycamore Mountain. I suspect Pearson's staying with her."

"Let's hope, because I'm getting a bad feeling about this job. If Rodeo and Tommy Boy couldn't find her..."

"All due respect to Rodeo and Tommy Boy, I've been doing this longer than either one of them. Hell, I've found people Fiddler couldn't find. You remember him?"

Byrd shook his head. "Never met, but heard he was a legend in his time."

"Damn straight he was. But he couldn't find Holly Schwartz."

"That girl in the wheelchair who killed her mama? You tracked her down?"

"I did. Turned out her visiting nurse was hiding her in a cabin outside Prescott."

"Well, all right, girl. Let's go find our fugitive."

As we reached the base of the mountain, the road straightened out. At a weather-beaten sign that read Sycamore Estates, I turned right.

The residential area was nothing like the cookie-cutter neighborhoods in Phoenix. The lots were sprawling, rustic, and rocky. The aroma of manure lingered in the air, suggesting someone nearby kept livestock. Mature mesquite, ironwoods, and sycamores offered shade to a brilliant palette of wildflowers and wildlife. A small ridge ran behind the houses on Stevens's street and up the side of the mountain.

Stevens's house sat second to last at the end of the lane. I backed the Gray Ghost into the driveway.

"Let's gear up." I opened the back of the SUV, and we pulled on our vests, weapons, and walkie-talkies. "I'll hit the front door. You cover the back."

"Roger that. What if no one answers the door?"

I surveyed the area. No one on the streets, but that didn't

mean some nosy busybody wasn't watching. "We'll make entry through the back, away from prying eyes. Grab the ram."

By law, we had the right to enter a building without a warrant, provided we had reason to believe that our fugitive was inside. Of course, that left a lot of gray area.

Byrd slung the thirty-pound ram over his shoulder and marched around the house. I gave him a couple of minutes to get into position.

"Any signs of life in back?" I asked into the radio.

"Negative. All quiet back here. No activity through the windows."

"Okay, keep your head on a swivel."

I pounded on the front door and gave the doorbell a few rings, then listened. No sounds came from inside the house. I waited a few minutes then knocked and rang again but without any results.

"Anything?" asked Byrd.

"Nada. Any evidence of a security system?"

"Negative."

"All right. Make entry, then let me in through the front."

"Roger that."

I waited for the thud of the ram and the satisfying crack of the doorframe giving way. It didn't come.

"Byrd? You in?" I heard the distant sound of voices.

"Uh...Jinx, we got a problem. You might want to come around here."

I trudged around to the back of the house to find a petite woman with pale skin and a gray bouffant hairdo, wearing a pale-pink-velvet housedress. A long-haired Chihuahua in her arms was yapping its pampered little head off.

"What are you people doing back there?" she demanded in a voice that was equal parts Catholic nun and Mommie Dearest. "You don't live here."

"Minding our own business," I replied. "I suggest you do the same."

She put a hand on her hip. "And what business would that be?"

A flashed her a confident smile. "None of yours."

"I'm making it my business. I'm Mrs. Collins, Shea's next-door neighbor. We look out for each other 'round here."

"Well, Mrs. Collins, I suggest you leave us to our work and go back to watching *Price is Right.*"

From a pocket in her housedress, she pulled out a cellphone. "I'm calling the cops. We don't take kindly to thugs." She glared at Byrd.

Byrd held up his bail enforcement badge. "Go right ahead, ma'am. We're here to return a fugitive to custody. We always appreciate help from local law enforcement."

Collins's face went blank for a moment, and she clearly was not expecting Byrd's encouragement.

"There ain't no one here! You two are up to something. I'm calling Shea."

Byrd gave me a look that said, "What now?"

I was really hoping to complete this job without violence. But I was not going to let Miss Jane Marple here or Shea Stevens keep me from doing what I was hired to do.

"You interfere with us doing our job, lady, and we'll haul you to jail as well." I pulled out my handcuffs to show her I was serious. To Byrd, I said, "Give me thirty seconds to get around front and then break it down."

"You don't scare me!" She held up her phone while her dog yapped away.

Just as I reached the front porch, a loud crack shook the house. Byrd opened the front door.

"Avon calling," I said with a wry smile, noticing a wooden baseball bat leaning against the wall next to the doorway.

"I suggest we get a move on," replied Byrd. "Got a feeling we're gonna have company real soon."

The front of the house had a large living room with a small kitchenette to the left. The floors were bare concrete slab with a rug in the living room. I pointed at a door next to the kitchen. "Check the garage. I'll search the bedrooms."

"Roger that."

I checked the first bedroom. Queen-sized bed. Minimal decor. A few photographs of Shea Stevens with other female bikers on one wall. A desk sat in the corner. On it lay a sketchbook, which had drawings of motorcycles, and a Mac laptop. A bookshelf on the far wall was filled with service manuals, motorcycle magazines, and some novels by Tammy Kaehler. The adjoining bathroom and closet held nothing of interest. No signs of another adult living here. Only a single toothbrush in the cup by the sink.

I moved on to the guest bathroom and then the second bedroom. A couple of plushies were on the bed with a Captain Marvel comforter. A vase of wilting carnations stood in the windowsill. On one wall, a Dua Lipa concert poster was tacked next to a few others for young male artists I didn't recognize.

A hemp net hung from the far wall, strung through with fairy lights and photographs of a young girl with a family resemblance to Shea. The bond agreement had mentioned Shea's niece, Annie Wittmann, lived with her, though I didn't know the story behind why. This must have been her room. No sign of Pearson anywhere.

Byrd returned to the living room. "Lots of motorcycles in the garage, but no evidence of Pearson."

"Shit. No joy on my end either. Let's get out of here before..."

The air rumbled with the thunder of motorcycle engines. I opened the front door to see four bikers pull up in front of the house and park their rides across the driveway, blocking the Gray Ghost. *Damn, they got here fast.*

Stevens pulled off her helmet and held it in one hand, drawing a pistol with the other. "What the fuck y'all doing in my house?"

The three other women gathered around her, holding their helmets like clubs. All wore matching biker vests with white and pink patches. Byrd and I drew our weapons. I held up my free hand in an attempt to de-escalate the situation.

"This house? The one you put up as collateral for the defaulted bond you signed for Pearson?" Okay, my mouth was clearly less interested in de-escalating.

"You had no right to break in."

"Once Pearson failed to show up to court, we had every right to search any location we believed she might be hiding. But if you tell us where she is or, better yet, get her to come down and surrender, we'd be happy to be on our way." Wishful thinking, but it never hurt to ask.

"And I'd be within my rights to shoot an intruder. This is Arizona, after all."

"Fine. Move your bikes away from my truck, and we'll leave."

"Make us," said a tall Latinx woman with long dark hair.

"Suit yourself." I gestured toward the Gray Ghost.

Byrd kept his pistol trained on Shea as we got in.

I started the engine and rolled down the window. "Last chance. Move your bikes."

"Fuck you, bitch!" said one of the other bikers, who was aiming a revolver at us.

I slammed the Gray Ghost into Drive and floored it, pushing the bikes off to the side. A couple of gunshots behind us made me duck. The SUV lifted up onto two wheels as we turned the corner at speed.

12

———

"You hit?" I asked as I took a hard right onto the main highway, heading south. I kept glancing in the rearview mirror, but so far there were no signs of our biker friends.

"No. Don't think so." His voice was as shaky as I felt.

I glanced over. Bits of foam rubber surrounded a hole at the edge of his seat that lined up with a corresponding hole in the glovebox. "Wow," he said. "That was close."

"You want to quit?"

"Aw, heck no." He shot me a grin. "It's just getting interesting."

"Awesome, because I really need your help."

"So where we headed now?"

"Ironwood."

"To Pearson's house? Rodeo and Tommy already checked out the place. Said Pearson's side of the closet was cleared out like she was on a long vacation."

"I want to talk to Pearson's employer, the Lambda Resource Center over by the university."

"No offense, Jinx, but Ironwood is back the other way. Why are we headed south?"

"I didn't want to drive up those switchbacks with bikers on our tail. We'd never outrun them. There's a state highway ahead that bypasses Sycamore Springs."

After a mile or so, I hooked a right onto the state highway. The purple and yellow wildflowers lining the roadside reminded me of my ex-girlfriend, Toni Bennett, a corrections officer from Scottsdale. She'd always said wildflowers were her favorite flower. Beautiful and wild, yet still tough enough to bloom in the unforgiving desert.

We'd started dating last February. She was fun and flirty, not to mention a goddess in the sheets. But our relationship didn't last. I was still damaged goods after losing Conor. Toni's attempts to pull me out of my shit failed. I sunk deeper into a funk, ignoring her calls and texts. In the end, she dumped me via voicemail. It was more a relief than anything.

Now I blamed myself for Conor turning himself in. What would happen if he was convicted? Would they imprison him for life? Behead him? Did they still do that in the UK? I had no idea.

The rolling hills rose into steep, forested peaks as we entered the Cortes National Forest. The road twisted through the mountain folds. A recent snowfall had left patches of black ice in the corners, forcing me to focus on the driving rather than my failed relationships.

"I haven't been here since I was a kid," I said, breaking the stifling silence.

"Yeah?"

"My folks used to rent a cabin every summer. I remember playing in streams, roasting marshmallows by campfire, dodging prickly pears that grew among the piles of fallen pine needles. Oh, and the maddening itch of poison oak."

Byrd stared out at the treetops stretching out below us. "My mama sent me to a Christian summer camp up here once after my dad got killed."

"Shit. I'm sorry. How'd he die?"

"A cop mistook him for a man who carjacked a Toyota like the one he drove. Shot him in the back."

"Geez, that fucking sucks, man." I didn't know what else to say.

Byrd shrugged. "Can't change it. It is what it is."

"So afterwards, your mom sent you to a summer camp?"

"Thought it might help. Gave me some father figures to fill the absence left by my dad."

"How was it?"

"Strange, but cool. It was my first time outta the city. Trees and shit everywhere. Animals, like you'd only see in the zoo or on TV, but just wandering around—bobcats, javelinas, and even a skunk. Oh and elk. They looked like deer on steroids. And the sounds, especially at night. Man! Coyotes howling, owls hooting, and all night long them crickets or cicadas or whatever they were. You'd think they'd get tired after a while, but no, they kept on going all day and all night like the Energizer Bunny."

"Nice to get out once in a while."

"Yeah. Your family still rent a cabin up here?"

"Not lately."

"My church has a thing up here every summer. Never gone, but being here now, remembering that time as a kid, I kinda miss it, you know?"

I nodded.

"You'd be welcome too, if you want. They're always encouraging us to invite visitors."

"Thanks, but I'll pass."

"You Christian?"

Ugh, here we go. "My mom is. Italian Catholic. I used go to Mass with her, but not since I came out as trans." I gave him a quick look. "You're not gonna try to recruit me, are you?"

He paused for a moment. "Naw, but I'm curious, how do decide between what's right and wrong?"

"Live and let live. Treat others how you want to be treated. I don't need some Bronze Age tome to tell me that. All them

Catholic priests raping children. Evangelicals doing everything they can to make life harder for queer people, acting like we're some kind of threat to society when they're the one's brutalizing us. Hell, look at the case we're on. That street preacher carrying signs saying women need to be raped and that queer people deserve to be murdered. If that's what you call morality, you can have it."

"Not all Christians act like that."

"What's your church's position on transgender people?"

He sighed. "Not as enlightened as it should be."

"There you go."

"How'd your folks react when you came out? They freak on you?"

"They were cool when I finally told them. I got to transition young, which is rare." The conversation lagged as we wound through the sun-dappled mountain curves. "You and your mom still close?"

"Yeah, pretty close. She hates what I do for a living. Keeps wanting me to become an engineer."

"Like on a train?"

"Mechanical engineer. Loved math and physics in high school. Got a football scholarship to ASU."

"You played football?"

"Until some guy sideswiped me sophomore year and tore up my knee. End of football. End of scholarship. End of college. So here I am."

"Shit. That sucks."

"Yeah, I think about going back. Got some money saved up. Just got so damn expensive, you know? Tuition's ten times what it used to be. Tried to qualify for a student loan but no luck."

"My mom worries about me doing this job too. Even offered to pay my tuition to law school."

"And you said no?"

"To being a blood-sucking lawyer? Not just no, but hell no."

After half an hour of zigzagging through the forested mountain roads, signs of civilization appeared. First a trading post, then a QT gas station, and finally the trees gave way to the businesses of downtown Ironwood. Cafes, hardware stores, and art galleries. Pickup trucks and cars dusted with frost filled the streets. A few hearty cyclists weaved their way between the vehicles, sending up clouds of water vapor in the chilly air.

We drove east to Ironwood's University District. The art galleries and gift shops of downtown were replaced by bookstores, frat houses, dormitories, and classroom buildings. The students lugging backpacks full of books brought back memories of when I attended Arizona State ten years earlier. My biggest worries then were turning in term papers on time and passing final exams. Now I struggled to stay sober and employed without getting killed.

We found the Lambda Resource Center south of campus on Red Tanks Trail Road. I pulled into the lot behind the small wooden building. In the lobby, rainbow flags and a gallery of event photos hung from the walls. The receptionist desk was empty.

"Hello?" I called.

"In here," came a voice down the main hallway. We followed it.

I knocked on a half-opened door which bore a plaque that read Director. A woman in a mauve suit and short dark hair looked up with a pleasant expression on her face. A nameplate on her desk identified her as Trina Lantz, Director of Operations. "Hi, can I help you?"

"Yes, we're looking for Zia Pearson. I understand she works here."

Lantz's smile faded a bit. "I'm sorry, she's not in today. My name's Trina. Perhaps I can assist you." She offered her hand, and I shook it.

"I'm Jinx Ballou. This is my associate Jubal Byrd."

Trina's smiled brightened as she shook Byrd's hand, clearly taking her time. "Love your name. So poetic."

"Thanks. I like yours too," he replied. The two of them were having some kind of flirty moment that bugged the shit out of me.

I cleared my throat. "Where can we find Ms. Pearson?"

Trina sighed and straightened her suit jacket. "Judging from your bulletproof vests and badges, I'm guessing this is about that murder case down in Scottsdale."

"She missed her court hearing. We need to find her before her bail gets revoked entirely."

"Have you tried her at home?"

"She wasn't there," answered Byrd.

"Well, I don't know what to tell you. She's on temporary leave from her position here. And...can I be honest?"

"Please," I said with a little more snark than I intended.

"I believe she's being framed. I've known Zia for a couple years now. She has a good heart. She's not a violent person much less a murderer. As vile as that preacher was, I don't see Zia killing him."

"And yet this model citizen is a member of a violent biker gang and has now skipped bail."

Byrd shot me a look that said ease up. I ignored him.

"The Athena Sisterhood," said Trina. "Yes, I know about them. But they're not violent."

"Really? Well the bullet hole one of them put in the back of my SUV would indicate otherwise."

"I can't speak to this bullet hole, but from what I've seen, the Sisterhood is a law-abiding, pro-feminist, pro-LGBTQ club. They've been active participants in several of our fundraisers. And they provide protection to battered women and children. They're nothing like those other biker gangs. I don't think the sheriff's office would work with Zia if they were."

"And yet now she's violated the terms of her bail agreement," I replied. "And the biker club has closed ranks around her."

"Can you blame them?" asked Trina. "After Zia was brutally

assaulted in a men's jail? What were they thinking to put her in there?"

"So you've spoken to her since she was arrested?" asked Byrd.

Her gaze hit the floor. "Yes."

"Where can we find her?" I pressed.

"I don't know. That's the truth. She sent me a text a few weeks ago saying she was going on leave for a bit and asking me to hold her job for her. But nothing about where she was or when she would return."

"Who is her contact at the sheriff's office?" I asked.

"Detective Toni Rios. She works in their Violent Crimes Division, but she's also a part of their Community Outreach Division." Trina flipped through a Rolodex on her desk, then scribbled a name, address, and phone number on a scrap of paper. "Not sure if she knows anything, but you can certainly try."

I took it from her and stuffed it in back pocket. "Thanks."

"And if you find Zia, please be gentle with her. She's been through a lot."

"We will, Trina," Byrd replied, taking her hand again. I felt like I was going to barf.

An androgynous person with purple hair knocked on her office door. "Hey, Trina! Sorry to interrupt, but Parker Davies with the Cortes Chronicle is on line two."

I gave Trina my business card. "If you hear from Pearson, call me. Immediately. The longer this drags on, the worse it will be for her."

Trina stared at the card. "Don't know when I'll hear from her. But if I do, I'll let you know." She looked up at me, then at Byrd.

"Thanks for all your help," he said, giving her a wink as I turned and walked out of the office.

"Geez, Byrd, since when is flirting part of the job?" I asked when we finally emerged into the sunlight. "I was half afraid you'd start humping her leg."

"Aw, that wasn't flirting."

"Yeah, right! 'Oh Jubal, your name is so poetic.'" I climbed into the driver's seat of the Gray Ghost, slamming the door shut.

"Hey, that was all her. Not my fault she likes what she sees." He flashed me a blinding white smile.

I started the ignition just to get the heat going as I planned our next move. "Maybe the two of you should get a room, and I'll track down Pearson myself."

"Aw, don't hate the playa, girl."

I rolled my eyes and pulled onto the street.

"At least we didn't get shot at this time," I said, trying to remain upbeat as we returned to Downtown Ironwood.

"You're setting a low bar for success, there, Jinx." Byrd replied.

"We'll find her. Just have to shake the trees till something falls out."

"We shake much harder, and the Athena Sisterhood's going to be putting us in the morgue."

"And here I thought you were a man of faith," I teased.

"Oh, I am. I have faith that the Athena Sisterhood is serious about not surrendering one of their own."

"Let's get some lunch. Maybe we can figure out another approach, one that doesn't involve getting shot at."

"I hear that."

I followed Prospector Avenue into Ironwood's Downtown Square, the heart of the city built around the old courthouse. Normally this time of year, the sidewalks would be bustling with Phoenicians escaping the desert heat. But with temps hitting near freezing at night, most pedestrians were students from nearby Central Arizona University.

I grabbed a parking space and looked along the street to assess our dining options. "Let's see, we got College Burger—very popular among the students. A few doors down, there's a Filipino restaurant called the Manila Grill. And across the courtyard, the Desert Star Saloon in one of the historic buildings. What's your poison?"

"Let's give the Manila Grill a try."

Byrd ordered a pork dish called crispy pata with a soda. I asked for a fried rice dish and a beer. While our server walked away to place our order, I caught Byrd giving me a look.

"What?" I asked.

"You often drink on the job?"

"It's a beer. I think I can handle it, preacher boy."

"I hope so, Miss Jinx. I hope so."

"So what kind of name is Jubal anyway?"

"It's from the Bible."

"I shoulda figured. Jubal Byrd, huh? Sounds like a creature from Greek mythology."

"Oh yeah? How'd you get the name Jinx? Sounds like a bad luck kind of name."

I chuckled. "Bad luck for whoever I'm chasing. It's a mash up of my first and middle names, Jenna Christine. A friend of mine gave me the nickname when I was a teenager."

He nodded just as our server showed up with our drinks. "Well all right, Miss Jinx. How we gonna put the jinx on Zia Pearson?"

I took a sip of my beer. "Not sure."

"Let me see if my skip tracer's got anything." I called Becca.

"I'll be honest, I haven't been monitoring Pearson this morning. I'll see what I can pull up as far as phone logs, emails, and social media, but it may take me a while," she explained. "I'm working on a tight deadline for a security client."

"I'm working on a tight deadline, too. I only have a week to track her down before Pima Bail Bonds has to cough up the rest of the bail money."

"I'll see what I can do."

"Also, pull the phone logs for Shea Stevens, the woman who put up the bail bond, and Pearson's wife, Chelsea Tucker. See who they're talking to. Check for common phone numbers they've been calling."

"Jinx..."

"I know it's a big ask. But who loves you more? Your bestie since junior high or this security client of yours?"

"I'll do what I can. Anything else you need? A massage? Your car washed? The dog walked." She teased, the frustration evident in her voice.

"Naw, Adam and Steve from next door should be walking Diana. Seriously, though, thanks, Becks! You're the greatest!"

After our food came, I flipped back through the job folder looking for anything that might suggest our next approach. "Pearson worked for the Lambda Resource Center as a liaison with the Cortes County Sheriff's Office. I want to talk with her contact at the CCSO, this Detective Antonia Rios. Maybe she knows how we can reach Pearson."

"Seems like a long shot."

"Every lead is a long shot until it pays off." But despite my optimistic words, I felt the same frustration. After the Penzler disaster, I wondered if I'd lost my mojo. Maybe I should find another line of work, one where people were less inclined to shoot me.

13

When we reached the CCSO's Ironwood Substation, I asked for Detective Rios at the front desk. The desk sergeant made a call, talked to someone, then hung up. "I'm afraid she's away from her desk at the moment. Can I leave her a message?"

I shook my head. "Thanks, anyway."

Back in the Gray Ghost, I called the phone number Trina had given me.

"This is Detective Rios. How can I help you?"

"Detective, this is Jinx Ballou. I work with Pima Bail Bonds down in Scottsdale. I'm looking for an associate of yours—Zia Pearson."

There was a pause at the other end of the line. "I haven't spoken to Ms. Pearson in over a month. I'm guessing this is connected to the homicide she was charged with in Scottsdale?"

"Yeah, she jumped bail. I could use your help bringing her back into custody."

"I'm wrapping things up at a crime scene at the moment. Meet me at the Ironwood Substation around three o'clock. We can talk then."

"I appreciate it." I hung up. "Now we're getting somewhere," I said to Byrd.

"She know where Pearson is?"

"Didn't say, but she wants to meet in a couple hours. I'll count that as a step in the right direction."

"What should we do in the meantime?"

"We tried Pearson's residence, workplace, and the woman who posted bail. Let's try her attorney, this Rebecca Li."

"Since when have you gotten any information from an attorney about one of their clients?"

"Not often, but right now, all we got are long shots. Besides, attorneys are still officers of the court. Attorney-client privilege does not extend to harboring fugitives."

I started the Gray Ghost and returned to downtown Ironwood. Rebecca Li shared a small professional building on Raven Rock Drive with another attorney. Despite our lack of an appointment, the receptionist escorted us to Li's office.

Li, dressed in a tailored black business suit, stood and shook our hands as Byrd and I entered. The room was small but tidy. Shelves of law books lined the wall opposite a modern desk. A familiar black leather vest with pink and white patches hung on a coatrack behind her desk.

"How can I help the two of you today?" Li asked with a bright smile.

"We're looking for your client, Zia Pearson," I said. "As I'm sure you know, she missed her hearing."

"Ah, I see." Was that a flush of embarrassment I saw for the briefest of moments? "Unfortunately, I don't know where she is right now."

"Really? No clue, huh? Why do I find that hard to believe? Maybe it's that biker vest you got hanging there."

"Ms. Li," said Byrd, "we understand your client had a rough time before she was bailed out. And we're willing to help get her bail reset..."

"No." I cut him off. "No more Ms. Nice Bounty Hunter. We

tried being nice to some of your fellow bikers, most notably your client's wife and that crazy bitch who runs the motorcycle shop. After being threatened and shot at, I have zero interest in helping your client reset bail. You and your biker gang are conspiring to harbor a fugitive wanted for murder. If you don't turn her over now, we will recommend you—"

"Don't threaten me, Ms. Ballou." Li's professional demeanor turned dark. "You don't know the law half as well as you think you do."

"You're an officer of the court," I replied. "You hiding her is a conflict of interest."

"If my client is staying with another member of the Sisterhood, I'm not aware of it. There's no conflict of interest."

"Of course not," said Byrd, giving me a look. "We're just trying to return her to custody so she can stand trial and put this unfortunate episode behind her."

"Sounds great," Li replied. "Provided they don't convict her for no other reason than being a trans woman of color."

"Look, we get it," I said. "But sooner or later, she has to face the charges."

"Like I said, I have no idea where she is."

I dropped one of my business cards on her desk. "If you see her, get in touch. We'd hate for anyone to be disbarred for hindering prosecution." I glared at her. "Come on, Byrd."

The two of us stormed out of there. Well, I stormed out. Byrd just followed.

"You sure do know how to make friends," he joked.

"Bite me. All this driving around is making me cranky." I swung open the driver's door of the Gray Ghost, hopped in, and slammed it shut.

"Oh, is *that* what's making you cranky." His goofy laugh only made me more frustrated. "I thought you were this super bounty hunter, capable of finding fugitives even the legends in the business can't find."

"Keep it up, Jesus Boy. You'll be walking back to Phoenix." I started the engine and drove out of the lot.

"All right, all right. That was rude of me. I apologize."

"Besides, I've got a plan to lure her out of hiding."

"If you're planning to use the old 'you just won a new cell-phone' trick, don't. Rodeo and Tommy Boy already tried that. She didn't take the bait."

"Huh, that usually works. Anyway, that's not the plan."

He cocked an eyebrow. "No? What is the plan?"

"We need to drive to the hospital."

"You hurt?"

"Nope."

"Then what?"

"You'll see."

I drove north to the upscale Shadow Hills district with its exclusive country clubs, overpriced condominiums, and gated neighborhoods. The Gray Ghost didn't blend in so well here, among the Ferraris, Bentleys, and Porsches. Still, we had a job to do, and at this point, I wasn't planning for us to hide in the SUV.

The Shadow Hills Medical Center's emergency department was on the back side of the building. I parked in the emergency visitors' lot.

I took off my vest and tactical belt, then stashed a pair of handcuffs in my back pocket. Byrd also disarmed. Even as licensed bounty hunters, we weren't allowed to carry firearms into a hospital. I hoped it wouldn't be a problem.

As we walked through the parking lot and past the sliding glass doors of the hospital, Byrd said, "You're not planning on doing what I think you're doing, are you?"

I smiled mischievously. "Depends on what you're thinking. I just need to make a phone call."

I strode past the check-in desk to where a courtesy phone hung on the wall. I dialed 9 to get an outside line and then Zia Pearson's cellphone number. It rang three times before a voice answered.

"Yes?"

"Hello, is this Chelsea Tucker's wife? A Ms. Pearson?" I asked.

"This is Zia Pearson."

"Good afternoon. I'm sorry to disturb you, but my name is Liz Windsor." It was a fake name I often used. "I'm a nurse in the emergency department at HealthCorp Shadow Hills Medical Center. Your wife has been in a serious accident. You need to get down here right away."

"What kind of accident? Is she okay?" The panic in her voice was evident.

"It's best we discuss this in person. Are you able to be here soon?"

"Y-yes, I'm leaving right now. Just tell me, is...is she still alive?"

"The last I checked she was, but really, you need to hurry."

"I'll be there in about fifteen minutes."

I hung up. Byrd shook his head. "You are diabolical."

"I have a reputation to uphold and a fugitive to return to custody."

We took seats in the waiting area near the door. People wandered in and out, many looking in pretty bad shape. More than one looked like they had a bad case of the flu, which I hoped I didn't catch. After ten minutes, a team of EMTs brought in a white man on a gurney. I caught a glimpse of blood-soaked bandages as they rushed past. A lot of people were having a bad day.

A few minutes later, a woman who matched the photo in the file I was given rushed in. Dark skin, long braids that looked like they could use some maintenance, and an Athena Sisterhood biker vest. She was a few inches taller than me and probably outweighed me by a good twenty pounds.

"Ding, ding, ding! We got a winner," I whispered to Byrd as we got up.

14

Pearson approached the information desk and gave the elderly volunteer behind the desk her wife's name to look up in the computer.

"Zia Pearson?" I asked from behind her.

I was tempted to snap the cuffs on her right away, but I had to confirm it was her. Otherwise, I risked being charged with kidnapping and a few similar charges. Byrd stood on the other side of her.

She turned. "Yes. Where's my wife, Chelsea Tucker?"

I snapped the cuffs on one of her wrists and was reaching for the other when someone shouted, "Hey! Leave her alone!"

I turned to see three other women in matching biker vests running toward us. "Aw, shit."

Byrd ran to intercept them while I struggled to get Pearson cuffed.

"Zia Pearson, you missed your court date and violated your bail agreement. I've been hired to return you to custody."

She slipped out of my grip, whirled around, and delivered a glancing blow to my jaw. Damn, she was fast! I blocked another punch and tried to get her into an arm lock. Someone grabbed me from behind and dropped me onto the linoleum.

"Get off me! I'm a licensed bail enforcement agent arresting a fugitive."

"Not today you're not," said a deep female voice.

I turned my head in time to see Pearson escape out the sliding glass doors with her fellow bikers. Byrd chased them.

"If you don't get off of me, I will have you arrested for aiding a fugitive. It comes with a mandatory two-year sentence." It was a bullshit threat, but it usually worked.

The woman got off of me. I pulled myself to my feet and glared at her. She was a stocky woman with a squarish face and short blond hair. The words Cortes County Fire and Rescue were stitched on her shirt. With a grim look on her face, she crossed her arms. Goddamn EMT!

"You have any idea who you let escape?" I screamed.

"Sure do. She's my wife."

Suddenly, I remembered. Chelsea Tucker was an EMT. Shit!

"She missed her hearing. I'm trying to help her get bail reset and her court date rescheduled."

"No, you're trying to take her back to the men's jail so she can be raped and assaulted again."

"I understand her predicament. I'm transgender. If I help her get her bail reset, she won't have to sit in jail for the remainder of the trial."

"You tell that prosecutor to drop the bogus charges, and it won't be an issue."

"Unfortunately, that's not within our power," said Byrd, walking up to us. "But we do care and will do what we can to help."

"Sorry. Not interested."

Two men in security uniforms approached. "We received a report of a disturbance."

"Hey, Hank! Dave!" Tucker said to them. "I think we got it

under control. Just make sure they leave." She shot us a glance and walked away.

"We're bail enforcement agents," I told them. "Her wife jumped bail. We are here to bring her into custody."

"Not here you're not," said the larger of the two security guards. "This is a hospital. Not a wrestling arena. You're going to have to leave, or we're calling the cops."

I exchanged a glance with Byrd. Pearson was gone. The cops wouldn't do anything about it.

"Fine, we're leaving."

We trudged back out into the parking lot.

"It was a good plan," said Byrd. "Would've worked if she didn't have her friends with her."

"This is looking like it may take a few days. Maybe we oughta check in to a motel before meeting with this Detective Rios. I've been seeing a lot of No Vacancy signs in town," I said.

Despite the late-May wintry weather, many Phoenix residents were already up here in the high country since most years it was already in the triple digits down in the valley.

"Just out of curiosity, who's paying for these rooms?" he asked. "I'm in this to make money, not shell it out."

"Relax, dude. I'll cover the rooms."

We sat in the Gray Ghost while I searched Google for motels in the area. I drove east and pulled into a Hampton Inn. They were full. Days Inn. Full.

After making several calls, I found a little mom-and-pop operation called the Montgomery Family Inn located not far from the Central Arizona University campus.

When I balked at the price of a single-occupancy room, the man behind the counter explained that those were the normal in-season rates. Decent rooms were at a premium.

"We could always double up," suggested Byrd. "Get one room with two beds."

"What would your fellow churchgoers say?" I teased. "You shacking up with a woman you're not married to."

"Hey, I ain't tryin' to get in your pants, Jinx. I'm just offering to save you some Benjamins."

"Fine." I replied and handed over my plastic. "One room."

The room was standard budget motel fare—clean and utterly uninteresting, especially the artwork, which had a theme of desert sunsets. I tossed my duffel bag on the double bed nearest the door and unpacked while trying to ignore the whirlwind of feelings inside of me. I could've used a little something to even me out.

Byrd had stepped into the bathroom when my phone rang. No name on the caller ID, but the number looked local.

"Ballou Fugitive Recovery."

"I think we got off to a bad start earlier," said a husky female voice that reminded me of Jodie Foster. Shea Stevens.

"A bad start? I'd call blocking my vehicle and shooting at me more than just a bad start. I'd call that aggravated assault and attempted murder."

"For the record, I didn't shoot at you. It was one of our younger members who's a little eager with her trigger finger. She's been properly chastised."

"She should be in jail."

"We want to make this right. We understand you're trying to do your job."

"Give me Pearson, and we'll be out of your hair."

I heard another voice in the background but couldn't make out what was being said.

"Let's meet."

"That's the first sensible thing I've heard all day. When and where?" I was intrigued by this sudden change in direction and duly suspicious. I didn't want to be walking into a trap.

"Eight o'clock. There's a bar in downtown Ironwood called Gertie's. Know where it is?"

"I've heard of it. Lesbian bar on the square."

"We'll be at the large table in the back. Can't miss us."

"If you and your biker gang are planning an ambush, I'd advise against it," I replied.

"No ambush. I've talked to Indigo. She wants to come in, but there are conditions."

"Which are?"

"That's what we need to discuss."

On the one hand, it was a public place. There would probably be a lot of witnesses on the square, especially college kids enjoying a last hurrah before final exams. On the other hand, I had a hunch Stevens and Pearson wouldn't be alone.

"See you at eight." I hung up and called Becca, hoping for some intel in case this meetup with Stevens and company turned out to be a bust. "Got anything for me?"

I heard a long exhale. "Jinxie, I'm sorry. By the time I got done with the job for my security client, I was out of spoons. I'm wiped, bestie."

I was frustrated with the situation, but I knew it wasn't her fault. Living with chronic fatigue was tough. "Easton still out of town?"

"Yeah, but they went grocery shopping before they left. I should be okay."

"Don't worry about the skip tracing for now. Get some rest and call me if you need me."

"I should be okay, but thanks. Good hunting, Jinxie. And be careful."

"Always."

Byrd walked out of the bathroom. I filled him in.

"Totally a trap," he said.

"Maybe. Or Pearson is tired of hiding and genuinely wants to turn herself in. Stevens said there are conditions but didn't specify what. If our meeting with Detective Rios doesn't pan out, we'll gear up and try to bag Pearson at Gertie's."

15

We returned to the Ironwood Substation. The same desk sergeant called and confirmed Rios was there. A few minutes later, a Latinx woman barely five feet tall walked into the waiting area. I guessed her to be in her mid to late thirties.

"Jinx Ballou?" she asked with a faint Central American accent.

Byrd and I stood. "That's me. This is my associate, Jubal Byrd."

"Come on back." She led us past the locked door, down a hallway to a small interview room. "Let's talk in here."

After we sat down, she said, "Honestly, all of this came as a shock to me. Wouldn't have guessed Pearson had it in her."

"You think she did it?" I asked.

"In nearly twenty years as a cop, I've learned that anyone is capable of just about anything. I've seen sweet little grandmothers who tortured children. A teacher of the year running a dog-fighting ring. I don't know whether Pearson killed Fitzgerald, but with the hateful rhetoric that *pendejo* was spewing, it was a matter of time before someone did."

"Any idea where Pearson might be hiding out?" asked Byrd.

"Well, if she's not at home, I'd guess she's laying low with one of her friends in the Athena Sisterhood. You familiar with them?"

"A bit," I replied.

"They're not a bad group of women, all in all. Helped us with a major drug bust a while back. Do a lot for the community, especially women in trouble. Just don't cross them. They are rather protective of their own."

Now you tell me.

"Any particular member she might be staying with, if you had to guess?" I asked.

"I couldn't tell you. They have about two dozen members locally. Could be any of them. The Sisterhood also has chapters in LA, Vegas, Denver. At this point, she could be anywhere."

"Would you have a list of names and addresses for their local members?"

"Unless they've got a jacket, which most of them don't, we wouldn't have a record of them. But if you want to wait a bit, I can check with our gang task force, see what they have. Can't guarantee anything, but you never know."

"I'd appreciate that."

"Okay, sit tight. Either of you need anything while you wait? A soda? Coffee? Bottle of water?"

Byrd shook his head. "No, we're good."

When she left, Byrd said, "I'm beginning to see why Tommy Boy and Rodeo couldn't find this chick."

Rios returned twenty minutes later with a small stack of papers. "We have sheets on eight of their members. Nothing recent and mostly minor offenses—reckless driving, possession, a domestic dispute, one with a DUI from six years ago."

I glanced through the printouts. "Thanks, I appreciate it."

We stood and shook hands with Rios.

"Hope you find her. And honestly, I hope she's acquitted. I enjoyed working with her. She was a good liaison with Lambda."

"We'll let you know," said Byrd.

We grabbed dinner at a local diner near the motel, then drove back to the Downtown Square, parking a few doors past Gertie's.

"Gear up," I said as I killed the ignition. "Vests, weapons, and backups. The works."

"Maybe this isn't such a good idea, Jinx. And me being a guy? I'll stick out like a sore thumb in a dyke bar."

"We'll be fine. Just keep a cool head."

Byrd shot me a grin. "Oh, trust me. I'm always cool."

A few minutes later, we walked into Gertie's and immediately drew stares from the patrons. The place was about half filled, including several women in Athena Sisterhood biker vests, sitting at a large table near the back covered with pitchers of beer, shots of booze, and baskets of pretzels.

The smell of alcohol called me like a siren. I only wanted a shot or two. Or three. Just enough to take the edge off. But I needed my wits about me if Byrd and I were going to get out alive.

Shea Stevens sat at the far end, her back to the wall, with Chelsea Tucker on one side of her and Rebecca Li on the other. The rest of the women looked familiar, from either the information Detective Rios provided or our tango at Stevens's house. Zia Pearson was nowhere to be seen.

We sat in a couple of empty seats across from Stevens. A patch on her vest read *Havoc*, her biker name. Under that was another that identified her as the club's VP.

"You showed. I'm impressed," Stevens said.

"Where's Pearson?" I asked.

"Indigo is safe," said Tucker.

"You said she'd turn herself in," Byrd replied.

"She will," Stevens explained, "after you locate the real killer."

"Excuse me?" I almost choked on a pretzel I'd snagged from a basket between us.

"Indigo didn't kill that preacher," Tucker said. Her name patch read Savage. "She shouldn't have to suffer just because the Scottsdale police are too stupid or too lazy to go after the real murderer."

A tall Latinx woman whose biker vest identified her as Fuego, the club president, put a calming hand on Tucker's shoulder. "Indigo's only crime was getting into a shouting match with the guy at Bike Week."

"Someone posted a video of that online," Byrd added. "The confrontation got physical. She made threats."

Stevens shrugged. "So they shoved each other a couple of times. Not that big a deal. No one got hurt."

"Police also got a DNA match," I said. "That's pretty damning evidence."

"Maybe some of her skin got under his nails in the tussle at Bike Week," replied Fuego. "She didn't shoot him or cut off his dick."

"And it was just coincidence that she was in a strip club next door to where the police found his body?" I asked.

"We had no idea that asshole was at the sleazy motel next door," Savage insisted. "The cops targeted her because she's a black trans woman. Kept calling her a tranny and a junkie whore. I wanted to put my fist through their teeth."

"Look, I understand y'all want to protect your friend," I said. "But I was hired to return her to custody, not to work as your private investigator."

"You used to be a cop. And you are licensed as a private investigator," Li said. Her name patch read Dragon. "Yeah, I checked up on you too."

I tried not to show my frustration. "I was a patrol officer for a year, and that was a long time ago. I was never a detective. As for being a private investigator, I only got the license because the bounty hunter I used to work for wanted me to. I've never investigated any cases beyond my capacity as a bail enforcement agent."

"That's the deal," said Shea. "Get the county attorney to drop the charges against Indigo, and she'll turn herself in to you."

"I sympathize with Indigo's situation. I'm a trans woman. I know what it's like to be brutally assaulted and what it's like to be arrested on bogus charges. Which is why I'm willing to help get her bail reset so she can stay out of jail for the duration of her trial."

Tucker held my gaze. "But you can't guarantee that."

"No."

Tucker shook her head. "Not good enough."

"If we got the charges dropped, then we'd lose out on the recovery fee," said Byrd. "Why should we work for free?"

"Exactly." I turned to Li. "You're her lawyer. Hire a professional investigator to track down the real killer."

"I've suggested it." Li looked at Stevens.

"We don't have the money," said Stevens. "We put up all the cash we had for the deposit on Indigo's bail."

"You're going to lose a lot more if Indigo doesn't come with us. You'll lose your whole house and all those pretty motorcycles you have in your garage."

"And *you'll* lose a whole lot more than the bounty if you try to take her by force." Stevens made an upward gesture, and the other members of the Athena Sisterhood suddenly stood and surrounded Byrd and me.

I eased to my feet, my hand resting on the grip of my Ruger. "You all need to back the fuck off."

Adrenaline roared into my system, sending my senses into overdrive. Li, I noticed, had disappeared. Plausible deniability, no doubt.

Well, here we go.

Byrd put a hand on my arm. "Everybody just chill before someone gets killed. It doesn't have to go down like this."

I kept my hand on the grip of my pistol and glared at Stevens. "You try anything, we'll put enough of you down to make you regret it."

"Leave Indigo alone." This from Fuego. "Everybody walks away in one piece."

"Sorry, can't do that. She skipped out on her bail bond. Law says she goes back to jail."

"And y'all get paid your thirty pieces of silver," said Stevens.

I shrugged. "We all have a job to do. No shame in getting paid for it."

"You want to get paid, find the real killer," said Fuego. "We'll make sure you get something for your trouble."

"We'll consider the offer," said Byrd, trying to be all diplomatic and shit.

"Like hell we will," I replied. "We're taking Pearson back to Scottsdale with us, willing or unwilling."

"Ever heard of the Confederate Thunder?" asked Fuego. "They used to rule this area. Tried to shut us down. Didn't want us calling ourselves a motorcycle club. Raped and murdered a couple of our members. So we took them down. They're all dead or in prison now."

I nodded. "Interesting. You ever heard of Milo Volkov?"

A self-satisfied smile curled the corners of Stevens's mouth. "Bastard kidnapped my girlfriend once. I shot him too."

"But you didn't kill him, did ya? I did. Him and several of his goons. And I didn't need a biker gang to do it."

"Enough of this." Fuego shot glances at her fellow bikers, and they put away their weapons. "I suggest you two leave. Now."

"Come on, Byrd. Let's blow this dive." We pushed our way through the bikers, ignoring the stares from the bar's other patrons.

When we stepped out the door, I let go of a breath I'd been holding, sending out clouds of water vapor. "Fuck me."

A chill was growing in the air. A ring of ice crystals encircled the full moon casting a silvery glow on the Downtown Square.

Byrd ran a hand over his close-cropped hair. "That coulda gone better."

"No shit, Sherlock." I shuffled along the crowded sidewalk back to the Gray Ghost.

"So what now?"

"Back to the hotel. Go over the paperwork Rios gave us on the Athena Sisterhood members with a record. Formulate a game plan."

"So you still intend to arrest Pearson?"

"I do."

"And when they come after us?"

"We'll deal with the threat as it comes." I unlocked the Gray Ghost and hopped in behind the wheel.

16

———

As we cruised out of the downtown area, the headlights of two motorcycles behind us caught my attention. "Looks like we got a tail."

Byrd turned in his seat. "Gotta give them points for moxie."

"Moxie? Geez, what century are you in? Been binge-watching *Mary Tyler Moore*?"

"I like to read. Gives me a rich vocabulary. So what you gonna do about our tails?"

"Nothing for now. The Ghost isn't exactly built for speed. They're probably just keeping an eye on us."

They followed us out of downtown, never more than a couple of cars behind. I drove into the pass-through of a Days Inn. The bikers pulled into parking spaces nearby facing the motel entrance. Neither got off their motorcycle.

"This isn't our motel," Byrd said.

"No, it's a diversion." I turned on my walkie-talkie. "Sit tight and keep an eye on them. If they get off their bikes, hail me on the walkie."

"I don't like this."

"Stay cool, man. You're good at that, remember?"

I gave the biker women a friendly wave and walked into the motel lobby. At the front desk, a white man in his late twenties with gelled anime-style hair greeted me. His name tag read Chuck.

"Do you offer room service?" I asked, knowing the answer. I pulled a brochure from a holder on the counter.

Chuck smiled. "I'm afraid not, but in your room, you will find a directory of nearby restaurants that deliver. Big Daddy's Smokehouse is a popular barbecue restaurant. There's also the Peking Palace, if you prefer Chinese. And the Ring of Fire is a fabulous Mexican-Asian fusion place. Of course, right now, we're all booked up."

I nodded appreciatively. "How far is it to the Grand Canyon from here?"

"Depending on your route, it should take you about two hours."

I asked a few more unnecessary questions, thanked him for his time, and walked out holding the brochure prominently as I climbed into the Gray Ghost. Our escorts were still watching from their bikes. I drove around behind the building. The bikers followed but maintained their distance.

"Why are we here? I don't understand," said Byrd.

"I was hoping they'd assume we were staying here and then drive on. Time for plan B." I jumped out and opened up the back. "Grab your bag."

"Did you get us a room here?"

"Not exactly." I led Byrd to a door at the rear of the building. Unfortunately, the back door required a room key card to open.

"Shit." I glanced through the window. A woman with two young kids was approaching the door from the inside. "Ah, here we go."

The door burst open as the kids raced through playing tag, followed by their haggard-looking mother. I held it open for her.

"Thank you," she said in a tired voice.

I smiled. "My pleasure." We stepped inside and turned down a corridor, out of view of the door.

"Would you mind explaining what's going on?"

I called up an Uber ride on my phone. The app told me the driver would arrive in ten minutes.

"I'm trying to lose our tail. I requested an Uber to take me back to the Square. The Goldstrike Saloon on Prospect Avenue has a rear entrance onto Orange Grove Boulevard. If I'm right, the bikers will follow me in the Uber. I'll lose them at the Goldstrike, and you can pick me up on Orange Grove."

The Uber car arrived shortly. I tossed Byrd my keys, stepped outside carrying my duffel, waved at the women on bikes, then hopped in. As expected, the bikers followed. When I kept glancing back at our tail, the driver, a young man originally from Benin, asked if everything was all right. I shot him a smile and assured him it was.

I hopped out at the Goldstrike and hustled in past the hostess station, saying my group was already waiting for me. Just past the restrooms, I found the back door. The sign had the words Orange Grove Blvd painted on it and a crooked arrow pointed downward. I stepped outside and took the staircase down to the rear parking lot. Byrd flashed the headlights to the Gray Ghost.

He laughed. "I honestly did not think that would work."

"My plans always work. Eventually."

We drove back to the Montgomery Family Inn, with a side trip to a liquor store so I could pick up a bottle of Cuervo. The thrill of losing our biker tail faded, replaced by the tendrils of depression and self-doubt wrapping around my brain. What made me think I could find this chick? For that matter, what was Deez thinking when he recommended me?

People had a tendency to get hurt or killed around me. Teammates, fugitives, and even innocent bystanders. I was a walking disaster. And now I was responsible for Byrd's safety. The more I thought about it, the more I wanted to chase him away so he didn't get hurt.

While Byrd stretched out on his bed and watched the TV, I poured some tequila into a plastic cup.

"Want some?" I offered.

Byrd shook his head. "Nah, I'm good."

"Why? Because Jesus?" I mocked.

"I don't drink when I'm on a case. But you do you, girl."

"Yeah." I was being a bitch. I didn't care. I poured more into the cup, then sat on the bed and dove into the paperwork Detective Rios had given us.

Two of the eight members were Shea "Havoc" Stevens and Zia "Indigo" Pearson. Nothing new there. Two were deceased. That left four others with rap sheets. While there was no guarantee any of those four were hiding Pearson, I figured they were our best bets.

My phone started playing the *Game of Thrones* theme song—Becca's ringtone.

"What's up, Becks. You okay?"

"Yeah, I felt bad about not running those checks for you."

"Geez, girl. You know your health takes precedence over any skip tracing work."

"I know. I just felt bad, so I ran the phone logs you needed. There's been no activity on Zia Pearson's phone. Nothing of interest on her wife's either. No unidentified numbers."

"Not surprising. Clearly laying low. I'd think they would be communicating somehow. No text messages?"

"A few people sent messages to Tucker asking how Indigo's doing. Tucker just responded that she was fine. Didn't elaborate. From what I could find out, most of the people sending the messages appear connected to the motorcycle gang."

"Damn. I was hoping for some direction. We don't have long to find her."

"How are things working out with Byrd?"

I glanced over at him. He was laughing at something on the television. "We haven't killed each other yet. We're sharing a motel room, if you can believe it."

"Ooh, sexy. I want details."

"It's not like that."

"Sure, sure."

"Honestly, sex is the last thing I want." I took a long pull on the tequila. "Kinda wondering if I lost my mojo."

"For sex?"

"No, for catching fugitives."

"Jenna Christine Ballou, you are a badass bounty hunter," Becca said matter-of-factly. "Don't let this rough patch let you forget you've caught a lot of fugitives."

"And a lot of people have been hurt along the way. Caden. Peyton. Rodeo. Deez. Conor. I don't want Byrd to be added to that list."

"It's a rough business. You know that. Byrd knows it, too, I'm sure. Everyone who does that job knows that. And for the record, Peyton's death is not on you. Those racist bastards with White Nation killed him. You'll get your mojo back, girl. Remember, smile."

The word *smile* was like a piercing ray of light into the murky black of my soul. The word was code, a reminder of the first time Becca and I had gone to the movies together as kids. We were eleven years old. I had recently transitioned and was still insecure about going out dressed as a girl, terrified people would laugh or worse.

We'd gone to see the movie *Anywhere But Here*. I was petrified when we approached the ticket taker in the lobby. Becca leaned in close and told me to smile. I did. And instead of mocking me, the ticket taker simply returned the smile and said, "Enjoy the movie, girls."

Since then it had been a code, a magical word that helped me rediscover my strength and courage.

"Thanks, Becca. You're the best. Now get some rest."

17

———

The next morning, I woke to a scratching sound. "Diana, cut it out."

The scratching continued. "Diana, if you don't stop scratching at that door, I'm gonna…" I realized I wasn't at home. Diana wasn't around. I looked up to see Byrd standing on his bed. The painting that had been secured above his pillow lay flat on the bedspread. Byrd had a pen and was drawing on the wall.

I rubbed my face to wake up. My head pounded, no doubt a result of my indulgence the night before. The bottle of tequila was half-empty. Or half-full. Whatever.

"What the hell are you doing?" I asked.

"SWT."

"SW-what?"

"Secret Wall Tattoo. You create your own art behind the awful pictures they mount on the walls."

"I believe the legal term for that is vandalism. You realize I'm paying for the room, right? I don't want to get charged extra just because you decided to express your subversive creative side."

"Don't worry. No one will know. Besides, there's already artwork on the inside of the toilet tank lid, on top of the bar for the shower curtain, and on the inside of the nightstand, behind the drawer."

I studied the image he was sketching with the ballpoint pen. It looked like a scene from an Avengers movie. "You're good."

"Thanks."

"You into comic books?"

"Marvel mostly for superheroes," he said, focusing on his work. "Though most of the books I read are more indie. I'm currently reading a pulp crime series called *Las Vegas Repo*. How about you? You into comic books?"

"Yeah, more DC than Marvel. I also read *Bitch Planet*, *Peepland*, and *Rat Queens*. Even got a signed first edition of *Tank Girl*. You ever cosplay?"

"Not really. You?"

"Wonder Woman. Sometimes Xena," I said, feeling a little embarrassed.

Byrd stopped drawing and turned to me with interest in his eyes. "I can see that. You'd be badass as Wonder Woman."

My face heated. "Thanks, I guess. So how'd you get the picture off the wall?"

"With this." He pulled out a little tool with a notch in it, then stuffed it back in his pocket.

"Huh." I couldn't think of anything else to say. We were both comic book geeks working as bounty hunters. Weird. "Well, be ready to go in thirty. I really want to wrap up this job today and go home."

"Roger that. Ready when you are."

I took a quick shower and threw on a fresh set of clothes. Just as I was putting on my tactical belt, my phone rang. It was Becca.

"Hey," I said. "Feeling better?"

"A bit. I may have found something."

"Really? What?"

"I was going back over Chelsea Tucker's mobile phone logs," she told me. "There is one number she calls a few times a day that belongs to another member of the Athena Sisterhood—a woman named Helen Butler. Her biker name is Rah-Rah."

"Butler. That name rings a bell. Hold on." I thumbed through the report Rios had printed out for us. "Here she is. Helen Butler. Six years ago, she served three months for a possession charge and having a fake MMJ card. You think she's hiding Pearson?"

"That would be my guess."

"Good work, Becks. Do you have a location for this phone?" I wanted to make sure the address listed in the printout from Rios was still current.

"I pinged it, but the phone seems to be off. No location. The calls seem to be at regular times. Seven o'clock in the morning. One o'clock in the afternoon and nine o'clock in the evening. Like clockwork."

I looked at my watch. It was seven forty. "Guess we missed the good morning call."

"Yeah. I'll monitor it and let you know if it pops up."

"You have an address for Helen Butler?"

She gave it to me. It matched the one I already had, located in Bradshaw City, twenty minutes north of Ironwood.

"Thanks for the info. I have a good feeling about this."

"Be extremely careful, Jinxie. I don't think they'll give up one of their own very easily."

"So I've learned. Don't worry. I got my head on a swivel. Talk to ya later."

I hung up. "Let's go track down our fugitive," I told Byrd.

I spent ten minutes scraping the frost off the windshield with an old Macy's charge card. Never saw the need for investing in an ice scraper. Even in winter, the temps down in the valley rarely dipped below freezing.

On the way to Bradshaw City, we stopped at a QT convenience store. I grabbed a couple of breakfast burritos. Byrd snagged a few power bars. Breakfast of champions.

Once we were underway, I filled him in on what I'd learned about Helen "Rah-Rah" Butler.

"Why they call her Rah-Rah?" he asked.

"Who knows? Maybe she was a cheerleader in school."

"Or maybe it stands for 'rambunctious radical,'" joked Byrd.

"Or 'random razor blade.'"

"Rational radiologist."

I struggled to think of another. "Raging racketballer."

"Weak. How about ravishing rabbi?"

"With a name like Butler, she doesn't sound Jewish. Radiant radish."

"Could be if she's a vegan," he said. "Raucous raccoon."

We continued on, coming up with sillier and sillier explanations for Butler's nickname. Despite a lingering headache from my drinking the night before, I felt hopeful about wrapping things up. For the first time, we had a solid lead. Whether we could bag our fugitive without bloodshed remained to be seen.

Bradshaw City was smaller and more rural than Ironwood. Plenty of used car lots, feed stores, Walmarts, and check cashers. Not many Starbucks or shopping malls. Pickup trucks with NRA stickers outnumbered Priuses with Coexist decals by a ratio of thirty to one.

The terrain in Helen Butler's neighborhood was hilly. Homes were small with single-car garages. Aging vehicles lined the street. Lawns were choked with weeds and wildflowers. The Gray Ghost fit in perfectly.

Three motorcycles sat in Butler's driveway and a few more on the street. Two women stood guard by the front door, and I recognized one of them as Shea Stevens, Ms. Iron Goddess herself.

"Shit." I drove past and parked several doors down.

"What's our strategy?" Byrd asked.

I stared at the house in my rearview mirror. "We go in and get our girl."

"How? They still outnumber us. I really don't want to kill anyone over a bounty."

"Roadhouse rules."

"Roadhouse rules? What? 'Be nice until it's time not to be nice?' Hasn't worked so far."

"Just follow my lead." We stepped out of the truck and geared up. I put a Taser in my right holster, my Ruger in the cross-draw. Walkie-talkies on. I handed Byrd the beanbag shotgun.

"Sneak into the backyard between those two houses over there, then find a spot where you can see the back door. If it's guarded, keep your distance. If not, approach cautiously. If Zia Pearson runs out, tell her to stop. Be nice about it. Use your cool charm. If she doesn't stop, hit her with a beanbag and cuff her. You have handcuffs?"

He nodded.

"If one of the bikers comes at you, tell them to keep their distance. Be nice. Try to de-escalate the situation if you can."

"So the complete opposite of your approach last night."

I sighed. "Yeah. If they keep coming and or look like they're about to hurt you, shoot them. And if you get into trouble, call me on the walkie."

"I'm really not liking this. We should have a bigger crew for a situation like this. I could call Deez, see if he can spare anyone else."

"No time. We got this." I had my mojo back. I could feel it. "Just keep your head on a swivel. Ready?"

"No."

"Relax. You got Jesus protecting you, right?" I slapped him teasingly on the arm. "Call me on the walkie when you're in position."

He raced like a deer into the backyard of the house three doors down from Butler's. I checked my watch, then kept an eye on the two women guarding the front door. They didn't appear to have noticed us. Yet.

A few minutes later, my radio crackled.

"I'm in position."

"What do you see?"

"No one on the backside of the house."

"Good. Can you see anyone inside?"

"The sun makes it impossible to see in."

"Do you have cover?"

"Yes."

"Hold position for now. I'm approaching the front door."

18

I took a deep breath. Despite the danger, this was the part of the job I loved. The hunt was a challenge, but the takedown was always the satisfying conclusion. I was pumped. I was ready. No one was going to stop me from doing my lawful duty.

When I started crossing over into Butler's yard, both Stevens and the other woman at the door were watching me. Stevens's companion looked more like a cheerleader than the typical biker chick. Slim, athletic build. Hair in a cute chestnut ponytail, perfect makeup. Her biker vest read Rah-Rah.

"You need to pack up and go home," Stevens announced as I approached. Her hand rested on a Glock on her right hip. "We gave you our offer, and you turned us down. You ain't taking Indigo."

"Ms. Stevens, I don't negotiate. I don't play detective. I'm a bounty hunter, pure and simple. Indigo has a chance to get back on track so she doesn't spend the rest of her life looking over her shoulder. Nobody wants to live like that."

"I done told you, you ain't gettin' her."

I placed a hand on the Taser. "Step aside. No one needs to get hurt."

A boom echoed from the backyard, followed by a second. Shit.

Shea went for her Glock. I fired the Taser and hit her in the chest. Her body seized, and she fell to the ground with a strangled cry. Her Glock tumbled under a nearby shrub.

Rah-Rah rushed me, drawing a pistol at the same time. I sent the gun flying with a roundhouse kick. She swung. I blocked and slammed her perfect perky nose with a palm-heel strike. When she came at me again, I dropped her with a boot to her solar plexus. She lay in a heap, gasping for air, blood trickling down her face.

I picked up Stevens's Glock and reached for Rah-Rah's pistol, a Ruger similar to mine. Next thing I knew, I was tumbling off the porch into the hard-packed dirt of the front yard. I rolled to keep Stevens from pinning me.

She came at me with a series of punches and kicks. We sparred back and forth, exchanging blows. She was a ruthless street fighter with fast reflexes—a fair match for my years of training in Krav Maga.

At one point, I had her pinned. Heaving, I said between breaths, "It's not...not worth it. Just stop."

Her weight shifted below me, and she tossed me sideways. I fell hard against a large rock and tasted blood. I blocked a series of blows and kicks, grabbing her boot and twisting her off her feet. I reached my Ruger, but she drove a knee into my eye socket before I got a grip.

As I lay on the ground, trying to clear the cobwebs from my mind, a thunderous boom made my heart skip a beat. Stevens fell to the ground beside me, moaning. Twenty feet away, Byrd stood holding the shotgun.

"Drop it!" Rah-Rah held the Glock on Byrd and her Ruger on me.

Byrd looked at me for instructions. I nodded while still catching my breath. He dropped the shotgun and raised his hands.

I rubbed my throbbing eye socket. The vision was blurred. My face felt swollen. Blood ran down my shirt. My fists were scraped and bruised. Stevens didn't look any better.

"So what now?" I looked up at Rah-Rah. "You going to kill us?"

The guns in her hands trembled. Her expression was that of a frightened child. Someone with less experience might assume she wouldn't shoot. But I knew better. Fear made people do stupid things.

"F-forget about Indigo, all right?" said Rah-Rah. "Just...just forget her."

Stevens pushed herself to her feet, moaning and wincing. To my surprise, she offered me a hand and pulled me to my feet.

"Or take our offer," she said through gritted teeth. "We'll find a way to compensate you if you don't get your bounty."

I didn't like other people telling me how to run my business, especially people protecting a fugitive, innocent or not. But it was clear that with a couple of dozen members on their roster, the Athena Sisterhood had Byrd and me outmanned. And that was just the local chapter. If they brought in help from outside chapters, who knew how many we would face. No wonder Rodeo and Tommy Boy threw in the towel.

"Fine. We'll take your offer," I said reluctantly.

Byrd's eyes narrowed. "Jinx, no."

I locked eyes with Stevens. "But I need every bit of information you and Rebecca Li have about the case. And it has to be the truth."

"We'll give you what we got. I'll have Dragon hook you up."

"Another thing. I have less than a week before the judge vacates the bond and demands the full amount of the bail. If that deadline passes, it's no longer up to me what happens. Pima Bail Bonds will file to take your house. I've seen it happen. The sheriff will show up with a whole lot more firepower than you've got and kick you and your niece out on the street. And your pal Indigo will spend the rest of her life on the FBI's Most Wanted list."

"We'll come down to Phoenix with you," said Stevens. "We'll work together on this."

A bitter laugh escaped my throat, causing me to cough and spit blood. "Thanks for the offer, but I don't work with people I don't know and can't trust."

"You can trust us to help find the real killer. That's what we want."

"I don't need a bunch of outlaw bikers getting in my way. Bad enough I'm playing private eye instead of dragging Indigo's sorry ass back to jail."

"Don't talk about Indigo that way," said Rah-Rah.

"We're not one-percenters," insisted Stevens.

"Whatever that means," I sneered.

"It means, we're a law-abiding club."

"Really? Is that why your buddy's on the lam while you're pointing guns at us?"

"We're working toward the same goal. That's all you need worry about. Or you can walk away."

Every instinct told me to do just that. Who knew what these bikers would pull, all with my reputation on the line.

I looked to Byrd, who shook his head. "Let's just walk, Jinx. No shame in it."

I thought about it some more. It was the sensible thing to do. Tommy Boy and Rodeo couldn't bag Pearson. Why should I risk my life trying? But if I didn't come through for Maurice at Pima Bail Bonds, I might never find work again.

"Fine, we work together." I wiped blood from my eyebrow onto my arms. Byrd's face fell in disappointment. I didn't blame him.

Stevens took her Glock from Rah-Rah and holstered it. "Meet me at Iron Goddess in an hour."

"Agreed." I waved to Byrd. "Grab the shotgun, and let's check out of the motel."

"The shotgun stays here," said Rah-Rah.

"Oh, so you're robbing us now? Is this the trustworthiness you were talking about?" I directed the question at Stevens.

"Rah-Rah, let them take the shotgun."

"But Havoc..."

"I'm club VP. I say give it back. You gotta problem with that, take it up with Fuego."

I held out my hand to Rah-Rah. "And my Ruger."

She looked to Stevens, who nodded. "Give it to her."

Rah-Rah let me take it from her. Byrd picked up the shotgun, and we shuffled to the Gray Ghost. I had no idea how Maurice was going to react to this latest development. But I hurt too much to care.

"What happened in the backyard?" I asked when we climbed into the Gray Ghost.

"Pearson ran out the back door with three other women. I hit one with a beanbag round. Tried to get Pearson but missed. The other women started shooting at me as they ran off."

I glanced at him. "You hurt?"

"No, I'm good."

I breathed a sigh of relief. "Glad to hear it." I started the SUV and drove off down the road.

"Jinx, all due respect, I don't like this. No shame in admitting we couldn't find her. Rodeo and Tommy Boy didn't get her either. Maybe Pima Bail Bonds just has to eat this one."

"You want to be the one to tell Maurice that?"

"Not really. But like you said, we're bail enforcement, not detectives."

"I guess there's a first time for everything. If you're not interested, I won't blame you for walking away."

Byrd grew silent, staring out at the passing landscape as I

drove south to Ironwood. I hated this tension between us. I almost wanted him to say he didn't want to join me on this ludicrous mission. At the same time, I wanted someone I could trust to do the right thing.

At the motel, I cleaned myself up and put on some clothes that weren't covered in blood. I tried some concealer and other makeup to make my face look less like an heirloom tomato. But there was no hiding the fact that I'd taken a beating.

"So what's it going to be, Jubal Byrd? You in or you out?"

He let out a long sigh. "I like you, Jinx. And I respect you as a bounty hunter."

Aw, shit, here it comes.

"Honestly, I think you're impulsive and sarcastic. You curse and drink more than I'd like."

"Oh, for fuck's sake, just spit it out. You're bailing on me."

He met my gaze. "No, that's just it. It's because I respect you that I'm willing to do this."

"Huh. Did not see that coming."

We packed up our stuff and checked out. It was nearly noon when we reached the motorcycle shop.

The skinny blonde behind the counter took one look at us, said, "I'll get them," and disappeared into the back. She returned a moment later with Stevens, Fuego, Savage, and Dragon. All four were wearing their biker vests.

"Well, look who shows up again, now that the fighting's over with," I said to Dragon.

Her face was unreadable when she handed me a thick manila folder. "These are copies of documents I deemed relevant from what I received in discovery from the Maricopa County attorney. You'll find crime scene reports and forensics—autopsy, fingerprint, DNA, and trace—as well as statements from my client and other witnesses."

"How do you explain Pearson's DNA on the victim?" I asked.

"The victim scratched Indigo when they got into a shoving

match earlier that day. I'm planning to impeach with an expert witness, but I can't count on that. Juries hear DNA, they assume the defendant is guilty. I need more to acquit my client."

"Like I said, you should hire a professional investigator." I thumbed through the paperwork.

"I'm already working pro bono on this case," replied Dragon. "The club has put up all they had for the bail bond, money they'll never get back even if Indigo is cleared. We need your help. Find the killer, Ms. Ballou, and get my client off the hook. She doesn't deserve this travesty of justice."

"We'll see what we can find out." I held up the folder. "This is a lot of information to sort through. Can you give me a highlights reel?"

"That is the highlights reel gleaned from the boxes of information the prosecution sent over."

I felt like I was competing in a marathon and was just leaving the starting block while everyone else was halfway to the finish line.

I looked to Stevens. "So who all's coming on this Quixotic adventure?"

"Just me and Fuego for now. If we need more, they'll be there."

I shook my head. This was going to be such a clusterfuck. "Okay, here's the game plan. I want to get my skip tracer, Becca Alvarez, looking into the victim's background, this Brother James or whoever he is. Hopefully, she can dig up something that will point us in the direction of the killer. If not, we'll check out the crime scene, talk to witnesses, whatever it takes."

I handed the keys to Byrd. "You drive while I get up to speed on these reports."

"I appreciate you doing this," said Savage as we walked to the front of the shop. There was a sadness and sincerity about her that I hadn't noticed before. "Indigo's the love of my life. And she's no killer."

I nodded. "I can't promise anything."

Byrd and I climbed into the Gray Ghost.

"Take it easy on the curves going down Sycamore Mountain. She tends to be a little top heavy."

"Easy on the curves. Got it."

We pulled onto the road. Stevens and Fuego followed on their motorcycles down the switchbacks. Trying to read as we wound down through the curves was all but impossible. I called Becca.

"How goes the hunt for the biker chick?" she asked.

My head still throbbed. "Things have taken a rather unusual turn."

"What's wrong? Are you okay?"

"More or less. Are you at the Hub by chance?"

"Yeah, why? You need me to skip trace more of Pearson's biker buddies?"

"Not exactly. Pearson's biker buddies have..." I struggled for the right word. "Let's just say they convinced me that she's innocent. They want me to find the real killer."

"I thought you always said you're not in the guilty or not guilty business..."

"I'm making an exception."

"Because she's trans?"

"Because Byrd and I are grossly outnumbered. Pearson has promised to turn herself in if I can come up with enough evidence to get her acquitted."

"This doesn't sound like you, Jinxie. Are you being held against your will? Do I need to call the Cortes County sheriff?"

"I'm fine. But I do need you to research the victim in the case, Brother James Fitzgerald. Personal history, financials, phone logs, social media, anything to point me to someone with the motive, means, and opportunity to murder him. I don't have much time before Pima Bail Bonds has to cough up the full bail."

"Got it. I'll see what I can find out."

I hung up and saw I had a voicemail message. I hit the play button.

"Hi, Ms. Ballou. Pete Stansfield again with Arizona Mutual Life Insurance. I really do need to talk with you about the claim we paid out on Conor Doyle. Please call me."

I deleted it. Dealing with that shit was so at the bottom of my list it deserved a gravestone.

Once the road straightened out, I was able to concentrate on the stack of papers in my hand. According to the crime scene report, Brother James, aka James Fitzgerald, was found dead in a room registered under his name at the Cactus Inn in Scottsdale.

The medical examiner's report listed cause of death as a gunshot wound to the head. The crime scene photos revealed a large man, probably over six feet tall, who looked like he'd lost a fight to a professional boxer, something I had personal experience with. His face was swollen beyond recognition. A trail of blood led from the body to where his severed penis was found in the toilet. A brutal but fitting end to a man who preached such filth against women and minorities.

A member of the motel staff claimed to have seen a tall African American female with long braids running from the motel room and screaming shortly before the body was discovered.

Patrol officers canvassed the area and questioned patrons at neighboring businesses. Members of the Athena Sisterhood had been drinking next door at Naughty's Cabaret. Zia Pearson fit the description of the woman leaving Fitzgerald's motel room.

When questioned by Scottsdale homicide detectives Atkinson and Torres, Pearson admitted to getting into a confrontation with the victim earlier that day at Scottsdale's Wild West event center, which was hosting Arizona Bike Week. Fitzgerald was reported to have been holding up signs that read "Women Deserve 2 B Raped" and "Put Homos 2 Death."

The police report noted Pearson's knuckles and forearms were scraped up, which she explained were due to her attempts to attach a luggage bracket to the back of her motorcycle while at the biker festival.

I flipped to the forensics reports. The room contained fingerprints from dozens of individuals, none matching Pearson's. DNA found under Fitzgerald's fingernails matched Pearson's, but no other corroborating trace evidence was found.

Pearson had two previous arrests, one for possession of controlled substances and one for solicitation. The controlled substance in question turned out to be estradiol, for which Pearson didn't have a prescription at the time. She received a suspended sentence. The solicitation charges were dropped after the arresting officer admitted he assumed she was a prostitute because she was black and transgender.

So if Pearson didn't kill the little hate-monger, who the hell did?

By the time we reached Phoenix, I had read or skimmed most of the documents in the file. I directed Byrd to go through the drive-through at Tres Leches, a downtown coffeehouse, where I picked up a regular latte for myself, an almond milk cappuccino for Becca, and a regular coffee for Byrd. I thought about getting something for Stevens and Fuego, who waited on their bikes on the other side of the parking lot, but considering the day's events, I wasn't feeling too charitable toward them.

With drinks in hand, I guided Byrd to the Hub's parking lot, having shed our winter coats to enjoy the more springlike weather of the valley.

"Where are we?" asked Stevens.

"The Hub. It's a coworking space where I rent a desk. Follow me."

I led them through the maze of desks while music from Dead Can Dance played on the Hub's sound system. I pulled up some extra chairs. Becca thanked me for the cappuccino.

"Becca Alvarez, this is Byrd, who's temporarily on loan from Viper. Becca is an IT security guru who handles my skip tracing."

The two of them shook hands.

"And these two"—I pointed at my biker guests—"are Havoc, aka Shea Stevens, VP for the Cortes County chapter of the

Athena Sisterhood and the owner of Iron Goddess Custom Cycles."

"You can call me Shea." She shook Becca's hand.

"And this is Fuego, the chapter's president."

"Nice to meet you, Ms. Alvarez." Fuego nodded.

Becca gave me a look that said, "What the hell?"

I shrugged. "What'd you find out about the late Brother James?"

Becca rolled her eyes. "What a piece of work that guy was. I'm surprised nobody murdered him sooner. Officially, he was a licensed minister in the Evangelical Light of the Messiah Church, which is run by Michael Vincent Wilkes, or Elder Michael, as he calls himself on their website.

"Of course, it's less of a church and more of a cross between a psycho religious cult and an extreme right-wing lobbying organization. No location or schedule of services listed on the website. Their 'disciples,' as they call themselves, show up at schools or large public events, spewing their bigotry. The Southern Poverty Law Center lists them as a hate group."

"No surprise there," I said.

"James Fitzgerald joined the organization in 2007. Prior to that, he worked as an elementary school teacher for a private Baptist school. The so-called church pays him three grand a month. He's divorced, no kids officially, though one woman claims he's the father of her special-needs child.

"He has accounts on most major social media. Shortly before his death, Twitter suspended his account for posting hate speech. He received a lot—and I mean a lot—of death threats.

"Late last year, he was charged with raping a teenager, copped a plea for misdemeanor assault. Sentenced to six months probation, no jail time, didn't have to register as a sex offender. He's been sued multiple times for harassment. Won most of those cases. One was settled for twenty thousand dollars, although the settlement remains unpaid.

"He routinely shows up at high school and college campuses

preaching hate against women and minorities. He also rents a room twice a month at the Cactus Inn, the same motel where his body was found."

"No doubt getting his holier-than-thou nob polished," Shea replied.

"Makes me sick," Byrd said. "Guys like him give Christianity a bad name."

"A year ago," Becca continued, "he was attacked by a lesbian teen with a two-by-four while he was protesting outside the fence by her high school."

"I remember that," said Shea. "The Athena Sisterhood raised money for her legal bills."

"So what's the bottom line?" I asked. "Who's the most likely suspect?"

"Bottom line is you're probably looking for a needle in a monster-sized haystack. Even in an ultraconservative state like Arizona, there were a lot of people who wanted this guy dead."

"Any of the death threats stand out, like whoever sent them intended to act on it?" I asked.

"Hard to say," Becca explained. "Most of the ones on social media were from accounts that have since been deleted or suspended. All I had were screenshots posted by Fitzgerald and his fellow 'disciples.' A few threats were from Wes Hancock, the father of the girl he raped. But that was last year. Nothing from him recently."

Stevens shook her head. "If Brother James raped my niece and got no prison time, I woulda dropped his ass down an abandoned mineshaft."

"We'll put him number one in the motive category," I said.

"So what's our game plan?" Fuego asked me.

"I want to talk to Detectives Atkinson and Torres, the ones who arrested Pearson."

Stevens scoffed. "Those fuckers wouldn't know their asses from a hole in the ground. They kept trying to get me to roll on

Indigo, claiming she had this big criminal past, which we all knew was bullshit." Her face colored with anger. "Talking to them is a waste of time."

Before I could reply, my phone rang.

20

———————

The number on the caller ID wasn't familiar. "Ballou Fugitive Recovery," I said.

"Is...is this Jinx Ballou?" asked a frantic female voice.

"Yeah, who is this?"

"V-Vanessa Colton. Used to be Vanessa Nealey. You...you took my husband back to jail a while back."

It took me a moment, but I remembered. Battered white woman giving me attitude when I showed up at her door, looking to arrest her then-boyfriend. I guessed she married the bastard.

"I remember. What do you want, Vanessa? I'm not looking for Freddie right now. If he's jumped bail again, I suggest you contact his bail bond agent."

"No, I...I need your help."

"*My* help? For what?"

She sobbed pitifully at the other end of the line. "I want out."

"Out of what?"

"Away from him. He...I'm so tired of being his punching bag."

"So why are you calling me?"

"I got no one else to turn to. Most of my friends, they don't want nothing to do with me."

"Oh for the love of bacon," I muttered. "Look, Vanessa, if Freddie's hit you again, call the police. Or get an order of protection."

"I tried all that. That order of protection didn't do shit. He just laughed and beat me up again. And when I called the cops, he was out on bail a day later."

"So change the fucking locks."

"Now that we're married, he says I can't."

"He says? Jesus fucking Christ on a cracker! What do you expect me to do about it? I'm not a bodyguard."

"Last time you were here, you told me to call if I needed help. You gave me your business card."

I didn't remember telling her that. I was pretty sure I hadn't told her that. But clearly that was what she remembered.

"What's going on?" asked Shea.

I put a hand over the mic while Vanessa sobbed in my ear. "Girlfriend of a fugitive I arrested a couple years ago. He's beating her up again, and she wants me to do something about it."

"Where is she?" asked Fuego.

"You still live in the same place?" I asked into the phone.

"Yes."

"Off Northern and Seventh Street," I told Fuego. "Why?"

"Is the abuser there now?" Fuego pressed.

"Vanessa, is Freddie there?"

"He just left."

"He's gone," I told Fuego and Stevens.

Fuego exchanged a look with Stevens. "Tell her we'll be there shortly."

"What? Wait a minute! The deal was you're here to help Byrd and me clear Indigo, remember? Now you want to go galloping off to save this damsel in distress?"

"This is what the Athena Sisterhood does—we protect women," Fuego insisted.

"Besides, you're going to talk to that cowboy Atkinson," said Shea. "Fuego and me had enough of that guy when he arrested Indigo. So while you're playing nicey-nice with the pigs, we'll help out this friend of yours."

"She is *so* not my friend, but whatever." I kicked myself for trusting them.

I turned back to the phone, fuming. "Vanessa, I'm sending a couple of"—I glanced at Shea and Fuego—"colleagues over to your place. They'll be riding motorcycles and have leather vests that say Athena Sisterhood. They'll help you deal with your asshole hubby."

"Thank you," she whimpered and hung up.

I gave Shea and Fuego Vanessa's address. "Have fun rescuing this princess, but don't say I didn't warn you. She's a piece of work."

"Call me when you're done talking to the heat," Shea replied. She and Fuego walked out.

"Jinx, what the hell's going on? You look like you lost a fight. What have you gotten yourself into with these bikers?" asked Becca.

Byrd nodded. "My thoughts exactly."

"I'm an idiot. I admit it. But there was no way we were going to arrest Zia Pearson. So I made a deal."

"And yet they're not holding up their end of it," said Byrd. "All due respect, Jinx, I think this was a mistake."

"Maybe so," I admitted. "No one's saying you have to do this with me. But I don't have a lot of options right now. Assurity Bail Bonds fired me after the Penzler fiasco. And now Conor's life insurance company is demanding I return the money they paid me, a lot of which I already spent on Caden's medical bills after he got shot while working for me. So if I need to track down the real killer to get Pearson to turn herself in, that's what I'll do."

Byrd held my gaze. I could see the calculations going on in his mind. I almost wanted him to walk away. To tell Deez what a head case and a failure I was. And he wouldn't be wrong.

"Let's see what those detectives in Scottsdale have to say."

"I'll keep poking around and see if I can't find anything more that'll point you to the murderer," Becca added.

I hugged her. "Thanks, bestie."

"I always got your back, girlie."

"Likewise. When's Easton get back from Denver?"

"They fly in tomorrow night. Can't wait. I'm in serious need of some cuddle time."

"Call me if you need help in the meantime." To Byrd, I said, "Thanks for doing this. For a Jesus freak, you're all right."

Byrd let loose a laugh. "I'll try to take that as a compliment."

Back in the Gray Ghost, I adjusted the driver's seat from where Byrd had moved it to accommodate his stilt-like legs.

"Despite walking out on us, it was mighty charitable of them to help that lady out," Byrd said while I pulled onto the I-10 heading east.

"I can't believe that dumb bitch married that asshole. It's a sick cycle with this woman. He beats her up. She calls the cops. They arrest him. She drops the charges and lets him back home. The one time she didn't drop the charges, he jumped bail, and I had to track him down. And then she goes and marries the son of a bitch. What'd she think would happen?"

"I had a cousin like that," Byrd replied. "Her boyfriend abused her, and she kept going back to him."

I shook my head. "No offense, but that's the definition of insanity. Doing the same shit over and over, expecting different results? Absolutely stupid."

"My cousin wasn't stupid. She was a biogenetics researcher. And hella beautiful. She just...I don't know, he was like her Kryptonite. He knew exactly which buttons to push to manipulate her."

"But why go back when he was so abusive?"

"She was convinced that if she loved him enough, he'd come around and treat her right. She was determined to figure out how to fix his abusive behavior, like he was one of her experiments."

"So did she fix him?"

Byrd got quiet. "He shot her in the head and then shot himself."

"Jesus Christ on a cracker! Couldn't just kill himself, could he?"

"I really wish you wouldn't use the Lord's name in vain like that."

"Sorry. It's just that relationships are so...I don't know. Maybe I should be celibate the rest of my life."

A half hour later, we arrived at the Scottsdale PD's main precinct.

"How can I help you?" asked the desk sergeant in the lobby, a woman with a sensible haircut, minimal makeup, and crow's-feet around her eyes.

"We need to speak with Detectives Atkinson and Torres, please."

"And you are...?"

"Jinx Ballou. This is my associate, Jubal Byrd. We're looking into a homicide case they handled recently."

"Let me check to see if they're in." She dialed the phone, spoke to someone, and hung up. "They'll be down shortly."

Twenty minutes later, two men came down the hall, both wearing detective shields on their belts.

Atkinson was a white guy in his late fifties and wore a grayish-tan suit badly in need of pressing. Below his Stetson, his curly hair hung in shades of silver, matching his barn owl of a mustache.

Torres was ten years younger, clean-cut with jet-black hair and penetrating eyes that left me feeling unsettled.

"Howdy, ladies. I'm Detective Wyatt Atkinson," he said in an exaggerated western drawl. "This here's my partner, Detective Marc Torres. How can we help y'all this fine afternoon?" He shook our hands, while his buddy gave us a nod.

I gave them our names. "We're looking into the case against Zia Pearson. You were the lead detectives."

"Are you reporters?" asked Torres.

"Bail enforcement." Byrd held up his ID and badge.

The two exchanged a glance. Atkinson beckoned with his long bony fingers. "Y'all come down the hall, and we can have ourselves a little chat."

Byrd and I followed them to an interview room nicer than most I'd seen. Instead of the typical broom-closet, bare cinder block aesthetic, this one had brightly painted walls, a window, and comfortable chairs. I figured the intent was to put suspects and witnesses at ease to make them chattier. Whether that worked or not, I couldn't say.

"So, y'all are bounty hunters, huh?" asked Atkinson. "I heard Pearson was a no-show at his hearing."

"*Her* hearing," I corrected. "We were wondering about other potential suspects for Fitzgerald's murder."

"Other suspects?" Torres raised an eyebrow.

Atkinson gave me a slow nod. "Y'all are working for the defense attorney, I reckon. As investigators, not bounty hunters. That it?"

"More or less." I shrugged.

"We thought maybe you arrested the wrong person," Byrd explained.

"Ya did, huh?" Atkinson stroked his mustache, like he was petting a bird. I half expected it to hoot. "With all due respect, boy, between Detective Torres and myself, we've been wrangling murderers, rapists, and other wrongdoers for a few decades now. We know how to work a case."

Torres glared at us. "We don't need a couple of two-bit bounty hunters with mail-order badges second-guessing our work."

"I used to be a cop too," I replied.

"Did you now?" Torres's patronizing tone was getting under my skin. "For how long?"

"A year," I admitted without enthusiasm.

"A whole year. Well, then you must have *all* the answers."

"Plenty of people had motive to kill Fitzgerald," Byrd insisted.

"Some with a lot more motive than Pearson. Wes Hancock, for instance—the father of the girl he raped."

Atkinson adjusted his hat and gave his bushy mustache a few more strokes. "Well, son, let me set your mind at ease. My partner and I don't turn a case over to the county attorney unless it's solid as granite. I assure you, this Pearson fella's the perp."

"She's not a fella." A vein in my neck twitched.

Atkinson laughed. "No offense, little lady, but bulls are bulls, and heifers are heifers. Never the twain shall meet, as they say. Just 'cause a man cuts off his johnson and puts on a dress, that don't make him a woman."

"And you putting on a Stetson doesn't make you a cowboy," I replied.

The sudden fire in Atkinson's eyes told me my jab hit home. "You best watch yourself, missy. Now I'm trying to be respectful to y'all. Torres and me, we interviewed a lot of folks, reviewed *all* the evidence, and put together a solid case against this Pearson *person*. They had a history of solicitation and drug possession. Not that big a leap to murder."

I was trying not to let these guys get under my skin, but I felt my hands ball into fists. "Those previous charges were bogus. The drug charge was for estrogen, not a narcotic. And the solicitation charge was dropped after the cop admitted it was bullshit. Or is a nonconviction only proof of innocence when it comes to cisgender men?"

"Enough of this nonsense." Torres stood up. "We have cases to solve. You two best leave before you get yourselves into trouble."

"What if we provide proof that someone else killed Fitzgerald?" asked Byrd. "Will you drop the charges against Pearson?"

"No," Torres said without hesitation.

"No?" I got to my feet, and Byrd followed suit. "You'd rather send an innocent woman to prison? Why? Because she's transgender?"

"Or black?" asked Byrd.

"We cleared the case and turned it over to the county attorney's office." Atkinson opened the door and stood there with an expression that said the conversation was over. "Our job is done. You want the charges dropped, talk to the prosecutor."

"And who would that be?"

"Wayne Prather," Torres said with a sneer. "I suppose you need us to give you his number too."

"Oh, would you, sir?" I said in my best Scarlett O'Hara voice. "That would be ever so nice."

"Get out." Torres looked ready to bite me in half. His partner didn't look too much more accommodating.

We got up and left without a word.

"That was a waste of time," Byrd said when we returned to the Gray Ghost. "What now?"

"Talk to the prosecutor."

I'd met Wayne Prather a few times over the years. Decent guy most of the time. If we came up with evidence that someone else killed Fitzgerald, there was a chance he'd drop the case. But it would have to be unimpeachable to counter the DNA evidence against Pearson.

I pulled out my phone, dialed the county attorney's office, and was directed to Prather's voicemail. "Mr. Prather, this is Jinx Ballou. I need to speak with you about your case against Zia Pearson." I left my number and hung up.

"Should we call Shea and Fuego?" asked Byrd.

"Soon. First, I want to check out the scene of the crime."

21

———

I headed south on Scottsdale Boulevard. Just past Oak Street, I pulled into the Cactus Inn parking lot, which was empty except for a 1990s-model Chevy Caprice and newer Kia Sephia. The paint on the street sign was peeling, giving the lettering a pointy, menacing style similar to the illegible graffiti tags on the sign's posts. A smaller, backlit sign by the front office promised rooms with free Playboy channel and other adult content.

The building's stucco exterior was pockmarked and yellowed from years of relentless heat and dust. Windows were dirty. Trash collected in corners.

To the north was a liquor store. To the south was Naughty's, the strip club where the Athena Sisterhood was hanging out when Fitzgerald's body was discovered.

"What do you hope to learn here?" asked Byrd.

"Not sure. I'd like to know why Fitzgerald rented a room every couple weeks."

My phone rang. Wayne Prather's name came up. "Thanks for calling me back, Wayne. I wanted to speak with you about your case against Zia Pearson."

"Pearson? The Fitzgerald murder, right?"

"That's right."

"You're the bounty hunter who was assigned to pick up Wilhelm Penzler. Isn't that correct?"

"Uh, yeah. But this isn't about—"

"You know he was helping us build a RICO case against the Volkov organization. That is until you got him killed."

"Now hold on a second. His death was accidental."

"Accidental, huh? Funny how anytime someone dares to testify against Sergei Volkov, they die in an unfortunate accident."

"About Zia Pearson..."

"Forget it, Ms. Ballou. I am not discussing that case or any other with you." The line went dead.

I looked at Byrd, feeling like I'd been sucker punched. "Grab the file. Let's see about this crime scene."

We walked into the rental office, a smallish room with a Plexiglass window that separated it from the office proper. The lobby, if it could be called that, held the faint scent of cheap perfume, taco sauce, and stale cigar smoke. I caught a glimpse of a security monitor that showed a camera view of the parking lot, including the Gray Ghost.

A man with a stubble-covered face sat on the other side of the window, eating a football-sized burro. A smear of salsa ran down his Hawaiian shirt. He stared at a computer tablet that was playing a video with cheesy music and a lot of moaning and groaning.

When I dinged the service bell on the counter, he grunted like we were intruding on his precious time.

"Hi, my name's Jinx Ballou." I flashed him my badge and my most charismatic smile. "What's yours?"

"Lenny. What's it to ya?" he asked with a mouthful of burro.

"I need some information, Lenny."

"Try Wikipedia," he replied without looking up.

"I need information on James Fitzgerald, otherwise known as Brother James."

"Never heard of him."

I laid a couple of twenties on the counter in the pass-through at the bottom of the window. "Heard of him now?"

Lenny glanced up at me, then down at the bills. "A fleeting memory. Don't recall no details."

I set down two more twenties. "Better now?"

He grabbed the cash, holding one of the bills up to the light to check the watermark. Like anyone would bother forging twenty-dollar bills. "Whaddya wanna know?"

"We know he rented a room a couple of times a month. We want to know why."

Lenny shrugged and returned his attention to the porno. The moaning was reaching a crescendo. "What people do in the rooms is none o' my business so long as it don't leave a big mess."

"Was he sleeping with hookers?" asked Byrd.

Lenny cast an eye in Byrd's direction. "That'd be illegal."

"Doesn't answer the question, does it?" I asked, matching his snarky tone.

Lenny didn't respond. Maybe he was waiting for me to shell out more money, which wasn't going to happen.

"Did he check in alone or with a lady friend?" asked Byrd. "Or male companion, for that matter."

"Not that I saw." He switched off the video and crossed his arms, glaring at both of us. "Anything else? I'm busy."

"How much for a room?" I asked.

"Forty-nine dollars. Checkout's at eleven."

"How much for just a few hours?"

Lenny tried to look indignant, but the result was more comical than he intended. "What kinda enterprise you think I'm running here?"

"A seedy motel crammed between a titty bar and a liquor store? But I'm sure the price includes numerous amenities. In-room Jacuzzi, perhaps? Michelin-rated restaurant? Open wine bar? Silk sheets?"

"Well, since you put it that way. For you, a special price. Forty-nine dollars. And I need an ID and a credit card." Lenny wiped his face and hands with a napkin, then dabbed at the spot on his shirt, which only spread the stain wider.

I laid fifty dollars in the pass-through. This was becoming an expensive fishing expedition. "I'm paying cash."

"State law says I gotta get an ID."

I held up a ten-dollar bill. "There's my ID. Hamilton. Alex Hamilton."

He looked at me like I was trying to pull a fast one. Or maybe he was trying to figure out if I was a vice cop. "You have to sign the register, *Ms. Hamilton.*"

I did so, and he grabbed a key and tossed it into the pass-through "Room 219. Upstairs, 'round back."

"I want the room Brother James's body was found in."

"Geez, you people into some kinky shit." He swapped the key for another one. "Room 149. North side of the building near the liquor store." He gestured with his thumb in the direction of the room.

"Thanks."

"Don't mess up the room, or you'll wish you hadn't. That means no physical damage, no bodily fluids on the walls. Or the ceiling. And no smoking. You got me?"

I waved as we walked out of the office.

"Why do you want to see the room?" Byrd asked when we walked around the building. "The crime scene techs would've already gone over every inch after the body was found. And who knows how many times the room's been rented since."

"Probably won't find anything. But maybe we'll luck out. I doubt the dearly departed Brother James was here for a Bible study."

"I was looking through the file Ms. Li gave us and found a photocopy of the motel register. Fitzgerald was signing in under the name Saul Tarsus." He showed me the photocopy.

"Saul Tarsus? Doesn't ring a bell."

"Saul of Tarsus was the name of the apostle Paul before he was converted."

"Well, isn't that clever," I said dryly.

We reached room 149, which had a lovely view of the strip club. I suspected the dancers were supplementing their income by providing more than lap dances to their customers. I inserted the key and had to jiggle it a bit to get the cylinder to turn.

Inside, the room smelled of a combination of mold and industrial cleaner with the lingering scent of decomp. The latter might have been my imagination. The place was small and dark. The floral wallpaper was peeling in spots, stained in others.

"We're not really going to stay here, are we?" Byrd looked a little green.

"Oh, come on, honey," I teased in an innocent yet seductive tone. "I did everything to make our little getaway special."

"What? I...uh...no offense, but I'm...I'm not..."

"What? Am I not pretty enough? Is it 'cause I'm trans?"

He looked like he was about to pass a kidney stone until I burst out laughing. "I'm just messing with you, man. No, we're not staying here."

He let go of a deep breath. "Oh, thank goodness."

"And lately, I prefer women, anyway. Mostly," I added.

He raised an eyebrow. "You're bisexual?"

"Bisexual, pansexual, who knows? After Conor disappeared, I dated this woman for about a month. A corrections officer, no less. Kind of a rebound thing."

"What was that like?" The curiosity in his voice was palpable. Like he wanted to know but didn't want to know.

"The sex was fantastic. But I wasn't in the right headspace for another relationship. I never called her. After a couple weeks of me ignoring her, she dumped me. Not that I blamed her."

"What did you two, you know, do in bed?"

I clapped him on the shoulder. "A lady has to have her secrets."

I opened the drawer in the nightstand. One standard copy of the Bible courtesy of the Evangelical Light of the Messiah Church, according to the stamp inside the cover.

"Maybe he really was doing a Bible study."

I laughed. "Here? Doubt it. But I'm sure God's name was called upon on multiple occasions. 'Oh God, that feels incredible. Oh God, don't stop. Oh God...'"

He was putting his fingers in his ears. "Please stop. I get it. Ha ha."

I was starting to like having him around. It had been a while since I had someone who was so much fun to torture.

I pulled back the bedcover and examined the sheets. They appeared relatively clean, but one never knew. Certainly not silk.

A cluster of reddish-brown, pinhole-sized dots on the edge of the fitted sheet caught my attention. "Ugh. Okay, I've seen enough."

"Why? What is it? Blood?"

"Sort of." I pointed at the dots on the bedsheet. "That is bedbug poop. They live on human blood."

"Bedbugs? For real?"

"Time to move on." My skin began to crawl, as if I was lying on an ant mound. We hurried out just as my phone rang.

"Jinx Ballou." I tried to ignore the creepy-crawly sensation.

"It's Shea. Where are you?"

"About to leave Scottsdale. How's your damsel in distress?"

"We checked with the domestic violence shelters around town. They're all full up with a waiting list."

"Oh, well, you tried." I should have been more sympathetic, but I still remembered how snotty she'd been the last time I'd seen her.

"We were wondering if she could stay with you."

"With me? Not just no but hell no! I do not need her drama in my life. I'm already trying to help out your buddy Indigo, remember?"

"Well, can you meet us over here? We need to discuss this."

I wanted to tell her there was nothing to discuss, but I didn't. "We'll be there in about half an hour."

22

———

We took the Loop 202 to the northbound Piestewa Freeway. A wave of sadness hit me like a sledge-hammer as we drove past where White Nation had set off a massive bomb last December. The memories and trauma drew me back into the emotional hell I'd been fighting.

At the Dreamy Draw exit, I turned west onto Northern and took that to Phoenix's Sunnyslope neighborhood. The enormous white *S* on Sunnyslope Mountain gleamed like a beacon against the dark green-gray of the craggy hillside. It was after four in the afternoon when we arrived at Vanessa's house. I parked behind Shea's motorcycle.

"Let's gear up," I said, "just in case Vanessa's husband shows."

Byrd nodded, and we pulled on our weapons and vests.

I pounded on the front door. From inside came the yapping of a small dog.

Shea opened the front door. "Glad y'all are here. You learn anything from those good ol' boys in Scottsdale?"

I shrugged. "No, but if you want me to exonerate Indigo, we need to work together. I don't need to be sidelined with this nonsense."

Shea nodded, guilt written on her face. "I know."

She led us through the living room to a small kitchen, where Fuego and Vanessa sat at a table that looked like a garage sale reject. One corner of the tabletop was broken, revealing layers of particleboard.

Vanessa looked much like the last time I'd seen her. Face swollen and bloodied, arms covered in a patchwork of purple, green, and yellow bruises. Then again, I wasn't looking much better.

She wore a pink Cinderella T-shirt, her hair a ragged mess. A Yorkie with a pink bow atop its head sat in Vanessa's lap, yapping its damn head off at Byrd and me.

"Don't mind Jasmine. She barks at anyone she doesn't know," Vanessa said with a self-deprecating chuckle.

"So what's the deal?" I asked Fuego.

Fuego glanced at Vanessa. "All the local shelters are currently at capacity. Vanessa left a voicemail for a friend of hers but hasn't heard back. We were hoping Vanessa could stay with you until her friend calls her back."

I barked out a laugh. "Are you shitting me? You want to stay at my house after being such a bitch when I was looking for your boyfriend last year? Not fucking likely."

Vanessa's face crumpled. "I know. I'm sorry." She sobbed into her hands.

"Why'd you marry that asswipe after all the shit he's pulled?"

"I...I thought if I married him, he would treat me better, that he would finally love me."

"Yeah, because that always works. Time to wake up from the fairy tale, princess. Freddie is no Prince Charming. I tried to tell you that last time."

"Jinx, ease up on the girl." Byrd put a hand on my shoulder.

"Hey, you want to take her in, be my guest."

"I would, but I don't think my pit bull, Peaches, would get along with Jasmine."

My old companion, guilt, tugged at my heartstrings like a

toddler yanking on a mother's sleeve for attention. Was it really my responsibility to deal with Vanessa's bad relationship choices?

"Where are you two staying while you're down here?" I asked Shea.

"Hadn't really thought about it. Any suggestions?"

"I don't spend a lot of time at motels unless I'm looking for a fugitive."

"The Desert View Inn's not far from here," said Byrd. "It's not too pricy, and it's clean."

Shea looked at Fuego, who shrugged. "Sounds okay."

"Great," I said. "The three of you can bunk together."

"Do they allow dogs?" asked Vanessa. "I can't go anywhere without Jasmine. She's my emotional support animal."

"Let's hope to hell they do," I replied. "Because that little four-legged tarantula is not coming to my place."

The quiet of the kitchen was disturbed by the sound of a car pulling into the driveway. Vanessa's eyes lit up with fear. "Freddie," she whispered.

"Stay with her," I told Fuego. "Shea, Byrd, let's go say hello."

Freddie Colton opened the front door to see us with our guns drawn. He was tan and tall and had a sexy bad boy look about him. From the bulge on the side of his jeans, I knew he had a gun tucked inside his waistband. And he wasn't alone. Freddie's companion had a Neanderthal look to him—heavy brow, jet-black hair that had been slicked back.

"Who the fuck are you? Vanessa!"

"We're Vanessa's book club," I said. "Unfortunately, you're not invited. Girls only. You'll have to come back later."

Freddie locked eyes with me. I saw the wheels turning in his mind as he worked out where he knew me from. "You're that bitch that dragged me back to jail. Threatened to blow my dick off if I didn't come along quietly."

I pointed my gun at his crotch. "After all this time, you still remember. What a romantic you are."

"You bitches best get out of my house or..."

"Or what?" asked Shea. "You gonna throw us out? I don't think so."

"Vanessa! Get your scrawny ass in here!" Freddie shouted.

"Vanessa," called Byrd, "you stay right where you are, darling. We got this."

"Boy, you best watch yourself. You think I'm gonna let a black man and a couple bitches come between me and my wife?" Freddie's hand hovered over where his gun hid underneath his shirt.

Byrd shook his head. "You and your friend should walk away and cool off before someone gets hurt."

"Don't you tell me what to do, boy. She's *my* wife. This is *my* house. You can't take what's mine."

"And if we do? Whatcha gonna do, dickhead?" I asked. "Call the cops?"

The anger in his face edged up a few notches. "I'll fucking kill you. Every one of y'all. Vanessa, too, that pathetic little bitch."

"Well, I'm terrified. How about y'all?" I asked.

"Absolutely trembling," Byrd said with dripping sarcasm.

"I may just piss myself, I'm so scared," added Shea.

"Come on, man," said the Neanderthal. "We can hang at my apartment for now."

"Yeah, man," I said. "You little boys go have a playdate at your buddy's apartment."

Freddie pointed at me and said, "Y'all gonna regret this." He and his lumbering companion turned and walked away.

I followed him outside with Shea and Byrd on my heels. "You threatened me the last time, numb nuts. How'd that turn out exactly? I can't remember."

He kept walking with his back to me and flipped me a bird. The tires of his Pontiac Trans Am squealed as they drove off. The three of us returned inside.

"They gone?" Vanessa and her overgrown rat both sat trembling.

"For now. I suggest y'all take Vanessa and get checked into

that motel. We can reconvene in the morning and refocus on finding James Fitzgerald's murderer."

"Agreed," said Shea, giving a look to Fuego.

"Y'all investigating that Brother James murder?" asked Vanessa. "I thought the police caught the killer. Some black tranny hooker."

My fist tightened at the slur.

"The cops arrested the wrong person," I muttered. "We're tracking down the real killer."

"And she's not a hooker," Shea growled. "She's a member of our club."

Vanessa looked from Shea to me and back again. "Oh, sorry."

"Enough chitchat," I said. "Y'all get checked in to your motel. I'm going home."

"How'm I supposed to take Jasmine and my stuff on the back of a motorcycle?" asked Vanessa.

I wanted to tell her to call an Uber, but we had no way of knowing how soon Freddie and his buddy might return. Possibly with backup.

"You can ride in my SUV. But if that little rat dog of yours pees or poops on the seat, you can fucking walk for all I care."

"Jasmine's very well trained," she replied, even as the dog resumed yapping at us.

Byrd helped Vanessa load her suitcase into the Gray Ghost. On the ride to the motel, the two of them chatted about dogs. Despite my ever-growing attachment to Diana, my appreciation for canines did not extend to yappy ankle-biters like Jasmine. I focused on dealing with the surge of rush hour traffic.

The Desert View Inn was located on the southbound access road off the I-17, just south of Thunderbird Road. The last time I was here, I'd been ambushed by a couple of fugitives fleeing a murder charge and ended up with a nasty concussion.

I pulled into the overhang by the front door. "Goodbye, Vanessa. Don't keep in touch."

"Thanks for your help, Jinx." She leaned over and planted a

kiss on my cheek. Jasmine started barking all over again and just missed giving me a nip.

I sat parked while Vanessa, Shea, and Fuego walked up to the front desk. I needed a second to clear my head before driving back into Phoenix traffic.

"What do you think's going to happen to her?" Byrd asked.

"Don't know. Don't care. As my dad says, 'Not my monkeys, not my circus.'"

"Sounds like a smart man, your dad."

"He is." I took a deep breath, let it out, and pressed Play on my sound system. Polythene Pam's "Tall Girl Posse" started playing. "Let's get out of here. I'm exhausted."

"Hold up." Byrd put a hand on my arm.

Shea was racing out of the lobby with Vanessa shimmying behind carrying the dog.

"What now?" I asked.

Shea came around to my side of the truck. I rolled down the window.

"What now?"

"The motel doesn't allow pets."

"Oh for the love of bacon, are you serious? Did he suggest a place that did?"

"He didn't know. Can she stay with you for the night?"

I was starting to think Wilhelm Penzler had the right idea. Just take a flying leap and end it all.

I scowled at Vanessa, who was cradling her dog and looking particularly pathetic. "Get in the goddamned truck." To Shea, I said, "You owe me big-time. I'll call you in the morning."

23

———

Shadows were getting long when we arrived at my place. I told Byrd to be back there at eight the following morning. "I'll find a way to make this pay for us one way or another."

"Copy that," he replied. "Good luck." I wasn't sure if he was talking to Vanessa or me.

While he drove off in his car, I escorted Vanessa and her dog into the house through the side door. Diana came bounding toward me. After showering me with kisses, she turned her attention to Jasmine, sniffing warily. The Yorkie yapped and growled at the much larger puppy. Diana replied with a couple of playful barks that seemed to say, "Nice to meet you! Let's play."

"You didn't tell me you had a dog," Vanessa said quietly. She tried to turn her body to keep the two dogs separated, but Diana was determined to get to know the little beast better.

"You didn't ask. But if you'd rather not stay, I'd be happy to call you a taxi."

"He won't bite her, will he?"

"It's she, and no, she probably won't. But if your little rat keeps growling like that, all bets are off."

Vanessa gave Jasmine's behind a gentle swat. "Hush or that giant dog will eat you."

If only. "Let me show you to the spare bedroom."

I led her to the room I used for a home office. There was a double bed, a weight bench, and a dusty set of free weights, with a window that was shaded outside by a shrub I couldn't identify. Some plant that grew red berries in the winter.

She set down Jasmine, who ran off to play chase with Diana.

"So what's the deal with you and the bikers?" Vanessa sat down on the bed.

"One of their members is being framed. I'm helping them get the charges dropped."

"I thought you only went after people who jumped bail."

"Me too," I admitted. "Look, I'm planning on ordering delivery. Your choice, pizza, Chinese, or Greek."

"I've never had Greek before. What do they eat?"

"I'll order a couple of gyros. It's like a gordita burrito but with a mixture of lamb, beef, and a cucumber-sour cream sauce."

"Sounds okay."

I placed the order, then went to my room to get cleaned up. The bruises looked darker, but my face was less swollen than it had been. A hot shower helped wash away most of the day's tension, though it still felt like a giant emptiness inside me was sucking out all my happiness. By the time I returned to the living room, the gyros had arrived.

After dinner, we were watching the latest news story about the string of fatal stabbings attributed to the Valley Slasher when a burst of gunfire erupted on the street.

"Get down!" I pushed Vanessa onto the floor as countless rounds plinked against the Lexan windows. Ducking under the coffee table, I grabbed the .44 Magnum revolver, holding it ready to fire, in case the shooter came through the front door.

As quickly as it started, the gunfire stopped, and the shooter's car roared off down the street.

"Stay put," I told Vanessa.

I raced out the front door and caught a fleeting glimpse of red taillights blazing into the night and around the block.

"Shit!" I hunched over to catch my breath. My heart thundered in my chest. The soles of my feet burned. I realized I was barefoot. I hobbled home to survey the damage.

My next-door neighbor, Adam, came rushing out of the house he shared with his husband, Steve. He was dressed in a T-shirt and shorts with his cell phone to his ear.

He stared at the large revolver in my hand. "Were you shooting at someone?"

"Not me. Some asshole just shot up my house. Y'all okay?"

He nodded. "I called the police. They're on their way. We were watching the *Game of Thrones* finale when we heard the shots. You think they'll be back?"

"Probably not. When the cops get here, send 'em my way. Oh, and thanks for taking care of Diana for me."

"Yeah, sure. This shooting—is it connected to why you were out of town?"

I shook my head. "Don't think so." The bottoms of my feet began to throb. "Have a good night, man."

"Yeah," he said nervously. "You too."

When I returned to examine the damage to the house, my nose twitched at the sharp smell of burnt powder in the air. A line of two-inch-wide snowflakes stretched across the impact-resistant polycarbonate windows, but none of the bullets appeared to have penetrated. Chips in the brick walls revealed a few more rounds had hit. They stopped just short of the door.

Had I been living in my old house, my houseguest and I would have been toast. Conor's renovations paid off yet again. "Thank you, Conor, wherever you are," I whispered to the night.

A trail of bloody footprints led up the walk to where I stood. I lifted my right foot. A smear of blood and grit covered the sole of my foot. Probably stepped on broken glass in the street.

I hobbled inside, trying to avoid bleeding onto my floor.

Vanessa lay on the floor, curled in a fetal position around her whimpering dog.

"You can get up now. Show's over."

"Wha...what was that?"

"A drive-by." I limped to the bathroom and washed the cuts on my foot with a soapy washcloth.

Vanessa followed me. "Who...who?"

"If I had to guess, I'd say that asshole husband of yours. Sounded like his Trans Am. He have any guns?"

"A few. But just for protection."

"Yeah, right. Protection."

I pressed a gauze pad against the wound and taped it in place, then pushed past Vanessa into my bedroom and slipped on a pair of ankle socks and my sneakers.

Vanessa continued to shadow me like a frightened child. "Maybe...maybe we should call the police."

"The neighbors already have." I sat on my bed and took a cleansing breath to clear my head. "Shit. Where's Diana?" I hadn't seen her since before the shooting.

"Who?"

"My dog." I ran down the hall, looking for her. "Diana! Where are you, girl?"

I checked under the bed, in the guest bedroom, the bathrooms, all the places she liked to hang out, but turned up nothing. *Shit!*

My heart started pounding again as worry set in. *Please be outside. Please be okay.* "Diana!"

I grabbed the Smith & Wesson again, along with a flashlight from my kitchen drawer, and rushed out the back. "Diana! Diana!"

The backyard was dark beyond the glow from the kitchen window. A security light on the patio wall had gone out a month ago, and I hadn't bothered to replace it.

"Diana!" Fear crept in my voice. "Where are you, baby?"

A shadow moved in the darkness near the six-foot block

fence. Was it her? Or another threat? I raised the revolver as I approached.

Her sudden bark sent my stomach lurching into my throat. It was a miracle I didn't pull the trigger. My night vision sharpened enough to spot her outline patrolling the edge of the fence. She looked at me and gave another bark, then fast-trotted over, tail wagging.

"You okay, baby?" I checked her over but didn't feel any blood. In the distance, sirens wailed. Right on time. "Come on inside."

She followed me into the house. Just as I returned the revolver to its holster under the coffee table, someone pounded on my front door.

I opened it to two uniformed officers. I answered their initial battery of questions. Twenty minutes later, a female plainclothes detective came in. She looked vaguely familiar. Her amber eyes matched the suit she wore, contrasting beautifully with her dark-brown skin. I wondered if we'd met before I quit the force.

"Ms. Ballou?" she asked. "I'm Detective Nicole Clifford from Phoenix PD's Gun Enforcement Squad. I understand you and your guest had some excitement this evening."

"Yeah, you could say that."

Vanessa was in the guest bedroom, speaking with one of the unis. I ushered Detective Clifford inside the living room.

"You have bulletproof windows?" From the armchair she was sitting in, she gestured to the pockmarked windows.

"I inherited the house from my fiancé," I said. "He was a cautious man, both of us professional bail enforcement agents."

She wrote in her notebook. "And where is he?"

A punch of emotion caught me off guard. Tears stung my eyes. "The Piestewa Freeway bomb." I didn't feel like elaborating any further than that.

"I'm sorry for your loss, ma'am." A grave nod of recognition. "Any idea why someone would shoot at your house?"

I put the finger on Vanessa's boyfriend. When pressed for other people with a motive, I provided her names and contact information for the past few fugitives I'd recovered, except for Penzler. Most of the fugitives I'd returned to jail weren't happy about it. But I explained to Clifford that I'd had my skip tracer scrub the Web of my home address. The shooter had to be Colton.

Maybe he had a way of tracking his wife's phone. He was enough of a control freak to do something like that. Or maybe he tailed us without me noticing. I was certainly pissed off enough when I drove her back here that I could have missed a car following me.

"I saw blood on the porch," said the detective. "Was anyone injured during the shooting?"

"I ran outside barefoot to try to see who was shooting. Probably stepped on some glass."

She wrote my answers in her notebook, then had me go through my story again, backward and forward, looking for inconsistencies. When she was satisfied, she told me to stay put while she coordinated with the rest of the investigators.

A peek outside my window revealed that the crime scene unit had pulled up. Intense floodlights lit up the yard like a Broadway stage, while techs scoured the scene, placing markers, taking photographs, and placing evidence in bags.

Three hours later, the circus left with all of the evidence they had found.

Detective Clifford stepped back inside. "We've recovered the brass from the street. Looks like the shooter was using a ten-millimeter semiautomatic handgun."

"Ten mill? That's an unusual caliber."

"Uncommon, but there are a number of models out on the street. Two of the six rounds embedded in the polycarbonate may be clean enough to compare ballistics, but no guarantee we'll find a match in our database."

She gave me her business card as well as the name and number of a local window repair company. I'd most likely call my brother, Jake, anyway, since he renovated houses for a living.

"You're going to pick up Colton, right?" I asked the detective when I walked her to the door to leave.

"Please," begged Vanessa. "Before he comes back and does something worse."

"We'll bring him in. If he's the shooter, we'll take the appropriate action. I promise. I'll let you know what we find out."

"Thanks." I shut the door behind her and collapsed on the couch. "Shit."

Part of me wanted to tell Vanessa to get the hell out of my house and my life. But even if she did, Freddie still might make an encore appearance. Underneath my frustration, I caught myself feeling sorry for her.

I grabbed a bottle of tequila and two glasses from the kitchen. When I returned to the living room, Vanessa was watching a cheesy Christmas movie on the Hallmark Channel. I would've told her to change it to something less insipid, but I was too exhausted to care.

"I'm sorry I got you into this," she said out of the blue, barely touching her tequila.

"Yeah." I didn't know what else to say.

"I'll pay for the damage. Somehow."

"I have insurance. I just want you gone tomorrow. Don't care if you're with one of your little girlfriends, at a motel, or on a park bench."

I drained my glass, enjoying the burn in my throat. After a couple of refills, I shuffled down the hall and collapsed onto my bed. Diana curled up near my feet, tail swishing back and forth. At least someone still loved me.

24

Despite my need for sleep, the incessant yapping and whining of Vanessa's rat dog kept me awake the rest of the night. On the rare occasions I did drift off, I was haunted with nightmares about drive-bys and intruders.

At four o'clock, I gave up the effort. I planted myself at my desk and pored over the case documents—criminal background checks, financials, phone logs, and news stories. On my laptop, I had links to online videos showing Fitzgerald in heated confrontations with passersby. The sick fuck knew how to push people's buttons.

I compiled a list of the most viable suspects for his murder. At the top was Wes Hancock, the father of the girl Fitzgerald had raped.

Below that I added Deneisha Love, the sister of Tamika Love, a trans woman who was murdered a few months back. Deneisha blamed Fitzgerald and his violent rhetoric for inspiring the murderer.

I also listed Gabby Tyson, a woman who claimed Brother James was the deadbeat bio dad of her special-needs child. There were dozens of others who might have murdered Fitzgerald, but I had to start somewhere.

The sky outside was showing morning's first light. I shuffled into the kitchen and started the coffee maker. While it gurgled and hissed, I poured myself a bowl of cereal and perused the news headlines on my phone.

The usual nonsense was going on at the federal level—legal wrangling between the White House and Congress, calls for impeachment, rumors of a potential war with Iran, and two more white men I'd never heard of had announced they were entering the 2020 presidential race.

I scrolled down to the local scene. More stories speculating about the Valley Slasher. One about a family of four killed by a wrong-way driver on the 101. The City of Phoenix was cracking down on dirty swimming pools after six more West Nile virus cases were discovered. And of course, a proposed bill in the Arizona state legislature to allow businesses to discriminate against LGBTQ customers. Same shit, different day.

I tossed the phone aside and realized the house was quiet. No more yapping. Rat dog must've finally worn itself out and gone to sleep after keeping me awake all night. *Mission accomplished, you little shit.*

Diana padded into the kitchen carrying her leash, her claws clicking on the Saltillo tile floor.

"I suppose this means you want to go for your run."

She gave me a look that seemed to say, "Yes, please, Mom." The soulful eyes of a puppy are more powerful than the Borg any day. Resistance really is futile.

I put my dishes in the sink, slipped on my running shoes, and took off with Diana toward Seventh Avenue. Leaving Vanessa alone in my house felt weird. But I needed to get out and burn through all the shit in my head, replacing it with some exercise-generated dopamine.

As my heart rate and breathing fell into their usual rhythm, my mind focused on the Fitzgerald murder. The more I thought about it, the more Wes Hancock, the rape victim's father, seemed the most likely candidate.

He had more motive than anyone. Not that I blamed him, if he'd done the deed. I half wondered if there was a way to get Indigo acquitted without sending Hancock to jail for his service to the community. Probably not.

I arrived home after seven thirty, sweaty and winded but mentally in a better place. Vanessa sat at my kitchen table spoon-feeding canned tuna to Jasmine.

"I hope you don't mind. You weren't here when I got up." She nodded at the empty tuna can.

"I'll just add it to your bill."

She gave me a confused, concerned look.

I shook my head to indicate I was kidding. "I gotta take a shower. You get ahold of your friend yet?"

"I called her again and left a message."

I shook my head in disgust. *How the hell do I get myself into these messes?*

Diana looked at rat dog nibbling the tuna, then at me with a wounded look on her face. I had a strict rule against feeding her people food. Sets a bad precedent. I reached into the pantry and offered Diana a few of her favorite treats, which she carried to her doggy bed in the living room.

The doorbell rang as I was drying off from the shower. I quickly pulled on a T-shirt and jeans. By the time I reached the living room, Vanessa was already letting Shea and Fuego inside.

Diana rushed in to meet the new houseguests. Shea knelt and made baby talk while scratching Diana's ears.

"She's such a cute dog. How old?"

"Nine months. You have one yourself?"

"Nope. Got a twelve-year-old cat named Ninja."

"You live with your niece, too, right?"

Shea turned and gaped at me. "How'd you know that?"

My face warmed from embarrassment. "Don't worry. Not a

stalker. Just came up in my background research when I was looking for Indigo."

"Right. Sorry. That makes sense."

"What happened to the front of your house?" Fuego's brow furrowed. "Looks like someone's been using it for target practice."

I jabbed a thumb at Vanessa. "Someone's unhappy husband."

Vanessa hung her head, looking like a kid who'd been sent to her room.

"Anyone hurt?" asked Shea.

"No, but I'm done playing referee in someone else's domestic violence shit." I turned to Vanessa. "You're not staying here any longer. There are motels that allow dogs. I suggest you find one."

"Actually, while you were in the bathroom, my friend Emma called back. I can move in with her for the time being. Problem is…I don't know how we're going to move all my stuff before Freddie gets home at four. So unless he's been arrested…" She clutched Jasmine closer to her chest.

"We can help with that," said Fuego. "We've done a lot of clandestine moves for women in abusive relationships."

"Hold on. Time out." I formed a T with my hands. "I agreed to prove your buddy Indigo innocent provided the Athena Sisterhood helps out. So far, all you've done is put me further in danger by dragging me into this little side drama. And now you're helping her move?" I glowered at Shea. "Maybe I should tell Pima Bail Bonds to revoke the bond and take your house."

Fuego exchanged a glance with Shea. "You're right. We're here because of Indigo. Shea, go with Jinx to find the murderer. I'll put the word out to the club to come down and help Vanessa with the move."

Shea turned to me. "Does that work for you?"

"I suppose so." To Vanessa, I said, "Grab your shit."

The doorbell rang. I checked the peephole and saw Byrd in full gear on my doorstep. With all the chaos, I'd almost forgotten he was helping out. I let him in.

"Uh, did you know that someone—"

"Shot up my house? Not at all."

"Do I want to know?" Byrd looked concerned.

I shook my head. "Not really."

"So what's our game plan?"

While Vanessa packed up her stuff in the guest bedroom, I led Byrd, Shea, and Fuego to the kitchen and laid out the case paperwork. "Wes Hancock seems our most likely suspect. Fitzgerald raped his daughter. Over Hancock's objections, the county prosecutor accepted a guilty plea for misdemeanor assault. No jail time. Didn't have to register as a sex offender. Hancock was furious."

"Can ya blame him?" asked Shea.

"Hancock has made a number of veiled threats on social media while ranting how the legal system protects rapists and does nothing to protect victims."

"How do we prove he killed Fitzgerald?" asked Fuego.

"It comes down to means, motive, and opportunity. He obviously has motive. Did he have the physical means to kill Fitzgerald? Possibly. Fitzgerald's official cause of death was a GSW to the head, but the crime scene photos show he was severely beaten and had his dick chopped off prior to the fatal shot. Fitzgerald was a big guy. Maybe Hancock is too. We won't know until we meet him.

"As for opportunity, he provided an alibi for the day of the murder. I don't see in the discovery documents that the police verified it. They arrested Indigo so quickly, they may not have investigated Hancock as thoroughly as they should."

Shea replied, "Sounds like a solid lead. Where do we find him?"

I pulled up his contact information. "Off Forty-Fourth Street and Camelback in Phoenix."

"Not far from Scottsdale," Byrd added.

"Exactly. Let me give him a call, make sure he's home. If so, we'll pay him a visit." I dialed the number, and Wes Hancock picked up on the fourth ring.

"I have no more comments to the press on that goddamned preacher's death."

"I'm not a reporter, Mr. Hancock. My name's Jinx Ballou. I'm a fugitive recovery agent working on a case related to your daughter's assault. I need your help tracking down a fugitive." I felt bad about dancing around the truth, considering what his family had been through.

"My daughter was *raped*, not just assaulted!"

"Of course, I'm sorry. But I could really use your help. The person I've been hired to track down has connections with James Fitzgerald. And the case is possibly tied to Alexandra's rape."

"Who are you looking for?"

"Unfortunately, I'm not at liberty to say. But I'm hoping you might provide me with some information that could lead to his capture. Could I stop by your home and ask you some questions?"

"You have questions, ask them now."

I didn't want to ask them on the phone because as soon as he got wind of my objective, he could just hang up. "Because of the sensitive nature of this investigation, it would be better if we met in person. And if at any time you want to end the interview, you say so, and I will leave."

There was silence on the line for a moment before he answered. "All right. I'm just sick of all this crap. Bad enough that sick son of a bitch raped my daughter. Then the whole pathetic excuse of a plea deal, not to mention being harassed by the media every time I turn around."

"I understand. You and your daughter have my sincere sympathies."

"I'll be home until ten this morning. Then I have to go to work. You have the address?"

"I do. I'll be there shortly. And Mr. Hancock, I greatly appreciate this."

25

———

Fuego and Shea convinced a half dozen of their fellow bikers to drive down to the valley and help Vanessa move to her friend Emma's place. Shea would stick with Byrd and me to solve Fitzgerald's murder.

Byrd, Vanessa, her dog, and I piled into the Gray Ghost and drove to Emma's, while Fuego and Shea followed behind on their motorcycles. The house wasn't far from Vanessa's but looked better maintained.

"Thanks for your help," said Vanessa as she climbed out with the dog under her arm. "Sorry about your house."

"Just stay out of my life, okay? And if you still got a brain in your head, you'll stay out of Freddie's." Without another word, I drove off.

The Hancocks lived in east Phoenix's Arcadia District in a white wood and brick ranch-style house trimmed with black faux shutters. A white picket fence with brick posts every ten feet encircled a perfectly manicured yard that was lush and green. A cobblestone walk led from the street to the front porch, where small flowering plants bloomed in ceramic pots.

Byrd and I got out of the Gray Ghost, leaving our gear inside but sporting our bail enforcement badges around our necks.

Shea parked her motorcycle just past the truck.

"Ditch the biker vest and sidearm," I told her. "I want to keep our talk with Hancock low-key and professional."

"What if he's the killer and realizes we're onto him?"

"Then concealed only. I don't want to further traumatize him if he's innocent."

Shea's expression told me she wasn't keen on the idea, but she stashed her vest and gun, holster and all, in a trunk on the back of her bike. "So what's the game plan, madam bounty hunter?"

"I want to establish a rapport with him if I can. Gain his trust before I start asking questions related to Fitzgerald's murder."

I felt out of my element. It had been nearly ten years since I was a cop. Even then, my experience looking into homicide cases was limited to canvassing areas near crime scenes and taking witness statements. No in-depth interrogations pressing suspects for confessions.

After I rang the bell, Mr. Hancock opened the door. According to his file, he was thirty-eight. But from the bags under his eyes, he looked ten years older.

"You Agent Ballou?"

"I am. These are my associates, Jubal Byrd and Shea Stevens. May we come inside?"

Hancock glanced at us. "Come on in."

The interior of the house was furnished with mid-century modern furniture and an abundance of metallic and glass artwork. He led us to a couch and matching chairs.

"Can I offer you some water or coffee?"

Byrd and I declined. Shea agreed to some water.

"Mr. Hancock," I said when he returned with a bottle for Shea, "let me say how sorry I am for what happened to your daughter, Alexandra. When I was a teen, I was brutally assaulted. The perpetrator fled the jurisdiction before he could be brought to justice. So I appreciate what y'all have been through."

"Thank you," he said, staring at his hands.

"Did James Fitzgerald know Alexandra prior to the rape?"

His body tensed at the mention of Fitzgerald's name. "No. He showed up one day outside her high school, shouting the most disgusting things and carrying hateful signs."

"He was protesting outside a high school?" Byrd asked. "How is that legal?"

"Parents complained, but the police told us that as long as he was outside the fence, there was nothing they could do. He was there for three days, shouting how girls who wore makeup were asking to be raped. Alex could hear him in her classroom."

"Disgusting pervert!" Shea muttered.

"When Fitzgerald was protesting, did Alex engage with him in any way?" I asked. It wasn't strictly relevant to our investigation, but I was curious.

"I don't know. Nothing to deserve being raped."

"Of course not. I just wondered why he targeted her."

"Who knows? When Alex..." Hancock's voice shook with equal measures of sorrow and violence. "She said he followed her home from school in his car. We don't live far, and ever since she turned thirteen, my wife and I agreed to let her walk home, provided she's with at least two of her friends."

His face darkened. "But that day, one of her friends stayed home with the flu. The other had an after-school activity. Alex was supposed to call me when she didn't have anyone to walk home with. But she...she didn't want to bother me at work." Tears ran down his face. I grabbed a tissue from a nearby box.

"Thanks." He took a deep breath and let it out. "Alex walked home alone. She was in the neighborhood when he pulled alongside her in his Volvo. He apologized for the things he'd said in front of the school and offered to drive her to Cold Stone Creamery to discuss their differing viewpoints. Despite our warnings about strangers in cars, she got in."

His fists were so tight, his knuckles were bone white. "He slipped Rohypnol into her drink. She woke up in some sleazy

Scottsdale motel where he...he hurt her." His head shook violently, and he rubbed at his eyes as if trying to clear the horrific images in his head. "He'd taken pictures of her...nude pictures. Said if she told anyone, he'd post the photos to the internet for all her friends to see."

"What a wicked thing to say," Byrd grumbled.

"How did she get back home?" I asked.

"He drove her. When her mom and I got home, we knew right away something was wrong. After a lot of encouragement, she told us what happened." He pounded a side table so hard a couple of knickknacks fell over.

Now we were getting somewhere. "What did you and your wife do, Mr. Hancock?" I asked.

"My wife took Alex to the hospital. I...I drove to the motel, but he was gone. I managed to get a home address from the little twerp in the front office. Fitzgerald's house wasn't far from the motel. I pounded on his front door till he opened it. God knows, I...I'm not a violent man, but..." He shook his head, clearly writhing in emotional pain.

"We understand, Mr. Hancock," said Byrd. "Any loving father would feel the same way."

Rage rolled off of Hancock in waves. I could almost taste it in the air. "I wanted to kill that man right then and there. Got in a few punches before the cops showed up. They took me to the Scottsdale police station. That damned Sam Elliott look-alike they call a detective kept asking ridiculous questions. Was Alex sexually active? What was she wearing? Did she ever drink alcohol or use drugs? Like getting raped was somehow her fault.

"When they finally found him guilty, I thought finally we'd get some justice. But no, that idiotic judge didn't send him to prison. Six months of probation, for God's sake. Didn't even have to register as a sex offender. After what he did to my daughter and who knows how many girls before that."

"I can imagine how that made you feel," I said. "I felt the same way when my attacker made bail and then disappeared."

"Pardon the profanity, but I wanted to fucking kill them all. Brother James, the cops, the judge."

I knew the time had come to ask the ugly questions. "Where were you the night that Fitzgerald was killed?"

"What?"

I could tell from his expression that the question had caught him flat-footed. "You think I killed that monster?"

"No, I don't. But for my paperwork, I need to put down something, or my boss will think I'm slacking off."

"I...I don't know where I was...I think the three of us went to dinner and then a movie."

"What movie did you see?"

"What difference does it make?"

"It doesn't, I just need it for my report."

"Um...that female superhero movie."

"*Captain Marvel*?" I asked.

"Yeah, that was it."

"Good. That helps. I know it sounds stupid. Where'd you have dinner?"

He gave me a quizzical look.

I held up my hands apologetically. "I know. I don't believe you killed him. My boss is a hard ass for details."

"Pei Wei, I think. Indian School and Forty-Fourth Street."

"And just so I can tell my boss I officially asked, did you kill James Fitzgerald?"

"No. I did not. But whoever did deserves the goddamn Medal of Honor. I heard the police arrested someone. Some hooker, I think."

"She's not a goddamned hooker," growled Shea. "And she didn't kill him either."

I put a hand on Shea's knee and gave her a look that told her to keep it together.

Hancock narrowed his gaze at Shea, then turned back to me. "All I know is what I heard on the news. I'm glad he's dead, but I didn't kill him."

I figured we'd gotten as much out of him as we were going to. I stood up. Shea and Byrd followed my lead. "Thanks for answering our questions, Mr. Hancock."

Hancock walked us to the front door. "I still don't understand why you're here. You mentioned a fugitive. What's this have to do with what happened to Alex?"

I stepped out into the warm sunshine. "I wish I could tell you, but I can't reveal the details for legal reasons. I can assure you, this will help bring them to justice."

"Well, good luck, I guess."

When the three of us reached the Gray Ghost, Byrd asked, "So, what do ya think? Did he do it?"

"Possibly," I replied.

"What about his alibi?" asked Byrd.

"I plan to check it out," I said. "If he's telling the truth, he probably charged the dinner and the movie. All we got to do is check his bank statement. If the alibi checks out, he's off the hook, and we'll move on."

I called Becca and told her the story. She agreed to double-check the alibi and get back to us within the hour.

"I found the two other people on your suspect list. Deneisha Love was the sister of Tamika Love, the trans woman whose murderer was inspired by Fitzgerald's rants. She moved to live with her father in New Jersey two weeks before Fitzgerald bought the farm. Also, she's only seventeen. I'm guessing she's not your killer."

"What about the mother of the special-needs child?"

"I did a little more digging into her. Gabby Tyson was in jail the night of Fitzgerald's death for possession of a controlled substance. Apparently, she has a heroin addiction. Right now, she's in a treatment center in Albuquerque and has been for the past forty-five days."

"All right. Thanks for the info. Let me know when you can confirm Hancock's alibi."

"Will do."

I hung up, frustrated. My list of prime suspects was getting short, but I wasn't any closer to finding the murderer.

"So where to now?" asked Shea.

"I want to see where Fitzgerald lived. I'm sure the cops already went over it with a fine-toothed comb, but as much as they were gunning after Indigo, maybe they missed something. Or more accurately dismissed something that might've led to the killer."

"How will we get in?" Byrd asked.

I grinned. "We'll find a way."

"Can we do that?" asked Byrd. "Legally, I mean."

"With Fitzgerald dead, who's going to complain if we pop in and look around?"

Byrd shook his head. "Maurice hired us to return Pearson to custody. Doing a little investigating is one thing, but you're talking breaking and entering. I don't know if I'm comfortable with this."

"Says the man vandalizing a perfectly good motel room wall."

I could have sworn he blushed, but with his dark skin, it was hard to tell.

Shea put a hand on his shoulder. "Look, Mr. Boy Scout, a friend of mine is being steamrolled for the murder of a piece-of-shit rapist. And you're uncomfortable looking through his house?"

"Fine," he replied. "How do we get in? Break down the door with the battering ram?"

"Too noisy. I got a better solution." Shea pulled a narrow leather case from her biker vest. I had a similar set of picklocks in the Gray Ghost. I was beginning to like this woman.

I gave Fitzgerald's address to Shea in case we got separated, then Byrd and I piled into the Gray Ghost.

26

Fitzgerald had lived in an upscale neighborhood near Pima Road north of Chaparral Road. The trees were mature, lawns manicured and green, the houses well-kept. Like something out of *Leave It To Beaver*, only in this scenario, Eddie Haskell was a pedophile rapist.

The house sat on the corner with a driveway and garage on one street and the front door on the other. The mailbox was shaped to look like a church. What a joke!

A late-model Buick sat in the open garage. Someone was home. My hope of sneaking in unnoticed evaporated. I parked past the driveway, next to an orange tree covered with star-shaped white blossoms.

"Did Fitzgerald have a roommate?" asked Byrd.

"Nothing in the paperwork mentioned it. I guess we'll go say howdy."

My phone started playing the *Game of Thrones* ringtone.

"Anything on Hancock's alibi?" I asked Becca.

"According to his bank records, he did purchase three tickets last month to see a movie at the Esplanade AMC Theater on the same day he purchased a meal at Pei Wei."

"So his alibi checks out."

"Not exactly. The dinner and movie tickets were charged two days *after* James Fitzgerald's body was discovered."

"So the alibi's bogus."

"So it appears."

"Okay, thanks for the 411. One more thing. I need you to run a plate for me." I read her the license plate off the Buick.

"Okay, let me log in to the database." I heard some key clicks. "The Buick belongs to Michael Andrew Wilkes."

The name sounded familiar. "The head of Fitzgerald's church of hate?"

"Yep." More key clicks on her end. "Let's see, ah, here we are, Michael Andrew Wilkes. Born in 1949, height five five, weight one thirty. Blah, blah, blah. What else do you want to know?"

"What's his background?"

Her fingers clicked away. "Checking NCIC. He has a sheet. Michael Wilkes, aka Elder Michael. A laundry list of misdemeanors—trespassing and harassment mostly—though he did a nine-month stint for assault back in the 1980s."

"Imagine my surprise."

"Currently listed as the head pastor of the Evangelical Light of the Messiah Church. Served in the Marine Corps during Vietnam. Ho, ho! Dishonorable discharge. Doesn't list why. Bummer. Registered owner of Colt .45, a Beretta 92, and an AR-15. Geez, what is it with Evangelicals and firearms? Let's check out his social media accounts... oh, wow! This guy is completely off his rocker."

"Why?"

"Wilkes's page is filled these dark, poorly Photoshopped memes depicting demons, torture, and hellfire but with provocative captions. Like Dante's *Inferno* meets the *National Enquirer*. He repeatedly calls women whores, refers to African Americans as mud people and jungle bunnies, and says queer people are children of Satan that must be destroyed before the Messiah will come again."

"Praise Jesus!" I mocked. "Sounds like a real charmer."

"Man, these memes are horrific. Here's one with a photo of an underwear-clad teenage girl in a suggestive pose. Caption reads 'Evil seductress falsely accused our Brother James of rape.' Misspelled the words *seductress* and *accused*."

"Funny how ignorant and hateful go hand in hand," I mused.

"There's another with a photo of Zia Pearson's face pasted onto a succubus body. Text claims Fitzgerald was murdered by the Negro whore of Babylon. Yowza! This guy takes toxic masculinity, racism, and radicalized Christianity to a whole new level."

"Why has social media not banned this guy?"

"You have to ask?"

I knew the answer. "Okay, thanks for the info."

"Watch your back, girl. This guy is seriously twisted. Old but twisted."

"Don't worry. I've got Byrd and Stevens with me. Wilkes would be an idiot to try anything."

Byrd and I got out of the Pathfinder and met Shea still on her bike, once again wearing her biker vest, a Glock on her right hip.

"So," she said, "I'm guessing breaking in is out of the question."

"The car and house belong to Michael Wilkes, a mental case who calls himself Elder Michael. Fitzgerald's boss, apparently. From what Becca tells me, this guy is like Brother James on acid." I opted not to share with Shea what he'd called Indigo.

"We going in?" asked Shea.

"Absolutely. I don't know if we'll find anything helpful, but we don't know unless we look." I glanced at the house. "Let's gear up. Wilkes is an old guy, but he's clearly off his rocker and may be armed."

With weapons, vests, and badges in place, the three of us walked around to the other side of the house. I checked the mailbox and rifled through what was there—a couple of utility bills, some Netflix movies, and the latest issue of *Playgirl* magazine addressed to Wilkes.

Now why would an old man get a porno magazine filled with naked men? Another closeted gay man consumed with self-hatred?

I picked up his copy of the *Arizona Republic* on the way to the front door and rang the doorbell.

A few minutes later, an art deco speakeasy grille in the door opened with a wrinkled face peering out.

"What do you want?"

"For starters, here's your mail and newspaper." I held them out to him. "I hear this issue of *Playgirl* has some really hot guys in it. You into hot guys, Mr. Wilkes?"

The speakeasy grille closed, and the door opened. A hunched man with no chin and pouty eyes stood with the assistance of a cane. He was dressed in a sweatshirt and sweatpants.

He snatched the mail and paper out of my hand. "My name is Elder Michael. And for your information, some pervert thought it'd be funny to send me a subscription to this filth. Now why are you people darkening my doorstep?"

I held up my badge. "We're looking into the death of James Fitzgerald."

"I thought the police already arrested someone. That Negro tranny whore."

"Fucking bigot!" Shea muttered under her breath.

I put my arm out to keep her from lunging at him.

"New evidence has come to light that exonerates the African American woman. So we are conducting a further investigation. You were Brother James's boss, correct?"

"I am the pastor of our church. Brother James, God rest his soul, was one of our disciples."

Byrd snorted. "Disciples, right."

I gave him a look that said, *Don't blow this.*

Byrd stood silent, looking like he'd swallowed a turd.

"And where is your church located? I couldn't find an address for it on Google."

"We are a private congregation. The location is kept confidential due to security concerns. We get a lot of death threats."

"Gee, I wonder why," said Shea.

"Brother James used to live here, correct?"

"Yes. Your fellow officers already tore up his room once looking for clues. What more do you people want?"

Impersonating an officer was illegal. But if Wilkes here mistakenly jumped to the wrong conclusion, I wasn't under any legal obligation to disabuse him of the notion.

"Because of recent developments in the case, we'll need to take a second look."

"Do you have a warrant?" Wilkes stood defiantly, or at least as defiantly as he could while using a cane for support.

"You do want Brother James's killer brought to justice, don't you?" asked Byrd. Good to see he was on board.

"Of course I do. What kind of stupid question is that?"

"Seems like you don't want us to look around again. Like maybe you have something to hide. Makes you look guilty, to be honest."

"Guilty? Me? How dare you!" He crossed his arms and engaged me in a staring match.

After a few minutes, he sighed. "Very well. You two can come in but not her." Wilkes stabbed a bony finger at Shea. "She looks like one of them hooligan homosexuals."

"Her? She's one of our undercover agents." Sounded legit, anyway.

"I don't want her in my house." Wilkes's jaw was set. "She can wait outside."

I took Shea aside. "Poke around the garage. See if you can find anything of interest," I whispered.

She nodded and walked off.

I turned back to Elder Michael. "So, give us the grand tour."

He harrumphed and slowly shuffled away from the front door, his cane clomp-clomp-clomping along the floor. Byrd and I followed him inside.

27

A hallway lined with artwork in gilded frames ran the length of the house. Most were copies of Renaissance paintings with a gruesome Biblical theme—crucified Jesus in agony, saints being martyred in horrific ways, and depictions of hell. I recognized a few from an art appreciation course I'd taken in college—Bosch's *The Garden of Earthly Delights*, Grünewald's *The Temptation of St. Anthony*, and David's *The Judgement of Cambyses*.

One, which was less gruesome, I identified as Rembrandt's *The Return of the Prodigal Son*. I suppressed a laugh as I passed it. It had always looked like a man giving a blow job to another.

An open door on the left revealed an office with an antique walnut desk and matching bookshelves lining the walls.

"This is my office," Wilkes said, shuffling past.

"Mind if we have a look?" Never hurt to ask.

"I do mind. It is private and has nothing to do with Brother James's untimely death."

We continued down the hall.

"He was renting a room at the Cactus Inn twice a month," I said. "Why exactly was he doing that?"

"Brother James conducted Bible studies with prospective members of our church. Part of our vetting process."

"Bible studies?" Byrd asked in a disbelieving tone. "At a motel advertising porn channels and frequented by hookers?"

Wilkes fixed him with a stern look. "We preach to sinners, not to saints."

"We'll need a list of the people he met with there over the past few months, along with their contact information."

"That information is strictly confidential."

"Someone he met with recently could well be the killer," replied Byrd.

"What motive would any of them have to kill Brother James?"

I scoffed. "Oh, let me think. He was a rapist, a homophobe, and a racist."

"Brother James was a godly man. And no one he was meeting with had any motive to harm him. We are very careful in our screening process."

"Nevertheless, I want those names," I pressed.

"I don't care what you want, young lady. I won't do it. Arrest me if you like. I know my rights."

I exchanged a glance with Byrd. "Show us Brother James's room."

We continued slowly down the hall past a spacious sunken living room with large windows overlooking the front lawn. On the other side was a kitchen, then a den with a couch set and an old tube television.

"What's here?" Byrd rapped on a closed door on the right.

"The garage."

I nodded and continued on until we came to an open door on the left. Elder Michael pointed inside. "This was Brother James's room."

I flicked on the overhead light. A double bed was bordered by a small bookcase on one side and a four-drawer upright dresser on the other. A small desk and a separate three-drawer vertical file cabinet stood at the opposite side of the room.

"Thank you," I said dismissively to Wilkes. "We'll let you know when we're done."

Wilkes glared at the two of us, then slowly clomped back down the hallway.

"Makes me sick the way he's perverted Christ's teachings," grumbled Byrd.

"Let's focus on searching this place. Maybe we'll get lucky and find something that implicates Wilkes." I gave him a wink, but he just frowned.

I opened the file cabinet; it was empty. The center drawer in the desk had also been cleaned out except for two paper clips, a ballpoint pen with no cap, and thirteen cents in change. Atop the desk sat a flat-screen monitor, a pencil cup, and a small framed print of Jesus with long blond hair. No computer, but there was a rectangular impression in the carpet underneath the desk.

"Looks like someone took Fitzgerald's computer," I said.

"Probably the cops." Byrd checked under the bed and between the mattress and box spring.

"There wasn't any mention of it in the discovery files Rebecca Li sent."

"You think Wilkes got rid of it before the cops showed up?"

I shrugged. "I wouldn't put anything past a man like Wilkes."

"I wouldn't put anything past those cops. That guy with the cowboy hat struck me like he was hiding something."

"Maybe he knows his case is full of holes and is afraid we'll expose them."

Byrd and I spent fifteen minutes searching the shelves, the closet, the bathroom, and every nook and drawer of the room. I checked all of the pockets in his clothes for notes. Inspected underneath drawers for clues. I did find a note with a list of what appeared to be computer passwords, but it was useless without the computer itself. I wasn't likely to be getting my hands on it. Still, I tucked the list away, just in case.

Despite our best efforts, we found nothing that might indicate who killed Fitzgerald.

I was about to suggest we wrap up our search when the ratcheting of a pistol hammer caught my attention.

Wilkes stood in the doorway, holding a .45-caliber Colt pistol in his trembling hand. "Who the heck are you people?"

I stood up, my back sore from stooping and snooping. "Like I said, we're investigating Brother James's mur—"

"Don't lie to me. I just spoke with Detective Atkinson. That case is closed. That Negro tranny's still charged with his murder."

"Mr. Wilkes, please put down the gun," said Byrd in a soothing voice.

"My name is Elder Michael, boy! And don't you forget it."

"Elder Michael, I understand you're upset." I shot him a reassuring smile. "We are independent investigators, and we have evidence that exonerates the woman that Scottsdale PD arrested. We are just trying to ascertain the truth."

"The truth is that tranny whore murdered my colleague. Her DNA proves it. I don't know what you people are up to, but you have no business being in my house, pretending to be cops."

"We never said we were cops. Only that we were investigating the murder, which is the truth. But seeing as how you're upset, we'll leave and get out of your hair."

"Oh no you don't. The real cops are on their way. You're not going anywhere. If you try to leave, I'd be within my rights to shoot you."

"Try it, ya little fucker." Shea pressed her Glock to the back of the old man's head. "I'll splatter your brains all over this room."

Wilkes's left eye twitched, and his mouth twisted into a snarl. After several long seconds, he laid the weapon on the nearby dresser. "You people will burn in hell for all eternity. And I will rejoice in your suffering."

"We'll keep that in mind." I grabbed the Colt from the dresser, ejected the magazine, and popped the round from the chamber, catching it in my free hand. I pocketed the magazine and extra round, then handed him back the unloaded pistol. "Until then, we're going to find out who really killed your little buddy and clear our friend."

We walked out the front door and convened between the Gray Ghost and Shea's motorcycle.

"Well, that was a waste of time," Byrd said.

"Not necessarily." Shea opened the top case on the back of her bike and pulled out a folder filled with papers.

"You find something?" I asked.

"A banker box in the garage contained some legal documents. Not sure if they shed any light on what happened or not." Shea handed me the folder.

I flipped through the papers. "There's a nondisclosure agreement and a severance agreement. Fitzgerald was leaving the fold. Wilkes didn't want him spilling any dirty secrets apparently."

"Could go to motive," added Byrd.

"Possibly. No doubt there was some bad blood between the two. But this parting of the ways seems mutual. Why kill Fitzgerald if he was already leaving? Doesn't make sense."

Shea's face fell in obvious disappointment. "Well, shit."

I clapped her on the arm. "Hey, it's another piece in the puzzle. Right now, Hancock's still our prime suspect, especially since his alibi was bogus. I say we press him, see if he'll crack and confess."

"And if he doesn't?"

"We'll keep digging until we come up with something more definitive. Any word from Fuego on getting Vanessa moved?"

"Yeah, she said a half dozen members of the MC showed up and moved her stuff to her friend Emma Kahn's house. No sign of the abusive husband. Quick and clean and no caffeine."

"Glad to hear it. Because if she spent another night at my place, I was going to strangle her and feed that little rat to my golden retriever. Let's go pay another visit to Mr. Hancock."

28

A green '70s-model muscle car parked on the street started up as we drove out of Wilkes's neighborhood. It was still a few cars behind Shea when I turned left onto Camelback Road.

"Looks like we got company," I said.

Byrd glanced back. "The '71 Nova? You think they're following us?"

"One way to find out." I made an abrupt turn south on Scottsdale Road just as the turn arrow switched from green to yellow. I glanced in my rearview. Shea squeaked through just as the light went red.

"They still tailing us?" I focused on the heavy congestion around Scottsdale Fashion Park. From behind us came a squeal of brakes and a blaring of horns.

"Yup. You think it's the guy who shot up your house?" asked Byrd.

"Freddie Colton drives a Pontiac Trans Am."

"Maybe it wasn't Colton last night. You said it sounded like a sports car."

A chill ran down my spine. "Who else would try to kill me? I haven't pissed anyone off lately."

"Other than the FBI, the county prosecutor, the Athena Sisterhood…" Byrd chuckled.

"I'm working with the Athena Sisterhood," I clarified. "And I don't think the feds or the Maricopa County Attorney's Office shoot up people's houses or drive classic muscle cars."

"The guy at the Cactus Inn."

"Why would he be after us? I paid him for the info and even rented a room."

"Maybe he doesn't like people asking too many questions."

I shook my head and confirmed the Nova was still behind us.

"Old Man Wilkes, perhaps."

"Doesn't track." I turned west on Indian School Road. The Nova stayed with us.

"Someone's interested enough to keep tabs on you. Maybe you have a rabid fan who likes when you dress up as Wonder Woman. Like a stalker."

A chill ran through me. I'd had a stalker once who had left a gift on my front doorstep in the form of a dead newspaper reporter. The stalker turned out to be Milo Volkov, the Chechen gangster whose brother, Sergei, was Penzler's boss. Maybe Sergei was looking to tie up some loose ends. Loose ends like me.

The Nova continued to tail us up Sixty-Fourth Avenue and back onto Camelback. I pulled into the right lane, intentionally getting stuck behind one of the city buses that was stopped while passengers boarded. The Nova sat a few cars behind us for a minute before jumping back into the left lane, cutting off a delivery truck. It happened so fast I wasn't able to catch a license plate.

As the bus resumed its route, my phone rang. I answered it in speaker mode.

"Ballou Fugitive Recovery."

"Is this Detective Ballou?" asked a familiar male voice with a western twang.

"This is Jinx Ballou."

"Well, howdy, Miss Ballou. This is Detective Atkinson with Scottsdale PD."

Aw shit. "How's it going, Detective?"

"Funny you should ask. I just had a most interesting conversation with a certain man of the cloth asking why a couple of my detectives had reopened the case into Fitzgerald's death."

"Is that so?"

"Miss Ballou, there's an old saying, 'Don't dig for water under the outhouse.' Last I checked, you're no longer a law enforcement officer, much less a member of my squad."

"I never told Michael Wilkes we were police officers. I simply explained that we were looking for Brother James's killer and had reason to believe that Zia Pearson was falsely accused."

"Tread softly, Miss Ballou. I don't appreciate people interfering in my cases. Neither does the county attorney's office. I suggest you and your little posse focus on returning Pearson to custody."

"I have a PI license, Atkinson. I'm well within my rights to track down exculpatory evidence that you and your buddy Torres missed."

"Watch yourself, little lady. Hate to see you sharing a cell with your tranny friend." He hung up.

"Goddamn that fucking man," I said when we pulled onto Hancock's street.

"Jinx..."

"Sorry...golly darn that f-ing man." In my mind, it still sounded like *goddamn that fucking man*.

"Better." Byrd sighed. "The more that guy Atkinson talks, the more I want to blow his case out of the water."

"You and me both," I replied.

I pulled into Hancock's driveway.

"You notice that green Nova behind me?" asked Shea after we got out.

"We noticed. May be nothing, but we need to be ready in case they show up again."

I rang Hancock's doorbell. When there was no response after a few minutes, I rang it again.

"Maybe he's not home," said Byrd.

"Should we let ourselves in?" asked Shea.

I pointed at the vertical window beside the door. There was just enough light inside to see a security panel on the wall. The lights told me it was armed. "Place is alarmed. We're here to talk to Hancock, not search his house."

Shea shook her head. "You're no fun."

I called Hancock, listening for a ringtone inside the house. The call rang a few times, but I heard nothing from inside. On the fourth ring, the call went to voicemail.

"Hi, Mr. Hancock. I hate to bother you again, but I do have a few remaining questions. If you could give me a call back, I'd appreciate it." I left my number and hung up.

Had I made a mistake in making the deal with the Athena Sisterhood? Finding fugitives was one thing. Solving a murder that the cops got wrong was a completely different skill set.

"When Fitzgerald was murdered, he obviously wasn't alone," I said to my colleagues.

"No doubt fucking one of the dancers from next door," said Shea.

Byrd looked like he'd been sucking on a lemon.

"Do the dancers at Naughty's moonlight as hookers?" I asked her.

"What do you think?" She smirked. "But I don't see a hooker murdering a john."

"Unless he got too rough," suggested Byrd, "trying to act out his little rape fantasies."

"So we have motive, potentially opportunity. But means?" I wondered aloud. "Brother James was a big man. A woman could shoot a guy like that. Even chop off his manhood. But from the crime scene photos, he looked like he'd gone twelve rounds with a heavyweight champ."

"Maybe her pimp did it. One of the bouncers from the club, perhaps," added Shea.

Byrd nodded. "Seems reasonable."

I looked at Shea. "Y'all spent a few hours at the club that night. Think we could speak to some of the dancers? Find out if any of them were doing sex work on the side? Or would know who might have been meeting Brother James next door."

"I don't know, Jinx. We were there, but honestly, I don't remember any names. Sapphire. Precious. Chastity. After a few rounds, the stage names all sound the same."

An idea popped into my head. I pulled out my phone. "Hey, Amber, it's Jinx."

"Jinxie! Oh my Godiva! How are you, girl? You know, I still owe you that lap dance for helping me out that time."

Amber Chaney and I had been close friends for years, having first met at the Phoenix Gender Alliance. At one point, the trauma and depression of transitioning got the best of her.

I found her after an attempted suicide and took her to the ER. In time, she found the determination to turn things around. She got work as an exotic dancer and earned enough money for her gender confirmation surgery.

For the past few years, she'd been attending Arizona State University during the day and dancing at night. How she found the energy to do both, I'd never know.

"You helped me track down those fascists last December," I told her. "I'd say we're even. How's school?"

"If I pass my finals next week, I'll get my degree and hang up my G-string for good. I already have a job offer from Hilton and Hodge Accounting."

"That's awesome, Amber!"

"You sure I can't interest you in a lap dance? Last chance!"

"I appreciate the offer, but you're like my little sister. It'd be a little awkward."

"Oh, poo! You never wanna play! How about that sweet Irish honey of yours?"

"You didn't hear? He...uh..." A wave of emotion blindsided me like a sucker punch to the solar plexus. "We're not together anymore."

"Seriously? I'm so sorry, sweetie."

"Listen, Amber, I'm calling because I need your help on another case."

"Really? At this rate, you may owe me a lap dance," she said with a chuckle.

"You know anyone dancing at Naughty's Cabaret in Scottsdale?"

"That slime pit? That's one of the clubs run by those Russian gangsters."

A knot formed in my stomach. "The Volkovs?"

"Yep. They own Naughty's and that sleazy motel next door."

"Shit." Not what I wanted to hear.

"Why the interest in Naughty's?"

"I'm working on that case with the preacher who was murdered next door. I suspect he was sleeping with one of the dancers, and things went bad."

"Wait, that preacher who's always saying queers should be put to death?"

"That's him. Or was until someone shot him. A trans woman is being framed for the murder. Got sent to a men's lockup. You can imagine what happened."

"I remember reading about that. Let me make some calls. I'll be in touch."

"I'd appreciate that, Amber."

"Take care of yourself, sweetie!"

"You too." I turned to Byrd and Shea, who were looking at me impatiently.

"A friend of mine may know a dancer at Naughty's."

"What do we do in the meantime?" asked Shea.

I looked at my watch. "Let's grab some lunch. There's a great place near my house."

29

Shea made a call to Fuego, and we all met up at Grumpy's Bar and Grill, around the corner from my house. It was a regular winner of *Phoenix Living*'s "Best of Phoenix" awards in the Bar & Grill category.

Grumpy Russell, the owner, was a pudgy Vietnam vet with silver mutton chop sideburns and an ever-present unlit cigar stub dangling from his lips.

He wasn't a fan of finicky customers. All those half-caf, no-foam, fat-free latte-type requests would elicit a string of vulgarity from Grumpy that could ignite wildfires. Even ordering dressing on the side was a risky move.

When Fuego, Dragon, Savage, and four other members of the Athena Sisterhood joined Shea, Byrd, and me, I feared Grumpy would have an aneurysm.

"Y'all couldn'ta called ahead o' time?" Grumpy growled, the cigar stub bouncing up and down from the corner of his mouth.

"Kind of a last-minute thing," I said. "Besides, we both know you don't take reservations."

He harrumphed. "Gimme a minute to clear out couple o' tables in back."

When we finally got seated and ordered, I filled in the bikers on our progress or lack thereof.

"I was hoping you'd have some proof by now." A worried expression hung on Savage's face.

"This was your idea," I snapped back. "You want this little whodunit solved faster, you're welcome to hire someone else."

"We're grateful," Dragon replied. "Savage is just worried about Indigo. Keep working to get evidence. Sooner the better, of course."

Yeah, whatever.

I was halfway through my Grumpy Burger and fries when my phone rang.

"Ms. Ballou? This is Detective Clifford. We met last night after the shooting at your home."

"I remember. You arrest Freddie Colton yet?"

"That's why I'm calling. Colton has an alibi for the shooting."

"Whatever he told you, he's lying."

"Unfortunately, his alibi's pretty solid. He was in the ER being treated for a knife wound from a bar fight when the shooting took place. I've confirmed with the attending physician and reviewed surveillance footage. He was not the shooter. We're still waiting on ballistics. If we find a match, I'll let you know."

I thanked her and hung up.

It was midafternoon by the time we paid the checks—which Grumpy agreed to split, though not without complaint. Between the lack of sleep from the night before and the lack of progress on the case, I was spent. Shea, Byrd, and I agreed to reconvene at my house in the morning. Shea headed off with her fellow bikers. I took Byrd back to my place, where he drove off in his Chevy Malibu.

The bullet-riddled front of my house reflected how I felt. I wanted to relax into Conor's arms, to tell him about my crazy day and hear about his own adventures chasing down fugitives. One advantage of dating another bounty hunter was that our war stories didn't freak each other out.

But Conor wasn't here. And it was my fault. If I had run away with him, he wouldn't have turned himself in to the Northern Irish police. I was shit. A shit girlfriend. And a shit bounty hunter who couldn't keep a crew together for more than a few months. One who gave up pursuing a fugitive at the first sign of trouble. Hell, now I was working for the very people who refused to give her up.

Determined to do at least something right, I laid out all of the paperwork on my antique kitchen table. It felt like assembling a puzzle with no idea what it was supposed to look like, half the pieces missing, and others that didn't belong. I arranged the reports different ways, hoping a new perspective might reveal connections I was overlooking. No insights came. Not so much as a tickle in the back of my brain. I was shit at being a private investigator.

At some point, I poured myself a liquid dinner from a bottle of cheap tequila, which I bought on the way home. I followed it up with a little sativa for dessert.

I lay on my bed and thumbed through photos of Conor on my phone, my brain unraveling like a knit sweater in a monsoon. When the phone rang, it slipped from my hand and dropped hard on my forehead. "Ow, fuck!"

I picked it up and looked at the caller ID. Pima Bail Bonds. *Fuck.* I tried to send it to voicemail, but in my impaired state, I hit the answer button by mistake.

"Hel...hello?" I mumbled.

"Jinx, this is Maurice Begay over at Pima Bail Bonds. I'd like a progress report. Where are you in locating Pearson?"

"I...uh...wow, you know." I tried to concentrate, but my thoughts felt like wisps of smoke swirling around me. "I am really, really close, man. So very, very close. Like it's almost inside me. You know? Maurice the man. Man-reece!"

"Jinx, are you okay? You sound...odd."

"No, no, no, I am totally cool. Just chilling out after a hard day of fugitive-ing. Fugitive catching. Chasing. Fugitive chasing.

That's why they call it fishing. 'Cause they don't call it catching. Or something like that."

"I've got a lot riding on this job and am paying double the standard rate. I expect results. And regular updates."

"I've...I've narrowed the suspect list down to a few people."

"Suspect list? What suspect list? You mean people who are hiding Pearson?"

"What? Oh yeah, that's what I meant. People who are hiding with person. Pearson. The Pearson person." A giggle snuck out before I could stop it.

"Is this funny to you, Ms. Ballou?"

"No." I guffawed. "No. This is..." An eruption of laughter burst forth so intense I couldn't catch my breath. Tears streamed down my face. The room was spinning, and even that seemed hilarious. By the time I got control of myself, Maurice had hung up. I laughed at that as well. Oh, I was so totally fucked, but at the moment, I didn't really care.

The next thing I remembered, Diana was licking the side of my face. I swatted at her blindly, but she was back a moment later. It took me a few minutes to realize I was lying on the tile floor of my kitchen. My head thundered like a late-summer rainstorm. A sharp beeping pulsed viciously in my ears. *Is this a hangover, or am I getting tinnitus? Or maybe it's a tumor. No, no, it's not a tumor.*

With considerable effort, I used the chair and then the kitchen table to pull myself in a near-vertical position. Baking ingredients, glass mixing bowls, sifters, and other utensils were scattered across the counter. *Have I been trying to bake? While baked?*

I caught a whiff of something burning. The piercing sound riveting my brain wasn't the hangover. It was the smoke alarm. The oven was on. What the fuck?

I turned off the oven and opened it. Smoke billowed into the kitchen. I opened the back door and windows and cranked the ceiling fan to high while coughing like a lifelong smoker.

Using a pot holder, I pulled a rectangular Pyrex dish from the oven and set it on the stove. An inch-thick layer of charcoal lined the bottom of the dish. *Brownies? Shit.*

I ran down the hallway and fanned the smoke detector. It refused to shut up. I tried to pull it off the wall to remove the batteries, but I couldn't figure out how to twist or pull it off. Finally, I grabbed a hammer from the junk drawer. After a few wobbly blows, the beeping stopped.

I collapsed into a chair and rested my throbbing head in my arms until I felt Diana pawing at me for attention. The rising sun was shooting death rays through the haze-filled kitchen straight through my eye sockets, intensifying the pain in my self-traumatized brain.

"Guess you need to go for a run, huh, baby?" I asked her.

Her tail thumped on the floor. She rested her head on my lap. I started bawling and hugged her. "You deserve a better mom. You know that? One who isn't such a fuckup."

More tail thumps. I wasn't sure if she was agreeing with me or reminding me she loved me regardless. I was still new at this whole dog-mommy thing.

I tumbled down the hallway to my room, pulled on a T-shirt and shorts that were only a little smelly, attached Diana's leash, and went outside into the furious light of morning. A ball cap and my wraparound shades barely sufficed to protect my brain from the golden rays of pain peeking through the trees. I shuffled along the sidewalk, Diana tugging me to go faster, jolting my concussed brain into new experiences of agony. But I couldn't scold her. This was my fault. I deserved to suffer.

As we waited at a light, I pulled my phone out of my pocket from habit. Another text from Maurice. Delete. A text from Vanessa. I was about to delete it as well, but something in her text caught my eye.

You still looking for Bro James killer? Emma thinks Simon knows whos involved. Call me.

Diana barked. The light had turned green, and fellow pedestrians pushed past me to cross the street.

Who the hell is Simon? I stepped into the street. An asshole in a pickup truck nearly clipped me while making a right turn.

Once I was safely across the street, I called Vanessa. It rang six times before going to voicemail. Figured.

"This is Jinx. I got your text. Call me."

30

I was in the middle of showering when my phone rang. "Thank Guinness!" I rinsed the shampoo out of my eyes before tossing the shower curtain back and picking up the phone.

"Vanessa?" I asked without checking the caller ID.

"Um, no. It's Shea. Something's happened."

"What? Where?"

"At Vanessa's friend's house. The police are here. Vanessa and Emma are both dead."

"Text me the address. I'll be right there."

I grabbed my gear and raced over to Emma's in half the time it should have taken.

A dozen police vehicles with lights flashing had blocked off the road, forcing me to park one street over. Crime scene tape stretched across the front yard. I found the Athena Sisterhood huddled just outside the tape.

"What the hell happened?" I asked.

Shea's face was dark. "Got a call a couple hours ago from Vanessa. Freddie was pounding on the front door."

"Fuck!" Another wave of guilt hit me. If I'd let her stay at my place, would she still be alive?

"I told her to call 911," explained Shea. "We drove over quick as we could but were too late. We found them both shot to death."

"Shit. Who's in charge of the investigation?" I asked.

Shea pointed at a group of unis gathered around a plain-clothes detective. "Black guy right there. I think he said his name was Hardy."

"Hardin. Detective Pierce Hardin."

"You know him?"

"He was my FTO when I joined the force. My field training officer."

Hardin turned toward us. His eyes narrowed when he spotted me. He shook his head and wandered over. "Don't tell me you're involved in this shitfest, Ballou."

"Vanessa Colton called me yesterday because her asshole husband, Freddie, kept beating on her. I let her stay one night at my place. After that, she moved in with her friend here." I was tempted to tell him about the drive-by, but since Detective Clifford had cleared Freddie, it didn't seem relevant to Vanessa's murder.

"How did you know Ms. Colton?" asked Hardin, taking out his notebook.

"I took her husband to lockup after he jumped bail two years ago on a domestic violence charge. She still had my business card from when I showed up looking for him."

"Anything else you can tell me?"

"That's it." I caught myself feeling angry as well as guilty. I should have done more to protect Vanessa, but so should the cops. This shit between her and her husband had been going on for years. "Hey, what kind of gun was used?"

"Ballou, you know I can't tell you that."

"Come on, Detective. Just tell me. Was it a ten-millimeter auto?"

"Why?"

"It's relevant to a case I'm working."

"No brass was recovered. My guess is it was a revolver, but we won't know the caliber till the slugs are recovered from the bodies."

"What happened to Vanessa's dog?"

"What dog?"

"Vanessa had a little dog. A Yorkshire terrier."

Hardin shrugged. "No one's mentioned finding a dog in the house. If we find it, you want I should call you?"

I shook my head. "No. I've got one. That's plenty for me."

"Well, thanks for the information." Hardin tucked away his pen and notebook.

As he turned to walk away, I asked, "Hey, wait! You ever work with a Detective Atkinson out of Scottsdale PD?"

"Atkinson?"

"Big cheesy mustache. Wears a Stetson."

That actually got a rare belly laugh out of Hardin. "That Wyatt Earp wannabe? Shit. I woulda thought he'd be retired by now."

"So you know him?"

"That white boy done seen too many westerns. Moved down here from Chicago 'bout twenty years ago. Thought putting on a hat and adopting a swagger made him seem like a local. Far be it from me to dis another officer, but I'm glad he ain't on my squad. What's your interest in him?"

"He arrested the wrong woman—a trans woman—for a murder. I'm helping out some friends to get the charges dropped. So far, neither Atkinson nor the prosecutor, Prather, will budge."

Hardin let loose with another belly laugh. "Damn, Ballou, how many times a fugitive tell you they didn't do it?"

"More than I can count. But this time I believe her."

"Because she's transgender?"

"That's part of it. It isn't the first time she's been falsely charged with something. I think Atkinson has it in for her. And

Prather, well, he's not exactly a fan of mine after what happened with Wilhelm Penzler."

"Jesus, you sure know how to step in it, don't you?" The look on his face told me he believed me. "I'm not saying you're wrong. But I'd caution you to watch your step. You cross Atkinson and Prather on this, you damn sure better be right."

"Noted."

"By the way, you remember an officer named Garza?"

"Luis Garza? He was my partner when I worked Patrol. Why?"

He let out a long, slow breath. "He's dead."

"What? How? When?"

"A few weeks ago. Couple of gangbangers held up a liquor store. Garza was there buying beer. Wrong time, wrong place."

"Shit. That sucks." I felt bad even though things between Garza and me had soured after he found out I was trans. "Camila and the kids okay?"

"Devastated. He'd recently made detective, assigned to the Assaults Unit. Jennings is working the investigation. "

"Shit. I'm sorry. If you see Camila, please give her my condolences." I thought about calling her myself, but it would be all kinds of awkward.

"Will do."

I returned to Shea, Savage, and the others.

A whimpering sound caught my attention. Savage was juggling a bundle under her jacket. "Shhh...it's okay."

"You took the dog?" I asked.

"Didn't know what else to do with her," Savage replied. "Poor girl just lost her mommy. Didn't want that murderous bastard to get her or for her to end up in the pound."

A lump formed in my throat. I hated the little rat, but I also felt sorry for her. I hoped they nailed Colton's ass to the wall. For good this time. "Glad she's got someone to care for her."

"You learn anything from your detective friend?" asked Shea.

"Not much." I told them about the text I'd received from Vanessa. "Any idea who Simon is?"

"A guy that Emma's been going out with," said Fuego. "She mentioned him when we were getting Vanessa moved in. Don't know his last name, though."

"All right. I'll see what Becca can dig up on him. He supposedly knows who killed Fitzgerald."

31

As it was only seven o'clock, I texted Becca instead of calling her, telling her what I knew and asking her to locate this Simon person for me.

"The rest of the Sisterhood's heading back up north. Not much else they can do now that Vanessa's dead." Shea's face was solemn. "What's our game plan, boss?"

I stared out at the sky smeared with streaks of thin clouds. "We need to track down Hancock and get a straight answer about where he was the night of the murder. I also want to speak to this Simon, since Vanessa thought he knew something about it. And I'm still waiting to hear back from my friend Amber regarding the dancers at Naughty's."

Becca returned my call. "Emma's Facebook account shows she's in a relationship with a Simon Benedict. Wow, this guy looks like a freakin' caveman. He doesn't have an account of his own, as far as I can tell. Doesn't pop up on any other social media. I've run a skip trace and located an address for his apartment off Northern and the 51. Works nights at a bowling alley on East Glendale Avenue. I'll send you what I have."

"He drive a green Chevy Nova by chance?" I thought about our tail from the other day.

"Let's see…" Keys clicked away like machine-gun fire. "I'm showing a 2007 Hyundai Excel, red, registered in his name. No other vehicles. Sorry."

"Thanks for getting back to me so quickly, Becks." I hung up and immediately called Byrd. "Dude, we've had some developments."

I filled him in on everything. "I want you to go to Hancock's place. If he's home, call me. If not, contact Becca and see if you can track him down. When you find him, let me know, and we'll show up."

"Roger that."

"So what're we doing?" Shea asked when I hung up with Byrd. The rest of the Sisterhood had taken off.

"Becca tracked down Emma's boyfriend, Simon Benedict." I pulled up the photo Becks had sent me. "Look familiar?"

"The guy with Freddie Colton. Vanessa's friend was dating him?"

"Apparently. Emma must've told him that Vanessa was staying over, and then he told Freddie."

Shea's hands balled into fists. "What a pathetic piece of shit."

"Yeah, but one who may know who killed Fitzgerald. What say we go have a talk with the guy?"

She pounded her right fist in her left hand. "I say we do more than talk."

"Talk first. We'll see about anything afterward. Oh, and this time, I'm taking the Charger in case our friend in the green Nova shows up again."

Simon Benedict lived in a faded-yellow apartment complex. Despite a fence enclosing the property, the automatic gate was wide open for anyone to drive through. Benedict's red Hyundai sat parked in one of the covered parking spaces, not far from his apartment.

When I stepped out of the Charger, I was hit with the smell of garbage and urine coming from an open dumpster. Small weeds poked through the crushed rock that once served as flower beds between the buildings. Everything about the complex was a study in neglect.

I pulled on my gear and met Shea by her motorcycle.

"How you want to handle this?" Her hand rested on the grip of the Glock on her hip.

"We don't know for sure he told Freddie where Vanessa was staying or why, if he did. But be ready. If things go sideways, remember we need him alive to tell us what he knows."

"I'll resist the urge to shoot him," said Shea with a mischievous grin. "But no promises."

We approached the door, and I rang the bell. Simon the Neanderthal opened the door a minute later looking barefoot and bleary-eyed. He reeked of alcohol and body odor. His T-shirt and shorts looked slept in.

"Simon Benedict?" I asked.

"Who wants to know?" Clearly, he didn't recognize us. I considered that a plus at this point.

"You're Emma Kahn's boyfriend, right?"

"Yeah. Why?"

"I'm afraid we have some bad news. Mind if we come in?"

He stood there a moment, as if sizing us up. "You cops?"

I tapped the badge hanging from a chain around my neck. "I work mostly fugitive cases, but this is in regards to a homicide."

Fear seemed to punch him between the eyes. He stumbled back, holding onto the wall for support. "Is Emma all right?"

I took that for our cue to enter. He lumbered to his kitchen table and collapsed into one of the wooden chairs.

"I'm sorry to inform you that Emma Kahn was found dead this morning, along with her friend Vanessa Colton."

He sat there wide-eyed and pale, meaty hands trembling while gripping the table. "No, no, no! Emma can't be dead. I saw her just last night. We were supposed to go out, but Vanessa was staying over."

"You mention seeing Vanessa to Freddie Colton?" asked Shea.

"Freddie? Sure, Vanessa's his wife. Why shouldn't he know?" He looked at Shea, then me. I could see him doing the calculations in his head, however slowly. "Wait, no! No way! I mean, Freddie gets a little rough with her now and then, but he wouldn't...."

"You were in their house a few days ago when he threatened to kill her," I said, dropping my comforting tone.

"But that's just the way Freddie talks. He'd never actually..."

"Oh, he would, and he did," insisted Shea. "Killed Vanessa and Emma both, thanks to you."

His anguish morphed into anger. "That motherfucker!" He knocked a napkin holder into the wall with enough force to shatter it, sending a cloud of paper napkins drifting to the floor like dandelion seeds.

He looked up at me. "Y'all...y'all were at Freddie's. Y'all ain't cops."

"Now he figures it out," Shea said grimly.

"I used to be a cop. Now I'm a private detective investigating a recent homicide. But if you'd like us to call the cops, we'd be happy to let them know you tipped off Colton to his wife's whereabouts. That makes you an accessory to first-degree murder."

Simon's face blanched. "I had no idea what he was gonna do."

"Yeah, right." Shea snorted.

"You're certainly welcome to tell that to the cops, Simon," I replied. "Or you tell us what we want to know."

"Whaddya wanna know?"

"We're looking for the man who killed James Fitzgerald," I said. "Vanessa sent a text saying you knew who did it."

"Fitzgerald? Don't know nobody by that name."

"Sure you do. That preacher who was murdered in Scottsdale a month or so ago. Went by the moniker Brother James."

"Him? Whaddya wanna know about him for?"

"That's our business," replied Shea. "Now spill, or we give your name to the cops."

"Fine. I was down at the Stone Horse Pub a while back. This guy Boris, kind of a regular there, he's drunk off his ass, bragging how he put a beatdown on some loudmouth preacher. A week later, I saw a story on the news about that preacher's body being found. Figured it was Boris."

"Did Boris have any dealings with a man named Wes Hancock?"

"Don't know nobody named Hancock."

"Where does Boris live?" I pressed.

"How the hell should I know? I see him every once in a while at the Stone Horse."

"What's Boris's last name?"

"Geez, I don't know. All them Russkie names sound alike. Starts with a *G*, I think, and ends in *O-V*. Garnov. Gorkov. Who knows? We just call him Boris because he speaks with an accent. Probably not even his real name."

"Any idea where he works?"

"From what he said, he ain't got a regular job. Beats people up for a living, but I don't know for who. Why are we even talking about him? My girlfriend's dead, man. Boris can go fuck himself for all I care." He broke into sobs. Who knew Neanderthals had such deep emotions?

I put my hand on his arm, remembering how I felt when I learned about Conor and the explosion on the highway.

I wrote down Detective Hardin's name and number on a piece of paper and handed it to him. "I'm sorry for your loss, man. This is the detective working the case. He'll help you out."

I nodded to Shea, and we let ourselves out. A text from Byrd told me that Hancock wasn't home, but he was in touch with Becca to track him down.

"What do you think?" asked Shea.

"Until now, my money was on Hancock, especially with his

bogus alibi. But in light of what Simon told us, maybe it was this Boris person, whoever the hell he is."

"Maybe Hancock hired Boris."

"Possible. But that still doesn't explain Hancock's bogus alibi." I looked up the Stone Horse Pub on my phone. "Stone Horse doesn't open until one. I'll have Becca see what she can dig up on Boris Gorkov or Garnov."

I sent Becca a text giving her what little I knew about the guy. I knew it was a needle in a haystack, but it was all I had.

She texted back, "Wasn't Gorkov a Cardassian in *Deep Space Nine*?"

"That was Garak, you goofball," I replied.

She responded with a goofy-faced emoji and a message that she'd look into the name.

My phone rang just as I was putting it back in my pocket. It was Amber.

"What's up, girl?"

"Friend of mine was caught up in Volkov's trafficking operation. Used to dance at Naughty's in Scottsdale. The girls there took interested clients next door to the motel for sex."

Bingo! No doubt Fitzgerald was one of those interested clients. Bible study, my ass!

"How do I get in touch with her?"

"Well, that's the thing. She's a little shy."

"She takes off her clothes in front of strangers, but she's shy?"

"Shy about speaking to strangers. You gotta understand, Sergei Volkov's people keep a tight rein on the girls. My friend was lucky she got out."

"I get it. But one of Volkov's clients was murdered in the motel next door, and a trans woman is going to take the fall unless I can prove someone else did it. I need to talk to someone who's been on the inside."

"If Volkov finds out she talked…"

"He won't, Amber. I swear."

I heard voices in the background. "You remember where I live?"

"Off Olive Avenue and Grand. Near Glendale Community College."

"Exactly."

"I'll be there shortly." I hung up and smiled at Shea. "We got someone who used to work at Naughty's. Follow me."

32

I navigated out of Simon Benedict's neighborhood and pulled onto Northern Avenue. A green muscle car behind Shea's bike caught my attention. Whether it was the Chevy Nova we'd seen earlier, I couldn't tell from the glare off the windshield, but it seemed the same emerald shade. So far, our dogged shadow hadn't made any aggressive moves. Maybe the driver was just keeping tabs on where we were going. Maybe they were biding their time, waiting for the opportune moment to strike. Either way, in light of Amber's concerns for her friend's safety, I didn't want to lead our shadow to her place.

At the last second, I turned hard onto the northbound I-17 on-ramp and floored it. Shea followed on her motorcycle, having no trouble keeping up. The Nova followed suit.

"Okay, girl," I said to Conor's old Charger. "Let's see what you can do."

Back in 1968, the 440 R/T was a helluva car, I was told. But after she'd had more than a half century of use in the dry heat of the desert, I wasn't sure she still had it in her.

I forced my way through the post-rush-hour traffic to the car pool lane. I put the pedal to the metal, the engine growled, and the speedometer climbed...60, 70, 80, 90. I checked my rearview. The Nova was behind me. Where was Shea?

I looked right and saw her next to me, crouched down to reduce wind resistance. She shot me a thumbs-up then ducked into the center lane to dodge a utility truck and put on a surprising burst of speed. The Nova changed lanes, clearly attempting to follow Shea.

When the Nova was next to me, I tried to catch a glimpse of the driver but couldn't see through the tinted windows. I turned the wheel to the right, gritting my teeth at the sound of metal crunching against metal. The Charger shoved the Nova, then the Nova shoved back. We swapped paint a few more times before the traffic thickened as we approached the Loop 101 interchange. I was forced to move back into the carpool lane or risk losing the Nova completely.

Shea was about a quarter mile ahead of us. Maybe she was trying to lead him off and lose him. She had mentioned that her bike had a high-performance motor. But I didn't like the thought of leaving her to deal with the asshole in the Nova by herself.

Once past the 101, my speedometer wobbled to a hundred miles an hour, then one ten as I took after the Nova that was pushing hard to catch Shea. The car shook with the increased speed. The world around me became a blur, leaving only the Nova in focus.

I jerked the wheel hard, barreling into the Nova's crumpled side panels and driving it onto the shoulder. I hoped that was the end of it, but the Nova swerved back onto the road, cutting behind me and ending up on my left.

I glanced over in time to see the passenger window rolling down. The barrel of a gun appeared. I rammed the car. My rear window shattered when the gun went off. I rammed again, even harder this time. Metal scraped. Tires screamed, but I kept pushing, driving it from the left lane, into the carpool lane.

Ahead, an RV was cruising along in the carpool lane. Some snowbird probably headed back to Canada or Minnesota. We were going a hundred and twenty. The RV zoomed toward us almost as if it were going the wrong way. At the last second, the Nova slid onto the left shoulder. The RV vanished behind us.

An idea popped into my head. A memory from the police academy's defensive driving course. I eased off the gas a hair. The Nova pulled ahead. I drifted into the right lane. The other car followed.

An arm emerged from the passenger side, holding a gun. I pulled in behind the Nova and rammed it as hard as I could from behind. The gun dropped from the shooter's hand and disappeared behind us.

I moved back into the right lane, then swerved into the Nova's rear quarter panel. The Nova spun around out of control in front of me as I jammed the accelerator to the floor. The combination of speed and rotational forces sent the Nova catapulting end over end in a flash of green paint, chrome, and smoke.

My heart was hammering faster than the pistons under my hood. A smile crept across my face. "See ya later, alligator."

I recognized the tiny dot in the distance as Shea. I floored it to catch up. The distance between us narrowed until she was on my left. I gave her a thumbs-up. She returned the gesture. I slowed to 80 miles an hour, then took the Carefree Highway exit and pulled into the Chevron and sat there.

"You all right?" asked Shea. I could hear the concern in her voice as she appeared outside my door.

"Think so." The door groaned when I got out. My knees were wobbly, and I leaned on the car for support.

"You should've let me lead them off," she said. "I could've lost them and doubled back."

"They had a gun. They could've shot you." I held her gaze for a moment. A lot of things passed between us, things I didn't have words for. "One thing's certain. It was the same Chevy Nova. And now I have a plate number."

I texted the info to Becca to pull up on the Motor Vehicle Department's database. She replied she'd pull it up when she could, but at the moment, she was tied up with a client whose entire network had been hacked and brought down. She hoped to have an answer within the hour.

I was tempted to tell her that our situation was also time critical, but she'd often put me ahead of her better-paying clients.

"I don't like this." Shea gazed south at the highway.

"Me either." I followed her sight line. A column of black smoke was rising in the distance, too far away to know if it was the Nova or something else on fire. "Hopefully, that's the last we see of them."

I walked around the Charger. The body panels looked like the car had been through a giant pinball machine. Green paint streaked across the dented black body panels. The front grille was cracked, though the radiator seemed intact. The bullet had punched though the backseat window and into the upholstery. I found what was left of the slug embedded in the spare tire in the trunk. I was glad Conor didn't have to see what I'd done to his beloved sports car.

"Let's go meet this former dancer."

33

The streets in Amber's part of town were cracked and riddled with potholes. Dollar stores outnumbered Starbucks. All of the buildings had a tired, dingy look to them, as did the pedestrians cruising down the weed-strewn sidewalks. Sprouting from street corners were homemade signs promising free cable and cash for houses.

A couple of streets south of Northern, Amber maintained a cute little three-bedroom, which she shared with a gay man named Ace and a single mother named Rebel and her two-year-old daughter, Sage. Only Amber was home at the time.

Amber was tall, sinewy, and tan. Her voice was husky but sultry in a Miley Cyrus sort of way, and the only hint of her being trans. She hugged me when she opened the door to let us in.

I introduced Shea. Amber introduced us to her friend Maricela Ramirez. She was shorter than Amber but busty with bronze skin and burgundy hair. Her eyes were large and lips full. She looked like she was hiding a basketball under her shirt.

We settled in around the coffee table in Amber's living room.

"Thanks for agreeing to talk to us," I told Maricela.

She looked worried, like she was on trial for her life. And maybe she was. The Volkovs were ruthless, as Shea and I already knew. The last thing I wanted was to put someone else's life in danger, even to save Indigo.

"If word gets out that I talked..."

"We know. We've dealt with Milo Volkov in the past. I'm sure Sergei's not much better."

"Not better but different. Milo treated girls like meat. He let his men rape us. Some women, he kept chained like animals. Sergei...he has a different approach. More businesslike. Only paying clients could have sex with us. And if a client gots too rough, Sergei's men put a stop to it. More protective, in a way, unless..."

"Unless what?"

"Unless we tried to escape."

"What happens to those who try to escape?" There was fire in Shea's voice. I felt it too.

"Bad things. Very, very bad things. Most girls were from other countries. Honduras. Nigeria. India. Sergei's men promised great jobs in America. But when we got here, we learned it was a lie. They kept our passports. Forced us to dance and have sex with clients. Some tried to escape. One lost an eye. Another..." She blinked back tears.

"But you left, anyway. Despite the risk."

Her arm wrapped protectively around her enlarged belly. "I discovered I was pregnant. It happen before. They forced me to get abortion. I don't want that again. I want this baby. I heard about a group who helps women like me, women who are forced to be prostitutes."

"The Human Trafficking Resource Center," Amber added. "I sometimes volunteer for their helpline."

"I called and talked to Amber. She helped get me out."

"Did you tell the police or the FBI about Volkov's operation?" I asked both Maricela and Amber.

"She's undocumented," Amber replied. "Volkov pays cops to

look the other way. The feds would've turned her over to ICE and stuck her in a cage before eventually sending her back to Honduras. Best if we keep quiet."

"You said when a client got too rough, Sergei's men put a stop to it. How?"

"Yuri would send his men to have talk with him. Andrei or one of the other bouncers at the club."

"Who's Yuri?" asked Shea.

"He is in charge of Naughty's and of the prostitution business."

"Just talk?" said Shea.

She shrugged. "Maybe not just talk."

"Would they kill a john who got too rough?" I asked.

"Never heard them do that. Usually just..." She made punching gestures in the air.

"Beat him up a bit?" asked Shea.

Maricela nodded. "Tell him to play nice, or he no longer a client. Sergei is more businessman than Milo was. Smart. Police look the other way for prostitution. But killing a client can bring the feds. Bad for business. Also drives away other clients. Easier to beat up a bad client or tell him not come back."

"You ever meet James Fitzgerald? The preacher?"

"Brother James? Yes, a few times." She stared down at the floor. "He got rough. Yuri sent Andrei to talk to him."

Shea's posture stiffened. "What'd that piece of garbage do?"

"He liked to pretend to rape us girls. Tie our hands and feet." Maricela rubbed her wrists. "Then he slap, punch, kick. Very rough sex. Broke my wrist and cracked two ribs. I could not work for weeks. I was afraid Yuri would do something bad to me, but he let me rest and get better."

"How long ago was this?" I asked.

"A year."

"What did Yuri do to Brother James?" Shea sounded angry.

"I do not know exactly. I never saw Brother James again."

I was getting a good picture of what went on. Shea and I

continued to probe Maricela's knowledge of Sergei's operation, asking how clients approached dancers for sex work, how money was handled, anything that might help clear Pearson. Unfortunately, what little Maricela knew didn't shed much light on the situation. And she had escaped long before Fitzgerald was murdered.

"You ever hear of a guy named Boris working for Sergei?" I asked finally. "I think his last name is Gorkov or Garnov."

Maricela's brow crinkled. "I do not know a Boris."

"Who took your place with Brother James after he hurt you? He was obviously sleeping with someone else."

"I don't know. I was happy it was not me."

"What are you doing now?" I asked. "For work, I mean."

"Amber helped me find a job working in a restaurant. At least till the baby comes."

"Amber's good people." I gave my friend a wink. She blushed.

My phone rang. Caller ID came up as Arizona Mutual Life Insurance. No doubt Pete Stansfield wanting to chat about Conor's life insurance policy. No thanks. Bigger fish to fry. I sent it to voicemail.

"Jinx, Maricela's looking a little tired," said Amber. "Think we can wrap it up?"

"Of course. Thanks for talking with us, Maricela. I hope everything goes well with your baby."

"*Muchas gracias.*"

Amber walked us to the door. "You get what you needed?"

"Hard to say. I appreciate your setting this up."

"Hope it helps."

Back at the vehicles, Shea asked, "What do you think?"

"Some good background on Sergei's operation. But nothing she said points to him or one of his minions being the killer."

"Not yet. But we both know what psychos the Volkovs are, no matter how 'businesslike' she said Sergei is. I'm sure they're mixed up in Fitzgerald's death somehow. Maybe not for beating up a ho. Maybe some other shit they had going on between them."

"Could be." I checked my watch. "Let's grab some lunch and then head to the Stone Horse Pub. Maybe we'll get lucky and find this guy Boris."

34

———

While we chowed down on a couple of burros at Filibertos, Becca called back.

"Sorry to put you off, Jinx, but this client was seriously shitting bricks. She runs a chain of sporting goods stores, and getting hit on a Friday..."

"I get it. You find anything out on this Boris fellow or the Chevy Nova that's been tailing us?"

"Nothing on Boris yet. No one named Boris Gorkov or Garnov that I can find. As for the Nova, it belonged to an eighty-year-old woman named Consuelo Silva."

"Eighty?" That caught me off guard. "Was it reported stolen?"

"Not at this time. You want a photo? She's cute. Reminds me of my *abuela*."

"I'm sure she's lovely, but I don't think she's the one who's been tailing us. She have any grandkids with a record?"

"Entirely possible. I'll run some face-recognition algorithms and see if a relative has posted family photos on social media. I can also run a search on her address. Maybe she's got family living with her."

"Thanks. Let me know what you find."

I hung up. Time to find Boris.

The Stone Horse Pub had seen better days. The illuminated sign on the street was so yellowed with age, I wondered if someone had scorched it with a flame. The building's plaster facade was made to look like flagstones, but the years had left the surface pockmarked and chipped.

A life-sized concrete horse stood outside the front door. It had been tagged with graffiti and patch-painted so many times, it made the poor beast look like a pinto. A jagged stub remained where the lower jaw had been.

Shea and I stepped inside the bar, geared up in case Boris was here. It took my eyes a moment to adjust to the low-lit interior. Not all that charming inside either. The barracks in the police academy had more character than this dive.

A bar with an oaken top ran the left side of the room. The bartender was a white woman with a bulldog face and crooked teeth. The Statue of Liberty had been inked on one of her arms and an M-16 along the other.

Four patrons sat at the bar, nursing drinks, occasionally glancing up at the baseball game on the TV above the bar. The Diamondbacks were pounding the Giants 10-1 in the bottom of the fifth. A handful of tables, all filled, and a jukebox with a cracked glass cover sat along the right wall. Welcome to Barfly Central.

"What can I get you ladies?" Bulldog the bartender asked when Shea and I approached.

"Information," I replied. "I'm looking for Boris. Speaks with a Russian accent. I hear he's a regular customer."

"Boris, huh?" The bartender had a deadpan expression. "You seem to know a lot about this guy. I hope you find him."

"He was here bragging about killing a guy a month or so ago," Shea added.

"Guys are always shooting their mouths off in here, bragging about one thing or another. How tough they are. How fast their cars are. How big their dicks are. It's the nature of the beast. I just sling booze. I don't keep track of who says what. You want booze, I'll line 'em up. You want information, try the library over by PV Mall."

Great, a tight-lipped bartender with a snarky attitude. Just what I needed. I set three twenties down on the bar. "Does this refresh your memory?"

She shrugged nonchalantly. "Not really."

The man on the stool next to me slurred something and slumped over. He would have face-planted on the floor if I hadn't caught him. I shoved him back up and flopped him onto the polished bar, toppling his glass.

"This guy's plastered." I took a photo of him with my phone. "I do believe over-serving is a great way to lose your liquor license. Maybe I should send this to the Department of Liquor Licenses."

"Leave Sam alone. His wife just died of ovarian cancer, for Chrissakes. You okay, man?" she asked him.

Sam mumbled something that sounded like "Okeydokey."

Bulldog shot me a stern look. "I've already called him a cab, all right?"

"Tell us what we want to know, or I report this."

She narrowed her gaze, perhaps gauging whether I was bluffing.

"Look, Boris comes in every so often. Drinks Stolichnaya. Talks a lotta shit. Claims to be some tough guy, but if you ask me, he's full of hot air. That's all I know."

"What's he look like?" Shea asked.

"Big guy. Short brown hair. Dark eyes. Kind of a bodybuilder type. Has some tattoos on his arms and hands. Skulls and stars, I think."

"He got a last name?" I inquired.

"Everybody does, but I don't know what it is. Starts with a *G*, I think."

"Garnov? Gorkov?" I pressed.

"Garnov sounds right. His first name's really Alexei. Boris is more of a nickname on account he's Russian."

"When's he usually here?" Shea asked.

"Do I look like I keep a schedule of my customers?"

"Fine." I held up my phone again, tapping on the screen. "Ah, here we are. Report a liquor license violation."

"Stop! I don't know when he's here. I honestly don't keep track. Best guess, middle of the week but late at night. Maybe ten or so. I could be wrong."

"You are useless," Shea told her.

Time for plan B. Crowdsourcing. I pulled a few twenty-dollar bills from my wallet and faced the rest of the room. "Good people of the Stone Horse, can I get your attention, please? I have sixty bucks to anyone who can tell me where to find Boris or Alexei Garnov. Has a Russian accent. Lots of ink. Likes to brag about killing people. Sixty bucks."

"You're wasting your time," Bulldog said with her arms crossed.

The people in the bar ignored me. I pulled out a few more twenties. "One hundred. One hundred bucks. All you gotta do is tell me where Boris is."

A couple of people looked up from their drinks but remained silent. Sam the Puddle mumbled something, but it was a slur of syllables.

Shea held up a C-note. "Make that two hundred dollars."

"Two hundred dollars," I echoed. "Easy money. Just gotta tell me where we can find Boris."

"Make it three!" said a guy nursing a glass of whiskey at a table.

Shea pulled out another. "Fine. Three hundred dollars."

"You know where we can find Boris?" I asked him.

"Your mama's house." That got a round of laughter from his fellow patrons.

"Good one, Joe!" said Bulldog, clapping.

"Last chance, gentlemen! When was the last time a woman gave you three hundred bucks?"

"Last time I fucked your mama," Joe retorted.

"That's real classy," Shea said, strolling up to him. "Last time I saw your mama, she was licking my pussy. I guess your father didn't interest her no more."

"Fucking dyke!" His face turned the color of a rotten tomato. He threw his drink at her. She popped him in his face with a quick jab. The back of his head smacked the jukebox like a gunshot. He collapsed to the floor, blood trickling down his face.

In the span of a heartbeat, the stale air in the bar crackled with anger. Men at both ends of the room jumped from their seats and converged on us.

I blocked the punch from one man and drove the heel of my palm into his nose. A second attacker swung a chair. I dodged left, feeling the breeze as it brushed my ear. My hand caught the chair, ripping it from his grasp, and I brought it down on his head.

Bulldog reached beneath the bar. I drew my Ruger before she could pull out whatever was under there. "Drop it! Now!" I demanded.

I heard the resonant clunk of a baseball bat hitting the floor.

Another man rushed at me from the side but stopped short when I glared at him. He held up his hands and took a step back.

"Get out of my bar," growled Bulldog.

"Tell us what we want to know, and we will oblige," I replied.

"We don't know where Boris is, all right? No one does."

"Fucking pigs," grumbled the guy Shea had punched. The other combatants were picking themselves up and returning to their duly appointed booze.

"Come on. Let's blow this joint. These people don't know shit." Shea grabbed a bar rag and held it to her bleeding nose, wincing when she pressed it to her face. Somebody must have gotten in a lucky punch, but from the looks of things, she'd had three guys to contend with. "The smell of bullshit and cheap beer's turning my stomach."

I tried to think of a clever parting remark to tell Bulldog off but drew a blank. Instead, Shea and I backed out without another word.

My phone rang. The caller ID revealed it was Byrd. "Yo, man, what's up?"

"I tracked down Hancock. He's working in the sales office of an equipment rental place."

"You there now?"

"Yeah, parked in the CVS lot next door. You want me to go in and press him on his bogus alibi?"

"Stay put. We'll be there shortly."

I hung up and turned to Shea, who still held the rag to her nose. "You okay to ride?"

"I'll manage. Just wanna get the hell outta here."

"Good. Byrd tracked down Hancock."

35

Hancock did not look happy to see the three of us crowding into his cozy equipment rental office. "I told you everything I know. Why can't you leave me and my family alone?"

Shea plopped her butt on his desk, glaring at him with her arms crossed. "Seems there's a discrepancy in your story, dude."

"What are you talking about?" From the look on his face, I thought he might bolt. I nodded at Byrd, and he blocked the door.

"Your alibi is bullshit," I said.

"Do you own a gun?" Shea pressed.

"No, I don't own a gun. I hate guns."

I glared at him. "Then where the hell were you that night?"

"I told you, my family and I went to the movies!"

"Two days *after* James Fitzgerald was murdered. We checked your bank records."

"You went into my bank records? What gives you the right?"

I tapped my badge. "A man was murdered, and a woman has been framed. No more lies, Mr. Hancock. Where were you the night of the murder?"

"None of your business."

"I beg to differ. Right now, you're our prime suspect. You had means, opportunity, and a helluva motive. So if it wasn't you, then you need to prove where you were."

"I could call my lawyer."

"And I can call *Phoenix Living*. They'd love to do a front-page story about the man who took revenge against his daughter's rapist. You'd still go to prison, but at least you'd have the support of the reading public as an avenging father."

His tough-guy act folded. "Look, I...I was at an AA meeting. Court-ordered."

"Can you prove it?"

"It's Alcoholics Anonymous. Emphasis on anonymous."

"How does the court know you went?"

He reached into his pocket and pulled out an aluminum coin. I examined it. The AA emblem appeared on one side with "60 Days" embossed in the middle. On the back was printed the Serenity Prayer.

"Doesn't prove anything," Shea said. "I have lotsa friends in recovery. You can buy one of these for less than a buck at the Sobriety Bookstore on Seventh Street."

"I also had the chairs at the meetings sign a sheet. After thirty days, I turned it over to the drug court clerk."

"You have a copy?"

He pulled out his phone, tapped the screen a few times, and held it out to me. An image of a document was on the screen. I zoomed in. The sheet had a list of signatures with dates and times and locations of meetings attended.

The night of the murder, he attended two meetings. One at eight p.m. in Central Phoenix and another at nine thirty p.m. in Glendale. According to the ME's report, Fitzgerald was killed sometime between nine and ten o'clock that night. Assuming the sign-in sheet was legit, Hancock would have either been at the meeting in the west valley or traveling to it. The complete other side of town.

"Can you forward a copy of that to me?" I gave him my business card again.

He snatched his phone out of my hand and tapped on the screen. His phone made a whooshing sound. Ten seconds later, my phone dinged. I forwarded the image to Becca to look into.

"Before you quit drinking, you ever hang out at the Stone Horse Pub?" I asked.

"This really is beyond the pale. I proved I was nowhere near Scottsdale when that piece of shit was killed. I don't need to answer any more questions."

"You lied once," replied Byrd. "Your credibility is shot."

"Just answer the damn question," insisted Shea.

"Yeah, I've been there once or twice. So what? It's not a crime."

"Is that where you met Alexei Garnov? Sometimes goes by Boris?" I asked.

"Garnov? I don't know anyone named Garnov."

"Come on," said Shea. "Russian accent. A regular at the Stone Horse. What I hear, he likes to tell tales when he drinks. He was heard bragging he killed Fitzgerald. Maybe you hired him. "

There was no recognition in his eyes. "I don't know anyone with a Russian accent. I didn't kill that goddamn rapist, nor did I pay someone to do it for me. I'm just glad someone did so no one else has to endure what my daughter did. Now get the hell out of my office."

"Gladly," I said.

"And if you harass me any more, I am calling my lawyer and suing you for harassment. How do you think *Phoenix Living* will write that headline? Cops harass father of rape victim."

"Cops?" I smirked. "No one said we were cops."

His jaw dropped, and his face flushed red. "Then who the hell are you?"

"Don't worry. If this thing about the AA meetings checks out, you won't see us again," I promised.

We stepped out into the parking lot, where tractors, lawn equipment, and hydraulic pumps were waiting to be rented.

"I was so sure it was him," said Byrd.

"I'm still not convinced it wasn't," replied Shea.

"I don't know much about these sign-off sheets," I added, "but Becca will let me know what she thinks."

My phone dinged. "That's probably her."

I unlocked my phone. I had a message. *Back off or you die.* It wasn't from Becca but from an unknown caller ID.

I glanced around the CVS and equipment rental parking lots. No sign of a green car.

"We seem to have ruffled some feathers." I showed them the text.

"Any idea who it's from?" asked Byrd.

"Not a clue. From what I've learned from Becca, a text message can be sent via an SMS service and completely anonymized."

Byrd hooked a thumb at the rental office. "You don't think it's Hancock, do you?"

I looked toward the office. "I wouldn't rule out the possibility, but my gut tells me no."

"Then who?" asked Shea. "Someone working for Volkov? This Garnov dude?"

"Quite possibly. First the drive-by, then the green Nova tailing us, now this. The question is, what do we do about it?"

"Rally the troops and go into lockdown," Shea replied.

I raised an eyebrow. "Meaning?"

"I grew up around my father's motorcycle club. Whenever the shit really hit the fan, such as a war with a rival club, they gathered everyone together at the clubhouse. Members, old ladies, and kids. Kept everyone protected until the threat could be neutralized. We've done that once or twice with the Sisterhood, too, as needed."

I thought about it. We weren't a motorcycle club, and we didn't have a clubhouse, but we did have the Bunker.

"You're both welcome to stay at my place. Safer than staying at a motel."

"Thanks for the offer," replied Byrd, "but I should be all right at my place."

I nodded. "Suit yourself, but watch your back. And keep your eyes peeled for a green Chevy Nova."

"You want me to get members of the Sisterhood back down here?" asked Shea. "A little extra firepower."

"I'd rather not turn my neighborhood into a war zone."

Concern hardened Shea's face. "Whoever sent that text may plan to do just that, whether you want it or not."

"Let's hold off for now." I turned to Byrd. "Meet back at my place tomorrow morning at eight."

"Tomorrow's Saturday, Jinxie."

"Yes, and we only have till Tuesday to either get the charges against Pearson dropped or get her back in custody."

Byrd nodded and gave me a half hug and a pat on the back. "For my cut of that sixty grand, I'll be there."

Shea followed me to the Willo District. The streets were clogged with afternoon rush hour traffic, which always seemed worse on Fridays. A block from my neighborhood, I pulled through a Culver's for a couple of butter burgers and vanilla malt shakes.

When we finally pulled into my driveway, the pockmarked window reminded me I hadn't called my brother, Jake, about repairing the damage. The Lexan had held up to the bullets from the drive-by but wouldn't take much more abuse.

Shea stared at the front of my house. "If Freddie Colton didn't do this? Who did?"

"Probably one of his buddies."

Diana greeted us when we walked in the door, nearly knocking the tray with the milkshakes out of my hand.

"Such a sweet baby," Shea cooed. I couldn't help smiling. Anyone who got along with my dog was okay in my book. And even with her face busted up from the bar brawl earlier, she looked sexy as hell.

We settled into the kitchen and dug into dinner.

"Tell me something," I said. "If the Athena Sisterhood is so gung-ho on protecting women, how come y'all were at Naughty's?"

"We weren't all there—just those of us who are into women. 'Course, if we'd known the club was owned by the Volkovs, we woulda taken our business elsewhere."

"Makes sense."

She hooked a thumb in the direction of the living room. "I notice you have a lot of comic books stuff. Movie posters, dolls..."

"Action figures, not dolls. But yeah, I'm kinda into the whole superheroes thing. You?"

"Not so much. You go to those conventions where people dress up in costumes?"

Embarrassment warmed my face. "Yeah."

"You dress up?"

"It's called cosplay."

"You're avoiding the question."

"Because you think it's stupid. I can see it in your eyes."

"Hey, we all have our own kink. I was curious. No judgment."

"I cosplay as Wonder Woman. Sometimes as Xena. I even won an award last year."

"That spiky thing on the table in the living room? Impressive. I'd like to see you in costume sometime."

I took a deep breath and tried to let go of my embarrassment. "I'll be at San Diego Comicon in July. Maybe you can come along."

"Maybe."

"Now it's my turn to ask questions."

"Shoot."

"How come your niece lives with you? The background check didn't say."

"Annie moved in with me after my sister and her old man

were killed." Her voice took on a somber tone. I was curious to learn more but didn't want to pry.

"Shit, I'm sorry. Must be tough."

"Never saw myself as the mommy type. But somehow it's working. The Sisterhood's helped a lot. They're like an extended family of aunties. Annie's staying with my friend Whiplash while I'm down here."

"How old's Annie?"

"Eleven."

"Almost a teenager."

Shea chuckled. "Yeah, so not looking forward to it. I was a hellion at that age."

"Me too."

An awkward silence settled in the room. I found myself endlessly fascinated with this hardcore biker woman. Strange considering two days earlier, we were trying to beat each other's brains out.

"Well, I better see about getting these windows fixed." I wiped the grease from my face.

"I need to check in with Annie. Make sure she's doing her homework."

Shea disappeared into the guest bedroom, while I dialed Jake's number.

"Wow, who is this?" Jake asked in a snarky tone.

"Very funny."

"Is this my long-lost sister? The one who hasn't shown up to Sunday brunch in forever?"

"All right. You made your point. I need to hire you to do some repair work on my house."

"Which one?"

"Conor's place."

"The Bunker? Why?"

"Someone thought it would be funny to redecorate the front of my house with bullets."

"You're kidding, right?"

"I need you to replace one of the Lexan windows and patch the holes in the brick."

"You're serious. Geez, Jinxie. What the hell are you into?"

"Just the usual. Tracking down somebody that doesn't want to be found. Not something you have to worry about." I hoped, anyway.

"I can stop by tomorrow morning and take a look."

"Thanks, bro."

"Provided you show up Sunday to Mom and Dad's."

Sunday brunch was a big deal at my folks' house and had been since we were kids. Last December, I'd missed once and got hit with major Catholic guilt from my mother. After I lost Conor, my attendance grew more sporadic until they stopped asking about me. But I knew my family. Just because they weren't guilt tripping me didn't mean they weren't concerned.

My mother especially was a worrier. My job as a bounty hunter didn't help.

"I'll try to get over there Sunday."

"Do or do not, there is no try," said Jake in a very poor Yoda voice that sounded more like Pee-wee Herman.

"I'll be there. Okay? Now will you fix the damage to my house?"

"I'll be there." I hung up.

Shea and I spent the next few hours going over all of the documentation we had, looking for our next lead. Time was running short. All we had were bits and pieces, none of which connected into solid proof that someone other than Indigo had killed Fitzgerald.

36

The doorbell rang at six o'clock. Diana rushed off the bed to the living room, barking excitedly.

I grabbed my phone from the nightstand and pulled up the security video feed for the front door. It was Jake, thank goodness, and not some eastern European mobster. Then again, assassins didn't usually ring the doorbell.

I pulled on a bathrobe and shuffled out of my room but not before Jake rang another couple of times and pounded on the door for good measure.

"Jesus Christ! I'm coming!" I shouted.

"Who is that?" asked Shea, coming out of the guest room in a black T-shirt and boxers. Her short spiky hair was flattened on the left side. My heart fluttered, and my face warmed at the sight of her. Even with her hair a mess, something about her made my pulse race. "It's my brother. Sorry to wake you."

I hustled into the living room. "Morning," I mumbled when I opened the door.

"Shit." Jake stared at me like I was something the dog threw up. It had been months since he'd seen me. "You look like crap.

You're nothing but skin and bones. And your face is all bruised. What happened to you?"

"Gee, thanks. You sure know how to make a girl feel pretty."

Regret crossed his face. He gave me a gentle hug instead of his usual hearty embrace, as if he thought I'd break. "I'm worried about you, baby sister."

I pulled back, and our eyes met. "I know. I'm doing better than I was. Working again, for starters."

He glanced at the snow flurry of pockmarks on my front window. "I can see that. You expecting whoever did this to return anytime soon?"

"No."

"Whose motorcycle's in the carport?"

"Mine." Shea stepped into the room, her hair once again perfect. Hubba hubba.

"Jake Ballou," said my brother, shaking her hand. "Pleasure to meet you. You a bounty hunter like my sister?"

"Shea Stevens. Jinx is helping a friend of mine out with a...a case."

"A member of Shea's biker club is being framed by Scottsdale PD," I explained. "I'm working as a PI to get the charges dropped against her."

Jake shook his head. "Looks like things are getting pretty crazy."

"Nothing I can't handle. When can you do the repairs?"

"Depends. Are we talking cash or labor?"

I occasionally helped him renovate homes he planned to flip when work was slow for me.

"Cash this time. Family rates, right?"

"Fine. I'll put together an estimate. Let me go outside and assess the damage." He stepped out the front door.

Shea and I retreated to the kitchen, where I poured each of us some coffee. Before sitting down at the table, I looked through the pantry. "Don't have much in the way of food. Cold cereal, okay?"

"It's fine."

I opened the fridge and remembered the milk was sour. "No milk, though. Sorry. I suppose we could go out."

"I got a better idea. Tell me where the nearest supermarket is. I'll get some groceries and make us some breakfast. It's the least I can do for all the trouble we've been putting you through."

"You cook?" I asked a little too earnestly.

Shea shrugged. "Not like gourmet. But I can do a decent breakfast. Whaddya like? Bacon, eggs, French toast, waffles? I can even do an omelet if you want."

"All of that sounds good. Whatever you feel like making." *But what I really want to eat is you.* I hoped I wasn't drooling. "There's a Safeway on McDowell just past Third Street. North side of the road."

After she finished her coffee, she pulled on her shades, boots, and biker vest. "Be back in a jiffy."

Moments after she roared off on her motorcycle, Jake stepped inside. "She's cute. You two...uh..."

Heat poured into my face. "We're just...working together." I swallowed hard.

A devilish grin curled the corner of his mouth. "Uh-huh. Right. I know things didn't work out with that prison guard, but I'm not blind. I can see you two have the hots for each other."

"You think she has the hots for me?" I was at once terrified and elated.

"Duh. Are you kidding?"

I poured him a cup of coffee as he sat down at the kitchen table, totaling his estimate. "How are things between you and Rodeo?" I asked. "Will we be hearing wedding bells anytime soon?"

"Geez, you sound like Mom."

"So, spill. Since he started working for Deez's crew, I don't seem him around very much."

"Things are good. Not talking about wedding bells, but he's helped me work through a lot of my...issues."

"Like holding hands in public?" I asked.

Now it was his turn to blush. "Among other things. That stunt you pulled last Christmas in the restaurant was the push I needed. Embarrassing as it was."

"Glad I could help."

He handed me the estimate, and I gasped. "What about the family discount?"

"Babe, that is with the family discount. It'd be thirty percent more otherwise."

It wouldn't have been a problem if I didn't have that damn insurance adjuster demanding I return Conor's life insurance money. I might be all right if we got paid on the Pearson job, but even that wasn't a sure thing.

"Okay," I said between gritted teeth. "When can you start?"

"I'll check with my suppliers to see if they have this grade of polycarbonate in stock. If so, I can get started this afternoon."

I hugged him. "Thanks, bro. I appreciate it."

"I better see your scrawny ass on Sunday. I'm telling Mom you'll be there. You don't show, she will be crushed." From the look in his eyes, I knew he meant it.

"You're as good at this Catholic guilt shit as Mom."

"I learn from the best. See ya later this afternoon."

"If I'm not here, you have a key and the security codes, right?"

"I do."

Shea showed up twenty minutes later with bags of groceries, including eggs, cheese, milk, and vegetables that didn't come out of a can. While she was whipping up something delicious, my phone rang. It was Becca this time.

"Hey, Becks. Whatcha got for me? You find Garnov?"

"Still nothing on this mystery man. But I have learned some interesting tidbits about the not-so-dearly-departed Brother James Fitzgerald. Turns out he had put down a deposit on a condo along the Central Corridor. One of those fancy high-rises."

"Are you serious? Those places are fucking expensive. Like

mid six figures. How could he afford that? Especially since he and Wilkes were parting ways."

"I found an alternative email address he was using. According to *Publishers Weekly*, he signed a seven-figure deal with Little, Brown a couple months ago."

"Who's Lil Brown? A rapper?"

"Little, Brown. A major book publisher. He was writing a nonfiction book on his experiences with the Evangelical Light of the Messiah Church. He also exchanged emails with an Olivia Sullivan at *Phoenix Living* about an interview."

"A tell-all book?"

"Looks like it. Not sure what all he was going to tell that was so scandalous. That's what I'm trying to find. So far, I haven't been able to track down any details."

"How did the cops not know about this?"

"The money from the publisher was wired to an account in Turks and Caicos. I just happened to stumble on it when I came across the other email address. Maybe once the cops found Pearson's DNA link, they stopped looking elsewhere."

"If Wilkes knew about this book deal, that might be motive to take out Fitzgerald. But I don't think he could have done it alone. Any evidence that Wilkes hired a hit man?" I started wondering about Alexei Garnov.

"I've looked into it but haven't found anything definitive yet. Wilkes's finances are a maze of shell corporations. Lots of money coming in from extreme right-wing organizations and individual donors, then getting shuffled around. The money trail is so convoluted, it makes my head spin."

"Keep looking. We need some solid evidence, and fast."

"Will do. Talk to you soon."

Shea brought a couple of plates to the table, each loaded with a beautiful omelet and two strips of perfectly crisp bacon. "Find out anything?"

"Fitzgerald was writing a tell-all memoir about Wilkes and his little church of hate. He's been talking to a reporter, Olivia

Sullivan at *Phoenix Living*. I have a feeling she's getting ready to write an exposé on Wilkes. I want to talk to her about this conflict between Fitzgerald and Wilkes."

Becca had texted me Sullivan's email address. I sent a message to Sullivan telling her I knew she was writing an article on Fitzgerald and that I, as an investigator looking into the murder, had information she might want to include. I stipulated I would only give it to her in person and it had to be today. Time was running out to resolve this case one way or another.

37

———

By the time Byrd arrived at eight o'clock, I'd received a response from Sullivan asking to meet at the *Phoenix Living* office downtown.

Despite its battered appearance, I opted to drive the Charger over the Gray Ghost. I had no reason to believe that whoever was chasing us before wouldn't do so again. I invited Shea to ride along with Byrd and me, under the premise of saving gas. Really, I just wanted to be closer to her.

"Thanks, but I'd rather follow on my bike. Not a big fan of riding in cages."

I tried to hide my disappointment, but it was probably for the better. I needed to focus on the task at hand. Having my head in a pink cloud over my newfound romance with Conor was what got Deez shot so many years ago. I didn't want history to repeat itself.

We drove down Central Avenue to the Sun Glow Building and parked in the underground garage. We geared up and hit the elevator. I didn't think we'd be ambushed, but I wanted to send a message that we meant business.

It wasn't the first time I had visited *Phoenix Living*. A year earlier, I had confronted Brian Hensley, one of their senior reporters, on a hit piece he'd done on me, outing me to their readers and getting me fired in the process. The problems didn't end there.

We took the elevator to the seventh floor. The glass doors to *Phoenix Living*'s office were locked, as Sullivan had told me they would be since it was Saturday. *Phoenix Living* was a weekly paper. I pressed the call button on a nearby intercom.

"Can I help you?" asked a staticky female voice.

"Jinx Ballou to see Olivia Sullivan."

"Be right there."

A moment later, a woman in her midforties wearing a sleeveless dress pressed a button to release the lock. Her lavender chalcedony earrings matched a pendant that hung from a gold chain around her neck. Sullivan had a tan face and a smart, above-the-shoulder haircut.

The lobby's style was understated elegance. The name of the paper was mounted in brass letters on the wall behind the receptionist's desk. A stack of the latest edition stood on a small table surrounded by comfortable armchairs.

"Jinx Ballou." Her eyes narrowed. "The transgender bounty hunter, right? I thought the name sounded familiar when you called."

"And you're Olivia Sullivan. Cisgender reporter. Now that we've established professions and gender identities..."

"Let's speak in my office, shall we?"

She led us down the hall, grabbed an extra chair from a conference room, and pulled it into her office. She took a seat behind her cluttered desk. The three of us sat down in front.

"So, Ms. Ballou. You're the one Jim Hensley wrote that story on. Right before he turned up dead on your doorstep."

"Milo Volkov killed Hensley. Probably pissed about the exposé Hensley did on his sex trafficking organization."

"Why did Volkov dump Brian's body on your front porch? Wrapped up in plastic like a sack of garbage."

My face flushed with heat. "Volkov was a psychotic stalker. He developed a twisted obsession with me thanks to Hensley's article. I wanted nothing to do with the sick fuck. And when push came to shove, I killed Volkov and several of his men. Think of it as avenging Hensley's death despite him getting me fired. You're welcome."

We held each other's gaze for what felt like an eternity. I hadn't anticipated getting blindsided like this, but I wasn't going to put up with the bullshit.

"Very well," Sullivan said at last, taking out a notebook and pen. "You have information about the James Fitzgerald murder. How'd you know I was working on a story about him?"

"I'm a bounty hunter, remember? Finding out information is my job."

"And what information can you tell me about Fitzgerald's murder?"

"The woman charged with the homicide is being framed. I suspect Fitzgerald's boss, Michael Wilkes, hired someone to kill him."

She leaned back in her chair, rotating slightly from side to side, twirling a pen in her hand. "Interesting. You have evidence to back up this theory?"

"Fitzgerald was moving out and leaving the cult they call a church. He also signed a major book deal with a whopper of an advance. A tell-all exposé. Clearly, Fitzgerald and Wilkes had a major split over something explosive. Something big enough to have him killed over. I was hoping you could tell us what it is."

Her eyes registered a hit, but she quickly regained her composure. "So you're here looking for answers, not providing them."

"We're looking to free a woman being framed for murdering that scumbag rapist," said Shea.

"But you're a bounty hunter," Sullivan said. "Did someone jump bail?"

"I'm also a licensed private detective. The defendant's attorney hired me to look into the case."

She studied us for a moment. "Since it comes out Thursday,

anyway, I might as well tell you. Wilkes is gay. Fitzgerald caught him in bed with a man hired from PoolBoy, an online male escort service. Thus the rift."

Shea snorted. "Fitzgerald raped a teenage girl but got his panties in a wad when he found out his boss is gay? That's one fucked-up religion."

Byrd shot Shea a look. "Don't paint all of Christianity with the same brush."

"Fitzgerald didn't just rape the Hancock girl," continued Sullivan. "Since his death, several girls have come forth alleging they were assaulted by Fitzgerald."

"Did Wilkes know about Fitzgerald's book deal?" I asked Sullivan, trying to get the conversation back on track.

"Possibly. I don't know."

"You might want to hold off on publishing that story, then."

"Why?"

"In the past week, someone has shot up my house. A green Chevy Nova has been tailing us. And yesterday, someone sent a text threatening to kill me if I didn't back off. Clearly, someone doesn't want us to expose the truth. Whoever killed Fitzgerald may go after you as well."

Sullivan shrugged. "We get threats all the time here at *Phoenix Living*. I think we can handle whatever Wilkes is capable of."

"I'm sure Brian Hensley thought the same thing about Volkov."

"We suspect Wilkes may have connections with Sergei Volkov's organization," Byrd said.

"Sergei Volkov?" Sullivan looked from Byrd to me. "Milo's brother?"

"Sergei runs the motel where Fitzgerald was killed, along with the strip club next door. We've talked to a woman who used to dance at the club. He doesn't like people interfering with his business."

Sullivan wrote furiously. "The dancer's name?"

I shook my head. "Confidential. Her safety's at risk if Sergei's people find out."

"So you think Wilkes hired one of Volkov's people to kill Fitzgerald? Any evidence to back this up?"

"Not yet. A Russian named Alexei Garnov was heard bragging about killing Fitzgerald at a Phoenix bar."

"How does that connect back to Wilkes?"

My phone dinged with an incoming message from Becca, asking me to call her. I slipped it into my pocket. "Wilkes had motive. Sergei's people have the means and opportunity. I have one of my people looking for a solid connection between the two."

"When you find it, let me know. I'll put it in my article. Could be some good publicity for you."

"I'd prefer to remain an unnamed source, if it's all the same to you. Considering what happened the last time I was mentioned in a *Phoenix Living* article."

I turned to Shea and Byrd. "I think we're done here. Let's go."

While waiting for the elevator, I called Becca. "What'd you find?"

"Turns out Wilkes is a closeted gay man. Fitzgerald found out about it and decided to move out."

"So we learned from Olivia Sullivan. He was hiring escorts from PoolBoy."

"Not just PoolBoy. ManSlave, Indiscreet, and several other escort services. But there's more. He was banned from PoolBoy after Wilkes offered five grand to an escort to kill Fitzgerald."

"That's it! We got him! Good work, Becks."

"Not so fast. According to a forum on PoolBoy, the escort, who uses the nickname Rodman, declined the offer. I don't think he killed Fitzgerald."

"But if Wilkes tried with one guy, he probably tried with someone else and got results. Any luck finding Garnov?"

"No Garnovs. But there are approximately eight hundred people with the last name *Garinov* living in the valley."

"That's got to be it."

"Only one Boris Garinov. He's an orthodontist working in Sun City. Originally from St. Petersburg."

"Russia?"

"Florida, actually."

"Don't think he's our guy. The Garinov we're looking for is from Russia, lots of prison tats."

"There is an Andrei Garinov who's a Russian permanent resident working for...wait for it...wait for it..."

"Just tell me already."

"Naughty's Adult Entertainment in Scottsdale, Arizona."

"That's got to be our guy. Think you can find a financial transaction that shows Wilkes hired Garinov to kill Fitzgerald?"

"I've been looking but so far haven't seen one. No financial transactions between Wilkes and Garinov, nor between any of Wilkes's business entities and Volkov's. I've checked all US banks, PayPal, even several offshore banks. If there's a payment for a hit, it's hidden deep. Possibly using cryptocurrencies, but Wilkes doesn't strike me as the type."

I blew out a breath in frustration. "Keep looking. It's got to be there."

I hung up and turned to Byrd and Shea as the elevator doors opened. "Time to pay another visit to the Right Reverend Wilkes."

On the ride down to where we'd parked, I shared what I'd learned. I felt a certain satisfaction knowing we were finally connecting some dots.

The instant we stepped out of the elevator and into the parking garage, the air exploded with a deafening barrage of gunfire.

38

I glimpsed a couple of figures wearing yellow bandanas across the way, between a white Ford passenger van and a black Pontiac Grand Prix.

The three of us ducked behind a concrete pillar as the shots echoed through the parking garage. My ears were ringing from the deafening sounds.

I pulled my Ruger. Byrd and Shea both drew their weapons as well.

"Cover me," Shea shouted above the din. She dashed past a couple of cars.

I stepped out from behind the column and fired a few rounds at one of the gunmen. My shots went wide and hit the van next to him, shattering a window and mirror.

He turned toward me. I ducked. Chips of concrete exploded in my face as bullets hit the pillar.

Gunshots with a different pitch punched through the air. Shea was five cars down, apparently trying to outflank our assailants. Byrd had worked his way in the other direction, returning fire.

I pulled off another series of shots and hit the first gunman in the shoulder. He vanished from view, his screams adding to the ungodly noise.

The second gunman ducked out of view. I stepped from the safety of the pillar and cautiously duckwalked toward them. The driver's-side door on the Grand Prix opened. The second gunman reappeared and raised his weapon.

I pulled my trigger first, but the firing pin hit an empty chamber. A bullet screamed past my ear. I hit the magazine release on the Ruger to reload. Pain exploded in my chest before I could grab a replacement magazine.

The garage spun. I slammed into the ground on my side. More shots ripped through the air.

"*¡Hijo de puta!*" someone screamed.

I struggled to get up, trying to ignore my throbbing rib cage.

A vehicle roared to life. The Grand Prix loomed toward me. I rolled out of the way while more gunshots thundered through the garage. Glass shattered. Tires squealed. The Pontiac raced up the ramp toward the exit. More gunshots followed and then a deafening silence.

My body trembled with pain and shock. I reached to my chest and felt three hot lumps embedded in the fibers of my ballistic vest.

Byrd and Shea appeared above me, their faces flush and anxious. Byrd's hands were all over me, no doubt checking me for wounds.

"Anybody hit?" I squeaked out.

Shea burst into laughter. "Just you, Wonder Woman. You hurt?" She helped lift me to my feet.

Awkwardly, I fumbled with the Velcro straps on my vest. Shea reached over and helped pull it off my aching torso. I reached under my shirt. Damp. I pulled out my hand, expecting a stain of scarlet but found only sweat, not blood. "I...I think I'll live."

I tried to cock my jaw and jiggle my ear canal with my finger to stop the ringing from the gunfire. Didn't help.

"Thought we lost you for a second," Byrd said.

"I'm harder to kill than I look." I shuffled to where the Grand Prix had been parked. Bright-red blood stained the dirty white pavement littered with spent brass. "Looks like we got at least one of them."

"I hit one of them in the chest," said Byrd. "But he could've been wearing a vest."

"They're Latino." I glanced around looking for witnesses but saw no one. "One of them cursed in Spanish."

"They were Jaguars." Shea's eyes had a haunted look. "A drug gang."

"How do you know?"

"Yellow bandanas."

I nodded. "Why are they after us?"

"No idea." Shea squatted down and stared at the blood. "They used to run heroin and weed up in Cortes County. Worked with the Confederate Thunder back in the day. But then one of the Jaguars kidnapped my niece. It got...ugly. A lot of folks died including my sister and her old man. The few Jaguars that survived moved down to Phoenix."

"Maybe they're after you." Byrd pointed an accusatory finger at Shea. "That why the Nova's been following us?"

"I don't know how they'd know I was here." But there was guilt in Shea's expression.

"Anybody get the license plate on the Pontiac?" I asked after an awkward moment.

"I did." Byrd rattled it off.

"Good. I'll have Becca run the tags. It's time we have another talk with Wilkes. If the Jaguars come at us again, we'll deal with them."

I sent a text to Becca, then glanced around looking for security cameras but didn't see any. "Let's get out of here before the cops show up."

We were driving north on Central when a couple of police cruisers with lights and sirens raced past us, heading toward the Sun Glow Building.

My phone dinged. I handed it to Byrd.

"Becca says the plate is from a silver Mercedes S55 AMG belonging to Sandra Levy," he said while I drove east on the I-10. "She's a fifty-two-year-old investment banker."

"The car we saw was a black Pontiac. You sure you got the plate number right?" I asked him.

"Absolutely. Becca says Ms. Levy reported her plate stolen yesterday while parked in the parking garage at Scottsdale Fashion Park."

"Scottsdale, again. Are the Jaguars and Volkov's organization working together?"

"No idea." He let out a harsh breath. "Speaking of working together, I don't like working with Shea."

"Why? Because she insulted your religious beliefs?" I asked.

"Not just that. After she and her biker gang refused to surrender Pearson, I had Deez do a little more digging. A few years ago, the Athena Sisterhood were suspected of dealing drugs and burning down several buildings including a bar popular with the Confederate Thunder. Now these Latinx gangbangers show up. And surprise, surprise, this chick has a history with them too. This is not the job I signed up for, Jinx. Not by a long shot."

I thought about it. Part of what drew me to Shea was her sexy bad girl biker image. "I hear what you're saying. Hopefully, we can get a confession from Wilkes, clear Pearson, and somehow get paid. You'll never have to lay eyes on her again."

Byrd didn't say anything, but the air between us rippled with tension. He wasn't wrong. The situation was getting way out of hand.

Thirty minutes later, we pulled up in front of Wilkes's house. When we got out, I handed Shea a walkie-talkie. "Go around to the rear of the house in case this little turd blossom decides to sneak out the back door."

"You got it, boss." She gave me a two-fingered salute. "Won't be hard to catch if he does. He moves kinda slow."

I turned to Byrd. "Keep an eye on the garage door. Don't need him driving away either."

He shot darts at Shea with his eyes as she walked away, then turned on his walkie-talkie. "Roger that."

I strode up to the front door and waited for everyone to get into position. "Y'all ready?" I asked into the walkie-talkie.

"Back door ready," replied Shea.

"Garage door ready," said Byrd.

"Showtime, kiddos." I rang the doorbell. When there was no response after a couple of minutes, I rang it repeatedly until I heard a shuffling on the other side.

The speakeasy grille in the door opened with a familiar face peering out. "What do you want now?"

"We need to talk, Wilkes."

"I'm not interested." The speakeasy grille snapped shut.

"You can talk to us," I shouted loud enough for him to hear me through the door, "or you can explain to the police why you hired someone to kill Fitzgerald."

"I...I don't know what you're talking about" came his muffled reply.

"It's why you got banned from the PoolBoy escort service, isn't it? You really think you could keep that secret? What are the police going to say when we tell them? Or maybe *Phoenix Living*? I'm sure they'd love to do a story on you."

"Someone must have stolen my credit card information."

"Is that what you're going to tell your Christian Coalition donors? You think they'll believe you? We have your posts on PoolBoy's forum. Should make for interesting reading."

"You wouldn't."

"Exposing a purveyor of homophobic hate as a closeted hypocrite? In a heartbeat."

"What do you want?"

"I want inside to talk."

"I don't believe you. I think you're here to kill me."

"If I wanted to do that, tempting as it may be, you'd already be dead. I'm here as a courtesy."

The dead bolt slid free with a snick. The door opened. "Where's your cohorts?"

"Coming." I keyed the walkie. "Everyone please report to the front door. Over."

I stuck my foot in the doorframe, making sure he didn't try to shut it on me again. Byrd and Shea arrived momentarily.

Wilkes led us into the kitchen. Swirling reflections of light from the backyard pool gleamed through the French doors, painting patterns on the ceiling. He slumped into a chair. The three of us stood around him.

I pulled out my phone and set the audio memo app to record. "You hired someone to kill Brother James, didn't you?"

"Yes."

"Why?" asked Shea.

"He...he found out I...I have an affliction."

"An affliction?" I asked. "What kind of affliction?"

"Sexual attraction to men."

"Being gay isn't an affliction, you twit," replied Shea.

Wilkes shook his finger at her. "It's an abomination. It says so in the Bible. You! I can tell you're a homosexual. Short hair, dressed like a man. The penalty for this evil is death and everlasting fire."

Shea grabbed him by the collar and drew back to punch him, but Byrd held her arm. "No."

"You think your God's going to forgive you for killing Brother James?" I asked. "Or don't the rules apply to you?"

"I...I didn't kill him."

"No," said Byrd. "You hired someone else to do it. Blood's on your hands. The sin is the same. So is the punishment."

"The guy I tried to hire, he refused. Said he doesn't do that kind of thing."

"But you hired someone else," I pressed. "A Russian named Andrei Garinov."

"No, no, I didn't. I repented of my sinful anger, and God has forgiven my transgressions out of his ever-flowing mercy."

"He's lying," Shea replied.

"Brother James and I came to an agreement. He was moving out. I agreed not to tell anyone about him raping those girls if he didn't tell anyone about my...my affliction."

"Affliction, my ass." Shea popped him in the face before I could stop her.

39

"You protected a rapist so your holier-than-thou sponsors would keep sending in the Benjamins," Shea screamed while she pummeled Wilkes.

He collapsed on the floor, pleading for Shea to stop and shielding his face from further blows.

Byrd pulled her off him and tossed her across the room. "Stay off him. We may not like the things he preaches, but that don't give us the right to physically assault the man."

"He's a fucking murderer, a bigot, and a liar," Shea growled. "He deserves a lot more than a beatdown. He deserves to be dragged behind a motorcycle until he's nothing but roadkill."

"Enough, you two!" I stepped between them. "Shea, back off. This isn't the way we do things."

Fire burned in her eyes. I knew that look and felt it too. The urge to kill.

I looked down at the pathetic little man while Byrd helped him back into his chair.

"I didn't have Brother James killed," Wilkes sobbed. "It was wrong of me to try, but I didn't. I swear upon the Holy Scriptures."

"For once, I think he's telling the truth," I said.

"Seriously?" Shea scoffed.

"Did you hire anyone to come after us?" I asked him.

He wiped his face with a tissue. "No, I did not."

"He's lying, Jinx. Let's just do what we came to do."

"We came to get the truth. Not kill a man, no matter how despicable or pathetic he is."

"You think we're going to get the truth out of him?" Shea kicked his chair leg. He bellowed, cowering and covering his head with his arms.

"Shea, stop."

I tried to think. This was all going off the rails. I had no reason to believe Wilkes about not hiring Garinov. But my gut told me he was telling the truth.

"I really should let her kill you," I said.

"No. Please, God, save me! I am your good and faithful—"

"Shut the fuck up!" I said. "And listen."

He shut up. His entire body trembled. I almost felt sorry for the little fuck. Almost.

"Who else would have killed Brother James?"

Wilkes looked at Shea. "That tranny Negro—"

"Wrong answer." Shea drew her Glock.

"No, please!" Wilkes wailed.

I put my hand on her gun and pushed it away. "Don't."

"Who else?" Shea shouted at him.

"I...I don't know who else. We get lots of death threats."

I stared at him. It would be so easy to look the other way and let Shea end his miserable life. For all the anguish that assholes like him had caused marginalized people. Encouraging rape, assault, and suicides. Wouldn't the world be a better place without him? But was it worth risking my own freedom?

"We're not going to get any more answers out of him." I locked eyes with Shea. "And we're not going to hurt him."

Shea holstered her pistol with a grunt. "This is such bullshit."

"If anyone asks, we were never here. Got it, Wilkes?"

He nodded vigorously. "I promise."

"And one other thing," said Byrd, who pulled the guy up by his front collar before tossing him back into his chair. "Stop preaching that women should be raped and queer people should be killed."

"I have a mission to preach the gospel."

Byrd leaned down into his face. "You do and we share everything with the press and the police. Your male escorts, your attempts to hire a hit man, everything. We will ruin you. All your donations will dry up when they discover what a hypocritical little cockroach you are. From now on, you preach only love, unity, and forgiveness like Jesus did. Understand?"

"I have the right to free speech," he said in a shaky voice with all the self-righteousness he could muster.

"So do we," I replied. "So does *Phoenix Living*."

His face clenched as if struggling with tremendous pain. "Fine. I will...tone things down a bit."

"See that you do." I looked at Shea and Byrd. "We're done here."

"You're going to let this piece of shit live?" Shea looked aghast.

"For now."

I led them out of the house.

The second I closed the front door, Shea turned on me. "That little shit weasel murdered his rapist buddy."

"Now listen here..." said Byrd.

I held up my hand to him and tossed him the keys to the Charger. "Go start the engine and get the AC going. Shea and I need to talk."

Byrd exchanged a tense glance with Shea then walked to the car.

"You and me, we want the same thing here," I told Shea. "I don't trust Wilkes any farther than I can throw him. But we need solid evidence to clear Indigo. And putting that asshole in the hospital, much less the morgue, won't accomplish that."

Shea blew out a harsh breath. "Maybe you're right."

I put a hand on her shoulder. Electricity crackled at the touch. From the look in her eyes, I thought she felt it too. I found myself falling into her gaze. Fear and excitement sizzled through me in equal measures. I wanted to feel her body close to mine.

"I need to know I can count on you, Shea."

"You...you can count on me." Her hand clasped mine.

It took every ounce of self-control I had not to kiss her.

I called Becca and asked her to look into the Jaguars street gang and also told her about Fitzgerald's other rape victims. This job was going to cost me a lot with all the skip tracing she was doing. I hoped I got paid somehow, which was looking less and less likely.

While I drove home, Byrd kept his eyes peeled for tails, in case the Jaguars decided on a rematch. But so far, there were no signs they were following us.

"I'm thinking we should handle this case just the two of us," said Byrd.

"Meaning without Shea."

"She just...she's not a professional. You saw what happened with Wilkes. That can land us all in hot water."

I pulled onto the Loop 202 headed to downtown Phoenix. "She knows she stepped over the line. Shouldn't be a problem going forward."

"Why even have her along? What does she contribute?"

"She's an extra set of eyes for starters. And I didn't mind having her when we were ambushed at the Sun Glow Building."

"For all we know, she's the reason we were ambushed."

On the ramp where the Loop 202 merged onto the I-10, an asshole trucker refused to let me over. I tried to get ahead of him, but he sped up. I slowed to get behind him, but he stayed in my way.

"Your objection has been duly noted, but I want her on the

team. That was the agreement. That at least one member of the Athena Sisterhood would work with us to locate Fitzgerald's killer."

"We should've just found some other way to bring in Pearson. It ain't right to let a fugitive suspect evade custody and then work with the people protecting her."

I forced my way in front of the semi and was rewarded with a long blast from his air horn. *Right back atcha, buddy!*

"Byrd, I appreciate what you're saying, but I'm in charge of the team. For now, she stays. If that doesn't work with you, you're welcome to leave."

Byrd didn't reply, but I felt his anger coming off him in waves.

I turned on my stereo and hit one of the playlists without looking. Lily Allen's "Fuck You" started playing. I stabbed at the Next Song button, worried that Byrd would think I was trying to tell him off. Tegan and Sara's "Goodbye, Goodbye" cranked up. *Next!* The Pink Trinkets' lead singer Wicked burst into a repetitive chant of "You so stupid! You so stupid!" at the beginning of the title song of their *Orange, You Stupid* album. I turned off the stereo.

"Sorry," I mumbled.

He didn't say anything until I exited onto Seventh Street. "You sleeping with her?"

"What? No!"

"Jinx, don't lie to me. I see how you look at each other."

"I'm not lying, Byrd, and I don't appreciate the accusation. Sure, maybe she's...she's interesting."

"Interesting...uh-huh. Yeah."

I pulled into a Filiberto's drive-through. Shea pulled through behind us on her motorcycle.

"You want anything?" I asked. "My treat."

Byrd shrugged. I ordered a few of their torpedo-sized burros, anyway, in case he changed his mind.

When I got to the window, I asked if Shea had put in an order. A teenage gal with a thick ponytail and a cheerful voice assured me she had. I paid for both orders. When the girl handed me the bag of food, I leaned out the window and shouted to Shea that I had her order. Shea responded with a thumbs-up.

As we drove the final half mile to my house, the aroma of meat and spices turned my hunger into a deep primal need so strong the saliva glands in my mouth ached.

By the time we got inside, I grabbed a burro and dug into it without bothering with a plate. Byrd reached into the cabinet and distributed plates and napkins, then took one of the burros and some chips and salsa for himself.

The burn of the spicy meat was equal parts pleasure and pain. The more it burned, the faster I ate with the ferocity of a piranha. I'd inhaled two full burros before I slowed down enough to grab us some drinks from the fridge.

40

———

When my ravenous hunger was sated, the fire lingering in my mouth, I grabbed my laptop. I ran a search, looking for links between Wilkes, the Volkov crime family, and the West Side Jaguars street gang, as they were officially known. Nothing definitive came up. The two organizations tended to stay in their own territory, with the West Side Jaguars' drug operation in the west valley, Volkov and his human trafficking ring in the east. No direct connections between Wilkes and either group.

Maybe the Jaguars' attack had nothing to do with Fitzgerald or Wilkes. Maybe Byrd was right in suggesting they were after Shea. I searched for news stories that showed connections between the Athena Sisterhood and the Jaguars. Even that was a bust.

Maybe I had arrested a bail-jumping member of the Jaguars without realizing his affiliation to the gang. Usually, something would have come up in the background check, unless the guy didn't have any priors. So many possibilities. Not so many answers.

"Goddamnit! It's gotta be here," I said, pushing away the

laptop. I took a long pull on a soda. I craved tequila, but after my last meltdown, I'd poured the last of it down the drain. I'd also tossed the last of my weed. I needed a clear head if I was going to work this shit out.

"Don't worry, Jinx. You'll figure it out," said Shea. "Sometimes when I'm working on a custom bike and it's not coming together, I focus on something else until inspiration strikes."

"Except we're running out of time. And I'm not building a motorcycle. I'm trying to solve a murder."

Shea shrugged. "I'm just saying, give your mind a break."

Byrd glanced at her, then at me. "Hate to say it, but Shea's right. You got to unplug."

I sat staring at the laptop, trying to let my mind go blank, using the meditation techniques my dad was always talking about.

"Don't fight the monkey mind, *chère*. Embrace it," he'd told me once. "It's part of the meditation process. We allow the junk into our consciousness. We acknowledge it. Only then do we let it go so more productive thoughts have room to flourish."

I still had no idea what he was talking about, but he was a psychologist, and I wasn't. I let the memory float away like a helium balloon.

Out of nowhere, I remembered Hardin telling me Detective Garza had been killed by a couple of gangbangers robbing a liquor store.

I pulled up a news story from a local TV station that included video from the liquor store's security footage. The anchor at the beginning of the video warned that some viewers might find the images disturbing. *No shit, Sherlock.*

I stared at the screen, my finger poised above the play button. Like a coked-out drummer, my heart pounded out a rapid rhythm in my chest.

Garza and I hadn't been all that close. For months, he was always flirting with me. Hell, he flirted with anyone with tits who came within ten feet of him. But when he learned I was trans, the innuendos and double entendres stopped abruptly.

I took a deep breath and clicked Play. Garza walked into the store, gave the cashier a wave, and strolled to the refrigerated case at the back of the store. Another camera shot showed a white woman with long dark hair and a black male companion in one of the aisles, apparently debating what to buy.

Two men wearing yellow bandanas—one bald, the other with spiky, dark hair—rushed into the liquor store with guns raised. The spiky-haired gunman stopped at the counter and pointed his weapon at the cashier, who raised his hands. There was yelling in Spanish, but the audio wasn't clear enough to make out.

Meanwhile, Baldy stalked deeper into the store. A second camera showed him searching the aisles, presumably for potential witnesses. When he spotted Garza, he immediately fired two shots. Pop, pop. The first hit Garza in the face, blowing out the back of his head. The second hit his chest.

Spike made threatening gestures. The cashier opened the register and handed him a stack of bills. Spike stashed the money in his pocket, then both gunmen rushed out of the store.

The burros I'd eaten felt like rocks in my gut. Garza was a womanizer, but he was good police and didn't deserve to be gunned down like that. He truly cared about the community we served.

Something about the video nagged at me, but I couldn't say what.

"Jinx, you all right?" asked Byrd.

"What's wrong, girl?" Shea put an arm on my shoulder.

I realized I was crying. "My partner...back when I was a cop." I swallowed hard. My throat felt like someone had a noose around it.

I turned my laptop so the two of them could see it.

Byrd furrowed his brow. "Jinx, I'm sorry."

"Yeah, that fucking sucks. And I don't like cops all that much," said Shea.

"Something's wrong…" I managed to squeak out.

"That's for sure," said Shea. "Fucking Jags. I hope whoever we shot in the parking lot dies."

I managed to get a handle on the anger and grief tearing at my insides. "Something's not right about the video."

"Like someone tampered with it?" asked Byrd.

It came to me. "No. The gunmen. Why shoot Garza but not the cashier or that couple?"

"Maybe they knew he was a cop."

I turned the laptop toward me and watched it again. It still felt like a punch in the gut, but I forced myself to study the interaction between Garza and the second gunman. Garza looked up as the gunman approached. Without a word, the gunman fired two shots and walked away.

I watched it again. And again. And again. I grew more and more convinced this was not a case of wrong time, wrong place.

When I managed to pull myself together, I called Detective Hardin. "It…it's Jinx Ballou." My voice felt raw, like a coyote's growl.

"I'm kinda busy at the moment."

"It's about Garza."

"What about him?" The change in his tone told me I had his attention.

"The gunmen, members of the West Side Jaguars. They weren't there to rob the store."

"What the hell you talking about?"

"I watched the security footage from the liquor store holdup. The bald gunman went right after Garza. No words, just shot him on sight. But they didn't shoot the cashier or the couple in the store. Not only that, the gunman up front didn't ask for the money in the drawer until after Garza was shot. It was a hit, Pierce, not a robbery gone bad."

"Goddamn. You sure about this?"

"Look at the security footage. Was Garza investigating the Jaguars for anything at the time?"

He let out a sigh full of frustration and bluster. I heard typing on his end. He must've been at his desk, working late on a case.

"At the time of his death, he had four open cases. Two domestic disputes. One sexual assault of a minor. One road rage incident. The only Latin name in any of the cases was the sexual assault victim."

"Who?"

"I'm not giving out the victim's name. She was a minor."

"What about the suspect in the case?" Could it have been Fitzgerald? Was that the connection?

"Barry Fields. The case has been turned over to the Maricopa County Attorney's Office."

"Had Garza investigated James Fitzgerald for anything?"

"Fitzgerald? Not that I...wait, hold on a minute. He was a suspect in a sexual assault case, but the status is listed as cleared by exceptional means. No arrest made."

It was a status that was supposed to be used only in rare cases, such as when the suspect was dead or there was another reason the suspect couldn't be charged despite strong evidence of guilt. But it was too often used to juice clearance rates on rape cases, even when no charges were filed.

"Exceptional means? Are you serious? He was already found guilty once for sexual assault on a minor. Why was he not charged again for this rape?"

"I don't know the details, Ballou. I'm telling you what I see in the system. I don't have the casebook in front of me."

"Who was the victim?"

"She was a minor. I can't divulge that information."

"Just tell me this, was she Latina? Could she have any connections to the Jaguars?"

"Ballou, I...aw, shit."

"I'm right, aren't I? Who was the victim, Hardin?"

"I can't give you that. All I can tell you is Garza interviewed Fitzgerald, as well as the victim and her father."

Something clicked in my brain. "The father got a rap sheet?"

More keyboard clicks. "Multiple convictions for aggravated assault and possession with intent to sell. Spent several years in Perryville. Suspect in several homicide cases but never charged.

"Who is he, Hardin? Who's the victim's father?"

There was silence on the line. I feared we'd been disconnected. Then Hardin said, "Juan Alfonso Cabrera. He's an enforcer for the West Side Jaguars."

"When did the rape take place?"

"March second."

"A few months after Fitzgerald got probation for raping the Hancock girl. And Garza refused to charge him?"

"Getting prior convictions admitted as evidence is tricky. You know this, Ballou. And when the victim's father is a violent gangster…"

"So you're saying the teenage daughter of a violent gangster can't be raped?"

"That's not what I'm saying, and you know it. The legal system's messed up. Rape cases are tough to prosecute, especially with a victim with family ties to a criminal organization. I'm not going to sit here and second-guess Garza's decision."

"Garza's decision got him killed, Detective."

"You don't know that."

"Yes, I do. And so do you. Can you send me that information on the Cabrera sexual assault case?"

"Are you kidding me? I shouldn't have even told you about it. I could lose my job."

"Hardin, I'm the one who clued you in on why Garza was really shot. It's looking more like the Jaguars killed James Fitzgerald as well. I'm trying to make sure an innocent person doesn't go to prison for that crime."

"I'm sorry, Ballou. I can't help you. Goodbye."

"Wait, wait, wait! At least tell me what caliber weapon was used to kill Garza."

Hardin let out an exasperated breath. "Ten millimeter."

"Thanks, Detective."

I hung up and grabbed Fitzgerald's file to check the ballistics report. He'd been shot with a ten mill as well.

"What are you thinking?" asked Shea.

"I think the West Side Jaguars murdered James Fitzgerald after he raped the daughter of one of their enforcers. They also killed my partner Garza because he didn't arrest Fitzgerald."

"Holy fuck!"

I repeated what I'd learned from Hardin. "I also think Cabrera shot up my house. Same caliber handgun was used in all three shootings—a ten-millimeter auto. I'd be willing to bet that's why they attacked us this morning. They don't want us looking into Fitzgerald's murder."

She looked at me. "How would the Jags know we were looking into the case?"

"Someone must have told them," replied Byrd. "Question is, who?"

"The other thing that's bothering me is this Garinov fellow. He was supposedly bragging about killing Fitzgerald. And he works for Volkov. Is he also connected to the West Side Jaguars?"

Shea shook her head. "The pieces don't exactly fit together, do they?"

I grabbed the police reports for the discovery of Fitzgerald's body. "The 911 caller used a pay phone at the liquor store next door to the motel and refused to give a name. Police interviewed a motel housekeeper named Camila Morales. She reported seeing a tall African American female with long braids leaving the room shortly before the body was discovered. Everyone assumed that woman was Pearson. But it wasn't."

I looked at Shea. "When you and the Sisterhood were at Naughty's, did you see a dancer who resembled Indigo?"

Shea let out a deep breath. "Shit, I dunno. We were there for a few hours. I got a little drunk. Hold on…"

Shea made a call. "Savage, that night at Naughty's, did any of the dancers look like Indigo? Yeah, yeah. I vaguely remember that. You get her name by chance? Oh, well, thanks." She hung up. "Savage said a couple of the sisters were teasing Indigo because one of the dancers looked like she could be her twin."

"So maybe that's who the housekeeper saw leaving the motel room right before they found Fitzgerald's body." I stood up. "Grab your gear. We're going back to Scottsdale."

41

It was three in the afternoon when we reached the Cactus Inn.

"We need to find this housekeeper, Camila Morales." I scanned the area, looking for a housekeeping cart or an open room door.

"We don't even know if she's working today," said Byrd. "You going to ask the guy at the registration desk?"

"Nope."

"Then what's the plan?"

"I'm going to talk to her." I pointed at a heavyset Latina woman stuffing bedsheets into a laundry bag attached to her cart. "Wait here."

I stepped out of the Charger and sidled up to Shea. "Sit tight. I want to talk with the housekeeper over there."

"I can come with you."

"I don't want to spook her."

"Spook her?" Shea smirked, giving her biker vest a tug. "Nothing spooky about me."

I figured she got my point and sauntered over to where the woman was pulling fresh sheets from a stack on her cart.

"Excuse me! Miss!" I said, trying to sound worried and desperate.

"*¿Si?*"

"I'm hoping you could help me," I said in Spanish, hoping that would put her more at ease. "Do you recognize this man?" I held up a photo of Brother James on my phone.

Fear glimmered in her eyes. She waved her hands, shook her head, and backed away. "*¡No se! ¡No se!*"

I knew she was lying. "Please, I need to know what happened to him. It's important."

"Front desk say I no talk to police," she said in English.

"Not police. Private investigator."

She pointed at the bail enforcement badge hanging on my chest. "*¡Policía!*"

She glanced toward the office. "I should not talk to you. I don't know anything. I never saw him," she insisted in Spanish.

I realized I was going about this all wrong. "I'm sorry. My name is Jinx Ballou. What's yours?"

"Camila. Camila Morales."

Bingo! "You are the person I need to speak to. You told the police you saw a woman leave this man's room."

"I...I was mistaken." She shuffled into one of the rooms and tried to shut the door, but I held it open.

"Please! A friend of mine is in trouble." I pulled up Indigo's photo. "She's being framed for that man's murder. She's a good woman. Do you think she should go to prison for someone else's crime?"

With some effort, she looked up at my phone. I offered it to her, and she held it. Tears glistened behind her eyes. "I...I saw that man. He was with a girl but not this girl."

"Who was he with?"

"I could get in big trouble."

I pointed at where Shea was leaning against her motorcycle. "You see her? She's a part of a group of women who can protect you." I didn't know if the Athena Sisterhood would help, but I was running out of options. "That's what they do. They protect women in trouble. Keep them safe." Most of the time.

Her face cycled through a series of emotions—fear, guilt, possibly anger. At last, she set the sheets in her hand on the bed. "I saw him with Scarlett. She dances at the club next door. She is also a prostitute."

"What does Scarlett look like?"

"Like your friend—black skin, long braids. But Scarlett has…" She gestured around her mouth.

"A more prominent jaw?"

"Yes, that is it."

"Was Scarlett with the man when he was killed?"

Sweat trickled down her dark face. "I cannot. I cannot say." I could tell she knew more.

"Please. Don't let my friend go to prison. We'll protect you."

"Yes, she was with him but ran out of the room screaming. She was bleeding. A man ran after her."

"A man? Who? Andrei Garinov? Did he kill Fitzgerald? Or someone else? Was he Russian? Latino?"

Her eyes grew larger. "I did not get good look."

"Was he tall? Short? Skinny? Fat? What color hair?"

"I do not remember." She was getting flustered. I was losing her.

"Is it common for housekeeping to work so late?"

She blushed. "Most customers stay only an hour or two. We must get rooms ready for the next customer. So we work sometimes at night."

"Was Fitzgerald still alive when Scarlett left?"

"I do not know." She looked away and gasped. "You must go now! Mr. Ivanov is coming!"

I turned toward where she was looking. Lenny, the skinny little pissant from the front desk, was striding toward us. *Shit.*

"Don't worry." I turned back to Camila and put a hand on her shoulder. She was shaking like a dog in a thunderstorm. "We will protect you."

"Not me I worry about. It's my daughter."

"Get the hell away from her," said Lenny. "Camila, get your fat ass back to work!"

"Camila," I pleaded, "come with us. I won't let them hurt you."

"Stay out of this, bitch. Camila, you know what'll happen if you don't shut your mouth and get back to work."

Shea and Byrd ran toward us.

I stepped between Camila and Lenny. "What's going to happen, asshole? You going to hurt her? Her daughter?"

"She knows." His voice was pure venom.

"It's okay, senorita," said Camila in a shaky voice. "I go do my job. I say nothing. I promise."

"No, it's not okay. You leave her and her daughter alone, you piece of shit. Or you'll wish you had."

He smirked. "You don't know who you're dealing with."

"Oh, I know exactly who we're dealing with. Sergei Volkov. Am I right? You can tell Sergei to kiss my ass. I kicked his brother's ass. I have no problem kicking Sergei's too. Now go back to jacking off behind the registration desk."

"What the hell's going on?" asked Shea.

"None of your goddamned business," said Lenny sharply.

"This little pissant's threatening this hardworking woman."

"Is that so?" Shea shoved Lenny back a step. "You like threatening women?"

"No, Miss Jinx," pleaded Camila. "Everything okay. I go back to work. You go now. Don't come back."

"See? Camila doesn't want you around. That means you're trespassing." Lenny had a smug expression that begged to be punched. Only question was whether Shea or I would do the honors.

"You gonna call the police?" I asked.

"Come on, Jinx," said Byrd. "Let's not make things worse than they are."

"Listen to your man, lady," Lenny replied.

It took all my self-control not to deck him. "If I learn you hurt Camila or her daughter, you will regret it."

"You won't hear nothing, bitch. If you come back, you will regret it."

I turned away from him only because Shea had grabbed one arm and Byrd the other. I shrugged them off and continued to the car. "I'm going."

When I climbed in the Charger, I made a call.

"Special Agent Lovelace. How can I help you?"

"It's Jinx Ballou. How's life at the FBI?"

"Ms. Ballou. I'm really surprised to hear from you after what happened to Wilhelm Penzler. We were counting on his testimony to bring down Sergei Volkov."

"Not my fault he jumped bail," I replied. "Nor was it my fault he threw himself off a three-story balcony rather than testify against Volkov."

"Why are you calling me, Ms. Ballou?"

"Trying to help you nail Volkov. I'm down at the Cactus Inn and just had a very interesting conversation with a woman from housekeeping named Camila. Sergei's people are holding her daughter hostage. The little turd bucket in the front office really doesn't like the staff talking to people with badges. You might want to send someone down here to investigate and maybe protect this poor woman."

"Okay, thanks."

"Just thanks? Are you coming down to investigate?"

"We will look into the matter."

"When?"

"Ms. Ballou, I appreciate your assistance in this matter. We will handle it."

"Don't you even want a description of Camila or the little shit running the registration desk?"

"We have it handled."

"Handled how?"

My phone beeped as the call dropped. "Shit."

"We should probably go," said Byrd. "We got enough trouble dealing with the West Side Jaguars. We don't need Volkov's men coming after us too."

"Not yet. Camila said the woman she saw leaving Fitzgerald's room was named Scarlett. She's a dancer at Naughty's. Looks like Indigo but with a more prominent jaw."

"What are you proposing?" asked Byrd.

"We go next door and try to find her."

"Into the dragon's den," said Shea with a wicked smile.

Byrd looked pale. "Volkov doesn't like people interfering with his business. If we get caught…"

"Relax, man." Shea slapped him on the arm. "We're just gonna have a drink and enjoy the entertainment. I'll even buy you a lap dance."

"That's the other thing. This isn't the kind of place I should go into."

"Why?" asked Shea. "Will Jesus send you to hell for looking at naked women?"

"Shea, ease up," I warned her. "Byrd, we're just going in there to locate Scarlett. This is the job. If we see her, we'll ask a few questions. Very low-key." I pulled off my vest and my tactical belt, then stuffed my Ruger in the concealment holster at the small of my back.

He let out a long sigh but didn't say anything.

"Or you can stay in the car. Your choice." I figured I might as well give the poor guy an out.

"And let you two ladies go in by yourselves? What kind of man would I be then?"

Shea rolled her eyes. "I think we can handle it, big guy."

"So you're in?" I asked him.

"I'm in."

42

———

I don't hang out in strip clubs very often. Not because I'm a prude or have a problem with women doing what they choose with their bodies. It just feels too much like window-shopping. You can look, but you can't touch. What fun is that?

But I needed some strong evidence to impeach Indigo's DNA. If Scarlett witnessed Fitzgerald's murder, I needed to find her.

I paid the cover charge for the three of us, and we stepped inside. The place smelled of booze, cheap perfume, and sex. The music was loud and bouncy. A dancer who looked all of sixteen spun around a pole on stage, leaving nothing to the imagination. Topless women with drop-dead gorgeous bods, in all sizes and colors, were giving lap dances and serving drinks. Middle-aged guys with an out-of-town-salesman vibe filled the tables crowded around the stage.

Shea pointed at an empty table. No sooner had we sat down than a woman with large, hypnotic eyes and olive skin offered to take our order. I asked for a bottle of water, Shea a Dos Equis, and Byrd nothing.

"Hey," I shouted to our server, trying to be heard over the music. "Is Scarlett dancing this afternoon?"

"Scarlett?"

"African American, long braids down her back."

"I think she's off today."

"When will she be back?"

Our server shrugged.

I nodded. "Okay, thanks."

After she walked off to fill our order, Shea leaned over. "What now?"

"Let's keep asking. Maybe we'll get lucky."

Shea eyed the new dancer on stage, who seemed a bit older and more busty, discarding piece by piece a sequined outfit inspired by the stars and stripes. "Maybe we will."

I sat staring blankly at the onstage entertainment as I contemplated our next move.

A different server brought our drinks. A flowering vine tattoo ran up her leg, around her torso, and out her left arm, with red hibiscus blossoms every six inches or so.

"You asking about Scarlett?" She handed me our drinks.

"Yeah. You know her?"

"She disappeared about a month ago. Right after that man was killed next door." The server looked around nervously.

"You know her last name? Or a phone number for her?"

She shook her head. "Sorry. I hope you find her. She was nice."

"Thanks for your help." I turned to Shea and Byrd. "I think this is a dead end."

"I told you," replied Byrd. "Let's get out of here."

"Aw, come on, guys. I'm thirsty. At least let's finish our drinks."

"Do what you want," I told her. "Byrd and I are leaving."

I gestured to Byrd, and he nodded. As we stood up, Shea took a long pull on her beer and followed along. We were almost to the door when a bouncer the size of a bulldozer stepped into our path. "Someone wants to see you." His accent was definitely Eastern European.

"You got the wrong person, pal." I tried to push past, but Bulldozer was hard to get around. I reached for my Ruger at the small of my back, but someone grabbed my arm and whirled me around.

The big guy holding me had a long face with lips like Mick Jagger's. He relieved me of my Ruger, phone, and wallet, then smiled, showing off his horse teeth.

Byrd and Shea were similarly disarmed by two hefty guys who reminded me of Hans and Franz, the comical bodybuilders from *Saturday Night Live*. It would've been funny if they didn't look so hostile. Four steroid-swollen bouncers against the three of us were not good odds.

Bulldozer pointed toward a hallway at the back of the room. Every cell in my body told me not to go wherever they were herding us. But now that they had our weapons, we didn't have much choice.

The bouncers frog-marched us across the room and down the hallway. Bulldozer led the way, followed by Hans pushing Shea. Franz drove Byrd a few steps behind her. Me and my buddy Mick Jagger brought up the rear, with him holding my arm tight enough to leave a bruise.

When a dancer emerged from the dressing room ahead of us, Bulldozer shouted, "Get back in room!"

She squeaked like a mouse and dove inside the dressing room.

Bulldozer turned right up a staircase. If we went up there, odds of us coming down alive were slim.

I pinwheeled with my free arm, breaking the bouncer's grip. Jagger returned the favor by driving his mallet of a fist into the side of my head. I dropped to my knees as the room spun like a carnival ride. He jerked me to my feet.

"Do that again, I snap your skinny little neck." He shoved me into Byrd, who helped steady me.

"You okay?" asked Byrd.

"Just peachy." I tried to shake away the cobwebs while being half dragged up the narrow staircase.

At the top, the bouncers led us down another hallway, where the doors were secured with large padlocks on the outside.

Bulldozer unlocked one of the rooms. Before I knew what was happening, Jagger tossed me inside like a sack of flour, crashing into the far wall. The door slammed shut followed by the snick of the padlock.

My temple throbbed. I rubbed it with my hand, and it came away wet. I didn't think it was sweat this time, but the room was near pitch dark. The only light came from a narrow slit under the door.

The stale air reeked of urine and fear. A quick search by touch told me it was empty and about the size of a small closet. *Fuck!*

I pounded on the door. "Let me out of here!"

"Shut your face, bitch, or I put bullet into your girlfriend."

"Shit!" I leaned against the back wall and slid down to the floor. *How the hell am I going to get out of here?*

My mother was right. I should have switched to something safer. Like being a bomb disposal technician, a stunt person, or a window washer for skyscrapers.

I lost track of time. All that was left was the darkness, the pain, and a highlights reel of reasons the world was better off without me. The thrum-thrum-thrum of the music downstairs was interrupted only by the occasional footsteps in the hallway.

Why do I even bother trying? I'm a goddamn failure. Bad enough I'm probably going to die. Now Shea and Byrd probably will too. I was a horrible girlfriend to Conor, only letting him get so close. I was a horrible daughter, a disappointment for a sister, a lousy best friend. A pathetic excuse for a bounty hunter, much less a private investigator. No matter what I do, people around me are hurt and killed.

The snick-clack of the padlock being unlocked caught my

attention. When the door opened, a blaze of light ripped through the room. I shielded my eyes with my arm.

A meaty fist wrapped around my arm and yanked me to my feet. "Someone wants to see you," Bulldozer muttered in a gravelly voice.

He dragged me down the hall and practically threw me into a large office. Jagger stood between Shea and Byrd, a pistol in one hand and my Ruger still stashed in his waistband.

A man with a rectangular face sat behind a wooden desk. Didn't look like the photos of Sergei Volkov that Becca had sent me, though his features were definitely European. He wore a black suit that looked a little heavy for this time of year in Phoenix. Our wallets and phones were on the desk in front of him.

"I hear you question my employees," he said in a thick Russian accent.

"Yuri Barayev," I guessed, recalling my conversation with Maricela.

"Impressive. And you are Jenna Ballou," he replied using my legal first name. "But you go by Jinx. Curious name. It means cursed, yes?"

"Only for people who get in my way."

"Why you poking nose where it does not belong?"

"You're going to have to be more specific. Poking my nose where it doesn't belong is what I do for a living."

"Why you look for Scarlett?"

I shrugged. "I heard she's a great dancer. Thought we'd come check her out."

Barayev nodded to Jagger, who punched Shea in the gut.

"Leave her alone, you fucking pig." That came from Byrd. I was shocked to hear him curse.

"Tell me what I want, or my friend here will do worse."

Jagger pressed the muzzle of his gun to Shea's temple. I needed a way to change the power dynamic and fast.

"All right! Here's the deal. Scarlett witnessed a murder we're investigating," I replied.

"The preacher man. Why you looking into murder? Police already make arrest someone."

"The wrong someone. We're looking for the right someone."

"Scarlett is not here," Yuri said. "She is gone missing. No answers here. Only trouble for you."

He glared at me, but I caught his gaze drifting down to my chest. My shirt was damp with sweat, making the outline of my nipples visible even through my bra. Fine. He wanted to look. I'd give him something to look at.

"You know, Yuri, I think we all got off on the wrong foot. I'm a woman. You're a man. This doesn't have to be an adversarial relationship." I took a step toward the desk.

Bulldozer aimed his pistol at me.

"Easy, big guy. I'm unarmed." I held up my hands and flashed Yuri a seductive smile.

He nodded. I stepped around the desk, pulling off my T-shirt. Yuri's eyes widened with want.

"I think we can come to a more amenable agreement."

I pushed him back in his swivel chair and straddled his lap. His dick was hard and pressing into my ass. "You know, back when Milo ran things, he and I..." I traced his jawline with my finger. "We had a little thing going. But now that he's gone, I haven't had anyone to entertain me. No one to...fill my emptiness. You think you could do that? Fill the empty hole inside me?"

He started to grind against me. "Da," he said in a breathy voice.

I leaned my chest against his. He stared down at my breasts peeking above my bra. I wrapped my arms around his waist and found exactly what I was looking for.

In a flash, I pulled the pistol from his waistband, pivoted off of Yuri, and pressed the gun against his head while using him as a shield. "Drop your guns, assholes!"

When Jagger looked at me, Shea snatched the gun out his

hand and kneed him in the crotch. The floor shook when he hit the ground, groaning. "Fucking asshole!" she said.

A bullet zinged past my ear. Bulldozer! Before I could return fire, Byrd twisted the gun out of the bouncer's hand and leveled it at him. "Don't shoot at my friends, please."

I stepped away from Yuri. "SIG Sauer. Nice. Always liked these. Thanks for the gift."

Yuri's eyes blazed with anger. "You just bought large trouble, bitch. You think you clever. Not so clever when you are dead."

"Don't threaten us, Yuri. We're just trying to solve a murder. Now where the hell is Andrei Garinov?"

"I am Garinov," said Bulldozer.

"I'm told you killed Fitzgerald."

The confused look on his face looked genuine. "I not kill goddamn preacher."

"Don't lie to me, asshole. You were heard bragging about it at the Stone Horse Pub. Guess you get blabby when you've had a few Stolis, huh?"

Garinov glanced at Yuri, a jolt of concern in his eyes. "I did not kill. I teach preacher lesson after he hurt our girl. But he was still alive. He come back, sleep with other girls."

"Including Scarlett, who just happened to go missing right after Fitzgerald turned up dead," replied Byrd. "Maybe you killed them both."

"Andrei did not kill preacher. We do not kill client, even when they are problem. Dead client is bad for business."

"You threatened to kill us," Shea snorted.

Yuri glared at her. "You are not client."

If Andrei didn't kill him, then who? Cabrera? I would need some sort of proof to get Indigo off the hook. But I wouldn't find it here.

"Well, I'm glad we got that cleared up. Listen, boys. It's been a lot of fun, but it's time we take our toys and leave. Stay out of our way, and we'll stay out of yours. Okay?"

"Not okay," growled Yuri. "You find Scarlett, you bring her back to me. Or we will…"

"Yeah, yeah, you'll kill us. Blah, blah, Russian blah. Here's the deal, Big Red. Come after us again, you'll wish you hadn't." I grabbed my wallet and phone from the desk, then handed Shea and Byrd theirs. "Let's go."

"Yeah, let's get the fuck outta here." Shea gave Jagger another kick.

We raced down the staircase and ducked out the back door, setting off a security alarm. We hustled into the dark alley outside and around the building to the front parking lot.

The alarm had dancers and patrons pouring out of the building like ants from a disturbed mound. Several of the men still held their drinks, looking around trying to figure out what was going on.

Shea, Byrd, and I filtered through the crowd, working our way to the Charger and Shea's bike.

"What now?" asked Shea.

"Back to my place. I've had enough of Scottsdale for one day."

Shea pulled on her helmet and threw a leg over her bike. Byrd and I hopped into the Charger.

The tension in the car was thick as butter. Every time we stopped at a light on Scottsdale Road, I pounded on the wheel and yelled at the light to turn green, then screamed at the cars in front of me to go.

Byrd silently stared out the window.

I started to settle down as we turned onto McDowell, passing between the wind-carved hills known as the Papago Buttes. As we crested the rise, the lights of Phoenix glittered in the night off to our left.

"You were right," I finally admitted. "We shouldn't have gone in there."

"I wasn't going to say anything."

"I know you weren't. That's why I did. You were right. I'm sorry."

"Sorry won't do us much good when the Russians track us down and kill us."

"I think they got the message to leave us alone." I hoped I wasn't wrong again.

"You think Garinov was telling the truth? That he didn't kill Fitzgerald?"

I turned left onto Fifty-Second Street, then right onto the Loop 202. "Simon heard Garinov brag about putting a beatdown on the preacher. Didn't specifically say he killed him."

"Because Fitzgerald got abusive with one of the dancers."

"If we track Scarlett down, maybe we can get the proof we need and wrap things up."

But clearing Indigo was only one of our problems. We had the Jaguars and Volkov's people after us. Our chances of getting out of this with our hides intact were looking slim.

43

———————

It was eight thirty by the time we reached my house. To my surprise, the damaged window had been replaced. When we walked in the door, Shea's phone rang. She rushed off to the guest room for some privacy.

"You want to stay here, or you headed home?" I asked Byrd.

"After what we just went through, I'd just as soon stay at my own place to Netflix and chill. I need some serious decompression."

"You want Shea or me to escort you home?"

"I'll be okay."

"All right, but keep your head on a swivel."

"Will do."

"See you tomorrow?"

"Sunday? I got church and...to be honest, I think I'm done playing private detective. Between the Russians and the Latino gangsters, this is a little more than I bargained for."

"Well, take care."

"Thanks." He gave me a hug. "Watch your back, Jinx."

I closed the door and called Maricela. I needed more information.

"*Bueno.*"

"Maricela, this is Jinx Ballou. We spoke yesterday about your dancing at Naughty's."

"*Sí.*"

"Did you know a dancer named Scarlett?"

"Yes, I liked her. Long braids. Very pretty. We used to talk a lot about our life before. She was from Haiti originally. Barayev found her, told her he could get her started in a modeling career."

"I think she was assigned to service Fitzgerald after he hurt you. She witnessed who killed him."

"*¡Ay, Dios mio!* Is she okay?"

"I don't know. She's disappeared. Do you know any way to reach her? A phone number? Her last name?"

"I...I have nothing to do with that world anymore. Too painful. Too risky." From her tone, I got the impression she was holding back. "I'm sorry."

"Please, Maricela. I understand you're scared, but I'm worried about her. Do you have any way to reach her?"

Silence filled the line, and I wondered if she'd hung up. "Yuri did not allow us phones. But Scarlett got one from a client. Before I escaped, she gave her number. Hold on. I will find it." She paused, then read me off the phone number. I wrote it down.

"Thanks. Could you call her? If I call, she might not talk to me, because I'm a stranger. But if you call..."

"I...I can't. Too risky. Yuri is smart. He might learn about phone. Track her down, then find out where I am. It is too much risk. I am sorry. Goodbye."

She hung up.

Shea walked into the living room with a smirk on her face.

"What's up?" I asked.

"Nothing."

"Nothing? You look like the proverbial cat who ate the canary."

"Club stuff."

I ordered us a pizza and turned on the TV for background

noise. Shea and I talked about everything from motorcycles to her adventures growing up in an outlaw biker family. My own life, even as a trans kid, seemed pretty vanilla and privileged by comparison.

She got me to talk about my decision to leave the police force to become a bounty hunter. We compared notes on our experiences with Milo Volkov.

"Kinda weird," said Shea before she finished the last slice of pizza.

I took a long pull on my soda. "What's that?"

"Me an ex-con, you an ex-cop. Opposite sides of the law, and yet here we meet in the gray, murky middle."

"Yeah, I suppose that is kind of weird."

"I heard about your ex-boyfriend, the Irishman who's on trial in the UK. What's his name? Colin?"

"Conor. It's…I don't know what it is. He was caught up in some bad stuff when he was younger. The Troubles, they call it. Ironic that he nearly died trying to stop a bomb here."

"The one that blew up on the Piestewa Freeway. Yeah, I heard that."

I felt the well of grief starting to open beneath me, calling me back into the all-too-familiar darkness. "I don't know if the Northern Irish cops tracked him down or he simply turned himself in, but now he's sitting in a cell somewhere in Belfast. I feel like it's my fault. If I'd…"

"Not your fault. He made his choices—both when he was a teenager and after the bomb blast here. We all make choices. I've made plenty of shitty ones. Spent seven years down in Perryville as a result."

"But then you turned everything around."

"Sometimes I wonder how much."

Something Byrd said popped up in my memory. "I heard that the Athena Sisterhood was involved with drugs and arson. What's that about?"

Shea's face darkened. "Who told you that?"

"Not important. Is it true?"

"Few years back, a couple of our members were involved with some bad shit. It wasn't a club thing. When we learned about it, well, we shut it down. I can't say any more. Not allowed to talk about internal club business. The Athena Sisterhood is a law-abiding club. We don't allow drugs or any other criminal activity."

"Good to know." My phone rang. "Yello."

"Jinx, it's Max." He sounded out of breath.

"Who?" The name sounded vaguely familiar, but I couldn't place it.

"Max Alexander. I'm a trans guy living at your old house with Ciara. We met a few days ago when you were…"

Flashes of memories flitted through my brain. Me arguing with someone about whose house it was. "Yeah, I remember. I was a little…confused. Sorry about that."

"This isn't about that. It's Ciara. Someone…someone took her."

"Took her? What do you mean 'took her'?"

"These big guys with accents. They showed up asking for you. We told them you didn't live here anymore. When Ciara refused to give them your new address, they kidnapped her."

"Did you call the police?

"They arrived a little while ago. I told them what happened. They want to talk to you."

"Sit tight. We'll be right there."

I hung up and looked at Shea. "We gotta go."

Five minutes later, we pulled onto my old street and parked a few doors away from my house. Patrol vehicles and unmarked cars, all lighting up the night in flashes of red and blue, blocked off the street. As we approached, I noticed uniformed officers canvassing the neighbors, no doubt looking for witnesses.

We found Max sitting on the curb outside the crime scene tape. He was wrapped in a foil survival blanket, holding an ice pack to his forehead and looking hopeless.

I introduced Shea, as we sat on either side of him. "What

happened?"

"I was..." He swallowed hard. "I was taking a shower when the doorbell rang. Ciara answered it. That's when I heard shouting."

"What were they saying?"

"I couldn't make out the words at first. I turned off the water and pulled on a shirt and shorts..." Max's androgynous voice cracked with emotion.

"There were three of them. Big, scary guys. Thick accents. Russian or Ukrainian, I think. They were looking for you and a woman named Scarlett."

"Assholes!" Shea said.

"Ciara tried to calm them down and explain you didn't live there. When she refused to say where you lived now, they punched her. I tried to save her, but there were too many of them. They punched me in the head. When I came to, the door was wide open, and they were gone along with Ciara."

"Shit."

A woman in a dark suit approached, carrying a small notebook. The shield on her waist told me she was a detective. "How you doing, Mr. Alexander?"

He shrugged again.

"These friends of yours?" she asked.

"Jinx Ballou." I offered my hand, which she shook. "I own the house."

"Detective Cooper, Violent Crimes Division." She glanced at her notes. "Ah yes, Ms. Ballou. Mr. Alexander stated the assailants were looking for you."

"Based on Max's description, the guys who took Ciara are part of Sergei Volkov's human trafficking ring. They're looking for a former sex slave named Scarlett who disappeared. They think I know where she is."

"And why would they think that?"

"Because I'm looking for her too. She witnessed a murder that I'm investigating."

Cooper raised an eyebrow. "You're a detective?"

"Private. Normally I work as a bail enforcement agent, but I'm also a licensed PI."

"Does Scarlett have a last name?"

"I'm sure she does, but I don't know it."

Cooper cocked her head. "Why would they look for you here?"

"We were at the club earlier this evening looking for Scarlett. They…uh…detained us briefly. Probably looked through our wallets. This address is still listed on my license."

I suggested she get in touch with Special Agent Lovelace at the FBI, since Lovelace was already working to shut down the human trafficking ring. Cooper asked several more questions, having me go back through my story repeatedly, before thanking me for my time and returning to the house to continue her investigation.

"What am I going to do now?" asked Max.

Guilt hung heavy on my shoulders. This was my fault. Again. "You're welcome to sleep on my couch until the situation gets resolved." I wasn't sure what *resolved* meant.

"He can have the guest room," Shea said. "I'll take the couch."

"Is it safe?" He looked at me the way a frightened child would.

"The place I live in now is very secure and not far from here."

"What about Ciara?"

"Sounds like Detective Cooper has a handle on things."

My phone rang, but the caller ID on the screen was blank.

"Ballou Fugitive Services."

"I have your friend." The Russian-accented voice was familiar. Yuri! A blood vessel throbbed on my temple.

"Motherfucker! You let her go. She's got nothing to do with any of this."

"Perhaps. Once you bring what we look for. You know of whom I speak."

"Look, man, I got no idea where Scarlett is. She's long gone."

"Find her. Return to me what is mine."

"She's not your property."

"Return her or your little friend dies. And not quick death. No, it will be slow. We take her apart piece by piece. She seem very healthy. Will last a long time before she dies."

"Hurt her, and you'll regret it. That, I promise you."

"Your little threats do not scare me. And do not involve police."

"Too late, dipshit. They were called right after you kidnapped Ciara."

"That is unfortunate, but maybe salvageable. This conversation stays between us. You deliver property back to us, we return friend. You have until two o'clock tomorrow. Or will not be much left for us to return."

I was about to say something when the line went dead.

"Who the hell was that?" Shea held my gaze.

"Take a wild guess."

"Yuri. That sick motherfucker!"

"We can discuss this later." I turned to Max. "See if the police will let you inside to pack a bag. Then we'll head back to my place."

Max hailed one of the unis, who escorted him inside the house.

"Yuri wants Scarlett back," I said once Max was out of earshot.

"Even if we find Scarlett, we can't turn her over to Yuri," Shea replied.

"I know." I wasn't sure what options that left us. "We still need Scarlett to testify on behalf of Indigo. I've left voicemail messages, as has Maricela. We only have another day or so before Indigo's bond is declared forfeit. That's serious."

"This is so messed up. I had no idea protecting Indigo would turn into such a clusterfuck."

Max returned fifteen minutes later dragging a black suitcase. I led him to the Gray Ghost, and we returned to the Bunker, where I set up the sofa with a pillow and sheets for Shea. I thought about inviting her to share my bed but didn't want to seem too forward.

44

———

What sleep I managed to get was haunted by nightmares of being pursued by men with rifles. I was a coyote.

I woke at six the next morning to Diana pawing at me, whining to go for a run. It felt like such a mundane task in light of all of the craziness going on. But I couldn't think of a more productive thing. Perhaps it would jiggle loose a solution for the problems we were facing.

I pulled on shorts and a shirt and quietly stepped out the front door and past a snoring Shea. At least someone was getting some sleep.

The ground was damp from an overnight rain. The cool air smelled sweet with the fragrance of palo verde blossoms and free of its usual cocktail of desert dust and car exhaust.

Diana insisted on stopping every hundred feet or so to smell a tree, a mailbox, or a street sign, and raise a leg to make her mark, the canine equivalent of graffiti, I supposed. While she did her thing, I sent a text to Becca asking her to put a trace on Scarlett's phone since calling and leaving messages wasn't getting us anywhere.

When I returned home, I found Shea and Max helping themselves to French toast and hot coffee.

"There's another couple of slices next to the stove," said Shea. "You didn't have any vanilla, so I had to make do without."

"I'm sure it's great. Thanks." I fixed a plate and turned to Max. "Any word from the cops?"

"The detective called. They searched that strip club, Naughty's, and the motel next door, but no sign of Ciara. The man who runs the place—Yuri somebody—had an alibi for last night, so they couldn't hold him. Jinx, you gotta do something. She's in trouble because of you."

"I know. Don't worry. We'll find her and bring her back," I assured him.

"How?"

"We'll find a way." Shea patted Max on the back. "We've got the Athena Sisterhood to provide backup if need be."

"I hope it doesn't come to that," I replied. "But we'll get her back, Max."

"Mind if I use your shower?" asked Shea.

"Go ahead. There's fresh towels in the linen closet in the hallway."

"Thanks."

I was halfway through my own breakfast when Becca called back. "I pinged the number you gave me. I got a hit."

"Where?"

"The Salt River wash just off Nineteenth Avenue."

"The Salt River wash? Why would she be there?"

"I don't know, but the phone hasn't moved in the twenty minutes I've been watching it. Jinx, I have a bad feeling about your girl."

"Yeah, me too. Last night, Sergei Volkov's goons kidnapped my friend Ciara from my old house so I would bring them Scarlett."

"Oh my Goddess, are you serious?"

"Seriously serious."

"That's going to be hard to do if my suspicions are correct."

"Only one way to find out. Shea and I'll drive to the wash."

"One more thing I thought you'd want to hear."

"What?" As if I wasn't dealing with a big pile of shit already.

"You were talking about Freddie Colton, the husband of that woman you were protecting."

"Trying to protect, anyway. He murdered her. Why?"

"Saw on the news that he was found dead."

"Freddie Colton is dead? How?"

"Shot twice in the face. Body found in his Trans Am parked behind Llantera Ruiz, a used tire shop on Hatcher Road."

"I swear this whole town's gone crazy. And it's not even summer yet." I wondered if Simon Benedict got his revenge for Colton killing Emma.

"Jinx, maybe you should walk away from this one."

"Too late. I'm already in too deep. Only way out is through. But thanks for the info, Becks. I'll be in touch."

"Please watch your back, Jinxie. You've been my bestie since sixth grade. I don't want to lose you."

"I'll be extra careful. Promise. You got anything fun planned now that Easton's back?"

"There's a farmers market they've been wanting to check out, and then we're meeting some friends of theirs for brunch at Queen Mary's. I'd invite you along, but it sounds like you've already got plans."

Queen Mary's was a restaurant on Seventh Street, known for its über-campy drag shows on Friday and Saturday nights and their elaborate buffet brunch on Sunday mornings.

"No worries! Have fun."

I hung up and called Byrd. When he didn't pick up, I left a voicemail asking him to call.

Max rinsed his dishes in the sink and excused himself to the guest bedroom. I got the impression all of the business talk was worrying him more. Not that I blamed him. Sometimes I forgot how crazy my work could get.

Shea walked in, her hair still damp from the shower. She smelled delicious. A surge of attraction crackled through each of my nerve fibers. I forced myself to focus on the situation. No room for distractions.

"We have a possible location for Scarlett. Or at least her phone," I told her.

She poured herself another cup of coffee. "Where is she?"

"Down on the Salt River, near the Durango Curve."

"That doesn't sound good."

"No, it doesn't. I learned something else from Becca. Our buddy Freddie Colton was found shot to death."

Shea stared out the back window, sipping her coffee, but said nothing.

"You knew, didn't you?"

She sighed but wouldn't meet my gaze. "Savage called me. The guy was a menace, Jinx. So don't expect any tears, all right?"

A chill ran down my spine. "Did the Athena Sisterhood murder Colton? Is that what that phone call was about last night?"

"We didn't kill him. But if we had, would it be the worst thing in the world? The man murdered two women in cold blood. Someone did the world a favor by taking him out of the picture."

"There's something you're not saying. I can hear it in your voice."

"The Athena Sisterhood did not kill Freddie Colton." She turned and faced me. "At least not directly."

"What's that supposed to mean?"

"Fuego, Savage, and Rah-Rah tracked him down to a dive bar on Dunlap Avenue, then passed the info on to Simon Benedict. But that's it. We didn't touch him."

"Why didn't you call the police?"

"All the times the police were called when he beat up Vanessa, and she still ended up dead. A different solution was called for."

A sick feeling formed in my stomach. I hated that she thought that was okay. And yet I wasn't entirely sure she was wrong. Fitzgerald had raped two teenage girls and didn't spend a day in prison. Was vigilantism the only option when the legal system routinely failed vulnerable women? I didn't want to believe it.

"We'll talk about this later. We need to see about Scarlett and somehow get Ciara back from Yuri. Let's grab our gear."

"What about me?" asked Max, walking into the kitchen.

"Stay put and keep Diana company. We'll be back shortly." I hoped.

45

———

When we stepped out my side door to the carport, I noticed a black sedan parked across the street in front of the Hendersons' house. The hairs on the back of my neck stood up.

"What's wrong?" asked Shea as she pulled on her motorcycle helmet.

"The car across the street. Something about it looks wrong." From the Gray Ghost, I pulled out a pair of binoculars I often used for surveillance.

The sedan was an old Crown Vic police interceptor model with a searchlight by the side-view mirror. But this one had gold-plated spinners on the wheels and dark-tinted windows. I had just enough of an angle to read the license plate—LDWENDE. Patrol cars didn't have custom plates. Someone had bought it at an auction and added the bling.

The Hendersons were a white couple with two young kids. Mrs. Henderson was the proverbial soccer mom with the requisite minivan. Mr. Henderson was an accountant who drove a used Volvo. A Crown Vic with tinted windows and spinners was not exactly their style. My gut told me the driver was a member of the West Side Jags.

I sent a text off to Becca to get the registration info on the driver when she had the chance, even though the last two I'd had her trace had been a bust.

She replied that she would run the trace as soon as she got back from Queen Mary's. I thanked her and said the sooner the better.

"You want me to draw them off on my bike then lose them?" asked Shea.

"If it's the Jags, I don't want you dealing with them alone. Dividing us up works in their favor, not ours."

Shea slapped the side of the damaged Charger. "I doubt you'll lose them in this old thing. No offense. She's fast, but a refurbished patrol car like the one out there has arguably more power and better handling. Better if we ride two-up on the bike. I got an extra helmet in my trunk."

"Never ridden on a motorcycle before." The thought sent a thrill of fear through me, coupled with a daring sense of curiosity.

She stepped into my personal space, making my heart flutter. "Then today's your lucky day, girlfriend."

I looked into her eyes, inches from mine. "While you go all Steve McQueen trying to lose them? Yeah, what could go wrong."

"Don't you trust me?" Her grin deepened.

"I...yeah, I trust you. It's just..."

"Don't tell me the badass Jinx Ballou is afraid of a little motorcycle."

I was still upset about the Sisterhood's involvement with Colton's murder. The thought of putting my life in her hands was a little unsettling. And yet...

"I...I'm willing to give it a try."

She unhooked her full-face helmet from the back of her bike and handed it to me. "Try it on."

I squeezed my head into it. My skull felt like it was being compressed in a vise. "It's a little tight."

She jiggled it. "Good. It's supposed to be." She pulled a half-dome helmet out from the trunk. "I'll make do with the party lid. Let me get the bike turned around so we can race straight outta here."

Using the Gray Ghost as cover from our stalkers in the Crown Vic, she turned the bike around to face the street and threw a leg over it. "Use the rear pegs to lift yourself up onto the bitch seat."

"The what?"

"Sorry. Old habit. The passenger seat."

With a hand on her shoulder for balance, I awkwardly hoisted myself onto the narrow cushion between her and the backrest. My body pressed against hers, as if we were spooning. I could smell the rich leather of her vest and the vanilla scent of her shampoo.

"What now?" I asked.

"Keep your feet on the pegs and hold onto me. When I turn, lean the way I do. And watch out for the pipes. They get fucking hot when the engine's warmed up. They'll burn you, even through your jeans."

My pulse raced as the engine roared to life beneath me. She gave me a thumbs-up. I returned the sign.

With a jolt, the bike accelerated onto the street and past the Crown Vic. My heart thundered in time with the rapid chut-chut-chut of the engine. I dared a glance back. The Crown Vic was making a U-turn.

"They're coming!" I shouted when we reached the Central Avenue intersection. A large pickup truck rumbled toward us on our left. An instant before the truck reached the intersection, Shea pinned the throttle and jumped out in front of it.

Brakes screamed and tires squealed. I pitched left, struggling to hold on to Shea's waist while we raced down Central. I felt like I was on the back of a roller coaster, while Shea nimbly wove between vehicles, splitting the lanes at times.

We leaned a hard right onto McDowell. The pavement loomed up toward us in the tight turn. I thought we would fall over until she straightened it up and accelerated further.

At Fifth Avenue, we hit a red light. Shea pulled into the left turn lane. The Crown Vic's horn blared somewhere behind us as it fought through traffic to catch us.

"Dammit, they're still following us," Shea growled. "Hold on!"

Despite the red light, Shea gunned the motor and turned onto Fifth Avenue. A light flashed. Stoplight camera. A ticket was better than getting killed, I supposed.

I chanced a look back when we turned onto the I-10 on-ramp. The Crown Vic was back a few cars but still in pursuit. Shit! With the velocity of a fighter jet, we surged down the ramp. The front wheel lifted and dropped.

Once on the highway, we whizzed past the other vehicles, the wind a thunderous rocket in my ears.

This must be what flying feels like. I realized I was laughing even as tears streamed down my face. My vision narrowed at the expanse of highway ahead of us. *Oh fuck yeah!* This was better than booze or weed or sex. Like an orgasm that wouldn't quit.

I'm Daenerys Stormborn soaring on the back of a dragon. If I survive this shit, I am definitely getting a motorcycle.

We merged onto I-17 South, taking the ramp at over a hundred miles an hour. My soul screamed with excitement, adrenaline coursing through my veins. I squeezed Shea tighter, pressure building in my groin. My face warmed at the thought of me with this ex-con biker chick.

It wasn't until we pulled off onto the Nineteenth Avenue exit and stopped at the light that I remembered we were running from the West Side Jags.

"I think we lost 'em," said Shea, sparing a glance in her side mirror.

"Thank goodness."

On Nineteenth Avenue, she returned to a reasonable speed. Shortly before we reached the bridge over the Salt River wash, she pulled into a small parking area on the side of the road. A hiking trail led down to the riverbed.

I shakily climbed off the bike and pulled off the helmet. My heart still thundered in my chest. My knees had turned to jelly. I put a hand on the backrest to steady myself.

The seat must have been pressing on a nerve because my clit tingled with a pins-and-needles sensation. One look at Shea, and my pulse accelerated even more. Maybe it wasn't a pinched nerve after all.

Shea hopped off the bike, took one look at me, and burst out laughing.

"Wh-what?"

"You should see your face." She slapped my shoulder and guffawed. "Like you just got your cherry popped."

"I...uh...feel like I did."

"And?"

"I think I...it's..." I almost said, *I think I'm in love.* "Helluva ride."

"Hells yeah." She put an arm around my shoulder. Her scent of vanilla and leather set my senses ablaze.

Unexpectedly, her mood turned somber. "Let's find Scarlett."

Using an app on my phone, we trudged down the trail to the coordinates Becca had provided for the phone's location.

Our boots crunched underfoot on the sandy ground. Aside from the road, the terrain was barren scrub desert. A few hearty shrubs—brittlebush, creosote, and tumbleweeds—dotted the landscape. Along the wash itself, green-barked palo verdes rose up, their yellow blossoms in full bloom.

When we reached the banks of the riverbed, the trail turned left following the Salt upstream. Large pools of water remained in the wash from the overnight rain.

"According to the coordinates Becca gave me, Scarlett's phone is on the other side of the bridge." I pointed past a fence with a No Trespassing sign.

"Then that's where we go."

We hopped the fence and continued on. I looked in the distance along the water's edge and spotted a figure on the ground. As we drew closer, the cloying scent of death hit us followed by the disquieting buzz of flies. I pulled the top of my T-shirt over my nose and mouth, but it didn't keep the stench away. Nor did it fend off the sense of failure that hit like a sledge-hammer to my chest.

The remains were those of a dark-skinned woman. The body was so bloated and discolored, I couldn't begin to guess age. She was dressed in a crop top and cutoff jeans. The gunshot wound above her left eye served as a gateway for insects seeking the decaying delights inside.

A halo of jet-black hair was matted with blood. Her hands were bound with wire. A weathered piece of duct tape clung loosely from her blistered lips.

A metallic glint in the sand to the right of the body caught my eye. A shell casing. I inserted a twig into the open end and lifted it up. The dimpled back of the spent round was stamped with the words "P M C 10MM AUTO." Same caliber used in the drive-by and to kill both Fitzgerald and Detective Garza. I eased the casing back into the same spot I found it.

"Shit. I had hoped…"

Shea's hands around my shoulders steadied me both physically and emotionally. "I know. Me too."

I gave myself fifteen seconds to grieve this poor woman's fate, then took a deep breath through my mouth and blew it out. I needed answers.

46

———

Was this Scarlett? If so, where was the phone? I pulled on a pair of latex gloves I carried in a Ziploc bag in a cargo pants pocket. On more than one occasion, I'd apprehended bail jumpers with open wounds, others covered in vomit, piss, and feces. Always best to be prepared.

Carefully, I searched the deceased's pockets, but they were all empty. *Where the hell's the phone?*

I reached into her bra and pulled out a flip phone. It was a pre-pay from the looks of it. When I opened the phone, the screen revealed three percent battery power remaining. I scrolled through the calls received and recognized my own number.

"No ID, but this has to be her." I stood and peeled off the gloves one into another, then stuffed them inside out into my pocket.

Shea's left arm wrapped around her face to fend off the odor of decay. "She doesn't really look like Indigo."

"Other than the fact that she's dead and Indigo isn't?" The dark sense of humor I'd developed as a cop emerged, a coping mechanism for situations like these.

"Indigo's more slender."

"Well, the body's bloated. Hard to really gauge."

"This woman's too short and doesn't have braids or dreads. Her hair's not even that long."

"What are you saying? That this isn't Scarlett? She has her phone."

"Scarlett could've tossed the phone, and this woman picked it up."

"You think Scarlett may still be alive?" I swallowed hard, trying to keep down the bile that threatened to rise up my throat. "Suppose anything's possible."

"What now?" Shea asked.

My mind searched for a solution. "Yuri wants Scarlett in exchange for Ciara. So let's give him what he wants."

I brought up the call history on the phone and deleted Maricela's calls. The former cop in me chaffed at my evidence tampering, but I had a life to save and didn't need anyone, cop or gangster, tracking down Maricela. Lastly, I used the phone's camera to take a picture of the dead woman.

"Jinx, what are you doing?"

"You're probably right. She isn't Scarlett. But she's bloated enough that it's hard to tell from a photo. Plus, we have the real Scarlett's phone, which shows I called her a few times. Maybe it will convince Yuri to let Ciara go."

"I fucking hope so."

I dialed the number from Yuri's recent call.

"Ms. Ballou. Do you have what I requested?"

I glanced at the woman's body lying on the sandy ground. "Yeah."

"This is good. Meet me two o'clock. Niko's Greek restaurant. Grand Avenue. Peoria. You can find this?"

"I know where it is." I had driven by the shuttered restaurant countless times. "Why wait? Let's meet now."

"I have other business to attend thanks to your friends in FBI.

Be at Niko's when I say. And no police, or your friend pays bigly. We are clear?"

"Crystal."

"Excellent." He hung up.

I called Byrd again but again got his voicemail. I left a second message, more urgent this time, to call me. He was probably at church, but I couldn't help worrying something had happened to him.

What about her?" Shea nodded toward the deceased woman after I hung up.

"I'll call 911."

Thirty minutes later, the place was crawling with cops, evidence techs, and people from the medical examiner's office. Patrol officers had escorted Shea and me back up to the main road and questioned us.

The story we told was that Shea and I were hiking along the trail when we spotted the body. I didn't mention Yuri, Ciara, the West Side Jags, or the phone I'd taken off the remains. No need to complicate things further.

When Detective Hardin showed up and took charge of the investigation, I gave him the same story.

"I wasn't aware you were such an outdoorsy person, Ballou," said Hardin.

"What can I say? I've let myself go these last few months. I figured, what with the nice weather, it'd be a nice day to walk along the Salt River."

"Do you always go hiking dressed like you're getting ready to knock down doors?" He nodded at my vest and gear.

"The weight of the gear is good training for the job."

"Uh-huh." He looked at Shea. "So this DB has nothing to do with the case you've been working. That dead preacher over in Scottsdale?"

"Scottsdale's, like, twenty miles away. Why would this have anything to do with that?"

"Don't you bullshit me, Ballou. I ain't got nearly the patience for this."

"I got an anonymous tip that the body of one of Volkov's former sex slaves was down here."

"Anonymous tip, huh? This girl got a name?"

"She went by Scarlett," I said. "Probably just a stage name."

"And why is this particular woman of interest to you?"

"She witnessed Fitzgerald's murder."

Hardin spit on the ground. "Dammit. I knew you were involved."

"Any progress on Garza?" I asked, desperate to change the subject.

His suspicious scowl softened. "Jennings is working the case. I filled him in on your theory. We'll see where that goes."

My phone rang. "Ballou Fugitive Services."

"Hi. Maybe you can find my sister. She's about five six, skinny as a rail. Supposed to show up at our parents' Sunday brunch, but there's been no sign of her. Think you can find her?"

"Aw, shit, Jake. I'm sorry." I looked at the time. It was ten thirty. "Things have been crazy. I'll be there in a bit, okay? And tell Mom and Dad I may be bringing a few guests."

"I'll tell them. Just get your butt over here. That was part of the deal with me fixing your fancy bulletproof windows. Remember?"

"I'll be there. Give me an hour." I hung up and locked eyes with Hardin. "My brother. I'm expected at my folks' place."

"Anything else I oughta know about the decedent?" Hardin asked.

"That's all I know, Detective." *Aside from the phone in my pocket.*

"Y'all get on out of here. I got any other questions, I know where to find you."

I called Max as we walked to Shea's motorcycle.

"Any updates from the detectives looking for Ciara?" I asked.

"No. You find the woman you were looking for?"

"Sort of. In a few hours, I'm supposed to meet with the people who took Ciara. With a little luck, I can get her back safe and sound. In the meantime, you're invited to my folks' place for Sunday brunch. You game?"

"Why not rescue her now?"

"If I could, I would."

"Guess it beats sitting around here all alone waiting for something to happen."

"Do me a favor. Look out the front window. Do you see any cars parked on the street? In particular a black Crown Vic."

"Hold on. Let me check," Max replied. "No, no cars parked along the street. Why?"

"Good. Take my SUV to my parents' house in Mesa." I gave him the address. "The spare key's in the drawer just left of the dishwasher. And lock the front door behind you."

"Thanks, Jinx," he said glumly. "For everything. You're not as bad as I thought you were."

"I'll see you in a little bit."

"You want me to have the Athena Sisterhood back us up when meeting with Barayev?" asked Shea.

I had thought about it. What I wanted was for Byrd to call me back. Someone who had experience in tight situations. Someone who I could trust to not lose their head when the shit hit the fan. After what happened to Colton, I wasn't keen on getting them involved.

"Let's hold off for now. I don't want this to turn into a bloodbath. If we can convince Yuri that Scarlett's dead and that we're not a threat to his business, we may be able to walk away with Ciara."

"Who says we're not a threat to that scumbag's business? I got nothing against consensual sex work, but this is human trafficking, Jinx. Nothing consensual about this. We can't let him continue to exploit those women."

"I hear you, but right now, our objective is rescuing Ciara. We can worry about shutting him down another day."

I was about to pull on the borrowed helmet when my phone rang again. Byrd calling.

"You're alive," I said.

"Yeah, why?"

I updated him on the situation, including finding the phone and our scheduled meeting with Yuri to rescue Ciara. "I need you, man. You in? I'll even treat you to Sunday brunch at my folks' house beforehand."

"Good food?" he asked with curiosity in his voice.

"You like Cajun and Southern home cooking?"

"Girl, you're playing my song."

I gave him the address, and he agreed to meet us there.

I pulled on the helmet and hopped onto the motorcycle behind Shea. We took the 17 north to I-10, then picked up the 202. Shea zipped along between cars with the grace of a ballet dancer.

Arriving in my parents' working-class neighborhood in Mesa was a time warp back to my childhood. Such a concentration of intermingled cultures—Native American, African American, Mexican, and Anglo. Brilliantly colored murals decorated the sides of buildings with urban flair and Aztec designs. Panaderías huddled between New York–style delis and galleries selling Navajo and Hopi artwork.

On the back of the motorcycle, I discovered the air was rich with the aromas of spices from around the world. Rap songs and Mexican love ballads played from the open windows of cars, evoking memories both joyful and painful from my childhood.

We passed the clothing store where I'd been caught shoplifting a dress at age eleven, back when I was still deeply closeted about my gender issues.

We turned the corner onto my parents' street. I recognized my friend Mirabella's house. As eight-year-olds, we played dress up with a box of her mother's old clothes. Such a whirlwind of fear, excitement, and joy that had been.

At last, Shea parked in front of my parents' house, a salmon-colored stucco structure my mother described as Mediterranean rose. To the rest of the neighborhood, it was the Pink House.

My brother's work truck, which was almost as battered and scratched up as the Gray Ghost, sat in the narrow driveway.

"Should we wait for Max and Byrd?" Shea asked.

I was a little concerned that Max wasn't already there, but then Shea hadn't exactly been heeding the speed limit on the highway.

"They know where we are. I need to say hello to my folks. Haven't seen them in a while."

The front door was unlocked. I ushered Shea inside. The air was filled with the sharp bite of cayenne and the indulgent aroma of bacon.

47

A conglomeration of Cajun, Italian, and Mexican artwork gave my parents' living room welcoming and comfortable style.

I led Shea into the kitchen, where the table was covered with dishes of strawberry crepes, poached eggs, grits, paella, French toast, boiled shrimp, beignets, and fresh fruit. A carafe of chicory coffee stood in the center of the table next to a spray of fresh-picked roses from my mother's garden.

My mother's eyes welled up with tears as a hand clapped over her mouth. "Oh...oh my dear sweet girl."

She was a petite woman with long graying hair that was once jet-black. She launched from the table and wrapped me in a hug so tight I could barely breathe.

"Oh, just look at you." She released me and planted kisses on my face.

"I've missed you too, Mom." I said when our eyes met once again.

I could see the hurt and sorrow roiling inside her. "Why have you stayed away so long? Did I do something to hurt you?"

I tried to hold back the tears pricking at my eyes. "No, Mom. It wasn't you. It was…I just needed some time after what happened with Conor."

She smoothed my hair and gripped my face in her wrinkled hands. "I have missed you so much. Every morning and every night, I prayed the Virgin Mother would send you back to me. I called so many times, but you…"

"I'm sorry." The dam broke, and tears streamed down my face. "I was messed up for a while, but I'm doing better."

"Truly? You're skinny as a stray dog. Are you eating?"

"I'm eating. More than I was, anyway." I caught my father striding toward the two of us. "Hey, Dad."

Tall and lanky, he hugged me and kissed my cheek. "Missed you, *chère*."

"I missed me too."

"You gonna introduce us to your friend?"

Shea stood next to me, looking awkward. "This is my friend Shea. She's helping me out with a case. These are my folks. And you remember my brother, Jake, over there stuffing his face full of cornbread."

"Mmmph," said Jake. "'Bout time you got here."

Shea gave a two-fingered salute. "Pleasure to meet y'all."

"Well, you two sit down and help yourselves," said my mom, wiping her face, a smile having replaced her grief. "And don't be shy. There's plenty more."

"I'm expecting a couple more, if that's all right."

"The more the merrier."

The doorbell rang. I opened the door to see both Byrd and Max on the front porch. I led them back to the kitchen and introduced them to my family.

After a few extra chairs were squeezed around the table, I fixed myself some grits topped with a poached egg, but I just picked at it. Max didn't look like he had much of an appetite either.

"What's with all the picky eaters? Something wrong with the

food?" asked my dad. "Jenna, you really oughta eat something. You, too, Max. No need to be shy."

"The food's great, Dad. We're just worried about...stuff."

"Oh? What pray tell?"

"Not exactly table talk," I replied.

My dad gave an understanding nod. He knew I didn't talk about work here if I could help it.

"Someone kidnapped Ciara," said Max, staring down at his plate, a strip of bacon hanging limply in his hand.

"Who's Ciara?" asked my mother.

"My roommate. We live at Jinx's old house."

"Kidnapped?" Worry deepened the wrinkles of my mother's forehead. "Jenna, what are you involved in?"

"Just a case, Mom. It's okay. We got it handled."

"Why would they kidnap her?" replied my father. "Do you need money for a ransom? Is this because of the life insurance money you got?"

"No. Just a misunderstanding. We just need to find the folks who took her and...talk to them."

The worry returned to my mother's face. "I wish you'd go back to school and get a law degree. You're smart. You'd make a great lawyer."

"And I'd hate it. I hate lawyers."

"But people wouldn't be trying to kill you."

"People aren't trying to kill me, Mom."

"Honey, she can handle things." My dad put an arm around her. "She's got Byrd and her friend Shea."

"Jinx is good at what she does," Shea added.

Byrd glanced at her then at me. "When she's going after fugitives."

"I hope so. If something were to happen to you..."

"Nothing will happen, Mrs. B," said Shea, clapping me on the shoulder. "Your girl can handle herself."

"What's that mean?"

"Nothing, Mom."

The conversation died, and we spent the rest of brunch in awkward silence. The grits sat like cement mortar in my stomach. I hated to see my mom all worked up.

When I couldn't stand to stare at my plate any longer, I helped my dad clear the table. Shea, Max, and Byrd followed Jake into the living room to watch the Diamondbacks game.

"Your mom's not the only one who worries." He dried the plate I'd just washed.

"Like Shea said, I can handle myself."

"I'm not as worried about your work as I am your mental health." My dad, ever the shrink. "You don't look well."

"I know I've lost weight. I was having a rough time of it, I won't lie. But that's behind me."

"You go to a grief counselor or a support group?"

"I tried. Not a good fit. Getting back into work helped."

"You still drinking?"

"You knew about that?"

"I'm a trauma therapist. I recognize the signs."

"I'm not drinking."

"Have you heard any more about Conor?"

"All I know is he's being held in jail in Belfast. I tried to get word to him but haven't heard anything back."

"Did you know he was alive?"

"Not till after Christmas. I went down to Mexico and saw him."

"Jenna, if the police or the FBI found out..."

"Dad, I needed closure."

"Conor was a good man. I admit, I was surprised to learn about his past. Sounds very...complicated."

"Yeah."

He took a bowl from me, dried it, and put it in the cabinet. "This case you're working...do be careful. And if you need help..."

"What?" I said with a laugh. "You going to show up on a white horse and rescue me?"

"I was going to say, call the cops."

"I will. I promise."

He hugged me. "You're irreplaceable, *chère*. You know that, don't you?"

"So are you."

The *Game of Thrones* ringtone played on my phone. "It's Becca, Dad. I gotta take this."

I stepped into my old bedroom for some privacy. "What's up, Becks?"

"I ran that plate. The Ford Crown Victoria is registered to Juan Cabrera. I ran a background on him. He's an enforcer for the Jaguars. His nickname is *El Duende*."

"What's *El Duende* mean?"

"*El Duende* is a goblin-like creature from Latin American mythology. When I misbehaved as a kid, my mom would warn me that *El Duende* would bite off my toes if I didn't behave."

"Ugh. How horrible."

"Cabrera has a brutal reputation, Jinxie. He once hacked off the hands and feet of someone from a rival gang."

"That's who's following us? Shit. His daughter was raped by Fitzgerald."

"And Fitzgerald was found with his junk chopped off. Be super careful. These guys are freakin' psychos."

"I get the picture. Thanks for the 411."

I looked at my watch. It was one fifteen. Time to get moving.

Back in the kitchen, my father was putting away the last of the dishes into the cabinet. "Everything okay?"

"Yeah. We gotta head out. You mind if Max hangs out here until...Shea, Byrd, and I can get back?"

"He's welcome to stay as long as he likes. But shouldn't you let the cops handle this?"

"I used to be a cop, Dad. I can handle it." I kissed his cheek.

He hugged me and held on for a long moment. When he released me, he looked me in the eyes. He was fighting back tears. "Don't be a stranger, *chère*."

"I won't. I'll see you soon."

I walked into the living room, and the place erupted in cheers. The Diamondbacks had just scored a three-point home run.

"Hate to break up the party, but we gotta go. Max, hang here until we get back."

"You need any help?" asked Jake.

"I think we got it, bro. But thanks."

48

———————

I pulled on my Kevlar vest and slipped my Ruger and Rossi into their respective holsters. The two of us climbed onto Shea's bike and took off down the road. Byrd followed in his car.

My mind marinated over how to convince Yuri to let Ciara go. I hoped telling him that the Jaguars had murdered Scarlett would give him someone else to direct his anger at. I wasn't sure it would work, but we were low on alternatives.

It was just shy of two when we pulled into the Niko's parking lot. The restaurant had remained vacant for a couple of years. The surrounding strip mall had similarly suffered from urban blight. Weeds grew through cracks in the parking lot. Signs for the stores had either been blacked out or flipped backward.

A black Lincoln Town Car sat by the restaurant's back door.

I stepped off of Shea's bike and adjusted the straps on my ballistic vest. My adrenaline was surging from the ride. Now, as I faced the daunting task of rescuing Ciara, my mind and body were firing on all cylinders.

"We ready for this?" I looked from Shea to Byrd.

Shea racked the slide on her Glock. "Time to kick some Russkie ass."

Byrd nodded. "We got some sort of strategy?"

"Tell Yuri that Scarlett's dead. Show him the photo and her phone. Point him to the West Side Jags as the ones responsible. Hopefully, he will give us Ciara alive. They are businessmen, after all."

"And if he doesn't?"

I took a deep breath. "Then we go with plan B."

"What's plan B?"

I drew the Ruger and chambered a round. "We take her by force."

Byrd didn't look convinced this was a winning strategy. "God help us."

I opened the rear door of the restaurant. The kitchen had been stripped of appliances, shelves, and equipment, giving the place an eerie, abandoned feeling, like the photos of post-meltdown Pripyat, Ukraine. The lingering aroma of Mediterranean spices was faint compared to the more prevalent stench of blood, sweat, and urine—the reek of cruelty and torture.

Andrei Garinov appeared across the room, holding a chrome-plated .50-caliber Desert Eagle.

"No weapons. Put on ground." Garinov pointed at the tile floor.

Three-to-one were odds I could live with. "We'll hold on to them this time, thank you very much."

Hans, Franz emerged from the office on our right, holding large-caliber pistols. Mick Jagger stepped out of the restroom on our left, carrying an AK-47.

An ugly sneer split Garinov's face. "No weapons or you and your friends die."

Déjà vu really sucked sometimes. "Fuck!"

I set my Ruger on the floor. Hans snatched it up and stuffed it in the front of his waistband. He frisked me and relieved me of the Rossi revolver in my ankle holster. Byrd and Shea were similarly disarmed.

"Where the hell's Ciara?" I tried to keep the anger out of my voice.

"Where is whore Scarlett?"

"That's between us and your boss."

"Bitch" was all Andrei said before he lumbered out of the empty kitchen. The three other Russian trolls prodded us to follow into what had once been the dining room. Plywood covered the plate glass windows. The only light came in from the glass doors. The carpet had been ripped up, exposing the bare concrete slab drizzled with dried glue. Wooden strips with exposed carpet nails ran along the edges.

Ciara sat slumped in a chair, a layer of plastic sheeting beneath her. She was topless and gagged, hands bound behind her back. Her face was swollen and bruised. Blood oozed from dozens of wounds across her body.

Yuri stood behind her, arms crossed, a displeased look on his face.

Ignoring the guns at my back, I rushed to Ciara's side. "You still alive in there?"

Ciara moaned and partially opened one eye. "Jinx?"

"Just hold on," I whispered. "We'll get you out of here."

I stood and glared at Yuri. "You fucking monster. Beating up a defenseless woman? Does it boost your fragile male ego, you fucking Russian snowflake?"

"I told you no police. And yet police and FBI show up at club. Question me for hours. Interfere with business. Try to shut me down."

"You don't like cops? Try not breaking the fucking law. Now let her go."

Yuri shrugged. "You say you find Scarlett." He spread out his arms and glanced around the room. "Yet I do not see her. This does not please me."

"We found her." I reached for my pocket.

Jagger and the boys swiveled their guns on me. I raised my hands. "Relax. Just getting a phone." I pulled out the phone we'd found on the dead woman, pulled up the photo I'd taken of her, and handed it to Yuri.

"What is this?" he asked.

"Scarlett's phone. That's her body in the photo."

His eyes narrowed. "You kill her? Why?"

"Wasn't us. It was the West Side Jaguars. We found her body in the Salt River wash."

"Fucking dirty Mexicans. Why they kill Scarlett?"

"Your former client, James Fitzgerald, raped the daughter of Juan Cabrera, an enforcer for the Jags. After the cops refused to prosecute Fitzgerald, Cabrera went on a killing spree. Killed the preacher, the cop, and Scarlett. Guess they didn't want any witnesses."

"How do I know this not trick? This black woman." He pointed at the photo on the phone. "She could be anybody."

"That phone was on her. Look through the call log. Some of those calls are from me trying to get her to call. It's Scarlett, all right, and she's dead."

He clicked through the call log, then said something in Russian that sounded like a curse. "Dirty Mexicans think they can interfere with my business? Kill my girls?"

I wanted to argue that Scarlett wasn't his, but it didn't seem like the right time. Getting out alive with Ciara was our priority.

He stood up and got into my face. He smelled of dollar store cologne and vodka. "I do not like people snooping at my club, talking to my people." He looked like a bull threatening to charge. "But I am businessman, Jinx Ballou. We make deal. You find this Juan Cabrera. Bring to me. Then we let your friend go."

"We already had a deal, man," said Byrd. "We're taking Ciara with us."

"No. Old deal is Scarlett for friend. No Scarlett, no friend, no deal."

"She's dead, you dipshit. D-E-A-D! Dead!" shouted Shea.

"What're you? Stupid? Your mother drop you on your stupid commie head? We're not bringing you nobody."

Yuri snatched Hans's gun from his hand, grabbed Shea by the collar, and pressed the barrel against her forehead. "Maybe I kill you all. Right here, right now."

At this point, we were down to plan F—fucking out of plans. I thought about my mother. I saw her tear-strewn face. Deep within me, a fire erupted. I was not going down without a fight.

From outside the restaurant came a deep, rolling thunder. But it wasn't a storm. Monsoon season was months away.

"What is that?" shouted Yuri. "What is going on outside?"

Andrei stood next to me, peering out one of the side doors. An endless stream of motorcycles roared past in flashes of chrome and leather. Jagger disappeared into the kitchen. Hans and Franz turned to the other side door, guns raised.

While Russians scrambled, Shea, Byrd, and I exchanged a split-second glance. I grabbed my gun, still in Andrei's waistband, and squeezed the trigger. A spray of blood exploded between his legs. He collapsed, bellowing in pain.

In the same instant, Shea disarmed Hans and finished him off with a double tap to the chest. Byrd grappled with Franz over his gun. Byrd drove his heel into the Russian's instep. Franz released the gun and fell to one knee. Byrd pressed the pistol to the man's head.

"I surrender," said Franz. Byrd lowered his weapon, but as he did so, Franz reached for it.

I raised my Ruger, but Shea was faster and pulled off two more shots, dropping the guy to the floor.

I turned my gun on Yuri. His narrow face colored with rage. "You stupid bit—"

Another pull of my trigger sent his brain splattering across the room.

A series of shots echoed from the kitchen, and the Athena Sisterhood charged in, guns raised. Jagger was no doubt dead.

"We're good! It's over," Shea told Fuego, who led the charge. The dining room filled with leather-clad women.

"Damn." Fuego shook her head as she surveyed the carnage. "We missed all the fun?"

At my feet, Andrei muttered frantically in Russian while blood oozed between his fingers pressed against his crotch. I'd hit his femoral artery. His eyes were wide with terror. I was tempted to finish him off but decided not to.

"Die slowly, asshole."

His muttering dissolved into moaning and then silence.

I moved to Ciara and cut her bonds. She collapsed into my arms. Savage appeared next to me and helped lower her to the floor.

"She's in shock," said Savage. "We need to cover her up."

I looked around for something to use—a blanket, a tablecloth, anything—but came up empty. Shea retrieved a jacket from the back of her motorcycle and draped it over Ciara. I pulled off my ballistic vest and used it as a pillow for her head.

"How'd you know we were here?" I asked Savage.

She nodded toward Shea. "She gave us a call. Sorry we were late."

"911 is on the way." Byrd turned to Shea. "Thanks for the save."

Shea snorted. "And I thought only Jesus saves."

I knelt down beside Ciara. "You're safe. Ambulance is on the way."

Her sobs were the only response.

As I studied the faces of the women bikers, I recognized one and approached her. "Zia Pearson, right?"

Her eyes narrowed. "Yeah?"

I slapped my cuffs over one of her wrists and then the other. "Jinx Ballou. Friendly neighborhood bounty hunter."

"Hey, wait a minute! Help!"

Savage, Fuego, and Rah-Rah turned toward me, weapons in hand. "Let her go!"

Dragon stepped between us and gestured for the others to lower their guns. "Jinx, do we have to do this now?"

"That was the deal. I find the real killer. Indigo turns herself in."

"These people?" Dragon indicated the dead Russians. "They killed Fitzgerald?"

"No," said Shea, joining us. "Juan Cabrera, aka El Duende, of the West Side Jaguars did. Jinx has the evidence we need to prove it. I'm no lawyer, but it should be enough to get the charges against Indigo dropped."

Approaching sirens screamed in the distance.

Indigo looked at Dragon, her face filled with terror. "I don't want to go back to jail. Not for another night. Not after what happened last time."

"I understand your fear," I said. "But I can keep you safe. A friend of mine's a CO in Scottsdale. She can put you in protective custody. No one will get to you."

Her fear turned to rage. "But I didn't do nothing wrong. Why should I suffer for what some *cholo* did?"

Our eyes met. She was right. If I took her in, knowing what she'd already endured, I was no better than that cowboy cop Atkinson who'd railroaded her. I uncuffed her.

The back door slammed open. Four uniformed officers from Peoria PD burst into the room, guns raised. "Police! Everyone down on the ground!"

I complied with their instructions to lie on the floor while the officers snatched up our weapons. "Oh, goody. The cavalry's here. We're saved."

"Just when things were getting fun," replied Byrd.

EMTs arrived and transported Ciara to the hospital. More unis arrived by the dozen, along with FBI Special Agent Lovelace and detectives from Peoria's homicide squad. I was allowed to call my attorney, Kirsten Pasternak, before Shea, Byrd, and I were herded into squad cars and taken to the precinct for questioning.

Kirsten arrived shortly after I was put in one of Peoria's interview rooms. After a brief consultation with her, I told Agent Lovelace and the Peoria detectives assigned to the case that I'd been contacted by Yuri Barayev and told to show up with Scarlett. We'd shown up with the phone as fictional proof that Scarlett was dead, whereupon Yuri threatened to kill all of us. Byrd, Shea, and I had consequently acted in self-defense.

Neither Agent Lovelace nor the detectives were happy about me removing evidence from the dead woman's body in Phoenix. I surrendered the phone to Lovelace, who agreed to forward it to Detective Hardin for his investigation into the dead woman's murder. I had no doubt I'd be hearing from Hardin and would get a thorough ass chewing. Whether he'd charge me with evidence tampering and interfering with a murder investigation was uncertain.

After several hours of questioning, I was officially released, though Lovelace warned me the investigation was still open pending ballistics and autopsy. She informed me that Ciara had been transported to Boswell Medical Center in Sun City.

While being escorted to the precinct lobby, I sent Max a text letting him know about Ciara and offering him use of the Gray Ghost so he could drive there from my folks' house.

Byrd, Shea, and members of the Athena Sisterhood were waiting for me in the precinct lobby.

"Thanks for your help," I told Kirsten.

"Try to stay out of trouble, Jinx." She gave me a hug. "Though if trouble finds you, you know who to call."

"Hey!" said Byrd. "How'm I supposed to get back to the restaurant to pick up my car?"

"I can give you a lift." Kirsten turned to me. "You coming?"

I looked at Shea, and she nodded. "Naw, I'm good. Watch out, Byrd. See that she doesn't charge you for the lift. Her rates are outrageous."

"Very funny." Kirsten stood in the doorway. "For that crack, I should charge you double for dragging me out on a Sunday night."

Me and my big mouth.

"So who's up for a victory celebration?" I asked the group.

Shea and her fellow bikers seemed in a rather somber mood considering we'd avoided multiple murder charges. "I think we'll pass," said Shea.

"We just rescued my friend from Russian gangsters. I'd say that calls for some sort of celebration."

"They took Indigo into custody," said Dragon.

Only then did I notice Indigo wasn't with the group. My enthusiasm fell. "Why? I let her go."

"A bench warrant had been issued," Dragon explained. "Peoria PD will be transferring her to Scottsdale lockup later tonight. I'm going to try to get her bail reset, but considering the circumstances, I'm not hopeful. At least she's being sent to the women's unit this time."

"I'll contact my friend at the Scottsdale jail. She'll make sure Indigo's kept safe until we can get the charges dropped."

"We'd appreciate that, Jinx." Dragon managed a weak smile.

"I wish I could have done more."

"You did enough." Shea's eyes met mine. "You risked your life. Several times. We couldn't have asked for more."

"Thanks. I'll—" My phone rang. The caller ID was unfamiliar. "Hold that thought." I answered the call.

"Hi, I think you've been trying to reach me," said an accented voice. "My name is Sophie Dujardin. I used to go by Scarlett."

Sophie agreed to meet with me the following morning. I made another quick call to my ex-girlfriend, Toni, at the Scottsdale jail and let her know about Indigo. It was an awkward conversation, both of us still regretting how our brief fling had ended, but she agreed to keep Indigo safe. Apparently, two COs had lost their job over what had already happened to Indigo.

I hitched a ride on the back of Fuego's bike, while Shea

doubled up with Dragon to pick up her bike at the old Greek restaurant.

When we arrived, the parking lot of the blighted strip mall was dark except for the motorcycle headlights. All of a sudden, I felt very alone. The thrill of rescuing Ciara and avoiding arrest had faded.

"You heading back up to Sycamore Springs?" I asked Shea.

"Not yet. We want to stick around until Indigo gets arraigned and hopefully released."

"Where you staying?"

"Desert View Inn." The corners of her mouth curled in a wistful smile. "Unless I get a better offer."

"Well, there's a cute little house down in the Willo District. Owner's not much of a cook, but it's homey, and there's a very friendly dog."

"I do like dogs," she added. She reached for my hand, and a jolt of electricity ran up my arm.

There was no sign of Juan Cabrera or any of his gangbanger friends on the street when Shea and I arrived at the Bunker. It was nearly nine o'clock when we walked through the door. I was beat and wanted to collapse into a coma for the next six months, despite a desire to get to know Shea on a more intimate level.

After I made a few quick phone calls, Shea and I tumbled into my bed, kissing, cuddling, and drifting in and out of sleep. Both of us were too exhausted for anything more.

49

O n Monday morning, Dragon called and informed us that Indigo's new hearing was set for Tuesday morning at ten. Indigo was miserable being in custody but safe for the time being.

I felt bad for her, but there wasn't much I could do except provide Dragon with what I had uncovered about Juan Cabrera and the trail of bodies he left following his daughter's rape.

"What's our game plan?"

"Sophie Dujardin, aka Scarlett, has agreed to meet with us this morning," I told Shea over coffee and cold cereal. "I'm hoping we can convince her to testify."

"Fingers crossed," she said. "How's Ciara?"

"Stable, but the doctors at Boswell Medical Center are still checking her for internal injuries."

"What are we going to do about the West Side Jaguars?"

"I spoke with Detective Hardin last night before we crashed. There's a statewide BOLO out on Juan Cabrera and Chuy Rodriguez, another member of the Jaguars. The ballistics from Garza, Fitzgerald, and the woman we found in the wash all matched, as did the ones from the drive-by. Hardin will provide Dragon with copies of the reports."

"He mad about the phone?"

"Can't you tell one of my ass cheeks is missing?" I joked. "Trust me, I got an earful. But he's not going to charge me with anything."

"So Cabrera and this other guy are still on the streets?"

"As far as I know. Hardin agreed to have a patrol car cruise by my house every couple of hours in case Cabrera shows up."

"How the hell did Cabrera know we were looking for Fitzgerald's murderer?"

"I don't know."

"Maybe that cowboy cop in Scottsdale and/or his partner are on the Jaguar payroll. Maybe that's why they railroaded Indigo—to cover up for Cabrera."

As a former cop myself, I didn't like to think of other cops as being corrupt. Assholes, yeah, but actively working with felons to throw a murder case? "So long as Phoenix PD puts Cabrera and Rodriguez away for killing Garza, I don't care how they knew." I stood up and set my dishes in the sink. "Before I meet with Dujardin, I want to visit Ciara. You care to join me?"

"I got nothing better to do." She smiled, and my insides melted.

Getting ready took longer than anticipated. Turns out, taking a shower with someone you're sexually attracted to doesn't save time or water. But it was enlightening. Turns out, Shea had very strong hands and knew how to use them for more than building motorcycles.

Once dressed, I pulled on my ballistic vest. Peoria PD had seized my Ruger and Rossi for evidence. Fortunately, I still had the SIG I'd taken off Yuri Barayev, which I tucked in a conceal holster at the small of my back, and a snub-nosed .38, which I tucked in my ankle holster. I offered Shea my spare vest.

She replied, "Nah. When it rains, I just run between the drops."

I gave her a look. "You serious? Cabrera's still looking for us, remember? Your bike may be fast, but I doubt it will outrun bullets."

"Kevlar vests are heavy, hot, and make it hard to move out of the way. Thanks for the offer, but I'll pass."

I looked out the front window. No cars on the street as far as I could see. Maybe they'd caught Cabrera after all.

Shea helped me onto the back of her bike, and we cruised toward Seventh Avenue. I spotted Cabrera's Crown Victoria parked on Fifth Avenue. The headlights flickered on as the car roared to life.

"That's them," I shouted to Shea.

"I'll lose them." She poured on speed, and we flew past Cabrera's car.

I hung on as best I could while Shea navigated through the labyrinth of streets in the neighborhood—up Fifth Avenue, onto Granada, twisting onto Third, around the island where Holly Street split with Monte Vista, then back west, headed for the ever-bustling traffic on Seventh Avenue. Cabrera bore down on us the whole way.

I felt the impacts a microsecond before I heard the triple crack of the gun. They hit like a sledgehammer to the spine. I slammed into Shea, smacking our helmets together.

"Jinx?" shouted Shea.

"All right," I wheezed through gritted teeth. "Kevlar."

More gunshots followed. Shea put on a burst of speed just as I reached for the SIG Sauer. I slammed hard against the backrest, another explosion of pain rippling through my body. The pistol slipped from my hand and disappeared behind us.

Shea wove sharply back and forth down the road, trying to make us harder to hit but forcing me to cling to her for dear life. The busy Seventh Avenue intersection rapidly approached. There was no way to make the turn without either getting creamed by oncoming traffic or stopping and letting Cabrera catch us.

"Hold on," Shea shouted.

Without slowing, Shea pulled a hard Hail Mary right turn. An air horn bellowed behind us followed by the wail of screeching tires, screaming people, and the sickening crunch of metal and glass.

Shea whipped onto a side street and stopped so suddenly that I tumbled forward and landed on my back. I was so stunned I barely noticed the asphalt scorching my arms and legs. Every breath felt like a power drill to my spine.

Shea rushed over to me. "Jinx, you okay?" The concern on her face nearly broke my heart.

"I'm...alive." I gritted my teeth and, with her help, wobbled into a standing position. I ripped off my vest and found three rounds mushroomed in the back.

Shea pulled up the back of my shirt. "Didn't break the skin, but you're gonna be feeling those hits a while. Guess I didn't do so well at driving between the drops, huh?"

I turned and caught her gaze. "Not your fault. And I'm not so easy to kill."

An unexpected chuckle escaped from her throat. "So I see."

I took a deep, painful breath and looked at what had become of our pursuers. Cabrera's car lay crushed between a cement truck and a bus shelter.

"Let's finish this," I growled, pulling the .38 from my ankle holster.

Fueled by adrenaline and rage, we pushed through a crowd of people gathered around the crash site. The cement truck had pancaked the driver's side of the Crown Vic through to the center console. Somewhere in the tangle of twisted metal, plastic, and glass were the flattened remains of Juan Cabrera. *El Duende* was now *Una Tortilla*. I approached the car's passenger side.

A man with a shaved head and an elaborate neck tattoo sat dazed with the door halfway open, one foot on the ground, a .45-caliber held loosely in his right hand. Blood trickled down his face. He looked up at me with glazed eyes and tried to raise his gun.

I pressed my revolver to his forehead. "Drop it, or I'll put one through that ugly face of yours."

The pistol clattered to the ground. I kicked it away.

"Who are you?" I asked.

"*¿Que?*" he asked in a deep growl.

"*Cómo te llamas, pendejo?*" I repeated.

"Chuy." A fine mist of blood sprayed from his lips as he mumbled his name. "Chuy Rodriguez."

"Who told you we were investigating Fitzgerald's murder, Chuy?" I asked in Spanish.

His eyes were dull and glassy. "*Pinche puta.*"

I pressed the barrel of the .38 harder against his skull. "*¡Digame! ¿Quien?*"

"*¡Chingáte!*" He started to cough up more blood.

With Shea's help, I dragged him out of the car and tossed him onto the sidewalk. I took a photo of his face with my phone, then cuffed him. "Fuck you, too, asshole!" I whispered into his ear.

The heavyset driver of the cement truck huffed into view. There was an abrasion and a dusting of white powder on his face from where his airbag had hit him. "I tried to stop, but that car, it just came out of nowhere. You gals police?" he asked, looking at the handcuffs on Rodriguez.

"Not exactly," I said. "But this man's wanted for murdering a cop."

"I...I called 911 and my corporate office. Geez, I sure hope I don't get dinged for this. I'll lose my job."

When the patrol officers and ambulance arrived, I explained that Chuy Rodriguez and the now deceased Juan Cabrera had murdered several people including Detective Garza. I suggested they contact Detective Oliver Jennings, who was assigned to the Garza case. He arrived not long after.

Detective Jennings always reminded me of a chunky Tom Skerritt. His salt-and-pepper mustache was bushier than the last time I'd seen him. The guy must've been pushing sixty at this point, and I wondered if he'd ever take his pension and retire.

"Ms. Ballou," he said genteelly, shaking my hand. "Getting yourself into a little dustup with some gangbangers?"

"Something like that."

I introduced Shea and gave him the rundown on the situation, filling him in on Cabrera's involvement in the murders.

"He shot at you?" Jennings asked when I told him about our most recent narrow escape.

I held out my vest and showed him the three hollow point rounds still embedded in the Kevlar fibers.

"I'd like to take that in as evidence, if you don't mind." Jennings was always polite. It was his friendly, I'm-your-best-buddy style that got him so many confessions from suspects.

Giving up my vest felt like surrendering my wallet or phone. I felt naked without it. But with Yuri and his guys in the morgue and Cabrera soon joining them, my need for it was less critical than it had been. I watched him put it in a large evidence bag.

By the time Jennings allowed us to go, I'd received a text from Max that Ciara had been released and was home resting. I replied that I'd check on her later. We didn't have much time before we were due to meet with Scarlett.

50

———

Shea and I pulled into my neighborhood, where I found the SIG still lying in the street. Maybe my luck was changing. Last thing I needed was one of my weapons ending up in the hands of one of the neighborhood kids.

At ten o'clock, we arrived at a small brick building on Thomas Road that served as the office for the Human Trafficking Rescue Center. We parked in a small lot behind the building and left our weapons in the top case on Shea's bike.

A sign by the back door read Entrance, but when I turned the knob, it was locked. I rang the doorbell.

A large black man with the physique of a bodybuilder opened the door. A semiautomatic pistol hung from his left hip. "Can I help you?" His voice was deep and gravelly but polite.

"Jinx Ballou and Shea Stevens. We're here to meet with Ms. Acevedo."

"Can I see some ID?"

We handed him our driver's licenses. The man inspected them, looked us over to make sure our faces matched the photos, and handed them back. "Right this way, ladies."

He led us past a break room into a reception area with couches and overstuffed chairs. The shades were all drawn.

A woman dressed in a tan summer-weight business suit sat on a sofa that looked like it had been picked up at Goodwill. She stood and shook our hands. "Welcome to the Human Trafficking Rescue Center. I'm Mariana Acevedo, the senior coordinator. I see you've met our security officer, Lewis Jackson." She nodded at the man who'd let us in.

Shea and I introduced ourselves.

"I really appreciate you meeting with us," I said.

Mariana's smile faded into formality. "Please sit. Would you care for something to drink?"

We both shook our heads and sat in armchairs across from Mariana.

"Do you know about the rescue center? What we do here?"

"Perhaps you could tell us," I said.

"I like to think of ourselves as an underground railroad helping people escape modern-day slavery. We operate a loose network of volunteer service providers and shelters. On occasion, we work with law enforcement, but many human trafficking victims are also undocumented immigrants. We often find ourselves having to protect clients as much from the federal government as from the criminal organizations."

"Makes sense," I said. "Wouldn't make sense to rescue a woman from human traffickers only to have ICE stick her in a cage."

"Exactly."

"We're here because a woman is being wrongfully put in a cage," I explained. "She's being framed for a murder she didn't commit. She's transgender and has already been raped once in jail because the idiots in Scottsdale stuck her in a men's facility. If she's found guilty, it could cost her her life."

"Yes, our client told me you are investigating the murder of that preacher." Mariana's face revealed a laundry list of emotions.

"Scarlett is the only eyewitness to the murder," Shea replied. "We need her to testify."

"That is out of the question. She is an undocumented refugee from Haiti. Not only would she risk deportation if she testified, but she would face reprisals from the men who trafficked her and from the men who murdered that preacher."

"Yuri Barayev and the men running the sex ring are dead," I replied. "Juan Cabrera, the man who murdered Fitzgerald, is also dead. She doesn't need to fear reprisals."

"If you already know who's responsible, why do you need her to testify?"

"If she doesn't, my friend will die in prison. Police found her DNA under the victim's fingernails." Shea's voice crackled with emotion.

When Mariana gave us a quizzical look, I added, "The two of them had a...scuffle earlier that day. She didn't kill him. But when juries these days hear DNA, they think guilty. Scarlett's testimony is crucial to prove our friend innocent."

Mariana appeared to process the information for a few minutes, then nodded at Lewis. He vanished down a hallway and returned with a woman dressed in a loose-fitting sweatshirt and jeans. She had dark skin, long braids, and a very nervous look. She could easily pass for Indigo's sister.

"Jinx Ballou, Shea Stevens, this is Sophie Dujardin, whom you know as Scarlett. I leave it up to her whether to assist you."

I shook her hand. "Thank you for calling me back."

We all sat down, and I explained Indigo's predicament to Sophie. "We really need your help."

Sophie shook her head. "I...I just want to live my life. Nine years ago, much of my family was killed in the earthquake near Port-au-Prince. Then my mama and brother Pierre died from cholera. I was alone. A couple years ago, a man told me I could be a model and actress in America. But he lied."

"He turned you into a sex slave," I said.

"*Oui.* I lost hope of ever being happy. The men were like animals. And then that horrible night..."

"I'd like to show you a couple of photos. Could you tell me if you recognize them as the men who murdered James Fitzgerald?"

Mariana looked to Sophie, who nodded. I pulled up a photo of Juan Cabrera that Becca had sent me, and handed my phone to Sophie. The moment she looked at the photo, she shuddered, then nodded before squeezing her eyes tightly shut. A tear streamed down the side of her face. "He's one of them." She handed me back my phone.

I pulled up the photo of Chuy Rodriguez I'd taken at the car crash a few hours earlier. "How about him?"

She took a deep breath and let it out. "*Oui,* he was the other."

"Thanks. That helps. Now if you could testify to this in court..."

Sophie's face tightened like a fist. She clutched her chest but couldn't tear her gaze away from the photo on the phone. "I... cannot. I am sorry."

"Please, Sophie," Shea begged. "You can't let my friend go to prison."

"I think we're done here," said Mariana. "You've made your case, but clearly—"

"Can I show you one more photo?"

Sophie wiped the tears from her face. "Okay."

I pulled up another photo and gave her the phone.

She gasped and covered her mouth, handing me back the phone as if it were too hot to hold. "I do not know this person."

"Her name is Zia Pearson. Her friends call her Indigo."

"What happened to her?"

"She was brutally assaulted at the Scottsdale jail. The men's jail," said Shea. "She's transgender, and those bastards stuck her in with the men. Didn't care that she's post-op. She, too, has been traumatized for a crime she didn't commit. And unless you help us prove she's innocent, they're going to send her back. She'll probably be raped again and eventually murdered. Even if you don't want to testify, we need to know exactly what happened in that motel room."

She closed her eyes, both arms now wrapped around her. "Okay, I will tell you."

51

Sophie went through her story. Yuri had ordered her to service Fitzgerald. She had no idea he had been violent with Maricela. Shortly after she entered the motel room, Fitzgerald got verbally abusive with her, calling her an ugly whore.

At first, she thought this was just playacting. But then he struck her with his fist. She tried to escape, but he was too big and powerful. He forced her onto the bed and was about to rape her when Cabrera and Rodriguez burst into the room. Both had guns. Cabrera had a machete stuck in his belt.

Fitzgerald yelled at them to get out, but Rodriguez pulled Fitzgerald off the bed and held his arms while Cabrera pummeled him, screaming at him for raping his daughter. Then Rodriguez dragged him into the bathroom while Sophie cowered in the corner. She heard a thunk followed by a bloodcurdling scream.

Sophie grabbed her clothes and headed toward the door. Cabrera spotted her and yelled, "Where you going, *puta*?"

Blood dripped from the machete in his hand. He lunged at

her, but she managed to escape. She recalled hearing a loud bang like a gunshot as she raced across the parking lot.

She took refuge in the liquor store next door. Turned out that Marco, the old man who owned the store, was an HTRC volunteer. He hid Sophie in the storage room. When Cabrera stormed in moments later, Marco claimed she had run out the back.

After Cabrera left, Marco contacted the HTRC hotline. Mariana picked up Sophie and brought her to an HTRC-affiliated shelter.

Sophie buried her face in her hands as she finished her story.

"Thank you for sharing this, Sophie," I said. "Is there any way I can convince you to talk to my friend's lawyer? No judge. No jury. Just the lawyer."

"I am sorry for your friend, truly I am. But I cannot risk going back to Haiti. And the man with the machete, he was part of a gang. They would come after me."

I nodded. "If you change your mind, please give me a call. Thank you both for your time."

"No, you have to testify!" Shea rose to her feet, the scars on her face deepening with emotion. "You want to be an American? Well, that means standing up to injustice."

"Shea!" I reached for her, but she swatted my hand away.

"No, I understand you're scared. We were scared, too, but we risked our lives to rescue a woman that Yuri Barayev and his goons kidnapped. We nearly got killed by Cabrera and his *cholos* because you refused to tell the cops what you witnessed."

Lewis Jackson, the security officer, reappeared in the room, looking very stern.

Mariana stood. "Ms. Ballou, Ms. Stevens, I'm going to have to ask you to leave now. Sophie has given you as much information as she is comfortable providing."

"No, you can't do this," insisted Shea.

"Shea, we got to go." I put a hand on her shoulder and steered her toward the back door. "We tried our best."

Shea began walking, but her rage continued. "I swear, if Indigo gets convicted, I will find you."

"Shea, stop," I whispered.

Mariana and Lewis stood stone-faced. Sophie sobbed on the couch.

Shea's shoulders slumped as we stepped outside into the parking lot. The dead bolt on the door clacked shut behind us.

"It's not right." She tossed me my borrowed helmet.

"I know. But we know the whole story now. We can piece together the evidence because we know what we're looking for. We'll have the ballistics and police reports to tie it all together."

"What if it's not enough? You know how juries are with DNA."

"Trust the process," I said.

"What the hell's that mean?"

"Something my father says. All we can do is what we can do. Then we have to trust that things will somehow work out the way they're supposed to."

"The way they're supposed to," Shea repeated derisively. "The way they worked out for my mother when my father murdered her? The way they worked out for your fiancé? The way they worked out for Vanessa Colton?"

I put a hand on her shoulder. "Let's talk to Dragon. She's a smart lawyer. With the information we have, she'll figure out a way to get the charges dismissed."

We left the HTRC office and met Dragon in her room at the Desert View Inn. I provided copies of my report that connected the dots between Fitzgerald raping Cabrera's daughter and the murders of Fitzgerald, Cabrera, and the woman found in the Salt River wash, as well as the drive-by at my house. I referred her to Detectives Jennings and Hardin for copies of reports from ballistics, autopsy, and whatever else she needed from the Phoenix Crime Lab to prove her case. I also gave her a copy of the audio file of Sophie's statement I'd secretly recorded on my phone.

"It's too bad Ms. Dujardin won't testify. I can try to get the audio file admitted into evidence, but it's iffy. We may have to make do with the other information you provided. I'll file for a dismissal first thing. Thanks for your work on this."

I glanced at Shea. "It's been interesting."

My phone rang. It was Maurice at Pima Bail Bonds. I stepped outside Dragon's motel room and answered it. "What's going on, Maurice? How come they issued a bench warrant for Pearson a day early? I was about to turn her in."

"Ms. Ballou, when I call you or text you for a progress update, I expect a response."

"Well, things were—"

He kept going as if I hadn't said a word. "I brought you in as a favor to Deez. But I expect a minimal level of professionalism."

"For which I—"

"Dodging my calls or telling me you're close when you aren't is not acceptable."

I stepped outside, and Shea joined me. The sunlight glittered in her eyes.

"Maurice, to be fair, I—"

"Now I hear you teamed up with the people hiding Ms. Pearson so you could play private eye? What were you thinking?"

I waited, not wanting to be cut off again. Plus having Shea so close to me all of a sudden felt very distracting. Images of the two of us in my bed doing more than cuddling played through my mind.

"Ms. Ballou, are you there?"

"Uh, yeah. I'm here."

"Did you partner up with the Athena Sisterhood to locate Fitzgerald's killer?"

"I did everything I could to bring Pearson in. It wasn't going to happen. Deez's crew couldn't do it either, by the way. So I gathered exculpatory evidence as an incentive for her to surrender voluntarily."

"I nearly lost my shirt on this deal."

"Look, Maurice, I—" The call dropped.

Shea stepped in close, sending a jolt of electricity through my body. "Everything all right?" she asked in that sultry alto voice of hers.

"Just the usual. Me getting fired. It's kinda my thing."

Looking into her eyes was like taking a hit off a joint. Waves of euphoria washed over me. A deep fire I hadn't felt in months blazed to life inside me. Before I knew what I was doing, I was kissing her.

After what felt like an eternity, I came up for air. "I...uh, you want to...um, head back to my place?"

She looked so deep into my soul I felt naked and yet unafraid. "Yeah."

We said goodbye to Dragon, then hopped on the back of her motorcycle. We blazed down the Black Canyon Highway, weaving between the cars, roared onto the Thomas Road exit, squeaking through yellow lights, and it still wasn't fast enough. We hooked a left so hard onto Central I literally saw sparks flying when her foot peg scraped the pavement.

While racing past a light rail train, I caught myself waiving at the passengers like a goofy teenager. I didn't care how silly I looked.

We stepped inside my house. Diana rushed up to greet me like I hadn't been there for a thousand years. The way she always did. I loved that about her.

"Hey, baby!" I said as she showered me with sloppy doggy kisses. "You keep the place safe from intruders?"

"She loves her mommy. That's for sure," Shea said.

I gazed into the furry face, reflecting over the past few months. "She's been my North Star ever since I got her. Even when everything went to shit, she was always there for me. Always loving me no matter how broken I got." Tears pricked my eyes.

I stood up and turned to Shea, mustering a smile for her.

She caressed my cheek. "What say you and me go to your bedroom and tear each other's clothes off."

I pretended to be appalled. "What kinda girl do you think

I am?"

"The kind who needs someone to tear her clothes off."

"Okay, you got me there."

"And who hasn't been properly fucked in a good long time." A sly smile crept across her face.

My knees almost buckled from anticipation. "Aw, shit, I'm in trouble."

We meandered down the hallway, hand in hand, looking at each other like a couple of shy, lovesick schoolgirls. I flopped down on my bed and winced in pain.

"What's wrong?" she asked.

"My back," I replied through gritted teeth.

"Lemme take a look."

I sat up, and she helped me off with my shirt.

"How bad is it?"

"Shit, girl, you got a lot of scars."

"Hazards of the trade, I'm afraid. What about from today? Where I got shot."

"Got yourself some hellacious bruises and a bit of swelling. Wait here." She stepped out of the room.

Diana started nudging my hand, wanting me to pet her and scratch her back.

"Diana, go lay down in the living room."

She gave me a pouty look that tugged at my heartstrings. But right now, my heartstrings would have to wait. "Lay down and we'll go for a run later." She whined, then hustled off, wagging her tail.

"This should help." Shea returned with a bag of frozen peas, pressing it to my bare back.

I gasped and sucked in a pain-riddled lung full of air. "Fuck. That's. Cold."

"Sorry." She nuzzled close so that I could feel her breath on my ear. The icy chill of the frozen peas suddenly didn't bother me so much. Her free hand slipped over the inside of my thigh. The words "fire and ice" took on a whole new meaning.

"I...I'm not...huh...not complaining," I managed through breaths as she nibbled on my earlobe. Shivers that ran down my spine had nothing to do with the bag of frozen peas. A needful ache grew between my legs.

I lay on my side, facing her. In the afternoon light filtering through the security blinds, I studied the scarred landscape of her face, softened by the warm glow of her eyes. I was still trembling—not from the improvised cold pack on my back but from the thrill of opening myself up, allowing this person beside me to see my most vulnerable self.

I traced the lines on her face. "You're so fucking beautiful, you know that?"

"You sure you didn't hit your head when you fell off my bike?" She chuckled. "Clearly, your judgment is impaired."

"We both have scars. Do my scars make me less attractive?"

"Fuck no." She pressed her forehead against mine. Waves of heat rippled between us.

My deepest fear bubbled up. I couldn't avoid it. "Does it bother you that I'm trans?"

She kissed me deeply. The pack of peas dropped with a smack onto the hardwood floor. I cradled her face in my hands, our tongues teasing and probing and caressing each other in a dance.

I rolled onto my back. She positioned herself on top of me, our legs intertwined.

"I'm not hurting you, am I?" she asked. The concern on her face was almost heartbreaking.

"No. I'm okay." I could barely register the throbbing in my back.

She bent down and kissed my breasts, gently sucking and teasing at first, and then grew more insistent. For the next hour, we explored each other's bodies, tracing war wounds and battle scars and bringing each other to much-needed climaxes over and over.

52

The next morning, I felt lonely and confused about the situation with Shea. Where the hell was this going? She lived up in Sycamore Springs, easily an hour's drive away. Maybe less the way she drove. But still, it wasn't like we could see each other on a daily basis. Things were crazy enough when I'd dated Conor, and he'd lived only a couple of streets over.

Was I even ready for a relationship? Was I making more of it than it was? Maybe it was just a friends-with-benefits situation. A friendly fuck between comrades in arms who'd survived some harrowing events. Suddenly, I jumped out of bed. Shit! I'd totally forgotten about Ciara.

I called Max. "Hey! How's Ciara doing?"

"Jinx. Hey." He sounded sleepy. The clock read six twenty. Shit. I'd woken him up. "Let me get her. Hold on."

A moment later, a raw, tired voice I barely recognized as Ciara came on the line. "Jinxie?"

"I'm sorry. I shouldn't have called so early. It's just, I meant to stop by yesterday, and well, things kept getting in the way."

"It's no problem. I'm...I don't know how I'm doing. Physically, docs said I should be okay. Mentally, I'm still trying to process everything."

"Yeah, I get it. I've been through some similar stuff."

"The hospital staff recommended some therapists who specialize in trauma. Your father was on that list."

"Not surprised. He knows his shit."

"Would it be weird if I went to see him? At least with him, I don't have to rehash all the transgender stuff."

"Not at all." I sighed, trying to push through the guilt. "Ciara, I'm so sorry for all of this. If I had known..."

"Not your fault."

I felt like it was. "If there is anything I can do, just ask."

"You rescued me, Jinx. You killed those bastards. I'm...I'm glad they're dead. Is that a bad thing to say?"

"No, I'm glad they're dead too. Not even sorry I killed some of them. I'd do anything to protect you. You're a good person."

"I'm gonna go back to sleep now. They gave me these meds. Just so tired."

"Sleep. We'll talk again soon."

"Hey, lover," Shea said when I put my phone back on the nightstand.

"Hey." I kissed her, soaking in the bliss of whatever the hell this was.

"You hungry?"

"For you or food?" I asked.

She shrugged. "Either."

Forty minutes later, we pulled ourselves from the sheets. I took Diana for her morning run while Shea showered.

The air was warmer than it had been. The cooler-than-usual spring was giving way to the first hints of the fury of summer. I didn't care. I felt whole in a way I hadn't in a very long time. Not just because of whatever this was between Shea and me. I felt like I'd broken out of the swamp I'd been living in for so long. I felt powerful.

An hour later, I was dressed in a blouse and slacks, even put on some makeup and did something with my hair other than pull it into a ponytail. I tried to convince myself that I wanted to look professional in court, especially if Dragon needed me to testify that Indigo should be released again on bail. Deep down, I knew why I was really going full femme. Shea.

She packed her stuff into her motorcycle's top case, and we drove separately to the courthouse. After all the time I'd spent getting ready, I didn't want to show up with helmet hair. I offered Shea a ride in the Charger, but she declined.

"Not a big fan of riding in a cage," she reminded me with a twinkle in her eye. "Besides, look at that thing. You drive like a maniac."

I arrived in the courtroom to see two dozen women sitting in the gallery, dressed in Athena Sisterhood biker vests, which I had since learned were called cuts. Guessed if I was going to become a biker, I needed to learn the lingo.

Byrd was there, too, looking quite dapper in a charcoal-gray suit. When I sent him the details for the hearing, I wasn't sure if he'd show up. I was glad he did.

The Honorable Alice Gwinnett, a woman with graying hair, walked in, her black robe swishing as she walked, and called the room to order. Wayne Prather started the proceedings by claiming that Indigo was a flight risk and should be remanded without bail. I wanted to smack the hell out of his smug little face.

Dragon objected, calling for the charges to be dismissed, explaining that she had ballistic reports that tied Fitzgerald's death to other murders in the valley. She further offered to have detectives from Phoenix PD testify that Juan "El Duende" Cabrera, recently deceased, was believed to be responsible for the murders of James Fitzgerald, Detective Luis Garza, and Bisi Awojobi, a Nigerian-born sex worker whose body was found in the Salt River wash.

Objections, counter objections, and all kinds of legal wrangling ensued. One reason I decided not to go to law school.

Justice was more like a high school debate than the pursuit of truth, all about cleverness and procedure. For all its risks, I much preferred my work as a bounty hunter.

After listening to all of the arguments and counter arguments, Judge Gwinnett issued a ruling. "After consideration of your motions, I—"

My phone rang. I had meant to silence it but forgot. The caller ID showed it was Sophie Dujardin.

"Whoever's phone that is needs to silence it immediately," demanded the judge.

"Hello? Sophie?" I whispered.

"Ma'am, you are disrupting this proceeding. Either—"

"Ms. Ballou, I have changed my mind. I...I will testify."

"Ma'am, do you hear me? Hang up that phone this instant or leave the courtroom. Otherwise—"

"I cannot let another innocent woman suffer because of what happened."

"Thank you, Sophie. Hold on just a moment." I squeezed past the other people sitting in my row and strode up the aisle toward Dragon.

"Ma'am, if you do not sit down this instant, I will hold you in contempt."

I ignored her.

"Bailiff! Please take that woman into custody."

I was almost to the defense table. Dragon looked at me as if I'd lost my mind. The bailiff charged toward me like a linebacker. I tossed the phone toward Dragon. She fumbled it, and it clattered to the floor the same instant the bailiff tackled me.

I was cuffed and frog-marched downstairs to a holding cell, which I shared with three other women, all wearing DOC coveralls. I ignored them.

For two hours, I sat there. Periodically, a bailiff would escort one of the other women out of the cell for her court appearance. I couldn't believe I'd come so close to getting Indigo free. My phone was smashed and useless. I might never get back in touch with Sophie, and even if I did, she'd probably have changed her mind. Indigo would spend the rest of her life in jail suffering who knew what horrors.

"Comfy?"

I looked up to see Dragon outside the bars, her briefcase in hand. A bailiff stood beside her.

"I've had better days."

"That was a bold move in court. Not necessarily smart but bold."

"What can I say? Not smart but bold is how I roll."

"I've got some good news and bad news. Which do you want first?"

"Rip off the bandage. Hit me with the bad news."

"You are being fined three hundred dollars for disrupting the court and ignoring Judge Gwinnett's demands. You will also have to personally apologize to her."

"So what's the good news?"

"The prosecutor and I met with the judge in chambers. She listened to Sophie's statement over your phone. The prosecutor didn't want her testimony admitted, but the judge heard her out. The charges against Indigo have been dismissed."

I took a deep breath and let go of a boatload of tension. "That is good news."

"Also, I spoke with Maurice Begay at Pima Bail Bonds and explained that you were instrumental in returning Indigo to custody. He's agreed to pay you your bounty and to keep you in mind for future jobs."

"Thanks, Dragon. You didn't have to do that."

"You really went above and beyond. It was the least I could do."

The bailiff let me out and escorted Dragon and me to Judge Gwinnett's chambers. She spent ten solid minutes chastising me for my disruptive behavior and schooling me on courtroom protocol. I stood there and took it, and when she was done, I apologized.

After paying my fine to the court clerk's office, I met the members of the Athena Sisterhood in the downstairs lobby.

Dragon handed me her business card. "If Mr. Begay doesn't hire you for any more bounty hunter work, look me up. I can always use a good investigator."

"Jinx," said someone behind me. I turned to see Indigo, arm in arm with Savage. "Havoc told me what all you did to help me. You put your life at risk multiple times. I...I don't know how to thank you."

"I got paid. I'm good." It sounded more mercenary than I intended, but I didn't know what else to say.

"I know I shoudn'ta run, but..."

"You don't have to explain," I said. "I probably would've done the same thing if I'd been put in men's lockup. I'm glad it all worked out."

"We got to celebrate!" insisted Savage. "Is it too early to drink in this town?"

I looked at my watch. It was just after noon.

"I'm sure it's beer o'clock somewhere," said Fuego.

"Let's head to Naughty's," Rah-Rah suggested.

"Let's not," said Shea, giving me a wink. "Jinx, you know this town better than we do. Where do you suggest?"

"I'm kinda in the mood for Grumpy's. And they have beer for those who want it." I thought about it. "'Course, he'll probably have a heart attack when he sees all of us show up at once."

My phone dinged. Ciara had sent me a text. *Please meet me at your house.*

I replied. *Which one? Old or new?*

New came the reply

What's up? I asked.

Not over the phone.

Meet you there shortly.

"Hey," I said to Shea. "I got to take care of something real quick at home. But I'll meet you all there."

"Everything all right?" she asked.

"Yeah. It's Ciara. Probably dropped the Gray Ghost at my place and wants a ride back. Shouldn't take long."

"You want me to come with?"

I wanted to say yes, but everybody was in such a celebratory mood. "Naw, I'll be along soon enough. Just save me a seat."

Shea gave me a peck on the lips. "Don't take too long, gorgeous."

I didn't see the Gray Ghost when I pulled into the carport. Aside from a black BMW parked down the block, there were no cars in sight.

I unlocked the door and found the security system wasn't armed. In my haste to get to the courthouse, I must have forgotten. But then I stepped inside, and immediately, something felt wrong.

"Diana?" Where was she? She always came running when I walked in.

"Dog is here," said a thickly accented male voice.

Fuck. Having just come from court, I didn't have any weapons on me.

I stepped into my living room. Two men sat on my couch. One, I guessed to be in his fifties with a long chin-beard but no mustache or sideburns. I recognized him from his photo—Sergei Volkov.

The other looked to be in his thirties and was built like a linebacker. Both had guns stashed in their waistband. Diana sat between them, getting her head scratched by Volkov.

53

"Fine guard dog you turned out to be," I told Diana. She gave me a confused look. I pointed toward the hallway. "Bed." I didn't want her getting hurt when the shit hit the fan.

After Diana had disappeared into the bedroom, Volkov gestured toward a stuffed armchair opposite the coffee table. "Sit."

"Why are you in my living room, Volkov?" But I had a good idea of the answer to my question. "And what are you doing with Ciara's phone?"

"You know of me. This is good. And this is Anatoly. He doesn't say much."

"Pleasure. Now get the fuck outta my house."

"You are Ballou, yes? Jinx Ballou, famous bounty hunter."

"That's me."

"Ballou is French, yes? *Parlez-vous français?*"

"*Nyet!*" I replied with a sneer.

"Oh, you speak Russian."

"'Fraid not, wise guy. Spanish and English only. Pretty much all I need in these parts."

"I am impressed you speak Spanish. Most Americans only speak English. Stupid, lazy. This is why you have clown for president. Me? I speak Chechen, Russian, German, French, and of course, very good English. I am polyglot. Because Russians are not lazy like Americans. "

"I thought you were Chechen."

"My family moved to Chechnya when I was child. But we are still proud to be Russian."

"Well, goody for you."

"Please sit. We discuss."

I stared at the gun in Sergei's waistband and complied. As I sat, my hand casually slipped into a pocket on the side of the chair.

"We relieved you of gun in chair pocket," said Sergei.

Anatoly held up the Glock I usually kept stashed there and pointed it at me.

My eyes drifted to the coffee table, where I kept the Smith & Wesson, but I had no way to get to it before Anatoly filled my body with lead.

Sergei pulled my .44 Magnum out of his waistband and aimed it at me. "Also this found under table. You have good taste in weapons."

"How'd you get in here?" I was sure now that I had set the alarm.

"Anatoly look dumb as bull, but he is good with technologies. Especially good bypassing security alarms."

"Fine. Anatoly's a fucking genius. What. Do. You. Want?"

"Several of my men are dead. Yuri Barayev. Andrei Garinov. You know of them?"

"Maybe if Yuri hadn't kidnapped my friend, your guys wouldn't be chilling in the morgue right now."

"Yuri could be a little..." He turned to Anatoly and said something in what I assumed was Russian or Chechen.

"Aggressive," said Anatoly.

"Yes, aggressive. But you show up looking for missing girl. I tell Yuri, have you bring her."

"Scarlett's dead. Murdered by Juan Cabrera of the West Side Jaguars. Same asshole who killed James Fitzgerald, one of your clients at the Cactus Inn. I tried to explain this to Yuri. He still wouldn't release my friend. Left us no choice but to get...*aggressive*. As far as I'm concerned, the slate's clean."

"Slate is clean. What means this?" Sergei asked Anatoly in whatever language. Anatoly replied.

Sergei nodded. "Ah, now I understand 'slate is clean.' Like balancing accounts, yes? I am businessman. I understand business language. But no. Slate is not clean. Accounts not balanced. I see on news Scarlett still alive. And my men are dead." He leaned forward. "But don't worry. I not kill you. Not yet. You want clean slate? You work for me now. First job, bring Scarlett to me."

"I don't think so. I don't work for human trafficking scum like you."

"I am scum? Your government, they lock up people looking for American dream. Put little childrens in cages. Me? I give women opportunity to work in America. Make money. Live American dream. But I am scum?"

"Don't bother giving me the sales pitch, asshole. I'm not buying. Just because our government is doing evil shit doesn't make what you do any better. You can take your job offer and shove it up your Chechen Russkie ass.

"And for the record, I told the feds all about your sex trafficking operation. They're going to shut you down—your club, the motel, and everything else you got going. If you were smart, you'd be getting the hell outta Dodge instead of stinking up my living room."

"You not hear? Club burned down. Many girls die. Very sad." From his exaggerated pout, I could tell he was behind it. "As for you, Jinx Ballou. You are not in position for to bargain."

"Let me give you a little history lesson, Sergei. Your brother, Milo, made me a similar offer. When I turned him down, he got aggressive too. I put him down like the rabid dog he was, along with several of his men. And now I've killed Yuri, Andrei, and those steroid-swollen sides of beef he used for bodyguards. So don't threaten me, unless you want the same."

"I see. Perhaps I kill you now." Sergei raised the .44 Magnum.

Out of nowhere, Diana lunged, sinking her teeth into Sergei's meaty hand. The gun went off right before he dropped the revolver, sending a bullet into my newly replaced window. The gunshot sent Diana bolting out of the room.

My ears ringing from the gunshot, I hurled my spiky cosplay trophy at Anatoly, nailing the silent security genius in the eye. He clutched the injured socket while blood trickled down his face.

I snatched my Glock from his hand and put two rounds in his chest. His chest bloomed scarlet. Sergei reached for the revolver. I kicked it away, pressed the pistol to his head, and pulled the trigger.

"Jesus fucking Christ." Shea stepped into the room, followed by members of the Athena Sisterhood, all with their guns drawn. "What'd I miss?"

I hugged Shea and realized my heart was racing. "How'd you know?"

"Know what? Grumpy's was closed. Gas leak of some kind."

We kissed. I barely noticed the hoots and hollers from the other members of the Athena Sisterhood.

Detective Jennings showed up, along with the uniformed crime scene circus. I was thoroughly interrogated, swabbed for GSR, and eventually escorted out of my home. It would be hours before they were done gathering evidence and I would be allowed back inside, even though it was a clear case of self-defense.

I was not looking forward to cleaning the ick off my wall. I would probably need to repaint and get another new window and a new couch. But knowing Sergei and his crew were gone forever made it worth it.

Was I a sociopath for not feeling bad about killing evil people? Would a sociopath worry about not feeling bad?

Shea and the rest of the Athena Sisterhood were getting ready to head north. A sense of dread, loneliness, and loss hung over me.

"Damn, I'm gonna miss you." I pressed my forehead against hers.

"Likewise. But I gotta get back to Annie and the motorcycle shop. Clarence, my business partner, probably thinks I fell off the face of the earth."

"Yeah" was all I could think to say.

"Jinx, I don't know where this thing between us is going, but I'd like to give it a chance. I know we can't see each other every day, but we got weekends. Take a vacation from this fucking heat and spend some time up in the bustling metropolis of Sycamore Springs. The *Cortes Chronicle* says we're getting a Tastee Freez soon."

I met her gaze. My insides turned to jelly. "I'm told there's a fancy shop up there that makes custom motorcycles for women."

"Come on up. I'll teach you to ride."

"I'd like that."

I pulled her in for a deep, slow kiss that sent the world tumbling. I came up for air only when my phone started playing the *Game of Thrones* theme. Becca.

"I probably should take this."

Shea pulled on her helmet. "I'll call you when I get to Sycamore Springs."

"Please do. I really want to see where this goes."

The Athena Sisterhood mounted their bikes. The air shook with the thunder of two dozen motorcycles. It was so gloriously fucking loud I had to wait until they were out of the neighborhood before returning Becca's call.

54

"Hey, Becks. What's up?"

"I found it."

"What?"

"The smoking gun. Wilkes didn't pay for a hit man. He posted a message on a website run by the West Side Jaguars."

"The Jags have a website? That's rather bold."

"No kidding, right? Even the drug gangs are going high tech. Thing is, Wilkes posted a comment on the site that he knew Fitzgerald raped Cabrera's daughter and told them where Fitzgerald would be on the night he was killed. He totally set him up."

Even though Indigo was already cleared, there was still some reckoning to be had. I suspected he was the one who sent the Jags after us as well. "Send me what you got. I want to see Wilkes's face when I tell him he's busted."

"Will do."

I hopped in the Charger and raced like a madwoman to Scottsdale. I wished I already had a motorcycle so I could split lanes and get past all the slow-moving cars. But finally I pulled up to Wilkes's fancy house, swelling with joy. I put a call in to

Atkinson, got his voicemail, and left a message that Wilkes was an accessory to Fitzgerald's murder. Maybe he could get a win out of this after all.

I waltzed up the walkway and found Wilkes's front door ajar. "Hey, asshole!" I called into the house. "You left your front door open." I walked in past the fancy paintings and sculptures.

"Guess what, dipshit? I got proof you had your buddy Brother James killed. You're going down, you piece of shit."

He wasn't in his office. Not in his bedroom. Something wasn't right. A metallic scent hit my nose.

I stepped into the kitchen and drew my pistol. Wilkes lay on the floor, blood pooling around him from two knife wounds in his back. A teenage girl with a buzz cut stood over him, a bloody kitchen knife in each hand.

"What the fuck?" I aimed the gun at her chest, in case she made a move toward me. But she simply stared at me like a deer in the headlights.

"You stabbed him?" I asked.

"He was always posting videos saying queer people deserved to die." Her voice was soft and raspy but with a resilience. "My friend Rainey was murdered by one of his devoted fans. I had to stop him."

"Yeah" was all I said.

"You gonna shoot me?"

"You planning on stabbing me?"

She shook her head.

"Then I'm not going to shoot you." I lowered the gun but didn't holster it. "What's your name?"

"Maggie. Friends call me Knife."

"You're the Valley Slasher, aren't you?" When I got no reaction, I said, "Well, uh, Knife, my name's Jinx Ballou."

Her eyes widened in recognition. "Jinx the bounty hunter?"

"You heard of me?" I must be getting a reputation in vigilante circles.

"You're trans. I am too." She looked down at blood dripping from the knives in her hand. "You here to arrest me?"

"Nope." I looked at Wilkes. "He killed one of his associates. I was coming for him."

"Huh."

She turned and nonchalantly rinsed the knives in the sink, then dried them, and slid them into sheaths in her waistband. I should have stopped her. But instead, I let her walk past me and out the front door.

I stood there looking at Wilkes's body. "I hope there's a hell. And I hope you're in it."

I stepped outside and called 911.

Soon Detectives Atkinson and Torres arrived. I told them I'd found Wilkes already dead, then showed them the proof of his involvement with Fitzgerald's murder.

They battered me with questions and even checked my pistol. They were disappointed to find it had not recently been fired.

"You didn't see anyone hanging around the house when you pulled up?" Atkinson asked in a disbelieving tone.

"Not a soul."

"Looks like the same MO as the Valley Slasher," said Torres. "Fucking brutal."

"Huh," I said.

I drove back to my old house to see if I could crash with Max and Ciara. It had only been two hours, and I ached physically to have Shea beside me in the Charger. I was tempted to drive up to Sycamore Springs to surprise her, but after what I'd just witnessed, I needed time to get my head straight.

55

Two months later, I arrived back in Phoenix on my Iron Goddess 1100cc cruiser motorcycle. She had black panels, shiny chrome, and indigo-blue accents. I had named her Storm, after the character from X-Men comic books.

The Athena Sisterhood had invited me to join them on a loop ride through Payson, up along the Mogollon Rim. Riding in the middle of a convoy of two dozen motorcycles was a thrill I never thought I'd experience.

The group ride ended at Gertie's in Ironwood's Downtown Square, where Shea presented me with a leather cut with a patch on the back that read Havoc's Old Lady. The recovery jobs I'd been doing for Pima Bail Bonds allowed me to keep my schedule flexible enough to spend a few days each week with Shea and her niece, Annie. Shea had even joined me at a few of my therapy sessions, which were helping me process the trauma of the past several months.

The only downside to riding with the Sisterhood was returning to the furious August heat of the valley all alone. A monsoon storm was rolling in from the southeast. I hoped to beat it home.

The first fat drops were hitting my visor when I pulled onto my street and spotted a figure sitting on my front porch. A nervous chill ran up my spine until I recognized the eyes twinkling in a ginger-bearded face. I didn't even pull into the driveway. I just parked on the street, scrambled off the bike, and raced up the path to my front door, tearing off my helmet as I ran.

"Are you really here?" My hands grasped his arms, wondering if I was dreaming or hallucinating.

"I am, love. In the flesh, such as it is." His warm hand cupped my cheek.

"But how?"

"The Honorable Mr. Justice O'Rourke found me not guilty, if ya can believe it," said Conor.

"I…I…" My head was doing somersaults. My heart felt like it was trying to tear itself in two.

"Ya just gonna stand there gawking, or ya gonna give your fiancé a hug?"

Ready for Another Adventure?

Download a free copy of "Kissing Asphalt", a Jinx Ballou short story, by subscribing to Dharma's newsletter, The Gritty Gritty at dharmakelleher.com.

This semi-monthly newsletter features interviews with up-and-coming crime fiction authors, book reviews, release announcements, giveaways, and more.

BOOKS BY DHARMA KELLEHER

Jinx Ballou Bounty Hunter series

Chaser

Extreme Prejudice

A Broken Woman

Shea Stevens Outlaw Biker series

Iron Goddess

Snitch

Blood Sisters

ABOUT THE AUTHOR

Dharma Kelleher writes gritty crime fiction with a feminist kick and is one of the only openly transgender voices in the genre.

She is the author of the Jinx Ballou Bounty Hunter series and the Shea Stevens Outlaw Biker. Her work has also appeared in anthologies and on Shotgun Honey.

She is a former journalist and a member of Sisters in Crime, the International Thriller Writers, and the Alliance of Independent Authors. She lives in Arizona with her wife and three feline overlords.

Learn more about Dharma and her work at https://dharmakelleher.com.

www.ingramcontent.com/pod-product-compliance
Lightning Source LLC
Chambersburg PA
CBHW031601180726
48284CB00005B/1352